Leaving the Fold

Leaving the Fold

TESTIMONIES OF FORMER FUNDAMENTALISTS

Edward T. Babinski

Prometheus Books

59 John Glenn Drive
Amherst, New York 14228-2197

Published 1995 by Prometheus Books

99 98 97 96 95   5 4 3 2 1

Library of Congress Cataloging-in-Publication Data

Babinski, Edward T.
    Leaving the fold : testimonies of former fundamentalists / Edward T. Babinski.
        p.   cm.
    Includes bibliographical references and index.
    ISBN 0-87975-907-0 (alk. paper)
    1. Ex-church members—Case studies. 2. Fundamentalism—Controversial
literature. 3. Evangelicalism—Controversial literature. I. Title.
BV820.B29   1994
270.8'2'0922—dc20   94-26945
                                                                      CIP

Printed in the United States of America on acid-free paper.

To Protestant fundamentalist Christians, who do not realize how liberal they have grown over the past few hundred years, and who may wish to consider alternatives to the "conservatism" they now embrace.

And also to my mother and father, who have loved me regardless of the correctness or incorrectness of my beliefs.

To free a man from error is to give, not take away.
—Arthur Schopenhauer

You can only go halfway into the darkest forest;
then you are coming out the other side.
—Chinese proverb

Contents

Acknowledgments

"I Just Lost Faith in Faith," chapter 3 of *Losing Faith in Faith* by Dan Barker, copyright © 1992 by Dan Barker (published by Freedom From Religion Foundation, Inc.), reprinted by permission of the author.

Excerpts from "With Perfect Hatred" by Dan Barker, which appeared in *Freethought Today*, October 1991, reprinted by permission of Dan Barker.

Excerpts from *The Heretic: A Study of the Life of John William Colenso, 1814–1883* by Jeff Guy, copyright © 1983 by Jeff Guy, reprinted by permission of University of Natal Press.

Photograph of Bishop John William Colenso with his daughter, Harriette Colenso, reproduced by permission of the Killie Campbell Africana Library, Durban, South Africa.

Portions of Dr. Harvey Cox's contribution to "An Ecumenical-Evangelical Dialogue with Harvey Cox," which appeared in *Right On,* June 1975, reprinted by permission of Dr. Cox.

Excerpts from *The World's Tragedy* by Aleister Crowley, copyright © 1985 by the B.M.I.T., reprinted by permission of New Falcon Publications, 655 East Thunderbird, Phoenix AZ 85022.

Portions of *Harpur's Heaven and Hell* by Tom Harpur, copyright © 1983 by Tom Harpur (published by Oxford University Press), reprinted by permission of the author.

Excerpts from "A Personal Note" by John Hick, which appeared in *Odysseys to Dialogue,* edited by Leonard Swidler, copyright © 1992 by Edwin Mellen Press, reprinted by permission of Edwin Mellen Press.

Photograph of Robert G. Ingersoll with his grandchildren, reproduced with permission of the Illinois State Historical Library, Old State Capitol, Springfield, IL 62706.

Portions of *Charles Templeton: An Anecdotal Memoir* by Charles Templeton, copyright © 1983 by Charles Templeton (published by McClelland and Stewart Limited), reprinted by permission of the author.

Excerpts from The New Inquisition by Robert Anton Wilson, copyright © 1987 by Robert Anton Wilson, reprinted by permission of New Falcon Publications, 655 East Thunderbird, Phoenix AZ 85022.

In addition to the above, whose permission made this book possible, I wish to thank:

All the book's contributors who composed and submitted testimonies especially for this volume.

The faculty and fellow staff members at the J. B. Duke Library, Furman University, Greenville, South Carolina: Dr. Edward A. Scott, Robin P. Lindsay, Douglas N. Anderson (whose expertise at transferring and reformatting computer data saved me many hours that I would otherwise have had to have spent at the keyboard), Lilli Ann Hall (who obtained materials for me via interlibrary loan), Nancy R. Lewis (who perpetually renewed the books I had borrowed for the project), and all the rest of the faculty and staff, whose understanding and encouragement were ever present.

Robert Anderson of Bob's Computers who (with less than twenty-four hours left for me to print out the manuscript and mail it to the publisher by the date specified in the book contract) installed a new hard-drive on my computer at a moment's notice.

My father, Edward T. Babinski, and mother, Winifred K. Stang, my "other father," Edwin R. Stang, and my aunt, Rose Kobylus, for their encouragement, understanding, and patience during the six or seven years I have spent collecting testimonies of former fundamentalists.

My "sister" Sally Stang, who told me over the phone about six or seven years ago that she would buy a book that contained testimonies of former fundamentalists. She pointed me toward an idea for a manuscript that was potentially marketable, as opposed to some of my previous ideas.

And lastly, my girlfriend, Lori Anderson, whose understanding, encouragement, and patience buoyed me up when I began to despair that I would "never be through with the !*@!#?! project."

Introduction

This book is primarily a collection of testimonies by people who were Protestant Christian fundamentalists and who later left fundamentalism (with the exceptions of Tom Harpur and Harvey Cox, who were moderate Christians whose views underwent a broadening similar to what some fundamentalist contributors experienced).

A hard-line fundamentalist may wish to warn the authors of this book's testimonies, and anyone reading this book, that "hell" is probably their "next destination." But he will have to do better than that if he hopes to convince his former brethren to rejoin him in his "straight and narrow" appreciation of the Bible and Jesus. He may even have to read this entire book to understand where his former brethren are "coming from" rather than simply predict where he thinks they are going.

I first tried marketing this book in parts. The testimonies of those who had left fundamentalism but remained Christians were to be published by a moderate/liberal Christian press; the testimonies of those who had left both fundamentalism *and* religion were to be published by an atheist or agnostic press. However, some testimonies, such as those by William Bagley and Ernest Heramia, did not fit easily into either category.

I contacted several moderate and liberal Christian publishing houses and found that none of them were interested in "testimonies." I think that is a defect of moderate and liberal Christian sensibilities. Perhaps they do not wish to "lower" their standards, so to speak, by copying confrontational evangelistic techniques used by conservatives and fundamentalists, one such technique being "testifying." (Can I hear an "Amen," brother?) Yet personal testimonies are remarkably effective at conveying feelings, not merely facts; deeds, not merely dogmas; and they incite people to act as well as to think. For many years evangelical Protestant Christianity has used the power inherent in a single person's "testimony" to win new converts and buoy the faith of old ones.

So, after several rejections from moderate and liberal publishing houses, I offered the testimonies to the largest free-thought press in America, Prometheus Books.

At first I was skeptical whether a "free-thought" press would print testimonies by people who had remained *Christians,* but I was assured that promoting genuinely *free* thinking was more important to the press than selectively chopping up every hundred-thousand-word manuscript they bought until it resembled a ten-page primer for atheism. Prometheus has published three full-length autobiographies of people whose faith in Christianity was shattered after they had witnessed the unethical or demagogic practices of church leaders and the naivete of their followers (i.e., *Salvation for Sale, Don't Call Me Brother,* and *Jesus Doesn't Live Here Anymore*). None of the authors of those books is an atheist. Furthermore, printing only testimonies advocating atheism would be to fall into the same error as that of the fundamentalists, who feel it imperative that everyone believe exactly as they do.

I suppose that the nearest that *fundamentalist* Christians ever came to advocating greater diversity rather than greater uniformity was when Jerry Falwell founded the Moral Majority, which, until its demise in 1986, focused on the moral (and political) concerns of Protestants, Catholics, and Jews. Considering what fundamentalist Protestants teach about the grave errors of Catholicism (not to mention Judaism), that was quite an amalgamation for a fundamentalist like Jerry Falwell to construct. But, as they say, "politics makes strange bedfellows." For that matter, so does "televangelism." (Chuckle.)

This book exemplifies how an even more diverse array of people (far more diverse than the Moral Majority) is willing to band together to speak out on an issue that has intimately affected all of them, hoping thereby to increase the volume and scope of their declarations.

Once you have read all the testimonies, certain threads linking them together become apparent: the dilemmas and fears each person faced in leaving fundamentalism behind; their gradually dawning courage to ask crucial critical questions, and to continue asking more questions; their discovery of how wonderful it can be to allow one's innate curiosity the freedom it craves; and the blossoming of their distinctive personalities and beliefs. Anyone who enjoys a novel with idiosyncratic and markedly diverse characters will enjoy reading what lies ahead.

Of course, people who have left fundamentalism can differ markedly in their reactions to it. At one end of the spectrum are those who bid fundamentalism a "fond farewell." They had fun as fundamentalists, particularly in their youth. They also remind us that belonging to a fundamentalist church is a healthy alternative to drug addiction, alcoholism, and crime. A fundamentalist church setting can provide some with the social and psychological context that helps them to legitimize and catalyze radical changes they wish to make in their lives. (Of course, individuals must also *want* to change in the first place. No mere context can do that *for* you, as groups like Alcoholics Anonymous have pointed out.)

At the other end of the spectrum are those who aim both barrels at their former fundamentalist lives and beliefs. They view fundamentalist organizations as robbing people of their money (through "tithing," "giving till it hurts," and phoney come-ons to garner more contributions than a television ministry knows what to do with); robbing people of their time (every minute involved in church activities); robbing people of their health (phoney promises made by "faith healers"); and robbing people of their individuality, their freedom of thought, or even their ability to appreciate life.

Both perspectives can undoubtedly be true, depending on each individual's personal experiences. It was left up to each contributor to discuss in whatever terms they chose their entrance into and exit from fundamentalism, and to explain where they are today.

If you are a Christian, you may be interested primarily in testimonies by former fundamentalists who remained Christians. If you are not a Christian, but open to non-Christian spiritualities (wiccan or eastern), then you may find testimonies of that nature more to your liking. If you "don't know" which part of the book you might enjoy reading first, try the testimonies of those who became agnostics. If you are an atheist, your curiosity may be peaked by that section. Or, if you are a historian, you may wish to flip to the final section of testimonies of historical figures.

Readers of all persuasions should peruse the annotated bibliography that lists further testimonies. Or, you may wish to advance directly ahead.

Part One

What You Should Know About Fundamentalism

Q.: What is fundamentalism?

A.: According to Protestant Christian fundamentalists, with which this book specifically deals, it is a belief in the "fundamentals" of the Christian faith: The truthfulness of events recorded in the Bible, miracles and prophecies described in the Bible, morality prescribed in the Bible, and Christian doctrines derived from the Bible, "rightly understood and interpreted in their intended sense." (For "intended sense," read, "fundamentalist sense.") It is necessary to maintain one's faith unwaveringly in these things—or else.

Q.: Who is a fundamentalist?

A.: According to some fundamentalist groups, only *they* are true Christians, and only *they* are going to heaven, while the rest of the world's "so-called" Christians, including those in other fundamentalist groups, are going to hell. That would be a very narrow definition of "fundamentalist," to say the least.

There is also the definition of "fundamentalist" used by evangelical Christians. To an evangelical, a "fundamentalist" is someone who strives very hard to obey the "law," a person who makes moral decisions based on a "legalistic" (almost a Pharisaic) interpretation of what God demands of each Christian believer. For instance, an evangelical (as opposed to a fundamentalist) might listen to Christian rock music, might drink and smoke, and, yes, might even dance.

Generally speaking, evangelicals, unlike fundamentalists, place greater emphasis on the *experience* of being "born again" than on the literal truthfulness of every "jot and tittle" in God's word. This experiential focus allows them to take some criticisms of the Bible's literal truth more lightly than fundamentalists do.

For instance, a moderate evangelical might admit that Scripture is "inspired . . . and good for teaching, for reproof, for correction, for training in righteousness" (2 Tim. 3:16, NASB), but without claiming that the Bible is necessarily free from *all* error. Even the Bible admits that Adam, the first man, was "inspired" (literally, "breathed in"), animated directly by "God's breath" blown "into Adam's nostrils." But that did *not* guarantee that Adam's mind and/or heart would be *free from error.* Adam still "fell from grace." In other words, the human authors of each biblical document were not "ventriloquist's dummies" whose writings were dictated by God word for word. They were men whose writings also reflected to some extent their limitations in knowledge, even the prejudices and preconceptions of their society and their day and age. If Adam could fall, the Bible could contain errors.

Of course, not all evangelicals are "moderates" in the above sense of the word. There are, for instance, many evangelicals who believe that where Scripture is concerned, "inspired" means, "without errors of any sort."

And there are probably many evangelicals such as I once was—I had no clear idea of my exact beliefs concerning the Bible, until a friend began pointing out a few discrepancies in the Good Book. Speaking for myself, I did not laugh off such discrepancies, but began studying books by fundamentalist apologists, and eventually learned how to construct tier upon tier of "alternative explanations" in an attempt to circumvent every single alleged error. That was when I began to realize that I was at heart a biblical literalist.

Q.: What percentage of Americans are fundamentalists?
A.: It depends on how you define "fundamentalist" (see previous question). If you include those groups that acknowledge being fundamentalist, along with many evangelical and pentecostal groups, then we would arrive at a sizeable percentage.

The American Institute of Public Opinion (the Gallup poll organization) "has collected data since 1976 which may fairly be said to constitute a scale of fundamentalist/evangelist orientation: (1) the experience of being 'born again,' (2) a literalist view of the Bible, and (3) a report of an attempt to encourage someone else to accept Jesus Christ as savior. . . . In 1976 18 percent of respondents gave positive responses to all three items; in 1984, this figure had risen to 22 percent [not a statistically significant increase—ED.]."[1]

These dedicated "fund-evange-costals" (to coin a term), therefore, constitute at least one out of every five Americans. Some polls indicate that this estimate may be too low.

According to a Gallup poll taken around 1989, "31 percent of Americans believe the Bible is 'the actual word of God and is to be taken literally, word for word.' "[2] That's nearly one out of every three Americans.

Nonfundamentalists need not be extremely alarmed by such figures since polls taken by the Gallup organization over a thirty-year period indicate that "the proportion of Americans . . . who believe that every word in the Bible is literally true—continues to decline."

For instance, "In 1963, 65 percent of Americans believed the Bible was literally true. This figure fell to 38 percent by 1978. The proportion of fundamentalists hovered between 37 and 39 percent between 1978 and 1984, but has begun to inch down again since then [down to 34 percent in 1985, and 31 percent in 1989]."[3] Over the past twenty-seven years, the percentage of people who believe that the Bible is "literally true" has fallen from 65 to 31 percent, and continues to decrease.

Nonfundamentalists ought not to be lulled into complacency by the thought that the number of biblical literalists continues to diminish. Biblical literalists still constitute about a third of the population. And the number of fundamentalist and conservative Christian believers engaged in local and national politics and judicial decisions is apparently increasing. If 30 percent of the country adopted a unified and militant political stance, their influence would be considerable. So fundamentalism is still far from going the way of the dodo.

Q.: In general, does a person's educational level have anything to do with whether they believe the Bible is literally true?
A.: That's the sixty-four-thousand-dollar question, isn't it? Answering that "polls show that there is an inverse relationship" is not going to prove anything to a genuine fundamentalist, who will respond that the "hearts" of "intellectuals" are "hardened," therefore they cannot perceive the "foolishness of the cross," which

is "wisdom unto salvation." "Ye must become as little children," and Jesus will melt your "hard heart," etc.

Of course, an intellectual, reproached in such a fashion, might be tempted to respond, "My heart is just as 'hard' as your head is 'soft.' "

The pollster, George Gallup, Jr., has recently verified that, concerning the "belief that the Bible is literally true. . . . Education is the major variable, with belief in the literal truth of the Bible decreasing according to the educational background. Literal belief in the Bible is 45 percent among those with less than a high school degree, 34 percent among high school graduates, 26 percent among those with some college, and 11 percent among college graduates."[4]

Of course, if a poll were taken only of graduates from *fundamentalist Bible-based colleges and universities,* then the percentage of college graduates who believe that the Bible is literally true would be much improved. Therefore, to help ensure that fundamentalist children maintain the literalist faith that their parents have instilled in them, many fundamentalist parents see to it that their children attend such colleges, especially ones where the professors sign a statement of faith that they swear to abide by for the duration of their employment. (However, that is still no guarantee that the students who attend such institutions will remain literalists, as a number of the testimonies in this book show. See the testimonies of M. Lee Deitz, Ernest Heramia, Conrad Hyers, Harry H. McCall, Dennis R. MacDonald, David K. Montoya, Robert Price, H. P. Smith, Farrell Till, and Mike Yaconelli, found in this book.)

A further embarrassing point for fundamentalists to ponder is that *all of the oldest and most renowned universities in America were originally founded to serve as conservative Christian seminaries*—Harvard, Yale, Princeton, and several others. Some of these early American seminaries were even founded in response to the "theological excesses" of other schools that had begun to shift a little to the left. In all cases, after decades and decades of settling only for the brightest students and professors these universities eventually grew so "liberal" that fundamentalists had to found entirely new colleges to send their children to. Thus, fundamentalist "Bible colleges" are all relatively youthful institutions. And as each fundamentalist institution grows older, more broadly experienced and wiser, it too runs the risk of growing more and more "liberal." In our own day, Fuller Seminary has undergone a gradual transition away from fundamentalism and toward liberalism. So has Calvin College in Grand Rapids, Michigan. Even professors at the academy founded by Calvin in Geneva, Switzerland, teach things today for which Calvin and his followers might have had them jailed, exiled or executed.

Q. Are fundamentalists correct in assuming that what's really wrong with America is "secular humanism," "evolutionary theory," and "new age thinking?"

A.: The problems that America and the rest of the world currently face will not be solved or even diminished by fundamentalists' efforts to combat "secular humanism," "evolutionary theory," and "new age thinking." The *real* problems we face today are far more diverse and concrete. A worldwide economic crunch is gradually widening the gap between the very rich and the very poor. Ninety-five million people are added to the world's population each year (or 10,800 per hour), breaking all previous records, and making it increasingly difficult to provide adequate food, shelter, education, and opportunities for employment for those living in less industrialized sections of the world (or in the inner cities of the industrialized sections). Such circumstances guarantee a general increase in human misery and criminal behavior. Moreover, in the industrialized sections of the globe radioactive wastes are piling up, and levels of air and ground water pollution continue to increase. The hole in the ozone layer above Antarctica is widening. New strains of old "germs," such as tuberculosis, are growing immune to the same antibiotics.

Today we require a wide variety of solutions to match a wide variety of present and future problems. Fundamentalists can preach about the evils of believing this or that, but their preaching does not help solve the problems outlined above, which we all share, regardless of our religious or ideological differences. Of course, if a fundamentalist believes that Jesus will solve all those "knotty" problems with the flagging economy, the population, and the environment "when he returns," and that every believer's job is to convert people and ensure that an increasing number of babies are born each year, then we have a *real* problem in trying to find any common ground.

Bertrand Russell once pointed out that the early church fathers busied themselves discussing "how to preserve virginity" while the Christianized Roman Empire continued to decline around them (the overall process took several centuries). The concrete "worldly" problems that contributed to the decline of the Christianized Roman Empire were not recognized and dealt with as they should have been. Instead, they were either blamed on Satan, praised as "signs of Jesus' soon return," or ignored. Today's fundamentalist and conservative Christians appear to be reacting in a similar fashion to many of today's problems.

I wish to stress here that Christians in ancient Rome took their beliefs as seriously as today's politically active fundamentalists, even more so. Once Christians held the governmental reins of the Roman Empire they began to persecute and massacre pagans; they outlawed pagan religious practices and pagan schools of philosophy; they destroyed pagan works of art and pagan temples; they burnt the Serapaeum of the Library at Alexandria; they forcibly baptized pagans in the tens of thousands; they made it illegal for pagans to leave a will; they separated pagan children from their parents in order to have the children raised in Christian homes; and they rioted in the streets, Christian declaiming Christian, over their theological differences of opinion (since "correct theology" was what "really" mattered). But even with all the prayers, activism, and governmental sanctions of the "religious right" during the days of the Christianized Roman Empire, that empire fell. So why should anyone believe that Christianizing America is the solution to today's complex problems? Only people ignorant of history can believe such a thing.[5]

And regardless of the insistence by fundamentalist ministers that "things are getting worse every day," and, "things were better in the good old days," on the contrary, many things have *improved* over the centuries (many such improvements having occurred relatively recently). For instance, in the "good old days" genocide was practiced on Indian tribes, blacks were enslaved and lynched, the

Civil War set "brother against brother," the Wild West flaunted its lack of law and order. At the turn of the century New York and other big cities had annual increases in crime that exceeded today's, poor families could not afford an education for their children, children labored in factories and mines, the child mortality rate was exceedingly high, wife-beating was an acceptable practice, the average lifespan was nearly thirty years shorter than today, heroin was sold over the counter as a sedative for coughs, and cocaine was sold as a toothache remedy for children. So when you compare the "good old days" with today, it becomes apparent that many positive changes (not merely negative ones) have accompanied the "liberalization/secularization" of American society.[6] Or consider the wise words of the Greek philosopher Theophrastus who wrote in his book *Ethical Characters* (circa 300 B.C.): "The idle chatterer is the sort who says that people nowadays are much more wicked than they used to be."

Q.: How do you explain fundamentalism?
A.: There are many reasons why Protestant Christian fundamentalism arose and why many still find it attractive. But to discuss them all would require a larger harddrive on my computer, so I shall focus on major characteristics of "fundamentalism" without limiting myself to the Protestant Christian variety.

> Characteristic of all fundamentalism is that it has found absolute certainty— the certainty of class warfare, the certainty of science, or the literal certainty of the Bible—a certainty of the person who has finally found a solid rock to stand upon which, unlike other rocks, is "solid all the way down." Fundamentalism, however, is a terminal form of human consciousness in which development is stopped, eliminating the uncertainty and risk that real growth entails.[7]

This calls to mind Mark Twain's gentle poke: "We have infinite trouble in solving man-made mysteries; it is only when we set out to discover the secret of God that our difficulties disappear."[8]

Another characteristic, not of fundamentalism, but of fundamental*ists* is their intellectual

> modesty, their almost saintly humility. Nietzsche said once that we are all greater artists than we realize, but fundamentalists are too timid to think of themselves as great artists. They take no credit for what they have invented; they assume they have no part in the creation and maintenance of the Idols they worship. Like the paranoid—very much like the paranoid, in fact— they devise baroque and ingenious Systems, and define them as "Given." They then carefully edit all impressions to conform to the System. There is no vanity, no vanity at all, in people who are so intensely creative and so unwilling to recognize their own cleverness.[9]

One clever Protestant fundamentalist Christian, Gleason Archer, has created a 480-page *Encyclopedia of Bible Difficulties* in which he ingeniously explains away a host of "apparent" contradictions found in the Bible. Critics have pointed

out that Archer's single volume "encyclopedia" is far too short. What he needs
to do is produce an enormous *set* of encyclopedias dealing with "Bible difficulties,"
along with a yearly supplemental volume to explain away the latest problems
raised by textual and archeological research.[10]

This unwillingness to recognize their own cleverness was also apparent in the
Plymouth Brethren (nineteenth-century Protestant fundamentalists who insisted the
Bible was literally true).[11] Aleister Crowley, who was raised in that milieu, recalls:

> They devised an elaborate system of mental watertight compartments. The
> contradictions of Old and New Testaments were solved by a Doctrine that
> what was sauce for the Jewish "Dispensation" was not necessarily sauce for
> the Christian "Dispensation." Cleverer than Luther, they made possible the
> Epistle of James by a series of sophisms which really deserve to be exposed
> as masterpieces of human self-deception. My space forbids.[12]
>
> So, despite all the simplicity of the original logical position [i.e., that
> the "Word of God" must be without error or contradiction], they were found
> shifting as best they might from compromise to compromise. But this they
> never saw themselves; and so far did they take their principle that my father
> would refuse to buy railway shares because railways were not mentioned
> in the Bible! Of course the practice of finding a text for everything means
> ultimately "I will do as I like," and I suspect my father's heroics only meant
> that he thought a slump was coming.[13]

If a fundamentalist searches diligently for something in the Bible, anything
in fact, they can almost always find it there. (It's just this uncanny "gift" they
have, which they take *no credit* for.) In fact, if Crowley's father had just searched
a little more, and with a bit more faith (and creativity) he *could* have found
railways mentioned in the Bible! Chaplain Tresham Dames Gregg did, and delivered a noteworthy sermon on the subject that was published as a booklet in
1863, *The Steam Locomotive as Revealed in the Bible. A Lecture Delivered to
Young Men in Sheffield.*[14] Gregg's sermon is a little gem of fundamentalist ingenuity and creativity in which he demonstrates that God gave the prophet Ezekiel
a vision of a steam locomotive. (Ezek. 1:4–25)

A fundamentalist not only believes that "with God, all things are possible,"
but, "with the Bible, all *interpretations* are possible" (except, of course, any that
disagree with church doctrine, or imply the existence of errors or contradictions).

So fundamentalists display at least two major characteristics: (1) absolute
certainty, and (2) an unwillingness to recognize all the cleverness employed in
keeping their "absolute certainty" afloat. There is also a third characteristic, namely,
grabbing the oars of the "U.S.S. Absolute Certainty" and using them to beat
the heads of landlubbers who refuse repeated invitations to join the crew.

As A. E. Van Vogt observed in his pamphlet *Report on the Violent Male*,
and Colin Wilson observed in his book *The Criminal History of Mankind*:

> The Violent Male—and almost all violence is committed by males—seems
> to be a man who literally cannot *ever*, admit he might be wrong. He *knows*
> he is right. . . .

His ego definition, as it were, demands that he is always Right, nearly everybody else is always Wrong. . . .

Wilson emphasizes that this model describes not only many, many infamous criminals, but quite a few of the more infamous statesmen and churchmen of history, who were not *called* criminals only because they were powerful enough to define what was "crime" in their society.[15]

This "Violent Male" model certainly describes two of the most "totally right" men in fundamentalist Protestant history, Martin Luther and John Calvin. They were not physically violent themselves (except for bursts of wrathful temper), but they incited Christian rulers and magistrates to perform acts of persecution and murder.

Crowley observed a similar characteristic in the Plymouth Brethren: "An irreligious man may have moral checks; a Plymouth Brethren has none. He is always ready to excuse the vilest crimes by quoting the appropriate text, and invoking the name of Christ to cover every meanness which may delight his vain and vicious nature."[16]

Having outlined fundamentalism's readily observable characteristics, I will now supply one possible explanation of the present worldwide resurgence of different fundamentalist religious movements. Trust is a product of familiarity, of repeated encounters with others that turn out well. The same goes for personal preferences. If children are repeatedly exposed, by both their parents and peers, to certain types of music, or to certain religious beliefs, the children tend by and large to remain comfortably immersed in their given milieu rather than journeying far from it intellectually or even geographically. Thus certain regions of the country remain primarily country music oriented, or Latin music oriented, or Catholic, or Baptist, and so on. The same goes for the various regions of the globe.

But geographic and linguistic barriers that once separated disparate cultures on this planet are being torn down at an accelerating rate via a growing worldwide information network. It is becoming increasingly difficult for many people, especially older adults, to integrate the barrage of "new signals" radiating from televisions and computer terminals, read in newspapers, and viewed on stage, screen, and video. Many require comforting links with the familiar, with the same old repetitions, to maintain their mental equilibrium.

Our minds, grown accustomed to the same old experiences, try to stuff new experiences within familiar mental compartments. But, lacking the ready-made compartment in which to store an experience of "unfamiliar" dimensions, a disruption occurs, a discomfiture, a mental irritation. New signals cannot be processed easily along the same mental pathways as the old signals. Effort must be expended to form new mental connections and interpretive matrixes to accommodate the new signals. It is easier to simply reject the new signals out of hand (or even, with a vengeance), and to maintain that the old repetitions (the old hypnosis) were the best. After all, they made us feel so much more calm and comfortable.

Sometimes it takes quite a while to *see* a new type of signal: which is why even "cultivated" Europeans once saw Chinese painting as "crude" and heard Chinese music as "weird."[17]

[And] it is ironic that the early European missionaries in Africa, unfamiliar with patterns of such rhythmic complexity, described the music as incoherent and its practitioners as lacking rhythmic sense! It is also worth mentioning that this West African practice of layering rhythmic patterns is one of its most important contributions to jazz and, later, to jazz's step-child, rock music.[18]

Hence it remains painful, threatening, and/or difficult for many to "see new signals," or to integrate the world's increasing number of them into their consciousness. This explains the efforts of some to reinstitute the "fundamentals" of their faith and/or culture to the exclusion of all other faiths or cultures. Such "fundamentalist" movements do not help ease mankind's problems. Instead, they magnify their members' misunderstandings of what those problems really are, and create new ones.

Q.: Since you *left fundamentalism, what have you found to take its place?*
A.: Since I left fundamentalism I have not discovered a new religious "creed" to believe in, but I have discovered a new attitude toward life. Today I would say that the most important factor in a person's life is not whether they are a Christian or an atheist (or anything else for that matter), but what *kind* of person they are.

Speaking of different *kinds* of Christians and atheists, I am familiar with the kind of Christian who looks down upon whomever does not belong to his particular faith or his particular church, who has such an ironclad preconception about the hereafter that he loses sight of the here and now, who is more interested in dogmas than deeds, and who may discipline his children and his wife in a relatively harsh fashion.

I am also familiar with the kind of atheist who is light-hearted, friendly, and compassionate. They are tacitly thankful for each earthly moment. And they help their neighbors without any thought of converting them. (Of course, if the subject of organized religion should arise, or religious fervor gets tossed their way, they may react apathetically.)

If I was forced to choose, out of the above two, which one I would prefer having as my neighbor, it would be the latter. And I think that many Americans, regardless of their religious beliefs, would make the same choice.

That is not to say that each atheist or Christian (or anyone else for that matter) should be viewed as being primarily good or bad. We each have different mixtures of faults and virtues within ourselves. My point is that it is more important to learn about a person as a whole rather than focusing on what his beliefs might happen to be. People are unique. Beliefs are ubiquitous, and may tell us little or nothing about the person who believes them (or who doesn't believe them).

What else have I learned since leaving fundamentalism? I have grown to recognize essential differences between "belief" and "faith," as Alan Watts, the writer on eastern and western spiritualities, once pointed out:

> Faith is an openness and trusting attitude to truth and reality, whatever it may turn out to be. This is a risky and adventurous state of mind. Belief, in the religious sense, is the opposite of faith—because it is a fervent wishing or hope, a compulsive clinging to the idea that the universe is arranged and governed in such and such a way. Belief is holding to a rock; faith is learning how to swim—and this whole universe swims in boundless space.[19]

Notes

1. Andrew M. Greeley, *Religious Change in America* (Cambridge, Mass.: Harvard University Press, 1989), p. 19.

2. George Gallup, Jr., and Jim Castelli, *The People's Religion* (New York: Macmillan, 1989), pp. 60–61.

3. Ibid., p. 61.

4. Ibid.

5. For those interested in the effect that Christianity had upon ancient civilization, viz., the Christianized Roman Empire, the following works ought to be consulted: Edward Gibbon, *On Christianity* (Amherst, N.Y.: Prometheus Books, 1991, a reprint of chapters 15 and 16 of *The Decline and Fall of the Roman Empire*); Joseph McCabe, "How Christianity 'Triumphed,' " in *The Myth of the Resurrection and Other Essays* (Amherst, N.Y.: Prometheus Books, 1993, a reprint of an essay first published in 1926), pp. 119–68. Madalyn Murray O'Hair, "Gibbon, The Historian, and Christianity," in *An Atheist Speaks* (Austin, Tex.: American Atheist Press, 1986), pp. 267–72; Madalyn Murray O'Hair, "The Establishment of Christianity," in *What on Earth is an Atheist!* (Austin, Tex.: American Atheist Press, 1969), pp. 123–27; Ramsay MacMullen, "Conversion by Coercion" and "Summary," in *Christianizing the Roman Empire* (New Haven, Conn.: Yale University Press, 1984), pp. 86–120.

"The [Christian] zealots for conversion took to the streets or criss-crossed the countryside, destroying no doubt more of the [pagan] architectural and artistic treasure of their world than any passing barbarians thereafter" (Ramsay MacMullen, *Christianizing the Roman Empire*, p. 119).

"To the contention by [the pagan philosopher] Celsus that Christians took children away from their parents, . . . Origen [the Christian apologist] could only respond that Christians did not lure children away from better things or incite them to worse things. This was a lame argument, one that could hardly have appeased a pagan who cherished family life and worked hard to give his children a good education and a place in society. In this case, Origen's near admission of guilt may only have confirmed many suspicions held by pagans that Christianity was by and large a disruptive force" (Stephen Benko, *Pagan Rome and the Early Christians* [Bloomington, Ind.: Indiana University Press, 1984], p. 157).

"The first time that 'Christians were put to death by other Christians' (S. L. Greenslade, *Schism in the Early Church* [London: S.C.M., 1953], p. 189) was right after the imperial peace, under [the first Christian emperor,] Constantine. . . . Even during the persecutions [of the Romans against the Christians], churches were cleft by rivalry and schism" (Samuel Laeuchli, *The Serpent and the Dove: Five Essays on Early Christianity* [New York: Abingdon Press, 1966], p. 48).

"[Murderous riots broke out between Christians over the appointment of Arian bishops who believed that Christ was the exact 'image' of God, but not of the same 'substance.'—ed.] Probably more Christians were slaughtered by Christians in two years (A.D. 342–43) than by all the persecutions of Christians by pagans in the history of Rome" (Will Durant, *The Story of*

Civilization, Vol. 4, *The Age of Faith* [New York: Simon and Schuster, 1950] Durant cites Socrates, *Ecclesiastical History* [London: 1892], ii, 7–11).

6. Otto L. Bettmann, *The Good Old Days—They Were Terrible!* (New York: Random House, 1974). Highly readable account with plenty of pictures that enlightens readers as to the terrible shape of society during the late 1800s and early 1900s.

Stephanie Coontz, *The Way We Never Were* (New York: HarperCollins Publishers, 1993). Examines two centuries of American family life and banishes the misconception about an "ideal" past that clouds the current debate.

Maeve E. Doggett, *Marriage, Wife-Beating and the Law in Victorian England* (1993). Not until 1891 was it illegal for a British man to beat and imprison his wife.

Patricia Miller, *The Worst of Times: Illegal Abortions—Survivors, Practitioners, Coroners, Cops, and Children of Women Who Died Talk About Its Horrors* (New York: HarperCollins Publishers, 1993). Today, fearing intimidation and harassment from pro-life protestors, the latest generation of medical students is reluctant to include abortion as part of their practice. However, old-time physicians, who recall what things were like before abortion was legalized, are not so easily intimidated. What they fear most is a return to "the worst of times."

Richard Shenkman, "The Good Old Days," an enlightening and entertaining chapter in his book, *"I Love Paul Revere Whether He Rode or Not"—Warren Harding* (New York: HarperCollins Publishers, 1991), pp. 158–64.

7. Heinz Pagels, *The Dreams of Reason* (New York: Simon & Schuster, 1988), p. 328.

8. Mark Twain, "As Concerns the Deity," essay, 1917.

9. Robert Anton Wilson, *The New Inquisition: Irrational Rationalism and the Citadel of Science* (Phoenix, Ariz.: Falcon Press, 1987), p. 91.

10. There are further "difficulties" that arise from the mere acknowledgment of "apparent contradictions" in the Bible. As my friend Robert M. Price has said, "an *apparent* contradiction is the worst kind," because no matter how many ingenious explanations you devise for explaining it away, it will always remain glaring at you there in the Bible, and you will not know if any one explanation you have devised is truer than another, nor whether all of them are failures, and the contradiction indeed exists exactly as it "appears."

Besides, if two verses "apparently" contradict each other, then the best a fundamentalist can do is accept one *or* the other verse's "apparent" meaning, and reject or alter the remaining verse's "apparent" meaning. But that means fundamentalists are "adding and taking away" from what the Bible is "apparently" telling them! In effect, to even admit the existence of "apparent" contradictions is a hopeless position for fundamentalists.

Take the case of Harold Lindsell's clever suggestion that Peter may have denied Jesus as many as *six,* or even *twelve* times, if that is what it takes to "harmonize" all the stories of Peter's denial of Christ that are found in the four Gospels [see Lindsell's *The Battle for the Bible*]. Of course he has to ignore the fact that all four Gospels *agree* in their separate tellings that Peter denied Jesus "three" times. So Lindsell has to *dis*agree with something all four Gospels *agree* upon, in order to preserve his preconception of the Bible's literal truthfulness! Apparently fundamentalists do not like the Bible they have.

11. The Plymouth Brethren happen to be quite important in the history of fundamentalism. If their weighty influence down through the decades were traced in the style of an ancient Hebrew genealogy, it would read something like this: The Plymouth Brethren "begat" John Darby. John Darby "begat" Dispensationalism (an elaborate chopping up of the Bible into discrete parts that was devised to help explain away contradictions). Dispensationalism "begat" Scofield. Scofield "begat" the fundamentalist's old friend, the *Scofield Reference Bible.* The *Scofield Reference Bible* "begat" Dallas Theological Seminary. Dallas Theological Seminary "begat" Hal Lindsey. And Lindsey "begat" *The Late Great Planet Earth,* one of the best-selling books of all time, containing many clever and creative explanations of Bible prophecy that Lindsey culled from generations of inventive fundamentalist minds. Unfortunately, things just haven't turned out as Lindsey predicted.

12. Martin Luther said: "The Epistle of James I account the writing of no Apostle," because it taught that "a man is justified by works, and not by faith alone," which contradicted Paul the apostle's teaching.

13. Aleister Crowley, *The World's Tragedy* (Phoenix, Ariz.: Falcon Press, 1985), pp. xii–xiii.

14. *The Steam Locomotive as Revealed in the Bible: A Lecture Delivered to Young Men in Sheffield* (London: Wertheim, Macintosh, and Hunt, Paternoster Row, 1863; reprinted in 1991 by Paradox Press, Burnsville, Minnesota, by Robert Schadewald).

15. Wilson, *The New Inquisition,* pp. 139, 198–99.

16. Crowley, *The World's Tragedy,* p. xiii.

17. Wilson, *The New Inquisition,* p. 200.

18. Dana Wilson, "The Role of Patterning in Music," *Leonardo,* vol. 22, no. 1 (1989): 104.

19. Alan Watts, cited without reference in Steve Allen, *Steve Allen on the Bible, Religion & Morality* (Amherst, N.Y.: Prometheus Books, 1990), p. 415.

Part Two

Fundamentalism's Grotesque Past

Moving to Greenville, South Carolina, has taught me that Protestant fundamentalist Christianity may be with us until either Jesus returns or, barring that, hell freezes over. Although it took only ten years to exhaust the fundamentalist phase of my life, for many, especially in the southern states of America, it remains a way of life. There are, I estimate, over two hundred Protestant churches in the county where I live, most of them Southern Baptist. (In 1985 the "Peace Committee" of the Southern Baptist Convention "found that most Southern Baptists . . . believe in direct creation of mankind and therefore they believe Adam and Eve were real persons.")

The two universities in Greenville both have Protestant Christian roots: Bob Jones University (founded and named after the famed evangelist), and Furman University (founded and named after the Southern Baptist minister and educator, Richard Furman). Bob Jones University is proud of its fundamentalist beliefs and orientation. Furman University only recently gained its political independence from the South Carolina Southern Baptist Convention, which used to elect its trustees.

Having spent my youth in New Jersey, I experienced a bit of culture shock upon moving to South Carolina. But I was even more shocked after learning about some of the more embarrassing episodes in southern and local fundamentalist history. Such episodes are worth sharing if only to demonstrate how liberal fundamentalists have become.

Take the issue of slavery:

> In the eighteenth century, defenders of slavery among men of the cloth were
> far more numerous than opponents. "For every John Wesley who was critical,"
> David M. Reimers wrote, "there were several George Whitefields who considered slavery a blessing."[1]

By the mid-nineteenth century, "not one of the major [Christian] denominations other than the Quakers held a strong antislavery position."[2]

The Bible mentions slavery often, yet the "God of the Bible" never condemned the practice. "The Old Testament clearly earmarked *strangers* and *heathens* for servitude and [in the New Testament] the Apostle Paul's admonitions to masters and servants were emphatic (if debatable)."[3]

Not surprisingly, in 1822 Richard Furman (then the president of the Baptist State Convention), wrote a letter to the governor expressing the proslavery sentiments of South Carolina Baptists. In it he eloquently and rationally argued:

> . . . the right of holding slaves is clearly established in the Holy Scriptures,
> both by precept and example. . . .
>   Had the holding of slaves been a moral evil, it cannot be supposed
> that the inspired Apostles, who feared not the faces of men, and were ready

to lay down their lives in the cause of their God, would have tolerated it for a moment in the Christian Church. Or if they had done so on a principle of accommodation, in cases where the masters remained heathen, to avoid offences and civil commotion; yet, surely, where both master and servant were Christian . . . they would have . . . required, that the master should liberate his slave. . . . But, instead of this, they let the relationship remain untouched, as being lawful and right, and insist on relative duties.

In proving this subject justifiable by Scriptural authority, its morality is also proved; for the Divine Law never sanctions immoral actions.[4]

Richard Furman's high appreciation of "Divine Law" reminds me of the fundamentalist bumper sticker: "God said it. I believe it. That settles it!" Perhaps Richard Furman skipped over the part where the Bible states that a master may beat his or her slave within an inch of the slave's life. If the slave dies "a day or two" after the beating, the master is not guilty of the slightest wrongdoing. That is "morality," according to "Divine Law" (Exod. 21:20, 21).

Since the Bible prescribed using "the rod" to discipline one's children, how much more must the whipping of slaves be necessary "to keep them in subjection, to correct them for the neglect of duty, for their vices and transgressions," and so on. In fact, Christian slaveholders could back up their whippings with the *words of Jesus,* who stated in a parable, "And that servant [the Greek word here is ambiguous and also meant, "slave"], which knew his lord's [that is, his master's] will, and prepared not himself, neither did according to his will, *shall be beaten with many stripes*" (Luke 12:47, KJV).

Frederick Douglass, an escaped slave who was raised a Christian and never forsook his faith in God, still had to admit, "Were I to be again reduced to the chains of slavery, next to the enslavement, I should regard being the slave of a religious master the greatest calamity that could befall me. For of all slaveholders with whom I have ever met, religious slaveholders are the worst."[5]

In one instance, Douglass recounted how a slaveholding family (who knelt and prayed together daily) expressed no concern at all that their slaves nearly froze to death every winter due to an inadequate supply of clothing and blankets. To mention another instance from Douglass' book:

In August, 1832, my master attended a Methodist camp-meeting . . . and there experienced religion.

He prayed morning, noon, and night. He very soon distinguished himself among his brethren, and was made a class leader and exhorter. . . .

I have seen him tie up a lame young woman, and whip her with a heavy cowskin upon her naked shoulders, causing the warm red blood to drip; and, in justification of the bloody deed, he would quote the passage of Scripture, "He who knoweth the master's will, and doeth it not, shall be beaten with many stripes."[6]

Furthermore,

Douglass is not the only witness to testify that Christians were the cruelest slaveholders. . . . Henry Bibb . . . lists six "professors of religion" who sold him to other "professors of religion." [One of Bib's owners was a deacon in the Baptist church, who employed whips, chains, stocks, and thumbscrews to "discipline" his slaves.—ED.] Harriet Jacobs, in her narrative, informs us that her tormenting owner was the worse for being converted. Mrs. Joseph Smith, testifying before the American Freedmen's Inquiry Commission in 1863 tells why Christian slaveholders were the worst owners: "Well, it is something like this—the Christians will oppress you more."[7]

Prior to the Civil War, when Richard Furman composed his defense of slavery, there was a single major Baptist denomination. Yet Baptists began to differ strongly over the issue of slavery, an issue that would soon erupt into war between the North and the South.

The proslavery Baptists met in Augusta, Georgia, in May of 1845—the same month that the proslavery Methodists met in Louisville—to found the Southern Baptist Convention. The Southern Baptist Convention, the largest Protestant denomination in the United States, with some fourteen million members, was founded for the sole purpose of defending the institution of slavery.

After the end of the Civil War, Southern Methodists, Southern Baptists, and Southern Presbyterians all continued to denounce emancipation as contrary to the will of God. . . . These three Evangelical denominations . . . taught Southern whites that the North had abused them and that life had been better before the Civil War. They comforted the Southern whites, not only by telling them that they were superior to blacks, but also they were morally superior to Northern whites, who were less religious than they. . . .

The three Southern Evangelical churches achieved great success with this message, and by 1890 they accounted for 95 percent of all Southern church members. And their heritage lives on. Today we are still confronted with Southern Evangelicals who claim that belief in the literal truth of the Bible, the subordination of women, the [harsh physical discipline] of children . . . have all been ordained by God. And none of them will acknowledge— nor do very many even remember—that their religion arose from the theological defense of slavery.[8]

After decades of denouncing the emancipation of the slaves many members of evangelical Southern Protestant denominations applauded the "magnificently constructed" walls of segregation that followed. As Clayton Sullivan recalls:

Blacks were viewed as inferior. They rode at the back of the bus, went to separate schools, lived in shanties on the other side of town, and attended black churches (called "nigger churches"). Nor do I recall from my . . . youth hearing anyone question the justice or injustice of segregation. . . . For a white Southerner to question segregation would have seemed as surprising as to question the existence of God.[9]

In the 1950s Clayton joined nonprejudiced seminarians at the Southern Baptist Louisville Seminary in wincing

> . . . when Dr. W. A. Criswell [the famous Southern Baptist preacher] in Dallas spoke to the seminary students in Alumni Chapel and said, "Fellows, things are changing down home. You used to be able to say 'chiggers.' But now you have to say 'CHEE-groes.' "

Two decades later, things had changed:

> The "impregnable walls of segregation" . . . were not, so it turned out, impregnable after all. . . . [For instance] Mississippi now has the highest number of elected black officials of any state. Negroes patronize motels, restaurants and libraries. The public schools have integrated and blacks compose the backbone of the Ole Miss football team. The only institutions left segregated are *churches,* funeral homes, country clubs, and chapters of the Daughters of the Confederacy.[11] [emphasis added]

Who was it that said, "Sunday morning is the most segregated time of the week in America"?

Here in Greenville, the fundamentalist founder of Bob Jones University, Bob Jones, Sr., cited the apostle Paul's statement in the book of Acts (17:26, KJV) in order to oppose interracial schooling and dating. Paul wrote, "And [God] hath made of one blood all nations of men for to dwell on all the face of the earth, and hath determined the times before appointed, and the *bounds of their habitation*" (emphasis added). Bob Jones, Sr., interpreted Paul's statement in this way:

> If you are against segregation and against racial separation, then you are against God Almighty, because He made racial separation in order to preserve the [Jewish] race through whom He could send the Messiah and through whom He could send the Bible. God is the author of segregation. God is the author of Jewish separation and Gentile separation and Japanese separation. God made of one blood all nations, but He also drew the boundary lines between races . . . [compare Paul's statement, above—ED.]
>
> Slavery was not right. . . . The colored people should have been left over in Africa, and we should have sent missionaries over there and got them converted. That is what we should have done. But we could not have converted them as fast that way; and God makes the wrath of men to praise Him. . . .
>
> We had planned to build a school, just like Bob Jones University, here in the South for colored people. . . . Where Christian colored people could get their education in an atmosphere where their talents in music and speech and art and all could be preserved and handed down. . . . We had that in mind until all this agitation started. . . . [Yet how did "all this agitation" *really* "start?" With the enslavement of a people.—ED.]
>
> No nation has ever prospered or been blessed like the colored people in the South.[12]

So spoke Bob Jones, Sr., in an address delivered over radio station WMUU, Bob Jones University, Greenville, South Carolina, April 17, 1960, transcribed and printed as the pamphlet *Is Segregation Scriptural?*

One Bob Jones University alumnus recalls how he was attending a Bible conference on campus in 1968 when the news arrived of Dr. Martin Luther King, Jr.'s assassination. The audience with few exceptions clapped and cheered on hearing that Bob Jones University would *not* be hanging its American flag at half-mast to honor Dr. King, who was viewed as an "apostate" (see the testimony of Dennis Ronald MacDonald).

Today *Is Segregation Scriptural?* is no longer seen on the shelves of the campus bookstore at Bob Jones University. Furthermore, a handful of *black* students now attend Bob Jones University each year. It seems that the university is gradually losing sight of its founder's original teachings, or, in the words of Bob Jones, Sr., they are going "against God Almighty!"

Another interesting little episode in Greenville's fundamentalist history took place during the 1920s, when the nationwide fundamentalist-modernist controversy was at its height. A revivalist preacher riled up a number of Protestant ministers and their congregations by denouncing the "modernist" teachings found in *Jesus and the Young Man of Today,* a book whose author was at that time the general secretary of the Central YMCA (Young Men's Christian Association) in Greenville, South Carolina. Even Greenville's *Baptist Courier* published several negative editorials, including a front-page exposé that denounced "Mr. Holmes' Teaching," adding, "The man who holds such views . . . HAS NO RIGHT UNDER THE HEAVENS TO HOLD AN EVANGELICAL POSITION THAT IS SUPPORTED BY THE CONFIDENCE AND GIFTS OF EVANGELICAL PEOPLE."[13]

The Directors of the YMCA called a meeting of the supporters of the Young Men's Christian Association and requested Mr. Holmes to make a statement of his belief, which was delivered at the Greenville Public Library, July 3, 1924 (and published as a booklet titled *My Christ*). In his address Holmes explained how he had been raised "in a most orthodox way," the son of a Methodist minister. He had "believed the Bible literally from cover to cover." Then, when he went to college to prepare for the ministry, "It was there that all my [literalist] beliefs were undermined." Holmes did not abandon his faith.

> I can appreciate the feelings of those who oppose me. I remember a few years ago, when I felt like throwing a secretary out of the window of a YMCA building because he stated that some scholars did not believe the Gospel of John to be historical in the same sense as the first three gospels. I said to him, "Does it not say that Jesus said to Nicodemus, 'Ye must be born again.' If you say that that book is not history then that is a lie, and the man who said it is a liar." That is the position which many of you now take. Perhaps I can explain how a man can believe that the Gospel of John is not history and yet can accept the great truth it contains.[14]

Holmes then outlined the full range of his beliefs. The author of the first chapter of Genesis, he said, was not concerned about when the world was created, or how the world was created, but by whom it was created. . . .

The story of the Garden of Eden is a parable to explain the origin of sin in the world. . . .

[Jesus was] a man . . . in whom God completely expressed Himself to the world. . . .

Jesus does not mention His Virgin Birth. Paul does not mention it and does not require belief in it for admission into the Church. . . .

I believe that the perfectly spiritualized body [not the physical body] of Jesus appeared to the disciples. . . . The Bible gives room for [that] interpretation.[15]

Christ reconciled men to God. Every Christian believes that . . . but I cannot accept the substitutionary theory of it. . . . Many of us still worship the God of old. The God demanding bloody sacrifices and gifts to appease his wrath, whereas Jesus said God was our Father and wanted our love and devotion. . . . Breaking rules does not necessarily have to have a penalty. I only punish my boy as I think it is good for him, not that I have any sense of justice to be appeased. GOD IS MY FATHER . . . [therefore] Christ's death was [not a "substitutionary sacrifice," but] an expression of love. His indwelling presence lifts us from sin.[16]

Since he was a member of an evangelical Methodist church, Holmes went on to quote Methodist Bishop Mouzon:

The Bible which we actually have was not verbally dictated. . . . This doctrine will not bear two minutes' investigation with the open Bible in one's hands. Compare, for instance, the history of the Hebrew people as contained in the Books of Chronicles with the history covering the same period contained in the Books of Kings. Compare the account of any miracle recorded in Matthew with the account of the same miracle in another of the Four Gospels. Compare the sayings of Jesus as given in Matthew with those given in Luke, or, for a more striking dissimilarity, with those given in the Gospel according to John. Then compare Paul's quotations from the Old Testament with the actual language of the Old Testament. No, the Bible was not verbally dictated. We make unbelievers out of intelligent people by saying things about the Bible which are not true.[17]

As someone else Holmes quoted once said, "If you do not let people think within the church they will think without it."[18] Holmes also cited Methodist Bishop Denny, who wrote, "A true Christian life is infinitely more valuable than a correct Christian creed without that life. As a matter of fact, what a man *really* believes he lives."[19]

In the end, Holmes was vindicated. In a statement issued by the Board of Directors of the YMCA soon after his speech, they "unqualifiedly endorsed" Holmes "as a man who . . . has few public servants in this community who are his equal and who combines to a rare degree qualities that make him a valuable citizen, an outstanding leader of boys, and a man who in his public and private life furnishes an exceptional example of Christian manhood and teaching."[20]

Of course the editor of the *Baptist Courier* shot back in an editorial (July 17, 1924) criticizing "modernism," that one must believe the "redemptive facts" of Christianity in order to call oneself a "true Christian." Such "facts" in his opinion, could only be affirmed or denied, they were not open to "modernist" interpretations. But that was about all he could say or do, and the matter was soon dropped because the majority of evangelicals who supported the YMCA also supported Holmes's admirable character and the right for him to disagree on matters of theology. Both the Holmes episode (1924) and the famous Scopes "Monkey" Trial held one year later in Tennessee turned into ludicrous failures for fundamentalists of the 1920s. To these must be added the famous "fundamentalist-modernist debates" held in New York City in 1923 and 1924, between Charles Francis Potter and Dr. John Roach Straton (see Potter's testimony elsewhere in this book).

If any lesson is to be gained from this perusal of fundamentalist history, it is that over the centuries fundamentalists have strayed from a forthright biblical defense of slavery and whippings, to preaching segregation, finally even to agreeing, more or less, with certain liberal ideals. That is not to deny that fundamentalists are conservative relative to many of today's "liberal" opinions, but look at how far fundamentalism has come!

And the differences between the majority of today's fundamentalists and their Bible-believing predecessors become even more pronounced the further you look backwards in time.

For instance, you might think that today's fundamentalists who insist that "creation science" be taught in public schools are total literalists when it comes to interpreting the Bible. But even *their* views of what the Bible teaches about creation are "liberal" compared to what Martin Luther and John Calvin (great-granddaddies of Protestant fundamentalism) insisted that Scripture taught. For instance, Luther and Calvin were both geocentrists, and insisted that no matter what Copernicus might say, the Bible says that the sun moves while the earth does not. Job 9:7 states, "He [God] can command the *sun* not to rise," i.e., rather than command the *earth* to stop spinning. Or, as Martin Luther pointed out, "Joshua commanded the sun to stand still and not the earth (Josh. 10:12)."[21]

The Bible also states: "The sun rises and the sun sets; And hastening to its place it rises there again" (Eccles. 1:5, NASB). "Rising" and "setting" may be easy to explain away due to one's earth-bound perspective, but speaking of the sun "hastening to its place" so that it may rise again is not so easy to explain away. It means the author of Ecclesiastes believed that the sun moved daily around the earth. Likewise, the Bible states that the stars "course" through the heavens, constellations are "led forth" in their season, and the constellation known as the "Bear" is "guided," and so on. (Judg. 5:20; Job 38:32, NASB). In reality, the "coursing" of stars through the heavens is an illusion produced by the earth's rotation. The "movements" of constellations in the sky "in their seasons" is another illusion created by the passage of the earth around the sun and the tilt of the earth's axis. Thus, *no one* "guides" the Bear or "leads forth" the constellations at all, even though it is *God* who is employing such language in his discussion with Job! This apparently makes God a liar, or it means that when "God spoke to Job," He deliberately reinforced Job's unscientific notions about the cosmos. Either conclusion produces problems for those who believe the Bible teaches literal scientific truths. (If it did, then God would have asked Job, "Can you 'lead forth' and 'guide' the *earth* in *its* seasons?")

John Calvin, like Luther, agreed that to take the Bible literally meant that one would have to affirm the immobility of the earth. In his commentary on Psalm 93, verse 1, Calvin wrote:

> By what means could it [the earth] maintain itself unmoved, while the heavens above are in constant rapid motion, did not its Divine Maker fix and establish it? Accordingly, the particle, aph, denoting emphasis, is introduced, "YEA, he hath established it."[22]

Calvin even preached that "those who asserted that 'the earth moves and turns' . . . were motivated by 'a spirit of bitterness, contradiction, and faultfinding'; possessed by the devil, they aimed 'to pervert the order of nature.' "[23]

Needless to say, a few fundamentalist Christians still defend geocentricity, based on the literal words of the Bible.[24]

Perhaps even more embarrassing to today's fundamentalists is Martin Luther's literal interpretation of the "firmament" depicted in Genesis:

> A firmament . . . [whose] Maker gives such solidity to this fluid . . . material. . . .
>
> Indeed, it is . . . likely that the stars . . . are fastened to the firmament ["set in" the firmament, Gen. 1:17—ED.] like globes of fire, to shed light at night. . . .
>
> Scripture . . . simply says that the moon, the sun, and the stars were placed . . . in the firmament of the heaven, *below and above which heaven are the waters*. . . .
>
> We Christians must be different from the philosophers in the way we think about the causes of these things. And if some are beyond our comprehension like those before us concerning the waters above the heavens, we must believe them . . . rather than either wickedly deny them or presumptuously interpret them in conformity with our understanding.[25]

Indeed, until the Renaissance both Catholic and Protestant theologians agreed upon and defended the Old Testament concept of vast waters lying above a solid "starry firmament."[26] That is where literal "Bible-science" led them.

But perhaps the greatest difference between today's fundamentalist Christians and their predecessors is their relative levels of tolerance. Today's fundamentalists are generally a *much* more tolerant bunch.

For instance, during the Reformation, Martin Luther argued strenuously for the persecution and/or cold-blooded murder of Jews, witches, Anabaptists, Papists (i.e., Roman Catholics), and peasants (who dared to revolt against their Protestant Christian lords, princes, and kings). What is more frightening, the secular authorities took many of Luther's arguments to heart, which led to the persecution and murder of many.[27]

John Calvin's record for inciting acts of persecution and murder is equally despicable, but not on as grand a scale, since he was the leading religious and moral authority in a single city, Geneva.[28] Nevertheless, the influence of Calvinism eventually extended far beyond the city of Geneva.[29]

The Protestant reformer Melanchthon was a friend of both Luther and Calvin. In Saxony in 1536, Melanchthon prepared, and Luther signed, a document *demanding the death penalty* for denial of any article in the Apostles' Creed. Melanchthon also spoke for many Christians of his day when he advocated the continued use of deprivation and torture on prisoners. As he put it, "Why should we treat them any better in this life than God is going to treat them in the next?" After all, does it not say in the Gospel of John, chapter three (KJV), "He who does not believe is condemned already . . . the wrath of God abideth on him"?

And then there was war.

The Thirty Years' War . . . began in 1618 when Protestant leaders threw two Catholic emissaries out of a Prague window into a dung heap. War flared between Catholic and Protestant princedoms, drawing in supportive religious armies from Germany, Sweden, France, and Italy. Sweden's Protestant soldiers sang Martin Luther's "Ein Feste Burg" in battle. Three decades of combat turned central Europe into a wasteland of misery. One estimate states that due to the war and resulting famine and pestilence, Germany's population dropped from eighteen million to four million. In the end nothing was settled.[30]

Compare the above estimate of deaths in Germany due to the Thirty Years' War, fourteen million dead, with the estimated number of deaths in battle during World War II, about fifteen million according to the *1991 Information Please Almanac*. Keep in mind that World War II was fought on several continents, so the havoc and misery was "spread out," while in the case of the Thirty Years War, all the deaths were concentrated in Europe and centered around Germany. This conflict of Christian kingdoms versus Christian kingdoms, of believers in Jesus' deity and the Trinity fighting believers in Jesus' deity and the Trinity (and of "creationists" fighting "creationists"—contrary to the belief that only "atheist evolutionists" slaughter people *en masse*), produced one of the most concentrated bloodfests in human history. Herbert Langer, author of *The Thirty Years' War,* reminds us that more than just fourteen million Germans perished. More than one quarter of Europe's population died as a result of those thirty years of slaughter.

It was also the first time that firearms were featured in battle. Thank heaven that machine guns, poison gas, and atom bombs had yet to be invented. The antagonists in this conflict would undoubtedly have used them, both sides feeling assured of their salvation in heaven, and their enemies' damnation in hell.

Later, on the North American continent, Puritan preachers referred to Native Americans as "Amelkites and Canaanites"—in other words, people who, if they would not be converted, were worthy of annihilation. Even Maryland's famous Act Concerning Religion, passed in 1649, which supposedly instituted "freedom of religion" for the first time in an American colony, stated in its first section that any person who blasphemed God, denied that Jesus was the Savior and Son of God, denied the Trinity, or uttered "reproachful" words concerning the Trinity "or any of the three persons therein," would be *executed* and their estates forfeited.[31]

A "liberal" fundamentalist of today might argue that the intolerance and murderous proclivities of Christians in the past are not a fair indication of the Bible's "true" teachings. Or, "Christians aren't perfect, just forgiven." So, "fallen human nature" is to blame for the imperfections of fundamentalist Christians, both past and present.

Such an argument is weak beyond belief. It is like admitting that Luther and Calvin, who had the aid of an inerrant Bible, who prayed for, and supposedly received, the wisdom and guidance of God's "indwelling" Holy Spirit, still advocated the persecution and/or massacre of witches, unbelievers, blasphemers, heretics, Jews, Catholics, Anabaptists, and others, without mercy. On the other hand, lesser known and less revered figures, living during the same time period as Luther and Calvin, advocated mercy for the same people whom Luther and Calvin sought to punish and destroy. These lesser known figures, such as Castellio, Erasmus, and Voltaire, voiced teachings on tolerance that have won the approval of the majority of Christians living today (even conservative Christians)! So, whose interpretations concerning these crucial matters were "more inspired"? Luther and Calvin's, or Castellio, Erasmus, and Voltaire's?

Moreover, there is no evidence that Calvin's "fallen human nature" was to blame for the atrocities that his theology commended. For instance, Calvin, "the man," exuded serenity, warmth, and sympathy toward his close friends and those with whom he was in theological agreement. But whenever Calvin "the man" became Calvin "the theologian," at that moment the kindly Dr. Jekyll turned into the evil Mr. Hyde. Acting under the influence of the Bible he let loose a torrent of wrath upon his fellows. In his theological treatises he argued for the death of heretics. He personally prosecuted witches, heretics, and other "disobedient" citizens before the Genevan council. And it was Calvin "the theologian" who employed "abstractions that relieved him of the need to recognize the humanity [of those who disagreed with Biblical truths—ED.]. They constituted 'the mob,' which could be dismissed as 'ignorant and stupid' and consigned to destruction."[32]

In the end, it cannot be denied that it is the Bible, *understood literally,* that is to blame for the monstrous teachings and practices outlined above. But you have to delve deeply into both the Bible and Christian history to discover *why* the blame lies there.

When Christians were in the minority they generally "obeyed the powers that be, which were instituted by God" as the apostle Paul taught. But once Christians constituted a majority the question arose, "What laws should Christian rulers decree for their kingdoms?"[33] Among Protestant rulers and kingdoms, the answer to this question lay ultimately in the Bible. What do the Bible's two Testaments say?

The New Testament contains Jesus' commands in his Sermon on the Mount. Individual Christians might be able to obey some of those commands, but if a *kingdom* of Christians were to decree only those commands it "would be necessary to put up with everybody's whim and insolence. Personal safety and private property would be impossible, and finally the social order would collapse," as Luther pointed out. So, the New Testament can't provide a *kingdom* with laws.

Furthermore, the New Testament defers to the Old when the subject of "law" arises. Jesus stated, "I have not come to abolish the Law and the Prophets . . . but to fulfill them. Till heaven and earth pass away, not an iota, not a dot, will pass from the [Old Testament] Law until all is accomplished. . . . Whoever, then, relaxes one of the least of these [Old Testament] commandments and teaches men so, shall be called least in the kingdom of heaven" (Matt. 5:17–19). And Paul wrote, "Do we, then, overthrow the [Old Testament] Law by this faith? By no means!" (Rom. 3:31). But *which* laws should be adopted from the Old Testament, and which should not?

According to the New Testament certain Old Testament laws were clearly no longer in force, such as animal sacrifices, since Jesus was the "final sacrifice"; nor certain dietary laws and cleansing practices, nor circumcision. Other laws of the Old Testament remained in force, such as the commands to punish thieves and murderers, whereupon Protestant theologians agreed that a Christian ruler ought to decree the punishment of "heretics" also, since their teaching "murders" a person's immortal soul. It states in the Old Testament that a father may kill someone who is directly threatening the life of his child. How much more so is killing justified in cases where the *eternal life* of a child (or adult) is being threatened by the spread of false doctrine? Such "heretic snuffing" logic is flawless *once you accept that "false beliefs" damn one's soul eternally.*

Further Old Testament laws unequivocally support such heavenly logic. Each Israelite is to "stone to death" their "brother, son, daughter, wife, or best friend" if that person tries to "entice them away to serve other gods" (Deut. 13:6–9). The same penalty applies to "blasphemers" (Lev. 24:16). Furthermore, "You must not allow a witch to live" (Exod. 22:18). And those who interpret omens, or practice divination, or sorcery, should be "driven out" (Deut. 18:10).

And if you accept the Old Testament's explanation of why the kingdom of Israel (and other kingdoms) were at times "cursed," it would be natural to assume, in a similar fashion, that the God-sustained safety of a kingdom was "at risk" once "false doctrines" or "heresy" were allowed to spread. After all, didn't God destroy the whole earth with a Flood because mankind displeased Him? And didn't God tell his chosen people to kill "everything that breathed" in the Canaanite cities that displeased Him? (Deut. 2:34, 7:1–2, 20:16–17; Num. 31:17; 1 Sam 15:3—not to mention what happened to Sodom and Gomorrah). So if anyone living in a kingdom with Christian rulers was foolhardy enough to "entice others to serve other gods," or "blaspheme," or, say or do things that could be interpreted as "displeasing to God," there was little doubt how Christian magistrates were going to react. Thumbs down.

Of course, when Christians were a powerless minority, Jesus' commands in the Sermon on the Mount more nearly fit their situation. It was only after Christians became rulers that they were put in the situation of having to decree "laws" for their *kingdom or nation*. In that case, God's "everlasting" holy laws found in the Old Testament provided "direction." So, *different parts of the Bible can be, and usually are, focused upon depending on whether or not Christians are a powerless minority, or "law-givers" of a kingdom or nation.*

Some readers may no doubt wish to ask how the Reformers, Luther and Calvin, could remain so blind to Jesus' emphasis on "love." The Sermon on the Mount may not decree laws by which a kingdom should be ruled, but it does contain lessons in *leniency*. However, the Reformers were quick to point out that Jesus was not "all that lenient" when it came to God's honor, and neither was there any reason to believe that the *laws of a kingdom* ruled by Christians ought to be "lenient" when the necessity of *honoring God* was at stake.

The New Testament warns against the danger of "false Christs" arising and "deceiving many." Therefore a Christian ruler, having been forewarned, should seek to protect his subjects from the spread of "false doctrines about Christ."

Even Jesus' teachings in the New Testament leave room for intolerant legislation to be passed by Christians against all others. For instance, the Bible contains sayings by Jesus that echo the command in the book of Deuteronomy to "kill" your "brother, son, daughter, wife, or best friend" should they attempt to "entice you away to serve other gods" (13:6–9). Jesus said, "Suppose ye that I am come to give peace on earth? I tell you, Nay; rather division: For from henceforth there shall be five in one house divided, three against two, and two against three. The father shall be divided against the son, and the son against the father; the mother against the daughter, and the daughter against the mother. . . . If any man come to me, and hate not his father and mother, and wife, and children, and brethren, and sisters, yea, and his own life also, he cannot be my disciple." (Luke 12:51–53 and 14:26, NASB)

As Luther and Calvin pointed out, Jesus' command to "love your enemies" meant to "love *your* enemies," i.e., personal enemies. It did not mean that you had to "love *God's* enemies." Did Jesus "love" the Pharisees who opposed his preaching? Or consider Jesus' command not to call anyone "*raca*" (Aramaic for "empty-head," or "good for nothing"). That command obviously did not apply to *God's* enemies, whom Jesus denounced in the most inflammatory terms, calling them names that were far worse than "*raca.*"

Luther pointed this out in his commentary on Matt. 5:44, "Love Thy Enemy":

Christ pronounces "Woe!" upon the Pharisees [He says, "You blind fools . . . you serpents, you brood of vipers, how shall you escape the sentence of hell?" (Matt. 23); "You are of your father the devil" (John 8:44)]. . . . Stephen reads a hard and sharp text to the high priests (Acts 7:51–53) . . . Paul says to Elymas: "You son of the devil . . . full of all villainy!" (Acts 13:10) . . . and Paul puts it all on one pile and calls everyone *anathema,* that is, excommunicated and cursed and sentenced to the abyss of hell, who does not preach the pure teaching about the faith (Gal. 1:8). . . .

That is how God's word proceeds . . . denouncing and cursing their whole way of life, something that is not proper for you or me to do as individual Christians except in our office and our teaching position. . . .

So far as his neighbor's person is concerned, a Christian will love and bless everyone. But on the other hand, so far as God and His Word are concerned, He will not put up with any transgression. He must give this precedence over everything else and subordinate everything else to it, irrespective of any person, be he friend or foe; for this cause belongs neither to us nor to our neighbor, but to God, whom it is our duty to obey before anything else (Acts 5:29, "We must obey God rather than men"). Consequently, I say to my worst enemies: "Where it is only my own person that is involved, there I am very willing to help you and to do everything good for you, in spite of the fact that all you ever do for me is to harm me. But where it is the Word of God that is involved, there you must not expect any friendship or love that I may have for you to persuade me to do something against that, even if you were my nearest and dearest friend. But since you cannot endure the Word, I will speak this prayer and benediction over you: 'May God dash you to the ground!' I shall willingly serve you, but not in order to help you overthrow the Word of God. For this purpose you will never be able to persuade me to give you a drink of water." In other words, our love and service belong to men. But they belong to God above all; if this is hindered or threatened, love and service are no longer in place. For the command is: "You shall love your enemy and do him good." But to God's enemies I must also be an enemy, lest I join forces with them against God. . . .

Therefore, even though personally they (i.e., Christians who serve as spiritual and secular officials) may be gentle, yet administering justice and meting out punishment (i.e., to "witches," "heretics," "blasphemers," etc.) is their official work; and it has to go on. It would be wrong if their pity moved them to neglect this; for that would be tantamount to helping, strengthening, and encouraging the evil . . . [of] our enemies, the pope, the bishops, the princes, and all the rest, who are persecuting the Gospel and trampling its poor adherents underfoot. . . .[34]

Calvin agreed with Luther:

"Love itself [ought] to abide under purity of faith." If both lay claims, we must not give in to pity.[35]

We should not set human considerations above God's service. We must forget humanity and spare not kin or blood when the matter is to combat for His glory. . . .

We ought to trample under foot every affection when it is a question of God's honor. The father should not spare the son, the brother the brother, nor the husband his own wife. If he has some friend who is as dear to him as his own life, let him put him to death if he is a heretic or false prophet. . . .[36]

[Civil government] . . . prevents idolatry, sacrilege against God's name, blasphemies against his truth, and other public offenses against religion from arising and spreading among the people. . . . In short it provides that a public manifestation of religion may exist among Christians, and that humanity be maintained among men. . . .

[T]hose laws are preposterous which neglect God's right and provide only for men. . . . [Therefore] let Christian princes and magistrates be ashamed of their negligence if they do not apply themselves to this concern.[37]

So, Christian "teachers and theologians" are empowered by God to denounce heresies and blasphemies in the harshest terms possible. And Christians who rule over a nation full of believers (like their Old Testament counterparts) ought to decree "holy" laws that maintain "God's honor," rather than laws that "honor" the heresies and blasphemies of "fallen" mankind.

Not surprisingly, the Bible continues to fuel the flames of behavior reminiscent of Luther's and Calvin's day. In Kanawha County, West Virginia in 1974, fundamentalist Christians protested the use of school textbooks that introduced "Godless" viewpoints, a protest that led to two men being shot, news crews beaten, a local minister praying for the pro-textbook committee to be struck dead by God, school buses being stopped enroute to school, cars set aflame, and schools dynamited.

Fundamentalist Bible believers, called "reconstructionist" Christians, have established a movement to return to Luther and Calvin's biblical views, and to remake America into a nation with "Scriptural" laws. For instance, they would like to see legal discrimination against homosexuals. Some fundamentalist Christians have even admitted that instead of mere legal discrimination they would be pleased to fully obey the Old Testament command to "stone" anyone caught practicing "homosexuality." But they admit that we would first have to become a "*very* Christian nation" before such a penalty had the least likelihood of being written into America's lawbooks. What do they envision beyond that? How about burning witches (or practitioners of "New Age" healing and meditative techniques)? Luther said, "I would have no compassion for a witch; I would burn them all."[38] In fact, in southwestern Germany, 3,200 "witches" were executed during the years 1562–1684.[39]

After the "heretic," Michael Servetus, was burnt at the stake in Calvin's Geneva, a book was published anonymously which raised the question, *Should Heretics Be Persecuted?* By way of reply Calvin composed, *A Little Book on the Duty of Civil Magistrates to Punish Heretics,* in which he repeated many of the arguments discussed above.

Regardless of the biblical purity of Calvin's replies, Christians in increasing numbers began to question the wisdom of persecuting heretics. The advent of the printing press was making the spread of "heresies" and new ideas in general, more difficult to halt, regardless of whether the authors of such books could be found and executed. Harsh experiences, like the Thirty Years' War, taught that wars fought in order to preserve the integrity of one's faith and Christian nation brought nothing but ruination and plagues instead of "blessings" from God. (Unfortunately for the Protestants, and their Bible-based faith, none of the walls of their enemies came "a tumblin' down" miraculously like the "walls of Jericho." Neither were they fortunate enough to engage in battles where their side "lost not a single man," as in some Old Testament tales.) With both Catholics and Protestants exhausted after the Thirty Years' War, and neither side able to persuade (or impose its will upon) the other, trade and travel gradually increased. This led to the consternation of merchants and travellers who often had to pass through several countries in the course of a single journey, each country having its own state-imposed religion, supported by princely decree. If intolerance were to increase rather than diminish, then every merchant and traveller who journeyed across Europe would have to "change their religion" as often as they exchanged their money at the boarders, making hypocrites of many.

Rising out of the ashes of bitter experience and biblical debate, the seed of "tolerance" took root and continued to attract intelligent, eloquent advocates. There were, for instance, the writings of the Christian humanist scholar, Desiderius Erasmus (who wrote *In Praise of Folly* and admired "Saint Socrates"), Castellio (presumed to be the author of *Should Heretics Be Persecuted?*), John Locke (author of *The Letter on Toleration*), Baruch Spinoza (who wrote a *Theological-Political Treatise*). And there was the wise and witty Voltaire, whose essay "On Tolerance," Benjamin Franklin adored.

Toleration was born of lengthy experience and reasoning, not divine revelation. Divine revelation taught men to both hate and love "with a vengeance." So naturally, many Bible believers for centuries abundantly loved all "insiders" (or those whom they were hoping to lead "inside"), and viewed all "outsiders" with suspicion or derision.

One consequence of literally believing the Bible involves psychologically projecting what one knows is worst about oneself onto "outsiders," (and blinding oneself to the existence of genuine goodness in "outsiders"). It also involves projecting what one knows is best about oneself onto "insiders" (and blinding oneself to the existence of evil in fellow "insiders").

One biblical belief in particular creates and magnifies the force of such "projections." Namely that, "Insiders are all going to heaven, while outsiders are all going to hell." So there *can't* be anything essentially wrong with "us" (we are "born again," we are "sanctified," we are "baptized in the Holy Ghost," we have the "correct faith," we are the "elect" and so on), while there *must be* something essentially wrong with "them" (otherwise they would not be "eternally damned," which they "obviously" are—just look at what they believe).

But, as Joseph Campbell pointed out concerning the growing human population and our increasingly fragile natural and political environments:

> We can no longer hold our loves at home and project our aggressions elsewhere; for on this spaceship Earth there is no "elsewhere" any more. And no mythology that continues to speak or to teach of "elsewheres" and "outsiders" meets the requirements of this hour.[40]

There is one further episode in the history of fundamentalist religion that I would like to draw to the reader's attention. All democratic nations owe a great debt to Europe's first major experiment in adopting the republican form of government and "liberal democratic" ideals, which took place in the Netherlands in 1579. At that time Europe was ruled by kings, queens, and princes. The king of the Netherlands, however, died, leaving a not-yet-born child as his heir. Partly due to this unforseen circumstance (and the growth of an educated and wealthy upper class) the Dutch "stumbled" into forming a republic. Soon thereafter, Amsterdam became the envied center of all who loved freedom in Europe. As the philosopher Baruch Spinoza wrote:

The city of Amsterdam reaps the fruit of this freedom in its own great prosperity and in the admiration of all other people. For in this most flourishing state, and most splendid city, men of every nation and religion live together in the greatest harmony, and ask no [religious] questions before trusting their goods to a fellow citizen. . . . His religion and sect is considered of no importance; for it has no effect before the judges in gaining or losing a cause, and there is no sect so despised that its followers, provided they harm no one, pay every man his due, and live uprightly, are deprived of the protection of the magisterial authority.[41]

Or, consider this description from a fellow of the Royal Society of London:

Here is the greatest Equality in the World. . . . Certainly when I do reflect upon the miserable condition of some Christians in Europe; as of the peasants in Lytuania, and almost all over Poland, where the Lords have the power of hanging them, when they run away from their tyranny; in Bohemia, and some other place of Germany; in Denmarke and Sweden, where the Gentlemen do highly abuse the Commons; I cannot chose but cry out, O Happy Holland, that hast preserved that precious jewel of Liberty; preserve it well, for with its loss, goes that of thy happiness![42]

People who live in democratic nations today cannot even begin to imagine the curtailment of liberties their ancestors suffered under, when state religions were imposed upon the populace of each nation and enforced by a king. And it should be remembered that this experiment in the Netherlands *failed,* because the Calvinist "fundamentalists" of that day grew appalled at how tolerant the upper classes had grown!

The Calvinist spokesman, Gybertus Voetius, Professor of Theology and Oriental Studies at the University of Utrecht, complained that the Dutch East India [trading] Company had made so small a number of converts in Asia. . . .
[Later] . . . the Calvinist consistory of Batavia reminded the Governor-General, Maetsuycker, that the Law of Moses forbade the tolerance of non-Christian religions . . . [to which] he replied . . . "The laws of the old Jewish republics have no force in the territory of the Dutch East India Company!"[43]

The tolerance extended toward the religious beliefs and practices of Hindus and Moslems who worked for the Dutch East India Company angered the Calvinists greatly. The Calvinists comprised the majority of the lower classes, and had leaders who wanted the Netherlands to resemble Calvin's Geneva. The upper classes were by and large "liberal democrats" who defended Arminian ["free will"] Protestantism, and who opposed Calvinist doctrines like "predestination to eternal hell" and "infant damnation." The Calvinists called these "liberals" by another name, "Libertines," a term used by Calvin to designate a religious sect, widespread in France and the Netherlands, which emphasized the "Spirit" over the "letter of the Law." These "Libertines" and their preference for a democratic form of government were portrayed by Calvinists as a peril to the nation's security. The Calvinists were adept (then, as now) at playing on everyone's fears. (The Netherlands had only recently broken free from Catholic Spain's rule, and the Thirty Years' War in Europe would begin in less than forty years.) The Calvinists felt the nation would be "securer" if it returned to a biblically acceptable form of government, a kingship. The Calvinists' ultimate wish, however, was that "there may be only one religion in the state; all heretics must be driven out; for better is a desolate city than a trafficking city full of sectarians."[44]

In 1618 the Thirty Years' War began and the Calvinists capitalized on the commotion by aiding a prince to take control of the state. They condemned all who opposed them, forcing them to "recant" or choose exile. They interrogated Oldenbarnevelt, an elder statesman and "liberal democrat," for several days, then hanged him. Thus the "little monsters of the new Holland inquisition"[45] took control. But the lesson in freedom taught by the Netherlands' republican form of government was not soon forgotten. It gave others the inspiration and courage to pursue liberal democratic and republican ideals, which eventually led to our own country being founded on such ideals.

By the way, one of the "liberal democrats" who lived in Amsterdam during the period spoken of above was Hugo Grotius, the founder of international law. He collected many passages of moral and spiritual worth in the Greek and Latin classics and published them beside corresponding biblical passages in his *Notes on the New Testament.*

Today the majority of American fundamentalists do not appear as eager as their predecessors to overthrow the government and install a king, no matter how "biblical" that concept may be. Neither are they in agreement with John Winthrop, a Puritan and the first governor of the Massachusetts Bay Colony, who called democracy "the meanest, and worst of all forms of government." In fact, many of the political and religious ideals of today's fundamentalists more closely resemble those of "liberal democrats" or "Libertines" of the seventeenth century!

Today's fundamentalists are also, in general, more "liberal" than their predecessors in spooning out doses of Jesus' love rather than filling up on hellfire sermons morning noon and night. For example, they are less likely to rush out and buy a copy of Jonathan Edwards's famous sermon, *Sinners in the Hands of an Angry God* (which went through eight editions in the later half of the eighteenth century). Nor are they likely to sing about the ecstasy of viewing the torments of the damned, a theme employed by the popular hymn writer Isaac Watts (1674–1748):

> What bliss will fill the ransomed souls,
> When they in glory dwell,
> To see the sinner as he rolls,
> In quenchless flames of hell.

Incidentally, Watts composed his hymns around the time of the "Great Awakening," a religious revival that swept through America's colonies from the 1720s through the 1740s. The philosopher-theologian Jonathan Edwards (who taught that Jesus would return "soon") was a leading light of the "Great Awakening." And it may have been Edwards's exposition of the Bible that inspired Watts's verses. Edwards elucidated the matter thus:

> The glorified saints will see the wrath of God executed upon ungodly men. This the scriptures plainly teach us, that the righteous and the wicked in the other world see each other's state. Thus the rich man in hell, and Lazarus and Abraham in heaven are represented as seeing each other's opposite states, in the 16th chap. of Luke. [The rich man sees Lazarus being comforted, and Lazarus sees the rich man writhing in pain.] The wicked in their misery will see the saints in the kingdom of heaven; Luke 13:28,29. "There shall be weeping and gnashing of teeth, when ye shall see Abraham, and Isaac, and Jacob, and all the prophets in the kingdom of God, and you yourselves thrust out."
>
> So the saints in glory will see the misery of the wicked under the wrath of God. Isa. 66:24. "And they shall go forth and look on the carcases of the men that have transgressed against me: for their worm shall not die, neither shall their fire be quenched." And, Rev. 14:9,10. "If any man worship the beast and his image, and receive his mark in his forehead, or in his hand, the same shall drink of the wine of the wrath of God, which is poured out without mixture, into the cup of his indignation; and he shall be tormented with fire and brimstone, in the presence of the holy angels, and in the presence of the Lamb." The saints are not mentioned, being included in Christ, as his members. The church is the fulness of Christ, and is called Christ, 1 Cor. 12:12. So in the 19th chapter, verse 2,3 the smoke of Babylon's torments is represented as rising up for ever and ever, in the sight of the heavenly inhabitants . . . [Furthermore, Jesus spoke a parable that ended with the words, "Bring them here and slay them *in my presence.*" Luke 19:27.]
>
> When the saints in glory, therefore, shall see the doleful state of the damned, how will this heighten their sense of the blessedness of their own state, so exceedingly different from it! When they shall see how miserable others of their fellow creatures are, who were naturally in the same circumstances with themselves; when they shall see the smoke of their torment, and the raging of the flames of their burning, and hear their dolorous shrieks and cries, and consider that they in the meantime are in the most blissful state, and shall surely be in it to all eternity; how they will rejoice! . . .
>
> How joyfully will they sing to God and the Lamb, when they behold this!
>
> [Psalm 58:10 "The righteous will rejoice when he sees the vengeance; he will bathe his feet in the blood of the wicked." And in Isaiah 30:27–33, the nation of Assyria is depicted metaphorically as a human figure being sacrificed and slain by Yahweh; this act being accompanied by festival songs, gladness of heart, the sound of the flute, tamborines and lyres.][46]

The popularity of this "abominable fancy" began to diminish during the age of the Enlightenment, at which time Thomas Burnet dared the sarcastic remark:

> What a theatre of providence this is: by far the greatest part of the human race burning in flames forever and ever. Oh what a spectacle on the stage, worthy of an audience of God and angels! And then to delight the ear,

while this unhappy crowd fills heaven and earth with wailing and howling, you have a truly divine harmony.[47]

In short, fundamentalists today appear considerably more tolerant, generally speaking, than their predecessors. Mind you, the change has taken time.

Even on an individual level, it sometimes takes years for a once zealous Protestant fundamentalist youth to learn the valuable lessons life and history have to offer. They must first pass through

> that bitter and heartrending period of youth which comes before we realize the one grand and logical basis of all optimism—the doctrine of original sin. The boy at this stage being an ignorant and inhuman idealist, regards all his faults as frightful secret malformations, and it is only later that he becomes conscious of that large and beautiful benignant explanation that the heart of man is deceitful above all things and desperately wicked.[48]

Thus sayeth the evangelical Christian "humanist," G. K. Chesterton. I agree with Chesterton, at least metaphorically. The "doctrine of original sin" should be looked upon as a "large and beautiful benignant explanation," rather than as a reason to despise or deeply distrust yourself or other people. It should open a fundamentalist Christian to consider the weaknesses and faults we *all* share (Christians included), and what forgiveness and tolerance we ought to extend toward one another, every day.

Or, put in terms that a secular humanist and evolutionist might agree with, none of us is perfectly "tame." We still have our "claws" and will use them (either physically or verbally) given enough provocation. So we all need to practice tolerance and forgiveness for the sake of the obvious benefits we can all enjoy in doing so. It seems an irrefutable truth to me, regardless of religious or philosophical differences, that joys shared are doubled, while sorrows shared are halved.

May this book add impetus to the age-old fundamentalist pilgrimage toward more liberal perspectives.

Notes

1. Forrest G. Wood, *The Arrogance of Faith: Christianity and Race in America from the Colonial Era to the Twentieth Century* (New York: Knopf, 1990), p. 292. It should be added that although John Wesley viewed the plight of slaves with compassion, he might have liked to see "witches" persecuted, perhaps even punished with death (the Biblical penalty that Puritans in Salem, Massachusetts enforced). As Wesley lamented in his journal, "The giving up of witchcraft is in effect the giving up of the Bible" (*Journal of John Wesley,* 1766–1768).

2. Donald B. Gibson, "Faith, Doubt, and Apostasy," in *Frederick Douglass: New Literary and Historical Essays,* ed. Eric J. Sundquist (New York: Cambridge University Press, 1990), p. 88.

3. Wood, p. 83. For verses in the New Testament endorsing slavery see Col. 4:1; Titus 2:9–10; Ephesians 6:5–8; 1 Peter 2:18–20; and 1 Tim. 6:1.

4. Richard Furman's entire letter appears as appendix B of James A. Roger, *Richard Furman: Life and Legacy* (Macon, Ga.: Mercer University Press, 1985), pp. 274–86.

5. Frederick Douglass, *Narrative of the Life of Frederick Douglass: An American Slave* (New York: Penguin Books, 1982, originally published in 1845), p. 117.

6. The Frederick Douglass passage was reproduced as cited by Steven Overholt in "God's Word," *The Frontline,* tract #28, April 1990. The original source is presumably Douglass' autobiography, *The Narrative of the Life of Frederick Douglass: An American Slave* (1845).

7. Gibson, p. 89.

8. James Hill, "How We Got the Bible Belt," *Free Inquiry,* vol. 12, no. 1 (Winter 1991/92): 36–37.

9. Clayton Sullivan, *Called to Preach, Condemned to Survive: The Education of Clayton Sullivan* (Macon, Ga.: Mercer University Press, 1985), pp. 141–42.

10. Ibid., p. 143.

11. Ibid., p. 154.

12. Bob Jones, Sr., *Is Segregation Scriptural?* (Greenville, S.C.: Bob Jones University, 1960), pp. 16, 19, 22, 24–25, 32.

13. "Mr. Holmes' Teaching," the editor of *The Baptist Courier* (Owned and controlled by the Baptists of South Carolina), vol. 55, no. 26, June 26, 1924, p. 15.

14. John M. Holmes, *My Christ* (Greenville, S.C.: Central Young Men's Christian Association, July 1924), p. 7.

15. Does the entire New Testament agree that Jesus' *physical* body emerged from an "empty tomb?" No. The *earliest* written testimony to Jesus' "resurrection" is found in the letters of the apostle Paul, which do not mention an "empty tomb." The most that Paul admits is that Jesus "appeared" to various brethren (1 Cor. 15). Furthermore, Paul considered his own testimony to Jesus' "appearance" as equal to that of the other apostles, in which case Jesus' "appearances," may refer to something as incorporial as hearing a heavenly voice and seeing a bright light (which was all that "appeared" to Paul).

In fact, when Paul states that Jesus "appeared" to "over five hundred brethren at once" (1 Cor. 15:6), that would have been to a far greater number of "brethren" than were said to have existed before Jesus' *physical* body supposedly rose into the clouds. (Only one hundred and twenty "brethren," "all of one mind," existed at that time—Acts 1:9, 14–15, 22.) So by the Bible's own admission, whoever or whatever may have "appeared" to "over five hundred brethren" could *not* have been a *physically* resurrected Jesus, since his body left the earth before that many "brethren" existed.

Moreover, in 1 Corinthians, chapter 15, Paul specifically addressed the question, "How are the dead being raised? With what kind of body are they coming?" and he answered that they would *not* be raised with an "earthly body," but a "*spiritual* body." "What you sow is *not* the future body but a *bare grain,* whether of wheat or of some other variety" (1 Cor. 15:37). Interestingly enough, once a "bare grain" is split open by the emerging plant, the seed invariably leaves behind its "husk" or "shell." Surely that fact was not lost on Paul. In fact, Paul's "spiritual body" lacks earthly flesh and blood *and* a stomach: "Flesh and blood cannot inherit the kingdom of God" (1 Cor. 15:50). "Food is for the stomach, and the stomach is for food; but God will do away with both of them" (1 Cor. 6:13). Thus, Paul's notion of a raised "spiritual body," and his lack of all mention of an "empty tomb" can be cited as evidence that Paul believed Jesus' *earthly body* remained buried.

It is *later* Gospel traditions that mention an "empty tomb" and have the resurrected Jesus appear *entirely physical.* According to the Gospels of Luke and John, Jesus plainly has a stomach, puts food in it, invites Thomas to touch his wounds, and asks, "Does a spirit have flesh and bones?" Neither does Jesus qualify that statement by adding that he now has "spiritual flesh" (and "spiritual bones"?!) as opposed to merely "earthly flesh." Rather, the raised Jesus is depicted as saying he has "flesh and bones" *exactly* like the apostles, and totally *un*like any "spirit's," and he eats a piece of fish (Luke 24:39–43)!

Here lies a knotty problem: If Paul is correct that earthly "flesh and blood *cannot inherit the kingdom of God,*" then what is Jesus doing in the Gospel of Luke eating *earthly fish flesh*? Did the fish miraculously change into "spiritual fish flesh" as soon as it passed Jesus' lips, so that he might digest it? What an odd miracle that would be for God to perform, just to "keep up the appearance" that Jesus was exactly like the apostles in his "flesh and bones."

And if the resurrected Jesus indeed ate the piece of fish, might he not also have *defecated* it? After all, if "flesh and blood *cannot* inherit the kingdom of God" how much less can "fish flesh" inherit it? Furthermore, did the resurrected Jesus have a "stomach" at all, or *no* stomach, as Paul says in 1 Cor. 6:13?

This represents a genuine problem for fundamentalists, who must "harmonize" the early Pauline notion of a raised "spiritual body" with the grossly physical conceptions found in the Gospels which were written at a *later* date.

Also consider these Pauline verses, which agree with the "spiritual body" idea, rather than a physical one: "If our earthly, tent-like house should be destroyed, we have a building from God, a house not made with hands, eternal in the heavens. . . . We long to clothe ourselves over with our dwelling which comes from heaven. . . . We have this treasure in earthen pots . . . in our mortal flesh . . . our outer person is being wasted away. . . . Indeed, while we are in this tent we are sighing under the burden, because we do not wish to unclothe ourselves, but to clothe ourselves over, that mortality may be engulfed by life. . . . For while we are at home in the body we are away from our home with the Lord. . . . We are resolved instead to get away from being at home in the body and to get on home to the Lord" (2 Cor., chapters 4 & 5).

"Mortal flesh" could "waste away" or be "destroyed" (or left in a tomb to rot) for all Paul cared. He focused instead on the "*spiritual* body," "the eternal dwelling *which comes from heaven.*" How unlike the way later Gospel writers emphasized the raised Jesus' physical earthly flesh!

The "empty tomb" is first mentioned in the Gospel of Mark, where it states that the ladies who discovered it "said nothing to anyone." That is how the earliest known copies of Mark's Gospel end. Notice that such an ending gives scholars exactly the reason they need to declare that the "empty tomb" story may have been a late legend, for if the ladies "told no one," then *no one* may have heard about such a tale until years later, perhaps even after the destruction of Jerusalem at which time the city was in such a shambles with so many people dead that no one could ever hope to trace the origins of such a story. Lengthier and more detailed "empty tomb" legends appear in the Gospels of Matthew, Luke, and John, all of which were completed *after* Mark.

There are also good reasons to suspect that the story of Lazarus' resurrection (found only in the Gospel according to John) was a later invention of the Christian community. It was born from the amalgamation of people, places, and parables from earlier gospels. The story, found only in John's Gospel, of Mary (the sister of Martha) anointing Jesus' feet and then wiping them with her hair (in the village of Bethany) is also an amalgamation of stories found in earlier gospels. According to those stories, Jesus was anointed in different towns by two different women (Mark 14:3; Luke 7:37-38). John's Gospel mixes together elements of those earlier stories to construct a third tale of Jesus being anointed! Only the *name of the town* in Mark's account ("Bethany") is used, where an unidentified woman anointed Jesus' head. It is combined with the *actions* of an unidentified female "sinner" who performed her anointing in a different town, "Nain." That "sinner" "anointed Jesus' feet and wiped them with her hair." And the town and action was then combined with the *name of a person,* "Mary." But this "Mary," found in Luke 10:38-39, lived in a town whose name was not mentioned, and merely "*sat* at Jesus' feet" without anointing them. Anyone can see that the name of the town, the action, and the name of the person given in Mark and Luke's Gospels have been mixed together to form a new "anointing" tale in the last written Gospel.

Likewise, the tale of Lazarus' resurrection is mixed together from names and circumstances found in a previous gospel, Luke. The sisters, "Mary and Martha" are drawn from Luke 10. But in the Gospel of Luke there is no mention of the sisters having had a "brother"—"Lazarus" appears not as the "brother" of Mary and Martha, but merely as *a character in one of Jesus' parables.*

In Luke, Jesus' parable of the rich man and Lazarus ended with the admonition, "neither will they be persuaded if someone rises from the dead." (The figure in the parable *does not* rise from the dead.)

Now compare the story found in the Gospel of John. "Lazarus" is no longer a figure in a parable, but depicted as a genuine person, the brother of Mary and Martha, who *does* rise from the dead, due to God's and Jesus' intervention. And, in accordance with the admonition at the end of Luke's parable, John depicts the Pharisees as not being "persuaded," even though someone named "Lazarus" does in this case "rise from the dead." In fact, they react yet more negatively, and decide to have Jesus crucified *because* of the unsettling nature of this "resurrection" that only the author of John's Gospel depicts Jesus performing! (The other gospels say that it was the "overturning of the tables in the Temple" that made the Pharisees finally decide to have Jesus killed. Instead, the author of John's Gospel placed the table–turning episode in the *beginning* rather than near the end of Jesus' ministry, so as not to take away from his invention of the miraculous tale of Lazarus' resurrection.)

John's Gospel is a *theological* creation, from its first chapter, incorporating Greek philosophy ("In the beginning was the Word [=Logos]"), to Jesus' long-winded prayer about "oneness," supposedly spoken by Jesus on the eve of his death (taking up all of chapter 17, twenty-six verses—and recalled exactly by "John" decades later?). Furthermore, Jesus' (and John the Baptist's) speeches suspiciously resemble the gospel author's own theological musings delivered in the first chapter of his gospel. The same metaphorical contrasts are employed by all three. And instead of Jesus' pithy sayings and parables of the kingdom of God found in the previous three Gospels, John's Jesus speaks primarily of and about himself, "I am the light of the world . . . I am the way the truth and the light . . . I am the resurrection and the life . . . I am the good shepherd." In John's gospel the prophet who announced God's words has become transformed into "the Word." The messenger has become far more important than the message. Belief in the messenger has become the whole point of Jesus' mission according to the Gospel of John. This does not agree with the first three gospels, in which Jesus stressed the connection between salvation and moral *actions*. Therefore, there is reason to suspect that John's Gospel is not the most accurate, but contains speeches and tales concocted at a later date. The "Gospel of John" even ends by stating that it was written "that ye may believe." How objective could such a work be?

16. Holmes, *My Christ*, pp. 13, 20, 22, 28, and 36–38.

17. Bishop Mouzon, "Contend Earnestly for the Faith Which Was Once For All Delivered Unto the Saints," *The Methodist Quarterly Review*, April 1923, as cited by Holmes, *My Christ*, p. 42.

18. Holmes, *My Christ*, p. 43.

19. Bishop Denny, "Some Functions of a Creed," *Methodist Quarterly Review*, April 1923, as cited by Holmes, *My Christ*, p. 47.

20. Holmes, *My Christ*, p. 4, "Statement of the Board of Directors of Central YMCA, Greenville, S.C."

21. Martin Luther, "Table Talk." *Luther's Works*, vol. 54, ed. and trans. Theodore G. Tappert (Philadelphia: Fortress Press & Concordia Publishing House, 1967), p. 359.

22. John Calvin, *Commentary on the Book of Psalms*, trans. James Anderson (Eerdmans, 1949), vol. 4, p. 7.

23. John Calvin, "Sermon No. 8" on 1st Corinthians, 677, cited in *John Calvin: A Sixteenth Century Portrait* by William J. Bouwsma (Oxford Univ. Press, 1988), p. 72.

24. "I would not be a geocentrist if it were not for the Scriptures," stated Gerardus D. Bouw at the 1984 National Bible-Science Conference. Dr. Bouw is head of the "Tychonian Society" a group of fundamentalist Christians who attempt to bolster their Bible-based geocentric viewpoint with "scientific" arguments.

25. Martin Luther, "Lectures on Genesis." *Luther's Works*, vol. 1, ed. Janoslaw Pelikan (St. Louis: Condordia Publishing House, 1958), pp. 25, 30, 42, 43.

26. See Hyppolytus, *The Discourse of the Holy Theophany*, 1, where water "obtains a seat" above "the highest vault of the heavens." St. Basil, *Exegetic Homilies* (Washington, D.C.: Catholic University of America Press, 1963), p. 42. St. Ambrose, *Hexameron, Paradise, and Cain and Abel* (New York: Fathers of the Church, 1961), pp. 52–56. St. Augustine, *The Literal Meaning of Genesis* (New York: Newman, 1982), 1.52. St. John Chrysostom, *Homilies on Genesis 1–17* (Washington, D.C.: Catholic University of America Press, 1985), p. 168.

27. In his early ministry Martin Luther spoke favorably of the Jews, and condemned their

mistreatment by the Catholic church. But when the Jews failed to respond to his preaching, Luther viciously attacked them. He may have been consciously following Jesus' example in that respect. (Read Jesus' condemnation of those who failed to respond to his preaching in Matt. 23.)

> We will believe that our Lord Jesus Christ was truthful when he declares of the Jews who did not accept but crucified him, "You brood of vipers and children of the devil." (Martin Luther, *On the Jews and Their Lies*)

Luther went on to declare in *On the Jews and Their Lies* that Christian rulers must see to it that the Jews' synagogues were burned "so that God might see that we are Christians, and do not condone or knowingly tolerate such public lying, cursing, and blaspheming of his son." Also, that their houses and sacred writings be destroyed, that their rabbis be forbidden to teach, and that "safe-conduct on the highways be abolished completely for the Jews." (So, as they fled from the desolation of their homes and former synagogues any highway-robber could murder them and steal what little possessions they had left.)

In 1525 when the peasants revolted against their cruel and corrupt landlords, Martin Luther sided unequivocally with the lords and rulers. He wrote "Against the Robbing and Murdering Hordes of Peasants," a pamphlet that he attributed to divine revelation. In it he stated that,

> To kill a peasant is not murder. . . . Crush them! Cut their throats! . . . Leave no stone unturned! . . .
>
> It is a trifle for God to massacre a lot of peasants, when He drowned a whole world with a flood and wiped out Sodom with fire. He is an almighty and frightful God. . . .
>
> If there are innocent men amongst the peasants, God will certainly prepare and keep them, as He did with Lot and Jeremiah.

Luther recommended the same treatment for the Anabaptists, who were "left-wing Lutherans" who preached and practiced a form of socialism in the sixteenth century. "Many Anabaptists were beheaded with the official approval of Luther, who regarded their heroism in the face of death as proof of diabolic possession."

For a concise collection of the inflammatory teachings of Martin Luther and the criminal actions his teachings inspired, see Peter F. Wiener's little book, *Martin Luther: Hitler's Spiritual Ancestor* (Austin, Texas: Gustav Broukal Press, 1985), copies of which are available from American Atheists Books.

28. For twenty-two years John Calvin headed the "Consistory" of Geneva, Switzerland, a body of men who militantly ordained the religious worship and moral conduct of everyone in Geneva. He also organized the pastors of Geneva into "the Venerable Company." Together these organizations held greater sway over determining the town's laws and their enforcement than the Town Council. People were fined or imprisoned for dancing too gaily at their own daughter's wedding, wearing their hair too high, wearing breeches (a popular form of pants in those days), etc.

On the darker side, more than twenty witches were executed in one year on the charge that they had persuaded Satan to afflict Geneva with plague. According to McNiell's *The History and Character of Calvinism,* "Calvin held traditional beliefs about witchcraft, was involved in the prosecutions, and did nothing to assuage this irrational cruelty."

Calvin's biblically persuasive arguments resulted in the executions of over a hundred people during the time he headed the Consistory. His laws, based on the Bible, included severe demands. In one instance, a small boy in Geneva was beheaded for having struck his father (i.e., based on the command to put to death anyone who curses their father or mother, Lev. 20:9).

> [And] in 1555 Calvin demanded that the council apply the death penalty to adulterers of both sexes (i.e., in accordance with the command found in Lev. 20:10). The Council balked, but five years later, in 1560, Calvin managed to have two unfortunate men . . . decapitated for having engaged in adulterous liaisons with married women. He also had a number of adulteresses tossed into the Rhone with great rocks tied round

their necks. Calvin also arranged for young unmarried girls who had lost their virtue to be imprisoned and heavily fined. Upon their release . . . their heads were locked in iron collars and the poor creatures were forced to stand for several hours, either at the Molard or at the Church . . . on Wednesdays—so that after the . . . Wednesday sermon, all those who departed from church might insult and revile them. But that was not all! Even if those girls married the men who had seduced them, the ministers who performed the wedding ceremony were obliged to publicly denounce their "shame" from the pulpit. (Soledad de Montalvo, *Women, Food and Sex in History,* vol. 3 [Austin, Tex.: American Atheist Press, 1988], p. 787.)

Yet even with an omnipresent Consistory keeping an eye on everybody, able to search anyone's house without a search warrant, and with Calvin preaching several times a week (attendance was compulsory), the records of the Council for this period nevertheless reveal a high percentage of illegitimate children, abondoned infants, forced marriages, and sentences to death.

There was a little excitement in Geneva when Calvin's brother's wife was apprehended in the act of adultery with Calvin's hunchback servant, Pierre Daguet. In her defense, we have to remember that opportunities for fun and games were scarce in Geneva, and she couldn't be too choosy. A little later Calvin's stepdaughter Judith was caught doing the same thing (with a different fellow). (Charles Merrill Smith, "John Calvin," a chapter in *When the Saints Go Marching Out* [Garden City, N.Y.: Doubleday & Co., 1969].)

Geneva's most prominent affliction (besides Calvin) was the plague, a particularly virulent strain, killing, by one estimate, nine out of ten people who contracted it. (See Montalvo's book, mentioned above.)

Regardless of their belief in the Bible as the word of God, and their implementation of many of God's holy commands, there remains no evidence that the Genevese of Calvin's day received miraculous "blessings" in return. Today, Geneva is no longer overwhelmingly Protestant, but 47 percent Catholic.

Those who would like to learn more about Calvin and his Geneva should consult (besides the books mentioned above):

J. M. Audin, *History of the Life, Works, and Doctrines of John Calvin* (Louisville, Ky.: B. J. Webb & Brother, undated [1890s?]).

David Cuthbertson, *A Tragedy of the Reformation: Being the Authentic Narrative of the History and Burning of the "Christianismi Restitution," with a Succinct Account of the Theological Controversy Between Michael Servetus, Its Author and the Reformer, John Calvin* (New York: AMS Pr., 1912).

Will Durant, "John Calvin: 1509-64," in *The Reformation* (*Story of Civilization,* vol. 6) (New York: Simon and Schuster, 1957), pp. 459ff.

Albert Rilliet, *Calvin & Servetus: The Reformer's Share in the Trial of Michael Servetus Historically Ascertained,* trans. W. K. Tweedie (New York: AMS Pr. reprint of 1846 ed.).

29. See for instance Franklin Palm, *Calvinism & the Religious Wars* (New York: AMS Press reprint of 1932 edition).

30. James A. Haught, *Holy Horrors: An Illustrated History of Religious Murder and Madness* (Amherst, N.Y.: Prometheus Books, 1990).

31. Madalyn Murray O'Hair, "The Christianity of Our Founding as a Nation," in *What on Earth is An Atheist?* (Austin, Texas: American Atheist Press, 1969), pp. 235–39.

32. William J. Bouwsma, *John Calvin: A Sixteenth Century Portrait* (Oxford, 1988), p. 101.

Calvin "the man's" warmth, and Calvin "the theologian's" coldness appear side by side in a letter Calvin wrote to Melanchthon (Geneva, March 5, 1555). [The letter in its entirety may be found in *John Calvin: Selections from His Writings,* ed. John Dillenberger (New York: Anchor Books, Doubleday & Company, 1971), p. 56.]:

Your letter, most renowned sir, was grateful to me, not only because whatever comes from you is dear to me, and because it let me know that the affection, which you entertained for me in the commencement of our intercourse, still remains unaltered; but above all because in it I find a magnificent eulogium, in which you commend my zeal in crushing the impiety of Servetus.

Servetus was condemned to death for the "heretical" beliefs and "impious" statements found in his books, and Calvin was the chief prosecutor at Servetus' trial. Notice in the letter above, Calvin's human side, his mutual "affection" for Melanchthon. But "above all," Calvin prized being "commended" for his "zeal in crushing impiety." In short, his theology triumphed over his humanity.

As a man he [Calvin] was not cruel, but as a theologian he was merciless; and it was as a theologian that he dealt with Servetus. (Unnamed "theologian" quoted by Paul Feyerbrand in *Farewell to Reason* [New York: Verso, 1987], p. 21.)

The serenity and warmth that characterize Calvin's letters to his close friends . . . contrasts strongly with the tone of his published writings or the record of his public office. (Suzanne Selinger, *Calvin Against Himself: An Inquiry in Intellectual History* [Hamden, Conn.: Archon Books, 1984], p. 104.)

33. For information on the history of *early* Christian civilization, i.e., the Christianized Roman Empire, see the previous section, "What You Should Know About Fundamentalism," footnote number 5.

34. Martin Luther, from his commentary on Matthew 25:44, "Love Your Enemies." *Luther's Works*, vol. 21, *The Sermon on the Mount (Sermons) and the Magnificat*, ed. Jaroslav Pelikan (Philadelphia: Concordia Publishing House), pp. 119–24.

35. John Calvin, cited in Suzanne Selinger, *Calvin Against Himself: An Inquiry in Intellectual History* (Hamden, Conn.: Archon Books, 1984), pp. 104.

36. John Calvin, *A Little Book on the Duty of Civil Magistrates to Punish Heretics*, 1554.

37. John Calvin, cited in William J. Bouwsma, *John Calvin: A Sixteenth Century Portrait* (Oxford, 1988), p. 213.

38. Martin Luther, cited without references in *The Heretic's Handbook of Quotations*, ed. Charles Bufe (San Francisco, Calif.: See Sharp Press, 1988), p. 173.

39. H. Erik Midelfort, *Witch Hunting in Southwestern Germany, 1562–1684* (Stanford University Press, 1972).

40. Joseph Campbell, *Myths to Live By* (New York: Bantam Books, 1982), p. 275.

41. Baruch Spinoza, *Tractatus Theologico-Politicus,* quoted in Lewis Samuel Feuer, *Spinoza and the Rise of Liberalism* (Boston: Beacon Press, 1958), p. 65.

42. W. A., Fellow of the Royal Society, quoted in Lewis Samuel Feuer, *Spinoza and the Rise of Liberalism*, pp. 65–66.

43. Lewis Samuel Feuer, *Spinoza and the Rise of Liberalism*, pp. 67–69.

44. Ibid., p. 74.

45. Ibid., p. 75.

46. Jonathan Edwards, *The End of the Wicked Contemplated by the Righteous; Or, The Torments of the Wicked in Hell, No Occasion of Grief to the Saints in Heaven,* Section I, "When the Saints in Glory Shall See the Wrath of God Executed on Ungodly Men, It Will Be No Occasion of Grief to Them, But of Rejoicing," and Section II, "Why the Sufferings of the Wicked Will Not be Cause of Grief to the Rightous, But the Contrary" (Posthumous Discourse, March, 1773). Reprinted in *The Works of President Edwards*, vol. 4 (New York, N.Y.: Burt Franklin, 1968 reprint of the London 1817 edition, 10 v.), pp. 506–507 and 512.

Elsewhere Edwards stated:

The sight of hell torments will exalt the happiness of the saint for ever. . . . (*The Eternity of Hell Torments* [Sermon, April 1739]].)

Can the believing husband in Heaven be happy with his unbelieving wife in Hell? Can the believing father in Heaven be happy with his unbelieving children in Hell? Can the loving wife in Heaven be happy with her unbelieving husband in Hell?

I tell you, yea! Such will be their sense of justice that it will increase rather than diminish their bliss. (*Discourses on Various Important Subjects,* 1738.)

Edwards also stated in *Remarks on Important Theological Controversies,* chapter 2, "Concerning the Endless Punishment of Those Who Die Impenitent" (reprinted in *The Works of President Edwards,* vol. 8 p. 339):

> They [the saints] shall not be grieved, but rather rejoice at the glorious manifestations of God's justice, holiness, and majesty in their [the damned's] dreadful perdition, and shall triumph with Christ; Rev. 18:20; and 19 at the beginning. They [the damned] shall be made Christ's footstool, and so they shall be the footstool of the saints. Ps. 68:23. "That thy foot may be dipped in the blood of thine enemies, and the tongue of thy dogs in the same."

Now I know why the apostle Paul spoke about God "doing away with the stomach" in the afterlife (1 Cor. 6:13)—because who could keep their food down while viewing such sights as Edwards gleefully depicted?

47. Thomas Burnett, *De Statu Mortuorum & Resurgentium Tractatus* (1720), cited in *The Decline of Hell: Seventeenth-Century Discussions of Eternal Torment* by D. P. Walker (Chicago: Chicago University Press, 1964), p. 32.

To be precise, Burnett was addressing a very early manifestation of the "abominable fancy," voiced by the Church Father, Tertullian (155-222 A.D.), who wrote with ghoulish anticipation:

> But what a spectacle is already at hand—the return of the Lord . . . and there are still to come other spectacles—that last, that eternal Day of Judgement . . . when this old world and its generations shall be consumed in one fire. How vast the spectacle that day, and how wide! What sight shall wake my wonder, what my laughter, my joy and exultation? as I see all those kings . . . groaning in the depths of darkness! and the magistrates who persecuted the name of Jesus, liquefying in fiercer flames than they kindled in their rage against Christians! . . . the philosophers blushing before their disciples whom they taught that . . . men have no souls at all, or that what souls they have shall never return to their former bodies! . . . and, next, the athletes to be gazed upon, not in their gymnasiums but hurled in the fire . . . [etc.] (*De Spectaculis,* XXX [from *Tertullian. Apology. De Spectaculis,* trans. T. R. Glover (New York: G. P. Putnam's Sons, 1931), pp. 297, 299].)

48. G. K. Chesterton, *Robert Browning* (London: Macmillan Co., 1914).

Part Three

Testimonies of
Former Fundamentalists
Who Are Now Moderate Evangelical,
Liberal, or Ultra-Liberal Christians

He drew a circle that shut me out,
Heretic, rebel, thing to flout.
But love and I had the wit to win:
We drew a circle that took him in.
——Edwin Markham

Photo by Chase Ltd.

Dewey M. Beegle: Journey to Freedom

One of the books prescribed by the Free Methodist Home Course of Study was *The Christian Faith* by Olin A. Curtis, professor of systematic theology at Drew Theological Seminary. For years he had wrestled with biblical data and sought some frame of reference to accommodate all the evidence. One day on a quiet hilltop near Marburg, Germany, there suddenly came to him "a vision of the full Christian meaning of the human race." The implications of that vision caught hold of me also, and I began to think in terms of a more ecumenical, mediating type of ministry, one that would more readily and effectively help "to obtain a race of holy persons."

—Dewey M. Beegle

Dewey M. Beegle is professor emeritus at Wesley Theological Seminary and an ordained clergyman of the United Methodist Church. He is also on the board of trustees and the translations subcommittee of the American Bible Society. His works include *God's Word Into English, The Inspiration of Scripture* (expanded and retitled *Scripture, Tradition and Infallibility*), *Moses: The Servant of Yahweh*, and *Prophecy and Prediction*. He has also composed articles on Moses for *Encyclopaedia Britannica* and the *Anchor Bible Dictionary*. The following was composed especially for this book.

Two of the greatest passages of Scripture come from Jesus and Paul: "If you continue in my word, you are truly my disciples; and you will know the truth, and the truth will make you free" (John 8:31–32, NRSV), and, "For freedom Christ has set us free. Stand firm, therefore, and do not submit again to a yoke of slavery" (Gal. 5:1). Both claims were made to counter the views of sincere legalists who believed that they were truly free. These insights are just as crucial and relevant today because human nature has not changed.

My journey from right-wing Christianity has brought me into contact with many others in their search for freedom. Our stories, with numerous similar experiences, reveal a basic pattern of actions by the elders whose traditions have been challenged.

Enlightened commitment, so indispensable for healthy growth, should be far more evident than it is. Unfortunately, zeal without knowledge and understanding seems to flourish and plague society, both secular and religious.

It is obvious that *fundamentals* are basic to success in all athletic activities and this is equally true of endeavors in society. The problems of right-wing *fundamentalism* are: (1) its failure to determine a coherent set of genuine fundamentals; and (2) its use of unethical means to defend its traditions.

What is not often recognized is that there are *left-wing fundamentalists* as well. In the circular spectrum of belief the two groups of extremists are back to back, facing in opposite directions while making their divergent claims. Yet in temperament, disposition, and attitude they are similar: they have the same psyche, being wired the same way. This is evident in the examples where rabid right-wingers flip over to the left while some left-wingers move the other way. Another difficulty with extremists is that being *one-eyed* (either left or right) they lose the accurate gauge of two-eyed depth perception, so crucial for a proper understanding of reality.

In assessing the reactions of the elders we have understood them as rising from insecurity or fear, yet this interpretation has been stoutly rejected. How else can devious means, "fighting like the devil," be explained? A very subtle transition has occurred in these people who began their religious journey with such sincerity and honesty. In defense of the faith, some ancient traditions were expanded to meet the challenges of our modern, scientific culture. Gradually these elaborations about Jesus and Scripture became the foundation for faith and displaced the earlier joy of personal relationship: "being in Christ." Since these views had become part of their egos, defense of God became defense of self, and faith shifted from the living Christ to human doctrines. This is similar to the religious idolatry the ancient prophets had to contend with.

The ultimate and perennial problem in right-wing Christianity is the failure to be inductive in its study of Scripture. This is no doubt a reaction to the findings of critical scholars over the last two hundred years. The frustration of trying to get traditionalists to examine the data of the Bible led some critics in the nineteenth and twentieth centuries to a negative attitude which delighted in undermining Scripture by exposing its defects. But many biblical scholars have had a genuine faith. They did not invent these difficulties: they were simply trying to explain how these problems, both explicit and implicit, happened to occur.

Some fundamentalists accept the insights of lower (textual) criticism, but in the area of higher criticism (who wrote the book; when, where, why, and to whom was it written) no findings are considered valid, even though formulated during millions of study hours over two centuries. Since few, if any, persons or institutions have been completely wrong, one wonders why right-wing scholars didn't have some uneasiness and twinges of conscience. Apparently, a gut-level fear wiped out such openness because acceptance of any critical conclusions would involve a radical change in orientation, even some denial of previous convictions. Since memories of encounters with critical data linger on, this is an appropriate place to begin the story of my journey.

My first protest was at birth in Seattle, Washington, on 17 January 1919. My parents, Burton Linton and Gladys Juliette (Smith) Beegle, were devoted Christians and active members of the Free Methodist Church. Mother had a desire to become a missionary and apparently influenced Father, professor of Mathematics at Seattle Pacific College, to accept appointment as a missionary in old Panama City, Panama. They had an effective ministry (1922–26) opening up new churches and maintaining an elementary school, but serious cases of malaria necessitated their return. I can remember the whole experience, even the trip to Panama via New York City. A very influential factor was having playmates of various races. Beyond the differences of culture and color I began to see them as human beings like myself. This basic attitude has been a blessing ever since.

When Father returned to Seattle Pacific College to assume his former position, I began a life oriented around a campus where I would complete grade school, high school, and college. Since school work came easily I was pushed ahead and became the campus pest or pet among the older students with whom I palled. On 6 June 1938 I received a B.S. with a major in mathematics and a minor in psychology, along with a diploma qualifying me to teach in the grade schools of Washington State. A rather unusual sidelight at graduation was a photo of me in gown holding my two-month-old daughter, Kathryn Nadine. As a freshman I was going with Josephine High and on hearing that our parents were thinking of breaking up our romance, we eloped on 12 May 1936 to get married. This episode was traumatic for the community, our parents, and us, but we all survived. With help I was able to finish college.

From August 1938 to May 1941, I was teaching grades five to eight at the Northwood School, north of Lynden, Washington, near the Canadian border. On 22 October 1940 Barbara Lee came to bless our home. While I enjoyed teaching, weariness set in with the necessary duties at the grade school level. As a possible way out I took a civil service exam for border patrolman in the U.S. Immigration and Naturalization Service. The results were satisfactory and I was interviewed for a possible appointment as an immigrant inspector. The expectation was an assignment at one of the small stations along the border. To my utter surprise and the consternation of Border Patrol friends who had taken tests for inspector, I was assigned to San Francisco, California, the largest port of entry on the West Coast.

It was an exceedingly interesting job involving a variety of duties: inspecting the crew and passengers of ships; holding warrant hearings; and deporting aliens convicted of illegal entry. A depressing experience was the afternoon and evening of 7 December 1941 (Pearl Harbor), spent fingerprinting hundreds of Japanese, some of whom had been classmates in college.

Although I had a family, in November 1942 I enlisted in the U.S. Coast Guard Reserve (under the Navy during the war), knowing full well that we were guarding many distant coasts. In spite of a college degree and teaching experience, the recruiting officer said that I was still too young to be granted officer's rank, therefore I was required to attend the four-month officers training school at the Coast Guard Academy, New London, Connecticut. I would not want to go through the experience again, but the benefits were invaluable. Because of my knowledge of the whole San Francisco Bay area, my first assignment was to the captain of the Port Unit there.

While I was on duty in San Francisco, the Free Methodist Church held a revival meeting with Nathan Cohen Beskin as evangelist. During the years in Seattle I had experienced repeated high-pressure revivals with numerous trips to the altar, so that I was not very keen about getting involved in another one. Moreover, the evangelist, whom I had heard while at Seattle Pacific College, majored in prophetic themes with predictions of Christ's imminent return. Nevertheless, in order to avoid criticism I attended the service on 13 January 1944.

I was amazed to see and hear a transformed Beskin. His former dogmatism and showmanship had been replaced with a warm message of God's love and care. Before I realized it, I was walking up to the altar, where I committed myself into God's hands. As a result of the difficult Depression years, with salaries so desperately low, I vowed that I would never go through the penny-pinching experiences of my parents. I had chided Father for not accepting a more lucrative teaching position, but he thought it better to rear his family in a Christian environment with some physical sacrifices than to move to a more secular situation with more money. Whereas the idea of the ministry had been a bitter prospect, the new relationship with Christ transformed that bitterness into peace and joy.

Even though I was in the military service, the California Conference of the Free Methodist Church took me under care, and I began a home course of study. I was promoted regularly in the Immigration Service during the years in the Coast Guard (Navy), but to certify my commitment I burned the bridges behind me by resigning as an immigrant inspector. My friends thought I had taken leave of my senses! During the tour of duty as line and gunnery officer on two ships in the Pacific, I served as an assistant or unofficial chaplain with a number of opportunities to witness by life and word.

After being discharged in April 1946, I intended to accept a church in California because I had acquired some distrust of theological education. However, a wise old minister convinced me to take advantage of the forty-eight months of GI Bill credited to me. Accordingly, in June 1946 I enrolled at Asbury Theological Seminary, Wilmore, Kentucky, since in 1945 the John Wesley Seminary Foundation of the Free Methodist Church had been incorporated within Asbury. I did not have a church appointment while at Asbury, but I substituted a number of times for some of my classmates who had charges in Ohio and Indiana.

One of the books prescribed by the Free Methodist Home Course of Study was *The Christian Faith* by Olin A. Curtis, professor of systematic theology at Drew Theological Seminary. For years he had wrestled with the biblical data and sought some frame of reference to accommodate all the evidence. One day on a quiet hilltop near Marburg, Germany, there suddenly came to him "a vision of the full Christian meaning of the human race" (p. 316). The implications of that vision caught hold of me also, and I began to think in terms of a more ecumenical, mediating type of ministry, one that would more readily and effectively help "to obtain a race of holy persons" (p. 317).

Some aspects of life at Asbury contributed to this vision, but I did not get a balanced presentation of theological and critical issues because the basic conservatism of the faculty fostered a negative, defensive stance. This changed in the fall of 1947 when Claude H. Thompson joined the faculty. He had studied at Drew University and Theological Seminary, where his intellectual life was stimulated by Edwin Lewis.

Concerning his favorite teacher, Thompson commented, "Here was a man who had struggled through the modernist fundamentalist controversy in America and had seen the seeds of decay in a kind of liberalism that had much academic respectability but little Gospel. . . . During my five years of study with him, I felt I was on a pilgrimage not only in intellectual pursuits but in a positively exciting spiritual endeavor."

Lewis had drunk from the well of Olin Curtis, and so Claude Thompson was the embodiment of the best in the Curtis-Lewis tradition. His lectures were a breath of fresh air that energized many of us. However, the right-wingers were alarmed and wanted to report the "so-called" heresy to other faculty members. Some of us seniors urged them to refrain from starting a controversy because we needed both points of view.

I had promised to return to California on graduation from Asbury and take a church, but some of my professors urged me to continue studying for the doctorate. It was a total surprise and took me a few months to accept the idea. Since they had received their Ph.D. at Harvard University, they recommended that I apply to study there because I would have Robert H. Pfeiffer as a teacher and could learn how to counter the views of his massive volume *Introduction to the Old Testament* (1941). I checked with Claude and he thought that would be a mistake. As at Asbury, a number of the dominant faculty members at Wheaton, Fuller, Gordon, etc. had earned their Ph.D.s at Harvard. This group of right-wingers picked safe topics for their dissertations, dodged all the critical courses they could and learned little in those they had to take because they reacted negatively. This core of professors controlled the thought of the National Association of Evangelicals and helped found the Evangelical Theological Society, based on belief in the inerrancy of the original documents of Scripture.

Claude was fearful that I might react similarly and so he urged me to study with William F. Albright at The Johns Hopkins University, Baltimore, Maryland. Since he was the son of a Methodist missionary to Chile, he would be far more helpful in making the transition to a critical methodology for Old Testament research. I applied to both schools, thinking that they would determine my fate, but in the spring of 1948 I received notice from each admissions office that I had been accepted and the scholarship offered was identical. Since I could not dodge the moment of truth, I chose Hopkins, and after graduation on 30 May 1948, Claude Thompson drove us to Baltimore to begin three difficult years. Our expectation was to return to Wilmore because the seminary had requested that I join the Old Testament faculty on completion of the program at Hopkins.

For the first year in Baltimore I was assistant minister at the First Free Methodist Church, then ordained deacon in July 1949. For the next two years I was pastor of the Sailor's Union Bethel Church in South Baltimore. The original church, on the old sailing vessel *William Penn,* was organized by Methodist businessmen as a spiritual home for sailors in port. The idea of a "Ship Church" originated with Methodists in the New York Conference and they founded *Bethelship* in Brooklyn, New York.

During the summer of 1949 I received news that after our more mature class graduated in May 1948, disenchanted students began reporting the contents of

Claude Thompson's lectures to other professors so that their classes became diatribes attempting to refute Thompson's views. It was time to organize a support group for Claude, therefore during Christmas vacation 1949 I returned to Wilmore to interact with my former teachers. In a sense I was also a former colleague because during 1947–48 I had the pleasure and challenge of assisting Harold Greenlee, professor of New Testament, in teaching two classes of Elementary Greek.

I pleaded for a broad-gauge view that would affirm the Gospel of Jesus Christ while being open to a view of inspiration that could be honest with all the data of Scripture. The usual rebuttal was a plea for a positive Gospel, implying that attention to critical matters was negative. I noted the far too high mortality rate of Asburyians who had gone out thinking they had the necessary answers only to drop out of the ministry in disgust because of the warped education they had received. Professor Albright was well quoted by the seminary faculty, but only when he agreed with their views. When asked whether the world-famous scholar could be correct in some areas where he disagreed with the Asbury agenda, the innocent (and arrogant) rejoinder was the assurance that eventually Albright would come over to their side.

After consulting with Thompson's friends I had a memorable chat with Claude. He urged me to stay out of the battle because the seminary needed me on the faculty. I assured him that I was with him all the way. If the seminary community could not tolerate such an honest, gracious Christian gentleman as he, there was no way I would accept the faculty appointment and bite my tongue for fifteen to twenty years hoping for *the day of freedom.*

I returned to Baltimore with a heavy heart. Later, news arrived that nine faculty had walked into a meeting of the Asbury Board *without* an invitation and threw down the gauntlet by announcing that they would resign from the faculty if Claude Thompson were not fired.

Claude loved teaching and thought that Asbury was where he belonged, but to avoid further distress in the seminary community he resigned. After three dedicated years Claude and Sue went out, like Abraham and Sarah, not knowing where they were going. Emory University in Atlanta, Georgia, realized the worth of this couple, and Claude spent the rest of his days teaching and counseling at Candler School of Theology.

In June 1951, after completion of the comprehensive written exams at Hopkins, I received word, as the result of an earlier interview with Eugene A. Nida, that I had been hired by the Translations Department of the American Bible Society to work on *The Comparative English Bible.* My task was to provide footnotes for the King James text indicating variant readings and renderings of the English Revised, American Standard, and Revised Standard Versions.

My wife had never been completely in sympathy with the decision to enter the ministry and after five difficult years during my graduate training she decided it was best to separate. In order to begin work on the new project at the Bible House, I moved to the Biblical Seminary, 235 E. 49th St., New York City, where I was to begin part-time teaching in September.

The year 1952 was climactic in many ways: I finished my dissertation on the complete Dead Sea Isaiah Scroll; was ordained as an Elder in the Free Methodist

Church; was married to Marion Ethel Butterworth by her father Edwin, with whom I had served in the Baltimore Free Church; passed the extensive German-style oral exam and received the Ph.D. degree from The Johns Hopkins University. Marion welcomed the girls as her own and helped educated them at Houghton Academy and College by working at the reception desk at the seminary. She has been a wonderful companion and supporter during the years of our theological journey.

Another key event in 1952 occurred in September when the complete Revised Standard Version (RSV) was published. While attending a session in a Brooklyn Church, I heard some right-wingers exploding with indignation when they found that the RSV had "young woman" (rather than "virgin") in Isaiah 7:14. "We must have our own translation," they declared.

That sentiment, expressed in many places, was the beginning of the New International Version (NIV). The furor that accompanied the publication of the RSV revealed a tremendous ignorance about the history of biblical manuscripts and translations, therefore I wrote *God's Word Into English* (1960) to help bridge the gap in knowledge.

In 1955, when the American Bible Society project was completed, I began full-time teaching at the Biblical Seminary (now known as the New York Theological Seminary). My relationship with the American Bible Society was continued, however, as a member of the Translations Committee and the Board of Managers (now the Trustees). The major task (1961–76) was checking the various drafts of the Today's English Version (TEV), the text of the Good News Bible, and serving during the last year as coeditor of the TEV along with Howard Clark Kee.

During the summers of 1957, 1960, and 1963 I taught at Young Life Institute, Fountain Valley, Colorado. In faculty discussions and counseling with students it became evident that the doctrine concerning Scripture was the most vexing problem. This was certainly true at Asbury and to some extent at Biblical. Many young evangelicals were being turned off by the doctrine of inerrancy and the dogmatic apologetics associated with it. I consulted with friends, suggesting that they tackle the problem.

Since no one took up the task, I decided to offer an alternative view of inspiration, following the lead of Olin Curtis and James Orr, who claimed that the term "inerrancy" was neither biblical nor defensible. The manuscript was revised a number of times to include comments by friends who had read it. On 9 May 1962 I signed a contract with the Westminster Press. In an attempt to keep the cost of the book down the text had to be shortened a number of pages, and so it was not as well balanced as the original text.

I had had a number of contacts with Carl F. H. Henry, editor of *Christianity Today*, and knew of his interest in the subject, so I wrote him on January 21, 1963, to announce that *The Inspiration of Scripture* would be published on April 15. I urged him to request page-proof for review purposes, and hoped that the *Christianity Today* review would be objective, thus helping contribute to the dialogue within evangelical circles. To reassure Henry, I commented, "I expect criticism, and in fact I welcome constructive criticism, so I do not want a blanket approval."

Henry's distress over the book was very evident in the April 26, 1963, issue of *Christianity Today*: it contained three reviews! Frank E. Gaebelein, Headmaster of The Stony Brook School, Stony Brook, New York, was asked to write the basic review. Since he had some of my former students on his staff he asked them for their comments. Accordingly, he made a number of revisions so the review (covering more than three pages) was less critical.

Henry was displeased with Gaebelein's review so he wrote one of his own, seven thousand words long, titled, "Yea, hath God said . . . ?" (six pages of fine print).

Gaebelein told me later that he asked to have his review removed since Henry was writing the major review, but Henry retained Gaebelein's review anyway.

David E. Kucharsky, news editor of *Christianity Today*, got into the act with a one-page, fine-print news report laced with critical comments which sounded like Carl Henry. He had phoned me to get some personal data and in the conversation he wanted to know why I had never joined the Evangelical Theological Society.

I explained that I agreed with the Society in its concern for the biblical Good News offering spiritual healing and a transformed life, but I could not honestly sign the creedal claim of "inerrancy" because it meant accepting the theories developed during the modernist-fundamentalist battle in the late nineteenth and early twentieth centuries. Some of my friends had reinterpreted the term and joined, therefore I knew what was going on. But I was never invited to any special sessions dealing with the authority and inspiration of Scripture because the Evangelical Theological Society did not consider my definition of "evangelical" valid. Kucharsky's label "sometime evangelical scholar" and over ten pages of reviews reveal how galling my book was for *Christianity Today* people.

Early in 1963 Marion and I decided to travel west, attending graduation exercises at Asbury since it was my fifteenth anniversary, then on to Seattle Pacific College for my twenty-fifth anniversary since graduation. Little did we dream that Carl F. H. Henry would be the graduation speaker at *both* schools!

I spotted him first while he was touring the Asbury Library and came up behind him. He was shocked to see me and wondered why I was there. I noted that I had come back for my fifteenth anniversary. Then he said he would like to talk with me. We agreed to meet at the Greenlee home after the evening service, 27 May. Others shared in our two-hour conversation, but my inductive approach with stress on the biblical data was parried by Henry's dialectical arguments and deductive approach. I asked him what "sometime" meant. When he was reluctant to define it as "former," I wondered why, as editor, he had not checked Kucharsky's report. He said that he was so busy working on his review *he did not have time,* but that was hardly a valid excuse because he could have checked one page of text while doing the review.

The answer to the problem came four months later. During the Lake Forest Consultation, an ecumenical discussion about Scripture held at Malone College, Canton, Ohio, 19–22 July 1963, I presented a paper, "The Authority of Extant Scripture." Frank Gaebelein, designated coeditor of *Christianity Today* to function while Carl Henry was on sabbatical, was in attendance and he was very active in the discussions. While he was reluctant to give up the term "inerrancy," he was a gracious Christian gentleman and thought that a number of the accusations Henry had made were uncalled for.

One of the first things Gaebelein did on assuming his new duties was to ask Kucharsky why he had called me a "sometime evangelical." He said that two weeks before his story was due, Henry had called him into his office and listed six reasons why I had put myself outside the evangelical camp. In essence then, Henry had determined a major part of Kucharsky's report. After Gaebelein's conversation Kucharsky wrote me a gracious letter offering to publish a retraction in *Christianity Today*. I thanked him, but declined his offer because that would not have been fair to him. It was Carl Henry who should have made the retraction.

The reviews in *Christianity Today* set off a series of shock waves. Free Methodist Bishop J. Paul Taylor, a friend of my father and Marion's parents, prepared an "Open Letter," which appeared in the 23 July and 6 August 1963 issues of the *Free Methodist*. It was a sincere attempt to get me to reconsider my views, but I thought it would be fair to have a chance to explain my position, therefore on 17 August I wrote Dr. James F. Gregory, editor of the *Free Methodist,* requesting space to reply. On 20 August he informed me that the Board of Bishops had authorized the "Open Letter." Then in his letter of 28 August he excerpted some quotations from the bishops' letter, the essence being: "Dr. Beegle stated his position in a book; we stated our position in two articles to make it clear that the two positions are completely incompatible." I wrote the book for people with some understanding of the issues involved, but most Free Methodists were not cognizant of the problem or prepared to deal with it. Therefore, the world-wide church membership was presented with an unnecessary choice: Bishop Taylor or Dewey Beegle. The proper place for the "Open Letter" was *Recent Books,* a quarterly sent to all Free Methodist ministers in order to acquaint them with the latest publications relevant to their task.

To get an accurate picture of the situation it is necessary to discuss a hidden agenda in this confrontation. Bishop Leslie R. Marston, senior bishop of the Board of Bishops, was a member of the Asbury Board when it dealt with the Claude Thompson issue. He had aligned himself with the views of Carl Henry and the National Association of Evangelicals, therefore he was strongly in favor of removing Thompson from the Asbury scene. Since I presented views similar to Thompson, I had to be dealt with as well. Thus the power behind the Board of Bishops' actions was Bishop Marston. One of the excerpted quotations from his letter was: "We do not consider that such an important matter as the declaration of the church's historical position requires the opening of our official organ to the advocates of a contrary position." If "inerrancy" was "the church's historical position," one wonders why Olin Curtis's *Christian Faith* was put on the list for the ministerial home course of study. Obviously other officials in the Free Methodist Church did not consider "inerrancy" as the official teaching of the church, and neither did its doctrinal statements. It was Bishop Marston who determined "the church's historical position."

Accordingly, I wrote Bishop Taylor directly (with carbon copies to the other bishops) urging that my request be reconsidered. Then I closed as follows: "If my request is not granted I will have no other recourse than to mail my answer, prefaced with your refusal and reasons thereof, to key men throughout the Church."

Again my request was denied. Therefore on the 4 November 1963 I wrote a fourteen-page statement: four pages explaining why I prepared it and ten dealing with issues in Bishop Taylor's "Open Letter" and George A. Turner's review in *Recent Books,* September 1963. Copies were mailed to all the bishops and personnel at headquarters as well as many superintendents, ministers, and school officials. Some friends on the scene reported that there was considerable embarrassment at Winona Lake. The Board of Bishops could have been spared this unpleasant ordeal if they had not locked themselves into Carl Henry's narrow agenda.

The December 1963 issue of *Eternity,* another evangelical journal, contained the results of their annual poll for "the most significant books of the year for readers of *Eternity* magazine." First Place was *The Inspiration of Scripture* by Dewey M. Beegle. Obviously, the evangelical movement was, and still is, schizophrenic.

Some friends of long standing urged me to remain a Free Methodist, but I felt that it would be many years before the Church as a whole would be ready "to live and let live" in issues concerning the authority, inspiration, and interpretation of Scripture. I needed a broader base where I could have the *freedom* to follow my research and conscience without causing so much controversy. Accordingly, I took action to become a genuinely *free* Methodist by joining the New York Conference of the Methodist Church in June 1964. I had friends and former students in the conference so I was well aware of its spiritual and ecclesiastical shortcomings.

Another shock wave from the *Christianity Today* reviews was felt at Biblical Seminary. When I began teaching full-time in 1955 I was not asked to take one of the required Bible courses. I was the only full-time person who had not studied at Biblical Seminary and apparently it was felt that I could do better with the Hebrew, Greek, and elective courses. At Asbury I had studied with George A. Turner, who had earned two degrees at Biblical, therefore I was not a novice when it came to "the inductive study of the Bible." My problem was that I defined "inductive" to include all the data in the Hebrew and Greek texts as well as the various English Bibles. None of the faculty at Biblical Seminary had any thorough training in the critical issues associated with Scripture and most of them were not able to use Hebrew and Greek. Thus most of their insights were limited to commentaries and study of the English versions.

For a number of years President Dean G. McKee would call me into his office at contract time, discuss problems arising from my classes, and then inform me that he would give me tenure when I quit upsetting the students. I kept reminding him that I had not written the Bible and should not be held responsible for its contents. My task was to help the students study the Bible *inductively.* In such courses as Biblical Archaeology and The Bible and Modern Science a knowledge of Hebrew or Greek was helpful, but many of the difficulties were apparent in the English text, so that I was able to teach them how to read critically and spot difficulties that most students would miss.

I gave a few informal lectures for some of the faculty in an attempt to illustrate what I was doing and to broaden their base for inductive study. Complications arose, however, when intelligent students who had been in my classes began asking valid questions that the other teachers were not able to handle.

In 1960 President McKee resigned to accept a faculty appointment at Columbia Theological Seminary in Decatur, Georgia. The president-elect was Edwin Rian. He had some good ideas for broadening the base of the curriculum as well as the constituency, but he never had a chance to accomplish them because the older faculty accepted as true some criticisms of personnel at a college where Rian had been president.

At first I knew nothing of this reaction, but when it became apparent I tried to mediate. All the old fear and feelings of resentment came to a head in a three-pronged attack against President Rian, Dean Alvin Ahern, and me. In the Asbury style, seven faculty signed a statement demanding my resignation or they would leave. This time, however, things were different. I did not resign, as Claude Thompson had done, and the Board had a hearing in which I was given time to explain my side of the various complaints. To the dismay of the accusers, the board cleared me.

The aftermath of the *Christianity Today* reviews was a series of letters from right-wing graduates of Biblical Seminary demanding my removal.

In November 1963, after the resignations of Rian and Ahern, I was called into the President's office to appear before the personnel committee. The new Dean, Norman Baxter, chaired the meeting and Robert A. Traina, leader of old faculty, was present although he was not a member of the committee. I was thanked for my service to the seminary and notified that I would be granted the sabbatical due me and be paid through May 1965. Then I was told that on my return I would have to look for another job. Chairman of the Board Ernest Inwood was present, but completely stunned by the committee's action because he had never been consulted on the matter.

After glancing around to the committee members, he looked directly at me and said, "Dr. Beegle, you have been cleared by the board of this seminary and you have every right to return to your post after your sabbatical."

Traina urged me not to report anything about this meeting, and Dean Baxter noted that if I didn't they would write recommendations to help me get a new position.

What strange actions for people who professed to be defending God's truth! I had not thrown down the gauntlet and demanded to meet the committee, so why should I have to be quiet about the proceedings in order to protect my future? Strange as it may seem, the "green light" turned on and with a new peace I determined to resign and move on.

The next day or so I went to see Ernest Inwood in his office. I informed him that I did not want to use the tactics of my accusers, but that I felt I should get paid through August 1965 because any new employer would begin my salary in September. He took immediate action and got board approval to extend the pay period.

I told some close friends in other seminaries what had transpired and they were dumbfounded. Some urged me to report the whole matter to the Association of Theological Schools so that the situation could be corrected, but I knew that such a report would mean the loss of accreditation at Biblical Seminary. I told them I did not want to pound the last nail into the coffin. Fear and insecurity had driven essentially good people to take actions that clouded their religious life. Their faces showed their misery: the loss of peace and joy. Enough harm had occurred already without adding further trauma.

On Tuesday, June 9, 1964, the New York and New York East Conferences of the Methodist Church met at Drew University, Madison, New Jersey, for the purpose of becoming the New York Conference.

On June 11, I was recommended for Elder's Orders and full connection in the Conference, then on Sunday I joined the robed procession to participate in the Ordination Service.

On Monday afternoon, June 15, we had Kathryn Nadine and Barbara Lee with us at Kennedy International Airport. At the end of our farewell visit I said, "We have worried about you all these years, now you can worry about us." We boarded our plane and headed to Jerusalem, making visits with friends and former students in Spain, Italy, Greece, and Lebanon.

We joined the excavation staff for a ten-week dig at Shechem (West Bank) under the direction of Dr. George Ernest Wright. Later, while staying at the American School of Oriental Research (now the W. F. Albright Institute) in Jerusalem, we visited various sites in the area and also in Jordan.

On New Year's Eve we crossed into Israel via the Mandelbaum Gate for five months of study at the Hebrew Union College Biblical and Archaeological School. In addition to many tours of archaeological sites, we participated in the dig at Gezer, also under Wright. He wrote many letters of recommendation, but no appropriate teaching position opened up.

In late May 1965 we left Israel and began a two-month schedule visiting former students and other friends in Europe.

On 15 July, at Lake Constance, we learned that Marion's mother Ethel had had a critical heart attack. My own mother died prematurely in 1947 and so Mother Butterworth, who loved me as her own, was loved as my own. This relationship and our schedule posed a genuine dilemma. However, when we learned that she was calling for us, it was clear that we should return at once. We flew to Washington, D.C., on 16 July, but as fast as we had come, death was swifter and Mother had gone to her rest.

After her funeral, I contacted President Norman Trott at Wesley Theological Seminary. He asked me to appear for an interview because Dean L. Harold DeWolf had just joined the seminary and was eager to start hiring more faculty. I met and was interviewed by the newly formed personnel committee. Dean DeWolf had read my books and the committee checked out my credentials, and so forth. Since most of the faculty had not had a chance to visit with me, nor I with them, I requested that, if hired, my title be Visiting Professor of Old Testament.

On 16 August, just three and a half weeks after phoning Dr. Trott, I joined the faculty to be the junior partner with Dr. Lowell B. Hazzard. Since the Butterworths had retired in Washington, D.C., Mother prayed earnestly that I would find a teaching post in the area. Little did she realize that her passing would be the immediate means of having her prayers answered.

The fall of 1965 seemed like a dream. At Asbury and Biblical I had been chided for upsetting the students. It was a different world at Wesley, where I was patted on the back, not below. Although I was white in color I was truly a minority in the religious communities where I was reared, trained, and employed. In a sense I could resonate with my black friends who had been delivered: "Free at last, free at last!"

In a November faculty meeting I was requested to leave the room for a minute. On my return I was informed that the faculty had voted to recommend to the board that I join them as a regular member. It was a thrilling moment and I expressed my emotions by confiding, "I feel that I have finally come home." In April 1966 the Board of Trustees voted to grant me tenure with the rank of full professor.

In order to relate my experiences with Harold Lindsell it is necessary to pick up the story of the Harper Study Bible, 1960–64, when I was at the Biblical Seminary. Eugene Exman, senior editor at Harper & Brothers, recognized the need of an RSV study Bible for laity, students, and ministers. Since Harold Lindsell had been one of the first conservatives to make consistent use of that translation, he was chosen as the editor inasmuch his name would open up a big market among conservatives. I had developed cordial relations with Exman while Harper was processing and publishing my book *God's Word Into English,* therefore he sent me some of Lindsell's work on introductions and notes for the Old Testament (December 1960).

At the same time, Robert G. Bratcher, translations department of the American Bible Society, was checking the New Testament material. Independently, we came to the conclusion that the material tended to be naive, with hardly any notes to point out and explain obvious critical issues; too similar to the Scofield Bible notes; skewed to support the doctrine of inerrancy; and prone to consider the Old Testament as prewritten history of New Testament views, thus failing to let the Old Testament speak for itself.

Exman requested Lindsell to meet with me for discussion of the notes I had prepared. On 16 January 1961 we met for seven hours in our apartment at Biblical Seminary. As we worked through the material in the first chapters of Genesis it became evident that he was no biblical scholar. I asked him where he had gotten his material. He explained that he had asked Gleason Archer to write some notes for him. I remarked that it seemed odd to quote such a large block of material without giving credit to the source, then I noted that he should have asked William LaSor, his other Old Testament colleague, to help him because he was an up-to-date, mediating-type scholar.

Lindsell seemed willing to accept my suggestions, but I sensed that he was between a rock and a hard place. Although he was willing to balance his conservative, inerrant stance with more objective, scholarly notes, he was worried that the new material might alienate the conservatives, especially the nine million Southern Baptists, thereby cutting out a big segment of the market.

Since I didn't have the time to check the whole Old Testament, I asked Charles F. Pfeiffer, professor at Gordon Divinity School, Beverly Farms, Massachusetts, to assist me. I would make recommendations for Genesis through Esther and Pfeiffer for Job through Malachi. As a double check for consistency we exchanged comments and then each of us had separate sessions with Lindsell. To ensure that the notes were fairly consistent, Exman requested Lindsell to go through his combined notes looking for contradictions and other inconsistencies, but in the early part of 1962 he was traveling a great deal in connection with his major concerns, Missions and Missiology, therefore he did not get around to a thorough check of the material.

Galleys of the introductions and notes for the Harper Study Bible arrived in July 1962 with instructions from Exman "to read them all with some care and list any things mentioned that seem to you to lie to the extreme right or extreme left of the broad stream of evangelical biblical scholarship."

This I did, but I was amazed that Lindsell had skipped over or failed to recognize glaring contradictions in the material. Conservatives who have doubts about the documentary (source) hypothesis will find evidence of it in the Harper notes: L (Lindsell) and B (Beegle) or P (Pfeiffer) strands in the Old Testament; while L and B (Bratcher) appear in the New Testament right next to each other, and sometimes even in the same note. Originally the title page was to indicate that the three of us assisted in the project, but I requested Exman not to mention my name, and the others felt the same way.

The finished product appeared in October 1964 and Exman sent me a copy and a letter of appreciation, noting, "What you have done will make the book a more significant contribution." In spite of its deficiencies, the Harper Study Bible was helpful in broadening the outlook of conservative Christians.

During the debate over *The Inspiration of Scripture,* some of my Roman Catholic friends noted that I had not dealt with their views of inerrant Scripture and an infallible pope. Since they were reluctant to deal with the issues openly, I agreed to expand my book by discussing the Roman Catholic problems along with the Protestant. William B. Eerdmans Publishing Company agreed to publish this revision and it appeared late in 1973 under the title *Scripture, Tradition, and Infallibility.*

In my discussion with Carl Henry during the 1963 visit at Asbury, I noted that the evangelical British scholar F. F. Bruce had expressed interest in my book, but Henry was convinced that, in spite of his cordial tone, Bruce really affirmed the doctrine of inerrancy. Bruce was a very gracious person who composed his books with an enlightened evangelical readership in mind. Accordingly, he placed most of his critical insights in footnotes, a feature which Henry failed to pick up and interpret correctly. Visits and correspondence with Bruce convinced me that he did not hold to inerrancy.

Accordingly, I wrote to Bruce (of blessed memory) urging him, like the person in Paul's vision (Acts 16:9), "Come over to Macedonia and help us!" He did so by writing a very favorable three-page foreword for the book.

Countering the idolatry of right-wing traditions, Bruce commented, "The role of tradition on the evangelical side, as Dr. Beegle shows, has been no less influential than in the Roman communion—perhaps even more influential from the very fact of its being so largely unrecognized for what it is" (p. 7). Then to remove any possibility of misinterpreting him, he added, "I endorse as emphatically as I can his deprecating of a Maginot-line mentality where the doctrine of Scripture is concerned" (p. 10). Carl Henry dared not label F. F. Bruce as "a sometime evangelical scholar."

On the other hand, Harold Lindsell became more insistent on drawing the line at a literal interpretation of inerrancy. He showed uneasiness while working on the Harper Study Bible, but as the shift to a moderate stance occurred at Fuller Theological Seminary, he became very agitated. Carl Henry, a member of the original faculty there, moved on to become the editor of *Christianity Today*. Later, in protest to further change, Henry brought Harold Lindsell to the staff.

During Lindsell's years as editor of *Christianity Today,* he felt compelled to alert evangelicals to the danger of rejecting the view of inerrancy. His book *Battle for the Bible,* which was published by the Zondervan Publishing House in 1976, set off another flurry of reviews and countercharges. In Henry's review he appreciates Lindsell's warning, but is concerned that "Lindsell promotes a division between genuine and false evangelicals within the evangelical community itself on the basis of the inerrancy/errancy issue."

Lindsell allotted fourteen pages to me and *The Inspiration of Scripture* dealing with errors noted there, especially "The Famous Case of Pekah." On the basis of an article by Edwin R. Thiele, he commented, "And Beegle's claim that Scripture has erred falls to the ground" (p. 172). Then he concluded, "And to all of this, it may be added that it is now time for Beegle to look at the facts and admit that he was mistaken" (p. 174).

I did take a look at the facts and found that Lindsell had misunderstood Thiele and failed to read the whole article. I wrote a nineteen-page rebuttal and phoned Lindsell to make a date for discussing it, since *Christianity Today* was still in Washington, D.C., at the time. He graciously took me to lunch at the Press Club, then we went to his office to go over my material (27 August 1976). He was rather chagrined when I pointed out his error, and so I asked him about publishing my comments to clarify the issue. He declined on the grounds that he had not used *Christianity Today* to push his book, therefore it would not be proper to use that magazine for my rebuttal. Then he noted that in two years or so he would publish another book dealing with the fallout of *Battle for the Bible*. There, he promised, he would make things right. But one looks in vain throughout *The Bible in the Balance* (Zondervan, 1979) to find any reference to Pekah, the problem in 2 Kings 15:27, or Lindsell's confession that he was the one in error. This is a crucial issue and needs to be treated carefully so as to settle the matter once and for all.[1]

The rest of my books and articles involve other aspects of my "Journey to Freedom." In *Moses, the Servant of Yahweh,* Eerdmans, 1972, I followed the lead of William F. Albright, my mentor at The Johns Hopkins University, by countering the excessive pessimism of some scholars concerning the historicity of Moses and early Israel.

The essence of the book appeared in the article "Moses" in the fifteenth edition of *Encyclopaedia Britannica* (1974). Critical reviews pointed out some defects and I had to reconsider the data. I had never had any thorough training in the form-critical method because Albright did not have any appreciation for it, and he seldom dealt with it except in a defensive manner. In reading and studying various form critics I learned that this method had made some genuine contributions. On the other hand, I was convinced more than ever that the extreme left-wing critics were far too iconoclastic. As in other areas, the truth is more likely to be found somewhere in the middle. Therefore, in the article "Moses (Person)," which appeared in 1992 in the *Anchor Bible Dictionary* (vol. IV, pp. 909–18), *I know less than I did when I wrote the book!*

The purpose of *Prophecy and Prediction* (Pryor Pettengill, 1978) was to counter the popular notion that prophecy equals prediction. While some prediction is involved, the mass of prophecy is proclaiming the word and will of God. The book ranges over the topics of eschatology, apocalyptic, and the second coming, with special attention to Dispensationalism, Seventh-Day Adventism, and Zionism. Because of our life and work in the West Bank, Israel, and Jordan, Marion and I have worked consistently for a just peace in the Arab-Israeli struggle so that the Palestinians would have their state in the West Bank as had been spelled out in the Partition Plan voted by the United Nations on 29 November 1947.

To inform the general public, especially the churches, how practically all our presidents, members of congress, and senators have thwarted the human rights of the Palestinians and stalled their journey to freedom, I included a chapter, "Modern Israel: Past and Future." I approached Harper, Westminster, and Eerdmans, with whom I had published, and seven other publishers. All of them appreciated the basic work of the book, but they would not write a contract until I deleted the chapter on modern Israel.

I refused, and so I had to seek financial support. A good friend who shared our concern for justice in Palestine put his wallet where his mouth is and gave us $30,000 to publish the book at a subsidized price. Another friend and I formed Pryor Pettengill, Publisher, to produce the book and reprint *God's Word into English, Moses, the Servant of Yahweh,* and *Scripture, Tradition, and Infallibility.*

It is interesting that a bulk of the sales over the years have been from fundamentalistic schools where the books were required reading. A friend, who was once enrolled at Dallas Theological Seminary, reported that he, along with the rest of the class, ripped me to pieces in their reviews of *The Inspiration of Scripture.* More serious, however, was the tendency to malign my character because I had obtained a divorce and remarried. My friend finally became disenchanted with this environment and began the move toward a moderate, mature faith.

Our twenty-one years at Wesley Theological Seminary were a challenge and a delight. Retirement activities occurred on 18 April 1986. Like one of the M.Div. seniors, I preached a "Senior Sermon" in Oxnam Chapel during a service conducted by my advisees. I presented the exaugural lecture, "In Search of Moses," at 5 P.M. in Elderdice Hall. Our daughters and families from the west coast shared in an exhilarating evening with a delightful dinner and program.

In June 1986 I retired from the New York Conference after twenty-two years of service. Actual retirement from Wesley occurred in August after summer school. This marked another phase of our journey: *freedom from* committee and faculty meetings, preparing exams, and correcting papers.

After cataloging and sorting our archaeological artifacts and slides, we presented most of them to Wesley and two other schools. Then we made one of the last stages in our journey: the big move on January 11, 1991, to our comfortable apartment at Asbury Methodist Village, Gaithersburg, Maryland, twenty-five miles northwest of Washington, D.C. This was *freedom for Marion* because we have dinner at the apartment center dining room and "play house" for breakfast and lunch.

I am continuing my forty-two-year relationship with the American Bible Society by remaining on the Board of Trustees and the Translations Subcommittee. The New Testament of *Bible for Today's Family* was featured at the 175th Anniversary of the American Bible Society in New York City, May 9, 1991. This translation, also known as *Contemporary English Version* (CEV), will appeal to all ages because it is in good common English. It flows with great clarity inasmuch as theological terms have been explained in current language. The New Testament with Psalms and Proverbs appeared in 1992. The task of checking and commenting on the translation continues so that the whole Bible will appear in 1995. The edition with Deuterocanonicals and Apocrypha is scheduled for 1997.

As long as life lasts we will keep up with our extended family; press for justice in troubled areas at home and abroad; continue to ease the pain of the world's oppressed wherever we can; and do our best to proclaim the Good News by deed and word.

Note

1. The Pekah problem came to my attention many years ago while reading *Revelation and Inspiration* by the respected evangelical scholar James Orr: "Pekah's twenty years in 2 Kings 15:27 . . . is shown by the Assyrian synchronisms to be a mistake" (p. 180). He did not explain further, and nothing was generally accessible to the layperson until Thiele's *The Mysterious Numbers of the Hebrew Kings* appeared in 1951. Then in his "Coregencies and Overlapping Reigns Among the Hebrew Kings," *Journal of Biblical Literature* (June 1974): 174–200, Thiele presented a more complete explanation of the problem.

A literal translation of the Hebrew in 2 Kings 15:27 reads: "In the fifty-second year of Azariah king of Judah, Pekah son of Remaliah reigned over Israel in Samaria twenty years." This is not a complete, coherent sentence, and so translators have expanded the text to make sense. In each case, however, the translations have understood that Pekah reigned twenty years in Samaria.

The Hebrew text of Hos. 5:5 reads, "Israel and Ephraim shall stumble in their guilt; Judah also shall stumble with them." While most translations drop "Israel and" as a scribal error, Thiele (correctly in my estimation) retains the whole text as evidence that "there were *two* Hebrew states in the north at this time" (p. 194). With this clue, Thiele reads between the lines of the garbled text in 2 Kings 15:27 to find a combination of *two* notations from the court records of Israel, the northern kingdom.

For the year which would be 740 B.C. (according to our chronological system) the scribe noted: "Pekah *began* to reign in Samaria." In 732 B.C. (only eight years later), when Hoshea assassinated Pekah, the scribe made the notation: "Pekah had a reign of *twenty* years." Accordingly, his total reign began in 752.

Thiele understands "Ephraim" of Hos. 5:5 as pointing to Pekah's previous twelve-year reign (752–740 B.C.) over Gilead in Transjordan. (And twelve years reigning in Gilead *plus* eight years reigning in Samaria would explain the "twenty" years given in the garbled 2 Kings 15:27 text.) Therefore, Thiele believes that when 2 Kings 15:27 is *properly understood* the verse should not be considered in error. It was this idea which Lindsell took as proof that I was wrong.

But when the two scribal notations are mixed, as in 2 Kings 15:27, *a different situation is created*. Readers, who know nothing of the recording system in Israel (including the scribal editors in Judah and all modern scholars up to Thiele's research), invariably assume that Pekah reigned "*in Samaria* twenty years" because this is what is clearly implied. It is for this reason that I have claimed since 1963 that the verse is erroneous.

But even if we grant, for the moment, that Thiele and Lindsell have a point in claiming that the verse is inerrant, this does not really solve the problem. The real difficulty is that some scribal editors in Judah took the beginning of Pekah's eight-year reign in Samaria (740 B.C.) as the start for his total reign of twenty years, going down to 720. Thus Hoshea, who slew Pekah (2 Kings 15:30), became the last king of the northern kingdom, Israel, reigning 720–711. This is impossible, however, because Israel was taken into exile in 722 B.C. (two years before Hoshea's reign had even begun!). The Judean editors continued the system of making cross-references between the kings of Israel and Judah, therefore they related Hoshea with Ahaz (2 Kings 17:1) and Hoshea with Hezekiah (2 Kings 18:1, 9–10).

If Lindsell *had read just one more page* (p. 196) in Thiele's article, he would have found quotations destroying his premature conclusions: "These synchronisms clearly reveal the fact that the late editors of Kings did *not* understand the exact years of Pekah's reign" so they "resorted to calculations of their own to provide what they thought were the synchronistic relationships between Israel and Judah for that time."

I made contact with Thiele in the early fifties and expressed great appreciation for his research. I asked him how his studies had impacted on his view of Scripture. He admitted that he had not really faced that issue, and so I kept pressing him on the matter. During our contacts at various scholarly meetings and two personal visits with him and his wife Margaret in Porterville, California, he was increasingly at ease with friends in following his research to its logical conclusion. However, as a Seventh-Day Adventist whose church believed in the doctrine of inerrancy, he was reluctant to use the term "error" in his writings or public lectures.

In a still later article ("An Additional Chronological Note on 'Yaw, Son of "Omri," ' " *Bulletin of the American Schools of Oriental Research* [April 1976], Thiele reiterated, "The late editors, finding certain desired data lacking, sought to supply them by their own calculations, and failing to understand the employment of dual dating for Pekah, they began his 20 years in 740, the 52nd year of Azariah, and the synchronisms of 2 Kings 17 and 18 came into being" (p. 22). This material, *in the autograph manuscript of 2 Kings,* is *proof of an error in the original scroll of 2 Kings.*

It is interesting that while my consistent attempt to stay with the data is interpreted by Lindsell as "Beegle is out for the kill" (*Battle for the Bible,* p. 170), he and his inerrancist friends justify, in the name of God's truth, claims that the proof is inconclusive or that there are valid alternate interpretations to solve the problem. Some have held that the original text assigned an eight-year reign to Pekah, but this is futile because the whole system of the synchronisms is based on twenty years for Pekah. In a joint article, "Chronology of the Old Testament," *The New Bible Dictionary,* pp. 212–23, K. A. Kitchen and T. C. Mitchell state that Thiele's interpretation of the four synchronisms is invalid.

In *Scripture, Tradition, and Infallibility* I dealt with this claim as follows: "They feel that the '12th year' noted in 17:1 refers to Ahaz' last year of a 12-year coregency with Jotham, rather than to the 12th year of his sole reign" (p. 185). Then I continue,

> To account for 2 Kings 18:1, 9–10, Kitchen and Mitchell have also to postulate a 12-year coregency for Hezekiah (beginning about 728, when he was thirteen years old). In other words, their solution necessitates 12-year coregencies for three successive kings: Jotham, Ahaz, and Hezekiah. This solution is *theoretically possible* but the probability is exceedingly remote. What Kitchen and Mitchell are really saying, whether they realize it or not, is that somehow Uzziah (who died at 68), Jotham (who died at 45), and Ahaz (who died at 36) happened to appoint their sons as coregents *exactly twelve years before each of their deaths.* This takes some credulity." (p. 186)

It would be so much easier and more honest for the inerrancists to acknowledge this evidence because that would relieve them of the burden of carrying around the large bag of unresolved mysteries. They dare not do so, however, because their "idol," inerrancy, would fall to the ground. They counter this fear with a naive hope, one that Lindsell has expressed to me a number of times, that when all the data are in they will be proven correct.

David Coffin:
Fundamentalism: A Blessing and a Curse

Today, while I don't see eye to eye theologically with fundamentalist churches, my own background has given me empathy for their cause. If mainline churches, middle-class community groups, or other agencies are unwilling to meet struggling families in the chaotic gutters they find themselves in, then I would prefer to see the fundamentalist churches come in to help out in reaffirming order and structure. But one word of warning. With the blessing of fundamentalist Christianity comes a curse.

—David Coffin

David Coffin is the pastor of Trinity Evangelical Lutheran Church in Malinta, Ohio. The following was composed especially for this book.

My early childhood memories are filled with sights and sounds of my mother and father violently arguing, throwing plates, slamming doors, and cursing. After their messy divorce I was shuffled from place to place, until my mother eloped with the man who became my stepfather.

Little did my mother realize that she had married another alcoholic with a temper. Again, echoes of lying in bed listening to my mother and stepfather yelling, banging furniture, and cursing, remain a nightmare that I still carry in my consciousness as an adult.

Fundamentalist Christianity entered my life and ended my childhood nightmares. My stepfather's bar buddies were converted at an independent Baptist church and made frequent evening visits to our living room to share Scripture with my stepfather. He was "saved" at a Baptist church altar call.

My mother, a former Catholic, took some correspondence courses from Moody Bible Institute to understand the fundamentalist Baptists. For my mother, brother, and myself this was a blessing.

Now we had structure, order, and a clear black-and-white set of rules to live by. For people in the lower working classes, relying on the meagerest economic opportunities and support systems, fundamentalist Christianity is the lesser of two evils, especially when alcoholism and violent uncontrollable tempers are the other option. Fundamentalism provides structure in an otherwise chaotic family life. It provides a clean, wholesome social support group for people living at the lower end of the economic ladder. It aids in instilling values, morality, social skills, and genuine concern for other people in an otherwise hellish nightmare of being poor with few voices of affirmation and tender care available.

As a child attending elementary school—and church three days and nights per week—I was thoroughly immersed in Baptist beliefs and practices. I could quote John 3:16 before I could write my name. I knew the first four books of the New Testament by name before I knew our street address or telephone number. It was within the damp, poorly lit, church basement Sunday school classes (and "Junior Church" held in the same basement while our parents worshipped in the church above) that I participated in "sword drills" with my Bible and sang songs about Jesus that I still recall as an adult. When asked to sing in front of my classmates, I would sing, "Do Lord," or, "When the Roll Is Called Up Yonder."

The important thing to remember is that fundamentalist church members will go down into any gutter, barroom of filth, or hellish nightmare of shattered family life and offer a viable alternative with strict rules, "black-and-white" categories of looking at life, and supply a ready-made community of support, friendliness, and interaction. Where else could a total stranger come in off the street to share in homemade foods at potluck dinners, uplifting singing, and people shaking hands and embracing each other? Contrasted with a life of drinking to excess and receiving low wages in a job the breadwinner hates, fundamentalist Christianity offers an opportunity for that person to have dignity, honor, and blessings. The shop worker who is a "cog" in the corporate machine with a foreman slavemaster is now "Brother So-and-So" who is one of Christ's soldiers in Christ's army in this "Devil's world."

My mother saw how the Baptist Church made my stepfather a loving, responsible, and conscientious husband and father. While he was no longer as jovial, happy-go-lucky or fun-loving as in times past, my mother thought this was the better of two options. Indeed, long altar calls, tent revival meetings, people standing up to give personal testimonies of what Jesus had done, potlucks, picnics, and performing gospel singing groups, were all a blessing to me as a child.

I recall one Sunday when a visiting evangelist pounded our small pulpit so hard that he broke it. Another Sunday, a preacher got so excited that he had a heart attack and an ambulance arrived (there was no altar call that day). My favorite line is from the preacher who couldn't get anybody to come up front for altar call, so he said, "I'm going to keep you here a bit longer. I know many of you have roasts at home in the oven. But it's better that your roast beef burns in your ovens than your souls burn in hell for eternity."

Back then, the hard wooden pews and restless children made things uncomfortable. Today, I cherish such memories. The structure and order had a positive influence on my life. I occasionally subscribe to *Sword of the Lord* for casual reading (though I'm not a fundamentalist by any stretch of the imagination).

Our family moved often because the number of my brothers and sisters eventually increased to five, and we had to find a suitable (and inexpensive) place to live. Furthermore, in order to provide for us, my stepfather (now my father, after he adopted me) worked six and seven nights per week on second shift at the auto factory.

After one move we found ourselves attending a small-town Free Methodist Church. But the only thing "free" about that denomination in those days was the name. Strict rules forbidding makeup, work on Sundays, card-playing, dancing, motion pictures, rock and roll music, and women wearing bathing suits were the order of the day. I got a note from my pastor excusing me from participation in square dancing at school gym classes.

My parents, struggling to raise their large family on shop wages and long work hours, found that these conflicted with their church's rules for frequent attendance and resting on Sundays. Furthermore, the church leadership felt that its members ought to vocalize nothing but conservative Republican ideals, while my father was an Automobile Union Democrat. These differences heralded the beginning of the end of my parent's days as active fundamentalist churchgoers.

In my junior high and high school years my parents missed attending church a few Sundays each month. Then months of absence became years. My sister and I continued to ask for rides to church. Today, my sister and I are the only two active church members in our family of eight.

The Free Methodist experience wasn't too disillusioning for me while I continued to live beneath the security of my parents' roof. Church camps, youth groups, witnessing, and Bible study proved to be a good "poor person's social life" and character-molding vehicle. But during my freshman year at the state college in northern Michigan while watching Christian television ministry programs, I had a major spiritual crisis!

I had been raised in a close "cocooning" Christian community and had left to attend a trade or technical college that would prepare me to make a living. It was the only college my parents could afford and I needed to learn a marketable trade. However, the people I met at college were busy with parties, alcohol, drugs, fraternities, and the like. In effect, I encountered a world that never knew I existed. Besides which, visits to my Free Methodist Church back home showed me that I was a "past event." Plus, the congregational makeup and small town were in a state of constant change. Many of the people I knew were leaving, or had left. So I was doubly lonely.

I reflect back on watching Richard DeHahn and "Day of Discovery" with its toothpaste-smiling "Christian Covergirl" gospel singers. Meanwhile, I was sitting on the cold dormitory floor eating beans and Spaghetti-Os with my dorm mates passed out from last night's alcohol and drug parties. The aroma of pot and incense still lingers in my mind.

Then I watched Jerry Falwell's "Old Time Gospel Hour." There he was, inviting young people like me to attend a college where *real Christian* love, nurture, and fellowship occurs. Again, in the 1970s, being a visible vocal voice for Jesus was strictly a minority report in an atmosphere of parties, panty raids, and Peter Frampton concerts.

If I wasn't feeling miserable enough about missing out on all the evangelical "cocooning communities," "Oral Roberts Presents" would then come on. Again, I saw friendly, well-groomed young men and beautiful college-age women singing, rejoicing, and hugging each other while praising Jesus. How different this was compared to the cigarette smoke-filled student lounges with the crack of pool tables and cussing of those players about to lose their money on a game of "eight ball."

The worlds of Richard DeHahn, Jerry Falwell, and Oral Roberts were not the world of my state college, which was genuinely and sincerely attempting to prepare me for the brutal, competitive, merciless, blue-collar printing industry. Competent skills and an ability to work closely with people of various backgrounds and beliefs, despite their personal problems and eccentric quirks, were the lessons I learned in college. I was being taught how to walk the jungle trails of the "secular world." Such invaluable worldly lessons contrasted greatly with the world depicted on Christian television shows.

Only time revealed to me that even the Christian cocoons required cold hard "secular cash" to *keep them going!* Until one realizes that, the wooing warmth is oh so tempting in the unfriendly, changing, individualistic American society we all inhabit.[1]

As I write this retrospective piece, it is ironic that the cover of a recent issue of *Christianity Today* magazine reads, "Will Bible Colleges Survive the '90s?"

At the state college I attended, my courses in introductory psychology, health, social science, and business all called into question my assumptions about life, my beliefs, and my way of organizing reality. For me, the 1960s movement, known as "Death of God" theology, occurred in the 1970s, while I was in college. The Christian television programs I watched were now seen in my eyes as almost mindless, superficial ways of avoiding life's ambiguities and gray areas. I was alone on weekends on the college campus with five dollars to spend. The God of fundamentalist Christianity had let me down. I was isolated and alone.

Desperately I shopped for campus ministries. Guess what I discovered? An animal called a "neo-evangelical" Christian. The churches they attended wished to distance themselves from legalistic fundamentalism, yet not "sell out" totally to secularism either. I got involved in a campus Christian Reformed church that was quite progressive.

Guess what? Those people claimed to be Bible centered Christians, yet they drank beer, went to motion pictures, played cards, danced, listened to rock and roll, and even cussed once in a while. Mind you, while at college I saw former fundamentalists leave the Christian faith *entirely*! I saw many who were bitter and angry about their strict church upbringing. I tried to stake some middle ground between no church and the strict fundamentalist churches.

The "curse" in this case was that fundamentalism was so rigid and strict that young people, especially those from low income families like myself, fell between the cracks by having to attend a state college. We underwent alienation from those of our own faith for having attended a secular institution. And we also felt alienated within secular society at college.

So, I joined the Christian Reformed church on campus (which was related to the Dutch Reformed Church). Predestination and the doctrine that the nonelect ("reprobate") individual was totally corrupt morally, spiritually, and mentally, were difficult for me to fully accept. Upon graduation from college I tried attending a small traditional Dutch Reformed church off campus. It was not *at all* like the one on campus. Instead of demonstrating an open welcome to any outsider, it seemed as though "If you're not Dutch, you're not much" was the implicit message I often detected being delivered. So I looked elsewhere. (I think those types of churches are working hard these days to change that image, so I do compliment them in their efforts.)

After relocating to a town where I had found a job, I joined a mega-church that was a conservative evangelical Presbyterian church. Theologically they were "Baptists in robes," but their ministry to all people regardless of their race, nationality, or previous religious affiliation was superior to excellent. I met my wife in that church. If I died and got to choose which years of my life I would like to relive throughout eternity, it would be those six years in the "cocoon" of evangelical entertainment, top-notch Christian speakers, air-conditioned churches, padded pews, and the like. There were more courses offered at that church than at many colleges. And the teachers, pastors, and counselors were brilliant.

But again, a "gray area" emerged due to the fact that my wife and I had to live in the decaying inner city due to our low incomes. Life in a city where explosions, flashing police lights, and yelling in apartment hallways were commonplace proved to be a challenging spiritual growth experience. But people in the mega-church who lived in suburbia displayed discomfort with us sharing this in small group settings.

So we prayed a lot, faced another spiritual crisis of being "left out," and joined a mainline Lutheran church that was involved in a grassroots ministry in the inner city we lived in. We developed close ties with the people in this church and I eventually applied to the bishop's office to attend the nearest mainline Lutheran seminary.

Today, as a Lutheran pastor, I love the confessions, liturgy, and sacraments. They supply the structure and stability I found appealing in fundamentalism. Furthermore, the existentialist theology and emphasis on a God who meets us and shapes us in our cross-bearing experiences adds meaning to my life while acknowledging the gray areas of thought and faith.

Today, while I don't see eye to eye theologically with fundamentalist churches,[2] my own background has given me empathy for their cause. If mainline churches, middle-class community groups, or other agencies are unwilling to meet struggling families in the chaotic gutters they find themselves in, then I would prefer to see the fundamentalist churches come in to help out in reaffirming order and structure. But one word of warning. With the blessing of fundamentalist Christianity comes a curse.

Notes

1. Maybe the lonely road I traveled is similar to that of the Jesus that Mark depicted—a mysterious, misunderstood figure marching down the lonely road to the cross. Isn't that what Luther's theology of the cross is somehow about?

In an age when mainline Lutheran churches like mine, an Evangelical Lutheran Church in America church, are mockingly called dying "sideline" churches, I cannot get too enthused about the emerging shopping mall model of the "mega-church." The reason? A Christian faith that is solid enough to live with daily is one that can maintain its own integrity, respect, and continuity in a secular world that rejects authoritarian appeals and rejects lures for close cocooning away from it all. Christ sent us *out* to make disciples!

2. "Fundamentalists are notorious for selectively dumping teachings, practices of faith, and doctrines when they don't accommodate where the church is now, or where the cash is flowing from.

"Mainline churches are up front about the ambiguities inherent in different' biblical interpretations and Christologies. It is the fundamentalists who keep moving the Rapture dates.

"My main point of critique is that *conservatives themselves have moved considerably to the left since the fundamentalist/liberal controversies of the early 1900s.*

"Next Sunday as Jimmy Swaggart points his finger at me calling me a 'liibraal' (I watch him as I put on my black clerical collar for church) my 'gut' response is that Swaggart himself would have been thrown out of the fundamentalist church I was raised in—so look who is the *liiibraaal* now!" (From a letter by David Coffin published in *The Door*, no. 114, November/December 1990.)

Harvey Cox:
An Ecumenical/Evangelical Dialogue

I went into the U.S. Merchant Marines in 1946. I travelled to Europe right after the Second World War, to Poland. I kept meeting people in the Merchant Marine who were from different social strata than I was. I saw the results of the Second World War. I was approached on the streets by fourteen-year-old prostitutes. As a seventeen-year-old who considered himself an evangelical Christian at that time, I had to deal with that.

—Harvey Cox

Harvey Cox is the Victor S. Thomas Professor of Divinity at the Harvard Divinity School, and author of *The Secular City, Turning East, Religion in the Secular City,* and *Many Mansions: A Christian's Encounter with Other Faiths.* What follows is Cox's 1991 version of a portion of the dialogue that first appeared in "An Ecumenical/Evangelical Dialogue with Harvey Cox" in *Right On,* June 1975.

Harvey Cox: I was raised in an evangelical church, a Baptist church in Pennsylvania. It belonged to the American Baptist Convention and had ministers from Eastern Baptist Seminary. Some of them were very suspicious of the literature that came from the then (allegedly liberal) Northern Baptist Convention. I was saved at thirteen, and baptized the same year. I was president of the Baptist Youth Fellowship. I think I used my experience in the Baptist Church to rebel against my parents, who I then regarded as merely conventional Christians. A lot of people rebel against their parents by throwing off religion— I did just the opposite. I outdid them in my piety.

I graduated from high school and went into the U.S. Merchant Marines in 1946. I travelled to Europe right after the Second World War, to Poland. I kept meeting people in the Merchant Marine who were from different social strata than I was. I saw the results of the Second World War. I was approached on the streets by fourteen-year-old prostitutes. As a seventeen-year-old who considered himself an evangelical Christian at that time, I had to deal with that. I came back out of the service and went to the University of Pennsylvania as what might now be described as a political radical. I began studying radical political literature. I joined the socialist group at the university. In 1948 I was a member of the Inter-Varsity Christian Fellowship there and I began working in the Progressive Party. (You don't remember what the Progressive Party is—this was the vehicle for Henry Wallace—the third party. *Not* George Wallace, but the "good Wallace," the populist Wallace.) I began wearing a Wallace button and going around organizing for the Wallace campaign in the fall of 1948. Then I was approached by some Inter-Varsity Christian Fellowship friends who had been praying about this matter and had come to the conclusion that no born-again Christian could possibly support that kind of socialist for political office. Truman was bad enough, though one could possibly vote for him, but preferably for Dewey, and certainly *not* for Wallace.

So, I had to struggle with this. It sounds funny now, but it was a very hard problem for me to face. If this had been in the days of *Sojourners* magazine I wouldn't have been faced with that choice, but it wasn't. It was in the days when that kind of ultimatum could be served on people; evangelical or radical. I labored over that for a long time and finally quit the Inter-Varsity group though I went back later.

A few months later somebody put into my hands a book called *Moral Man in Immoral Society* by [Christian theologian] Reinhold Niebuhr, and I date my second conversion from that point. I read the book straight through that night. I really dived into Reinhold Niebuhr at that time, not realizing all the things that I have learned since—that he was "neo-orthodox" and not orthodox and things like that, and that at certain points his theology is very questionable. But at that point Niebuhr really saved me. I went on to a career that included Yale Divinity School, then being chaplain at Oberlin College, then coming to Harvard. And after finishing my Ph.D. at Harvard, I went to Berlin and worked in the first stages of what since has come to be called the Communist/Christian Dialogue.

This was in 1962. I started working for the World Council of Churches, living in West Berlin and being in touch with people in East Berlin, Czechoslovakia, and Poland who wanted at least to begin a conversation between Christians and Marxists. Again, it is very hard for people in the middle of the 1970s to realize that in those days some of us thought we were headed for a real Armageddon, with the Soviet Union and the United States on a collision course with nuclear weapons aimed at each other and with lots of people saying God was on our side and the devil was sponsoring their side. The world was headed for disaster. People were digging bomb shelters and there was very little communication.

But some people thought we needed to take some steps in getting people from the two sides of that curtain to talk with each other, to listen to each other. So I volunteered. I worked for a year with some dedicated, courageous people— some German Lutherans, a couple of Swiss Reformed people—living in West Berlin and traveling through the wall four or five times a week, meeting Christian pastors and others in East Berlin, getting up little clandestine conversations, and getting something going that has produced at least a different mood when Marxists and Christians meet each other. We weren't interested in any kind of synthesis. We were interested in dialogue.

In Berlin nobody could possibly call the Christians that I was working with—

on either side of the line—"liberals." Most of them were Barthians, and Bonhoeffer had a lot of influence on them, but whatever else you might want to call them, they certainly were not liberals. So they reaffirmed a theological perspective that meant something to me: when you are talking to Marxists, better that you should have some position. Better that you should have something that you are talking from, that you are committed to, that you believe in—not only from your point of view but from their point of view. Then something happens. I learned that and it was important for me to learn.

When I came back from Berlin in the fall of 1963, my wife Nancy and I and our three children bought a house in Roxbury, which is the black district of Boston. We lived there from 1963 until 1970, the only white family on the block. Our kids were the only white kids in the school. We were nearly the only white people in the church we went to. There I learned that in some ways the black churches have always maintained this integration of biblical perspective, biblical faith, and solid, critical, unsentimental, unmystified awareness of the oppressive structures of the American capitalist racist society. They weren't liberals either.

My family eventually had to move out when things got too tough, after the eleventh burglary of our house, after the drug traffic started, and after our middle-class black friends started moving out. We decided maybe it was time to go somewhere else, and we moved to Cambridge. . . . And I want to report to you something that you may not be aware of, that after the influx of Roman Catholics at Harvard Divinity School, after the Second Vatican Council, and the large increase in blacks in the late sixties, the enormous increase of women (I believe now 50 percent), the newest kind of visible presence is people who no longer are "closet evangelicals." They are people who call themselves Pentecostals or evangelicals and who want to be there with everybody else, not secretly or clandestinely, but really entering into conversation. And I'm grateful for that. I found to my amazement that I click with those people better than I click with most Unitarians and I must say most Congregationalists. I find that with most of the latter there's just something missing. And I think that "something missing" has to do with a kind of experience that one has, even though one's theology may change eleven times in the meantime: the *evangelical experience.* I don't like the phrase "evangelical *background*" because it seems like something you left behind. I mean the evangelical formation (let's use the Catholic term) that enables you to talk with people like that in a way in which something real is going on.

So . . . I am interested in "ecumenical/evangelical dialogue" for very personal reasons, because it is something I am still working at. I don't have any wonderful intellectual reasons to work with, it is just that I think *I* need it. And I do not think I am going to be completed in my own development (we never are completed) until all that gets worked out. . . .

What I think theology is really all about . . . is constantly looking at how the proclamation of the gospel is distorted by idealogical, racist, sexist, classist, and other kinds of pollutants, so that what is coming out is almost unrecognizable as the gospel. . . .

If "to be a Christian is to believe that Jesus Christ is the normative revelation of God" causes a problem in relating to other people, then . . . the whole business of Eph. 2, that in Jesus Christ the separating wall is broken down, doesn't make sense to me. That's my favorite text, by the way. Now, why can't it be that a Christologically centered theological perspective *facilitates* conversation and openness to other people? . . .

I don't think there is any divinely revealed *doctrine*. Christian truth is precisely the person of Christ and not any specific code, creed, confession. All of these are more or less acceptible, more or less criticizable. We don't really *need* creeds. We have Jesus Christ and that is all we need. . . .

I am very uncomfortable with theological relativism, which I am surrounded with: "All religions are equal; inherently the core of experience is the same, etc." I think this is intellectually reprehensible, that it is a sellout to a kind of bourgeois idealogy—which is that there aren't any real differences in life.

But I also have a problem with the notion that people who have never become disciples [of Jesus Christ] are going to be in worse shape than people who have heard this gospel all along. I am uncomfortable with both of those positions and I do not know where to go yet. I wish I could tell you that I knew, had some clues, I just don't. I don't know where to go with that, I think it is the most serious issue that my schizophrenic evangelical/ecumenical inner self has to deal with. Because I am just not content with the people who say they are disciples.

And I meet so many people who won't claim to be disciples but seem somehow or other to be closer in some ways to what I think disciples should be than others.

Jim Daane: Don't you see any that claim to be disciples that you acknowledge to be disciples?

Harvey Cox: Yes, and thank God for those.

Tom Harpur: Heaven and Hell

I have interviewed every notable religious figure of our time, from the pope to Billy Graham to Mother Teresa to the dean of Canterbury Cathedral, and examined every kind of cult as well as all the major religions. And as a result I can say that my views on religion and faith have been profoundly changed. After seeing the grace and glory of God at work in saintly men and women of other faiths, I could no longer believe in only one right and true faith.

—Tom Harpur

Tom Harpur is a syndicated columnist on ethics and religion with the *Sunday Star* of Toronto, Canada. He is currently seen daily, Monday to Friday, for one hour on Vision TV's Canada-wide network, which goes by cable to six million homes, and he has hosted over fifty-six hours of religious profiles, also on Vision TV. His works include *Always on Sunday, For Christ's Sake,* and *Life After Death: A Study of the Evidence.* He writes, "I still consider myself a Christian, but in the early New Testament sense of a follower of Christ, not a follower of later orthodoxy so-called." The following was excerpted from *Harpur's Heaven and Hell.*

The year was 1967. An ordained Anglican priest lecturing on the New Testament and teaching Greek at Wycliffe College in Toronto, I preached every Sunday at an active downtown evangelical parish.

I had had a successful parish career—a year as curate at the posh Anglican Church of St. John's in York Mills, Toronto, and then seven years building up my own suburban parish, including a new rectory and a large sanctuary, at St. Margaret's-in-the-Pines in West Hill. I had even had the luxury of a year's postgraduate work back at Oxford, studying under some of the great theological minds of our time. Moving to the seminary in 1964, I had thought I would be at the center of things, shaping the minds that in turn would shape the new, more relevant church of the future. But things didn't quite work out that way.

I found to my surprise that the majority of theological students were ultra-conservative, so afraid of new ideas that they were unwilling to be influenced, let alone shaped, by anybody. (Recent conversations with theological professors suggest that would-be ordinands today are, with notable exceptions, much the same—perhaps not surprisingly, given the conservative mood that seems to have fallen over most denominations and religions with regard to basic beliefs.)

The academic life itself, rather than sparkling with wit and discussion about the great theological and practical issues being raised out-of-doors, so to speak, seemed almost incestuous, bent on a holding operation—anything to avoid the radical change that was to my mind essential. I felt bored and frustrated.

In the spring of 1967 I met with the only media person I knew, the co-owner of radio station CFGM in Richmond Hill, just outside metropolitan Toronto. I proposed an hour-long talk show on religion, with me as host, to commence that fall. He called back the next day to say he thought we should begin the following week! I felt rather the way Peter must have when Jesus told him to get out of the boat and walk to him on the water: a radio show seemed much safer to talk about than to do. "By the way," the owner said, "I've already got a name for the program: 'Harpur's Heaven and Hell.' " The title did little to ease my fears. Friends and colleagues, mostly clergy, urged me to back off. It was bad enough for a theology professor to broadcast on a country-and-western music station—a name like "Harpur's Heaven and Hell" was downright un-Anglican. I almost took their advice when I heard the show's first promo, after which the disc jockey jauntily announced the next record: "I won't go huntin' with you, Luke, but I'll go chasin' women."

However, after a faltering start, the show became a success and eventually evolved into a five-nights-a-week format. Sometimes we had guests, including a stripper who had found God, and Beatle John Lennon, who made a lengthy appearance by phone from his famous "Bed-In for Peace" in a Montreal hotel. Most often, though, there was no one but me, facing a microphone and a line of telephone buttons, and talking to anyone who cared to call about whatever was on his or her mind.

The show lasted for five years. As the owner had predicted, the title was effective: once people heard it they never forgot. There was plenty of controversy; some listeners were so offended they tried to pressure my bishop to have me "unfrocked" (to use that quaint term). I even received bomb threats—notes left under the windshield-wipers on my car—because of my stand against the war in Vietnam.

Eventually I was to "unfrock" myself, voluntarily laying down the exercise of my ordained ministry in 1979, partly because of a conflict of interest in doing my job as a journalist (would I counsel people as a preacher or interview them as a reporter?) and partly because of my diocese's new strictures on what one could or could not preach as a loyal subject of the bishops. But that is another story.

The point is that because of "Harpur's Heaven and Hell," I was soon asked to write opinion pieces for the *Toronto Star* and other papers, and to appear regularly on various radio and television shows to discuss religious trends and events. Before long I realized that what I was doing freelance, as a hobby, was really much more stimulating and fulfilling than my teaching career. And so in 1971, after a talk with the bishop, I left Wycliffe College to become the religion editor of the *Star*.

Now, after a dozen years of travel—to Italy (including over ten trips to the Vatican), India, Japan, the Middle East, Africa, Central America, Scandinavia, France, the British Isles (many times), the High Arctic, and most of the principal cities in North America—I have covered two papal elections and three papal tours, interviewed every notable religious figure of our time, from the pope to Billy Graham to Mother Teresa to the dean of Canterbury Cathedral, and examined every kind of cult as well as all the major religions. And as a result I can say that my views on religion and faith have been profoundly changed.

After seeing the grace and glory of God at work in saintly men and women of other faiths, I could no longer believe in only one right and true faith. I could no longer hold that one denomination's view of Christianity was the unique reflection of what Paul calls "the mind of Christ," when I'd seen at first hand the havoc each denomination, in its own way, is capable of wreaking in people's lives. It is significant that in South Africa, where there are more orthodox believers in the dominant Protestant church, more people who give to missions, more people who attend prayer- and Bible-study meetings, and more who take the Bible to be the inspired, inerrant word of God, than in most other countries of comparable size, the worst forms of racism and injustice reign supreme, fully supported by selected biblical texts. In the United States the battle for racial integration and equality found its bitterest opposition in the "born-again" Christians of the so-called Bible Belt. And in Guatemala, where born-again Christianity has been growing faster than anywhere else in the world, the rate of official terror and massacres—especially of the Indians—under the "born-again" former dictator Efrain Rios Montt was second only to that of El Salvador.

I could not look with equanimity on religion's claim to bring peace and unity when I had witnessed the tragic controversies and divisions it is capable of producing. (I will never forget walking the streets of strife-ravaged Belfast in the fall of 1979, investigating the effects of years of sectarian violence and hatred upon the children.)

I could not simply accept Christianity's claims to relieve guilt when I knew the inside story—how much unnecessary guilt can be incurred by its often cruelly rigid dogmas. (I cannot restate Dietrich Bonhoeffer's words emphatically enough: the church must stop trying to act as a kind of "spiritual pharmacist"—working to produce acute guilt, and then in effect saying: "We just happen to have the remedy for your guilt here in our pocket.")

I began to grow both sad and angry at the number of people in most major faiths who want to compel everyone to jump through the same verbal hoops.

What is most distressing to me, as I look back on my experience as a reporter, is the sharpness with which religion continues to divide people into different camps, even to the point of violence and bloodshed. You can see it in Ireland or in Iran, but there is plenty of *odium religiosum* (religious hatred) much closer to home. I have a special file for the most extreme forms of hate mail I receive—all from people professing to be deeply religious—and much of it is filled with latent violence. Broadcaster Gordon Sinclair and others who have dared to question or criticize religious institutions and their doings tell me they have found the same thing. Tragically, each sect, cult, and denomination seems convinced that it alone is "The Truth" in its entirety. All others are heretics.

If every one of the world's one billion Christians could agree and resolve, even just for one twenty-four-hour period, to jointly perform the will of God they all profess, the planet would never be the same. Imagine if they were to join with the nearly one billion Muslims in the same commitment, and then with the Jews, and then the Buddhists.

Protestant Christians are divided into myriad camps because most of them have mistakenly elevated the Bible into an infallible "paper pope." Taking a view of the New Testament that would have astonished its authors—whose only Bible was what we call the Old Testament—they have to an alarming degree become Bible worshippers. The Bible has become an idol, assuming the place reserved for God alone; in their mistaken zeal, they have broken his first commandment. Yet the New Testament authors themselves adapted or changed the Old Testament passages they quoted, and at times Matthew and Luke quite cavalierly altered the materials they found in Mark. There is no suggestion that they believed every line of Mark's work to be sacrosanct or infallible.

The more trendy temptation today, especially among young people, is to attribute infallibility to a particular mystic, sage, or guru. But this tendency, like the attitude of fundamentalist Muslims to the Koran, of Jehovah's Witnesses to the *Watchtower* publications, or of the Mormons to the writings of Joseph Smith, stems from a single basic illusion: that absolute objective certainty is possible about eternal things. If it were, there would be no room whatever for faith or trust. That kind of certainty doesn't require faith: it demands, even coerces, total acceptance and obedience. The truth cannot be stated boldly enough: God is not a Fascist, and his followers are required to use their own minds, consciences, and wills. It may seem less secure, but it is an exciting and liberating experiment in human responsibility.

Conrad Hyers: The Comic Vision

In one of his tall tales Mark Twain tells how exercised he had become over the considerable discord among God's creatures and how he had decided to take the matter in hand.

> So I built a cage, and in it I put a dog and a cat. And after a little training I got the dog and the cat to the point where they lived peaceably together. Then I introduced a pig, a goat, a kangaroo, some birds and a monkey. And after a few adjustments, they learned to live in harmony. So encouraged was I by such successes that I added an Irish Catholic, a Scotch Presbyterian, a Jew, a Muslim from Turkestan, and a Buddhist from China, along with a Baptist missionary that I captured on the same trip. And in a very short while there wasn't a single living thing left in the cage.

The endemic weakness that accompanies the intensity of our most sacred concerns is a predilection for translating that intensity into intolerance, aggression, and violence. In this lies the seriousness of humor. The barbarous chronicle of inquisitions, heresy trials, witch hunts, book burnings, religious persecutions, political imprisonments, holy wars, and even acts of genocide—justified by the most respected elements of society and sanctified by pious interests—is sufficient testimony to the stark possibilities of sincerity without humor.

—Conrad Hyers, *The Comic Vision and the Christian Faith*

Conrad Hyers is professor of the history of religions at Gustavus Adolphus College, St. Peter, Minnesota. Among his special interests are science and religion, humor/comedy and religion, and the Taoist and Zen traditions of China and Japan. He has lectured widely, both nationally and internationally, on these themes in a variety of religious contexts, including among fundamentalists. He has written one book on creation/evolution: *The Meaning of Creation: Genesis and Modern Science* (Westminster). He has recently published a book on the phenomenon of "born-again Buddhism": *Once-Born, Twice-Born Zen: The Soto and Rinzai Schools of Japan* (Longwood). He is best known for a number of books on humor, comedy, and religion, the more recent being *The Comic Vision and the*

Christian Faith (Pilgrim), *And God Created Laughter: The Bible as Divine Comedy* (Westminster), and *The Laughing Buddha: Zen and the Comic Spirit* (Longwood). All of Hyers's interests and publications have their roots in the fundamentalism of his youth. He has chosen here to retrace some of the steps leading to his interest in the religious importance of humor and comedy.

We are all defined not simply by where we have come from but also by where we have arrived; not just by what we have been given but also by what we have done with it. In my own case, the "given" of my childhood and youth in the forties and fifties was fundamentalism in all directions. My father and mother were a fundamentalist Baptist minister and Christian education director respectively. Aunts and uncles were fundamentalist Baptist and Brethren, including one aunt and uncle who were missionaries to Taiwan. My grandfather was a fundamentalist Methodist minister, and grandmother a Bible school teacher. My other grandparents didn't talk religion much—they were chicken farmers— but they staunchly supported Billy Graham and disliked John R. Rice, who said unkind things about him. In our family, at least, it was fundamentalism all the way down—except for one black sheep in the family who was a "liberal" Methodist college professor and for whom we all prayed.

The religious context was further defined by the "fundamentalist/modernist controversy" of that era, which had led to deep divisions and animosities in many Protestant denominations, with new churches, colleges, seminaries, denominations, and nondenominational groups being organized over against the "modernist take-over." My grandfather taught at one of these new Bible colleges and my father succeeded in withdrawing a succession of Baptist churches from the then Northern Baptist Convention into nondenominational fellowships, though in one case the church split occurred primarily over a fifty-fifty division in the congregation between those who wanted a new Baldwin organ and those who couldn't imagine singing to anything but a Hammond.

It was no great surprise, then, that I was enrolled at the age of seventeen in a fundamentalist university in the South where, for a time, I became even more ultrafundamentalist and politically ultraconservative than my parents. I became convinced that they had already taken a few steps down the slippery slope toward the apostasy of the mainline churches. They also were mildly supportive of desegregation, whereas my alma mater had given an honorary doctorate to the leading segregationist and states rights advocate, Strom Thurmond. Unlike some who rebelled against fundamentalism, my departure from this environment was gradual, based on what I slowly came to realize were a number of "fundamental" inconsistencies in fundamentalist beliefs, attitudes, and practices.

The first inconsistency to strike me forcibly was the common sacrifice of Christian love to Christian belief. That is, disagreements over doctrines and moral codes (whether with fellow fundamentalists or others at greater distances) frequently and almost inevitably led to a breaking off of fellowship—and a breaking in of outright hostilities. The movement from friend ("brother" and "sister") could occur suddenly and irrevocably. Not only love and friendship but anything and everything could be sacrificed to "the fundamentals"—whatever these were said to be and however interpreted—and even to matters that could hardly be said to be fundamental, but which became part of the "slippery slope" or "domino" theory. An incident of this latter sort occurred during my sophomore year at the university. It so dramatized this issue that I could not avoid it.

Lifelong friends of the founder (and chairman) of the university had retired and moved across the street, with much fanfare made of this enduring association and their reunion. The couple were placed on the board of trustees, were invited to lead and accompany the singing at daily chapel services whenever in town, and even had a dormitory named after them. The same academic year an administrator of the institution—who also had a long affiliation with the school as student, teacher, and administrator—was accused of violating a school rule that required staff members to patronize the school physician. The reason for this infraction, it was later learned, was that the man's wife was pregnant and had an Rh-blood-factor problem that they felt needed the services of a specialist. The punishment for this tear in the seamless garment of institutional policy— all biblically based of course—was that the administrator was summarily fired and given twenty-four hours to get his family and their belongings out of faculty housing. When the lifelong friends of the founder/chairman of the institution learned of this they offered to let the unfortunate couple store some things in their basement until they were relocated. When the founder/chairman of the institution learned of this act of mercy, he severed all further relationships with his lifelong friends. They were removed from the board of trustees; they were no longer invited to share in the chapel program; their name was stripped from the dormitory facade; and they were unwelcome to set foot on campus again!

Being quite well-versed in the Bible—having been required as a child to memorize large amounts of Scripture, so as to be armed against the Evil One— two verses came to mind. The first was from the book of Acts: "Behold, how they love one another!" The second was from 1 Cor. 13:8–9 "Love never ends; as for prophecies, they will pass away; as for tongues, they will cease; as for knowledge, it will pass away. For our knowledge is imperfect and our prophecy is imperfect." Despite the fundamentalists' loud claims to be faithful to Scripture and New Testament Christianity, the history of fundamentalism is replete with violations of such plain teachings. Though Corinthians insists that love—indeed the highest kind of self-sacrificing and unconditional love, *agape*—is to be placed above all other considerations, fundamentalism lays down a plethora of conditions and places all manner of considerations above love. In 1 Corinthians love has the first and last word, relative to which other virtues and concerns must give way, whether claims to knowledge, prophetic understandings, tongues of the spirit, righteous acts, even faith itself—let alone belief systems, moral codes, rules of behavior, or institutional regulations!

I began to understand the readiness of fundamentalism to sacrifice love and its attendant virtues (patience, kindness, mercy, gentleness, long-suffering, grace, etc.) to almost anything, from definitions of "the fundamentalist" to trivial points of disagreement and infraction (as in the above story). This led to another realization. One of the central motivating forces behind fundamentalism is a spirit that militates against love and its virtues. Despite the frequent tirades in fundamentalist preaching and literature against "the self-righteousness of the Pharisees," self-righteousness simply comes in the back door in the form of *self-rightness.* The only sustainable love possible to the spirit of self-righteousness or self-rightness is love in the sense of loving those who love you, are like you, agree with you—somthing Jesus called his disciples to go beyond in the Sermon on the Mount: "If you love those that love you, what reward have you? Do not even tax collectors do the same?" (Matt. 5:46). Fundamentalism is moved by the alien spirit of pride and the false promises of dogmatism. Those who share the correct interpretations of theological, moral, and political matters are to be loved and fellowshipped with; those who do not are to be cut off under the rubric of "come out from among them and be separate, says the Lord."

Fundamentalism is not well-known for its claims to have imperfect knowledge and prophecies that will pass away. Nor are fundamentalists well-known for their openness, humility, or love toward those who disagree with them. Not surprisingly, also, fundamentalists are greatly exercised over having an inerrant Bible in the original documents (even if nobody has them), and thus having a bedrock foundation for access to the final knowledge of good and evil (which belongs only to God). In the biblical context, the inerrancy of which is such a passion, this spirit is none other than that old demon "pride," which leads to the idolatry of wanting to be "like God" and thence to a long train of human evils.

Even those who would teach the biblical priority of love, citing authorities no less than Jesus and Paul, are anathema, as I soon learned when I defended the actions of the retired couple who befriended the fired administrator and his wife. The final break came for me when I was asked to deliver a devotional to a university student organization and chose to meditate on 1 Cor. 13. The ironies of those verses in that context were too much, and I discovered that students too could be given twenty-four hours to clear themselves and their belongings out of campus housing!

These experiences were later to lead my professional career in at least one unusual direction: an interest in exploring the importance of *humor* relative to "faith, hope, and love." I have since gone on to write a number of articles, then books, on this set of issues: *The Comic Vision and the Christian Faith* (1981), *And God Created Laughter: The Bible as Divine Comedy* (1986), and *The Laughing Buddha: Zen and the Comic Spirit* (1989). I owe all this indirectly to my early life among fundamentalists who helped me to understand—albeit negatively—that people with a well-developed sense of humor about themselves and their humanity are more inclined to love one another and less inclined to despise and dismiss one another.

There is, of course, a form of humor that laughs at others who differ from us or otherwise threaten us. Such humor reinforces our sense of pride, legitimizes our beliefs and practices, and justifies our animosities. And there is plenty of this kind of humor in fundamentalist circles. But humor at its best is a confession, not of everyone else's foolishness or unworthiness, but of our own. Through humor we confess that we, like all other human beings, are finite, fallible, mortal, sinful, and frequently foolish. We confess that we, too, "see through a glass darkly" and "know in part, and prophesy in part." Otherwise we become like the theologians of the sixteenth-century comedy *Des cris de Paris,* who have "such profundities in their minds that, if you were to believe their writings, you would think they were God's first cousins!"

Dennis Ronald MacDonald:
From Faith to Faith

During my early years faith was credulity . . . God said it. I believed it. That settled it. The curse of credulity, however, is defensiveness . . . nothing must be allowed to challenge the system. No theological domino so carefully stood on end could be allowed to fall. All of life had to fit into place; no ambiguity could be tolerated; mystery was outlawed; doubt exiled. All who believed differently were a threat; therefore, we had to keep up our guard against them and their father the Devil, or better, to convert them to our way of thinking. . . .

Never mind that so many who once found it now have lost it.

—Dennis Ronald MacDonald

Dennis Ronald MacDonald is professor of New Testament and Christian origins at Iliff School of Theology, Denver, Colorado, and author of *There is No Male and Female: The Fate of a Dominical Saying in Paul and Gnosticism*, *The Legend and the Apostle: The Battle for Paul in Story and Canon*, and *The Acts of Andrew and the Acts of Andrew and Matthias in the City of the Cannibals*. What follows is a newly edited version of MacDonald's autobiographical address, "From Faith to Faith: My Journey from Credulity to Awe."

My father was pastor of a Conservative Baptist church on the south side of Chicago; my mother a converted Jew, the daughter of a Russian emigré. They first met at what then was Bob Jones College in Cleveland, Tennessee. I spent most of my growing years in Illinois, Minnesota, and Michigan, where Dad served as pastor of various fundamentalistic Baptist churches.

My life was filled with the Bible. Our parents regularly read the Bible to us four kids after supper. Our church conducted what we called sword drills—contests to see who could look up Obadiah 10 the fastest—Bible memorization, Bible schools, Bible conferences, Biblical preaching, and so on. I remember my father rising at 5:30 every morning to walk to the office to read the Bible, and—as he put it—to be with the Lord. My mother's last act most days was to read the Bible. For them Bible reading was not simply devotional exercise: it issued in loving and sacrificial service for others. I remember how my Dad would regularly spend hours caring for a mentally handicapped woman and her grown mentally handicapped son, doing their wash, buying groceries, and cleaning house. Only our family ever knew Dad did this.

When I graduated from high school in 1964 I applied to Bob Jones University in Greenville, South Carolina. My parents were stalwart alumni, even though they opposed the school's policies on race. In part my parents' liberalism on this issue grew out of my mother's Jewish past. Her father's back bore a vicious scar, the work of a Cossack's sabre received during a pogrom against his *shtetl* when he was a schoolboy.

My first semesters at Bob Jones were routine: adjusting to college studies, learning how to bend rigid rules without breaking them, writing home for money, improving soccer skills, and satisfying my interests in the school's female population. When it came time to declare a major I decided on Bible, in part because I had a good background, but mostly because I considered the Bible the Word of God, and thought that the better I knew it the surer I would be of God's will for my life.

We "preacher boys," as Bible majors were called at the time (there were no "preacher girls"), were required to take Greek in our sophomore year. Greek allowed me to read familiar texts as though I had never done so before. It slowed me down and forced me to attend to previously ignored details. But most importantly, Greek gave me the confidence to interpret the New Testament independently and to analyze how others used it.

I soon discovered that even though speakers and teachers at Bob Jones claimed the New Testament as their ultimate authority, their theology and practice corresponded little to what I read for myself. How could I harmonize the school's narrowness and legalism with the New Testament's emphasis on freedom from law and the life of the Spirit? How could I harmonize the school's racial policies with the New Testament's articulation that in Christ there "cannot be Greek and Jew, barbarian, Scythian, slave, free" (Col. 3:11)? How could racism have anything to do with the New Testament message of the love of God and the command to love one another?

This dissonance between my life at Bob Jones and my study of the New Testament fascinated me but it also made me retreat silently into my studies. I found it dangerous to express my concerns openly, uncomfortable to share my disquiet with any but my best and likewise alienated friends. Though dangerous and uncomfortable, my intellectual awakening was thrilling. Had Bob Jones not been so extreme, I may not have had the motivation to get in touch with the joys and freedoms of intellectual discovery. My body was captive at Bob Jones, but my spirit began to soar.

My spirit crashed on April 4, 1968, ten weeks before graduating. It was Bible conference week at Bob Jones—that time every spring when three times each day we were required to listen to sermons and lectures from visiting speakers. The speakers during that week included Ian Paisley, the militantly anti-Catholic Ulster Presbyterian, and John Stormer, author of *None Dare Call It Treason,* an anti-Communist alarmist. Stormer gave the keynote address Saturday night, at the end of which Bob Jones, Jr., then president, came to the podium and announced that Martin Luther King, Jr., had been shot and killed in Memphis, Tennessee. He also said in words tattooed on my mind: "The president has asked all to fly the flag at half-mast. We'll not fly the flag at half-mast for an apostate." The audience, with few exceptions, clapped and cheered. Never in my life had I seen, never in my mind had I imagined, such an outpouring of racist hatred, and this at the end of a Bible conference!

We left the meeting to return to our dorms, and, as was the custom, several rooms assembled together for evening prayers. I refused to let our group pray until we had talked out what we all had witnessed just minutes before. Not another person in that prayer group saw the slightest immorality or even ethical ambiguity in the school's response. Early the next morning someone must have tattled on me. I spent most of that day bounced from one administrator to another. Over and over I was asked how a Christian could have responded the way I did to the death of Dr. King. Over and over I asked them how a Christian could have responded any other way.

I am certain that those administrators wanted to "ship" me, but they did not. To this day I do not know if the reason was my parents' longstanding loyalty to Bob Jones or the flimsy grounds for expulsion. In any case, they accused me of having a "bad attitude" and gave me 125 "demerits," just short of the number for dismissal. They moved me into a room occupied by one of their most reliable stooges, stripped me of my positions of leadership, and restricted my movement to the campus. By the grace of God—and by hiding in the library where I couldn't get into any more trouble—I graduated.

I had been given a scholarship to attend Princeton Seminary the following fall, but I knew I was too wounded to continue my education immediately. Instead, I decided to take a job for one year as a youth pastor in a Conservative Baptist church in Salinas, California, and use the year to translate the New Testament from Greek. During that year I did indeed translate the entire New Testament, but doing so helped little in resolving my disquiet with fundamentalism. I was baffled by inconsistencies in the New Testament itself. Neither simple-minded harmonizing nor elaborate explanations were able to satisfy my curiosity.

More troubling to me than these inconsistencies were the incongruities between the New Testament and the behavior of those in my church. Salinas is the heart of the "lettuce bowl" of northern California, and childhood home of John Steinbeck, who long before had written about the region's exploitation of agricultural laborers in *The Grapes of Wrath*. When I lived in Salinas, it was a center for labor protests of Cesar Chavez and the United Farm Workers, largely composed of Hispanic migrants. Although about one-third of Salinas's population was Hispanic, none of them attended church. We did, however, have our share of lettuce growers. The only Christians in Salinas I saw working actively among Hispanics were Catholics and Episcopalians—both of which Bob Jones and my parents would have considered apostate. Why was it that we fundamentalists, who claimed the Bible as our ultimate authority and Christ as Lord, were doing so little to live out the gospel? Something was wrong, terribly wrong.

After that year I went to Princeton Seminary, still trying to correlate my reading of the New Testament with the needs of the world I saw around me.

I thought that at last, in the serene ivy-clad buildings of the seminary, I would find shelter from the world and be able to pursue my quest. I did indeed pursue my quest, but not in serenity.

I entered Princeton in the fall of 1969, the year Ivy League students, including those at Princeton, nearly shut down the universities to protest the war in Viet Nam. From my youth I had been taught racism was wrong, and at Bob Jones and Salinas I worked out my views on racism. But it never occurred to me to question the war in Vietnam. After all, we were there to help the Vietnamese, right? The war was America's sacrificial attempt to aid free peoples withstanding godless Communists, right? America was a Christian country, founded on biblical principles, called by God to enforce justice and protect freedom and the gospel, right? In light of what I was learning about the war in Indochina, I was no longer able to convince myself that the war was justifiable or that America's intentions were unambiguously noble. Furthermore, my reading of the New Testament made it difficult to see how the ethics of Jesus could in any way support such carnage. Both in the classroom and out I was becoming even more alienated from my fundamentalist past.

It occurred to me that perhaps I was rejecting conservative Christianity because what I knew of it was a caricature, so I decided to attend Trinity Evangelical Divinity School in Deerfield, Illinois, which I had heard was evangelical but more liberal on social issues than Bob Jones. After one year there I would return to Princeton, so I thought.

At Trinity during the fall of 1970 I met several other seminarians seeking the same correlation between a faithfulness to the New Testament and appropriate responses to the crises of the time. Since there had been no peace activity at the seminary, we set up what we called a "peacetable," where we provided information and talked about the war and American imperialism. We were appalled at the hostility we faced because of that table. To be sure, several other students and a few faculty were sympathetic to our concerns, but we also were spat upon and administratively bullied. The school did its best not to let its constituency know that protests against the war had reached Trinity's own sacred shores. My faculty advisor refused to sign my course selection card and told me the school was not big enough for the two of us. He's now academic dean there. So much for Trinity's legendary social liberalism!

It became clear to a few of us students that Evangelicalism needed a new dose of New Testament ethical radicalism, and for that reason seven of us, one of whom was Jim Wallis, published the first issue of the *Post American,* the prototype of the magazine now known as *Sojourners.* We were overwhelmed by the response. Letters and checks streamed in from other disgruntled evangelicals encouraging us to continue our publication.

We rented a house not far from the seminary and formed a community, a kind of live-in house-church from which we wrote, published our little paper, organized protests and resistance groups, and even studied from time to time. The New Testament became for us a document of social criticism, no longer an icon of American civil religion. The qualities of the Roman Empire so vigorously denounced in the book of Revelation seemed all too apt descriptions of the American empire. America was the beast rising from the sea, whose mouth dripped the blood of the righteous.

The kingdom of God became for us a political ideal, a vision of human life permanently in tension with the kingdoms of this world, a vision for the future that required absolute obedience. The teachings of Jesus became for us a mandate for valuing the poor and for denouncing wealth, power, and arrogance, whether national, racial, or sexual. It was during those years that I returned my degree to Bob Jones—partly to protest the school's immorality, but mostly to purge myself from any symbolic identification with it. It was during these years too that I married Diane Prosser, who likewise had grown up in fundamentalism and whose pilgrimage was much like my own.

But gradually I also became disillusioned with the way we in the Sojourners community were using the New Testament. The issue came to a head for me in 1973. As the *Sojourners* magazine became more ecumenical in its constituency and awareness, we on the editorial board had to decide how much latitude we could tolerate without losing our distinctive perspective. One issue before us was how best to use critical scholarship on the New Testament.

Someone had contributed an article we wanted to publish, but which did not treat the Gospels as we did. The author argued in good Bultmannian fashion that it was impossible to be certain that the teachings of Jesus actually had been spoken by him. They were instead products of early Christian reflection on the significance of Jesus. This was a crucial issue for us insofar as we had appealed to these teachings to anchor our ethic. I was selected to deliver a presentation on the state of the art on the historical Jesus "problem" and to make suggestions concerning how to deal with it editorially.

I insisted that we recognize the complexity of the transmission of Jesus' sayings in the early church and be willing to admit that some sayings dear to us were in fact inauthentic, though not for that reason false or unusable. The rest of the board disagreed. For them it was crucial, for example, that Jesus himself and not the early church said, "If anyone would come after me let him take up his cross daily and follow me." But I was convinced that the reference to the "cross" here derived from post-crucifixion reflections on the death of Jesus. Jesus himself could not have uttered it. But for the board, such an assessment concerning the dominical authenticity of this saying and others was thought dysfunctional and rhetorically powerless.

Many such conversations followed and it appeared to me that once again the truth about the New Testament was compromised in order to serve ideological commitments allegedly derived from it. Though this commitment was noble, my years at Bob Jones had taught me the dangers of appealing to the New Testament uncritically in order to footnote one's own social or political agenda.

That same year the Sojourners community moved from Chicago to Washington, D.C., and Diane and I became students at Harvard—she in theology; I in New Testament. These graduate studies freed me at last to study the New Testament without the burdens of a dogmatic, fundamentalistic theology as in my Bob Jones days, but also without a rigid, radical social agenda, as in my Sojourners days.

That was seventeen years ago, and I have gone through still other transformations: becoming a father twice and teaching at Goshen College, the Iliff School of Theology, Harvard Divinity School, and Union Theological Seminary (New York). Faith for me now has a very different meaning from what it had in my youth, or even during my years with the Sojourners. My journey from faith to faith to faith has been a journey from credulity to deconstruction to awe.

During my early years faith was credulity, uncritical acceptance of my own religious heritage girded by an uncritical reading of the Bible. God said it. I believed it. That settled it. Credulity indeed has its rewards and virtues. I lived in a closed, comfortable symbol-system, one which inspired me to kindness, personal sacrifice, loyalty, and honesty. I knew what was expected of me and was assured of divine blessing in my life if I were faithful. The lives of my father and mother witnessed to the beauty of faith as credulity. Their devotion to help others, their unwavering commitments to the values they cherished, and their love of God are all rich fruits of their confidence about the rightness of their fundamentalistic worldview. At Bob Jones too I admired many students who had devoted their lives to sacrificial service and were unswervingly committed to honesty and integrity.

The curse of credulity, however, is defensiveness. At Bob Jones it was clear that nothing must be allowed to challenge the system. Its world was too fragile and had to be protected at any cost. No theological domino so carefully stood on end could be allowed to fall. All of life had to fit into place; no ambiguity could be tolerated; mystery was outlawed; doubt exiled. All who believed differently were a threat; therefore, we had to keep up our guard against them and their father the Devil, or better, to convert them to our way of thinking. Surely it is not accidental that fundamentalist groups who think their truth is besieged on all sides by the forces of evil, including that greatest of all putative evils—secular humanism—are fiercely evangelistic. One way of proving one's worldview correct is to see others who once did not share that view now convert to it. We can't be wrong if so many believe what we do. Never mind that so many who once found it now have lost it.

I believe in evangelism, but I am concerned that we may rejoice in others' affirmations of belief because they shield us from potential though necessary discomfirmations of our own comfortable beliefs.

At some point, however, we find that honesty requires us to question the correctness of our symbol-systems. For me the first cracks in the system came from reading the New Testament in Greek, and that crack became a chasm with the murder of Martin Luther King, Jr., and the war in Vietnam. My symbolic world construction was collapsing; my dominoes of dogma were dropping; I was alienated from my parents and from many friends. I know of few people for whom the study of the Bible has resulted in such cognitive rebellion, but I know of many for whom the study of science, or psychology, or anthropology, or philosophy had the same effect. For others it was not studies at all but experience that destroyed their old worlds—experiences of racial hatred, or of sexual exploitation, or of hypocrisy. For many, such disillusionment issues in cynicism and the wholesale rejection of religion.

For me it led to my time as a member of the Sojourners community. During those years faith no longer was credulity but deconstruction. Our religious life was a life in reaction to America's social sins and Evangelicalism's tacit complicity with them. We thought of the kingdom of God as a world-deconstructing ideal that could never be fully created on earth. Christians were called to be perpetual revolutionaries inasmuch as no political system, no society, no institution could embody our utopian ideals. Our community espoused a counterfaith for the counterculture of the late sixties and seventies. Whereas faith as credulity is uncritical cultural acceptance, faith as deconstruction is critical cultural rejection. Instead of reading the Bible for support of American civil religion, we read it for idealogical critiques of it.

There is much to be said for faith as deconstruction. It allows one to view life critically, to reexamine dominant cultural conventions, to seek alternative symbolic worlds and behaviors. But there also are dangers with faith as deconstruction. Like faith as credulity, it can absolutize itself. A fluid countercultural idealism easily freezes into a new cultural ideology, demands its own kinds of conformity, and denies ambiguity and complexity. We considered ourselves true Christians, the few faithful who lived only for the kingdom of God while others sought personal happiness and were controlled by uncritical conformity. We nonconformists, however, were white, predominantly male, middle-class graduate students who wore blue jeans, flannel shirts, and sported various outrageous arrangements of facial hair. We all liked Bob Dylan, Joan Baez, and "M*A*S*H," and identified with Archie Bunker's son-in-law, "Meathead." Without knowing it we, too, had constructed and now were defending a fragile symbolic world. We were certain this world was not our own creation but the necessary result of faithfulness to the teachings of Jesus.

Once again it was my study of the New Testament that eroded my confidence in this symbolic world construction. For others, including many of those still with the Sojourners community, this erosion proceeded from the loss of our original optimism. We, too, were getting divorces; we, too, found it difficult to raise our children to cherish our values; we, too, failed to approximate the ideals of the kingdom of God; we, too, were sinners. Our symbolic world was deconstructing under the weight of life.

For many of us, faith as deconstruction has become faith as awe. By saying faith is awe I do not mean to imply that one must stand mouth agape before the vastness of the universe, petrified by complexity, dizzy from ambiguity and absurdity. By faith as awe I mean that we recognize how we construct our religious meanings against the backdrop of mystery. Faith always seeks order in the midst of disorder; it builds habitable worlds in jungles of absurdity. Faith as awe takes responsibility for its own construction and knows that growth may require its deconstruction. Faith as awe refuses to absolutize itself and accepts ambiguity as the blessed curse of life.

This definition of faith also corresponds with my discoveries as a New Testament scholar. It seems to me that the New Testament is not the revelation of a divine plan for humankind that can be captured somehow in a system, be it conservative or radical. The New Testament is a witness to how some early Christians themselves constructed meaningful symbolic worlds against the backdrop of mystery. The very diversity of the New Testament is its greatest theological contribution. That is, the New Testament functions as a resource for us not in any perceived and systematized unity but in its elusive pluralism. But like the other definitions of faith, faith as awe also has its dangers. It can lead to cynicism about religion inasmuch as most religions claim for themselves absolute truth. Worse, the recognition of ambiguity can lead to nihilism. The challenge of faith as awe is to believe in the midst of doubt. It is significant, I think, that for Paul the opposite of faith was not doubt but self-righteousness.

Self-righteousness and uncritical smugness about one's own theology have nothing to do with faith. Doubt is not faith's rival; doubt is faith's twin sister.

Perhaps faith is best understood as that confidence in God that allows our fragile theological systems to collapse into new ones. "Unfaith" is the insistence that our thoughts are the same as God's thoughts. The apostle Paul understood this when he wrote: "Oh the depth of the riches and wisdom and knowledge of God! How unsearchable are God's judgments and how inscrutable God's ways! Who has known the mind of the Lord, or who has been God's counselor? . . . From God and through God and to God are all things. To God be glory for ever. Amen" (Rom. 11:33–34, 36).

David Montoya: The Political Disease Known as Fundamentalism

For people coming out of the 1960s and the 1970s, out of the relativism, out of the drug culture, fundamentalism can be a wonderful kind of "life jacket." It gives you some security. It makes things black and white. It allows you to feel a sense of forgiveness for the guilt and the things you've done to your body during those times. But it quickly changes from a "life jacket" to a "straitjacket." And it becomes just as addictive, just as destructive, as anything that was ever proposed by Timothy Leary and Tom Wolfe.

—David Montoya

David Montoya is the pastor of University Baptist Church, Wichita, Kansas. He is a graduate of the Criswell Center for Biblical Studies, and also of Southwestern Baptist Theological Seminary, where he received his master of divinity degree. In October 1990 at Stanford University, Montoya debated one of the key figures responsible for the fundamentalist takeover of the Southern Baptist Convention (SBC), Judge Paul Pressler, on the topic, "Hope for Reconciliation?" The following is based on a sermon Montoya delivered at the Broadway Baptist Church in Fort Worth, Texas, on July 22, 1990, on a written testimony, "The Tape," and on a phone conversation Montoya shared with the editor.

My story focuses on the [conservative versus moderate] struggle within the Southern Baptist denomination. But viewed in a wider perspective, it deals with every Christian denomination facing the political disease known as fundamentalism.

In 1979 I entered the Criswell Center for Biblical Studies, having had that school recommended to me by the staff at a Dallas church where I was a member. I entered Criswell with little prior knowledge of theology.

From the day I set foot in that school I was barraged with the declaration, "Our convention [i.e., the Southern Baptist Convention] is in trouble!" I was told, "Liberals are everywhere," and, "We have a divine destiny to save the SBC." It was our job to "turn the great ship of Zion around, to get it back on course." We couldn't trust our national leadership. We couldn't trust our state leadership. We couldn't trust our associational leadership. We couldn't trust the Sunday school board literature. We couldn't trust anyone. We were at war and we must win!

In 1980 my wife and I began working on a volunteer basis with Richard Land at Criswell Center, supporting the pro-life movement. I was the first Baptist to serve on the board of directors of Dallas Right to Life. And I was introduced, through the school, to several political leaders of the state.

Finally, I was recruited by the Texas Roundtable, a New Right organization, where I served as activities director. I helped put on the Rally for Life in Dallas, the stated purpose of which was to promote the Human Life Amendment. But in reality the purpose was to put pressure on Ronald Reagan to not nominate Sandra Day O'Connor to the Supreme Court. [O'Connor was nominated and confirmed, becoming the first woman to serve on the Supreme Court.]

The president of the Criswell Center for Biblical Studies, Dr. Paige Patterson, would commonly have political spokesmen address students on issues like, "High Frontier" [i.e., the "Star Wars" missile defense program], "South Africa," and other geopolitical issues. In our classes there were not many times when we did *not* get into the agenda of the New Right.

I graduated from Criswell in 1982,[1] then decided to attend Southwestern Baptist Theological Seminary. But before I went I met with Dr. Patterson, and he said, "I would appreciate any information that you can obtain for us on any professors over at Southwestern that are teaching liberalism. Watch yourself. You're going to be exposed to it. It will be good for you to go over there and get your 'credit card' [master of divinity degree], but don't let them change the way you are thinking."

At Southwestern Seminary I taped my professors' classes in order to collect for Dr. Patterson all the "evidence of liberalism" that I could.

However, I only attended Southwestern for *one* semester. As a fundamentalist, that was about all I could take. The noted British theologian John A. T. Robinson delivered a lecture there in which he made the statement that "Jesus Christ is *not* the only way to heaven." And that made me so angry, I left the seminary.[2]

Then I returned to Dallas, where I helped found "Salt and Light" ministries, which was at that time no more than a political action organization formed to aid some local politicians. We also tried to halt the Dallas city council's plan to divest its interests in South Africa. We argued that the South African government was totally justified in enforcing apartheid and maintaining their "rigorous" control over the black populace, otherwise, tribal warfare would reduce the country to total anarchy. Therefore, we should support the white Protestant leadership of that country in all they do. (I don't believe that today. I've seen *Cry Freedom* since then!)

I also worked with some pro-life people at that time. We showed the film *Silent Scream*.[3] I also supported vigorously the "Star Wars" agenda of Ronald Reagan.

Then, with the help of some friends at Criswell, I received my first call to pastor a church. Prior to leaving, Dr. Patterson called me into his office once again. Upon his wall was a map of the United States, and on this map were little red pins everywhere. He explained that these were his "children," the graduates that made up part of the network. These were the ones who were going to help him turn this great Baptist Zion around.

He showed me where I was going to go on the map, and said, "David, you're not going to get much support down there. But here's what you do. Be polite to the director of missions, but don't have much to do with him. And be very careful of whom you associate with down there, because many of the Baptists there are in the 'other camp.' "

So, I went down to that area and began my ministry as a young pastor in his first church. But when I got myself into trouble, as I was inevitably destined to do, it was that director of missions who came to me, supported me, guided me, and loved me. And if I had listened to him, and some of the sound advice from those senior pastors in the "other camp," I would not have had near the number of problems in my ministry that I had.

I should have realized then the untruths, the deceptions, the overpromotion of the "problems caused by liberalism." But we were "fighting for the faith," weren't we? We were "battling for the Bible," weren't we? After all, that's what the letters that I received from the Judge [i.e., Paul Pressler, a Houston appellate court judge, and one of the founding fathers of the political takeover in the Southern Baptist Convention] told me. That's what the *Southern Baptist Advocate* told me every time I sat down to read it. Was not our position being confirmed year after year by the votes of the Southern Baptist Convention? We *must* be right!

And then my ministry moved me to Arkansas.

I had not been in Arkansas two weeks when I received a phone call inviting me to Little Rock, to participate in a planning session of "conservative pastors" (as they were called in that state), to help put together an organization that would "get the vote out" for Arkansas. That meeting was the embryonic stage of what was to become a political machine that within a few years would attempt to take control of the Arkansas Baptist State Convention.

About a week and a half later the judge phoned and instructed me that a young northwest Arkansas pastor was to be the leader in that state. The young pastor called me less than a day later and asked if I would serve as one of his eight district leaders. *I* was given a position. I was also told that I could ask others within the associations that were within my district if *they* would serve as my associational whips, and I could give each of *them* a position. We were going to show those moderates!

As I began to attend the private planning sessions, became involved in conference calls, and was granted privileged information because of my position within the organization, it dawned on me what we were really doing. We were pursuing and getting positions.

The conservative machine in Arkansas put out its own newspaper, *A Conservative Voice*. In this paper they defined "a conservative." They didn't say it was someone who believed in the inerrancy of Scripture, or someone who had conservative theology, or someone who has upheld Baptist principles and practices steadfastly over many years. Their definition was someone who has voted for the man that the new Baptist bishops—the cardinals of control—had blessed that particular year.

Then the leaders in the state of Arkansas began to single out and attack men who I knew were more godly, who loved God's Word as much as, if not more than, the fundamentalist leaders. Godly men were labeled and attacked, not because of their theology, but because they wouldn't go along, nor bow the knee, or because they were perceived as a "threat." Then I decided, this thing has gone way too far.

But why generalize when I can quote chapter and verse of my last day as an active supporter of the fundamentalist Baptist movement. Here's the story of the straw that broke the camel's back.

Joe Atchison was the director of missions of Benton County Baptist Association in the Arkansas State Convention. He was employed by an association of Baptist churches to help them coordinate their mission efforts on a local level. However, he was using this paid position ($65,000 or more per year) to carry on a large part of his political activity in the SBC and in Arkansas. For he was also the coordinator of a political network constructed by fundamentalists to achieve the takeover of the Arkansas Baptist State Convention. (This has been well documented and is easily verifiable.)

I objected to Joe's practices of blackballing and labeling fellow Baptists in the state convention. He lied and misrepresented them, pursuing personal vendettas. He employed veiled and overt threats, planted nominations, and offered positions in exchange for support. I went to Joe and challenged him face to face about his activities.

Joe responded, "David, you're young, you don't understand. This is the way things are. This is the way they're going to be. Don't criticize, just go along. Don't worry. You've got your position sewed up. You just do what we want you to, and you'll go far in this organization."

Attempting to follow what I thought was a biblical pattern of confrontation, I took another pastor along with me and approached Joe a second time. When that didn't work I tried going to other conservatives in the Arkansas network with my concerns. When these individuals called Joe to ask him if what I was saying was true, Joe would either tell them that I was a pathological liar, or he would refer to my young age and say, "David just misunderstands what is going on."

So, I phoned Ronnie Floyd. Ronnie was one of Judge Paul Pressler's hand picked "golden boys." The Judge had put together a group of young right-wing fundamentalist pastors and was grooming them to be future leaders of the SBC, thereby guaranteeing the Judge's continuing influence and control of convention matters. Evidence of Ronnie's chosen status could be seen in the positions he had been given. He had been in Arkansas barely over a year when he was placed on the powerful executive committee of the SBC, representing Arkansas. His appointment preceded that of conservative pastors who had been in the state much longer, primarily because Pressler wanted him to have a key leadership role. Pressler himself told me that Ronnie would be leading the conservatives in Arkansas. In fact, Ronnie was to be the fundamentalist organization's candidate for president in the Arkansas Baptist State convention that year.

Ronnie was also the pastor of the First Baptist Church in Springdale, Arkansas. By the time this account is published I am sure he will have moved on to greener pastures if a bigger and better opportunity has presented itself. He emphasized more than once to several people that Arkansas was but a stepping stone for him. Such is the nature of the new young, upwardly mobile fundamentalist preachers in the SBC.

I recognized I was taking a chance by calling Ronnie, but I had tried just about everything else. He was the only person in the state with enough clout to deal with Joe Atchison. I also trusted Ronnie to be politically astute enough to recognize the pragmatic aspects of my concerns, such as the negative reactions that could result from Joe's behavior if it became public knowledge. Hopefully, Ronnie might listen to reason and use his position to halt, or at least limit, Joe's political and moral abuse of power.

Evidently, after our phone conversation was finished, Ronnie called Joe and told him what I had said. Joe then called me and asked me to come to a meeting at *Ronnie's* office *that* afternoon. He said he understood I had some concerns.

I told him, "You know what my concerns are."

Joe responded by stating our need to get together and work things out, adding that I had "much to lose" by my continued effort to push this issue. After this came a rhetorical plea to remain steadfast in supporting the fundamentalist cause. He reminded me how important the cause was and how my attitude could damage all our efforts. According to Joe the best way for our differences to be handled was for me to get in line, do my job, and keep my mouth shut.

Being treated this way made me angry. Still, I knew I had better not lose my cool. I let him know I wanted to get these things settled as soon as possible, but not this afternoon. He said fine and then hung up.

Now I had a decision to make, either *not* go to the meeting, in which case I might be one of the topics discussed, or *go,* in which case what good would it do? It seemed obvious that Ronnie was going to support Joe. Either he approved of Joe's activities or else he had been instructed to support him by the Judge.

Then a thought came to me. I needed evidence to prove what I was saying was true, evidence of what was going on in the leadership of the political organization in Arkansas. I needed something that Joe could not just explain away or deny. I would attend the meeting and obtain the evidence I needed to prove my point.

I had purchased a voice activated micro-cassette recorder a few days earlier. I put the recorder in my coat pocket and asked my wife, Juanell, if she needed anything from Springdale. I related to her the content of the call I had received from Atchison and how I felt the need to attend the meeting. She agreed with my assessment of the situation, so off to Springdale we went.

Speaking of my wife, Juanell, she surrendered to the ministry at the same time I did, soon after our marriage. Due to the fundamentalist indoctrination I had received at Criswell, and its negative orientation toward female ministers, her ministry was forced into the background. Juanell sensed the destructiveness of the political aspects of the fundamentalist takeover from the very beginning. If I had not been so stubborn and listened to her, we probably would not have gotten into this mess in the first place.

While I drove to Springdale, the demons of doubt and despair began working their malevolent mischief on my mind. Who did I think I was, challenging these men of God and the tactics they were using to "defend the Bible"? Did not I realize what could and would most certainly happen? Joe would retaliate against me. Time after time I had seen Joe cause trouble for pastors within their own churches, and within the association if they dared to oppose him. What right did I have to subject the church I served to that kind of suffering because of my actions?

Also, if the *network* supported Joe's behavior, I could be blackballed, making it difficult to obtain another pastorate. The network had become very good at "putting out the word" on those who were labeled "liberal" or who did not agree with their political agenda.

Lastly, I had to struggle with the ethics of recording people's words without their consent. Why not just leave the organization and let them do whatever they wanted? Other pastors did that, simply serving their particular congregations, refusing to get involved.

Then I remembered a quotation I had read a few days earlier, "The only way for evil to prevail is for good men to do nothing." I might not have been a good man, but I wanted to be. To me, there was no doubt that what was being done in Arkansas was evil. I had to tape the session if I were to live with myself. Once I firmed up my decision a strange sense of peace calmed my thoughts.

My wife dropped me off at the First Baptist Church in Springdale, and I asked her to return in two hours. I turned the recorder on before entering the building. Ronnie's secretary informed me that the meeting had already begun.

Upon entering I was greeted by Ronnie Floyd and two other political activists in the state, Mark Brooks and Bob Foster.

Brooks was pastor of Elmdale Baptist Church in Springdale and also editor of *A Conservative Voice,* a party propaganda newsletter that functioned regionally in a fashion similar to the way Paige Patterson and Paul Pressler employed the *Southern Baptist Advocate* nationally.

For those unfamiliar with the type of journalism carried out by the *Advocate,* perhaps the following analogy will help. If I said that the *Advocate* was as truthful as the *National Enquirer* I would be sued by the *Enquirer* for defamation of character. The *Advocate* has been used to spread slander and lies, all in the name of "inerrancy," without fear of being held legally accountable. They are smugly secure in printing whatever they wish since their board of directors remains a secret, covered by a trail of paper and the money of a certain judge (other powerful right-wing fundamentalists afford added protection).

The other fellow, Bob Foster, a former soft drink executive, had recently become the pastor of a small church in Siloam Springs, Arkansas. Bob served for several years as a non-seminary-trained, bi-vocational pastor before becoming a full time pastor. Bob was consumed with hatred for anything labeled "liberal." It was Bob who was used by the network to acquire press passes for fundamentalist activists, granting them access to the pressroom during the Southern Baptist Convention. One of Bob's major desires was to be placed on the board of directors of the Arkansas Baptist *Newsmagazine* in order to have the editor fired, whom he disliked with a passion. This was a goal shared by the majority of fundamentalist leaders. The fact that the editor was probably more conservative in his theology than they were did not matter. He would not acquiesce to their demands, therefore he was a "liberal."

Bob has since gone on to work for a foundation in Arkansas whose founder's ideology has been described as extreme right wing and has been accused of being racist as well as anti-Semitic—a common proclivity among fundamentalists. (Adrian Rogers, a key leader of the fundamentalist movement in the SBC, when asked by a nonfundamentalist pastor how he interpreted a particular biblical passage that apparently condoned slavery, responded, "I feel slavery is a much maligned institution. If we had slavery today we would not have such a welfare problem.")

Joe Atchison was also in the room, seated at Ronnie's desk. He was talking on the phone with Johnny Jackson, an evangelist who was in charge of the Little Rock district of the fundamentalist organization.

I knew why Joe was calling Johnny Jackson. In my earlier call to Ronnie Floyd, telling him of my concern over Joe's behavior, I had mentioned both Johnny Jackson and John Wright as two ministers, besides myself, who were discontented with the fundamentalist status quo. My sources in Little Rock had indicated to me that Johnny Jackson was *not* doing all he could to ensure that Ronnie was elected president of the state convention that year. The other discontented minister, John Wright, had objections to Ronnie's candidacy. Ronnie must have shared this information with Joe, who was now on the phone applying pressure to Johnny.

A word about John Wright. He was the pastor of one of the largest churches in Little Rock and carried a lot of influence among many of the nonpolitical conservatives in Arkansas. John felt Ronnie had not paid his dues in Arkansas. There seemed to be an unwritten rule in the state that required an individual to have served in Arkansas for at least ten years before they would be considered for the presidency of the state convention. Ronnie had been in the state only a couple of years. Also, Wright felt that too much of the conservatives' power was localized in northwest Arkansas. He wanted to see the influence spread around a bit more. In other words, he wanted to see some control retained in the Little Rock area.

So, Joe Atchison thought he could kill two discontented birds with one stone, by asking Johnny Jackson to see what he could do about stopping *Wright's* criticism! If not, Joe made it clear that he would turn the matter over to Judge Pressler. Joe stressed that they needed to do whatever was necessary to ensure that Wright would get back in line and support Ronnie Floyd.

In fact, at a later date, when John Wright's criticisms were silenced, Joe boasted how he had used Adrian Rogers to put pressure on Wright. He said Rogers told Wright that if he ever wanted to hold a position in the national convention he had better shut up and support Floyd.

After Joe got off the phone he indicated to everyone in the room how he would make sure the John Wright problem would no longer be an issue. Joe gave me a semi-cool greeting.

So, the five of us, Joe Atchison, Ronnie Floyd, Mark Brooks, Bob Foster, and I, began the meeting proper. The conversation turned to potential challengers that could be nominated to run against Ronnie.

Joe mentioned that Johnny Jackson thought Dan Grant, the recently retired president of an Arkansas Baptist university, might be urged to let his name be put into nomination. This was a concern because it was feared that Grant might be able to rally alumni support behind his nomination.

Mark Brooks did not feel Grant or the alumni of the school posed much of a threat. Mark was an alumnus and stated that he knew many alumni didn't care for Grant and would never vote for him. Mark added how easy it would be to stick Grant with the "liberal" tag that had been used so successfully in the national elections. If Grant ran and the network could tag him as a "liberal," it would make our work easy. Besides, we could also play upon the liberal reputation of the university to turn out the "redneck vote" in the state.

The "redneck vote" was a term employed by the leadership of the fundamentalist network for those pastors who served rural churches. Such pastors were usually bi-vocational and not college-educated. The fundamentalist leadership viewed those people as being easily manipulated. Also, they did not have to be rewarded for their loyalty. All you needed to turn them out to vote was to push the right emotional buttons. The word "liberal" was one of those buttons.

Someone asked what would happen if Grant would not run. What if the moderates found a pastor who was willing to be nominated?

Joe spoke up and shared with us a statement Johnny Jackson had made when they were talking on the phone. Johnny felt that if the opposition found a pastor who was willing to be nominated, then we would have no trouble winning because no pastor in the state could put together the type of organization we possessed.

Someone in the room responded, "Yea, we can beat anybody given the fact that we're going to get the people there."

The discussion shifted to the vote count. As with any political machine, the bottom line is the ballot box. The key strategy of the fundamentalist takeover has been to get enough supporters to the conventions, either national or state, in order to elect their predetermined candidate to the presidency. The president would then use his power to appoint fundamentalists as trustees, who would then design the bureaucratic policies needed to carry out the fundamentalist political machine's objectives. In Arkansas it was estimated that this task could be accomplished in six years by electing just three presidents to consecutive one-year terms. Ronnie was to be the first president in this grand strategy, which imitated the one used to take over the national SBC. All we needed for certain victory was to get out the vote.

Part of my job was to check with other conservative leaders around the state to see how our campaign to get out the vote was progressing. Each district leader contacted his associational whips to get a vote count. Each associational whip surveyed the churches in their association to discover how many messengers [voters] each conservative church was sending to the convention. This provided a semiaccurate vote count projection for the election. Based on previous election totals, we estimated that a vote of six hundred could easily win Ronnie the presidency.

I knew the organization was in good shape, having checked with leaders across the state. I also had a plan (that I had learned from watching Judge Pressler at work) that could increase the vote count even more, ensuring victory. You simply have to draw a circle on a map with a fifty-mile radius centered on Little

Rock and then work with all the fundamentalist pastors within that area to produce a drive-in vote. This would activate a lot of lay people who would show up just in time for the election of the president and then leave. That way they would not even need to take the whole day off from work. I felt confident that such an activity could produce at least two hundred more votes.

So, I submitted an optimistic report to everyone present, even though I was as nervous as a cat in the middle of a dog pound. I certainly did not want anyone to become suspicious that I was taping every laugh, every off-color comment, every insult toward other Baptist brothers and sisters that was being uttered. I wanted those who would hear the tape to understand that this meeting was the norm, not the exception.

Then the conversation shifted back to who the opposition might be. Rich Kincl's name was mentioned. I had been asked to dig up anything I could on Rich earlier that year. It had been rumored that he supported the ordaining of women deacons. This would label him a "liberal" in Arkansas. Though the rumor proved untrue, the fundamentalist leadership decided to keep circulating the rumor to insure that Rich would be viewed as damaged goods.

At this time I was still under the impression that the "liberal element" had a similar organization that was trying to do the same things we were doing! I later found out that no such organization existed in Arkansas. The "liberal political machine" was a straw man that was used to manipulate naive pastors and lay leaders in the state. It was employed as a tool to rationalize the creation of the fundamentalist political machine.

Those who were not insiders were led to believe they were "defending" the Bible against an "organized onslaught." Actually, the fear and paranoia the uninformed fundamentalist masses suffered from was caused by their own political machine's creation of the myth of a "liberal machine."

Mike Huckabee, a pastor in Texarkana, was mentioned as a possible opposing candidate. Joe Atchison reiterated Johnny's assessment that a candidate who was merely a pastor would not be a threat.

Ronnie Floyd then said that it did not matter who the opposition nominated, he [Ronnie] had better win. He wanted no chance of being embarrassed by being on the losing end of the vote. Then Ronnie told us how he had spoken with Freddy Gage, who promised to bring the "Rapha strategy" to Arkansas.

Freddy Gage is a well-known Texas evangelist noted for his rough manners and his Machiavellian maneuverings within the SBC. Prior to his conversion he was a professional street fighter in Houston. Many believed that God had saved his soul, but his approach to the ministry and to politics was still guided by a different master. Freddy served with James Robison until the latter fell from grace in the eyes of SBC fundamentalists. Freddy now sells his services to Rapha, a profitable counseling/management corporation that has been used to promote SBC candidates.

The Rapha strategy consisted of booking a large dining room at an elite hotel in the city where the convention was being held. Then pastors and messengers were invited to a free, top-notch luncheon. Those who attended were given free tapes and books. The candidate of choice would be seated at the lead table with other convention movers and shakers. The strategy then called for the candidate to be endorsed by the keynote speaker of the luncheon. Ronnie bragged how Freddy promised him four hundred votes based on the Rapha strategy.

After I made my break with the machine, and the contents of the tape became public knowledge, including the "Rapha strategy," the luncheon for Ronnie was not nearly as well attended as the fundamentalists had hoped. In fact, they didn't even bother to have the keynote endorsement delivered at the end of the luncheon.

In a quirk of fate, I later overheard Freddy Gage talking to one of his aides at the state convention concerning the failure of the Rapha strategy they had employed for Ronnie. Freddy was trying to blame the failure on Floyd's choice of hotel.

Then Ronnie voiced his concern that Don Moore might exert undue influence on the outcome of the convention. Don Moore is the executive director of the Arkansas Baptist State Convention. Indisputably a conservative in theology, he has even declared himself to be an inerrantist. But Moore would not bow to the political objectives of the Pressler-Patterson juggernaut. This made him a "threat" to be neutralized or replaced if necessary.

Ronnie also mentioned that someone who was a part of the fundamentalist political machine was leaking information to those outside the organization. Evidently, I was not the only individual who saw corrupt practices being condoned. This anonymous individual apparently had access to the same information I did, and leaked his/her information to pastors who were opposed to the takeover. (This individual has never been identified. After what happened to me, I'm sure they were glad that they had remained covert.)

Based on information supplied by this individual a "fact sheet" had been circulated that outlined the political agenda of the machine. The sheet mentioned that the machine planned to apply pressure to Moore to cave in to its demands. The conservative leaders denied this to be true, but the fact sheet was completely accurate.

Ronnie decided that the best thing to do would be to hold a day of "appreciation" for the convention staff at Floyd's church (one of whom may have been leaking the information), and to write letters praising the leadership Moore had shown in serving as the executive director of the state convention. In other words, build a smoke screen so no one would suspect what the fundamentalist machine's true objectives were. Joe Atchison and Mark Brooks were placed in charge of "spin control." The plan was to convince the conservatives who were not insiders of the spurious nature of the "fact sheet" and how the central issue was still the conservative cause and not politics. It was a manipulation of the masses as usual.

The topic then turned to rewards and positions. A bit of background is needed here. I had been appointed to serve on the powerful Committee on Committee Nominations, which chose who would fill nearly every position in the national Southern Baptist Convention! Furthermore, it was widely known that the people serving on this powerful committee always later received prestigious and lucrative positions at Baptist colleges and seminaries.

Originally I had refused the appointment when the Rev. Delton Beal had phoned to offer it to me. I did not want anyone to think that my active support of the fundamentalist political machine was fueled by a desire for personal gain. Soon afterwards, during a meeting at Ronnie's church to plan a rally, Ronnie told me that he was the one who told Delton to place me on the nominations committee!

When I told Ronnie and Joe that I had turned Delton down, Joe told me, "You have spoiled everything! Delton wanted to appoint a friend of his who might *not* do what he was told. And Ronnie and I didn't want to take that chance." They needed a yes-man on this committee so that they could guarantee their ability to reward others who had served them loyally.

Joe then ordered me to call Delton back and say that I had changed my mind. Ronnie said I could call from his office, so I called Delton's secretary and told her that I had been "advised" to change my mind and accept the position. I am sure that Joe and Ronnie have been haunted by this mistake in their scheme time and again. When I broke with the network this position helped give my accusations credibility.

As the positions and rewards conversation progressed, Joe told me he wanted Dale Thompson placed in one of the positions that would come open. Dale was one of the district leaders of the organization and had not yet been awarded with a national position. This was an oversight Joe needed to correct. Joe wanted Dale put on a seminary board as a trustee even though Dale had never been to a seminary. In fact, Dale received his bachelor's degree through the mail from a Bible college in Florida.

Ronnie also wanted an individual appointed to a position as a reward. It seems one of his key laymen expressed a desire for a position should something good come open. Evidently, Ronnie owed a favor to the layman.

Here I challenged Joe and Ronnie. "Doesn't this type of activity open the movement to the accusation of replacing one good ole boy network with another? If that's our goal, then aren't we prostituting the issue of inerrancy for political power? Were we defending the Word of God or political opportunism?"

Joe just sighed and made some remark about my obsession with this issue. He reminded me of the positions I had been given and how grateful I ought to be to him.

I reminded him, "I never wanted any position, and my concerns do not arise from ingratitude, but from my commitment to what I feel is right. Why not appoint other conservatives who are doing good work within the convention, but who are not politically motivated, to these positions? If we gave such men a chance to serve, we could avoid the accusation of being strictly a power-pursuing organization."

Joe laughed. A comment was then made on how these men had not "been burned enough" by the present moderate convention establishment and thus would not be mean enough to do what was necessary to change the base of power in the state! It was not yet time to "throw some of these boys a bone." These non-network conservatives would get their chance only if they became more active politically, i.e., aligning themselves with the network and its objectives.

What I suspected had been confirmed. The real issue had to do with obtaining and maintaining control. It had to do with threat, reward, and loyalty to leaders of a supposed cause. It had to do with the very nature of fundamentalism.

I thought to myself, "Boy, how gullible can a person be?" I had played a part in setting up the smoke and mirrors for the fundamentalists' manipulative machinery, which kept its ugly divisiveness, corruption, and methods of coercion hidden, while it professed righteousness and truthfulness. I grew so angry I wanted to yell at them, and at myself. If this was a lie, how much else in fundamentalism was a lie? But rather than stomping out of the room I decided it was best to remain seated and let the tape player record what was happening.

Then Bob Foster, who had been with me a few days earlier when I bought the micro-cassette recorder, reached toward me and pulled it out of my pocket. He held it aloft and said, "Look what David bought. It's voice activated." Bob just loved gadgets.

My heart stopped. Then I smiled, reached out, and took the recorder from Bob, adding, "Yes, Bob, it is voice activated." And putting the recorder back in my pocket I continued a conversation I was having with Ronnie Floyd. Through a miracle of chance or design, no one became suspicious.

Ronnie turned to Joe and asked how things were going with the Mid-American Seminary people. Joe said he had talked with Jerry Vines and the situation was being dealt with.

Jerry Vines was the president of the Southern Baptist Convention at that time. According to Joe, Vines was concerned that the activity on the state level was not moving fast enough. Joe capitalized on this by getting Vines to make calls for him to put pressure on others to see things done Joe's way. Joe helped Vines pick his Committee on Committee Nominations personnel, all of which had been previously approved by Judge Pressler.

Mid-American Seminary is located in Memphis, Tennessee. It was founded by Gray Allison as a fundamentalist Baptist seminary. Because of its proximity to Arkansas, many of its students and graduates served in Arkansas churches. It is no secret that fundamentalist schools use their alumni connections as a political power base. Paige Patterson's map of the United States with the little red pins indicating where his "children," his politically motivated graduates, were being sent, was one such example.

According to Joe, Jerry Vines and the Judge would be in touch with Grey Allison, Mid-American's president. It would be too risky for Allison himself to make contact, being located in a different state, but he would assign a staff member to help coordinate the activities of the seminary's alumni in Arkansas, making sure they got the vote out.

Within the Arkansas network, the person assigned to make sure everything was being done right was Ronnie Mays.

Ronnie was an Arkansas pastor who was president of the Mid-American Seminary alumni association in Arkansas. He would contact all the Mid-American graduates and lobby them in Ronnie's behalf. This would help with the vote count in a big way.

After this the conversation drifted back and forth between vote counts, old vendettas, rewards and favors, till someone suggested we bring the meeting to a close. We had worked to save the convention from "liberals" enough for one day.

Plans were made for a lunch meeting the next day between Joe, Mark, myself, and a new recruit I was to contact for the network. I reluctantly agreed to attend. I was still shaking from having the recorder yanked from my pocket. I also thought it would be wiser for me to continue to play the part of loyal soldier until I had decided what to do with the evidence in my pocket. Ronnie asked me if the guy being recruited was a rookie. Mark assured Ronnie the guy was no rookie. Mark added that this person had provided information on the activities of Don Moore's staff to the network. This information proved valuable to the network in countering Moore's attempts to limit our faction's influence.

We then exchanged the usual pleasantries and parting bits of bland humor as we exited the office and went in our own directions.

Thinking back on this meeting I recall that not one prayer was shared asking for God's guidance and blessing. Not one prayer was offered in intercession for those whom we called our enemies. In fact, there was never a prayer offered of any kind.

There were many names mentioned during the meeting. Most were either spoken of in terms of what they could offer or the nature of the problem they presented. There was, however, one name that was never mentioned. That was the name of Jesus.

As I walked outside to wait for my wife, I reached into my pocket and turned the recorder off. Knowledge itself is a powerful thing and I knew that what I held in my hand was political dynamite. It was dynamite that might destroy the fabled fortress constructed by Ronnie Floyd, Joe Atchison, and the minions they manipulated. Power can also have a negative effect on the individual who employs it and the shock of the blast that would be created by this tape would certainly affect me as well.

After my wife picked me up we drove back to Gravette in reflective silence. As we pulled into the driveway of our home I told her I was going to break completely with the fundamentalist organization.

"Thank the Lord!" she exclaimed.

"You know they will come after me," I told her. "They will make things difficult for us."

"I know." she replied, "But we have faced tough situations before and the Lord has always led us through the storms."

We prayed. After our prayer we discussed what I should do with the tape. At first I wondered if I should call the individuals involved and tell them what I had done. Not a good move, I decided. If they knew, they would find some way to discredit the tape before it could be used. A little more reflection lead me to conclude that I should not be the one to use the tape publicly. If I was the one who released it they would say I set them up for personal reasons or to blackmail them. Finally, I made the decision to send the tape to an individual in the state who was noted for his moral commitment and was beyond reproach. This person was also known for having a level head concerning political activities.

As it turned out, Mike Huckabee, the pastor in Texarkana whom we had mentioned at our meeting as a possible opposing candidate, and whom Joe Atchison was convinced would not be a threat since, as Johnny Jackson had said over the phone, "a candidate who was merely a pastor would not be a threat," actually won the election for president of the statewide Baptist convention. Ronnie Floyd lost! Mike accomplished this feat not with another political machine, but through the angry response of Arkansas Baptists to what the machine was attempting!

Naturally, after the tape became public, the fundamentalists released all their fury against the church I served, my friends, and my family. God was gracious to us during those times. I resigned from the church and re-enrolled in Southwestern Baptist Theological Seminary where I would have the opportunity to learn and not just be indoctrinated. I joined a church that allowed people to think and to question. I plan to again serve a congregation of Christians who seek to grow in faith without the need for a fundamentalist fence to keep challenging ideas at bay.[4]

However, I still worry about the creeping darkness that seems to be enveloping America and the rest of the world, a darkness that is becoming ever more diabolical as it seeks to merge its religious-political system with the political system of secular government. I hope this testimony will help others understand that my fears are well founded.

Notes

1. I made the "mistake" while I was at Criswell of reading *The Gospel of the Kingdom* by George Eldon Ladd, and his book changed my views from pre-millennialist pre-tribulationist to post-tribulationist. That was almost an unforgivable sin at Criswell. My oral examination at Criswell for my B.A. in biblical studies took three hours, two hours of which was spent "dealing" with my post-tribulationist viewpoint, as they tried to get me to switch, but I couldn't.

I have a large library. Reading is my hobby. And, as I went out into the pastorate and I began to read some of my books written by authors other than those approved at Criswell, I began to ask further questions.

2. One of the great ironies of the situation was that John A. T. Robinson had been invited to speak by the most fundamentalist professor at Southwestern, L. Russ Bush, who had hoped Robinson would talk about *Redating the New Testament* [a work by Robinson that had prompted Professor Bush to attend Robinson's lectures in England]. In that work, Robinson argued that all four Gospels could have been written prior to the fall of Jerusalem in A.D. 70, and therefore *nearer* to the time of Jesus' life than most "liberal" scholars had previously deduced.

[See also the critique of Robinson's theory that appeared in *The Journal of Biblical Literature*, vol. 97, no. 2 (June 1978), by the historian Robert M. Grant (author of *Jesus: An Historian's Review of the Gospels*).—ED.]

But, instead of addressing the subject of when the New Testament was written, Robinson spoke in favor of universalism [the belief that after death, everybody might eventually wind up in heaven]. His books with universalist themes are indeed more numerous than his works dealing with the date of New Testament documents. His universalistic works include: *Honest to God; In the End, God; The Human Face of God;* and also the book he had completed at that time, *Truth Is Two-Eyed,* which demonstrated that Christian, Buddhist, and Hindu spirituality overlapped.

Ironically, I bought a copy of *Truth Is Two-Eyed* and had Robinson autograph it, although I was also so angered by his point of view that I left the school soon afterward.

I should add that during the semester I spent at Southwestern as a fundamentalist I took a class in ethics taught by Professor Bob Adams. He required his students to read books by authors whom I had been taught at Criswell to regard as "snakes." However, one book really got to me, *Christ and Culture*. It consisted of a series of lectures delivered by a man named H. Richard Niebuhr at Austin Seminary. I remained a fundamentalist, but this "liberal" made *sense*. I began to read others.

I read *The Unfettered Word: Southern Baptists Confront the Authority-Inerrancy Question*, edited by Robison B. James, and I was shocked to discover that J. I. Packer and others who are the "fathers" of the doctrine of inerrancy (i.e., of the "Chicago Statement on Biblical Inerrancy"), were *not* inerrantists! Not according to Paige Patterson, the president of Criswell Center for Biblical Studies.

I remained with the fundamentalists in spirit because my philosophy at that time was based upon my belief that there needed to be an inerrant Bible. "Inerrancy" as I define it, I still hold to, but I can no longer use that word as my brethren use it. I would have to say that they believe in a "perfect" Bible.

I also had a little problem with the idea of the "Kansas City Resolution." I have never believed that "a pastor is to rule the church." Goodness sakes! I'd make a terrible dictator. So I did not see eye to eye with my fundamentalist brethren concerning that issue.

In 1989 I was part of a group that was sent to "trap" Dr. Vestal [a moderate who agreed to run against the fundamentalist candidate that year] at the Southern Baptist Convention in Las Vegas. We tried to get him to say something that could be damaging, that could be used.

But when Vestal said, "I have come to the position that women can be ordained, and can serve as ministers," I thought, "That can't be right." I mean, I had read Hurley's book that argued against female minsters, a fundamentalist work. But then I read Susan Foh's work, and the arguments that she set forth, and I began to look at my understanding of what Christ does in man and woman, and the fact that the spirit of Christ indwells us no matter what our gender. That spirit gives us all "gifts." And I looked at the spiritual gifts and it says that the gift of being a pastor could go to anyone. So I had to change my theology there.

Eventually I began to question dispensationalism and I began to ask hard questions regarding the issue of inerrancy.

I began to doubt that any special "inspiration" lay behind the process that decided which books would and would not constitute the canon of Scripture.

The Protestant inerrantist says that the canon of the Bible has been preserved, meaning that God inspired men to make sure they decided exactly which books would constitute the biblical canon.

But if He inspired the council that gave us the canon, well, you would have to look at what *else* those men gave us. Things like the pope, celibate priests, church order, attending confession, and the "transubstantiation" interpretation of the Eucharist. If those men who decided which books would constitute the canon were inspired in one area, why would God have neglected to inspire them in all those other areas?

3. The film *Silent Scream* consists of the ultrasound image of a three-month-old fetus being aborted. Regardless of my rejection of fundamentalism, I am still pro-life. However, I think the issue is a political football.

I am pro-life in the sense that, if we are going to protect the fetal life, then we also need to protect the life of the fetus after it is born. . . . Will the people who are pushing through laws that force women to have more children than they want or need also take upon themselves the responsibility of raising those children, caring for them, or at least paying for them?

If pro-lifers like myself are going to deal with this issue in an ethical fashion we can't halt our concerns at the point where abortion is stopped. We need to take into account the *social factors* that caused the woman to seek an abortion in the first place. . . .

Pro-lifers also need to be the strongest proponents of birth control.

4. After recently completing a ninety-semester-hour master of divinity degree, my views have broadened considerably. For instance, I continue to consider myself an evangelical, but only as long as I have the right to define what an evangelical is. I have a *relational* theology, a theology of hope. I have a theology that does not have to be black and white, a theology that does not have to make God "all powerful."

I have become what you would call an "inclusivist" in my approach to understanding faith.

I don't think a person has to believe in the name of "Jesus" to come into the grace of God. I think that His grace transcends that one little social political entity called Israel [i.e., ancient Israel].

Relational theology gives me room to deal with many kinds of people. And when I do "evangelism," what I am sharing is the dynamic of what God has done in my life, and saying, "This might be something you want to check into."

I find myself in agreement with Catholic theologian Hans Küng in his recent book *Global Responsibility*. His view is that we are going to have to accept the "fundamentalists" of all the world's religions, and find some way to love them, but the future is going to belong to those who can come up with an ecumenical ethic we will all be able to share. In fact, Küng says, that's the *only* way we will survive.

Fundamentalism takes God and changes Him into a presuppositional idol. And by worshiping that idol built of presuppositions a person's faith is turned into easily repeated clichés. This is a faith for and of "sheep," sheep who are ready to follow any dictatorial "shepherd" that comes along. That was exactly what I saw the fundamentalist shepherds doing, and so I broke with them.

I have to stress that for people coming out of the 1960s and the 1970s, out of the relativism, out of the drug culture, fundamentalism can be a wonderful kind of "life jacket." It gives you some security. It makes things black and white. It allows you to feel a sense of forgiveness for the guilt and the things you've done to your body during those times. But it quickly changes from a "life jacket" to a "straitjacket." And it becomes just as addictive, just as destructive, as anything that was ever proposed by Timothy Leary and Tom Wolfe.

My latest research is in Christian spirituality, the history of spirituality—how we Baptists have lost it. I am focusing on the contemplative side, going back to Ignatian disciplines and trying to utilize those tools in a holistic-personal approach. Spirituality remains my focal point, the reason why I am still a Christian after going through all that I have gone through.

Marlene Oaks:
Old Time Religion Is a Cult

"I must be crazy," I began to think. "None of this [fundamentalist teaching] makes much sense." And I sure got different conclusions from reading my Bible than I got from the old time religionists.

—Marlene Oaks

Marlene Oaks is the minister of the First Church of Religious Science in Fullerton, California. After successful careers as mother and educator, Oaks trained to become a New Thought minister. She was ordained in 1978 in Hawaii by Drs. Marcus Bach, Roco Errico, and William R. Parker. Oaks has served churches in Hawaii, Colorado, and California. She was cohost of a popular weekly radio talk program for two years in Hawaii; of a radio program in Southern Colorado for a year; of a television program in Hawaii and one in San Jose, California. She consults with local businesses in stress management, communication and rapport, and self-esteem. She speaks at meetings, conventions, and classes, nationally and internationally. The following is excerpted from her book *Old Time Religion Is a Cult*.

My family wanted to do a good job with this tiny life entrusted them. And they did. I'm a healthy, happy, sane, creative, caring, giving, forgiving person. And, in their inexperience, they taught me a lot of garbage, much of which they believed, and much of which came directly from the post-hypnotic suggestions they lived within.

We prayed, "Now I lay me down to sleep, I pray the Lord my soul to keep, if I should die before I wake, I pray the Lord my soul to take." I didn't want to die. I wondered what kind of a Lord is this that wants my soul? Doesn't he have a soul of his own?

We went to church and Sunday School. The minister and teachers said things like, "You are a miserable sinner, a worm in the dust. You are damned by original sin to burn in hell eternally." Terror began to emerge in my soul.

Everyone seemed so big and I so little. It made me very susceptible to whatever they said and wanted. I know that my family and other teachers did their best.

137

. . . But I see from the vantage point of adulthood that much of what they taught in the course of a day was infected with a fearful religion. . . . They wanted to protect me, for life seemed fearful to them too. After all, they had been steeped in the notion of an angry god a lot longer than I had.

The preacher said, "God is watching you every minute. He knows everything you do, everything you think, every unkind word. He keeps track of it forever and you will have to pay. He'll get even with you."

I felt inside, "There is this god following me around everywhere and he wants to hurt me." I was afraid and imagined things in the shadows at night. If you can't trust God, who or what can you trust? I think it could be called paranoia.

He said, "You must get down on your knees and beg forgiveness for being such a sinner. You must beseech God to help you. You must promise God you will bargain with him if only he will consent to listen to you."

My heart prayed, "Dear God, pleeeaassse forgive me. Do you want me to give up candy? Is that my sin? Do you want me to stop drawing pictures? Is that my sin? Do you want me to hide so no one will have to be upset by me? The whooole world is my fault, I'm sorry. How could anyone love such a bad little girl?"[1]

The authority in the black robe told me more, "God sent his only son to save you. He let him do wonderful miracles and healings of all kinds, then he had him killed in the most painful way on the cross. He let him sleep in a tomb in the dark all by himself for three days and then he brought him back to life. His son, Jesus, went back to heaven shortly after that. If you talk to Jesus, believe everything the preachers are saying about him, particularly believe the preacher's interpretations of what Jesus said and meant (especially my interpretation), and if you ask in just the right way—Jesus might intercede with the Father for you, and you might be saved. You must take Jesus as your personal savior and worship him and forget the passages where he seems to say not to do that."

My heartfelt pleas emerged, "Jesus, I want to believe you and love you and hear you. Pleeeaaasse save me from these sins they say I have committed. Pleeeaaase save me from your Father who they say is so angry at me that he wants to hurt me like you were hurt—only I'm so bad that he won't ever stop, he'll hurt me forever and that's a long, long time. Oh, Jesus, where are you? With all of my heart I want to find the answer."

It became clear that if this god loved Jesus more than anybody else, boy was *I* in trouble. . . .

"I must be crazy," I began to think. "None of this makes much sense." And I sure got different conclusions from reading my Bible than I got from the old time religionists. I won a little New Testament in a Bible-reading contest. It grew to be underlined in a rainbow of colored pencils. I read and reread, seeking, searching. I prayed daily and tried to talk with Jesus. Sometimes my prayers were almost constant. This little New Testament is one of my treasures of today. It opened many inner doors for me that others could not open. The thousands of hours I spent contemplating its words were one of the most powerful ingredients of my freedom. . . .

Some "old time religionists" select the passages of anger to prove the god of ugliness and then say the Bible is inspired so you have to believe these passages. Most of these passages conflict with the positive ones such as the ones that have spoken to my heart. . . . If the passages do not agree with one another, which do we select?

I selected the love-filled passages because I know that God is love. Certainly there are negative passages. I agree that much of the Bible is inspired, and there is a lot of garbage that has been inserted by various people and groups, by ignorance, by error; and there have been ignorant interpretations that do not take into account the times, the culture, and the language and idioms of the people writing. There are many passages of violence, rape, incest, war, murder and other such things that are not by any stretch of the imagination inspirational or inspired. Just because someone has the nerve to stand on a high platform, wearing a robe, pounding a black book, saying that every word in it is the inspired work of God does not make it so. . . .

"Subconscious panic" is most evidenced by the teachings of hell, eternal damnation, the whole brimnation, firegod syndrome. Sometimes I bellylaugh to think that anybody could believe such a fairy tale about the Intelligence of God. But other times, I feel sad. I feel sad to see souls tortured—suffering pains of anguish, real pains—over far-fetched stories.

A life that could be used reaching out in love and caring, in discovering cures and new ways to develop foods and education, and the like. is stifled by the fear of the end of the world and spending eternity in hell. A child that could be laughing and playing and discovering the wonder of God's universe is crying and racked with fear, saying things like "I'm soorry. I don't want to be a sinnner and suffer in hell. Help meee, helllppp meee." Talk about resources being wasted. I wonder how many billions of hours have been wasted on suffering over imaginary tortures by this imaginary god. And I wonder how many billions of hours and dollars have been spent with psychologists and other counselors to try to recover. . . .

The old time religionists fear those who teach love, forgiveness, joining, oneness, self-responsibility, introspection, awakening, and brotherhood unless these things are taught in the "acceptable manner." That is, they must be encased within a teaching of fear, judgment, separation, outside responsibility, looking to theology for answers, and they must have an investment in staying in the trance.

[Today] I am a New Thought minister. That means I teach Oneness and Love. I teach a gospel of the inner Kingdom, a loving Presence, an elder brother who encouraged us to do better than he did, to practice forgiveness, growth, light, joy, peace, brotherhood and life-affirming ideas. I am complete with the old time religionists calling us cults and getting away with it without a peep from us. The old time religions are the biggest cults of all! . . .

Am I Now in a Cult?

Please answer the following questions . . . and be as honest as possible with yourself—the only thing you have to lose is your trance!

Does my group try to control me with guilt?

Are you blamed for the fall of man, for the crucifixion, for anything that went on in the past that you cannot possibly have any control over? Are you supposed to suffer for your mistakes way beyond the consequences of the mistake itself? Are you asked to be responsible for the eternal lives of not only yourself, but also of others the world over? Is it made clear to you that because of your sinfulness, your lack of trying to help spread the word, or other reasons, that you are guilty of something and should ask forgiveness?

Does your group suggest that somebody who is worthy had to be murdered two thousand years ago to save you from your inherent unworthiness?

Do the leaders give you ridiculous things to do to build worthiness in the eyes of their god? Do they tell you that you have to drink the blood and eat the flesh of someone who is dead in order to be made okay? Do they fill your mind with morbid pictures and control you as a result?

Does my group teach that other groups are not as good, will not be blessed, will suffer, etc.?

Do they suggest that by belonging to their group, you become special, but that without their teaching/authority you are a hopeless sinner? (Are they not the same group that seeks to instill and maintain that "hopeless sinner" sense of unworthiness in the first place?)

Do they look at others as people to be brought into the fold in whatever way necessary? Do they appear desperate, acting as if all's fair in love and war? Do you get to allay your feelings of inferiority by feeling superior to those in other groups? After all they aren't "saved" or converted.

Does it serve you to believe in a god who would harm his own creations? Would you destroy one of your children if they disagreed with you? Are you supposed to be better than God?

Does my group teach that ours is the only way?

Does it disregard thousands of years and millions of religious experiences that are not within its own narrow theology? Does it believe that God can be contained within one creed, one doctrine, one theology? Does it believe that God is not everywhere, inspiring, expressing in and through all of His children?

Could it be that there is only one acceptable flower, one acceptable tree, one acceptable kind of dog or cat—God is only in one flower and the others are doomed? Could it be that the Infinite Creativity that unfolded the vast array of flowers only allows for one religion?

Does my group imply that God has given us the final word(s), and that our interpretations are the only correct ones?

Do the leaders of your group give you explanations that puzzle you concerning the contradictions in the Bible, the references to very unholy behavior such as incest, rape, pillage, and murder?

Could any one person or group understand all of the scriptures?

Who really knows who wrote the Bible, when it was written, why they wrote it, why certain things were added and others deleted, how the Bible got into its present forms? How do you know which is the most accurate translation? Which particular scrolls did they use? Why did they use those scrolls and not all of them? Where are the original scrolls?

What if all the Bibles disappeared? Could you still know God? What if all of the theology disappeared? Could you still know God?

Does my group put restrictions/boxes around God and then around me?

Have you ever played in your mind with the word "infinite"? Is it bigger than could be described? Being finite, could you completely know "infinite"? Could you speak for God completely, assured that you knew it all? Neither can anyone else. At best we are vessels, channels of God's love and light. To the degree that we are out of harmony, are into fear, have unhealed issues ourselves, we distort the Voice of God coming through us. Since we know this about ourselves, it assists us to fall prey to others—they must surely know more than we do, we conclude!

Most of us are doing the best we can—and some of what we do is ignorant.

Have I ever suspected that they were not telling me the Truth but were trying to control me?

So many people report to me that they have sat in one old time religion meeting or another and have suddenly begun to awaken. They have had the experience of suddenly knowing that what was being said was not the Truth.

Some have feared that they were going crazy because everyone else seemed to believe the stuff being said and done. Some have walked out and begun a search for a better way.

I believe that God is within you and within me. I believe the Voice of God in us is continually, softly urging us to freedom and awakening. I believe that everyone, even the most entranced by old time religion, have had moments of doubt. The next moment of doubt could be your door out of the trance.

Hypnosis Class

Hypnosis is a fascinating study. My husband and I studied it in order to see what we could do to assist ourselves and others in awakening from the trance. At first we thought we were simply studying in order to understand how the mind works, and then we discovered the mass trance. It was the trance of suggestion from so many avenues of society, history, church, media, family, etc.— the trance of accepting whatever we were told as if it were the truth, without examining it. . . .

Whatever happens to those delightful, questioning, wetkiss-giving, explorers of life, ages two and three and four? Where did the excitement go? Where did the energy, the zest for living go? Where did these walking dead adults come from? The trance got them. . . . We have to wake ourselves up. We have to step outside the lines a bit in order to do it. Inside the lines may seem safe— however, it is the prison of the trance.

I'm not suggesting we run naked through the local shopping mall. I am merely suggesting doing some outside-the-lines-of-how-it's-been things. Be creative and break up the ruts, the routines, the blind patterns that rob us of aliveness. Stop and see that beautiful flower patch you pass every day. Smell it, feel it, experience it, appreciate it. Be present for your life. . . .

Feed your mind positive, life-affirming reading materials, movies, and other entertainments. Refuse to feed your mind, your life, the junk of negative input. Turn off that awful TV program. Don't go to the violent movies. . . . Start a branch of Fundamentalists Anonymous. Find a positive church. . . . Do not spend any significant time in the past. Move your thoughts to now. How can you make now wonderful? What can you do here and now?

If you start to hear the old tapes play and say awful things in your head, don't just sit there and let them root. Get up. Take a walk. Sing a song. Do something. Move around. Take charge of your consciousness. This can be such an exciting time.

Note

1. Marlene's traumatic childhood encounter with fundamentalism is echoed in the following admission:

My daughter is five years old and—people say how inhumane—I let my daughter lay and cry herself to sleep for a week straight about the flames of Hell. See my daughter personally lay at night and said, "I don't want to go to Hell, I don't want to go to Hell," and she'd be laying there crying.

I could have ran right in there and gave her the Gospel and she could have made a profession of salvation, but I let it get deep into her memory. Know what I mean? That there is a Hell. And that will affect her whole life. That's why she's an obedient child. (Barry Weaver, street preacher, quoted in Jim Naughton, "The Devil & Duffy Strode: In Marion, North Carolina, a Boy Preacher's Hellfire Gospel Alarms a Quiet Community," *Liberty* [January/February 1989]: 27).

Photo by John Skillin

Robert M. Price: Beyond Born Again

I had to swallow hard after twelve years as an evangelical, but almost immediately life began to open up in an exciting way. I felt like a college freshman, thinking through important questions for the first time. The anxiety of doubt had passed into the adventure of discovery. It was like being born again.

—Robert M. Price

Robert M. Price is the pastor of the First Baptist Church of Montclair, New Jersey. His published works are many and varied, including an article in the *Evangelical Quarterly* (vol. 55, no. 3 [July 1983]), "Inerrant the Wind: The Troubled House of North American Evangelicals," and one in *Playboy,* "Born Again Sex" (Price's candid review of Christian sex manuals). Price created and edited an H. P. Lovecraft journal, *Crypt of Cthulhu,* that had subscribers worldwide, and also published and contributed to *Churchyard: An Anthology of Christian Weird Tales.* From 1990 to 1991 he produced "The Freethinker's Bible," which aired on public-access cable television in his town and surrounding areas. What follows is the preface to Price's *Beyond Born Again,* to which he has appended some appreciative reflections on his fundamentalist past.

At age eleven, having begun to attend Sunday School at what turned out to be a hellfire-and-brimstone Baptist church, I was prompted to a sudden and serious desire to make sure I was safe ("saved") from the flames. After a couple of years I became increasingly involved with church activities until what other interests I had gave way almost entirely to religious activism and introspection.

I learned to pray and read scripture, and to "witness" to my friends (and to feel pretty guilty if I didn't do these things). An acknowledged "spiritual leader" among the youth fellowship, I found the peer-acceptance that all teenagers so desperately need.

Church activities were not enough, so I joined a student group called "HiBA" (or "High School Born-Againers," if you can believe it!) in order to see as many as possible of my classmates "come to the Lord." Eventually, several did. Just think, I was a father (spiritually at least) several times by age seventeen! My Campus Crusade for Christ training in evangelism served me in good stead.

Of course, winning others to Christ was only half the picture. After all, I could only help my converts to mature spiritually as much as I myself had. I must be a true man of God. Reading devotional works such as Robert Boyd Munger's *My Heart, Christ's Home,* and even C. S. Lewis's *The Screwtape Letters* considerably advanced my progress in piety. But never had I found so much spiritual wisdom as in Bill Gothard's "Institute in Basic Youth Conflicts," a week-long seminar on God's (and Gothard's) unbeatable principles for a successful Christian life. I took all this amassed lore with me when I went to college.

It did not take me long to become a leader in the campus chapter of Inter-Varsity Christian Fellowship. My knowledge of biblical doctrine and evangelistic techniques was welcome there. As I encountered new influences (though not too many, sheltered as I was), my Christian life grew in new ways. As I let down old barriers, I began to erect some new ones. I resolved to beware of the "unsaved professors." One should avoid religion courses offered by such people. Who knows what disturbing things one might hear? But eventually I was ready for combat on this enemy turf. I had become interested in "apologetics," the fine art of defending the faith. With stakes far higher than any mundane exam, I "crammed" with the writings of such knights of the truth as Francis Schaeffer, Josh McDowell, John Warwick Montgomery, and Os Guiness. Ready to do battle, I'm sure I irritated my professors no little.

In the great battle for the souls of students, one must close ranks with the like-minded. Within the circle of Inter-Varsity, I soon encountered new varieties of evangelical belief and lifestyle. I learned to tolerate and even welcome different ideas on eschatology, predestination, and the like. Wider horizons were a pleasant discovery. Eventually, I became a convinced and enthusiastic "neo-evangelical," going to movies (after the long cinematic abstinence of my teenage fundamentalist period), qualifying biblical inerrancy (recognizing tiny errors in this or that insignificant corner of the Bible), even going so far as to teach the Bible in a Catholic charismatic prayer group. My commitment to Jesus Christ gave me an exciting and satisfying sense of purpose. The Bible was a thing of constant fascination, and I learned to exult in the love of Jesus, and of my brothers and sisters.

During my college years I read voraciously, becoming familiar with "our" (evangelical) literature on most subjects. Not satisfied with encountering the writers only through their works, I took several opportunities to visit other cities, where I sought out and conversed with various evangelical leaders. In Wheaton, I met Carl F. H. Henry, Merril Tenney, C. Peter Wagner, and Billy Melvin (president of the National Association of Evangelicals). At a conference in Ohio, I met my favorite inspirational writer, Peter Gilquist, author of *Love Is Now* (Grand Rapids, Mich.: Zondervan, 1973), in which he points the way beyond legalistic, introspective fundamentalism to a freer, more spontaneous evangelical faith, a real breath of fresh air at the time. On a trip to Berkeley I stayed with the Christian World Liberation Front (later the Berkeley Christian Coalition), talking with Sharon Gallagher and Jack Sparks (now, with Gilquist, a bishop of the Evangelical Orthodox Church). In Chicago, I met David F. Wells and Donald W. Dayton. I talked with Dave Jackson of Reba Place Fellowship and Jim Wallis of *Sojourners.* I discussed ministry and theology with these fascinating people and finally decided to go on to seminary.

I chose Gordon-Conwell Theological Seminary, specializing in New Testament. I didn't feel drawn to the pulpit ministry and sought to prepare for a teaching ministry in my own way by concentrated biblical study. Also, I could continue my apologetical attack on liberal, unbelieving biblical criticism and theology. Though I didn't have definite plans for the future (being confident of God's eventual guidance), what eventually happened still surprised me.

One often hears the paradoxical statement that many enthusiastic students lose their faith while in seminary. As the story goes, the wide-eyed seminarian finds his faith in the Bible undermined by the destructive biblical criticism of his theologically liberal professors. Let me say that there is very little chance of this happening to anyone at my alma mater, where the commitment to evangelical thought and practice is and remains unswerving. My experience does not therefore fit the stereotype, but I did undergo quite a change, thanks to my own studies outside the recommended reading lists. I found to my unpleasant surprise that by my second year I was unable to affim much of that upon which I had spent my life up to that point. I might add that I was dragged to this conclusion kicking and screaming.

As I have said, one of my greatest interests was in apologetics, which in turn greatly contributed to my interest in New Testament studies. The reading of stalwarts like John Warwick Montgomery and Francis Schaeffer convinced me that the stakes indeed were high: if evangelical Christianity were not true, and based upon historically true events, why then life really held no significance at all! On the other hand, I must be honest. I could not try to convince an unbeliever with an apologetical argument I would not myself accept. My enthusiasm for the true faith, and the secret fear that the faith might not be true, were sources of fuel that fed each other. My zeal was great, but it was interrupted by periods of doubt that might last for months. The more terrible the doubt, the more zeal was needed to make up for it. As the zeal grew greater, the stakes grew higher, and the fear in turn grew deeper. Naturally, I was reluctant to find any weaknesses in the various arguments in favor of the resurrection of Christ, or the historicity of the gospels. Yet if there were weaknesses, I had to know! Eventually, I believe, I found them in the course of my own research.

At the same time, suspicion was beginning to mount in me concerning the viability of the way I had been told to interpret life's experiences. I encountered typical personal disappointments which I piously assumed God must have sent "for a purpose." Praise the Lord, I figured. Still, I just couldn't help but notice that I didn't need "God's will" as an explanatory factor. Human failure and immaturity seemed adequate explanations. Besides, what did it imply about life if every major experience was significant only as a "test" sent by God? And could you be sure you had discerned God's will, since the last time you thought you had it, everything fizzled anyway? I began to wonder if my picture of life was adequate for the increasingly ambiguous world I lived in. Born-again living seemed to me just a crutch which no longer facilitated healing and growth, but actually protracted immaturity.

During this period, I did not let my doubts and dissatisfactions stop me from sharing the good news of Jesus Christ. But evangelism began to present difficulties of its own. One cold night in Beverly, Massachusetts, I trudged out with a handful of other seminarians to witness to local sinners. As I sat conspicuously in a tavern telling a stranger about the abundant life Christ offered her, I suddenly found myself at a loss for words. Behind my evangelistic rhetoric, what did it all mean? Just *how* would her life change if she "accepted Christ"? Well, she would begin to seek guidance daily in God's Word, and go to church, and . . . uh . . . well, basically, to take up new religious habits, I guess. This woman already believed in being kind, loving, and honest. She didn't need religion for that. What *did* she need it for, I had to ask myself?

Around the same time, I found myself in a Cambridge cafe having supper with some friends before going to a lecture by Harvey Cox. As I looked at the secular students gathered there, I suddenly thought, "Listen, is there really that much difference between 'them' and 'us'?" I had always accepted the qualitative difference between the "saved" and the "unsaved." Until that moment, it was as if I and my fellow seminarians had been sitting in a "no damnation" section of an otherwise "unsaved" restaurant. Then, in a flash, we were all just people. My feeling about evangelism has never been quite the same.

I had to reevaluate my faith. I had some idea of what other theological options were like. But since I had always read them only to refute them, it was going to take some adjustment to be able to give them a sympathetic hearing.

In the summer of 1977 I took course work at Princeton Theological Seminary, learning from Donald Juel how valuable a tool for understanding the gospels form-criticism could be. It was not quite the demoniac heresy Josh McDowell made of it. The next fall, I went to Boston University School of Theology and Harvard Divinity School (member schools of the Boston area consortium to which I had access as a Gordon-Conwell student). There I had the privilege of studying with Howard Clark Kee, Helmut Koester, and Harvey Cox.

I had to swallow hard after twelve years as an evangelical, but almost immediately life began to open up in an exciting way. I felt like a college freshman, thinking through important questions for the first time. The anxiety of doubt had passed into the adventure of discovery. It was like being born again.

Now, thirteen years later, I have arrived at what I suppose would best be called "left-wing neo-orthodoxy," much influenced by Bultmann and Tillich. I believe I have found a synthesis that is satisfying both intellectually and spiritually. I do not believe the gospels are accurate histories, but rather legend-laden icons of the Christ of faith. For me theology and the Bible are sources of powerful catalytic symbols communicating the wonders of worship and spirituality. And after earning the Ph.D. in theology, and teaching in a college religion department for some years, I wound up in the parish ministry after all.

There are many ways to view one's departure from fundamentalism. Those still within the camp may see you as one expelled from Eden for daring to eat of the Tree of Historical-Critical Knowledge. You may be more inclined to think that you "put away childish things"; that is how I view it. But having put them aside, does anything abide? Yes, I still owe a debt of gratitude to my fundamentalist background. This is not to say that I don't often find myself looking back and wincing at the zealous and pathological excesses of my past, but I am grateful for other things. Here are a few:

If possible, fundamentalism may be more Bible-centered than Christ-centered. At any rate, my close acquaintance with and continuing love for the Bible (I'm now pursuing a second doctorate, in New Testament) is the most important legacy of fundamentalism in my life today. In fact it was the passionate love of the text, with its minutiae and its difficulties, that led me to find a greater understanding of it in nonfundamentalist perspectives. I may not take all the dispensations and harmonizations very seriously any more, but I still hanker for good exegesis. And my Bible knowledge gained from Bible-thumping days, needless to say, has served me in good stead.

Witnessing, though I always hated it, is an interesting experience to have under one's belt. I used to go door to door, hand out evangelistic tracts in shopping malls, take "religion surveys," accost people in the park, and manipulate conversations to "turn them toward spiritual things." I earned many, many funny looks, but also a good handful or two of converts, some of whom have continued in fundamentalism to this day. Since I myself haven't, how should I feel about this? Well, any commitment to Christ, even on terms I no longer accept, can't be too regretful a thing. But regardless of the results, the witnessing experience itself did steel me to go out on a limb and do what I thought right, people's opinions be damned.

And speaking of experiences, fundamentalism provided many good ones. There are few other ways, it seems to me, to feel for oneself the same apocalyptic urgency that characterized the New Testament church. Process theology sure doesn't provide it! I no longer imagine that such fervor proves the truth of anything, though— any cultist feels the same fire.

Fundamentalism was in many ways a fine place to spend my adolescence. In other ways it wasn't, since it sheltered me from facing important issues for myself at a crucial time. But, it did provide an alternative to the degenerate pursuits of other teenagers, with their drugs, acid rock, and sophomoric cynicism. Maybe I just hit on the right group of compatriots, but my fundie friends and I discovered that "good clean fun" actually *was* fun as we played softball and Risk and (believe it or not) sang "Old Man River" at the player piano. This is a lesson I have not forgotten. I have given up the ban on movies, but I still get a self-righteous charge out of turning down booze, tobacco, and pot.

What about my old "personal relationship with Christ" and the familiar struggle of "spiritual growth"? On exiting fundamentalism I laid down my burden of morbid introspection and "up-to-the-minute confession," but I have never lost the sentimental love for Jesus that fundamentalism fostered. And the "Christ-like" character-ideal of approachability, openness, kindness, and unpretentiousness has continued to be my goal, even when the "quest of the historical Jesus" has made me wonder how we can know what is or is not "Christ-like." And without the neurotic strictures of pietism it all seems so much more natural and spontaneous.

A few years back it was "in" to read Herman Hesse's *Siddhartha*. The novel tells of a young spiritual seeker in India at the time of the Buddha. His career parallels the Buddha's in some respects, as when he leaves home to join a brotherhood of ascetics and eventually finds it a dead end. He returns to the secular world, seeking in it clues to enlightenment. He gradually learns to take his place within it, but his earlier period of separation and austerity gives him a unique perspective on the world. He is still able to see it as an outsider. His past enables him to view the whole rat race as something of a game, taking it less than seriously while he decides just what parts of it he wants to embrace. I am not sure what I think of the vague metaphysics that the book winds up promoting, but I do identify with *Siddhartha* in one respect. Fundamentalism provides the same sort of valuable critical distance when it comes time to reenter the world. And this means, in my view, that one puts fundamentalism behind oneself not in the sense of repudiating it, but rather progressing beyond it as one does with any starting point.

Arch B. Taylor, Jr.:
The Bible, and What It Means to Me

I gradually moved away from the simplistic view of my childhood days, but I was not at all familiar with the disciplines of textual, historical, or literary criticism applied to the study of the Bible. After a term on the mission field divided between Taiwan and Japan, I returned to Louisville Seminary for a degree in master of theology. I read voluminously about the various views of inspiration and authority of the Bible, all within the field of doctrinal theology. I concluded that I could not conscientiously go along with the literalist/inerrantist view.

—Arch B. Taylor, Jr.

Arch B. Taylor, Jr. is the assistant director of the Kentucky Interfaith Task Force on Central America (KITCA). He was born, raised, educated, and ordained in the Presbyterian Church in the United States (the "Southern" church), which placed a high value upon the authority of the Bible as the word of God. Taylor obtained his master of theology degree at Louisville Presbyterian Theological Seminary. Most of his career as a missionary in Japan of the Presbyterian Church was devoted to teaching the Bible to Japanese students at Shikoku Christian College (Shikoku Gakuin University). He also edited the *Japan Christian Quarterly,* from 1956 to 1957.

"While being a teacher of the Bible, I have constantly striven to be a student of the Bible, regularly reading and studying it on my own, besides seeking to learn from a broad range of biblical scholars of proven ability and piety. I have never once doubted that the Bible *is* the Word of God. However, I constantly wrestle with the question, *how* is the Bible the Word of God? This question of *how* is one on which sincere Christians, all acknowledging the Bible as authoritative, can differ widely and sometimes very bitterly. Some fifteen years ago I wrote an essay entitled 'Ancient Scripture and Modern Life: A Conciliatory Suggestion Concerning the Inspiration and Authority of the Bible.' The essay was written at a time when a schism was threatened in the 'Southern' Presbyterian Church in which this question of biblical authority was held up as one of the most seriously controverted issues. It also was a time when I had reached a certain degree of self-assurance concerning my own understanding of *how* the Bible is God's Word. In the years since then, my knowledge of the Bible has increased in both width and depth. I have learned more about its original languages, and I have become better acquainted with the cultural and historical milieu in which the Bible was produced. Therefore, some revisions of that essay would be necessary to bring it up to date, but my basic position is still approximately the same. Copies of that essay are available, and I will be glad to share it with any interested readers. What I hope to do in this paper is give some biographical background to explain how I reached my particular position, and to indicate what I see as the direction in which my thinking and understanding of the Bible are moving. I hope also that I can be of help to others who are wrestling with the questions: How is the Bible the Word of God? and, What does the Bible as the Word of God have to say to people today?"

Ancestors on both sides of my family for a number of generations have been Presbyterians, including some in its ordained ministry. My parents were faithful and active members of the First Presbyterian Church of Charlotte, North Carolina, where I was born. The pastor, Dr. Albert Sydney Johnson, was a devout biblical student who was attracted to the system of doctrine known as dispensationalism. My parents attended lectures by well-known teachers of that doctrine invited to the church, and they used the Scofield Bible, which prints notes explaining the system right along with the biblical text itself. I remember as a child being fascinated by the graphic pictorial representations of the great tribulation and other scenes of the second coming of Christ and the end of the world, contained in books on dispensationalism that we had in our house.

However, before I was old enough to know a great deal about it, my parents had moved away from Dr. Johnson's congregation in Charlotte to the First Presbyterian Church of Winston-Salem, where there was apparently less fervor for dispensationalism. Not only so, but a close college friend of my father's who had become a minister had brought about controversy and division in several churches he served over the question of dispensationalism. From observing this kind of result from that doctrine, my parents concluded that there must be serious flaws in it, so they gave it up.

Still, we kept our Scofield Bibles, and the general attitude toward Scripture in my home was that it is all God's Word, to be accepted and believed in its entirety. Every night at family prayers we read a chapter from the Bible, each one reading a verse in turn from his or her own Bible. In the course of this reading, difficult questions might arise: the total annihilation of enemies, or a statement in one place that seemed to be inconsistent with a statement in another. My parents would attempt some explanation, and I don't remember that I ever questioned that, in spite of such problems, this really was God's Word and we accepted it as such, including belief in the literal Genesis story of creation and the Garden of Eden.

Nowadays this attitude toward the Bible may be referred to as "noncritical." It considers the Bible divinely inspired and not to be studied like other literature with a view to determining the dates and authors or the sources which went to make up the various writings included in the canon of Scripture. The answer given in the Child's Catechism was sufficient for our purposes: the Bible was written "by holy men who were taught by the Holy Ghost." Nothing that I heard in church, or sunday school, or even in two years of required Bible courses at Davidson College challenged this view of the Bible on which I was nurtured at home. Therefore for me everything only served to affirm it.

When I went to Louisville Presbyterian Seminary, things were not much different. Some of the faculty members, the so-called "liberals," were acquainted with the more critical approach to Bible study and made some references to it from time to time; there were other faculty members, the "conservatives," who openly or tacitly disagreed with biblical criticism. In those days there was no course in biblical introduction that would have dealt with the questions in such a way as to put them into the total context of church history and doctrine.

I was naturally more attracted to the "conservatives" than to the "liberals," who seemed to challenge my presuppositions. By far the staunchest "conservative" was Dr. Andrew K. Rule. In his courses on apologetics and church history he made clear his antipathy to the critical approach to Scripture and promoted the very conservative "plenary verbal" theory of biblical inspiration championed by the famous Dr. Benjamin B. Warfield of Princeton Theological Seminary. J. Gresham Machen, second-generation member of the Warfield faction, was leader of the group that left the Presbyterian Church in the United States of America (the "Northern" church) to form the Orthodox Presbyterian Church and to establish Westminster Seminary in Philadelphia. Dr. Rule was a native of New Zealand who had come to the United States expressly to study under Warfield at Princeton. Theologically he was very close to the "Machen Group," but he was not schismatic, and out of loyalty to the greater unity of the church he remained in the "Northern" church.

I consulted Dr. Rule about possibilities for doing graduate study, and he suggested that I consider the University of Chicago. At that time, Chicago was thought to be a "hotbed" of destructive criticism. Yet Dr. Rule told me that the rigor and depth of scholarship there was commendable, and he was confident my faith would not be undermined while my intellect would be stimulated. During our conversations, Dr. Rule alluded to the question of biblical criticism. He took special care to inform me that although many critical scholars had abandoned belief in the uniqueness and authority of the Bible—those "unbelieving critics" who were anathema to so many devout Christians—there were honorable and reputable scholars who were "believing critics." Dr. Rule suggested that I read a book written by one of them, Dr. Crawford Howell Toy. I did read the book, but I had too little knowledge of the whole subject to benefit greatly from it, and at that time it did not change my noncritical views. Neither did I go to Chicago. In fact, I was still attracted to Warfield, owned a complete set of Warfield's works, and subscribed to the *Westminster Journal,* all of which tended to solidify my views.

Dr. Rule's generosity in acknowledging that men with a different approach to the Bible could be faithful Christian believers worthy of study impressed me somewhat at the time. It was only later in retrospect that I came to understand the full importance of his irenic attitude. For in the course of my ministry I encountered fervent fundamentalists who took an unbending position on the uniqueness of Scripture as the very "God-breathed" Word that must be studied with totally uncritical acceptance. I came to see that with them it was "all or nothing at all."

The touchstone of orthodoxy was to deny the evolutionary hypothesis and insist on a literal interpretation of the Genesis accounts of creation and the Garden of Eden. For, they said, if one thinks the Bible doesn't mean what it says about the world being created by God in six days, then there is no obligation to take the Bible seriously when it says "Thou shalt not commit adultery" and "Christ died for our sins according to the Scriptures." Therefore, to take a critical approach to the Bible is in itself a denial of the faith—with them "critical" is equivalent to "unbelieving." Although I was not ready to accept the evolutionary hypothesis, I could not agree with the fundamentalists' rigorous absolutism. They were unwilling to recognize a third category, those Dr. Rule called "believing critics" or "critical believers."

I have come to see that there is a fourth category of people, the "noncritical unbelievers." They have been brought up on or confronted by a literalistic view of the Bible that they cannot honestly accept, so they simply reject the Bible. I once saw a pamphlet produced by an atheistic society. Of course the centerpiece of their argument was evolution versus creationism. Who knows how many potential believers there may be who are repulsed by an antiintellectual approach to Genesis and give up before they get to "Christ died for our sins according to the Scriptures"?

In my own experience, I gradually moved away from the simplistic view of my childhood days, but I was not at all familiar with the disciplines of textual, historical, or literary criticism applied to the study of the Bible. After a term on the mission field divided between Taiwan and Japan, I returned to Louisville Seminary for a degree in master of theology. I read voluminously about the various views of inspiration and authority of the Bible, all within the field of doctrinal theology. I concluded that I could not conscientiously go along with the literalist/inerrantist view. Though I was not able to articulate a satisfying statement of my own position on the subject, that did not in the least weaken my confidence in the Bible as uniquely inspired and authoritative. When I came to write my thesis, instead of approaching the question from the doctrinal/theological standpoint, I decided to examine all of the places in the Gospels where Jesus had quoted from the Old Testament. My approach was uncritical. I never questioned whether any of the words attributed to Jesus were products of the early church or of the gospel writers themselves. I didn't go into the very complex linguistic problems involved in the differences between the Greek rendering of some of Jesus' words and the original Hebrew of the passages he quoted. Nor did I go deeply into the questions raised when some of Jesus' quotations followed the Septuagint or Greek translation of the Old Testament rather than the Hebrew. I took note of these matters, to be sure, but I lacked the linguistic competence to deal with them. There was an undeniable superficiality to my work, but it was well organized and presented, and my faculty committee awarded me the degree "with distinction."

From this study I gained three unshakable convictions: First, the Bible is really one book, with an organic relationship between the Old and New Testaments that must not be ignored. While the increase of knowledge and discovery necessitates specialization in "Old Testament" and "New Testament" fields, to say nothing of further specialization in subfields within them, I must never lose sight of the canonical wholeness of One Bible comprising Two Testaments.

Second, in Jesus' quotations from the Old Testament, I could not find any instance in which the meaning depended upon the crucial significance of a single word. Rather, a study of the quoted words in their broader Old Testament context provided a deeper and fuller insight into what meaning they had in the New Testament setting.

Third, the text of the Bible as we have it is not susceptible of absolute determination. Even a relatively superficial study of the New Testament quotations from the Old reveals a bewildering number of variations. Not only so, but there is a large number of manuscripts of the Bible with many differences among them. For me, these facts by no means deprive the Bible of its authority, but it convinces me that biblical authority resides elsewhere than in a literal, "inerrant" text.

Benjamin B. Warfield of Princeton is the one person above all who has provided fundamentalist Christians in the United States with the strongest formulation of the doctrine of inspiration and authority of the Bible. I myself have benefited greatly from studying his writings. But Warfield was first of all a textual critic of the New Testament. His aim was to search out among the many manuscripts the text that was most nearly like the original "autograph"—that is, as written down by the hand of the first author.

Unfortunately, many fundamentalists are not willing to follow their mentor in this pursuit. Many refuse the results of textual criticism and cling tenaciously to the inadequate Textus Receptus, the Greek text that underlies the King James Version of the Bible. There are even some who go so far as to insist that the English translation of the King James is the infallible Word of God.

I can understand and to some extent sympathize with people who think in this way. We all prefer certainty to uncertainty. We all would like to have an authoritative voice to tell us: "This is the way; walk ye in it." At one time I was very close to the fundamentalist position because of that desire. But it hasn't been granted to us to see God or to hear God's voice in our ear. Therefore some people feel they have to look for divine certainty in the Bible. I heard a young fundamentalist missionary say, "If I thought there was even one error in the Bible, I would have to give it all up." That was long ago, and I didn't know then how to respond. But as I think back on it now, it seems so sad. His one hope for certainty was the Bible. If he couldn't be sure of the Bible, he couldn't be sure of anything. Now I see that really and truly the Bible was his God. Without an inerrant Bible, he would have nothing.

 : Within the divine plan, God has withheld that kind of certainty from us. Indeed, to give us such certainty would be to remove the necessity of faith. For faith is an attitude of trust in God, a personal relationship of trust which leans in confidence upon God in the midst of uncertainty. Faith is the kind of trust Abraham had when he answered God's call and went out "not knowing whither he went." Faith is that personal relation of trust exemplified by the Servant of the Lord described in Isa. 50:10, "who walks in darkness and has no light, yet trusts in the name of the LORD and relies on his God."

Our weak human nature shrinks from this kind of uncertainty, and abso-lutizing the Bible is one attempt to overcome it. In the early years of my teaching Japanese students, I found myself wishing for certainty. Most of my students were not Christians, had no knowledge of the Bible nor interest in it. Coming to the Bible from an attitude of total indifference, they could look at it with an objectivity lacking to one like me, brought up on the faith of the Bible. When these students asked hard questions and pointed out inconsistencies, I found myself struggling to harmonize and smooth over things, and I sensed that I wasn't convincing the doubters. Reflecting on one unsatisfactory session I thought to myself, "If I could only convince these young people that this is God's Word, then we wouldn't have such problems."

That thought had hardly entered my mind when I recalled that young minister who said, "If I thought there was even one error in the Bible I'd have to give it all up." I realized that I was being tempted to fall into that same trap. I was wanting to give highest priority to the Bible: just convince them this is God's Word, and your problems are solved. I realized that even if I could succeed at that, I would not be converting them to the living God, but to one shut up in the pages of a book.

In my study of the Bible, I kept running across references to books and authors who were clearly "critical," yet who were undeniably "believers." Perhaps the most significant of my discoveries was a second-hand copy of George Adam Smith's commentary on Isaiah. Folded into it was a yellowed newspaper clipping containing a review of the book. The reviewer, obviously disagreeing with Smith, wrote, "Tradition has it that the prophet Isaiah was sawn in two by King Manasseh of Judah. The modernist scholar George Adam Smith has just repeated that atrocity with his commentary." That is, Smith proposed and defended the view that chapters 40–66 were written by an anonymous prophet called "Second Isaiah" a century and a half later than chapters 1–39.

But for me, Smith's commentary opened a whole new world of powerful meaning, letting the light of God's Word flood into my faith and life. Understanding the political and historical times in which Isaiah of Jerusalem and "Second Isaiah" of Babylon had lived, and the contemporary situations into which God, through the prophets, inserted words of warning and comfort, was thrilling to me. The Bible was coming alive! I avidly read all of Smith's commentaries on the prophets. I sought other books and other sources by means of which I could educate myself in the critical approach to the Bible that had not been formally offered me in seminary, and that I had avoided by distancing myself from the "liberals." I read the myths of the Sumerians and Babylonians and Canaanites, noting the similarities but especially the significant differences in the biblical material. I saw how, in the stories of creation and the flood, the biblical writers had faced a pagan world, had accepted the general outlines of their worldview, but had boldly claimed it all for the God of Israel.

Could the author of Gen. 1, some exiled Jewish priest, far from home, and surrounded by the paganism of victorious Babylon, take on its mythology, accept its general description of an orderly three-storied universe, and declare, "Not by Marduk and his multitude of gods and goddesses, but by the God who redeemed

Israel from Egypt"? Then I too could accept the general description of the emergence of life through an evolutionary process and be bold to declare: "Not by blind chance, but by the God and Father of our Lord Jesus Christ and through the Living Word without whom "was not anything made that was made" (John 1:3)!

This process of learning took time, and I did not again experience such an immediate flood of joyous insight as I had gotten from George Adam Smith. But it was all part of a pilgrimage toward liberation! Not that I was being liberated from faith in God or from my commitment to God as both child and servant; I was liberated from bondage to my mistaken ideas of a little god shut up in the pages of a book. I enjoyed the freedom that comes from knowing the living God who is Creator and Lord of all. I finally understood that I had been trying to shut God up in a book, and God had finally made me understand that that was impossible.

I know, of course, that evolution is still not "proven," that in a certain sense it is a hypothesis which will undergo change and revision as time goes on and further scientific discoveries are made. For now, it seems to offer a framework which explains more of the universe in which we live than any other. But my belief in God is not dependent on whether evolution can be "proved" or not. My faith is in God who can, and I believe most probably does, use this sort of process in the ordering of the universe He created. If in the future some totally unforeseen "paradigm change" should occur necessitating a total revision of the evolutionary hypothesis, I won't find my conception of God threatened in the way inerrantist/literalists feel their conception of God threatened by the evolutionary hypothesis. If the new hypothesis should be more "elegant," as the scientists say, then by that much shall my understanding of God be more elegant.

Being able to accept evolution within a larger conception of God was liberating for me in other ways. I was at last able to recognize my dishonest use of the Bible in trying to "prove" the traditional doctrine of creation. While claiming to "believe the Bible" I had not really paid attention to what the Bible actually said.

For example, I ignored the fact that the "firmament" [Hebrew *raqia*'] which God made to separate the waters above and below the heavens (Gen 1:6), was really something solid like metal hammered out by a blacksmith. The same linguistic root occurs in the story of the punishment of the two hundred associates of Korah who challenged the priests' monopoly of offering incense and died (Num. 16:35–40). God commanded that the bronze censers they had used be collected and hammered into broad plates as a covering for the altar. Such is the conceptual background of the author of Gen. 1: God made heaven like a solid bowl turned upside down above the earth to keep the heavenly ocean from inundating the land. It is similar to the thought underlying the Babylonian epic *Enuma elish,* where likewise the dome of heaven is conceived of as something solid: Marduk split the body of the monster Ti'amat in two and used half of it to restrain the waters above. Despite the similarity in basic conception, the biblical declaration of faith stands out all the more clearly.

I knew the sky was not solid, so even when I got some idea of what "firmament" literally means, I just ignored it. As a child I had memorized Psalm 24, in which it was said that God founded the earth on the seas and established it on the floods, but I saw no conflict between that and knowing that planet earth is a sphere in space. I could compartmentalize my knowledge of the solar system and the Bible. I could still insist on the literal Genesis story of a six-day creation without honestly facing up to the obligations that a literal interpretation would lay on me.

Formerly, I had not honestly faced the differences between the creation accounts in Gen. 1:1–4a and 2:4b–2:25. The first describes a creation process extending over seven days. The second mentions only one, "the day that the LORD God made the earth and the heavens."

Furthermore, the order in which various things were created is different in the two accounts:

Genesis 1

God separates dry land out of watery chaos.
God causes vegetation to grow out of the earth.
God creates fish in the sea and birds on dry land and in the air.
God causes the earth to bring forth wild and domestic animals.
God creates humankind, male and female, in the divine image.

Genesis 2

Dry land, no vegetation or rain, only mist.
God forms a male human out of the dust of the earth.
God plants a garden and causes vegetation to grow.
God forms animals from the ground.
God makes a female human from a rib taken from the male.

I had conveniently ignored the details in the two accounts that were mutually inconsistent: the difference in the numbering of the days and the order in which God was said to have created various things. In keeping with the children's story Bible on which I had been brought up before having my own Bible, I had unquestioningly assumed that the story about Adam and Eve was just a more detailed description of what had taken place when, as chapter 1 had said, God created them in the divine image on the sixth day. The Bible doesn't say that; it obviously says something different. We do children (and adults too) a great disservice if we teach them such an erroneously conglomerated creation story as though it were the infallible Word of God. If we honestly pay attention to what the Bible itself actually says, we must face up to the obvious inconsistencies and decide how to deal with them.

Noncritical believers, who have already decided on prior grounds that the Bible is literally true and "inerrant," are forced into a sort of intellectual dishonesty to make it appear that everything is quite harmonious. They will quote Isa. 40:22— "He that sitteth upon the circle of the earth"—as "proof" that the Bible teaches that the earth is a sphere. What it literally says is that God sits on top of that inverted bowl of the heavens and looks down upon the circle which is formed by the circumference of a flat earth. It is the same word which appears in Prov. 8:27, "He set a compass upon the face of the depth."

Rigorous-minded noncritical unbelievers, confronted with the above "proof" of the Bible's scientific accuracy (Isa. 40:22), will not be impressed, and, like the writer of the atheistic pamphlet, will despise the apologists and simply reject the Bible. Only a critical believing position is adequate to deal with matters of such complexity. The critical believer does not think that the Bible is full of errors. Only the noncritical ones, believers and unbelievers alike, are concerned about errors, for they debate whether the Bible does or does not teach infallible truth about questions of natural science and historical events. The debate seems to focus primarily on the Bible, but for an inerrantist like the young missionary in Japan, that really means God, for they think that if the Bible contains error, God is not dependable.

The critical believer is concerned with God but in a different dimension. Such people do not believe that God, even by divine choice, has limited His actions to what people can discover by a literal reading of the Bible, and particularly of the book of Genesis at the beginning and the book of Revelation at the end. God is far greater than that!

I gained valuable insight into the greatness of God and concurrently the greatness of the Bible from learning more about the Canaanite culture and religion against which biblical faith struggled. As I studied more from devout scholars, and as my understanding of the original languages improved, my joy and pleasure in studying and teaching the Bible grew.

The faith of the people of Israel rested upon their salvation from Egypt by the gracious power of YHWH. Settled in the land of Canaan, the Israelites were tempted to adopt the fertility rites of the indigenous people. The discovery of clay tablets at Ugarit has made possible a fuller understanding of what those rites involved. They consisted in the worship of the storm god Hadad, familiarly called Baal, (which means "owner" or "master" or "husband") and several goddesses with which he was related. Baal as god of heaven was husband, and the earth mother goddess was his wife. Seasonal rains meant that Baal was fertilizing earth. Human worshipers engaged in sacral sexual intercourse as a form of sympathetic magic to encourage the deities to promote production of crops and herds.

In the days of King Ahab and his Tyrian wife Jezebel, Baal worship was aggressively promoted in Israel (1 Kings 16:29-33). It was not that the Israelites abandoned YHWH—they still revered YHWH as their savior from Egypt. King Ahab, indeed, gave his children names including the element "iah" or "yah" indicative of his reverence for YHWH. However, he and his people believed that agriculture was a realm in which YHWH had no authority, so they must look to Baal for assistance in this aspect of life.

It was this dualistic approach to religion that the prophet Elijah challenged: "How long halt ye between two opinions? If the LORD be God, follow him: but if Baal, then follow him" (1 Kings 18:21). In the contest to pray for rain in time of drought, Baal failed to act, but YHWH answered Elijah's prayer and sent fire and rain from heaven. In this either/or situation, Elijah succeeded in winning the day for YHWH, but the war did not end. There were still those who recognized YHWH as the deliverer from Egypt but Baal as the giver of fertility.

Jehonadab the son of Rechab became leader of a faction that made the absolute choice for YHWH. He joined forces with Jehu to annihilate the family of King Ahab and all the overt worshipers of Baal (2 Kings 10:15–28). As we learn from Jer. 35, over the next 250 years the Rechabites followed a strict policy of worshipping YHWH only. They continued to live in tents as their ancestors had done when they left Egypt; they would not plant fields; nor would they plant vineyards and drink wine. These Rechabites kept themselves separate and pure from the temptations of fertility religion by totally avoiding agriculture. What this meant was that they acknowledged that YHWH was not concerned with agriculture and fertility, so they abandoned all that to Baal.

The majority of the people, however, despite Elijah's temporary victory, continued the syncretistic practice of honoring both YHWH and Baal. They even applied the title Baal to YHWH. In one sense, they were perfectly justified in doing so, for Baal means "owner" and "lord," and certainly it could be claimed that that was what YHWH was to Israel. In the popular mind, YHWH and Baal began to merge into one. The result was that the sexual immorality of the fertility cult so widely pervaded Israelite life that the marriage commitment of husband and wife meant nothing, and the whole fabric of society and even the natural environment were deteriorating (Hos. 4:1–11). While paying lip service to YHWH, the people in reality had taken the other alternative Elijah had offered them. Baal was their choice, for they believed Baal was the source of their grain, their wine, and their oil. Syncretists made up by far the majority of the people, while the Rechabites were a small minority.

Fortunately for the development of biblical faith, the prophet Hosea was able to break out of the either/or choice Elijah seemed to have demanded. The God Hosea worshiped was not simply the God of the exodus and the desert but also the god of fertility who, as Elijah taught, could send or withhold rain. With Hosea, it was not a choice of YHWH or Baal, but YHWH alone taking over from Baal the realm of fertility. Instead of retreating from the fertility cult and avoiding agriculture as the Rechabites did, Hosea boldly took over the very terminology of pagan fertility and made it do service for YHWH.

YHWH is the husband and Israel is the wife, said Hosea (chapter 2). Participating in fertility religion's worship of Baal, Israel had betrayed her husband and committed adultery. Like any betrayed husband, YHWH became angry and chastised the wayward wife. Specifically, the punishment consisted in natural disasters reducing agricultural production, so that Israel would realize that YHWH, not Baal, was the giver or withholder of fertility. "Then shall she say, I will go and return to my first husband; for then was it better with me than now" (verse 2:7). It didn't work; she didn't return. So more punishment was in order (2:12–13): "I will destroy her vines and her fig trees, whereof she hath said, These are my rewards that my lovers have given me: and I will make them a forest, and the beasts of the field shall eat them. And I will visit upon her the days of the Baalim, wherein she burned incense to them, and she decked herself with her earrings and her jewels, and she went after her lovers, and forgot me, saith the LORD."

The very next verse comes as a complete shock to the unprepared reader: "Therefore, behold . . ." what? More punishment, of course, one would be inclined to say. But listen: "Therefore, behold, I will allure her, and bring her into the wilderness [i.e., a condition devoid of fertility gods], and speak comfortably unto her. And I will give her her vineyards from thence, and the valley of Achor for a door of hope: and she shall sing there, as in the days of her youth, and as in the day when she came up out of the land of Egypt" (2:14–15).

Punishment did not bring about reformation. Therefore, behold, the betrayed husband will begin again with courtship, allurement, speaking comfortably to her (literally "to her heart"). In the context of the development of Israel's understanding of God, Hosea opens a new window on to the character of God, not primarily as judgmental and punishing, but first and last as loving. And this understanding of God comes about at least in part because Hosea dared to use the pagan terminology of the fertility cults and apply it to YHWH.

As if to reinforce this deeper insight into the nature of God, Hosea comes at it from a different angle, namely that of the betrayed father who will not abandon an obstinately rebellious son. This is the message of Hosea 11:1ff: "When Israel was a child, then I loved him, and called my son out of Egypt." But the child spurned the loving care of the parent—Israel went after Baal. The father punished the child, as the husband did the wife, but to no avail. But the conclusion of this story is the same as the first: "How shall I give thee up, Ephraim? how shall I deliver thee, Israel? how shall I make thee as Admah? how shall I set thee as Zeboim [two cities destroyed with Sodom and Gomorrah]? mine heart is turned within me, my repentings are kindled together. I will not execute the fierceness of mine anger, I will not return to destroy Ephraim: for I am God and not man; the Holy One in the midst of thee" (11:8–9).

Humanly speaking, we would consider a husband justified in divorcing permanently a wife who persistently betrayed him. We could understand the frustration with an incorrigibly delinquent child whom the parents finally turned over to the juvenile authorities. But not YHWH; "I am God, and not man; the Holy One in the midst of thee."

Christians who are familiar with the idea of God our Heavenly Father as taught by Jesus the Savior may be surprised to know that in the Old Testament, the fatherhood of God was rarely mentioned. In pagan religions, there was a good deal of mythology about the gods actually begetting human children through sexual intercourse. Such an idea was not compatible with belief in the transcendent God YHWH whose acts of creation were totally devoid of sexual activity. Prophets were careful to avoid giving the impression that there was a physical relationship between God and humankind. But here again Hosea was bold enough to use the pagan terminology to stress the character of God in relation to Israel. Hosea broke new ground. In 14:4 the prophet transmits this word from God emphasizing the divine initiative: "I will heal their backsliding, I will love them freely: for mine anger is turned away from him." Hosea was a pathfinder on the way of faith that led finally to the sublime declaration, "God is love" (1 John 4:8 and 16).

I found this groundbreaking message of Hosea when I saw the prophet in his own historical context, in conflict with contemporary pagan polytheism, and in the broader biblical context represented by the stories of Elijah and of the Rechabites. For me, there were three heartwarming effects.

First, my confidence that the Bible is not inimical to the quest for truth in extra-biblical realms of study was strengthened. Already I had learned from the author of Genesis 1 that Darwinism or evolutionary theory, when viewed from the standpoint of biblical monotheistic faith, is not a threat but may even be an ally in understanding that the One True God is the God of all truth. One can go further: Is there any validity at all to Karl Marx's insights into the force and influence of economic factors upon human life? Then Christians can accept such valid insights as gifts of God, without adopting Marx's dialectical materialism. Does Sigmund Freud have anything worth listening to about the pervasiveness of human sexuality and the power of the subconscious? Then Christians can accept such valid insights as gifts of God, without adopting Freud's atheism and the total moral relativity that some Freudians teach. Do oriental religions contain any insights, such as, for example, a holistic view of the relation between humankind and the rest of creation? Then Christians nurtured in the adversarial relation between "man" and "nature" can certainly profit from such insights as gifts of God without adopting the pantheistic milieu in which such insights may be embedded.

The Bible I have found to be not an infallible collection of words, but the revelation of the living God, the God who became incarnate in Jesus Christ, crucified, risen, and reigning as Lord of all of life. United to God through faith in Jesus Christ I am set free from bondage to fear of the unknown. I need not fear new discoveries that might call in question old presuppositions based upon the pre-Copernican, pre-Darwinian, pre-Marxian, pre-Freudian views tied into a totally noncritical, literalist interpretation of the Bible. With Paul I can say, "He that is spiritual judgeth all things, yet he himself is judged by no man. For who hath known the mind of the Lord, that he may instruct him? But we have the mind of Christ" (1 Cor. 2:15–16).

Having the mind of Christ, then, I can go on and gladly accept what Paul says further in 3:21–23: "Therefore let no man glory in men. For all things are yours, whether Paul, or Apollos, or Cephas [or Calvin or Luther or Aquinas or Darwin or Marx or Ghandi], or the world, or life, or death, or things present, or things to come; all are yours; and ye are Christ's; and Christ is God's." Hallelujah! Praise the Lord!

Second, Hosea provided a focal point from which I could understand other references to the divine initiative in forgiveness and restoration scattered elsewhere in the Old Testament. God threatened our first parents with immediate death if they ate the forbidden fruit, yet God spared their lives and even provided covering for their nakedness (Gen. 2:7; 3:21–24). The fratricide Cain was driven out to become a wanderer, yet God placed a mark upon him to protect the murderer from human retribution (Gen. 4:1–15). In the Genesis story of the flood (in contrast to extra-biblical flood stories) God had a moral purpose in sending this catastrophe as judgment upon human sin: "And God saw that the wickedness of man was great in the earth, and that every imagination of the thoughts of his heart was only evil continually" (Gen. 6:5). Yet once the flood was past, it became abundantly clear that no change had taken place in the human heart. Therefore, "The LORD said in his heart, I will not again curse the ground any more for man's sake; for the imagination of man's heart is evil from his youth" (8:21).

Punishment didn't change the human heart. What changed, as we see in the Bible, is God's attitude. In view of the persistent rebellion of humankind, God called one family, Abraham and Sarah and their offspring, with the promise, "in thee shall all families of the earth be blessed" (Gen. 12:3).

I found in Ezekiel 20:1–44 one of the most persuasive arguments for the ineffectiveness of punishment and the grace of God transcending all human sin. Hosea and Jeremiah had viewed the period of Israel's wilderness wanderings as a sort of "honeymoon" when she was alone with her husband YHWH without the temptation of Baal (see Hos. 2:14, 9:10; Jer. 2:2–3). Ezekiel, however, sees the whole history of Israel down to his own time in the Babylonian exile as an uninterrupted tale of ungrateful apostasy in the face of God's grace. In Egypt Israel was stubbornly rebellious, and God determined to pour out his fury on them there (20:5–8). "But I wrought for my name's sake, that it should not be polluted before the heathen, among whom they were" (v. 9). So God brought them out of Egypt into the wilderness and gave them the law. Still they rebelled and disobeyed, and again God was ready to pour out wrath upon them (vv. 10–13). Yet God relented, "for my name's sake" (v. 14). The story continues in the same vein, over and over, with God ready to destroy Israel, yet each time relenting "for my name's sake."

The climax is reached when Ezekiel foretells that God will gather the people from all the places where they are scattered and bring them again into their land: "And there shall ye remember your ways, and all your doings, wherein ye have been defiled; and ye shall loathe yourselves in your own sight for all your evils that ye have committed. And ye shall know that I am the LORD, when I have wrought with you for my name's sake, not according to your wicked ways, nor according to your corrupt doings, O ye house of Israel, saith the Lord GOD" (Ezek. 20:43–44).

Ezekiel is telling us here that God's dealings with humankind are not based upon the principle of well-deserved retribution for human sin but according to the goodness of God. As any parent who has dealt with children knows, punishment may well harden defiance, self-defense, denial of wrongdoing. Even if punishment forces obedience, residual resentment may linger in the heart of the offender. In God's dealings with us sinners, it is not punishment but grace that wins us. We realize the enormity of our sin only when we have experienced the forgiving love of God. The whole Bible contains the story of how people came to learn that God deals with us not according to our sin, but according to God's own gracious nature.

The prophet Amos (probably a slightly prior contemporary of Hosea) provides further evidence of the inability of punishment to bring about regeneration. Verses 4:6–12 contains a list of calamities God had visited on the people. First was famine, "yet have ye not returned unto me, saith the LORD" (4:6). In succession there follow drought, agricultural blight, pestilential disease, war, and destroying fire. After each item in the litany comes the refrain: "Yet have ye not returned unto me, saith the LORD." So how does this section of Amos's message continue? "Therefore thus will I do unto thee, O Israel: and because I will do this unto thee, prepare to meet thy God, O Israel. For, lo, he that formeth the mountains, and createth the wind, and declareth unto man what is his thought, that maketh the morning darkness, and treadeth upon the high places of the earth, the LORD, the God of hosts, is his name" (4:12–13).

I used to assume that when Israel did meet God, it would be the God of final and complete punishment. Indeed, as a child, I used to see signs along the country highways proclaiming "PREPARE TO MEET GOD," and everyone was certain it was meant as a threat. But Amos doesn't say that. Amos goes on to speak of the Creator God, "who declareth unto man what is his thought." This is a personal God, taking the initiative in personal communication with humankind. What is the "thought" God wishes to declare? In the total context of canonical Scripture, we meet God in the person of Jesus Christ, the Incarnate Son. The thought that God would declare is stated in John 3:16–17: "God so loved the world that he gave his only begotten Son, that whosoever believeth in him should not perish, but have everlasting life. For God sent not his Son into the world to condemn the world; but that the world through him might be saved."

In the days of his flesh, the Incarnate Son condemned not the woman taken in adultery but her accusers (John 8:3–11). He received publicans and sinners in table fellowship, and he answered those who criticized such behavior, saying, "Go and learn what that meaneth, I will have mercy and not sacrifice." Jesus was quoting words from Hosea, the Old Testament prophet of love (Matt. 9:13; Hos. 6:6).

Third, I came to have a greater appreciation for the study of the original language of the Bible. Faithful and reverent Hebrew scholars have pointed to the fact that the text of Hosea is one of the most difficult, and apparently most damaged, of all the Old Testament writings. I myself lay no claim to being a Hebrew expert, but I have learned enough of the language to be able to benefit from works produced by recognized scholars.

I was brought up on the King James Version of the Bible, and whenever I quote from memory it is the KJV that comes naturally to my lips. But despite the fact that it is still the most popular and widely used English version, it has serious drawbacks. It contains some mistranslations, but greater understanding of Hebrew itself and discoveries of related or cognate Semitic languages make possible greater accuracy. Since the publication of the KJV in 1611, the English language itself has undergone change to such an extent that many expressions are either unintelligible or misleading and require revision.

For people who know only English, the KJV sometimes presents puzzling barriers to understanding. For that reason the trend toward translating the Bible into more accurate, intelligible English is to be welcomed and encouraged. In this way, those who are not competent to compare the original languages for themselves can at least benefit from the efforts of those who are. Strangely enough, people who are most insistent on the literal and inerrant truth of the Bible are the very ones who would limit the study of Scripture to the KJV alone. It is not enough for them to reject outright such modern translations as the Revised Standard Version and the New English Bible, claiming that the translators are "unbelievers" because they are also "critics." The inerrantists reject all other translations, including, for example, the NIV—New International Version—whose preface plainly states: "The translators were united in their commitment to the authority and infallibility of the Bible as God's Word in written form."

I cannot escape thinking that what the champions of inerrancy are really defending is not the authentic Word of God, but a system of belief and practice of their own devising. Then they search the Scriptures to find proof texts that support their particular view. They make the leap directly from the Bible to their current debate, without considering what the Bible really says. Is the translation they are using an accurate one? Is the original text on which the translation is based dependable? What did those words mean in the time and context in which they were first spoken or written? How do those words fit into the total context of the biblical canon, including both Old Testament and New? What is the meaning of those words in the light of the full revelation of God in Jesus Christ? When they pull a prooftext out of context and say: "The Bible says . . ." they may not be teaching what the Bible—the whole canonical Bible—says, but only what they are forcing one small bit of the Bible to say.

The Bible has such a vast variety of material in it that careful search can probably find a text to support any possible view. The Bible is like a statue with a nose of wax, it used to be said—one can twist and shape it any way one wishes. It's well known that when the devil tempted Jesus, he did so by taking a Bible verse out of context (Matt. 4:6; Luke 4:10–11). I do not mean to imply that only the "inerrantists" or those who use only the King James Version are guilty of specious arguments based on simplistic "prooftexting." Every single one of us is tainted with self-centeredness, and none of us is completely free of some bias in interpreting Scripture. Still, I firmly believe that the reverent exercise of free inquiry, anchored in faithful devotion to the God supremely revealed in Jesus Christ, is the surest way to learn what the Bible really says.

From the death of Ahab in 869 B.C. to the fall of Jerusalem in 587 B.C., the Rechabites faithfully observed the instructions of their founder to avoid agriculture and the temptations of the fertility cult. Jeremiah gave them well-deserved praise for their ceaseless loyalty in keeping the commands of their founder (Jer. 35:12–19; note that the prophet does not say these were commandments of God). Jeremiah relays God's promise that they will survive. Fortunately for us, however, the Rechabites' viewpoint did not govern the final statement of the biblical faith, for they achieved their adherence to YHWH at the tremendous cost of leaving Baal and pagan fertility cults supreme in the realm of agriculture.

It seems to me that inerrantists who reject evolution and try to force the creationist point of view not only on their own adherents but also on the general public through controlling school textbooks are the modern counterparts of the Rechabites. They are trying to achieve loyalty to God at the cost of abandoning to the skeptics and atheists the whole realm of human inquiry by means of natural science.

In the early days after the publication of Darwin's *Origin of Species,* the skeptics set the terms of the debate: Either evolution without God, or literal biblical creation. Too many Christians, scholars as well as lay persons, accepted these terms and undertook to defend the Bible. The relatively few theologians who tried to follow a mediating "both/and" way were soon overwhelmed by the conservatives, and it took many decades before such a position could gain respectability.

It is unfortunate that in the United States there are still so many people fighting the battle, alienating honest inquirers, and limiting not only the realms of inquiry for humankind but, worse, limiting God to their own small minds.

Thanks to Hosea and his successors, the faith of Israel reached out to absorb whatever there was of value in the fertility cults and make it serve the authentic faith. Indeed, it is my firm belief that this is precisely the basic pattern that can be discerned throughout the canonical Scriptures—monotheistic faith reaching out into every realm of life and thought and laying claim to it in the name of the One True God who created it all and to whom it all belongs.

But that is the theme of a book I hope to write some day. Suffice it here to say simply what I hope I have demonstrated in this essay: All my life long I have been loyal to the Bible as the Word of God. I have tried to live by the Bible, and the more I have studied and taught the Bible, the more I think of myself as living in and through the Bible. This has been the gift of the Living God to me, mediated through Jesus Christ my Savior, and enabled by the Holy Spirit.

Mike and Karla Yaconelli: Behind the Wittenburg Door

My journey out of fundamentalism and into an authentic relationship with God and Christ was a long one. The fundamentalist indoctrination scarred me for many years. . . . It was difficult to trust anyone who said they were a "Christian." Basically, I didn't discuss my relationship with God with anyone—including Mike—for a long time because the ways and areas of my life in which *I* encountered God didn't seem to fit the "rules" of Christianity as I understood them. Slowly but surely, God Himself revealed His character to me—and surprise! I discovered He wasn't anything like what I'd been told He was.

—Karla Yaconelli

I would say that the major influence that caused me to move out of fundamentalism was . . . working for Forest Home Christian Conference Center. . . . That was the first time in my life that I realized there were Congregationalists who were Christians, there were Episcopalians who were Christians. . . . That was when I realized this Christian world is a whole lot bigger than I thought it was.

—Mike Yaconelli

Mike Yaconelli is cofounder of Youth Specialties, Inc. The San Diego–based company has been going strong for about twenty-four years, holding seminars nationwide, and publishing books, like *Play It!, High School Ministry,* and *Greatest Skits on Earth.* Mike is also cofounder, copublisher, and senior editor of *The Door* (formerly, *The Wittenburg Door*), a magazine that combines humor with hard-edged scrutiny in its focus on Christianity—a sort of *National Lampoon* for Christians, or for anyone with a keen sense of the ridiculous and the sacred. Karla Yaconelli, formerly a dancer, and former owner/operator of a school of classical ballet (Ballet Northwest), is *The Door*'s managing editor. Mike is also the author of *Tough Faith,* a book about evangelical Christianity's reluctance to face difficult issues and unanswerable questions posed by suffering and paradox, and editor of *The Door Interviews.*

The Yaconellis, married in 1982, have five children (four are Mike's, one is Karla's) all of whom lived with them as a "blended family." As of 1993 the oldest boy, Mark, has graduated from college, married, and been working as a youth minister in Portland, Oregon. Trent is finishing his teaching credential and plans to be a history teacher. Lisa, who is between high school and college, recently finished a period of missionary work in Philadelphia's inner city. Jill is a college freshman. And Jessica is a high school sophomore. Together, Mike and Karla run *The Door,* Grace Community Church, and a local Young Life Club, through which they sponsor a mission trip each year to build homes in Mexico for poverty-stricken families. Over the past eight years $210,000 has been raised in support of this endeavor, all the contributions coming from a community of less than seven thousand people with an unemployment rate of 22 percent. Over seven hundred young people have participated in building forty homes, one school, two churches, and a health clinic in Mexico. Mike speaks worldwide 30 to 40 percent of each year. The following is based on a phone conversation the editor had with Mike and Karla.

Karla Yaconelli: I was raised in the United Methodist Church, and I don't remember a bit of it, except that I was bored most of the time. When I was fourteen, some guy I thought I wanted to date invited me to a revival in a neighboring town (held by a Berean fundamentalist church in Weed, California). I went, got humiliated and felt real guilty, did the weeping, crying, going forward thing, and as a result became involved in the youth group that this guy was a part of, as well as in their singing group, the Abundant Life Singers, which tried to evangelize neighboring communities. During the concerts we high school kids would tell the adults who attended that they needed to accept Jesus before they walked out of the room or they were going to go to hell.

The Berean fundamentalist group I had joined was also into "end times" stuff. According to them, Henry Kissinger was very likely the antichrist. We could not go to dances. High school proms were out of the question. If your bra strap could be seen through a white sweater, it was considered immoral and you were told that you were tempting the boys beyond their ability to resist.

Most of us in the group led a dual life. We would jump through the fundamentalist hoops at the youth group and while we toured as the Abundant Life Singers. Then we would go to high school and live a different life. I went to parties, drank, and danced. In fact, contrary to what I was taught as a fundamentalist, dancing (classical ballet, in particular) proved to be a major lifelong pursuit, and it ultimately enhanced rather than diminished my Christianity.

After high school, I went to college at the University of Oregon in Eugene, majored in dance, and tried to get involved with Campus Crusade. I went to one meeting and got so disgusted I walked out and never went back. At the beginning of the meeting they passed around a scorecard with different columns. You filled in your name, and next to your name were several columns, labeled, "Number of times I witnessed to someone this week," "Number of times I prayed with someone this week," "Number of times someone was led to the Lord through me this week," "Number of times . . ." this, "Number of times . . ." that. I got so furious, I filled in zeros in all the columns, put a giant "X" through my name, threw the pad down on the desk, and walked out. I hadn't witnessed to a single soul . . . at least not in the manner *they* advocated.

Basically, I got to a place in college where my life wasn't working the way I knew it ought to. I had graduated from high school a year earlier than most and went to college at age sixteen. I was upset with some of the decisions I had made and was getting kind of messed up. And the words of my mother echoed in my ears: "If you ever feel like you need help, you can always count on your church."

So I looked for a church in Eugene and ended up at a Church of God. I began meeting with the pastor and attending their functions. I entered into a counseling relationship with the pastor, and told him all about my struggles and that kind of thing. It went okay for a while, but eventually this much-older-than-I, married minister turned out to be a pervert and started putting the moves on me.

My parents were thrilled that I was involved in a church. So, when I came home from college the next summer, I didn't tell them that I'd sworn off the church and that the minister was a creep.

I returned to Eugene to have some surgery that summer. So my parents, of course (unbeknownst to me), called the pastor of the church and told him that I was going to be in the hospital and suggested that maybe he should visit me there. And the little weasel would come by at 7:30 in the morning or 9:30 at night, when nobody else was apt to be visiting, and lean over the bed to kiss me on the forehead, and gosh, gee, his hand just happened to "accidentally" land on my breast *every single time.*

The following school year, he found out where I lived and started dropping by unannounced and became much more blatant with his intentions. It got pretty ugly. It's amazing to me that I'm still a Christian today.

This was the second minister in my theretofore young life who had pulled that kind of thing with me. These days, that kind of conduct has some pretty hefty legal ramifications, but back then, you just had to get yourself away from it any way you could.

Before I realized this guy was weird, and shortly after I began counseling with him in my first year of college, I went through an immersion baptism at his church. It was a wonderful experience (truly) for me. Little did I know at the time, it was probably a wet T-shirt thrill for him.

I didn't return to church until several years had passed. I was married and pregnant, and couldn't face the prospect of bringing a child into the world without some sort of Christian influence besides my own. My then-husband was radically opposed to church, so I went alone.

Mike doesn't remember meeting me back then, but I began attending Community Bible Church, where Mike was preaching. The church was founded by the same family whose youth group I had attended in high school. They were never quite satisfied with any church they joined, so they eventually founded their own, and Mike became their pastor. No one can tell *me* that God doesn't have a sense of humor! I didn't go often, but I went enough to meet some people, and I tried to get involved in a couple of Bible studies, which were the typical women's coffee-klatch type done out of some stupid little book. I've never been much into women's tea parties, so I couldn't endure those.

By the time my baby was born, my marriage was falling apart. Probably one of my deepest encounters with God occurred in the process of my divorce. It's almost blasphemous to say something like that in a lot of Christian circles:

"Gosh, where did you encounter God?"

"Oh, while I was getting a divorce."

"And you still got one?"

"Yes."

"Then you must not have *really* met Jesus."

"I sure did."

And they think to themselves, "She isn't *really* saved, she hasn't *really* surrendered, and she isn't *really* a Christian like we are."

Because of some of the fundamentalist indoctrination, I was terrified that if I got out of that marriage relationship (which involved both physical abuse and alcohol abuse) and divorced, I would fall from grace and wind up in hell. Of course, I couldn't understand why God would want me to stick it out no matter what and lose my soul *that* way, but fundamentalist doctrine portrays divorce as the *absolute* unpardonable sin, so there I was.

I remember being on my face (literally) on the living room floor, praying, "God, God, if this is what you want me to do, if this is my form of the crucifixion, so be it." But everything inside of me was screaming, "This isn't the way it's meant to be! This is insane!" Actually, I believe I screamed, "This sucks!" God was strangely silent for a very long period of time. I gave in to the "evil" pursuit of a divorce, and it was only afterward that I was able to recognize God's silence as not approval, but as assent, acquiescence.

Eventually I came to a place where I understood that, as *earnestly* as I was praying, God would not turn a deaf ear and say, "Tough bananas, cutie pie, you figure it out on your own. I'm outta here." Does that mean God wants people to get divorced? That divorce doesn't matter? That marriage vows are inconsequential? Of course not. But it *does* mean that God *is* a personal God who interacts with you *in the midst of your life.*

It was during that time that my relationship with God became my own, became a personal thing that was definitely Him and me.

During the process of deciding to divorce, my father died of cancer. It was a nine-month, rapidly progressing horror. I was basically one screwed-up individual at that time on almost all fronts. Of course, I don't know that I've now arrived at any great plateau! A good friend of mine recommended that Mike make an appointment with me. He did, and he tried to counsel my ex-husband and me two or three times. Unfortunately, Mike was in over his head in his own marriage, which was on the skids, so he called and said, "I can't help you with this. I'm not qualified . . . my own marriage is falling apart." He sent us on to a flaming fundamentalist counselor. This counselor was a real nutcase who wanted nothing more than to put another notch on his marriage belt of relationships that had been "saved." He tried to sell us an exercise trampoline to help us improve our marriage. I am *not* kidding. I got a divorce instead.

I was a classical ballet instructor, and Mike's daughter was taking lessons from my partner, so I would see him periodically in that context, as well as when I would attend his church. His marriage ultimately fell apart and he resigned. The rest was an obvious progression of events, and Mike and I were married two years later.

In terms of my Christianity, my journey out of fundamentalism and into authentic relationship with God and Christ was a long one. The fundamentalist indoctrination scarred me for many years, even after Mike and I were married. It was difficult to trust anyone who said they were a "Christian." Basically, I didn't discuss my relationship with God with anyone—including Mike—for a long time because the ways and areas of my life in which *I* encountered God didn't seem to fit the "rules" of Christianity as I understood them. Slowly but surely, God Himself revealed His character to me—and surprise! I discovered He wasn't anything like what I'd been told He was.

Mike Yaconelli: I was raised Catholic . . . in name only. My folks never went to mass. When I was around ten or eleven years old, my folks walked into my room at night and they said, "We've been born again, we've become Christians. We poured alcohol down the sink last night. We don't drink anymore." The guy who led them to the Lord was an old missionary Baptist preacher.

I didn't know what the heck they were talking about. All I knew was that the preacher didn't wear a priest's collar and his wife didn't wear a nun's habit. They met at a house for awhile. Eventually they ended up in a church in Santa Ana, California. And they sang. There was a lot of life to it. I kind of liked it. Then my folks started having Bible studies at our house. It was incredible. I wouldn't go to the movies with my friends just so I could stay home on Friday night to be there. And they'd sing and have fun and laugh, get into giant debates, theological discussions. As a result of my folks becoming Christians, they led about eighteen people to the Lord all around the neighborhood.

The missionary Baptist preacher at the church would shout and scream, and he had long invitations. People would go up and talk to you and invite you down to the altar if you were new. I became a Christian then, around age eleven. I remember walking down the aisle. I got baptized. It was an incredibly emotional experience.

But after a couple years my folks couldn't handle the style anymore. They weren't that kind of people. Everybody in the church was from the South. To be honest, it was just a little too "southern" for my folks. So we left and went to a Presbyterian church. That's really where I found my roots.

Then when I was fifteen or sixteen, my folks moved to Anaheim, and they started going to Central Baptist Church . . . real conservative, huge, and growing like mad. The pastor was Bob Wells, a fundamentalist. As soon as we moved in, my Dad was teaching Sunday school and he was on the board.

When it came time to go to college, pastor Bob suggested to my dad that I attend Bob Jones University. I wanted to go to another Christian college, but a few of my friends were also planning to go to Bob Jones, so I decided to go there.

Then I heard about the rules they had—like the "eighteen-inch" rule: you were not allowed to get closer to a girl than eighteen inches—and curfews, and so forth. So I wrote the public relations department asking about these things, and I got a letter back saying that it was just Satan trying to keep me from going to BJU. At that time (believe it or not), that reply made sense to me.

So my friends and I jumped in the car and off we went. I was seventeen. The two other guys were eighteen and nineteen. I'd never been out of state by myself. We drove straight to New Orleans because we decided that before we went to this school we'd experience a little bit of the world. One of the wildest thing I'd done up to that time was buy a case of beer with some friends. I drank two cans and hated it. We dumped the rest.

Another time, the parents of one guy I was driving to Bob Jones University with put on a before-prom "Coke"-tail party (named after the soda, not the drug). Champagne was also provided. I'd never had champagne, so I drank seven glasses of it and thought it was terrific. Didn't think it affected me at all. However, walking out of there, I was bombed. So I got in my Dad's car and drove to the prom. It's amazing we didn't get killed. I had a reputation for being a "good" Christian, and I was an idiot at the prom—totally blitzed—which ruined my testimony. Later, I had to get up in front of my high school's Youth for Christ club and announce that I had been drinking and apologize, which I did. I also had to resign from being the club's song leader.

So, back to my journey to BJU. We arrived in New Orleans and decided to visit a nightspot on Bourbon Street, buy drinks with forged IDs obtained from a friend of one of the guys, and watch hookers dance. Afterward, one of them came to our table. We thought we were looking so cool. She was buying drinks like mad . . . which we were paying for. We were hemming and hawing and looking all around. Finally we all said, "Ahhh . . . we were wondering, you know, how much it would cost, you know, for a night for the three of us." I forget what she said. It was a bit too much money. More than we had. So we said, "Nice meeting you." And we were out of there.

We arrived at Bob Jones U—and they had all these rules. You couldn't talk to girls before 9:00 in the morning or after 6:00 in the evening. You could never visit the girls' dorms, which were off limits. You had to wear a tie on certain days. And you couldn't gripe. You could be "shipped" for doing anything wrong.

For about a month I was doing okay, loving it. Then, they had a talent show. Four of us decided to sing, 'cause I sang a lot. The group consisted of people from my church and some people we'd met at BJU. We were going to do a song called "Moonglow." The Four Freshmen made it famous in the 1940s, and we copied their arrangement. We practiced for hours—tight harmonies. We sounded hot. We auditioned, and this teacher came up afterward—this little Hitler (which nearly every BJU teacher was like)—and he said, "You will not be able to sing that for the talent show. You really did a good job. In fact, you won the audition. But you will not be able to sing that song."

And we said, "Why not?"

"It's too night clubbish."

"What?" I said.

"It's too night clubbish—like a song you'd hear in a night club."

I didn't know what he was talking about. I got so infuriated I was hysterical. I called Mom and Dad and said, "Get me out of here!"

And they said, "I'm sure there's a good reason for this. . . ."

I ended up staying.

During the first semester I was dating a girl who was kind of wild, and I went to a basketball game with her. The bleachers were packed.

One of the great things about BJU is that everybody has to be in a society instead of a fraternity, so you had all these intramural games 'cause they won't play with any "pagan" people. So, the game was packed, and I was sitting real close to this girl.

As I was leaving, along with thousands of other people, a teacher came up to me and said, "I saw you during the games sitting next to her and you were touching. Don't ever do that again. And I want you to move right now back to eighteen inches away from her."

Since I was still fuming over the song incident, I turned and looked at him and said, "Hey, you son of a bitch, why don't you go to hell, and you can take your goddamn school and shove it!" As I walked away you could hear a pin drop.

Everybody around me was going, "Mike, shut up, get out of here—go on, get out of here."

So, I put my arm around the girl and walked her all the way back to the dorm. And all the time this teacher is chasing after me, yelling, "You're gonna get in trouble, you're gonna be. . . ."

I was immediately called into the dean's office and permanently "campused." I received 140 demerits, 10 shy of the number necessary for expulsion. I was also forbidden all female contact and competition in intramural sports. In other words, the only thing I was allowed to do was study.

So, I stuck it out till the end of the semester, and at semester break my folks came to visit. By that time, I was getting a little more streetwise. They were having the weekly prayer meeting involving everyone on my floor, so I said to these guys, "My dad is coming to visit the school, I just want all of you to pray for him because I think he's a member of the Mafia. He owns a vacuum cleaner company, but when I'd go in to work last summer, I'd hear him talking about people on the phone and the next day I'd read in the newspaper that they were dead. I just think my dad is involved, and I'd really like you to pray for him."

Well, this spread like wildfire, of course, people saying, "Did you hear about Yaconelli?" My motive was not to get out of school, but just to smoke 'em— although it worked out better than I thought.

My dad had just purchased a lavender Buick convertible, and for this trip he'd bought a neat little hat, and he came on campus, driving that convertible with the top down and smoking a cigar. It was perfect. Everybody in the whole place believed it. So, I told my dad. He laughed. My folks were there about four hours and said, "Pack your stuff, let's get you the hell outta here. This school is weird."

But for some crazy reason I said, "No, I'd like to stick it out." So they left and I stayed.

I'd see if I could stay up past the 11 P.M. curfew by standing on the toilet seat and hoping they didn't check. Then I'd try and sneak out. Or, I'd see the shadow of some upperclassman outside my door, who used to listen for any sound within, and I'd throw a shoe at the door where I was sure his ear was planted. You understand prisons when you're at Bob Jones. You learn exactly what time the gestapos are coming, what they sound like, what their shadows look like, etc.

Everything worked fine until the very end of the year when the girl I'd dated at the basketball game told me she was not coming back to BJU the next year. I decided to meet with her and try to talk her into staying, primarily because I liked her. She was spiritual without being weird.

She agreed to talk with me on a Saturday, and I said, "Well, let's meet in the dating parlor." I'd never been in it because there were a million chaperones in the place and you couldn't do anything. So we walked up the stairs to the dating parlor together. There were three girls sitting on the stairs. We said "Hi," and they said "Hi" back, and we walked in and sat down. I noticed that there was nobody in there. It was empty. But I figured, it's Saturday morning, how many couples are gonna be at the dating parlor?

While we were talking, I heard someone scream, "Get out of here! Get out of here right now!" It was the dean of women. And she was screaming at the top of her lungs.

I said, "What?"

She said, "You know the dating parlor is closed. No one is supposed to be up here until 1:00 in the afternoon. I want you to leave immediately."

I replied, "What are you talking about? We passed three girls on the stairway. They didn't say a word."

"They're the ones who told me! You get outta here!"

So, she made the girl go out on one side, and me go out the other. and I was so mad I was ready to start swearing again. Instead, I decided to whistle. So, I'm whistling all the way out and I went downstairs and into the snack shop, which was underneath the dating parlor. The girl I was with went down the other stairs, after which she, too, walked into the snack shop. Then the dean of women walked into the snack shop, too, saw us together, and said, "Aha! You were going to meet her, weren't you! You were totally disobeying what I said!" She went berserk.

I said, "No, I was not planning to do that."

And she said, "You're lying!"

And I said, "*You're* lying!"

And she said, "Go to the dean of men immediately!"

And the dean of men said, "You are a liar!"

And I answered back, "No, *you're* a liar!"

For the second time, I was permanently campused. I was also not allowed to participate in the college Shakespeare production in which I had obtained a stand-in part. Returning to my room, I was determined to leave BJU, but the dorm resident told me to stick it out 'til the end of the year, which wasn't far off. So I did. *Then* I left. There was a notice put in my file stating that I would never be allowed back.

Next, I went to BIOLA College—the Bible Institute of Los Angeles, California, and was kicked out in six months. I wasn't allowed to wear shorts in the library.

I would say that the major influence that caused me to move out of fundamentalism—besides the Bob Jones experience—was my experience right after that, when I was working for Forest Home Christian Conference Center. I wound up working there for ten summers, beginning with the time I began attending BIOLA. That was the first time in my whole life that I realized there were Congregationalists who were Christians, there were Episcopalians who were Christians, etc. I heard Helmut Thielicke speak. I heard guys from Princeton, and Earl Palmer, and Donn Moomaw. It just blew me away. That was when I realized this Christian world is a whole lot bigger than I thought it was.

After BIOLA I attended Fullerton Junior College, which was nearby, and majored in theater arts. Then I majored in speech at California State Fullerton, and ended up working for Youth for Christ in San Diego.

Along with two other guys, I developed a new program for Youth for Christ, called "Campus Life." We came up with the name, the notebook, the philosophy, the whole deal. I wrote the first director's manual. That was around 1963–64. Campus *Life* is not to be confused with Bill Bright's Campus *Crusade* group—the one with the Christian scorecards that Karla walked out on. Of the three cocreators and founders of the Campus Life program, one of them, Ken Overstreet (who was also a big-time Youth for Christ San Diego area director), died recently of AIDS.

After my stint with Youth for Christ, I kind of floundered around and became sort of antichurch, and Wayne Rice and I started a company in 1968 called Youth Specialties, which was anti-institutional, antiestablishment. We wanted to work with kids and provide materials for people who worked with kids—materials that were not written by a bunch of retired ministers. We also held conventions. At our second National Youth Workers Convention, we had Francis Schaeffer, Hal Lindsey, Jack Sparks from the CWLF. . . . It was the most exciting, unbelievable conference you've ever seen. Hal's book, *The Late Great Planet Earth,* had just come out. I was blown away by Schaeffer and went to L'Abri, Switzerland, where he taught and lived. The three months I spent there proved to be a life-changing experience. I left with some good theological underpinnings. I returned home with a renewed love for the Church, or at least I began to feel like there was hope for the Church. We were publishing the *Wittenburg Door*—which is now just *The Door*—at that time. The magazine was very cynical and satirical, and I thought the Church was doomed, which, frankly, I still believe. But back then, after L'Abri, I thought that maybe there was some hope for the Church.

I ended up speaking at a conference at Mount Herman Christian Conference Center. I addressed five hundred ministers on "Why I Don't Go to Church." I said that there was no hope for the Church if it continued to move in the direction it was going, namely, institutionalized, established, insensitive to the needs of her people, unreal, dishonest, spending money terribly, like, wasting it on huge buildings, etc.

I met some people from Etna, California, at the conference who were running a church, and they said, "You need to see what we're doing, because we're doing the very thing you're talking about. Churches shouldn't own any buildings, ministers should not be paid."

So I visited Etna. The people introduced me to a group of people from a nearby town, Yreka, California. These people met on Sunday afternoons for their church, after going to Sunday morning services at different churches in the area. They had me come speak, and after hearing me they said, "How would you like to be our pastor?"

Well, I hadn't been to seminary. I'd been in Youth for Christ and had studied some stuff, but I certainly wasn't seminary trained. Even so, my wife and I decided to try a seven-hundred-mile move from San Diego to Yreka, California (my wife at the time was not Karla). We had four children and, two months after we put our house up for sale, we discovered that our nineteen-month-old daughter had cancer. I phoned the folks in Yreka and told them we weren't coming, because there were great hospitals where we were and nothing up there.

They said, "That's all right. We'll wait."

They waited two years while my daughter, Lisa, underwent surgery, radiation treatments, and chemotherapy. The doctors thought she had a pretty good chance and there was nothing more they could do, so we moved to Yreka, and I started pastoring Community Bible Church. After four or five years, there were a couple hundred people coming. Then I got a divorce. At that point I resigned from the church. I am still kind of the amazing guilt monster of the universe over my failed marriage. The church didn't want me to resign, but I'm glad I did.

Karla Yaconelli: Do you begin to get the picture of why we were attracted to one another?

Mike Yaconelli: After two years of recovering, of asking myself, "Can I still be a Christian? Can I talk about commitment any more? Do I need to go sell insurance?" Karla and I met and we eventually got married. After we'd been married for a year or so, we started a Young Life club—a nondenominational, Christian-oriented club for high school kids that emphasizes building relationships with kids. After we did that for two or three years, a number of the parents came to us and said, "We don't go to church. We haven't been to church for fifteen or twenty years, but if you guys started a church, we'd go." In the meantime, the church that I was previously the minister of had folded.

Karla's reaction was, "You are out of your mind. I'm *not* going to be a pastor's wife."

Karla Yaconelli: I (still) smoke—it's an addiction I haven't whipped yet. My language can be "earthy" at times. All the pastors' wives I'd seen were mousey, led Bible studies, taught Sunday school, played organ. . . . I was still a dancer. I had my own thing going. Young Life was fine, but there was no way I could see myself fitting the mold of a pastor's wife, and I refused to allow people to put those kinds of expectations on me. Plus, with Young Life, we were dealing with lots of kids who had problems. I wasn't willing to add just as many adults to the "people we *have* to help" list.

Mike Yaconelli: Anyway, we came across Brennan Manning's books and we interviewed him for our magazine. He's a Catholic priest who has written a number of wonderful books, including *Lion and Lamb: The Relentless Tenderness of Jesus* and *The Ragamuffin Gospel.* We read his stuff and, through a number of uncanny events, decided we'd say yes, and start this church, which happens to meet in the same building in which I had previously preached. We invited Brennan to be the first speaker, which he accepted. We sent a letter out to everybody we knew in town who didn't already go to church. We started a church that we loosely described as "a church for people who don't like to go to church." The first meeting we had eighty people show up. After the first year, we dropped down to about twenty-five. It's been six years now, and on a "big" Sunday, we have about a hundred people there [a considerable number, considering Yreka's small population of 6,000 or so.—ED.]. Our church owns no building, has no budget, no committees, I'm not paid, there is no staff. We don't take a formal offering, and we don't even have a membership list. We don't advertize *ever,* anywhere. It's called Grace Community Church, and there's a reason. We wanted to say, "This is a church of grace. We believe in the grace of God, and that's what you'll be hearing a lot about. You're not going to hear a lot about sin, because we figure you already know about that."

It was actually a very liberating experience to be divorced, because in a small town like this—with one traffic light (soon to be two traffic lights), and one high school, and six or seven thousand people—everybody knows everything. So everybody knew about our divorces and remarriage.

Karla Yaconelli: And the rumors were a-flyin', oh Lord, they were a-flyin'.

Mike Yaconelli: So it was great to walk into church and know that everybody knew. Like Will Campbell likes to say, "We're all bastards, but God loves us anyway." They knew that about us. There were no illusions.

Karla Yaconelli: And the "statement" I made in response to becoming a pastor's wife was this: For the first year, after church was over, I would walk immediately out of the building and light up a cigarette. It was like saying, "If there's anybody here who has a real big *doctrinal* kind of problem with this, then you're at the wrong place." After the first year I didn't feel the need to do that anymore. The church has been great. The people have accepted me—flaws and all.

Mike Yaconelli: It *is* a great church. Most of the folk don't have any idea what I do for a living. Most of them have never heard of the *Door.* And that's okay too.

Part Four

Testimonies of Former Fundamentalists Who Are Now Adherents of Non-Christian Spiritualities

The Divine was expansive, but religion was reductive. Religion attempted to reduce the Divine to a knowable quantity with which mortals might efficiently deal, to pigeonhole it once and for all so that we never had to reevaluate it. With hammers of cant and spikes of dogma, we crucified and crucified again, trying to nail to our stationary altars the migratory lights of the world.

—Tom Robbins, *Skinny Legs and All*

Photo by Ava Peterson

William Bagley:
Reflections on a Christian Experience

I found a passage in a Sufi book that stated, "Religion is like a garment. One has to know how it fits before one can take it off." The key was to study fundamentalism very deeply until one knew exactly how it fit in one. When clarity is reached, one does not have to even take it off, it falls off.
—William Bagley

William Bagley is the author of *The Easy, Rapid, and Peaceful Pathway,*[1] and is presently working on volume three of the *ERP Pathway* series. He has been exploring "energy work"—trying to achieve integration of repressed unconscious material within a nontraumatic process. The work combines brain wave research, Jungian psychology, bioenergetic methodology, rebirthing breathing techniques, acupuncture meridian theory, and classical aura balancing. He has been Westfield Chess Club champion, and also attained the highest individual score in the North Jersey Chess League. He has demonstrated his chess ability blindfolded, facing as many as five challengers at once, winning all five games, and then replaying them from memory. He has an undergraduate degree in philosophy and taken additional courses in psychology and computer science. He is also trained in various schools of martial arts. In 1984 he became a licensed massage, colonic technician, and hydrotherapist.

It was during the first year of my college curriculum that I found myself being preached at by fundamentalists. I did not know what to make of all their attempts to persuade me. I recall especially one time a person read the Bible to me and asked me to accept Christ as Savior. It sounded to me like nonsense. But I heard a deep and quiet voice within simply say, "Do it." Hearing the voice was a shock and I knew I was going to surrender to Christ even though my mind rebelled. There was something deeper at work. . . .

A week or so after the event, I read a fundamentalist book that had a prayer of surrender at the back and I prayed it three times. I ran off to a class I was late for and then, all of a sudden, a gentle opening took place. The sunlight doubled in brightness, the grass became luminous green, and the sky had a rich blueness. I felt a quiet but overwhelming joy fill me and any sense of difficulty about life dissolved completely. I felt I touched in the experience the natural state that humans were meant to always live in. An intuitive understanding came from the experience. I saw that no effort was required to be in this state and that humans were doing something to not be there. I felt "surrender" was the key to crossing over into this state.

The intuitive understanding was complete within the experience and still feels valid to me now. But when the event happened, sides of myself were still too philosophically immature to fully integrate the implications of the experience. There are sides of the mind that need some kind of conceptual framework to make sense of our experience. Since I related the experience to "surrender to Christ," I drew from my fundamentalist surroundings the framework for my experience.

I began to study the Bible, pray, fellowship with Christians, believe the dogmas, and follow the Commandments. I was baptized. I also felt many unresolved and contradictory feelings within. The old mind did not vanish, but slowly resurfaced and began to question the newer Christian mind. The old mind was naturally inquisitive and had a desire to understand everything via a process of thoroughgoing questioning. My intense intellectual investigations were not always welcomed by those with whom I fellowshipped. Doubt was considered a sin or a door through which Satan could enter to confuse believers. There were times I felt tormented inside because I did not want to be a heretic. There was a point where I actually prayed to get rid of my doubting mind.

One day, however, I realized that the more I got into fundamentalist/born-again Christianity the more unhappy I became. I had not entered the fold driven by despair. I had been happy with my previous non-Christian life. What I understood was that, for me, Christianity meant only one thing—the joy of "surrender to Christ." That was where I felt I had touched the truth of life. The rest seemed built around the experience, but was not essential to it.

I found too that many Christians had not shared my experience. Christianity meant something different to them. They felt that the experience I had was proof that Christianity was correct and that I had needed such proof. But to me the experience was not proof of Christianity's truthfulness, it was the essence and heart of what Christianity was meant to be. I had touched something that seemed meant to be for all. I could not believe that God would withhold the experience from anyone who was truly open.

I became determined to test every element of Christianity in terms of whether or not it helped me return to the original experience. In adopting such a method of investigation I had planted the "seed of science" within me. The seed took root, becoming stronger, more organized, and clearer over time. It was and still is a more flexible and experience-oriented approach than the rituals of conventional science, but its vital core was that of testing hypotheses against actual experiences.

I decided to begin with a deep study of the words that Jesus was reported to have spoken. I wanted to get as close as possible to the historical person who seemed related to my experience. The connection between the experience I had and the historical Jesus was only in the name of the person I invoked in my surrender. But the link made sense to me. If I called on a friend and he came by, responding to my use of his or her name, then I could imagine an advanced individual soul who worked invisibly doing the same. This gave me a place to start.

I found, while studying the Sermon on the Mount, a feeling akin to the original experience. I understood something about what was possible for humans through feeling the words of Jesus in the sermon. I saw that if everyone lived by its spirit then we would find peace on Earth. The unifying theme was unconditional love and the practical work was letting go of anger, condemnation, jealousy, fear, arrogance, lust, greed, and more subtle negative emotions.

I chose to concentrate on only one commandment, "Judge ye not." I watched my thoughts and words, and would stop any thoughts of condemnation.

The first day went by fairly easily. I caught myself and released the condemnation.

The second day was one of intense struggle. I would find myself condemning, and then condemn myself for condemning, and then condemn myself for condemning my condemnation. I felt as if caught in a revolving door. Condemnations would try to persist by disguising themselves in more acceptable words. They would mimic more impartial tones. But they began to be recognized by a characteristic feeling. What I saw was that all negative emotions have the same flavor and that I could simply step out of them. I found the secret was simply accepting that one is negative and choose to not be.

The third day I accepted and stepped out of each negativity with relative ease. Late in the day, I felt a mass of intense darkness rise from within. It wanted to condemn anyone for anything. There was a senseless irrationality to the mass of energy I felt. I could see it was only looking for an excuse to condemn. I kept stepping out of its energy and at one point it dissolved. A burst of love radiated from my center and touched everyone all around me without exception.

I felt I had arrived back in the Kingdom of God and was at peace. I had found one clear foothold that I could use to return to the original experience. What I learned was that there is a difference between seeing a fault in another and condemning a fault. We need to take into account the faults of others in our dealings with them, but we never need to condemn a fault. When we do not condemn, we are at peace with the world. We can encourage people to improve and change, but without the negative emotional feeling that they should not be who they are. Faults then become like weeds one learns to pull. They are nothing special, just something to work on when possible.

After the breakthrough, I had the raw elements to organize an experience-oriented approach to spirituality. These elements became more clearly defined over time and seemed to purify my Christianity in progressive stages. I still experienced myself as a fundamentalist Christian, but the gap was growing wider as the inner seed began to grow. I started reading books by the Christian mystics [Meister Eckhart, John of the Cross, Teresa of Avila, Jacob Boehme, William Law, Evelyn Underhill, Thomas Merton]. They had an experience-oriented approach that resonated with my own. They seemed to point to the heart of what I felt was important in the teachings of Christ. They talked less of the Trinity, the Atonement, and Hell, and more about loving your neighbor as yourself, creating a heart filled with devotion, communing with the living Presence of God, trusting God to support oneself even economically, learning how to be guided from within, purifying the heart of negative emotions, and learning how to allow divine grace to transform one. The understandings shaped during this period have had a profound and steady influence in my life. They are still with me as a living sense which puts everything into balance.

I began to expand my horizons beyond conventional and mystical Christianity. I studied Zen Buddhism and did *zazen* [sitting meditation]. This seemed a very pure practice uncontaminated by words. The teachings of Zen seemed to embody a deep sanity about life. It did not get dogmatically rigid, but always focused on what one was actually learning from present experience. When confusion would enter my mind, I would ask, "What did I really know from my own experience?" Conditioned thoughts would burn away in the light of this kind of inquiry and gradually a clarity would be generated that would resolve the issue. I had found a tradition that grew faith through intense doubting. This satisfied a deep part of myself. I drank deep from the well of Zen.

I began to meditate daily, making a commitment to meditate at least one hour every day no matter how tired I was. This expanded eventually to about four hours a day. I would also try to meditate during every available spare moment. I would meditate between classes at college or whenever I had a few spare minutes. There were many transformations that occurred inside. Many understandings came from weeding my inner garden of negative emotions. The very challenge of remaining aware in the present generated an intense struggle. It seemed as if I had never been taught to live here and now, but instead, to live in an inner world of nostalgia, regrets, forlorn hopes, and fears that kept me preoccupied with the past and future. This struggle continued until an illuminated thought said, "Let it be aware for you." A sense of grace entered me and I found that my back became erect and I could be naturally aware without strain.

Somewhere in the committedness to meditation I broke through to *satori*. This deep and profound insight-experience touched something very vast and wonderful. I saw that I had not really been free before *satori*. My life had been reactions to reactions of reactions. It was as if we were all billiard balls bouncing off each other in mathematically predictable ways.

Secondly, I saw that I was always free in another sense. I could always simply choose to do whatever I wanted. I could step out of reacting any time I wanted and simply live.

The third thing I understood was that everyone was always free and always doing what they wanted. People had made their minds too complicated to see how they were always doing what they wanted to do, because the mind had divided against itself and pulled oneself in many directions, but each direction represented something each person wanted to do.

When we understand our mind, then we simplify our inner life and just choose to do one thing at a time. We do what we want in a focused way and complete our desires. Some desires vanish because we see we really do not want them anymore. Others naturally fulfill themselves without our doing much. Others become dormant until events allow their fulfillment. Some we explore within the living present.

The intuitive understanding communicated within the *satori* was a whole sense. The three intellectual sides mentioned above emerged from one whole sense about the nature of freedom. *Satori* expanded to touch all the sides of myself. I understood that God simply created the world out of freedom, and for the same reason an artist grows through painting one picture after another. We grow through participation in life and expressing our nature. The sense of freedom communicated in *satori* continued to expand within me and enrich my life. The process is still going on. It is as if I discover freedom in more and more places and more and more ways.

Many other profound experiences were to come, but the *satori* would be the most deeply cherished. It seemed to complete the circle with the "surrender to Christ" experience. I had found my way back and remained. Even though difficulties sometimes come, a permanent intuitive understanding has become strong, can work through whatever arises, and find peace. We need to burn out all our *samskaras*. These are embedded thought impressions that do not resonate with the purpose of life but still have a root in us.

The transition from fundamentalism to nonfundamentalism took place over a long time. One result of the journey was a deeper sense that we are not our minds. When I became a fundamentalist I took on a different mentality. When one has felt two minds within oneself, then the concept that one is neither the new one nor the old can be felt. This was a gift that eventually enriched my meditation, since Zen in particular preaches that we are a no-mind awareness. Our thoughts come and go, but we remain.

The most difficult part of my fundamentalist experience was getting past the feeling of being victimized. It felt as if I had been forced to accept an alien mind and then had to overcome it. When I studied the psychology of mental manipulation I found that conditioning pressures were indeed used by Christian groups and preachers. Although many people study these effects from the outside, to actually feel the mind succumbing to the pressures is a very interesting journey into a kind of madness. One gets split inside and is ambivalent toward the new mind. Part of oneself wants to believe in it and does, while another part wants to let it go but feels it cannot.

When one studies the process of conditioning and its roots, then one finds that conditioning interferes with the study of conditioning. The art of meditation is to help one move past the double bind. The key I found was a passage from a Sufi book that stated, "Religion is like a garment. One has to know how it fits before one can take it off." The key was to study fundamentalism very deeply until one knew exactly how it fit one. When clarity is reached, one does not have to even take it off, it falls off.[2]

People who did not argue, but who were simply honest, proved particularly helpful during my transition. One professor simply said he did not believe Christianity was the only true way. This seemed to strike a chord deep inside, and I saw that it was true. When I read the *Tao Te Ching* there was such a deep sense of its truth that it abolished any last traces of Christian exclusivity.[3]

What I found interesting is that throughout all the transitions I kept redefining Christianity in my mind. The interpretations became wider and more inclusive.

I think one strength of Christianity is its symbolic nature. The symbols allow one to grow and find deeper meanings in biblical stories. The older literal interpretations give way to more archetypal human truths. When these truths are found in other religions we should be able to express joy in their universality rather than feel threatened by a loss of our exclusivity and elitist impulses.

Although I do not feel Christianity has any exclusive claim to the truth, I feel Christianity can make a positive contribution to world religious culture. Not because Christianity can teach anything that is not found in other religious traditions, but because the healthier sides of Christianity have focused on a message of love and made it real in human experience.

I think that much of Christianity has lost this focus and substituted a more literal and dogmatic message in its place. The substituted message lacks the wholesomeness of what I felt Jesus originally taught. The Great Commission was not to preach a gospel based on convincing people to surrender to a few dogmas, but to teach the nations everything that Christ taught his disciples. This means that the gospel includes understanding, faith, trust, hope, and love based on a living experience of Jesus and those inspired by his light.

After having studied what Jesus taught, and practiced contemplative prayer, what I have learned still seems relevant to the modern world. One learns to not get caught in greed, but to feel the prosperity of having enough each day because of divine grace.

We begin to understand that the inner is more important than the outer. When we take care of the inner, then the outer falls into place also. When the outer becomes more important, then we are already lost no matter what is done.

Even though Christ taught these things, not all sides of Christianity or even the New Age have fully integrated the radical simplicity of finding peace in God. To me, prosperity is feeling one has enough, knowing the universe is supportive, and living in peaceful trust of this inner fact.

Yet in spite of these teachings, many people continue to worry and are propelled by greedy ambition. Many have translated this urge into religious terms and are trying to manipulate God into giving them money. The paradox is that what force cannot do, surrender to life can. Pulling a bulb open does not create a flower, but gentle attention and care can. But unlike other kinds of teachings, one cannot grasp this within ready-made slogans and dogmas. One cannot go to a seminar and have it crammed into one. This kind of understanding can only grow within the climate of a life devoted to spirituality. This is a life based on simplicity, trust, compassion, study, fellowship, and prayer. Having ears to hear the teachings means understanding its life and letting it gently take root in one. There is no church one can join to get it.

Margaret Mead once said, "The best thing one can do for oneself is to have a religious experience and then get over it." This seems similar to falling in love the first time and then putting the experience into perspective. Other loves come and each is similar yet different when compared with the first one.

Part of forgiveness seems to be to "overlook" faults. This means to look past the dogmas, arrogance, and ignorance of fundamentalism and to see what is truly worthwhile. Part of the fundamentalist journey was like a nightmare, feeling pressure to conform to what does not feel right, suppressing doubts, and feeling guilty. Other parts seemed more joyful, praising God, feeling the heart open in love, and understanding worthwhile teachings from an advanced soul [Jesus]. I think, like all mixed blessings, we eventually learn to sort out what we feel, forgive the bad parts, and feel gratitude about the good parts.

If a fundamentalist is "born again," then one who leaves fundamentalism and conquers bitterness is "born even again." A circle is completed. One returns to ordinary life and understands the place for the first time.

Notes

1. A few points where *The Easy, Rapid, and Peaceful Pathway* contrasts with fundamentalist religious traditions:

Obeying morality, or feeling guilty, versus honoring personal values and making them consistent.

Effort to believe and obey versus wish to explore and understand.

Motivation by fear of hell versus motivation by love of truth.

Meeting with people of a common creed versus universal kinship with all seekers of truth.

Obeying rules versus applying principles.

Repressive control versus expansive integration.

Focusing on disagreements versus expanding on agreements.

Making dogmatic assertions versus using questions to help a person discover things for themselves.

Helping people to become liberated or saved versus communicating the prior existence of genuine freedom and grace.

Trying to reform the world versus encouraging it to grow further.

Religion as a creed versus religion as restoring inner peace.

2. On his attempt to "try on religion to see how it fit him" Bagley has this to add: "I spent not a few years trying to decide which seminary of which Christian denomination I might attend. I studied koine Greek [the language in which the Christian Scriptures were composed], investigated every major denomination and their theologies, and intensively studied Christian history. I poured through book after book and was devoted to prayer and living according to the best understanding of Christianity I could obtain.

"But the more I studied, the less likely fundamentalism appeared. Contradictions emerged out of the Biblical text. The canonization of the Bible did not appear like an 'inspired' endeavor. (At the Nicene council they said the three synoptic Gospels would balance out the errors in the Gospel of John, and they refused to canonize the Apocalypse of Isaiah, because one apocalypse was enough. At another council they drew swords over their disagreements.) Translations were deliberately altered to enforce theological points (like the Trinitarian passages added to one of the Epistles of John). The history of Christianity is mired in bloodshed (the Romans killed Christians by the thousands, but the Christians killed their opponents—oftentimes, other Christians—in the hundred thousands).

"Or consider the Atonement, the central doctrine of Christianity. It assumes that God 'held a grudge' against Adam and all his offspring and then took it out on the least deserving person.

"Anger therapy teaches people to take out their frustrations on a pillow. But God does not seem able to do this. He must pick something that can feel pain. If Jesus was God it amounts to God taking out His frustration by beating on Himself.

"Further, after heaping on one man all the sins of the world, this God will still throw people in hell if they do not 'believe' properly, 'accepting' what God did to a poor innocent lamb (the 'Lamb of God').

"I feel that a sacrifice is not necessary for an act of forgiveness to occur. 'Forgiveness' is *not* holding the sins of someone against them. The highest compassion is found in the idea that God can forgive *without any shedding of blood.* [See Ps. 32:5 and 51; Mic. 6:6–8; Jon. 3:8–10 and 4:11; and Zech. 1:3 for examples *from the Bible* where God directly forgives the sins of those who repent, i.e., without the need of a blood sacrifice. The most striking example being found in the Our Father, a prayer that Jesus taught, "Father . . . forgive us our trespasses as we forgive those who trespass against us."—ED.]

"Unfortunately, I can recommend no one book containing all the relevant criticisms of fundamentalist Christianity. *The Faith of a Heretic* by Walter Kaufmann is not a bad volume with which to start. Its bibliography refers to other works. *The True Believer* by Eric Hoffer is short and clear, focusing on the psychological traits exhibited by all 'true believers,' whether they be Communists or Christians.

"Even more important than simply reading books is to deepen one's self-knowledge, because if you are conditioned, then that conditioning will determine what you read and see, and even the best material will do no good.

"The reason religious conditioning is so difficult to overcome is because it is invested with so much authority. This authority is rooted in the way some Christian denominations strive to make you distrust yourself. They label people 'sinners' and even 'born in sin.' They try to convince you that you need them in order to be 'saved,' but first they create in you the notion that you are irrevocably 'lost.'

"People feel lost because they do not feel at home in the world, but how can you feel at home when you think the real life is in heaven? I think people feel lost because they have gotten out of touch with life. When awareness breaks through conditioning, the doors of resistance swing open, and life floods in, welcoming you home. That has been my experience."

3. The *Tao Te Ching* is an ancient work of Chinese religion/philosophy antedating Christianity by about five hundred years. Yet it contains teachings similar to Jesus' on non-resistance and doing unto others. It espouses such wisdom as the following: "Because the Tao never claims greatness, its greatness shines brightly. . . . The truly wise live for other people and thereby grow richer. . . . Money or your mind, which is more valuable? . . . Whoever makes a show of himself cannot shine." A few early Jesuit missionaries to China were so startled to discover a pagan book that contained such teachings that they considered having the book added to the Bible!

Ernest Heramia:
The Thorn-Crowned Lord/
The Antler-Crowned Lord

> I began coming into contact with more and more Wiccans (Witches), and
> Neo-Pagans at this time, and began reading books on their beliefs, so I
> could witness to them about Christ. While reading Margot Adler's *Drawing
> Down the Moon,* I ran across a couple lines that would later affect my
> overall view of God and religion. They went something like, "Monotheism
> is theological imperialism" and "Faith is the smoke of failed magic."
>
> —Ernest Heramia

Ernest Heramia is a graduate of a well-known New England Bible institute. He
has traveled as an evangelist throughout Hawaii in association with the Filipino
Assemblies of the First Born. He was a founding member of Christian Science
Fiction (and Fantasy) Fandom and editor of its newsletter, *Radio Free Thulcandra.*
He has worked with various evangelical ministries in concert with the Assemblies
of God, the PTL Club, and the 700 Club. He is presently working as a freelance
writer, and is forming an Urdic Wiccan coven devoted to letting The Weirdness in.

When I was six years old, my mother told me the story of Jesus and how
He had died for me. Being a city kid, I didn't know what a "crown of
thorns" was, and so when she came to that part of the story, I asked her. She
explained that it was like a hat made of pins that they pressed down on His
head to hurt Him. That stuck in my mind (pardon the pun).

When my mother asked if I would like to invite Jesus into my heart, I said,
"Sure." If Jesus had taken all that cruel treatment in my place, the least I could
do was give Him a place to stay in my heart.

We attended the Church of God. The services didn't impress me. No wonder.
They focused on adult matters. Father God was an adult. I politely endured
it all in hope of learning more about Jesus, His son.

I had heard the church referred to as "the House of God," and took it literally.
After the services, while everyone was downstairs getting refreshments, I would
go back up to the sanctuary to see if I could meet God in person. I knew He

could make Himself invisible, so I was not terribly disappointed when I did not actually see Him.

As I sat there in the quiet empty church, with sunbeams shining through the stained glass windows and a soft breeze carrying the scent of flowers, pine trees, and fresh-cut grass, I came to feel His presence. I did not need to see Him, I just knew He was there.

I figured He must like music a lot, because He had a big pipe organ in the corner of His house, instead of a TV. I wondered why they didn't let Him play the organ for services, wasn't He good enough? You would think God would be a great organist.

It was the quiet times with God that were the most meaningful to me. As I grew older, became a youth leader in my church, a Bible student, and then an evangelist, I became interested in ethics and theology. But it was always the quiet times with God, the mystical experiences, rather than the theological, that formed the cornerstone of my faith.

In time, my experiences came into conflict with my theology, and so I began to amend my theology. The doctrine of scriptural inerrancy was the first to go.

The Holy Bible speaks of the heroes of the faith as being men of like passions as we. If this is the case, then those who wrote the Bible must have been just as vulnerable to personal bias and self-deception as we. This would certainly explain the presence of so much "divinely sanctioned" genocide, racism, and sexism in the Bible. The Jesus I had come to know and love wasn't a racist, a sexist, or a killer of children.

The more I studied the Bible, the more I found that pointed away from it being unique and inerrant. (For instance, I discovered that the book of Esther had been based on the Babylonian myth of Ishtar and Marduk.)

With the loss of the Holy Bible as an inerrant theological yardstick, I found myself totally dependent on my own experiences of God for the basis of my religion.

Being raised in Pentecostal Holiness, the majority of my most intimate, meaningful, and transforming experiences of the Divine have been via the Holy Spirit, and so I trod in that spiritual direction.

The more time I spent with the Holy Spirit in devotional prayer, the more I became aware of a divine femininity. Theoretically I had always thought of God as being both masculine and feminine in nature, but now I encountered an overwhelmingly real impression of a female deity, as real and undeniable as any of my previous spiritual encounters, i.e., with Jesus or God the Father.

This scared me at first, as thoughts of self-delusion or satanic deception danced through my mind. But there was always this still, small voice (a girl's voice!) saying, "You know better than that."

The more I thought of it, the more sense it made. The various manifestations of the Holy Spirit (a dove, tongues of fire, etc.), and the nurturing work of the Holy Spirit are feminine. Pentecostals never actually refer to the Holy Spirit as a "She," but more often than not, they relate to the Holy Spirit as a feminine entity. We would speak of the Holy Spirit in much the same manner as Roman Catholics speak of the Virgin Mary.

Looking back on my spiritual life, I found far more women being an influence on me than men.

When I was in high school, one of the teachers pulled the "She is Black" routine on the class. Since a black woman preacher was the most godly person I had ever known, the idea of a black female "God" didn't come as that much of a shock to me.

One day I ran across several interesting Hebrew words, *Hokmah, Shekinah,* and *Ruach Hakodesh,* feminine names for Divine Wisdom, Divine Presence, and the Holy Spirit. So I wasn't the only one who has ever been impressed by the femininity of God.

This change in turn caused me to rethink my dualistic view of the world. If "The Female" was a coequal part of the Godhead, what else might not be a part of God? About this time I began to seriously look into the Taoistic, Animistic, and Holokai heresies I'd been carrying around in the back of my mind.

I began coming into contact with more and more Wiccans (Witches), and neo-pagans at this time, and began reading books on their beliefs, so I could witness to them about Christ. While reading Margot Adler's *Drawing Down the Moon,* I ran across a couple lines that would later affect my overall view of God and religion. They went something like, "Monotheism is theological imperialism" and "Faith is the smoke of failed magic."

About this time, too, things in my home church and alma mater began getting ugly, destroying what little confidence I had in organized religion and the clergy.

For twenty-seven years our pastor had served the church and its affiliated Bible institute. From the fifties to the early eighties, he had faithfully served the church and the school, and continued its founder's vision of providing a first-class ministerial education to those who couldn't afford seminary training. The sons and daughters of working-class families, bush missionaries, and the people of the Third World passed through the school, and returned to their communities to be of service.

As a child, our pastor had been hunchbacked and crippled. The church people kept praying for his healing, and as he grew, he was healed. He became a man of considerable intellect, acquiring degrees from various colleges and universities.

While at Harvard, a friend told him that he could go far if he stopped hanging out with "that Pentecostal crowd." He replied, "When I was a hunchbacked child 'that Pentecostal crowd' prayed for me. I'm going to stay with them until the day I die." Unfortunately, some people would not allow him to follow through with his wish.

With the eighties came bouts with diabetes. Our pastor began entering the hospital for longer and longer periods of time. And with each homecoming, less of him returned. First a toe was taken by diabetes, then a foot, then a leg, and then his strength. The rich, booming baritone of his voice became a faint, fragile whisper. The Thunder of Summer was gone, replaced by the Autumn sound of falling leaves.

While he was in the hospital, we prayed for him. At first the prayers were passionate. Some people set aside days for fasting and prayer, fervently believing he would be healed, just as two other church people had been healed of cancer.

But as the months became years, the passion faded. We kept praying for him, but as time went by, his name went from the top of the prayer list to the bottom, until he was remembered in prayer with the same mediocre feeling with which we prayed for "the peace of Israel."

The various department heads, teachers, and deacons filled in for him at the services. More and more often, Brother A. was preaching the Sunday sermons rather than our pastor.

Brother A. had been a missionary in Africa, a "Johannesburg missionary." Later he returned to America, became an evangelist, and would travel around regaling people with tales of his adventures in the bush and songs sung in Swahili. His main claim to fame, though, was all the novel ways he had of taking up offerings. Rumors started going around the church that the big contributors and the people on the board of directors were thinking of putting our pastor out and installing Brother A. in his place.

By this time everybody in the church knew that, barring a miracle of healing, our pastor was going to die. Most of us felt that he should be allowed to continue as the pastor, and his successor as "assistant pastor," until God Himself removed him from the pastorate. To forcibly remove the man from his office after a quarter century of service, when he was dying, seemed cold-hearted and barbaric. We did not throw our old and sick on the scrap heap. We cared for them until God called them home, or so I had been taught as a student.

I expressed my concern to Brother A. about these rumors. He assured me that they were just rumors, and that he would never do such a thing to his old friend.

The rumors continued to fly. The annual church business meeting was coming up. If the board was going to kick our pastor out, it would be legitimized by a vote at the business meeting. The deacons rallied the church people to oppose the board if they attempted to do such a thing.

That Sunday morning Brother A. announced that the annual business meeting had been rescheduled to take place in the middle of winter. That pretty much confirmed everyone's fears. The board was definitely planning something underhanded.

One Sunday morning, Sister B., wife of Brother B., came padding up to me, took my arm, and lead me with grandmotherly grace to a quiet corner of the church.

"Ernie dear, I know you care about me and Billy, and wouldn't do anything to hurt us, so could you please just not get involved in the matter about the pastor. There are things you don't know."

"Oh!" I said, trying to hide my amusement at this attempt at emotional manipulation. "What kind of things?"

"Well dear, I really didn't want to disillusion you, but you see . . . ah . . . the pastor and Maria have been doing improper things."

At first, the sheer absurdity of the picture she was trying to paint amused me. The pastor didn't even have the strength to raise his voice above a whisper, never mind an anatomical structure vital to "doing improper things." However, as the particulars grew from the abstracts, I realized that this sweet old lady was trying to carry out a very nasty bit of character assassination.

Church politics being what they are, I could understand her taking a cheap shot at a preacher she wanted to get rid of, but such a stupid and vicious shot! It was bad enough that she was saying such things about the pastor, but to slander Maria showed that she and the people on the board did not care whom they had to destroy to get their way.

Maria was a quiet, sweet-spirited young woman who never had an unkind word for anybody.

"Oh dear!" I said, "We can't have that, can we?"

I patted her hand and excused myself. She was just an obedient minister's wife doing her husband's dirty work. There was no point in arguing with her. As I walked away, a sadness settled around me—I did care about her.

Maybe when the board rescheduled the church business meeting for winter, they were hoping that people wouldn't bother leaving their nice warm homes to attend a "dull old" church business meeting. They were wrong. A lot of people loved the pastor, and were not about to let him get put out like so much garbage.

The meeting began with the same old dull business that usually constitutes a church business meeting. Stuff like Sister C. reading a report on how many children attended Sunday School that year, how much money was raised by this and that project, how much money was spent on this and that project, how many children attended that year's Daily Vacation Bible School, that Pastor had offered his resignation, how much money was spent on the Sunday school picnic and how many children attended it . . . stuff like that.

Having already sat through the minutes of the last business meeting, a church treasurer's report, and a youth group report, we seconded and accepted Sister C.'s report, eager to get to the new business of whether our pastor would remain in office.

Brother D. was chairman for the meeting, and asked if there was any new business to be considered. Brother E. stood and made a motion that Brother A. be made pastor.

A number of people stood and spoke against the motion, reminding the church that our pastor had literally given his life to the service of the church and the school, and should not be dishonored by being removed from the pastorate. Rather, Brother A. should be made assistant pastor, and carry out the pastor's duties until God either returned our pastor to the pulpit or "took him home."

One young man stood up and as he began to defend our pastor, Sister F. started speaking in tongues, walked up to the young man, and tried to force him to take his seat. Being a small woman, and not really in the Spirit, Sister F.'s efforts were in vain. The young man simply stood there and prayed while she tried to force him back to his seat. Eventually she tired and returned to her seat, and the young man went on with his defense of the pastor.

Later that evening, this same young man was replying to something that had been said, again, in defense of our pastor, and Sister D. started speaking in tongues, and ran up to him yelling, "You are rebellious, you are a rebel, repent and stop your rebellion against God."

This "prophecy" struck people as rather odd, since this young man was known for his quiet compliant nature, having never once gotten in trouble during his years as a student. This was perhaps the first time in his life that he had refused to submit to authority. It troubled him. Human decency told him he should defend the pastor. He had prayed much about the matter, and felt assured in the rightness of his actions in opposing the board. Being denounced by two of the church's prophetesses, though, caused him some doubt.

The young man closed his eyes while Sister D. was "prophesying," and prayed, "God, what's going on here? Am I being rebellious? If I am in your will, let her be quiet."

He raised his hand, and Sister D. stopped speaking in midsentence. She just stood there shaking and unable to speak.

"She will remain paralyzed and unable to speak until you put your hand down," God said to him.

He finished what he was saying, put his hand down, and Sister D., quite crestfallen, slunk back to her seat.

There were no further prophetic utterances that night. I wondered why the prophets who were on our pastor's side had not prophesied. Then it was pointed out to me that the board had ignored Sister D.'s having been paralyzed and struck mute by God. If they could ignore that, they were not about to listen to an opposing prophesy. The board was going to do what they wanted to do, regardless of what God and the church wanted, and God was going to let them do it, in accord with Psalm 106:13–15.

The debate on whether or not Brother A. would replace our present pastor continued for several hours.

About midnight a motion was made that the matter be tabled, since the church was clearly divided on the issue and to force a vote now would damage the harmony of the church.

Brother D. said that a motion was already being considered and had to be resolved before a new one could be considered, and so called for a vote.

Somebody rose to a point of order, and said that the motion being considered had been improperly made. First we should formally remove the pastor from the pastorate, and then elect Brother A. to take his place. Brother E. stood at this point and said we had already.

"What?!" said the church people. "This is the first new business we've had all night."

"We have already accepted Pastor's resignation," said Brother E.

"What?! We did no such thing," said the church people.

Brother E. then called for a portion of Sister C.'s report to be reread. Sure enough, we had accepted our pastor's resignation. I couldn't help but admire the Machiavellian beauty of that move.

Later I congratulated Brother C. on the cleverness of having his wife hide mention of Pastor's resignation in a Children's Ministries report. Being a modest man, he said he did not know what in the world I was talking about.

The board had accomplished what they wanted, so there was no point in fighting anymore that night. A vote was taken, and the motion was passed. This surprised us too. Looking around the church we noticed that a lot of "part-time church people" and people from a big evangelical denomination had come to the business meeting to vote in support of Brother A. The board had covered every angle.

Some of us thought about challenging the right of these people to vote, but dismissed the idea as futile given the lengths that the board had so far gone to.

When we went to visit Pastor, we asked him if he had submitted his resignation. He said, "No." Later the relative of a board member said that Brother B. had forged Pastor's signature on the resignation papers.

Some of us kept up the opposition to the board's actions, but one by one the board found ways to keep people quiet. Students could be expelled, young preachers and would-be missionaries could be given bad references, people who worked for the school could be fired, retired teachers and staff could be turned out on the streets or have their pensions taken away.

Being a "street preacher" I thought I was beyond the board's reach. Surprise! The jewelry shop my sister and brother-in-law worked for was owned by a board member. It's nice to know the price of your silence.

The deacons were able to do some back-room negotiating with the board, and in return for their cooperation, and that of the church people, our pastor would get his pension and be "pastor emeritus." It was about what we had wanted in the first place. Why the board went through all their intrigues, I can only attribute to vindictiveness. Maybe some of them wanted to get back at our pastor for having been chosen by our founder to head the ministry. Maybe Brother A., a white South African missionary, wanted to put the black preacher in his place and get some revenge for his supporting indigenous ministries over the white missionary machine. I like to think that some of them, like Judas Iscariot, sincerely thought they were doing some good by forcing matters.

Our pastor was not allowed to retire to one of the campus houses, as was the usual practice with us. Diabetes, gossip about him and Maria, and loss of the prestigious pastorate had ended his marriage. (Being the wife of a powerful and influential man was very important to his wife.) So he no longer had a family. A lot of people were afraid to associate with him, lest they get on the bad side of the new administration.

Ultimately, it was Maria and her family that took our pastor in to live with them. Brother A.'s administration had branded her a whore, there was not much more they could do to her.

The pastor lived for about two years as "pastor emeritus." He had a big funeral at the church with thousands of people in attendance, saying many wonderful things about him. I could not help wondering where all these people were when he was alive and needed them.

I had intended to keep attending church there, but it was like a woman trying to have a normal friendly relationship with the people who had gang-raped her. I tried attending a couple of other churches, but I did not feel at home in them.

Then came the televangelist scandals, and similar incidents at other churches, and I started to wonder what was going on.

A Wiccan friend I had met while out street-preaching introduced me to Starhawk's book *Truth or Dare,* and I found out what was going on. "Satanic assault"?

No, it was just human greed, ambition, vindictiveness, status-seeking, self-deception, and the like. It was the clergy, not Satan, that was destroying the churches.

For a while I thought I could start a Christian church, using some of Starhawk's ideas about immanence and cooperative government. The more I worked at it though, the more I found tyranny woven throughout the warp and woof of Christianity. It was not just a matter of corrupt clergymen, or an administrative structure that encouraged the rise of corrupt clergymen; it was Christian theology itself. It was just like somebody sat down and purposely designed a religion to enslave people to the clergy and the building of a religious empire.

I mentioned this to a former rabbinical student, and he said something to the effect of, "Sure, the Old Testament was put together by Jewish clergymen in Babylon to discredit the clergymen back in Israel. Reread the Old Testament, it's all one big power fight between the Levitical priests and the priests who didn't belong to the tribe of Levi. 'Baal' means 'Lord,' just like 'Adonai.' The Baal worshippers were actually a Hebrew sect rivaling the Adonai worshippers."

I did not want to think about the implications of all of this. I loved Jesus. He had been there for me, through all the crises of my life. He was not just my god, He was my best friend. Also I had trained all my life to be a Christian minister. To serve God and share His love was my reason for being. I didn't want to think about the implications, so I didn't. Then, one day, something weird happened.

I was sitting with some friends, talking about the British pop singer Kate Bush, when one of my friends quoted the line, "We let the weirdness in," from the song, "Leave It Open." This phrase struck me as being very profound, but I didn't know why. So I looked up the origin and development of the word "weird," and discovered that it came from the Germanic word *Urd.* Urd was the elder Norn in Norse mythology. It was Urd's job to water the world tree, *Yggdrasil,* and to cut the life threads of all beings, even the gods. This discovery radically changed my world view and my life.

According to the Yggdrasil myth, the material universe is a great tree, and the immaterial universe is a great well. The tree needs the water in the well, but can not get it itself. The tree needs Urd, the goddess of fate, to water it. The well in turn needs Urd to move its waters in cycle, to keep it from stagnating.

It then dawned on me that everything is an ever-changing whole. We tend to think of the universe as being made up of isolated "things," but the "things" are not really isolated. This sentence is part of this page. This page is part of this book. This book is a part of the material universe. The material universe is a part of the ever-changing whole that I call "The Weirdness."

Why "The Weirdness?" Because it *is* weird, and no matter how familiar we become with it, there is always going to be something that scares and disturbs us about the universe and the force that moves it.

The Weirdness is very big and complicated. So big and complicated that we can not grasp it all, so we grasp small parts, or *seemingly* isolated areas of it. We name these areas for mental ease of handling, thus making them appear "familiar" via an easily repeated name. Concentrating only on a few "familiar" and fairly well-understood areas, we feel safe and comfortable with the little we know.

But this creates problems. We do not realize that we have deluded ourselves into thinking that the areas familiar to us alone are equivalent to the whole. Based on that delusion we set up our areas as ideals ("good," "truth," etc.), and try to force all other areas to conform to ours, or be branded as "imperfect," "evil," or "false."

What does it mean to "let The Weirdness in?" Well picture your life, your mind, your heart, etc., as a house with a stout front door. As an infant, everything is weird, and your "house" is empty. As you grow older, you begin bringing things into your "house" and making them yours. The things that you like you call "good," while the things you dislike you call "bad." We try to shut out of our "house" the "bad" things, the weird things, The Weirdness.

But that "stout front door" is also an area of The Weirdness, and sometimes "bad" things can get through. The division between "good things" and "bad things" is a delusion. By "letting The Weirdness in" we throw open that "stout front door" and welcome into our "house" all that The Weirdness is. We welcome as honored guests our greatest fears, as well as our greatest hopes.

We fear want, because want brings illness. We fear illness, because illness brings death. We fear death, because it brings the unknown, The Weirdness. By "letting The Weirdness in" we befriend all that humankind fears. By befriending them, we become at peace with them. By being at peace with them, we nullify their power over us. Like Lao Tzu, when Life is sweet, we can smack our lips and say, "This is delicious wine!" and when Life is bitter, we smack our lips and say, "This is delicious vinegar!"

What had happened at my church and alma mater was just an area of The Weirdness. Those Machiavellian brothers and sisters were only following their nature. We who had defended the pastor were following our nature. The pastor was following his nature, and the pastor's diabetes was following its nature. The televangelists were following their nature. Christian theology was following its nature. It was all The Weirdness to be let in.

Having found The Weirdness in Norse mythology, I began reading more books on mythology, and keeping closer company with my neo-pagan friends. I was surprised to find so many similarities between the various Bible stories and the myths of other cultures. One that especially caught my attention was the similarity between the Gospels and stories of dying gods/sacred kings, (Osiris, Dionysus, Mithras, Cernonnos, Krishna, etc.). The teachings and actions of the Jesus I loved had been preceded by the teachings and actions of others who lived long before the events depicted in the Gospels.

Things started to come together: my belief in divine femininity, Animism, Taoism, and The Weirdness; my distrust of clergy, organized religion, and authoritarianism in general.

My Christian friends became scarce. And I noticed that most of the people whom I now began to recognize were my "true friends" were not Christians. When my mother had a heart attack, it was my Wiccan friends who came by to comfort me.

One autumn night, I looked up at the moon, thought of Hecate, and felt comfort. It then occurred to me that many things had changed. I had changed. The Holy Ghost had become the Triple Goddess, my Lord's crown of thorns had become Cernonnos's antler crown, and I had become a Witch.

Part Five

Testimonies of
Former Fundamentalists
Who Are Now Agnostics

Agnostics know accepted "facts"
have often been disproved.
So they will not conclude before
the doubts have been removed.
—Lewis Price, "Those Pesky Agnostics"
(from *Pensive Poems,* issue no. 1)

It is often difficult to hear in church because the agnostics are so terrible.
—An answer given by a child in a confirmation class at
All Saints Episcopal Church in Birmingham, Alabama

Edward T. Babinski:
If It Wasn't for Agnosticism,
I Wouldn't Know *What* to Believe!

The arguments that I had used to defend the truth of Christianity were peeled away from me like the many layers of an onion's skin. I put up all the intellectual resistance I could, and winced at each layer's removal. I suffered through dark nights of the soul pondering whether my beliefs might not be too narrow or even wholly false. Imperceptibly, my fears, doubts, and grief blossomed into relief, relaxation, and joy.

—Edward T. Babinski

Edward T. Babinski has produced two manuscripts dealing with the question of what the Bible says about creation, *Does the Bible Teach "Scientific Creationism?"* and *The Creationist Quote Book.* His article, "Varieties of Scientific Creationism," appeared in the journal *Faith and Thought.* From 1985 to 1988 Babinski dialogued with creationists in his self-published periodical, *Theistic Evolutionists' Forum.* Ivan Stang's *High Weirdness by Mail* (New York: Simon and Schuster, 1988) contains the following review of *TEF*: "Once a Young-Earth Creationist, the editor now prints this big amateur magazine in which Evolutionist cranks and Creationist troglodytes can rant and rend and tear at each other. Compares Flat-Earth, Geocentric, Heliocentic, Young-Earth, and Old-Earth Creationist views, proving why the Bible will never allow them to agree with each other. Oozes with personality. . . . Also publishes *Monkey's Uncle,* a *satire* of both atheism and fundamentalist foolishness . . . the price is worth it for its potential weaponry value in psychological warfare."

I recall strolling down a shaded path when I was perhaps ten years old, improvising a tune that revolved around my love of God. I was a happy once-born Christian, a Roman Catholic. However, I was not entirely satisfied with that arrangement. I nearly fainted during mass a number of times when I was young and the church was so crowded that my mother and I had to stand along the walls. During my early childhood the Mass was a bit longer than it is today and the priests recited it in Latin (and later, in English). Although I was raised a pious child and recall viewing my faith as both mysterious and intriguing, I eventually grew bored with its repetitiveness in both prayers and rituals.

At my confirmation the bishop was not familiar with the obscure French saint whose name I had picked out of a comprehensive book of saints, namely, St. Roch (pronounced, "Rock"), the "patron saint of pestilence and skin diseases." In front of the congregation he solemnly dubbed me, "Roach." My mother placed no pressure on me to continue attending church after I was confirmed so I ceased attending church at that time.

As a freshman/sophomore in high school I subscribed to a psychic book club and read some books by Edgar Cayce and Ruth Montgomery, the lady who was famed for her "automatic writing" messages from the spirit world. I tried to receive messages from the spirit world, sitting for a time at a desk with a blank mind, just scribbling away with a pen. I never received any messages. I also read Plato's dialogues concerning the trial and death of Socrates, which impressed me immensely.

While I was a sophomore in high school, my best friend, Art McEvoy, encountered an alluring charismatic Christian girl. His attraction to her overflowed into a love for what she loved, for he became "born again" soon afterwards, but didn't quite know how to tell me about it. He had also become, as I was to find out later, very concerned over the state of my soul since I had told him about the psychic book club I'd joined. So he invited me one night to a meeting at a house where he and some others had gathered to pray. Once I arrived no one paid much attention to me. I sat in the kitchen a while and remember picking small cards with Bible verses written on them out of a little plastic loaf-shaped container that was labeled on the side "The Bread of Life." Then, when the meeting was about to begin, Art ushered me out of the house. This was all apparently planned. The group inside was going to pray, including prayers for my salvation, while Art was supposed to ask me politely to recite the "sinner's prayer" and invite Jesus into my heart to become my Lord and Savior. We walked to a deli on the corner, I ordered a sandwich, and on the way back, we sat on the curb that was lit by a streetlamp. He asked me to pray with him, repeating what he said with meaning. So I prayed the sinner's prayer for salvation *with heartfelt meaning* (at that time I had no qualms about believing what I had been taught by the Catholic church, and there was nothing particularly "un-Catholic" about my friend's prayer). Afterwards my friend's previously cautious manner shifted to relief and happiness, as if a weight had been lifted off of *his* back. I felt that nothing special had occurred. Ah, but more persuasive influences were soon to follow. . . .

Immediately after this experience my high school history teacher, having apparently heard from Art that I had been "born again," gave me a copy of a Modern English New Testament to read, *The Greatest Is Love,* challenging me to finish reading it before he did. I loved reading the Gospels more than the letters to the churches, and I cried upon arriving at the end of each, at which point Jesus was scourged and crucified, then resurrected. Such behavior was not unusual for me. I was very taken with Plato's dialogues, as I'd mentioned, above, in which Socrates died at the end. But, having been raised on the story of Jesus all my life, and now reading it for the first time in the oldest extant church documents, it touched something deep inside me. That same point was also touched, later, as I read the fictional novel *The Robe,* and by C. S. Lewis's story of Aslan's death and resurrection in *The Lion, the Witch and the Wardrobe.* It was even touched by certain movies, such as *E.T.* or *Short Circuit,* where the beloved main character is believed to have died, yet survives. In a more general sense, I've always been a big fan, like most people, of tales where the hero must "beat the odds." It may require a genuine (or merely apparent) "miracle" for them to succeed, but succeed they do!

After I had finished reading the Modern English New Testament, Art gave me an entire Modern English Bible to read, which I proceeded to gobble up, cover to cover. I loved it. But boy was the book of Numbers boring! And all those laws in the Old Testament. And as for all the curses and stuff in the prophets, I couldn't understand what all the ranting and raving was about. They didn't appear to be thinking very clearly, if they were thinking at all, and not merely reacting against this and that injustice perpetrated upon their nation by larger nations and armies. But I plowed on, always keeping my eyes focused on anything in the Old Testament that resembled the New, my first love.

For a while Art and I began attending Catholic mass (something I would not have imagined I'd ever do again) on Sundays, and even during the week! We actually enjoyed it, played the part of altar assistants once, and got more out of mass, having read the Bible for ourselves by now, and having personally committed our lives to serving Jesus. Not long afterwards we switched from attending Catholic mass to strictly Protestant services in order to learn more about the Bible via those long sermons that Protestant ministers deliver, filled with Bible quotations we could reread for ourselves as we sat in a pew and absorbed everything like the little Christian sponges we had become.

My history teacher was apparently the only evangelical teacher in my public high school, and quite unashamed of the fact. Besides the New Testament, he plied me with gruesomely illustrated miniature Christian comic books published by the Chick tract organization, with titles such as *This Was Your Life, A Demon's Nightmare,* and *The Gay Blade.* I also read various books he would give me from time to time, such as Richard Wurmbrand's *Tortured for Christ* and Brother Andrew's *God's Smuggler.* They were about people in communist countries who were tortured for boldly expressing their beliefs, and/or for smuggling Bibles into their countries. I ate them up wholeheartedly, and one night I even recall getting into a tizzy with my mother after declaring that I too would like to try and smuggle Bibles into Communist countries. She called my dad and asked him to try and talk some sense into me. I recall that I cried over the fact that my parents were pressuring me to avoid what was perhaps my "calling" in life. After all, were they not good Catholics? Did they not believe the promises in the Gospels? Was not serving God the most important part of being a Christian, even if it meant risking pain and death to "spread the good news"?

As my knowledge of Christian doctrine grew, so did my fears that many of my friends and relatives were headed for eternal destruction, not to mention just about everyone I saw in person, on television, heard speaking on the radio, or read about. I prayed for the salvation of specific people and for hordes of humanity, like all the atheists in Communist China, not to mention all the dozens of toll booth operators I asked God to "save." It was very difficult at that time to *refrain* from handing a toll booth operator a tract (with the money inside, of course), since their outstretched hand was just waiting to be filled).

Only I had the antidote, the magic potion, the truth that would set people *free,* even if I had to *corner them* to administer it. For instance, I handed out tracts at my mother's second wedding. I didn't think that the minister of the Reformed Church in which they were being married was saved, or that anyone in my family was. She married a very nice gentleman (who liked singing hymns in church, but not hearing preachers broadcast exclusivistic teachings—he was a former Alcoholics Anonymous member who believed in "God" in a very broad sense) with whom she was to share a very loving relationship for eighteen years before he passed away. His tolerance toward me and my views eventually proved an inspiration to me.

As a fundamentalist Christian I was corrupted by having what I thought was the "absolute knowledge of life and death," like Dr. Frankenstein. And just like him I suffered much at the hands of my own creation, though in my case what I suffered most was continual anguish over the fate of "the unsaved world."

I soon learned things that added to my inner apprehension and increased my sense of evangelical urgency. After reading Hal Lindsey's phenomenal bestseller (over eighteen million copies sold by 1984), *The Late Great Planet Earth,* I began seeing the pieces of biblical prophecy fitting into Lindsey's picture puzzle. I heard God's time bomb ticking in my ears. And I kept an eye on the sky, for I sensed my salvation "draweth nigh."

I attended end-time evangelistic crusades that featured Jack Van Impe (author of *Revelation Revealed*) and David Wilkerson (author of *The Vision*). They focused on the evil days ahead and scared the be-Jesus *into* you.

At one prophecy conference I was given a piece of "lignin" (compressed wood) that one preacher said "could replace metal in the fashioning of weapons of war. Rifles, cannons, and tanks could be made out of it."

It felt hard, yet light. I did not question at the time whether it might *not* be as strong as metal, or how wood (even tightly compressed) could avoid being scorched or shattered by the force of gunpowder explosions. I simply took the preacher at his word. Why? Because the preacher swore that the existence of "lignin" demonstrated the "truth" of Ezekiel's prophecy: "Israel shall go forth [following a ferocious *end-time* battle], and shall set on fire and burn the weapons [of her enemies] both the shields and the bucklers, the bows and the arrows, and the handstaves, and the spears, and they shall burn them with fire *seven years*: So that they shall take no wood out of the field, neither cut down any out of the forests; for they shall burn the weapons with fire" [Ezek. 39:9–10, KJV].

The preacher continued, "Could iron and steel burn for seven years? No. But weapons made of lignin could burn for seven years, if there were enough of them!" I took the piece of lignin with me to high school and told others of the prophecy and its "miraculous fulfillment."[1]

But I couldn't keep my engine idling at such an "end-times" peak indefinitely. I eventually stopped thriving on mental pictures of raptures, A-bombs, anti-christs, God turning seas to blood, and final judgments. I stopped trying to match up the latest news from the Middle East with verses from the Bible.

After a few years I realized that the further my fellow fundamentalists and I ventured into such head trips, the further we withdrew from the person we were expecting to see. His arrival became another date on the calendar and not a date with a heavenly bridegroom.

I read an interview with the Anglican theologian Robert F. Capon in which he stated, "Predicting dates is only important when the immediacy of a present relationship is lost. When people start haggling about whether Jesus meant ten minutes or fifteen, they have lost the connection with the person they are expecting."[2] I agreed.

While in high school the books my teacher kept plying me with included Henry Morris's *The Twilight of Evolution* and *Many Infallible Proofs,* which advocated young-earth creationism. Since I had not read very widely at that time, I took everything that Morris said as "gospel truth." The fact that he cited Scripture to prove his points only made his views seem more attractive to me. My wish became to study biology at Christian Heritage College, which was closely affiliated with Henry Morris's Institute for Creation Research. I wanted to become a "creation scientist," spreading the good news of "creation evangelism" across the land, defeating evolutionists in public debates, like Duane T. Gish was apparently doing, according to the literature I was then reading. I phoned Henry Morris about attending Christian Heritage College, but he suggested that it would be better if I studied biology at a secular university so that my criticisms of evolution would come from within the scientific establishment instead of from without.

Five months after graduating from high school I was baptized as an adult believer in Christ at Jacksonville Chapel, Lincoln Park, New Jersey, November 24, 1974, by Pastor Earl V. Comfort, a man with a magnetic personality who used an overhead projector to illuminate his sermon points—in-depth analyses of the books of the Bible, mostly Romans, which included comparing and contrasting the views of the apostle Paul and Sigmund Freud! During the years I attended that church it grew considerably, including a brand new building, a brass ensemble, a gym, etc. It was in the vestibule there that I bought my first books of Christian theology, Paul Little's *Know Why You Believe,* John Stott's *Basic Christianity,* Francis Schaeffer's *Escape from Reason,* and C. S. Lewis's *Mere Christianity.*

I majored in biology at Mercer County Community College in Trenton, New Jersey, arguing all the while with my professors. I attended a creationist convention in Philadelphia. I obtained copies of slides that Duane T. Gish used in his debates with evolutionists, and on two occasions I used them to present the "case for creation"—once, during a college science seminar, and another time before a group of Ph.D. chemists at Hoffman-La Roche, where I worked as a lab assistant. My presentation only converted one lab technician. The Ph.D.s remained unimpressed.

While at Mercer County I joined the most "on-fire" Christian campus group I could find, Chi Alpha (meaning, "Christ's ambassadors," the campus outreach division of the Worldwide Assemblies of God Church). In 1976 I was elected president of our little Chi Alpha group. We brought Christian rock groups to campus, showed a film that questioned evolution (after which I fielded questions from the audience), and pursued other avenues of evangelism. Although we had thirty names on the membership roll only about half that number showed up regularly at weekly meetings, probably about the same number of people who attended the gay group's meetings on campus. Like them, we were a distinct minority.

This brings me to a revealing tale. After learning that a gay group was posting sheets informing other gays to come out and join their group, I posted my own sheets (without prior permission from the dean) containing the apostle Paul's railings in Romans against homosexuality, at the end of which I stated that "we" at my Christian group "loved" homosexuals, and invited them to hear the "good news" at our meeting. The dean spoke with me about my illegal postings, and told me that "Bruno and Melissa" of the gay group wanted to speak to me personally on campus that evening. I sweated out the pre-meeting time in prayer and met only Melissa (Bruno couldn't make it). We two met alone in the quad as the sun was going down. She was incensed at my callousness and intolerance and blissful ignorance. She recounted some heartrending stories of what she had had to suffer due to her sexual orientation. I smiled and listened as she went on and on. Finally it was my turn to speak and I told her that I was just repeating what the Bible said, and showed her the passages in question. She quieted down, realizing, I guess, that I was not interested in "battling homosexuality," but was unintentionally causing her grief by blindly repeating age-old "wisdom" from God. She shed some tears toward the end of our discussion, while I smiled blissfully at her. But my blissful example wasn't strong enough to hook her into my belief system and she let me know that I was "not going to convert" her.

I cringe a bit today, knowing what my illegal postings must have represented in her mind, how it rekindled her memories of previous acts of prejudice and pain, etc. Come to think of it, my one-dimensional interactions with "nonbelievers" (i.e., parroting "what Scripture sez" instead of dipping into the full range of my own thoughts and perceptions, and without ever really listening to other people) served two purposes: (1) to isolate me from being understood by them, and (2) to isolate myself from perceiving their unique personhood. Such a one-dimensional way of interacting with "nonbelievers" helped keep me faithful. It kept the blinders on my true believer's eyes.[3]

The overseer of our Chi Alpha group was a Church of God minister, Bob Wittick, who could speak in tongues, although I only distinctly remember him doing so once.

My increasing interest at that time in charismatic gifts of the spirit coincided with my heartfelt wish to know Jesus, and discover for myself the depth of the truth of Christianity. I read pro-charismatic books, sold in the Lamplighter, a Christian bookstore in Princeton, New Jersey, that told about speaking in tongues, and why you shouldn't be afraid to ask for such a gift from God, and biblical reasons why the gift still existed, despite biblical interpretations by fundamentalist Christians to the contrary.

I began attending living room sermons and prayer meetings at Leon Kastner's farm with a couple of friends. Leon had attended a Charismatic Christian seminary, and his living room was his church. There we lifted our hands and praised Jesus. During one such session I experienced the hoped-for bliss of what I then termed "baptism in the Holy Spirit."[4] It was a great flow of joy raining down on me from head to toe, a joy to cast out fear and make me want to laugh. I barely resisted laughing, and wish to this day that I *had* simply let go and laughed. But I was much more serious then than now. I hugged everyone afterwards, and felt for the first time that such hugging was natural and not a feigned gesture.

Two weeks later, I moved my lips "in faith," and repeated one or two nonsense syllables over and over until others appeared. I was soon forming entire "words" out of those syllables. I can still "speak" in that "tongue" whenever I wish. No preparation, meditation, or trance is required.[5]

For a year or two after being "baptized in the spirit" the mere memory of that moment was enough to maintain my utmost devotion to the "truth of Christianity." But eventually the memory dwindled and my ability to rekindle even a spark of the original bliss, through intense prayer and praise, ceased. That is not to say that my faith in Christ and belief in Christian doctrines waned at that time. It did not.

It was during my first year in college that I began reading all the Christian works of the Oxford English professor, C. S. Lewis. In his autobiography, *Surprised by Joy,* Lewis mentioned how great an influence G. K. Chesterton's book *The Everlasting Man* played in his decision to become a Christian. So I read just about everything that Chesterton (who may be called an "evangelical Catholic") wrote on Christianity, including nearly all his fiction. I also read George Mac-Donald's Christian fantasy novels, *Lilith* and *Phantastes,* since Lewis prized both of those novels highly, and called MacDonald "my spiritual mentor."

My heart ached with unspeakable yearning upon reading *Lilith,* which depicted how one could be both a Christian and a universalist. I was impressed by Mac-Donald's perception of God's unfailing compassion. He depicted ordinary sleep and dreams as avenues of God's healing and grace. And in his *Unspoken Sermons* MacDonald portrayed the flames of hell as the fingers of God reaching out to touch His children who perceived His touch as "painful"—the pain of spiritual awakening. Yet God continued to reach out to them, and would succeed one day in awakening every last child of God.

Later I tied together the universalistic threads that linked Lewis to his two Christian mentors, Chesterton and MacDonald. But for the moment, there was still another branch of Christianity I was to encounter and reject before proceeding along the path toward Christian universalism.

After receiving my associate's degree in biology, I transferred to Fairleigh Dickinson University in Rutherford, New Jersey, where I hosted two "Book Table Give-Aways." Standing to the side, I prayed for my fellow students to take and read some of the material on the table. I also sent twenty-five dollars a month to Pat Robertson, to spread the Gospel over the airways.

At one of my give-aways I met a girl at FDU who later introduced me to her brother, a theologically conservative Calvinist, who shared with me Rush-dooney's, Van Til's and Gordon Clark's works, published by the Presbyterian and Reformed Publishing Company. I even made two "pilgrimages" to Westminster Theological Seminary during this period, where I caught a fleeting glance of Cornelius Van Til, talked with a few students, and visited the bookstore.

You might think that I would have trouble getting along with someone who believed that miracles (like the gift of tongues) ended with the age of the apostles, and who handed out tracts that stated on the front in bold green print, *Mourn! God Hates You!* But Calvinism intrigued me.

I attended the brother's church twice, and spoke briefly with his minister. What a "solid" faith, I thought. God "made some vessels for eternal honor and *made others for eternal dishonor*" simply to bring glory to Himself and embody His attributes of eternal "compassion" and eternal "justice." Conversion was up to God. He either bestowed upon people the "gift of saving faith," or damned them.

In a sense it was a relief, knowing that you were not responsible for anyone else's salvation. You did not have to plead with anyone, or devise clever gimmicks to entice them toward the faith, like many Christian youth ministries utilize. The "absoluteness" of God's will was emphasized. If someone did not agree, such was God's will, let them be damned.

It was also a demanding faith for those already in it. They had to avoid unclean associations, i.e., anything that might intrude on the "purity" of their theology and behavior. From thence have arisen "Reconstructionist" Christians who would like to see ancient Hebrew laws writ into America's Constitution.

I rejected Calvinism after realizing that, unlike the believers I had met, I could not relinquish the "nonelect" to God's eternal "justice." Heaven would not be heaven for me if that were true. Neither could I conceive of any reasonably good person maintaining an eternal concentration camp, let alone God Himself. And I could not accept the doctrine of "total [spiritual and mental] depravity," nor the Calvinist rationalization that any and all righteous behavior manifested by the nonelect was merely "common grace," without which the world would be a "living hell."

John Calvin's teachings appear in their most blunt form in his *Institutes* [Bk. II, chapt. xxiii, sect. 7]: "Whence does it happen that Adam's fall irremediably involved so many peoples, together with their infant offspring, in eternal death unless because it so pleased God? . . . The decree is dreadful [*horribile*] indeed, I confess." I had to agree that worshipping a God who was pleased by such things *was* horrible!

Martin Luther, another advocate of the biblically based view known as "predestination," wrote in his classic defense of that view, *On the Bondage of the Will*:

This is the acme of faith, to believe that God, who saves so few and condemns so many, is merciful; that He is just who, at his own pleasure, has made us necessarily doomed to damnation, so that He seems to delight in the torture of the wretched and to be more deserving of hate than of love. If by any effort of reason I could conceive how God, who shows so much anger and harshness, could be merciful and just, there would be no need of faith.

I agreed with Luther that worshipping a God who "seems to delight in the torture of the wretched" would take more faith than I had.

I would sooner side with Voltaire than with Calvin and Luther on such matters. For Voltaire in his *Philosophical Dictionary* had the guts to stand up and say:

> The silly fanatic repeats to me . . . that it is not for us to judge what is reasonable and just in the great Being, that His reason is not like our reason, that His justice is not like our justice. Eh! how, you mad demoniac, do you want me to judge justice and reason otherwise than by the notions I have of them? Do you want me to walk otherwise than with my feet, and to speak otherwise than with my mouth?

Even Christian apologist C. S. Lewis was too smart to fall for Calvin's "horribile decree" and Luther's "acme of faith":

> [There are dangers in judging God by moral standards, but] believing in a God whom we cannot but regard as evil, and then, in mere terrified flattery calling Him "good" and worshipping Him, is still greater danger. . . . The ultimate question is whether the doctrine of the goodness of God or that of the inerrancy of Scripture is to prevail when they conflict. [Lewis was replying to the Biblical accounts of what he called "the atrocities (and treacheries) of Joshua" and the account of Peter striking Ananias and Sapphira dead, called "Divine" decrees by those who believe Scripture is without error.—ED.] I think the doctrine of the goodness of God is the more certain of the two. Indeed, only that doctrine renders this worship of Him obligatory or even permissible. . . . To this some will reply "ah, but we are fallen and don't recognize good when we see it." But God Himself does not say we are as fallen as all that. He constantly in Scripture appeals to our conscience: "Why do ye not *of yourselves* judge what is right?"—"What fault hath my people found in me?" And so on. . . .
>
> Things are not good because God commands them; God commands certain things because he sees them to be good. (In other words, the Divine Will is the obedient servant to the Divine Reason.) . . . If "good" means "what God wills" then to say "God is good" can mean only "God wills what he wills." Which is equally true of you or me or Judas or Satan.[6]

> The real danger is of coming to believe such dreadful things about Him. The conclusion I dread is not "So, there's no God after all," but, "So, this is what God is really like. Deceive yourself no longer."[7]

In college I also read nearly all of Francis Shaeffer's works (popular apologetics in the Reformed Church tradition), and found him interesting, yet not as fine a writer as Lewis or Chesterton. For me, learning is exemplified not only in what you say, but how you say it. Perhaps that helps explain why after five or six years of avid church attendance and intense reading, I found it increasingly difficult to sit through a sermon. Most of them seemed dull and superficial in comparison to what I was reading at the time, and as repetitious in their focus and emphases as I had earlier found the Catholic prayers and rituals to be.

Generally, ministers find it superfluous to address questions. They stand in the pulpit, "three feet above contradiction." Preachers, like politicians, are taught to embody, via a variety of rhetorical and nonverbal means, their utter conviction of the truth of whatever they happen to be preaching, regardless of how much they may know, or not know, about the subject. This reminds me of the story of a minister who wrote in the margin of his sermon notes, "Weak argument here. Shout louder." As I grew to recognize the *diversity* of opinions among Bible scholars and theologians (even just among evangelicals), the *rhetorical posture* of preachers (and politicians) increasingly appeared to me to be suspect in its own right.

Furthermore, I began to realize that large groups of people are better at being *manipulated* by rhetoric and bald assertions—getting caught up in the "crowd atmosphere"—than they are at making logical inferences concerning the preacher's (or politician's) statements. That is the primary reason I chose at that time to conduct several one-on-one dialogues with nonbelievers through the mail. Such dialogues take more thought, more time to cook up and digest. And I thought that in such an atmosphere, the truth of Christianity would be irrefutably self-evident.

It was right after four years of college, and before I began a full time job, that I began swapping lengthy letters with William Bagley and Robert Price (former fundamentalists whose testimonies are contained in this book). Lists of books were exchanged during our letter debates. Both of my friends were already familiar with evangelical Christian literature. So, they patiently explained that it was up to me to try reading at least one of the books that *they* had suggested, and discuss it with them, in order for the debate to continue.

Up to that time my knowledge of what others believed had been gained almost totally via books written by Christian apologists. In fact, about the only "critiques of Christianity" that I had heard about were those whose notorious infamy had led to them being briefly mentioned and summarily dismissed by some of the Christian apologists I had read.

The few times that I *had* read books critical of Christianity (i.e., before I had begun my correspondence with Will and Bob), they were books that two in-the-flesh friends of mine had badgered me to read. One libertarian chess buddy suggested I read Thomas Paine's *Age of Reason,* and lent me his copy. My philosophy professor was friends with Walter Kaufmann, and suggested a few times that I read Kaufmann's *Faith of a Heretic,* and some of Nietzsche's works Kaufmann had translated. I only read them to try and demonstrate to my friends and to myself how easily I could refute them. My mind by some miracle of double-think blithely disregarded what I would today consider to be the authors' most compelling points. As a Christian I would challenge each authors' arguments on a few particulars, though I soon found myself stretching the Bible's meaning to accomodate even the widest gaps in its truth content, and thinking that I had thereby discredited the nonbelieving authors' arguments *in toto.* I wasn't seeing the forest for the few trees I had chopped down, and the wide-angled blinders I was wearing.

Furthermore, those two books were not ones that dealt with matters that most concerned me as a *fundamentalist.* For instance, it would have been more of a challenge had I begun by reading Thomas Paine's smaller and more focused critique of specific Bible passages, *Examination of the Passages in the New*

Testament, Quoted from the Old, and Called Prophecies of the Coming of Jesus Christ,[8] rather than his *Age of Reason.*

In our letter exchanges, Will Bagley challenged me to view Christian symbols and sacraments, like "the Blood of Christ," "the Cross," even "the Resurrection," as pointers toward more universal truths, and not the Truth itself.

While corresponding with Will I first learned of C. S. Lewis's friend, Bede Griffiths, who was mentioned briefly in Lewis's autobiography, *Surprised by Joy.* Griffiths was one of Lewis's pupils at Oxford and converted to Christianity about the same time Lewis did. Afterwards they "kept up a copious correspondence." Griffiths became a Catholic monk and far surpassed Lewis in his ability to perceive a similar spiritual center lying at the heart of all the world's major faiths. Griffiths died the same year and month I'm writing this, at eighty-six years of age, while living in a Christian-Hindu *ashram* that he founded in India. The titles of his published works illustrate his mystic universalist approach to knowing God, beginning with his autobiography, titles like *The Golden String, The Marriage of East and West, Return to the Center, River of Compassion, The Cosmic Revelation: The Hindu Way to God,* and his final work, *The New Creation in Christ.*

Dom Bede Griffiths's obituary in the *National Catholic Reporter* (May 1993), by Tim McCarthy, stated:

> As late as 1990, Griffiths was forced to defend Eastern spirituality against the Congregation for the Doctrine of the Faith's December 1989 response to the challenge of Buddhist and Hindu spirituality.
>
> Discussing the CDF's warning that certain forms of Eastern prayer tempt people to try to overcome the necessary distance between creator and creature, God and humankind, Griffiths wrote in *NCR,* "As if God in Christ had not already overcome that distance and united us with him in the closest bonds. St. Paul says, 'You who were far off, he has brought near—not kept distant—in the blood of Christ.' Jesus himself totally denies any such distance, 'I am the vine,' he says, 'you are the branches.' How can the branches be 'distant' from the vine?" . . .
>
> We must "never in any way seek to place ourselves on the same level as the object of our contemplation," the CDF document insisted. "Of course, we don't seek to place ourselves on the same level," Griffiths countered. "It is God who has already placed us there. Jesus says, 'I have not called you servants, but friends.' And to show what such friendship means, he prays for his disciples, 'that they may be one, as thou, Father in me and I in thee, that they may be one in us.'"

In a letter published in the *National Catholic Reporter,* beneath the headline, "Vatican Letter Disguises Wisdom of East Religions," (May 11, 1990), Griffiths drew attention to several Christian movements in ages past that endorsed mystical prayer, then added, "This is not to say that Hindu, Buddhist, and Christian mystics all have the same experience. But it is to recognize an analogy between them and to look upon the Hindu and Buddhist experience as something of supreme significance, not to be lightly dismissed by a Christian as of no importance."

Naturally, if my friend Will Bagley resembled Griffiths, then I resembled

Lewis. For I found it very difficult at first to widen my religious perspective. *Christian* universalism seemed attractive, but not a universalism in which the truths of all the world's faiths overlapped to varying degrees. It was during my dialogue with Will that I began tying together those universalistic threads I spoke of earlier.

G. K. Chesterton, in his book *Orthodoxy* stated, "To hope for all souls is imperative; and it is quite tenable that their salvation is inevitable." He also had many positive things to say about the non-Christians whom he debated and remained friends with. For instance, in his book on George Bernard Shaw, Chesterton stated, "In a sweeter and more solid civilization he would have been a great saint." And when H. G. Wells was seriously ill, he wrote Chesterton and said, "If after all my Atheology turns out wrong and your Theology right I feel I shall always be able to pass into Heaven (if I want to) as a friend of G.K.C.'s. Bless you." To this Chesterton replied, "If I turn out to be right, you will triumph, not by being a friend of mine, but by being a friend of Man, by having done a thousand things for men like me in every way from imagination to criticism. The thought of the vast variety of that work, and how it ranges from towering visions to tiny pricks of humor, overwhelmed me suddenly in retrospect: and I felt we had none of us ever said enough. . . . Yours always, G. K. Chesterton."[9] Talk about being ecumenical!

C. S. Lewis himself seems to have had second thoughts about the dogma of the eternity of hell's torments. In his novel *The Great Divorce,* Lewis named a major character after the universalist Christian minister and novelist, George MacDonald, and has that character escort a visitor from hell around heaven, where the visitor eventually chooses to remain.

In *The Problem of Pain,* a work published before *The Great Divorce,* Lewis had assumed that the orthodox Christian doctrine of hell had "the full support of Scripture." But in *The Great Divorce* it becomes evident that Lewis had begun to reconsider his earlier wholehearted avowal of that church doctrine. He even has the George MacDonald character in his novel *deny* that the orthodox Christian doctrine of hell has the "full support of Scripture," by having MacDonald say, "St. Paul talked as if all men would be saved." Neither did Lewis have the angel (whom George was speaking to in the novel) deny George's interpretation of St. Paul's words, but only reply that it was not for man to ask such questions. Yet Lewis felt strongly enough about that possibility to *raise* that question in one of his novels for all his readers to ponder.

It was in a little book called *Salvation and Damnation* by a Jesuit priest named Dalton that I first learned about the verses written by St. Paul that suggested "all would be saved." That little book by Dalton opened my eyes to a universalistic view of salvation that has ever after seemed a superior moral view.[10]

Still more revelations concerning my Christian faith were forthcoming. Bob Price was a professional biblical scholar. He was immune to my pot shots fired at his "liberal" faith. His replies to my letters consisted of in-depth analyses of verses in the Bible, keeping in mind their historical contexts. I requested a book list. What I received was a neatly typed annotated list of about sixty titles, arranged according to various categories: "New Testament Studies . . . Old Testament . . . Theology . . . Apologetics. . . ." I began wading through the scholarly tomes.

The contention that Bob introduced me to that threw me for the biggest loop was that *Jesus* had *incorrectly* predicted that the Son of Man would come "with his angels; and . . . reward every man according to his works" before "some standing" *there with Jesus* had "tasted death" (Matt. 16:27–28)—a prediction that Jesus reiterated, stating, "*This* generation [meaning his own] will not pass away" until the Son of Man has arrived. (Matt. 24:30–34).

The attempt to overlook Jesus' error by citing Jesus' other saying, namely that, "No man knows the day or the hour," does not make Jesus' prediction any less false. "Days" and "hours" imply *nearness* in time and lie *within* a "generation's" span of time. To quote the famous German biblical scholar, David F. Strauss: "[Naturally there is a distinction] between an inexact indication of the space of time, beyond which the event will not be deferred (a "generation"), and the determination of the precise date and time (the "day and the hour") at which it will occur; the former Jesus gives, the latter he declares himself unable to give."[11]

Furthermore, look at what the apostle Paul has to say about the nearness of Jesus' "day" and "hour":

The sufferings of this present time are not worthy to be compared with the glory that will be [literally, *is soon* (Gk. *mello*) to be[12]] revealed to us. . . .

The whole creation groans and suffers the pains of childbirth *until now.* . . .

We . . . groan within ourselves, waiting eagerly for our adoption as sons, the redemption of our body. . . .

Knowing the time, that it is already the *hour* for you to awaken from sleep; for now salvation is nearer to us than when we believed! The night is almost gone, and the *day* is *at hand.* . . .

The God of peace will *soon* crush Satan under your feet. (Rom. 8:18, 22–23; 13:11–12; 16:20 [NASB])

Paul was even more explicit about the imminence of Jesus' return in his letter to the believers at Corinth:

These things were written for *our* instruction, *upon whom the ends of the ages have come.* . . .

The rulers of this age . . . *are* passing away [i.e., they will not last much longer]. . . .

Do not go on passing judgment before the time [i.e., "before the time" of final judgment, which Paul taught was close at hand—ED.], but wait until the Lord comes who will both bring to light the things hidden in the darkness and disclose the motives of men's hearts. . . .

The time has been shortened so that from now on both those who have wives should be as though they had none [i.e., Paul preached that the time was so "short" that married Christian couples ought to abstain from having sex, keeping themselves pure for their soon-returning savior—ED.]; and those who weep, as though they did not weep; and those who rejoice, as though they did not rejoice; and those who buy, as though they did not possess; and those who use the world, as though they did not make full use of it;

for the form of this world is passing away [="This world, as it is now, will not last much longer" (TEV)]. . . .

Proclaim the Lord's death *until he comes* [i.e., *not* "until the day you die," which means that he taught Christ's coming was nearer than the time when the believers he was writing to would all be dead—ED.]. . . .

We [Paul and the first-century believers being addressed] *shall not all sleep.* . . .

At the last trumpet . . . the dead will be raised . . . and *we* shall be changed.

Maranatha ["Come Lord"]

(1 Cor. 2:6; 4:5; 7:29–31; 10:11; 11:26; 15:51–52; 16:22)

That's a "day" and an "hour" that both Jesus and Paul predicted was going to arrive *very soon!*[13]

Even when I first encountered it, this problem was not new to me, having read C. S. Lewis's acknowledgment of it in his book *The World's Last Night.* Lewis attributed Jesus' erroneous prediction of his "soon return" to the limits imposed by the Incarnation, i.e., that Jesus, being fully human (as well as being fully God), could err in some of his knowledge and expectations, as humans do.

But, Bob also made me aware, contra Lewis's "God-man" defense, that "if we admit Jesus to have been in error on a very important factual/doctrinal claim like the near end of the world, then we must at least potentially think twice about his other teachings."

Debating Bob and studying books on his list I learned many other things about the Bible that I might have remained a happier Christian not knowing.

I read books that critiqued the idea that Jesus "fulfilled" Old Testament prophecies.[14] I read books that critiqued the notion that present day events were "fulfilling" biblical prophecies.[15] Meanwhile, doubts crept into my fervent *creationist* beliefs after reading "The Impossible Voyage of Noah's Ark"—the title of a special issue of *Creation/Evolution,* a journal devoted to answering creationist claims. (The article was written by Robert Moore, a former fundamentalist whose testimony appears elsewhere in this book.) That particular issue of *Creation/Evolution* was chock-full of embarrassing questions for creationists, and made me realize for the first time that well-informed critics of creationism *did* exist, contrary to what the creationist press had led me to believe.

Then I read articles by Bob Schadewald in the *Skeptical Inquirer* in which he mentioned Bible verses that implied their authors' view of the earth was *flat.* Two primary verses were Daniel 4:10–11, "I saw a tree of great *height* at the center of the earth . . . it was visible to the earth's farthest bounds," and Matthew 4:8, "The devil took him [Jesus] to a very *high* mountain, and showed him all the kingdoms of the world and their glory." In both cases such visiblity presupposes a flat earth, since on a spherical earth, no matter how "high" you were, things would remain beyond your vision, i.e., those areas on the earth's opposite side.

Thus, I was awakened to the shocking thought that the authors of the Bible may have taken for granted that the earth was flat! And the more I studied the matter (at first to debunk it) the more Bible verses I found that implied a strictly horizontal view of the cosmos.[16]

The arguments I had used to defend the truth of Christianity were peeled away from me like the many layers of an onion's skin. I put up all the intellectual resistance I could, and winced at each layer's removal. I suffered through dark nights of the soul pondering whether my beliefs might not be too narrow or even wholly false. Imperceptibly, my fears, doubts, and grief blossomed into relief, relaxation, and joy. I realized that my God was too small. I caught myself using the Bible as a paper idol. (My experience at that point resembled that of John William Colenso, whose testimony appears in this book.) I became a very moderate, but not quite "liberal" Christian. My favorite authors included Conrad Hyers (whose testimony appears in this book), Robert Farrar Capon (who wrote somewhat like G. K. Chesterton would have if he'd had a seminary degree), and Alan Watts (the *early* Watts, who, while still a priest in the Anglican church, wrote, *Behold the Spirit*).

I began to consciously admit that perceptions and questions raised by *non*believing thinkers agreed with some of my own, and I sought out further correspondences of that type. My former distrust of skeptical literature dwindled merely to a hesitancy in continuing to read more. But even that hesitancy eventually vanished. I found myself thinking at a greater depth, and admitting how I really felt about certain aspects of my faith, instead of repeating my old fundamentalist response, which was, "Yes, that seems to make some sense, but not if the Bible is 100 percent accurate and authoritative." I even grew *hungry* to read all sorts of intellectual materials I had previously denied myself.

I certainly owe a debt to my friends Bob and Will. Their learning, their tact, their tolerance and patience induced me to pursue three years of what was then the most intense reading, correspondence, and introspection of my life (though the entire process is perpetual, ongoing).

After reading yet more books on biblical criticism and the development of Christian doctrine, and after studying evolutionists' criticisms of "scientific creationist" arguments, I became disenchanted with Christianity *in toto,* and became an agnostic with theistic leanings of the Martin Gardner variety. Gardner is the prodigious author of skeptical articles and books (and former puzzle columnist for *Scientific American*). He believes in a benevolent (non-Christian) "God," and in immortality, but *not* because a preponderance of evidence exists to support those conclusions. Rather, he argues that there may be just enough scientific, philosophical, and heartfelt reasons to *not* simply abandon such an alternative to atheism. I found his book *The Whys of a Philosophical Scrivener* very helpful during this period. Gardner was once a fundamentalist Christian, and lived in Tulsa, Oklahoma, home of Oral Roberts University. The basic outlines of Gardner's own spiritual and intellectual odyssey appear in his novel *The Flight of Peter Fromm.*

Where am I at today? I have not been able to regain any sort of faith in the Bible as the "highest" authority on spiritual matters. It contains some "inspiring" passages, as many books do. But I have also learned that many of the ideas it contains owe a significant debt to the cultural milieu out of which they arose. There are in the Bible some plagiarisms from other ancient works, lessons in morality (along with some stories that picture God committing wholesale acts of slaughter that would stain even the devil's character), some history mixed with some legend and myth, Old Testament verses lifted out of context and misapplied to Jesus' life, contradictions, redundancies, omissions, and passages that fundamentalists would brand as "obscene" if they ran across them in any other book except the Bible. Those who say that they believe everything in the Bible from cover to cover don't know all that lies between the covers. A few self-evident examples should suffice to make my point:

And the Lord said . . . "With thee will I break in pieces old and *young*; and with thee will I break in pieces the *young man and the maid*." (Jer. 51:22 [KJV])

And the Lord said . . . "Go and smite Amalek, and utterly destroy all that they have, and spare them not; but slay both man and woman, *infant and suckling*." (1 Sam. 15:3)

"The Lord delivered him before us; and we smote him, and his sons, and all his people. And we took all his cities . . . and utterly destroyed the men and the women, and the *little ones*, of every city, we left none to remain." (Deut. 2:34)

And Moses said . . . "Kill every male among the *little ones*, and kill every woman that hath known man by lying with him [including pregnant women]. But spare the virgins for yourself." (Num. 31:17)

"*Happy* shall he be, that taketh and dasheth thy *little ones* against the stones." (Ps. 137:9)

And the Lord said . . . "I will cause them to eat the flesh of their sons and the flesh of their daughters." (Jer. 19:9 and Deut. 28:53, 57)

And Jesus said . . . "Suppose ye that I came to give peace on earth? I tell you, Nay; but rather division: For from henceforth there shall be five in one house divided, three against two, and two against three. The father shall be divided against the son, and the son against the father; the mother against the daughter, and the daughter against the mother. . . . If any man comes to me, and hate not his father, and mother, and wife, and children, and brethren, and sisters, yea, and his own life also, he cannot be my disciple." (Luke 12:51–53 and 14:26)

And the Lord said . . . "I will bring evil upon the house of Jeroboam, and will cut off from Jeroboam him that pisseth against the wall." (1 Kings 14:10 [KJV])

"The righteous shall rejoice when he seeth the vengeance; he shall wash his feet in the blood of the wicked. So that a man shall say, Verily there is a reward for the righteous." (Ps. 58:10–11)

"Noah took . . . of every clean beast and fowl, and offered burnt offerings on the altar. *And the Lord smelled a sweet savour*." (Gen. 8:20–21)

"In six days the Lord made heaven and earth, and *on the seventh day he rested, and was refreshed*." (Exod. 31:17) [According to learned editors of a Bible published in 1774, the true meaning of the Hebrew is, "on the seventh day He *rested,* and *fetched breath."*]

And Abraham said to his male servant . . . "Put, I pray thee, thy hand under my thigh: And I will make thee swear by the Lord. . . ." (Gen. 24:2–3 and 47:29) [Since God was the author of the mystery of reproduction and had blessed Abraham's "seed," the Hebrews took a sacred oath by putting a hand "under the thigh," that is, on another man's testicles. This type of "swearing in" is biblical and literal, unlike today's "liberal" practice in courtrooms of merely placing your hand on the Bible.]

"This thy stature is like to a palm tree, and *thy breasts to clusters of grapes.* . . . I will take hold of the boughs thereof: now also *thy breasts shall be as clusters of the vine."* (Song of Sol. 7:7–8)

"My breasts like towers: then was I in his eyes as one that found favor." (Song of Sol. 8:10)

"Let us get up early to the vineyard . . . there will I give thee my loves. The mandrakes give a smell and at our gates are all manner of pleasant fruits, new and old, which I have laid up for thee, O my beloved." (Song of Sol. 7:7–8) ["Gates" refers to genitals. And the two-pronged "mandrake" root is crotch-shaped. Even in earliest biblical times "mandrakes" were related to sexual potency. In Genesis 30 Jacob's barren wife tells him she has "hired him (a child) with *mandrake."*]

"Your *vulva* a rounded crater, may it never lack punch! . . . The smell of your *vulva,* like apples." (Song of Sol. 7:2, 8) [The *Anchor Bible* translation. The scholar who did the translation, Marvin H. Pope, concluded that the word "navel" has been the accepted unscholarly euphemism for an obscure term in the Hebrew. As he elaborates in his notes, the Hebrew much more likely refers to a woman's vulva.]

And the Lord said . . . "She doted upon their paramours [her illicit sexual partners], *whose flesh is as the flesh of asses, and whose issue is like the issue of horses."* (Ezek. 23:20) [It is plain that "the Lord" is describing men with "donkey dicks, who come like horses." Yet when was the last time you saw *that* translation in a modern English translation of the Bible?]

Recently, my agnosticism was shaken by the testimony of one man in particular, Howard Storm, a former hardened agnostic and chairman of a university art department, whose description of his long, involved, near-death experience roused me from my doubts and fear that there may be no afterlife, to positively hoping there may be one.

I am presently studying a number of books on near-death experiences, and have "confirmed" several aspects of Storm's story by comparing it with the stories of those who have had remarkably similar experiences. Few stories I've run across are as long and detailed as his. After his experience, Storm's life changed radically. He quit his well-paid position at the university and attended seminary. Today he is a minister in a liberal Christian denomination, United Church of Christ. He is much happier than he was before the experience and does not fear death. He continues to assert that his near-death experience was "more real" than waking reality, and that extraordinary experiences accompanied him long *after* he had it.

Moreover, I've discovered that my personal happiness has increased with my renewed interest in an afterlife. After studying only a few books on near-death experiences, and reading several skeptical pieces on them, I am still no expert on the phenomenon. However, I am no longer the skeptic I once was. There *does* appear to be some evidence for life after death. It wouldn't be much fun being a "skeptical inquirer" if there were absolutely no claims to "inquire" about, would it?

> Life is a "racket," so get a few laughs, do the best you can, take nothing serious, for nothing is certainly depending on this generation. Each one lives in spite of the previous one and not because of it.
>
> Believe in something for another world, but don't be too set on what it is, and then you won't start out that life with a disappointment. Live your life so that whenever you lose, you are ahead!
>
> —Will Rogers

Notes

1. It never occurred to me, blinded by my faith in "miraculous-maybe" interpretations of Scripture, that perhaps Ezekiel was not "inspired."

He depicted his "end-time" battle exactly as any ancient Near Easterner might, being fought with wooden shields, bucklers, bows, arrows, handstaves, and spears, instead of with today's metallic arsenal. How much inspiration would it take for an ancient Near Easterner to prophesy the employment of such weapons? None.

Furthermore, in the same prophecy Ezekiel mentioned "not needing to take wood out of the field, neither having to cut down any out of the forests; for they shall burn the weapons with fire." Ezekiel took for granted *the need to burn wood* for cooking, heating, etc. But, like prophesying the use of spears and arrows, how much inspiration would it take for an ancient Near Easterner to speak prophetically about wood-burning fires, as opposed to today's gas and electric? None.

Looking back, I should have noticed how "literalists" only take a literal interpretation as far as *they* want, no further. For instance, Ezekiel's "end-time battle" and "seven years burning of weapons" are interpreted literally, but his "shields, swords, spears and arrows" are not!

What about Ezekiel's end-time adversaries, "Rosh, Meshech and Tubal"? Hal Lindsey and other prophecy-mongers insist that Rosh equals Russia, Meshech equals Moscow, and Tubal equals Tobolsk (Moscow and Tobolsk being cities in Russia). Thus they interpret Ezekiel's prophecy to mean that present-day Russia will invade present-day Israel.

Not so, according to Edwin M. Yamauchi, professor of history at Miami University and author of *Foes from the Northern Frontier: Invading Hordes from the Russian Steppes* (Baker Book House, 1982). Yamauchi explained on the basis of documented archeological evidence how Ezekiel was "inspired" by the precarious situation of his own era.

In Ezekiel's day, invading hordes, like the Urartians, Manneans, Cimmerians, and Scythians, occupied parts of what are now Armenia, Turkey, and Iran, as well as the Russian steppes. These "invaders from the north" were the ones Ezekiel (and Jeremiah) feared, and prophesied against.

"Meshech" and "Tubal" have been clearly identified as kingdoms/provinces that used to lie in areas of ancient Anatolia (roughly equivalent to our present-day Turkey). They do *not* refer to Moscow and Tobolsk.

Yamauchi also explained why "Rosh" could not possibly be related to "Russia," and how archeological evidence was being ignored by end-times preachers, who, apparently, only read each other's books, thus perpetuating their collective blindness, passing it off on their listeners as the "God-breathed truth."

Take for instance, end-time preacher Hal Lindsey, who stated in *The Late Great Planet Earth,* "[I do not] believe that we have prophets today who are getting direct revelations from God, but we do have prophets today who are given special insight into the prophetic word." Undoubtedly Lindsey considers himself one of these "prophets." So, let's see how "the special insight" he claims to have been granted by God stacks up with reality.

In *The Late Great Planet Earth* (Grand Rapids, Mich.: Zondervan Press, 1970), Lindsey specified "an extremely important time clue" in Scripture, namely, Jesus' parable of the fig tree putting forth its leaves, letting you know that summer was near—after which, Jesus added, "when you see all these things, recognize that He is near, right at the door" (Matt. 24:32, 33). According to Lindsey, "This is the most important sign in Matthew."

"The figure of speech 'fig tree' has been an historic symbol of national Israel. When the Jewish people . . . became a nation again on 14 May 1948 the 'fig tree' put forth its first leaves. Jesus said that this would indicate that He was 'at the door,' ready to return. Then Jesus said, 'Truly, I say to you, this generation will not pass away until all these things take place' (Matt. 24:34). What generation? Obviously, in context, the generation that would see the signs— chief among them the rebirth of Israel. A generation in the Bible is something like forty years. If this is a correct deduction, then *within* forty years or so of 1948 [i.e., *before* 1988], all these things [including, according to Lindsey, the Temple being rebuilt, people fleeing to the mountains to escape the world's final battles, and Christ's return] could take place. Many scholars who have studied Bible prophecy all their lives believe that this is so."

Well, it ain't so. What *is* so, is that Lindsey must now admit that a "life" of conservative/ inerrantist "Bible study" can lead to erroneous "beliefs"!

Moreover, the "extreme importance" of this particular "sign" and "time clue" was reinforced by Lindsey in his later books. Note their titles: *The 1980's: Countdown to Armageddon* and *The Terminal Generation.*

In *The Terminal Generation* (Old Tappan, New Jersey: Fleming H. Revell Company, 1976), Hal stated another of his "prophetic insights," namely, "Based on biblical prophecy, I believe that there will continue to be *an increase* in major earthquakes. . . . In a recent book called *The Jupiter Effect,* written by two astronomers . . . amazing things are predicted to occur in *1982.* . . . The 'Jupiter effect' is a rare planetary lineup which occurs every 179 years. . . . According- ing to the authors, a result of the effect will be that great earthquakes will be triggered."

Again, it wasn't so. In fact, even fellow fundamentalist Christians, like the folks at the Institute for Creation Research, have acknowledged that since 1900, data regarding the frequency and intensity of global earthquakes has followed *no clear pattern of increase or decrease* [*Impact,* no. 198, December 1989].

Not surprisingly, Lindsey's enthusiasm inspired others to get into the "prophetic insight" business, including televangelist and presidential contender Pat Robertson, who stated just as unequivocally as Lindsey that, "If I am hearing Him right . . . I believe in the next two years, I would put it at '82, but the dates are risky, there is going to be a major war in the Middle East. . . . The Soviet Union is going to make the move, and that's what God is saying: we've got a couple of years . . . from now on it's going to be bloodshed, war, revolution and trouble" (Robertson speaking at a Christian Broadcasting Network staff meeting, January 1, 1980, as recorded by Gerard Straub, one of Robertson's producers [Wayne King, "Robertson Looks at God and Politics," *New York Times,* December 27, 1987]).

Robertson also announced during a Christian Broadcasting Network broadcast, June 9, 1982, "I guarantee you by the fall of 1982 that there is going to be a judgment on the world, and the ultimate judgment is going to come on the Soviet Union. They are going to be the ones to make military adventures, and they are going to be hit . . . by the fall [1982] undoubtedly something like this will happen which will fulfill Ezekiel."

"1982" was over ten years ago, and "1988" is over five years past. Meanwhile, what Robertson and Lindsey's "prophetic insight" told us to expect before then *did not happen.* Regardless of the fact that they approached Scripture with the utmost reverence, and prayed to receive wisdom from God to "interpret his word rightly," it is now apparent that either God did not answer those prayers, or God did not speak clearly enough to be rightly understood. (What might this imply about the claim of some fundamentalists that "God does not hear or answer the prayers of unbelieving Jews"? Does this put Robertson and Lindsey in the same category?) How many other interpretations of the Bible by its most fervent believers might be equally lacking in God-given "insight"? This may only be the tip of the iceberg!

2. Mike Yaconelli (ed.), *The Door Interviews* (Grand Rapids, Mich.: The Door/Zondervan Publishing House, 1989), interview with Robert Capon, p. 233.

3. Today I believe that the Hebrews, who depicted their laws as a "revelation" from Yahweh to Moses (just as the Babylonians depicted their laws as a "revelation" from the god Shamash to King Hammurabi, which "divinized" any and all local human prejudices by having them arise directly out of the mouths of "the gods") were wrong in unilaterally condemning homosexual activity, and equally wrong in their judgments concerning a number of other matters. The apostle Paul's exclusion of homosexuality from the realm of "natural behavior" was likewise an assumption on his part that is questionable today, and which in his day was likely to have been an argument from "natural philosophy" that he had plagiarized from some Roman philosophers who had used it before him. So, as I see it, neither the ancient Hebrews nor Paul were perfect and unlimited in knowledge with respect to what they wrote. The Bible is a book exemplifying what was believed then, and not necessarily what must be believed today.

Is the origin and spread of AIDS an example of "God's condemnation" of homosexual behavior? Many fundamentalists feel that it is. But, think again. There are other explanations. Male homosexual contact involves abrasive skin-to-skin contact and intermingling of bodily fluids, which *automatically* increases the likelihood of *any* contagious disease being transmitted from one person to another. The same is true of intravenous drug users who share needles, people who receive blood transfusions, and health care workers who accidentally get stuck with the needles they have put into other people's arms. Obviously, if male homosexuals practiced strict monogamy, or used condoms "religiously," and drug addicts used only their own needles and syringes, and no one sought a blood transfusion, AIDS would not have spread as it did.

A comparison may prove helpful. Say a Christian congregation all placed their lips one Sunday morning on the same communion cup. Now say that many of the Christians who sipped from the cup had lips with miniscule sores or cuts on them. In that case, AIDS (or some other disease) could conceivably be spread among a congregation of Christians. That may seem an unlikely scenario. But notice that the majority of Christian churches in America (even the fundamentalist ones) dropped the practice of drinking out of the same communion cup quite a number of years ago, due, I suppose, to warnings from health officials (although the Catholics still employ "germ baths" filled with "holy water" at the entrances to their churches that everyone dips their hands into and anoints their faces with). So Christians who drink out of many little separate cups at communion, instead of a single cup, are practicing "safe sacraments," regardless of the fact that Jesus probably shared the same cup with his disciples. So even fundamentalists choose less dangerous methods of doing what *they* want to do most, instead of curtailing their activities entirely.

If AIDS *was* some form of "judgment from God" sent to wipe out homosexual behavior, it has not had the desired effect. It has only made homosexuals more aware of the necessity of maintaining monogamous, long-term relationships, not of abandoning their inclinations altogether. It has done little toward discouraging lesbian behavior, which remains at a relatively lower risk for AIDS, perhaps even lower than the risk that heterosexuals run in catching the disease.

Besides, if AIDS represents "God's condemnation" of homosexual behavior, what do the host of *other* sexually transmitted diseases represent? "God's condemnation" of *hetero*sexual behavior? And what about the "plague" that subsided about A.D. 594, after killing "about half the population" of Europe (*Information Please Almanac,* 1991)? Not to mention Europe's "Black Death" during the Middle Ages, which killed twenty-five million people. Did such plagues represent "God's condemnation" of *Christian* civilization?

And what about the barrage of illnesses that children contract: small pox, measles, mumps, chicken pox, etc. These used to claim far more lives than they do today. According to Buffon, the French naturalist, only half the children that were born two hundred years ago ever reached the age of eight. Did such a high mortality rate due to killer diseases represent "God's condemnation" of *children?*

And what about any major outbreak of a *killer* disease, transferred not by genital contact but merely by breathing the same air, drinking the same water, or touching the same objects, diseases like influenza, tuberculosis, polio, and others? Do they represent "God's condemnation" of everyone who touches the same objects, drinks out of the same cup, and breathes the same air?

The trouble with AIDS is that many people wish that homosexual behavior and traits would cease, and AIDS is making their dream come true, by killing homosexuals.

Ipso facto, they rejoice at what is happening, some of them even stooping so low as to rejoice at what's happening in their deity's name. A similarly barbaric form of jubilation is evident in certain Psalms [58:10, NASB and 137:9, KJV]: "the righteous will *rejoice* when he sees the vengeance; he will wash his feet in the blood of the wicked," and, "Blessed [or *Happy*] shall he be, that taketh and dasheth thy little ones against the stones." "Beautiful" songs sung to Yahweh.

On the other hand, biblical literalists who believe that AIDS is a "happy" or "blessed" occurrence worthy of "rejoicing" over, should also meditate on Proverbs [17:5, 24:17 and 25:21, NASB]: "He who rejoices at calamity shall not go unpunished. . . . Do not rejoice when your enemy falls, and let not your heart be glad when he stumbles. . . . If your enemy is hungry, give him bread to eat; and if he is thirsty, give him water to drink." (I leave it to ingenious fundamentalists to "reconcile" the conflicting attitudes and messages being broadcast in the Psalms and Proverbs, cited above.)

Just how "flattered" God must feel with being credited for AIDS is anyone's guess. Too bad the people who praise God for AIDS don't praise Him for all the other rampaging illnesses that have plagued children and Christians throughout history. (See A. Nikiforuk, *The Fourth Horseman: A Short History of Epidemics, Plagues, Famines and Other Scourges.*)

Ironically, fundamentalist Christians cannot maintain their numbers without some form of "evangelism" coupled with "teaching and training" in church doctrines that no one is born believing. Compare that with the fact that throughout history and in different cultures homosexuals have comprised a fairly stable few percent of nearly any given population. As the most recent genetic, historical, sociological and genealogical studies have shown, we will probably have the same proportion of homosexuals with us for as long as people continue to be born. That means that a solid few percent of the world will remain homosexual for generations to come. On the other hand, a recent Gallup poll indicates that the number of Americans who believe the Bible is the *literal* word of God has continually and radically diminished since the 1960s. So homosexuality, even with the AIDS epidemic claiming the lives of many, may have a greater chance of outlasting fundamentalism in the long run.

4. Today, I think that what I experienced may have parallels in other religious traditions, such as the Buddhist's *satori,* or the Hindu's *samadhi.* Perhaps certain drugs (naturally produced in the brain, or synthetically produced) might duplicate or help rekindle the ecstasy. I have no idea, except to say that the experience was one thing, while the meanings and interpretations I attached to it at that time, and in that setting, were another.

5. Although I prayed in tongues for years, my "vocabulary" remained limited to certain syllabic patterns: "Kiddy-ya-say, bed-aloo-way, amiddy-ya-kay . . . etc." The "words" were each about four or five syllables long (longer if I took a deeper breath), with the accents on the first syllable and childish, sound-alike endings. The "gift of tongues" appears to be neither eloquent nor miraculous. I can still perform this "miracle," without the "faith."

I am even less impressed by the "gift of interpretation of tongues." I have attended meetings where a brief tripping of the tongue was "interpreted" quite lengthily.

6. July 3, 1963, letter from C. S. Lewis to John Beversluis. Letter quoted in full in John Beversluis, *C. S. Lewis and the Search for Rational Religion* (Grand Rapids, Mich.: Eerdmans, 1985), pp. 156f.

7. C. S. Lewis, *A Grief Observed* (New York: Seabury Press, 1963), pp. 9–10.

8. Thomas Paine, *Examination of the Passages in the New Testament, Quoted from the Old, and Called Prophecies of the Coming of Jesus Christ* (first published in 1807). Recently

republished, with added notes as *The Age of Reason—Part Three—Examination of the Prophecies,* ed. Frank Zindler, (Austin, Tex.: American Atheist Press, 1993). A briefer, edited version appears in *An Anthology of Atheism and Rationalism,* ed. Gordon Stein (Amherst, N.Y.: Prometheus Books, 1980), pp. 125–43.

9. December 10, 1933, letter from H. G. Wells to G. K. Chesterton. Undated reply from G. K. Chesterton to H. G. Wells. Letters quoted in full in Maisie Ward, Gilbert Keith Chesterton (New York: Sheed & Ward, 1943), pp. 604–605.

10. William J. Dalton, S.J., *Salvation and Damnation* (Butler, Wis.: Clergy Book Service, 1977).

11. David F. Strauss, *The Life of Jesus Critically Examined* (Philadelphia: Fortress Press, 1972), ch. 115, "The Discourses of Jesus on His Second Advent: Criticisms of the Different Interpretations," p. 587.

12. A. J. Mattill, Jr., in *The Art of Reading the Bible* (Gordo, Ala.: Flatwoods Free Press, 1988), p. 12, stated,

> I made an exhaustive study of the Greek verb *mello* and found what is seldom recognized, and even seldomer proclaimed by preachers and professors, namely, that *mello* in the New Testament is used again and again to indicate the speedy coming of the end of the world: "Before long" God "will judge the world" (Acts 17:31); "before long there will be a resurrection" (Acts 24:15); "the age which is about to come" (Matt. 12:32; Eph. 1:21; Heb. 6:5) to give a few examples. Needless to say, this imminent expectation failed to materialize.

Mattill's "exhaustive study" can be found in his book *Luke and the Last Things* (Dillsboro, N.C.: Western Carolina Press, 1979), ch. 4, " 'Before long' (Acts 17:31): The Imminent Expectation in Acts," pp. 41–54, and in his article, "Naherwartung, Fernerwartung, and the Purpose of Luke-Acts: Weymouth Reconsidered," published in *Catholic Biblical Quarterly,* vol. 34, no. 3, July 1972, pp. 276–93.

In personal correspondence, Mattill has also pointed out, "It's interesting to note that in the Jehovah's Witness interlinear Greek NT they translate *mello* in the interlinear as 'about to,' but then in the English text to the right ignore their own translation . . . that would appear to be their way of escaping the imminent hope as expressed by *mello.*"

No doubt, many fundamentalist and evangelical Bible translators employ the same mental gymnastics as the Jehovah's Witnesses.

13. I am composing "The Lowdown on God's Showdown," a lengthy essay examining the many New Testament predictions that Jesus would return in the *days of the Apostles,* not in our day.

14. Michael Arnheim, *Is Christianity True?* (Amherst, N.Y.: Prometheus Books, 1984), ch. 6, "Fulfillment of Prophecy?"; David Berger and Michael Wyschogrod, *Jews & Jewish Christianity* (New York: Ktav Publishing House, 1978); Gerald Sigal, *The Jew and the Christian Missionary: A Jewish Response to Missionary Christianity* (New York: Ktav Publishing House, 1981); Farrell Till, *Prophecies: Imaginary and Unfulfilled* (Canton, Ill. : Skepticism, 1991); Charles C. Hennell, *An Inquiry Concerning the Origin of Christianity,* 2d ed. (London: T. Allman, 1841), ch. 12, "On the Prophecies," ch. 13, "On the Prophecies of Isaiah," ch. 14, "On the Prophecies of Daniel," pp. 325–403; John E. Remsburg, *The Bible: I. Authenticity II. Credibility III. Morality* (New York: The Truth Seeker Company, 1930?), ch. 22, "Prophecies," pp. 293–305; Edward J. Barrett, "Can Scholars Take the Virgin Birth Seriously?" *Bible Review* (October): 10–15 and 29; Dennis McKinsey, various articles on "Messianic Prophecy" published in *Biblical Errancy* (see especially, no. 7 [July 1983], no. 24 [December 1984]; no. 30–31 [June-July 1985], and no. 76 [Apr. 1989]).

15. Dewey M. Beegle, *Prophecy and Prediction* (Michigan: Pryor Pettengill, 1978); Colin Chapman, *Whose Promised Land? Are the Ancient Promises of the Bible Relevant Today?* (Belleville, Mich.: Lion Publishing, 1983); Grace Halsell, *Prophecy and Politics: Militant Evangelists on the Road to Nuclear War* (Westport, Conn.: Lawrence H. & Company, 1986); Dwight Wilson, *Armageddon Now! The Premillenarian Response to Russia and Israel Since 1917* (Grand Rapids, Mich.: Baker Book House, 1977).

16. For instance, Scripture speaks of God at creation inscribing a "circle" on the (assumedly flat) "*surface* of the waters" (Job 26:10 and Prov. 8:27). Could this be a description of God's creation of a pancake-shaped earth and the limits of its flat circumference? It seems likely. The biblical earth is often described as having "ends," and also a "center," where Jerusalem is said to lie (Ezek. 5:5; 38:11, 12, and Ps. 22:27 and 59:13). A flat, circular earth would square well with such speech.

Notice also the use of the phrases, "from *one end* of the earth *to the other*" (Deut. 28:64–65); and "from one end of the heavens . . . to the other end of them" (Ps. 19:4–6). The writers of those passages were obviously thinking in terms of *opposite* "ends" of a flat surface. This is further corroborated by Isaiah 11:12, "Gather [them] from the four corners of the earth," and Revelation 7:1, "I saw four angels standing on the four corners of the earth," which demonstrate that four *flat* directions (north, south, east, and west) remained the norm for the ancient Hebrews, even to the extent of a psalmist rejoicing, "He removes our transgressions from us, as far as the east is from the west" (Ps. 103:12), which, on a *globe,* is not irreconcilably distant. For on a globe, "east" eventually *meets* "west."

According to Genesis the earth was created *before* the sun, moon, and stars, which were *afterwards* "set" above the earth to provide light for the earth below. Likewise, as only on a flat earth, all the stars "fall to earth" when the heavens are shaken. "And the stars . . . fell unto the earth, even as a fig tree casts her untimely figs, when she is shaken by a mighty wind" (Rev. 6:13). "And the stars will fall from the sky . . ." (Matt. 24:29 and Mark 13:25). Only on a flat earth with tiny stars hung above it to "light the earth," would their descent cause only negligible damage. This also explains why, according to Revelation 21, a "new heaven" has to be created to replace the one that "fell down" earlier.

Throughout Scripture the shape and construction of the earth is assumed to resemble that of a building (or a tent), having a firm, immovable foundation built by God, and a roof (or canopy) "stretched out" by God, overhead: "He established the earth upon its foundations, so that it will not totter, forever and ever" (Ps. 104:5). "The world is firmly established, it will not be moved" (Ps. 93:1). "For the pillars of the earth are the Lord's, and he set the world on them" (1 Sam. 2:8). "It is I who have firmly set its pillars" (Ps. 75:3). "Who stetched out the heavens . . . and established the world" (Jer. 10:12). "Who stretches out the heavens like a curtain and spreads them out like a tent to dwell in" (Isa. 40:22). "Stretching out heaven like a tent curtain" (Ps. 104:2). "In the heavens . . . in the true tabernacle [tent], which the Lord pitched, not man" (Heb. 8:2–3). "The One who builds his upper chambers in the heavens, and has founded his vaulted dome over the earth" (Amos 9:6). "Praise God in his sanctuary; praise him in his mighty firmament [i.e., sanctuary-shaped heavens]" (Ps. 150:1). Why no ball-shaped, or sphere-shaped descriptions of heaven or earth?

Also, why no mention of the earth's movement, except in terms of an "earthquake?" And why was the shaking of the earth equated with a shaking of the heavens and the stars above? "The earth quaked, the foundations of heaven were trembling" (2 Sam. 22:8). "The earth quakes, the heavens tremble" (Joel 2:10). Those were not mere "earthquakes," restricted to the surface of one relatively small planetary sphere. The biblical authors were attempting to depict a simultaneous convulsion of both halves of creation, God shaking the whole of creation from its roof to its foundation (namely, shaking the flat earth, and the heavens stretched out above the flat earth). "I shall make the heavens tremble, and the earth will be shaken from its place" (Isa. 13:13). "There was a great earthquake . . . and the stars of the sky fell . . . as if shaken from a tree" (Rev. 6:12, 13).

Of course, the book of Job does state, cryptically, that, "He hangs the earth on nothing, or, literally, without anything" (26:7). But that doesn't deny that God also hangs it solidly. Neither does such a verse suggest that the earth moved, or was spherical. Ancient Egyptian iconography, for instance, depicts *ka,* a personal power, directly supporting a flat earth disc. And, as Jeremiah 10:12 states concerning the mystery of the earth's ultimate support, which was an insoluble problem for ancient man, "He (Yahweh) . . . established the world by His wisdom; and by his understanding he has stretched out heaven."

Apropos of any discussion of the book of Job is the fact that later in the book, God rebukes Job for having said, "He hangs the earth upon nothing," because such a statement is more than any man has a right to declare with certainty. God replies to Job sarcastically, "Where were *you* when I laid the foundations of the earth? . . . On *what* were its bases sunk? . . . Have you understood (or examined) the expanse of the earth? Tell me, if you know all this!" (Job 38:4, 6, 18). Jeremiah also declared that the mystery of the foundation of the earth was one that only God would ever know the answer to, "If the . . . foundations of the earth (can be) searched out below, then I will cast off . . . Israel" (Jer. 31:37). In other words, just as Israel will never be totally "cast off," the foundations of the flat earth are portrayed as ever remaining a mystery to man.

Furthermore, neither does the author of Job, in other passages, refrain from presupposing the earth's "flatness." For instance, "[God's] measure is *longer* than the earth, and *broader* than the sea," "Who *stretched* the *line* on [the earth]?" and, "He looks to the *ends of the earth,* and sees everything *under the heavens*" (Job 11:9, 38:5, and 28:24). Not to mention Job 38:13, which speaks of dawn grasping the earth by its "extremity or hem" (Heb. *kanap*; cf. Num 15:38 and 1 Sam. 15:27) and shaking the wicked out of it. The picture is metaphorical, comparing the indubitably *flat* earth to a blanket or garment picked up at one end and shaken. In Job the flat earth's immobility is also asserted: God "leads forth" the constellations in "their season," instead of "leading forth" the earth in "its season." The earth, therefore, was considered immobile (Job 38:32), which agrees with the book of Joshua, where the sun, and not the earth, is commanded to "stand still"; and the book of Ecclesiastes, which says the sun must "return to the place from whence it arose" before it can "rise and set" again (Josh. 10:12–13 and Eccles. 5:1).

Against this vast array of scriptural evidence, inerrantists cite a single verse in Isaiah that they claim states the earth is a sphere, Isaiah 40:22, "He sits above the circle of the earth."

But there is an obvious link between Isaiah's "circle of the earth" and the "circle" inscribed at creation on the "surface of the waters" in Job and Proverbs. So, a *flat* circle appears like the most likely interpretation.

Moreover, if Isaiah had wished to write "*sphere, globe* or *ball* of the earth," instead of "circle," he could have done so, since he wrote elsewhere about a man being "rolled up tightly like a *ball*" (Isa. 22:18).

And in discussing the creation of the earth Isaiah did not say that God "rolled it up," but that God "spread out the earth" (42:5), the Hebrew word for "spread" being used elsewhere in the Bible to depict a "pounding" or "flattening."

This "spread out" earth also lies beneath tent-shaped heavens. According to Isaiah 40:22, "He stretcheth out the heavens as a curtain, and spreadeth them out as a *tent* to dwell in" (the last part of the very same verse inerrantists cite in favor of "sphericity").

Thus, I became convinced that Isaiah also viewed the earth as flat.

Finally, I discovered that the notion of a *flat, circular* earth also appeared in ancient Babylonian, Egyptian, and Greek iconography and literature.

In fact, so clear are the biblical verses concerning the earth's shape that many of the fathers of the Christian Church—Lactantius, Diodorus, Severianus, and Chrysostom, to name a few—insisted that Scripture taught that the earth was flat. Such a view was also defended by the Christian geographer, Cosmas Indicopleustes, in his sixth-century work, *Christian Topography.*

As late as 1935 in Zion, Illinois, Wilbur Glenn Voliva, the first Christian preacher to own his own radio station, advocated the biblical view of the world's flatness in contrast to "modern astronomy."

Lastly, according to a study conducted by the Harvard Smithsonian Center for Astrophysics during the 1980s, almost one-half of children aged ten years and younger in the United States and other countries believe the earth is flat. And those who say it is round picture "round" as a giant pancake or a curved sky covering a flat ground. One in four thirteen-year-olds also believes the earth is flat.

In other words, people living during the infancy of observational science, could hardly have avoided perceiving the world as flat. Indeed, it was so obvious to them that they never bothered to state outright that "the world is flat," until the idea of sphericity arrived contesting the notion of flatness. But, their figures of speech and iconography reveal what their view of the world's shape was.

17. Quoted in Bryan B. Sterling and Frances N. Sterling, *Will Rogers' World: America's Foremost Political Humorist Comments on the Twenties and Thirties—and Eighties and Nineties* (New York: M. Evans and Company, 1989).

Joe Barnhart:
Fundamentalism as Stage One

Our views and theories develop by raising difficulties and meeting those difficulties by explicating and qualifying our views. My fundamentalism eventually died the death of thousands of qualifications. . . .

After growing beyond it, I do not recall having any desire to return to it. Like influenza, it is something of which to be cured.

—Joe Barnhart

Joe Barnhart is professor of philosophy and religion studies at the University of North Texas, Denton, Texas, and author of *The Billy Graham Religion, The Study of Religion and Its Meaning, Religion and the Challenge of Philosophy, The Southern Baptist Holy War, The New Birth: A Naturalistic View of Religious Conversion* (coauthored by Mary Ann Barnhart), *Jim & Tammy: Charismatic Intrigue Inside the PTL,* and *Dostoevsky on Evil and Atonement* (coauthored by L. L. Kraeger). Barnhart is also the author of numerous articles, which have appeared in such publications as the *Harvard Theological Review, American Philosophical Quarterly,* and *Free Inquiry.* Barnhart is currently working on two novels.

It is important to distinguish fundamentalism as a worldview and perhaps as an attitude from individuals whose lives in varying degrees come under the control of the worldview.

As a youth I happened to come under the influence of fundamentalism and of adults who had come under it. Some of those people were exceedingly kind and supportive, and I am to this day grateful to them. Around the globe, children ordinarily find some nourishment within the sociocultural womb they happen to enter after leaving the maternal womb. If they are fortunate, the society they grow up in will provide numerous resources that make their lives reasonably enjoyable and meaningful.

I was fortunate in that some of the fundamentalists of my youth came under the partial influence of humanist ethics and were exposed to views of human nature that were not excessively burdened with categories of demons and original sin, convenient categories that some of the clergy have found useful in their drive to control the lives of others.

As a high school student I felt the need to attend at night the Southern Bible Institute in Knoxville, Tennessee, in order to deepen my understanding of the fundamentalism that I had embraced. Even though I was by far the youngest student in the institute, I felt warmly accepted and somewhat challenged.

As far as I can remember, two doctrines in particular became crucial to my developing young mind and heart.

At the age of perhaps sixteen I came to believe that without an error- free or infallible Bible to serve as the foundation of the Christian structure, the structure would collapse and possibly morality along with it.

A number of youths in the fundamentalist circle were and are today forced by a variety of circumstances to wrestle with the exceedingly painful question as to whether they are *really* saved and whether they can *remain* saved. The writings of a fundamentalist evangelist named John R. Rice convinced me as a struggling teenager that assurance of salvation was possible. Rice guided me to my first truly moving and exciting grasp of the Protestant doctrine of *justification by faith*. Also at that time, Rice convinced me that the Bible taught that once an individual repented and accepted Christ as Savior, he could never fall off the Ark of Salvation. Far from turning me into a libertine, however, this doctrine of *eternal security* freed me from the neurotic preoccupation with gaining and holding onto salvation. I came to feel sorry for Church of Christ friends who could not know from one week to another whether they were saved or were once again among the damned.

A few years later, when I learned Greek and was in seminary translating the Epistle to the Hebrews into English, I came to believe that the unknown author of that epistle did not lend support to the doctrine of eternal security. This did not greatly disturb me, however, since by then the doctrine of eternal security did not seem to me to depend upon the doctrine of the Bible as a wholly self-consistent document. To me, it seemed more honest and logical to trust in God for security of salvation than to tie my faith up with an increasingly entangled and dubious theory of the infallibility of the Bible. Eventually it became clear that some fundamentalist apologists had painted themselves into a corner by implying that it was easier to accept an infallible Bible than to accept the existence of a loving God. I spent considerable time and thought on this chicken-or-egg problem in epistemology.

Before going to seminary, I had studied some theology both in college and on my own, enough theology at least to allow me to wrestle personally with several of the major historical controversies. Looking back, I now conjecture that a number of the works that I read in English literature courses sowed seeds that slowly took root in my mind and conscience. For example, in *Paradise Lost* the Puritan poet John Milton raised almost in passing the profound question of why the Creator did not "find some other way to generate Mankind" rather than bring "innumerable disturbances on earth through Female snares." Over-looking Milton's male chauvinism, I could see that a profound point had been raised. Could not Omnipotence and Omniscience have found a better means of starting a new race? Why start with Adam and Eve, that notoriously flawed experiment which, according to orthodoxy's crowning speculation, had infected not only the entire human race for ages to come but the entire planet? Neither Milton nor orthodoxy succeeded in answering this simple question.[1]

The persistent enemy of fundamentalism is education. In the Southern Baptist Convention in which I grew up, fundamentalist preachers made perpetual war on the Baptist centers of higher learning. They professed to fear and abhor "liberalism," but their real fear was, and is, education. Even while earnestly denying it, fundamentalist preachers have consistently shown by their actions that they want Christian colleges and seminaries to become indoctrination centers. After graduating from a Baptist college, I remained theologically orthodox. But no longer was I a fundamentalist. I believed in the virgin birth, the physical resurrection, and so forth. But I also believed in *education*. As a Baptist, I had grown up with a fierce belief that each believer was a priest and that each person must seek truth for himself or herself. Others could help in the journey, I believed, but no one had a right to deny me or anyone access to views and arguments that promised to challenge me.

The Southern Baptist Theological Seminary in Louisville, Kentucky, was in the mid-fifties a remarkable center of learning. I was free to study, to challenge, to question, and to be challenged without fear of penalty, intimidation, or loss of fellowship. That air of freedom no longer exists at the Louisville seminary, however, for the fundamentalists have taken control of the board of trustees. Fundamentalists like Paige Patterson and Paul Pressler do not see themselves as enemies of education. Indeed, it might very well be that they regard education to be nothing other than indoctrination. Hence, since they believe in indoctrination, they honestly think they believe in education.

During my college years the difference between education and indoctrination became increasingly clear to me. During my first year at seminary I asked one of my professors for permission to do for credit independent research on the doctrine of the virgin birth of Christ. He encouraged me to study various views, and I remember how delighted I was to find and study in the seminary library J. Gresham Machen's highly acclaimed defense of the doctrine of Christ's virgin birth. Indeed, after graduating from the seminary I still believed in the virgin birth and continued to do so until my views shifted in another direction a number of years later, after considerably more reading and thinking. Today fundamentalist preachers regularly denounce the seminaries for undermining the faith of students, but the ultimate enemy of fundamentalism is still *literacy in an open environment,* one in which people are at liberty to think without fear of intimidation.

During my three years of intensive study at the seminary, I wrestled with the critical issue of the fate of the damned. Somewhere along the way my view of salvation modified and grew, so that the idea of salvation as fire insurance was no longer central. During my junior or senior year in seminary Calvinism strongly appealed to me, primarily because it promised to offer a plausible resolution to the free will vs. determinism issue, which had taxed my brain considerably during my college days. It was Calvinism's emphasis on divine sovereignty, however, that recommended itself to me primarily.

Often a solution to a problem creates new problems, which is what happened to me when I embraced Calvinism. How could I reconcile hard-core predestination with genuine divine love and the Golden Rule? (The latter rule seemed to make some fundamentalist preachers uncomfortable.) If my memory serves me well, I recall graduating from seminary as a Karl Barth Calvinist; that is, I embraced divine sovereignty, salvation by grace through faith, the theory of evolution, higher criticism, and probably either conditional immortality (unbelievers are permanently extinguished) or universalism.

After seminary, I was free to go to either (1) the University of Chicago to continue studying Greek and New Testament literature, (2) Princeton to specialize in theology, or (3) Boston University to study philosophy. I elected to pursue the Ph.D. in philosophy at BU. About a year into the program the problem of evil (theodicy) became once again important to me, so much so that I would eventually write half my dissertation on that thorny problem. The dissertation excited me greatly, for it allowed me to do a comparative study that was personally important to me. I compared the theodicy and epistemology of a leading evangelical scholar with that of a leading liberal scholar: E. J. Carnell versus E. S. Brightman. It became increasingly clear to me that the evangelical worldview was virtually bankrupt. Today, J. I. Packer and others are once again attempting to pump up the inerrancy of the Bible hypothesis, but it is a corpse that will not breathe on its own.

Brightman's approach to theodicy struck me as being a truly profound and morally heroic effort to embrace theism while at the same time facing squarely the problem of evil. While I have read a number of caricatures of Brightman's position, I have never found any other version of theism that measured up to it both intellectually and morally. It turned out also that Brightman's developmental view of the person offered a rather clear resolution, at least in my own mind, of the abortion controversy.

During my pilgrim's progress inside the fundamentalist territory I kept hearing that Bible-believing Christians, unlike liberals and others, took the Bible literally. Over the years, however, I came to see that C. I. Scofield and various other fundamentalist luminaries were highly selective in what they regarded as literal. In some cases the liberals, the neo-orthodox, and others proved to be more literalistic in interpreting early Hebrew and Christian literature. A fundamentalist pastor from Memphis indicated that every verse in the Bible should be taken literally unless there was a good reason not to. But what standard does a believer use to judge what is a "good reason"? It turned out that the Memphis pastor and others had an *a priori* belief system that they used to interpret biblical texts. This of course, raised the problem that continues to serve as fundamentalism's epistemological nemesis—the chicken-or-egg problem. Recently, some Southern Baptist pastors have affirmed *themselves* to be the authoritative interpreters of Scripture, as if the popes had not centuries earlier beaten them to the draw. The pastors' personal *a priori* belief system appears to have been fed by many sources, even though at times they seem to take it to be the original epistemological source, with the Creator presumably serving as the Original Source ontologically.

For several years after my fundamentalist phase I continued to believe in the *physical* resurrection of Jesus. A bit uneasy, however, with Christ's physical assumption into heaven, I sometimes wondered aloud if Jesus in heaven were still growing a literal beard and fingernails. Billy Graham had once remarked on national TV that one of the members of the Trinity could be distinguished from the others by the nail prints in his hands. Being something of a literalist myself, I later wondered about the following. Let it be supposed that while fasting, Jesus had permitted a physician to take a sample of his blood and a sample of his urine. Then sometime after the resurrection Jesus permitted a physician to take a sample of his blood and another of his urine. Would the postresurrection samples have matched biochemically with the preresurrection samples? Fundamentalists insist that the resurrected body of Jesus could walk through walls because it was glorified. With an inclination toward literalism, I could not help asking about the fish that, according to the Gospel of Luke, Jesus in his glorified state ate. When the fish entered his stomach, did it remain temporarily literal fish, or did it become instantly glorified? When Jesus appeared in a room whose doors were shut, did his clothes and sandals also pass through the barrier?[2]

Our views and theories develop by raising difficulties and meeting those difficulties by explicating and qualifying our views. My fundamentalism eventually died the death of thousands of qualifications. In addition, the steady process of translating biblical passages from either Hebrew or Greek eventually dissolved for me, although not for everyone, the hypothesis of an infallible book. I came to use the phrase *epistemological primitivism* to label the claim that a reader might simply pick up the Bible, or any large book, and read it free of all presuppositions, theories, and philosophical categories. I came to see in my seminary days that there is no such phenomenon as "simply reading" the Bible as if one were reading bathroom scales. The astounding advances of biblical scholarship during the past sixty-five years make it impossible for even modestly informed readers to say simply that they "believe the Bible." It must always be asked, What exactly about the Bible do I believe? And in what respect? When I read Plantinga and some of the modern philosophical defenders of evangelicalism, I keep wanting to urge them to talk with their own biblical scholars in order to understand that so-called "biblical Christianity" is not the simple and definite phenomenon that some once thought it to be.

Space prohibits going into further detail regarding my growth beyond fundamentalism. On the whole, fundamentalism as a worldview is, in my view, a truly miserable option, one that promises to leave most of the human race in torment in the Eternal Concentration Camp, the macabre "Final Solution" for Jews and all other non-Christians.

I came to see fundamentalism also as, at root, an anti-woman ideology. After growing beyond it, I do not recall having any desire to return to it. Like influenza, it is something of which to be cured.

Notes

1. Although much later the would-be theologian Alvin Plantinga could generate what appeared to be new arguments in, unfortunately, a rather tortured, first-draft style of writing. Eventually, his speculations proved to be largely less clear and cogent than some of those offered

by Leibniz, C. S. Lewis, Augustine, and the like. (It now appears that Plantinga has settled for becoming part-time custodian in the haunted house of orthodoxy, using entangled new ribbons and strings to prop up decayed theological carcasses. Stated in another way, he does Campus Crusade ontology in an idiosyncratic style that sometimes utilizes esoteric symbols.) [See Barnhart's paper, "Theodicy and the Free Will Defence: Response to Plantinga and Flew," *Religious Studies*, vol. 13, December 1977, pp. 439–53.—ED.]

2. In an interesting exchange between fundamentalist Norman Geisler (now at Falwell's Liberty University) and the evangelical New Testament scholar Murray J. Harris, the former raises the question of the latter's orthodoxy by charging that Harris does not believe in the physical resurrection. J. I. Packer and other fundamentalists have come to Harris's rescue. Apparently, Harris wants to say that the *essential* state of the postresurrection Jesus was one of customary invisibility and therefore immateriality. Harris then concludes that Jesus occasionally made himself "visible to the physical senses" of his disciples. Geisler of course wonders if Harris is not serving up a fancy form of gnosticism or at least docetism. I would like to know what Harris and Packard would say about the biochemical nature of the visible appearance. How much was mere *appearance*? My little experiment is of course designed to draw blood in more than one way.

Editor's note: In the *Expository Times*, 1990, the Rev. G. T. Eddy replied to the argument that Jesus' "body" was raised from the dead, by asking:

Did Jesus eat and drink after his resurrection? If so, what became of the food? Was it metabolized, with the obvious sequel of evacuation? And if the body, though "the same body as was crucified," was yet so transformed as to be able to appear and disappear, and enter and leave a locked room, did the fish and the honeycomb undergo instant transformation along the same lines as soon as they entered his mouth? . . .

Reflections upon questions such as these may well lead some, who wish to share the Christian faith in the Resurection, to conclude that the undoubtedly earlier account we find in 1 Cor. 15, with its simple verb *ophthe*, "he was seen," takes us nearer to the original experience than do the more colorful and conflicting narratives in the gospels. ("The Resurrection of Jesus Christ: A Consideration of Professor Cranfield's Argument," *The Expository Times*, vol. 101, no. 11, August 1990, p. 328)

Photo by Yvonne Henke

Kevin R. Henke:
A Little Horse Sense Is Worth
a Thousand Inerrant Doctrines

I was beginning to see that it was not primarily Christianity that had eventually transformed me into a better person. Emerging from adolesence, I became less selfish, more understanding, more patient, kinder, and nicer. My Christian friends wanted to attribute these virtues to my "growth in Christ" and "the Holy Spirit changing my life." However, I noticed that these virtues were also developing in many of my nonfundamentalist friends and family members. I began to realize that these changes were not supernatural, but rather we were all simply growing older and more mature. . . . I also began to notice that there was very little in the lives of nice Christians to distinguish them from nice non-Christians. . . .

[After] reading and rereading most of the Bible for many years, I had difficulty becoming enthusiastic about sections of the Bible that I had been through so many times before. I began to see less and less new and exciting insights in the Bible and more and more exciting and wiser things in secular books. Although my fundamentalist faith refused to admit it, the Bible appeared to offer few new ideas and solutions to the numerous issues and problems that I was beginning to face as a young adult. . . .

I also began to question myself: "What right did I have to upset other people's lives with a faith that did not make my life anything special?" I saw so many people leading happy and productive lives as either non-Christians or Christians. I saw miserable non-Christians, but I also saw miserable and chaotic Christian lives. Again, there did not seem to be much difference between nice Christians and nice non-Christians.

—Kevin Henke

Kevin R. Henke, a former young-earth creationist Christian, is presently in the Ph.D. program of the geology department at the University of North Dakota. The National Center for Science Education in Berkeley, California, sells diskette copies of two of Mr. Henke's extensive critiques of scientific creationism, *Science/ Creationism Reviews* and *The Origin of Theses*. The latter work takes a close and critical look at two "high quality" theses advocating a young earth that were composed for the master's degree program in "geology" at the Institute for Creation Research in San Diego, California. In the following piece Henke explains how even a Nebraska farmboy with plenty of horse sense and nonfundamentalist parents can be socially and psychologically intimidated into becoming a fundamentalist Christian, and how, in the end, common sense and freedom of thought can prevail.

I was born on April 17, 1957, in Friend, Nebraska. During the first eighteen years of my life I was raised on a farm about eight miles north of Friend, near the town of Beaver Crossing, Nebraska. I was baptized into the Beaver Crossing United Methodist Church as an infant. However, my parents were never very religious. They would occasionally send my younger brother and me to Sunday school and summer Bible school. Our family would also periodically attend church on Sunday mornings. However, at home we never read the Bible. Prayer was also very rare. My maternal grandmother or nieces would lead the family blessing at holiday dinners. When my paternal grandparents babysat my younger brother and me, my grandmother would pray with us before bedtime. My mother may also have led us in a generic "Now I lay me down to sleep" prayer when we were little, although I'm not certain about that. My maternal grandmother would occasionally talk to me about Jesus.

In late October 1963 my seventeen-year-old cousin was killed in a car accident. Now, my family, like most families in my hometown, had members from a number of different Christian denominations, including Roman Catholicism, Methodism, and Lutheranism. My cousin was Catholic and my mother had to explain death, heaven, and purgatory to my younger brother and me. Since I loved space programs on television, my mother explained to me that my cousin had become an angel and that heaven and purgatory were other planets that dead people go to. It was especially difficult for her to explain purgatory to a six-year-old. The way she explained it to me, I came to believe that purgatory was a brief layover for Catholics before going onto heaven, while Protestants, for some reason, did not get to go to purgatory.

At my cousin's funeral, I was told by my mother to do everything that the priest requested, except kneel. According to her, when the Catholics knelt during certain parts of the funeral, the non-Catholics were expected to sit. At six years of age, I did not understand all of the differences between the various churches. I noticed that the priest had a lot prettier clothing than our Methodist pastor and that the Catholics got to do some things during their church services that the Protestants did not get to do. However, I got the strong impression from my parents that people joined a particular denomination simply because their parents went there or because it was a matter of preference. We would all end up in heaven anyway.

In the early 1970s, my younger brother and I joined the local Methodist church. We went through the confirmation proceedings at the request of our parents, although they gave us the option to delay joining the church if we wished. However, because everyone in our confirmation class was joining, including my brother, I also decided to join.

About the same time I remember seeing a Billy Graham crusade on TV.

I "committed" my life to Christ because of the program. However, any changes in my behavior because of this commitment did not last for more than a couple of days.

In 1973 a couple of high school classmates of mine were reading apocalyptic books in school during the lunch hour, such as *The Late Great Planet Earth* and *666*. I was fascinated by the idea that the Bible could predict the end of the world and how books like Salem Kirban's *666* were "informing" people about the "end times." I bought a copy of *666* and read it. I again "committed" my life to Christ by signing the confession at the end of the book on my sixteenth birthday in 1973. However, once more, my life did not permanently change.

Church attendance for our family became a rare event and eventually ceased once our church became divided between the "traditional," almost secular Methodists, like my parents, and the "born-again" crowd that really took their religion seriously. This schism in the church occurred in the mid-1970s, when I was in high school. My parents detested the "born again" Christians and thought of them as a bunch of hypocrites, extremists, and self-righteous idiots. Our community consisted of a harmonious mixture of Roman Catholics, Lutherans, Methodists, other Christian groups, and nonbelievers. There was little or no tension between these groups. The Protestants helped the Catholics build their new church and the Catholics helped the Protestants with their projects. Except for the fundamentalist Christians, everyone respected each other. The traditionalists never attempted to evangelize each other or the minority of nonbelievers in our town. My parents and many other traditionalists looked upon the born-again Christians as bigots threatening decades of peace and tolerance in our small Nebraska community.

During my youth I feared the born-again Christians because I knew that they were much more Bible-literate than I was. I was afraid that they would misquote the Bible and use it against me or perhaps they would actually find valid verses to condemn me and other traditionalists. I actually decided not to attend a nearby conservative Lutheran college because they required that I take religion courses and I was afraid that my ignorance of the Bible would be exposed to ridicule. Furthermore, I was afraid that the courses would brainwash me into an ascetic, miserable, fundamentalist freak. So, in the fall of 1975 I ended up attending a United Church of Christ college in another nearby town. This college was secular, except for its deceptive motto: "We build on Christ." It was so secular that while I attended the school, there was not even a professional chaplain on campus. (This is really surprising since most secular universities, like the University of North Dakota, allow several organized ministries on campus!)

Although philosophy and religion courses were offered at this "church-run" liberal arts school, they were not required and they were all very liberal and nonsectarian. During the spring semester of my freshman year (1976), I took a philosophy course on classical religious and philosophical documents. This course included selected studies from the Bible. The professor was an extremely liberal Protestant. I remember while studying the Psalms that he would tell us which Psalms were well written, which were bad and self-righteous, and which had a mixture of good and bad intentions. His attitude surprised me. How could anything in the Bible be bad? Although I was never encouraged by my family to read the Bible, I was always given the impression by Sunday school teachers, television evangelists, and some family members that it was the "infallible, perfect word of God." My professor's attitude toward the Bible both worried and relieved me. I sometimes wondered if he and the entire class would be condemned to hell for blasphemy. At the same time, I was relieved that this book did not have to be used as an undefeatable weapon against me. According to this professor, the book had its faults just like any other book.

Around 1976–77, my parents received *The Watch Tower* and *Awake!,* which are periodicals from the Jehovah's Witnesses. I read these magazines, but I was not drawn into the Jehovah's Witnesses camp and neither were my parents. I was especially dissatisfied with the Jehovah's Witnesses' opposition to Catholics, American patriotism, and the possibility of miracles in the twentieth century. Again, part of my family was Catholic and so were many of my friends. I disliked the Jehovah's Witnesses' insensitive attacks on the Roman Catholic faith. I also found their "we're the only true Church" doctrines to be repulsive to the way that I was raised.

Conservative patriotism is also very strong in my family. My father and all of my uncles were veterans of the Second World War. So I did not like the pacifistic policies of the Jehovah's Witnesses. In my opinion, their pacifism was unrealistic and blindly dogmatic. Furthermore, I liked the idea of praying for miracles. I enjoyed hearing the "miraculous" testimonies of the television evangelists. However, from my point of view, the Jehovah's Witnesses seemed to be limiting the power and mercy of God by rejecting the possibility of miracles in the twentieth century.

During my sophomore year at college (1976–77), I had a roommate that attended a campus Bible study and informal worship group of born-again believers. My roommate used the tactics against me that I had long feared. Basically, he said that if I was a real Christian, I would seek fellowship. He suggested that I attend the meetings of the fundamentalist campus group with him. I kept putting him off. Again, I was afraid of ridicule.

In the summer of 1977, we took a family vacation to Colorado. While there, I heard an atheist on a radio program and I became very upset over the possibility that God might not exist. Up until then, I had never heard anyone preach against the existence of God. Although there were nonbelievers in my hometown, they never tried to evangelize me out of my theistic beliefs. I purchased several born-again testimonials and other religious literature during the trip to shore up my doubts. The reading materials convinced me to become born again. So, I did in June of 1977. This time I began to treat Christianity seriously.

During and after the summer of 1977 I read more of the Bible. While I was home from college on the weekends and during the summers, I was afraid to go into town and attend church. I did not want my parents to think that I was a "religious freak." However, I felt guilty about not attending church, so I frequently read the Bible on Sunday mornings.

In the fall of 1977, my old roommate dropped out of the conservative Christian culture and I joined it. At the invitation of a young woman, I started to attend the meetings of the campus fundamentalist group. This woman and I developed a romantic relationship that lasted from 1978 until the early 1980s. I also became deeply committed to Christian fundamentalism. This trend greatly disturbed my parents. They thought I was in a cult. During the late 1970s they would periodically send me newspaper articles about Jonestown and the Moonies and warn me about the dangers of the cults. I basically ignored them.

I finally began to read the Bible in its entirety. By the end of the 1970s, I had read and studied most of the Old Testament books at least once and most of the New Testament books several times. Much of what I read disturbed me, especially the violent parts of the Old Testament. Basically, I ignored the problems and told myself that the "apparent" contradictions and irrational verses were really not important issues. Jesus, I argued, would explain everything in the afterlife and fully compensate all those innocent children that had suffered in the times of the Old Testament. These arguments, along with the fear of God's wrath and the attractiveness and simplicity of fundamentalism, led me to accept the inerrancy and infallibility of the Bible. However, I continued to periodically have doubts about the reliability of the Bible as I read more of it. I tried very hard to suppress these doubts and ignore the contradictions and errors that I saw. Furthermore, I actually felt sympathy for the nonbelievers who faced the nagging evangelism of my fundamentalist allies, as my old roommate and others had nagged me. Such doubts, however, did help me to begin to understand how some people could be critical of fundamentalist Christianity.

The hypocrisy of fundamentalism was beginning to really annoy me by the late 1970s. I thought about becoming a liberal Christian, but liberalism seemed too subjective and heretical. The idea of abandoning Christianity altogether was simply too frightening to consider. I thought to myself: "How could I live without God and the promise of eternal life?"

Throughout the late 1970s I was also disappointed by the fact that God had not spoken to me in a clear and audible voice. Often I needed answers to questions that were not found in the Bible. These ranged from "What should I do for a career?" to "When should I go to bed tonight?" The Bible said that Jesus was my Lord, so why wasn't he giving me orders? How could I be a slave of Christ if I did not know what he wanted me to do? How were my prayers to be answered? My fundamentalist friends finally convinced me that I was too impatient and that God would reveal his desires to me when the time was right. Furthermore, they argued, I needed to concentrate on learning the basics of God's will from the Bible.

My reading of the Bible during the late 1970s and early 1980s created some problems between other fundamentalists and me. Particularly, my saved-by-grace-only fundamentalist friends did not like me finding and quoting the saved-by-works verses in Matthew, James, and Revelation. They quickly attempted to demonstrate to me that my personal Bible readings had not effectively emphasized the "right" parts of the Bible and properly "played down" the "less understood, more difficult, and seemingly contradictory" parts. They were also very creative at explaining away or "reinterpreting" the verses they did not like. In most cases, I submitted to their arguments, since I felt that they were more knowledgeable about the Bible than I was. Furthermore, in the case of grace versus works, I definitely preferred the doctrine of saved by grace only.

When I was a fundamentalist, I noticed that some fundamentalist preachers and teachers would build entire sermons or doctrines from single verses or even one or two words from the Bible. For example, creationists frequently use the word "circle" from Isaiah 40:22 to proclaim that "Isaiah" was miraculously told by God that the Earth was a "sphere" and therefore the entire Bible supports the notion of a spherical, rather than a flat, earth. These "word picking" fundamentalists justify such interpretational practices by saying that every word in the Bible is "inspired" and has "meaning." Therefore, one can rely on the "authority" of the Scriptures on a word-by-word basis (2 Tim. 3:16). Although not every fundamentalist would approve of building doctrines by emphasizing one word in the Bible or even an entire verse (notice 2 Tim. 2:14), the practice did have some support from the New Testament writers (e.g., in Gal. 3:8–16: the emphasis is on the word "seed" ["Christ"] rather than "seeds"). Verses like Galatians 3:8–16 clearly encourage "word picking" fundamentalism.

Of course, while my fundamentalist friends might admire a "creative" orthodox sermon based on one word from the Bible, they did not like me using single words from the Bible or even a series of verses to support "unorthodox" doctrines, like purgatory. In particular, I noticed that 1 Corinthians 13:13 seemed to support the existence of purgatory or at least the potential of a noneternal hell. The verse states that faith, hope, and love will remain or last forever. Now, according to fundamentalist Protestant traditions, everyone would either be in some sort of eternal heaven or hell after the Judgment Day. However, 1 Corinthians 13:13 suggests that hope will also last beyond the Judgment Day and forever. I immediately thought: "How could hope last forever? Hope for whom?" I finally concluded that the eternal hope could only refer to those in hell. Why do people in heaven need eternal hope? The saved have everything. They don't need to hope for anything. This verse was clearly indicating to me that those in hell had the eternal hope of eventually being freed from God's torment. Except for my new conservative Catholic roommate, my fundamentalist friends did not like my interpretation of this verse and they did not like me finding additional verses in 1 Peter to support purgatory or some sort of a noneternal hell.

In the late 1970s I did not realize that defining doctrines on the basis of one word was probably bad theology for everyone. Back then, I could not understand why my fundamentalist opponents were justified in using a single verse or word from the Bible to support their views, while I couldn't use the same "word picking" procedure to support nontraditional ideas. For me, the actions and biblical interpretations of my fundamentalist critics simply dripped with hypocrisy and inconsistency.

Between 1977 and sometime in 1981, my views of the Trinity were not always quite right for my picky fundamentalist friends. For example, at one time I had the tendency to view Jesus as being part of God rather than God. These views did not deny the deity of Christ or the existence of the Trinity. But, according to my fundamentalist friends, they were not quite consistent enough with traditional Trinitarian Christianity. My "errors" resulted from my exposure to the doctrines of the Jehovah's Witnesses and my own readings of the Bible. However, my fundamentalist friends eventually "corrected" my "heretical" views of the Trinity and "opened my eyes" to the "cultic" nature of the Jehovah's Witnesses.

In 1977–78, I became interested in geology after taking a couple of college courses. At that time, I strongly opposed biological evolution and was sympathetic and open to fundamentalist creationism with its young-earth and flood geology. I even defended fundamentalist creationism during a field project in Colorado in the summer of 1978. However, by 1979 I had studied enough geology to see that the version of creationism taught by fundamentalists was bogus. I become an old-earth creationist, but kept my anti-evolution views until the mid-to-late 1980s. Although as an old-earth creationist I no longer took Genesis 1–11 and some other parts of the Bible literally, I still strongly believed in the inerrancy and infallibility of the Bible. Furthermore, I remained very impressed by the biblical creation account. To me it represented a generally "accurate" geological description of how the world was created, told in poetic fashion.

In May 1979 I graduated with a B.A. in the physical sciences with minors in geology and physics. During the summer of 1979 I spent so much free time reading and memorizing Scripture that my parents really started to worry about me. In August I moved to North Dakota to attend graduate school at the University of North Dakota and to get my M.S. in geology. Once I arrived in North Dakota, I became very active in Inter-Varsity Christian Fellowship, which had a chapter on campus. Contrary to many misconceptions, this group has nothing to do with athletics. Instead, it is a largely fundamentalist interdenominational group that stresses evangelism. During the meetings of this group, fellow students would often rise up and read Bible verses that commanded us to evangelize. They were especially fond of citing Matthew 28:19–20, but doing it the way the National Rifle Association quotes the Second Amendment of the U.S. Constitution, i.e., just in part.

For instance, in the case of the Second Amendment, the NRA cites the last part, which states, ". . . the right of the people to keep and bear Arms, shall not be infringed." It forgets about the first part of the amendment, which explains the *reason* why this right was important. When such a right was first proposed in 1791 the government had no army to speak of and relied upon a "well regulated militia" to ensure our nation's security from external foes. Instead of taking a good long look at the entire Second Amendment—comparing the need for a nationwide "militia" in *early* America with today—the National Rifle Association only fires off part of the amendment, thus bypassing rational discussion, so that they may continue to oppose sane legal limitations on gun sales and ownership in modern-day America.

Similarly, evangelicals would read and emphasize the first part of verse 19 (in Matt. 20:19–20), which commands the disciples to go to all of the nations and preach, but largely ignore the rest of the verse and verse 20, which talk about the necessity of baptism and teaching obedience to the commandments of God. Obviously, the University of North Dakota Inter-Varsity chapter did not want to upset the Lutherans and Catholics within the group by promoting adult-believer baptism. Although the members of the group often talked about obeying the Bible, they clearly preferred to stay away from denominational controversies. I was again disturbed by their inconsistent use of the Bible and their unwillingness to oppose denominational practices that were clearly unbiblical.

From 1978 to 1985 my faith underwent several periods of turmoil. I had little peace with fundamentalism. Although I was tempted to reject the inerrancy and infallibility of the Bible and become a liberal Christian, I still looked at liberal Christianity as being heretical and even more inconsistent and hypocritical than fundamentalism. I became a pentacostalist for awhile. However, this did not improve things. Too many of the activities of the pentacostalists seemed to violate the Bible, and, as a fundamentalist, I did not like that. For example, it was not unusual for several pentacostalists to begin praying out loud in tongues during worship services, which seemed to violate the commands of 1 Corinthians 14. I even brought up this issue at a pentacostalist conference and a preacher ordered the "tongue speakers" to stop on my behalf. I was surprised, since it was not very often that I successfully got my fellow Christians to seriously consider my quotations from the Bible.

Some pentacostals also claimed to have the "gift" of prophecy, which means that these individuals could supposedly provide authoritative statements directly from God during a worship service. This "gift" bothered me as a fundamentalist. If people are acting as mouthpieces for God, why shouldn't we record these words and add them to the Bible? If they are statements from God, shouldn't they be included with the rest of God's Word, i.e., the Bible? However, I found the idea of stapling new verses onto the Bible to be completely unacceptable. I, like most conservative Christians, interpreted Revelation 22:18 as a likely prohibition against adding any words onto the Bible. The prophecy problem was another pentacostal dilemma that I could not deal with.

During the 1980s I was also beginning to see that it was not primarily Christianity that had eventually transformed me into a better person. Emerging from adolesence, I became less selfish, more understanding, more patient, kinder, and nicer. My Christian friends wanted to attribute these virtues to my "growth in Christ" and "the Holy Spirit changing my life." However, I noticed that these virtues were also developing in many of my nonfundamentalist friends and family members. I began to realize that these changes were not supernatural, but rather we were all simply growing older and more mature. I began to recognize that there were fewer and fewer miracles in my life. Most of the pleasant and surprising events in my life or in the lives of most of my friends could be attributed to ordinary, natural events. I also began to notice that there was very little in the lives of nice Christians to distinguish them from nice non-Christians.

Most of the time, I did not like nagging people with evangelism. Nevertheless, I obeyed the commandments to evangelize, since I wanted no one to go to hell. I evangelized on bus trips to Nebraska, in my dorm, on geology department fieldtrips, and elsewhere. Although I tried very hard to convince myself of the importance of evangelism, I simply could not become enthusiastic about evangelizing people into a religion that was becoming more and more of a disappointment for me. I also led prayer meetings and Bible studies. However, none of these activities seemed worth it. For example, in the prayer sessions, any answers to prayer seemed like coincidence and too many suffering people were not being helped by prayer. There were simply no miracles.

By the mid-1980s I had been reading and rereading most of the Bible for many years. I had difficulty becoming enthusiastic about sections of the Bible that I had been through so many times before. I began to see less and less new and exciting insights in the Bible and more and more exciting and wiser things in secular books. Although my fundamentalist faith refused to admit it, the Bible appeared to offer few new ideas and solutions to the numerous issues and problems that I was beginning to face as a young adult.

I continued to feel bad about evangelism. My evangelism frequently upset non-Christians and created resentment rather than a desire for Christ and his Church. I was told by the student leaders of the University of North Dakota chapter of Inter-Varsity Christian Fellowship that non-Christians are curious about our faith. They watch our Christian behavior and are drawn towards having the peaceful relationship with God that we "enjoy." However, with one or two exceptions, I saw little interest in fundamentalist Christianity by non-Christians. I also began to question myself: "What right did I have to upset other people's lives with a faith that did not make my life anything special?" I saw so many people leading happy and productive lives as either non-Christians or Christians. I saw miserable non-Christians, but I also saw miserable and chaotic Christian lives. Again, there did not seem to be much difference between nice Christians and nice non-Christians.

My romantic relationship with my fundamentalist girlfriend, who remained in Nebraska, eventually ended about 1981. I was rebaptized by full immersion around 1981 or 1982 during a trip to Nebraska. This was something that I had wanted to do for some time. In 1983 I met and married Yvonne and began my present job at the Energy and Environmental Research Center at the University of North Dakota. I graduated in May 1984 with an M.S. In the fall 1984 our daughter, Erin, was born.

In the mid-1980s the hypocrisy of Christian fundamentalism became totally unbearable to me. I ran into a group of Mormon missionaries. I read part of the Book of Mormon and tried to gather together as many criticisms of Mormonism as possible. It was easy to find books by fundamentalist Christian authors that contained useful and effective arguments that exposed the irrationality of Mormonism and the Book of Mormon. However, these anti-Mormon authors also unwittingly exposed many similar flaws in their own faith and the Bible. For example, fundamentalist Christians attacked the scientific inaccuracies in the Book of Mormon. However, the scientific inaccuracies of Genesis 1–11 were either ignored or defended with irrational creationist arguments. What was the difference between the scientific absurdities of the fundamentalist creationists and those of the Mormons? The Mormons were also attacked for using the lame excuse of "Well, Jesus will explain everything in the afterlife—just trust and believe in our faith." Again, the same excuse was frequently used by fundamentalists to brush off criticisms of the Bible and their version of Christianity.

Fundamentalist Christians complained that Mormonism is a prime example of a religion that started with a handful of followers and went on to deceive millions of people in less than 150 years. But couldn't the same claim be made against Christianity? The "prophecies" in the Book of Mormon were called forgeries made after the fact. However, didn't liberal Christians and skeptics have evidence that said the same thing about the book of Daniel? Mormonism was attacked as being emotional and subjective. But fundamentalist testimonies were often filled with the benefits of having a "peace that passes all understanding." Isn't that emotional and subjective? Fundamentalists were also fond of pointing out the parts of the Book of Mormon that were clearly plagiarized from the King James New Testament (e.g., Moroni 10:8f and 1 Cor. 12). However, it did not take much effort to see that part of 2 Peter was plagiarized from Jude; Revelation from parts of Daniel and Ezekiel; and the genealogies of 1 Chronicles 1 were copied from Genesis 5, 10, and elsewhere. Although the Bible, unlike the Book of Mormon, contains some historically accurate materials, I was beginning to see that the Bible and Christianity were far from perfect.

Finally, in 1985, I became courageous and intellectually honest enough to reject the inconsistencies and hypocrisy of fundamentalism. I became a "liberal" Christian. I believed that the Bible contained the word of God, but that some parts were fallible and human made. Supposedly the Holy Spirit and the Christ-like mind would help the believer to identify which verses of the Bible were reliable and which were not. This approach seemed to work well for a while. As a liberal, I argued that certain verses applied to everyone (e.g., 1 Cor. 13:1), some verses applied to some people (e.g., Matt. 28:19), and some verses were not good for anyone to quote (e.g., Ps. 109:10).

A few years after my liberal conversion, my views were sharply attacked by my moderately conservative Southern Baptist pastor. He criticized me for placing my mind above the Bible. He advised me to resubmit my mind to the authority of the Bible. I considered taking his advice. That is, I seriously thought about reaffirming the infallibility of the Bible and becoming a fundamentalist again. However, I could not. I never wanted to go back to the hypocrisy, misery, in-effectiveness, and disappointment of Christian fundamentalism.

Some of my fundamentalist acquaintances warned me that I would soon completely abandon Christianity. They said that by rejecting part of the Bible, I would soon reject the entire book and the Christian faith. One woman even suggested that I would be better off not reading "certain" books and magazines. I cringed at the thought of this "ignorance is bliss" attitude. What good is a faith that cannot stand up to simple questions and criticisms?

Now, I certainly recognize that many liberals can reject part of the Bible and retain a stable faith that will last for the rest of their lives. However, for me, this was not the case. The fundamentalists were right: my liberalism eventually evolved into disbelief. In the late 1980s, I began to read more literature that was skeptical of the virgin birth, the resurrection of Christ, and other Christian doctrines. Much of this literature came from Ed Babinski and his ex-fundamentalist friend, Bob Price [both of their testimonies are in this book—ED.]. I began to recognize that just because God could do something, that does not mean that he did.

I also did an indepth study on the book of Revelation, called "Revelations on Revelation." I was surprised how easily Revelation could be interpreted once it was read as a piece of poorly edited fiction from the middle to late first century A.D. Obviously, the book was largely plagiarized from Old Testament and apocryphal works.

Notice that the New Jerusalem of Revelation 21:16 has the dimensions of

1,500 miles by 1,500 miles by 1,500 miles. This means that the length of the sides of this cubic "city" is approximately one fifth the diameter of the earth! How can a 1,500 miles × 1,500 miles × 1,500 miles cube fit on a spherical earth with a diameter of only 8000 miles? Either the cube, the earth, or both must be severely deformed. Under natural conditions, a "cube" that size would create all kinds of structural, geological, and meteorological problems. "John" apparently realized that such a huge cube could not land on an earth with mountains and deep oceans, so they were eliminated (Revelation 16:20; 21:1). However, "John" was, no doubt, a flat-earther, since he ignored the problems relating to the curvature and spin of the earth. Interestingly, the distance between Rome and Jerusalem is roughly 1,500 miles. For "John," such a huge cube was clearly meant to crush the Roman Empire and especially the two major cities of the "known, flat" world. Revelation is a very interesting story about the culture of that time, but the contradictions and errors definitely show that the book has little or no divine inspiration in it.

Soon after my rejection of the inspiration of Revelation and several other New and Old Testament books, I began to realize how mythical and unreliable Genesis was. Genesis was no longer the beautiful poetry that reflected the facts of geologic history, but rather ancient campfire stories that were no more accurate or inspired than other mythologies.

The death of my grandmother in 1989, several months before the birth of my son, Kyle, also increased my skepticism about an afterlife and helped me to move into agnosticism. My grandmother had been very senile for a number of years. Although her last years were painless, I saw her die slowly over almost eight years of conspicuous senility. As her brain died, she began to forget her short-term memories. She kept asking us the same questions over and over again when we would visit her. Eventually, she failed to recognize even her closest relatives, like my father (her only surviving child). I began to ask myself: "How can a soul restore memories after death that have been lost by the brain during life? If my grandmother no longer remembered her own family in the late 1980s, how could she remember them in heaven? Where was her soul and its copy of her memories during her lifetime? How is the soul different than the brain?" I finally concluded that there are no souls or spirits, only brains; and when a person's brain dies, his or her personality is permanently extinguished.

In 1990, I began to realize that I really did not have any outstanding "miracles" in my life. Everything that happened to me had a natural explanation. I could no longer find impressive evidence for the existence of God that outweighed the arguments of the atheists. So I became an agnostic. Now, some people might consider agnosticism to be a confused, cowardly, and noncommittal position. However, I don't look it at that way. Agnosticism is an intellectually honest position, because it states that there is not enough evidence to commit oneself to a faith that is based on accepting the existence of deities that cannot be readily seen or even detected. On the other hand, the agnostic is not so bold as to deny the possibility that one or more deities may exist somewhere in our largely unexplored universe.

As an agnostic, I am now free from having to defend or believe in other people's inconsistent and illogical doctrines. I have finally found the peace and consistency that I had been wanting for many years. My basic philosophy is to treat others as I want to be treated. Unlike the elaborate claims of Christianity, this universal golden rule works very well for me. My philosophical outlook on life is now based on logic and argument rather than hypocritical and subjective holy books, church doctrines, faith by fear and habit, and the words of theologians. I am free to pursue beauty and accuracy and to accept whatever is logical and good. I can reject the hypocritical, the tyrannical, and the dogmatic, no matter where it exists. I can also move into atheism or back into theism, if the evidence demands it. I have returned to the democratic socialist values that I had before I became born again. I joined the Democratic Party and now I support secular and mostly liberal policies. However, I am also free to remain a strong secular pro-lifer and to oppose the abortion-tolerant views of most other secular humanists. (I became an advocate of the unborn for secular reasons around 1969.) Unlike the fundamentalists, most secular humanists that I know are not issuing doctrinal commands or threatening to brand me as a heretic if I do not agree with them on every issue. I can also watch whatever I want on TV, listen to rock music instead of hymns, and sleep in on Sundays. I enjoy this freedom. The freedom to think for yourself, without limitations, is the most precious "good news" that I can give to my children or anyone else who asks!

Sam Keen: To a Dancing God

The crisis came in the early hours of a February morning within view of the Harvard Yard. The armies of the Lord faced the army of Truth. On the one side was all that I had believed about heaven and earth and my dazzling aspirations toward purity, sanctity, and obedience to a known God. On the other side a restlessness in the loins, a handful of facts that would not be denied, and a wilderness which hinted of both terror and adventure.

—Sam Keen

Sam Keen has described himself as "a lover of questions, a freelance thinker, a man rich in friendship and, in a former life, a professor." A popular lecturer and prolific writer, his works include *Apology for Wonder, Gabriel Marcel* (Makers of Contemporary Theology Series), *The Passionate Life: Stages of Loving, The Faces of the Enemy: Reflections of the Hostile Imagination* (which he also made into a film that appeared on PBS), and *Hymns to an Unknown God: Awakening the Spirit in Everyday Life*. The following was excerpted from Keen's autobiographical odyssey, *To a Dancing God.*

It was in Tennessee that I first learned about the history of my native land, in . . . Sunday school rooms covered with pictures and maps of the Holy Land. Before I was six I had walked through Judea, Galilee, Capernaum, Bethlehem, Jerusalem, sharing a dusty road with Jesus and the disciples, finding at day's end the comfort of a footbath, bread and olives in a humble home.

And what a rich time and place it was to which I belonged! Over these hills and desert places my forebears—Abraham, Isaac, David, and Solomon—had roamed, killing the enemies of the Lord and establishing a kingdom for the children of promise. From papier-mache models I learned the architecture of the Holy Land, and from bathrobe dramas its way of dress. . . . I learned of Deborah's heroism (but not of Molly Pitcher's) and of the judges and kings the Lord raised to lead and chastise his people (but not of the judges of Blount County who helped to keep whiskey illegal and bootlegging profitable).

I knew the topography of Judea before I could locate the Cumberland Plateau, as I knew the road from Damascus to Jerusalem before I could find my way from Maryville to Knoxville.

Sitting astride the Holy Land was the figure of Jesus, my model, my savior, my judge, and my Lord. Jesus loved me, this I knew. I had a friend in Jesus who could walk with me in Tennessee and give me guidance, succor, and assurance.

Although I sang "It may not be on a mountain top or over a stormy sea, it may not be on the battle front, my Lord will have need of me," I had every good hope that I would be permitted the privilege of manning a post where the battle with the enemies of the righteous raged strong. I longed to be counted with the heroes and saints. I prepared for the place Jesus would assign me in history by arming myself with the Word of Truth (the Bible—King James Version—Scofield notes) and by keeping in frequent contact with headquarters by way of prayer.

There was not often doubt in my mind about what Jesus required, although there was frequent resistance when I suspected that the enemies I was called upon to love and convert to the faith were none other than the dreaded Long boys, whose depravity was obvious (they smoked real cigarettes filched from their father's store while the rest of us were limited to rabbit tobacco and corn silk).

I was sometimes fearful that the final test of discipleship might confront me—the choice between my parents and the Lord. Although the evidence suggested they were among the most loyal disciples of Christ, I knew that someday a decisive moment would come when I would have to demonstrate my total commitment in some mysterious and unnatural way. "Once to every man and nation comes the moment to decide. . . ." For the time being, Jesus required only gentleness and abstinence from the obvious sins (smoking, lying, stealing, swearing, going to the movies, questioning orthodox theology, sex, and a frivolous enjoyment of the world).

With all seriousness and commitment I prepared for the hard task of living as a heavenly exile in the midst of a sinful world. A wayfaring stranger traveling through this world of woe must be armed against the seductions of this age. There was always the danger that cheerfulness might break in and dispel the serious truth that all men are sinners whose only hope is in casting themselves on the mercy of Jesus Christ.

Of course I constantly fell short of the ideal of Jesus, repented, and renewed my resolve to follow in the footsteps of the Master. Although I knew the sanctity required of me was not within range of my will power, there was the ever-present possibility that the kingdom of God would arrive momentarily and purge me of my unholiness.

In the small towns of Alabama, Florida, and Tennessee in which I lived it was common knowledge among the righteous that we were living in the Last Days before the end of the world. There was widespread disagreement about the details of the coming kingdom. Some considered Mussolini to be the beast with 666 upon his forehead who, according to the book of Revelation, would usher in the kingdom of evil that was to arrive shortly before the triumph of the saints. Some accorded this honor to Hitler. Not a few staunch Republicans were certain that Franklin Delano Roosevelt was the Antichrist.

In my childish mind the situation was vastly confused because 666 was also the trade name of a widely advertised headache remedy. Each rival candidate for the Antichrist had loyal followers who could prove their claimant's case with cryptic quotes from Daniel, Revelation, or Mark 13.

I seem to recall that once in a fit of anger I announced that my brother was the "abomination of desolation" (as indeed he could be). There was lively controversy whether Jesus was to establish his dominion immediately or only after defeating the Antichrist and overthrowing his one-thousand-year kingdom. To the pagan or worldly-wise this may seem an academic issue. But to those who were awaiting the immediate conclusion of history it was of some concern whether they were to be ushered into the premillennial reign of the Antichrist or the kingdom of God.

Whatever minor differences in interpretation clouded the picture, the outline was clear. The present age was the decadent conclusion of history. Evil had progressed in its dominion over history to the point where God was forced to intervene. Christians were exiles and pilgrims in this evil age of creeping socialism, modernism, loose morals, and increasing leisure. Salvation belonged only to those who were willing to forsake the ways of the world and live for the coming kingdom.

It was strongly implied that the only authentic vocation for the born-again Christian was preaching the gospel to the pagans and bringing the saving knowledge of Jesus Christ to the world. The future belonged to those who planned for it, who turned their present into a quest for sanctity. Anything less than total allegiance to Jesus was betrayal. The authentic life combined disdain and suspicion of the present age with nostalgia for the Holy Land and longing for the kingdom which was to come.

As I approached puberty my nostalgia for ancient Israel and for the New Jerusalem came into conflict with a dark longing that was born in dreams of ecstasy. The voice of the body called me back into the present. The contest between Jesus who was Lord of the past and the future and the life-sap that rises in the green body of adolescence proved unequal. My loyalties split.

Even as my spirit hoped for the triumph of holiness, my body prayed that the kingdom would not arrive and find me still a virgin. It was impossible to rejoice in the promises that "in Christ there would be neither male nor female" and that in the kingdom of God there would be no marriage when I had not yet enjoyed the mystery of sex.

It was some time after my body began to demand satisfactions more immediate than those promised by the kingdom of God that my mind also joined the rebellion. With rising anxiety I discovered that the history I had taken as the basis of my identity was fallible. Historical and textual criticism of the Bible yielded a high degree of probability that many of the old, old stories were only that. The evidence suggested that many of the "mighty acts of God" did not happen and that the whole schema of promise and fulfillment which was the heart of the Christian idea of history was superimposed by the biblical authors *ex post facto*.

I learned of messiahs before and after Jesus who died as martyrs; and of the long process of political and ecclesiastical infighting which only gradually created the orthodoxy I had believed to be inseparable from the events. And I learned of gnostic redeemers who came to earth (or almost to earth) and died and rose again. As the conclusion became inevitable—my history as an Israelite had been constructed by men and not by God—my mind joined with my body in demanding that I leave Israel and come home to America.

The crisis came in the early hours of a February morning within view of the Harvard Yard. The armies of the Lord faced the army of Truth. On the one side was all that I had believed about heaven and earth and my dazzling aspirations toward purity, sanctity, and obedience to a known God. On the other side a restlessness in the loins, a handful of facts that would not be denied, and a wilderness that hinted of both terror and adventure.

The issue was so drawn for me, that the choice was between remaining a Christian or becoming honest. The armies defending the Holy Land fought to the last before yielding. Exhausted, I slept. I awoke at noon in Cambridge, Massachusetts, U.S.A., and after coffee and rolls, began to create the world. . . .

I have a growing conviction that the Christian presence in Western civilization has perpetuated a disease in order to offer a cure. It has encouraged schizophrenia by insisting that man is a sinner (estranged from self, others, nature, and God) who can do nothing to save himself. Indeed, all attempts at self-help are [viewed as] indications of pride which only deepen sin. . . . Nor is it possible, as liberals attempt in every generation, to remove the idea of vicarious atonement from the heart of the gospel. The hard core of Christian tradition has always insisted upon the impotence and bondage of the human will. It has said loud and clear— "You can't. You can't heal yourself. Your only hope is in accepting *the* physician sent from God" (whose credentials are certified by the church).

There is increasing (soft) evidence which suggests that reliance upon an exterior medium of salvation (whether the nostrum offered be church, state, psychiatrist, astrologer, drug, or some guru recently arrived from the East) fosters a passive-dependent style of life in which the responsibility for personal growth is evaded. This we know about psychopathology—at the heart of "illness" is the impotent child who is still crying, "I can't. You do it for me." And it is clear that the moment in therapy when the patient begins to "get well" is when he says, "I am responsible for my feelings, my actions, and my style of life. In spite of parents, family, friends or the surrounding culture, I alone can make the decision to outgrow my dis-ease and to establish a way of life that is satisfying."

[Furthermore,] Christian theology subtly devalues . . . feeling and sensation in favor of obedience to the authority which preserves the crucial memory. . . . Unless we are able . . . to get away from the idea that obedience (intellectual or moral) to some external authority . . . is the prerequisite for healing, we will not be able to understand that grace which comes from the viscera and which is available wherever beauty or tenderness may be found—in a flower in a crannied wall, or in the morning sun on a California beach . . . that grace which sometimes overtakes me in looking at the sea, or in making love. . . .

There is an element of succor and healing in certain sensuous experiences. There is grace in the harmony of color and in caressing winds as well as in words of friendship and the conversation of flesh and flesh. . . .

Nor is it the case that the instinct for self-preservation dictates that each man should protect only his own flesh. The normal visceral reaction to carnage is to be nauseated and want to vomit. This constitutes the deepest possible witness to the reality of universal identification.

The viscera is not separated from the imagination, except by the inhuman decommissioning of the conscience which national governments undertake to perform in time of war.

The healthy imagination creates a visceral connection between the self and other selves. Note, for instance, how the young mother flinches when her child is given an injection. The stomach knows that what happens to one happens to all, even if the mind tries to deny it. Its indigestible outrage is an index of the ability of the flesh to locate sacrilege.

Thus a categorical imperative issues from the viscera: "Reverence the flesh of all men as you reverence your own." This imperative rests upon compassion or dramatic identification with the flesh of another. It is this identification which is the basis of ethics. Obligation arises out of feeling, the categorical imperative out of compassion (contrary Kant). Men with any feeling for the inviolability of their own bodies would not tolerate the violation of other men's bodies. . . .

I think I would like to define the philosophical position I prefer at the moment as *trustful agnosticism*. I accept my life in wonder as a gift to be enjoyed responsibly, but I remain ignorant about the totality which is my ultimate context. I aspire to trust myself to the happenings which interweave with my energies to form an incarnate and situated person. I am not uncomfortable in saying that my trust in the ultimate context of my life is invested in God, provided the word "God" is not used more than once a year and is then handled like the Ark of the Covenant.

Austin Miles: Don't Call Me Brother

The break [with the ministry and the church] had been difficult, but once it was done, I felt free . . . like a captive released from prison . . . reborn—into real life. . . .

—Austin Miles

Austin Miles is an internationally known ringmaster who appears in selected circus engagements. In addition to his involvement with the Assemblies of God ministry he has been a lecturer, entertainer, producer, and television, stage, and film actor. The following excerpts have been compiled (with some altering of the original material to comply with space constraints) from Miles's autobiography, *Don't Call Me Brother: A Ringmaster's Escape from the Pentecostal Church*. Due to the enthusiastic response that volume received, Miles followed it with another, *Setting the Captives Free: Victims of the Church Tell Their Stories.*

Sunday in 1938 in Evansville, Indiana. . . . The North Park Presbyterian Church was filled. . . . Sunday school children were singing, "Jesus loves me, this I know, for the Bible tells me so. . . ." [I] seemed particularly to enjoy the words. . . .

Most of the congregation kept their distance from my mother and me [her five-year-old son]. As we [left the church] some conversations dropped to whispers and others stopped altogether. One congregant was heard to say, "There *she* is . . . she's nothing . . . she's *divorced* you know!" . . .

My mother stopped at Garvins Park. . . . [She] was saying, almost frantic, "The church regards me as a *fallen woman,* a *Jezebel!* because I am divorced. And I couldn't even help it—he left us! . . .

My mother, crushed by the separation and ensuing divorce . . . had turned to the Christian church for comfort. Now, she was in a worse state than ever. . . .

[At fourteen Miles joined the Tom Packs Circus and became "Kokomo" the clown.] The circus provided me with the first place of emotional security I had ever known. . . . A strong sense of family prevailed in the circus. What's more, they were positive, energetic, good people in every sense of the word. Not at all like they were portrayed in the movies. . . .

[Miles appeared in] a Broadway smash . . . "The Littlest Circus." [Afterward] I was billed as "Kokomo, the World's Greatest Clown." . . . I set my professional sights on becoming a ringmaster . . . and [became] the official ringmaster for the most prestigious Shrine Circus engagements in the United States and Canada. . . .

[During a performance a person in the audience had a heart attack. Miles had someone radio for an ambulance and asked if there was a doctor or nurse in the audience.] A nurse felt his pulse, then put her head to his chest. She began to massage his chest, then pounded on it. [She checked his pulse and chest again] . . . looked up and shook her head. Some men . . . pounded his chest desperately. The nurse checked again. They all shook their heads. . . .

The audience grew restless. . . . To prevent the audience from standing up and leaving—losing them to the fair going on outside the Big Top—I made a sudden expansive gesture and intoned, "I'm going to ask now—that everyone here who has the faith—please bow your heads—and in your own words, and in your own way—pray earnestly for this man."

The atmosphere in the tent turned into an eerie, intense silence. A strange tingling sensation went through my body like a mild electric shock. It unsettled me for a moment. Out of the corner of my eye I saw the ambulance attendants arrive, put the man on a stretcher, and take him out. . . . Into the microphone, I said, "Amen." . . .

The next afternoon . . . Ruby Landrus [the dwarf clown], told me she was "standing right next to the chap. . . . I bowed me 'ead, but kept one eye on 'im. . . . Things got tremendously quiet. Then, I felt a power go through me whole body! And the chap started breathin' again. . . . Oh, the chap completely recovered and they sent 'im 'ome from the 'ospital." . . .

It seemed as if every person who had been in that circus tent the night before had come back, just wanting to talk. They all agreed that at that precise moment they felt a strange tingling sensation. . . .

Had the man actually been dead, or had he only appeared so? Did the emotion of the moment that swept the crowd create a false impression of the situation, magnifying what had actually happened out of proportion? A steady stream of believers were proclaiming to me that God had performed a miracle. Even if one rejected that view, it had still been an extraordinary experience.

After the last performance that day . . . my eyes settled on a Gideon Bible on the dresser. . . . I flipped it open. My fingers came to rest on James 5:15: "And a prayer of faith shall save the sick, and the Lord shall raise him up. . . ."

I flipped some more pages, as if trying to bury the scripture I had just read and never see it again. . . . My fingers came to rest on Matthew 18:20: "For where two or three are gathered together in my name, there I am in the midst of them." . . .

[Soon afterward] I went to a Christian Businessmen's luncheon. . . . I prayed "the sinner's prayer" . . . and became a "born again" Christian. . . . [Miles began walking around the circus with his Bible in full view.] I pushed my chin out piously. . . . It was a defensive but strong posture. . . .

After that, it got easier. I did feel a strange new confidence and strength. I shouldn't have worried what nonbelievers thought of me. . . . If anything, they were to be pitied. Hopefully, one day they too would realize the truth and be saved. . . .

I received the Baptism of the Holy Spirit . . . at a Full Gospel Business-men's meeting. . . . I had gone through the ritual several times. Finally, I let out a string of unintelligible syllables. I had not felt anything earthshattering within or outside my body at the time, but the evangelist Robert Thom declared that I had received it. After receiving that "second blessing" I was recognized as a Pentecostal Christian. . . .

I [began appearing on radio and at churches] . . . I basked in the tremendous outpouring of love and acceptance by Pentecostal Christians . . . which served to draw me to the Assemblies of God church. . . . Many spoke of my "anoint-ing." . . . [One woman said she saw an aura around Miles's head as he spoke.] . . .

[One minister asked about Miles's wife.] I had spoken affectionately of Rose Marie in my talk that Sunday. . . . "Is she saved?" he asked.

"No," I said.

"Hopefully that will change," he answered. "We'll pray for her" . . . implying that she was now our spiritual inferior.

The more Christian teaching I took in, the more stricken I felt about the "self-centered" life I had led. . . . [Simultaneously, Miles's faith made him feel superior.] . . . It was the perfect antidote to my lingering childhood sense of rejection that had left me feeling unsure of myself despite my successes. It was the ultimate acceptance. It would induce me to display my Christianity more and more, and to give larger and larger cash gifts. . . .

To my own surprise, I found myself explaining how, even with all my worldly successes, something had seemed to be lacking in my life. I had been sold on the idea that my previous life, before I was "born again," had not been an entirely happy life. . . .

[One pastor phoned after Miles had testified at his church to tell him that a man was completely healed after his prayer.] "His doctor has confirmed it and is astonished. He said that Mr. Clark had the worst case of prostate cancer he had ever seen in a fifty-year-old man, in his twenty-five years of practice." . . .

The Assemblies of God is one of the fastest-growing denominations in the world. . . . In 1987 they were increasing at the rate of 307 churches per year. . . . They wanted to do an [evangelistic] booklet on me . . . [titled] "The Ringmaster Meets Jesus." . . .

[One of their previous booklets] was titled, "J. Edgar Hoover Testifies." . . . Christian testimony? Hoover, the late head of the FBI, was the most ruthless, power-mad individual who ever inhabited Washington, D.C. Suspicions about his bizarre sexual perversions were confirmed by the revolting pornography collection found in his home after his death. . . . He had been an unbridled homosexual! . . . With difficulty I squelched my negative thoughts for the time being. . . .

[After one service] a couple told me, "We just saw the movie *Marjoe* about an evangelist fraud, and decided on the spur of the moment to come to your meeting for a few laughs. But we saw something real here tonight, and want to give our hearts to Jesus!"

How ironic! Marjoe Gortner's grandparents helped found the Assemblies of God in 1914. They had the money-making potential of such a movement figured out well in advance. The family made Marjoe into a child evangelist with "special gifts." They put glitter in his hair, sewed extra-deep pockets in his clothing to hold the money, and pushed him mercilessly as they merchandised God. Marjoe grew up to be sick of the fraud and got out of the Assemblies of God altogether, but not before making the scathing documentary *Marjoe,* exposing the movement's more tawdry aspects. The documentary won an award, and Marjoe later had a degree of success as a movie actor.

By the time I saw *Marjoe* I had been so totally swept up in Pentecostalism that the message of the film escaped me. I had accepted the stock explanation for such things: It was just one more attack by the devil to try to stop the Word of God. . . .

Rose Marie was distancing herself from me. Still worse, I did nothing about it. Being a man called of God, I was to keep my eyes on Jesus only. Besides, the acclaim I was *receiving* proved that God's blessing was upon me. . . . Nothing else mattered. . . .

[Assemblies of God insiders saw to it that wherever Miles's secular career took him—Miles was now the announcer for the famed Royal Lipizzan Stallion Show—he had invitations to speak in nearby Assemblies of God churches.]

Gradually, I stopped reasoning things out and stopped looking beneath the surface of events. Passively, I let my thoughts be programmed into that unquestioning, blind faith that the pastors carefully instill in the faithful as the only way to know God. That narrowing of my view, that closing of my mind, had become a vise that choked off free will and intelligent action. Instead, I let them fill my mind with stereotyped thoughts and falsified feelings. The displacement of my true thoughts and feelings produced a euphoric state and a sense of release from the evils, cares, and responsibilities of this world. It was like sweeping all those things under the rug. There was no room to question or challenge; such thoughts were simply enemies of faith. The pastor to whom one should submit would always be there to assist, to guide, and to have the last word.

Like most believers I never bothered to think through the significance of likening the pastor unto a "shepherd" and his congregation to "sheep." Had I considered the matter with any degree of intelligence, it would have occurred to me that a sheep is one of the dumbest animals on four legs. Sheep don't even know enough to come in out of the rain. If one runs off a cliff, the others will blindly follow, to their deaths. The shepherd controls them completely, and however kind he may be in the meantime, his purpose is to shear them or, worse, lead them to the slaughter. . . .

As with many Christian groups, the Pentecostals are constantly "encouraged" to "tithe" 10 percent of their income to the church faithfully. They are also expected to give generously for "missions" and various "special offerings" over and above the tithe. There is much talk of giving "sacrificially."

I, too, was "moved" to give large cash gifts with, as one minister so delicately put it, "some of the money God has entrusted you with." I learned to equate giving money to "touching God." . . .

Everyone agreed that . . . I should be officially recognized as a minister of the Assemblies of God church. This would authenticate my ministry, since it would signify that I had submitted myself to the discipline of a body of godly men to oversee my work. . . .

Reverend Ernest Steffensen questioned me for six straight hours regarding my suitability for Assemblies' ordination. . . . I was approved to take the examination and assigned sixty-four short essays. . . . I passed the exam and my essays were approved. . . . I was then presented before the Presbytery—seventeen dour-looking men seated around a long table. . . . [They] put me through a rigorous verbal examination about the Bible. . . .

"What about the Song of Solomon?" [one Presbyter asked].

[Miles answered] "It's an expression of the intense passion Solomon had for the Shulamite girl. It's quite clear."

The Presbytery unanimously disagreed. "It is an allegory of the love Christ has for the church. Would you consider enrolling in the Berean Bible School if we ordain you?"

This astonished me. Even in my compliant frame of mind at that time, I knew that the Song of Solomon had been written 1,014 years before the birth of Christ. It took an overactive imagination to find a parallel. The idea of comparing the steaming sexual lust of Solomon to the love of Christ offended me. Couldn't Christians just accept that God's Word contained a candid acknowledgment that one of the Bible's "stars" was turned on by a woman? I stood my ground, and suspecting there would be other differences, I agreed to take the Berean Bible course by correspondence. . . .

Rose Marie flatly refused to come with me to my ordination ceremony. . . . "I did not marry a minister. . . . I vould nefer haf married a minister!" . . . [Not that Rose Marie was irreligious, but, as she told a reporter not long afterwards,] "I am not comfortable with the exuberance of the Pentecostal religion. I come from a different background in Europe, of the quieter, more traditional church."

A distinct "martyr" quality was evident in many Assemblies of God ministers, and I was beginning to take on the same mentality.

I became resigned to the prospect that Rose Marie would be part of the price I would have to pay. It was something I would just have to accept in good spirit, without complaining. The counsel I was receiving from various ministers led up to this, but I still had difficulty accepting it. I loved Rose Marie and the home we had together very much. . . .

[Before the ordination ceremony one minister asked Miles to pray for his healing.] He said he had a brain tumor, and there was a noticeable swelling on the upper side of his head. His eyes winced from the pain that could no longer be controlled by medication. . . .

With the other ministers . . . I laid hands on him and prayed. Everyone present gasped as the swelling appeared to go down. The pain left him, and his eyes relaxed. Everyone in the room shouted and clapped. . . .

[Asking about the minister who had questioned Miles for six hours concerning his suitability for ordination, Miles was told that he had been dismissed from the Assemblies for committing adultery. He had been carrying on with the organist in his church "for some time." He even had a direct telephone line to his married lover installed in his church office.]

Rose Marie attended a service with me . . . [after which] a woman told her, "I'm going to keep you in my prayers, Sister Miles. I know it's difficult for you when your husband is away. He *is* very good looking, and you never know exactly what he's doing when he's away from you." Rose Marie pulled her hand away and stared at the woman for a moment. . . . What a thoughtless, if not downright vicious comment for that woman to make. . . .

Back in our apartment Rose said, "Don't ever ask me to go to one of dose places with you again." . . .

I was asked by Reverend Zimmerman—the general superintendent of the entire Assemblies of God—to speak at the People's Temple in San Francisco, where the minister was Jim Jones. . . . Knowing nothing about Jim Jones . . . I preached in a different church. . . .

I began keeping a journal of my experiences in the ministry. It shows that in one year, I narrated 256 Lipizzan shows in 125 cities, preached 109 times in 70 different churches, appeared on 107 telecasts [including Jim and Tammy Bakker's "PTL (Praise the Lord) Club" and the Canadian Christian program, "100 Huntley Street"] and 250 radio broadcasts, and gave innumerable newspaper interviews. I also taped 100 religious TV spots and carried on full responsibility as chaplain minister to the Lipizzan company. . . .

On March 16, 1971 . . . I made the following journal entry: "My work with the Lipizzan Show . . . and my ministry is propelling me into national prominence—a position I frankly detest! . . . Never have I met so many forward, pushy women as I have since becoming a minister. It was never this bad in show business. They have out-and-out propositioned me after services and many have sought out my hotel and motel room numbers—some finding my whereabouts under the pretense of an 'emergency.' . . . Happily—my wife impressed by radio sermon by Unitarian Church—and now interested more in the purpose of being 'born again.' Praise God!" . . .

There were frequent news accounts of ministers of the Gospel getting caught in sin. The latest was Billy James Hargis, a high-powered Baptist televangelist who denounced homosexuality, extramarital sex, drinking, and drugs from his pulpit. His enterprises included a Bible university and traveling choir groups. He was also an extreme right-winger. Anyone who disagreed with his politics or theology was denounced as a Communist. He took in millions of dollars from the faithful each year, until he was caught engaging in every one of the sordid practices he preached against—with his own students! . . .

I became increasingly aware of the . . . prevalence of homosexuality among Assemblies of God ministers. . . .

In one large church, the pastor was standing next to the handsome young song leader, near where I was sitting on the platform. During an exuberant congregational song, the pastor glanced over at the young man, winked his eye, smacked his lips, and said, "Oh, you're so gorgeous I could just eat you up!"

During a regional ministers' convention, within earshot of me, a pastor sidled up to a boy who belonged to the Royal Rangers, an Assemblies youth organization. He said to the boy, "My wife will be gone for the next four days. Why don't you come over and sleep with me?" . . .

The prevalence of Assemblies of God ministers committing—and getting away with—child molestation is a horror of the first magnitude. Reverend E. R. Schultz, district secretary of the Florida District of the Assemblies, told me of a seventy-five-year-old pastor in his district who had recently been caught molesting a twelve-year-old girl. . . . Schultz transferred him out of the district. . . . Later, I learned that the offending pastor had been transferred to Florida from yet another district, where he had been involved in a similar incident. . . .[1]

[Rose Marie moved out of the house, and began filing for a divorce.] This was a matter of extreme concern to the Assemblies of God. The sin of divorce *might* be accepted in my life, so long as I was repentant, adhered to a life of celibacy, and never remarried. I assured them that I would do exactly those things. . . .

Word spread far and wide about my sudden singleness. Church women were literally coming out of the woodwork to offer me their companionship, and making no bones about their intentions. . . .

On January 13, 1977, following a "PTL Club" appearance . . . [I opened the door to the steam room in the studio basement.] I closed my eyes and opened them again in disbelief. There were Jim Bakker and three of his male staff members frolicking about in the nude.

The four were so absorbed in playing with and massaging each other that they did not see me by the door in the feeble light. Jim had one of the naked young men stretch out on the table and began massaging the prone man's legs, working his hands up over the knees and thighs.

The expression on my face probably revealed the rest of the story, as effeminate giggles and a falsetto "whoooeeeee" filled the room. Suddenly, Jim looked up and saw me. There was a moment of deafening silence. Regaining his composure, Jim reached for a towel, wrapped it around him, and became very professional and formal. . . . [He announced to one of his naked aides that he wanted me booked on his program "every month."] . . .

"Right, Jim," I said uncomfortably. "I'll see you later." . . .

I stood outside the door for a few moments. . . . Hearing footsteps, I ducked into a shadowed area. . . . Tammy Faye was storming across the room. . . . She banged her fist on the steam room door. "Jim Bakker, you come out of there right now! . . . GODDAMMIT!" She leaned against the door and started to cry. . . .

[After leading] a crusade [one night] . . . a woman came up to me and told me she "definitely saw Christ standing behind" me while I was praying. . . . Another woman verified it. . . . Many people "testified" to miraculous healings. . . .

Perhaps this was a "sign" . . . [that Miles ought] never to leave the ministry. . . . I had been considering leaving. I had felt that the main problem in my marriage was my involvement with the church and Christianity. But there was, after all, nothing wrong with Christianity. Or was there? I was thinking about the PTL steam room. . . .

As I mentally inventoried the pastors who had impressed me, Reverend Jim Jones came quickly to mind. I had been reading and hearing good reports about him. . . . An Indiana farm boy. . . . He opened the doors of his first church, the Christian Assembly of God, in Indianapolis in the late fifties . . . moved to Ukiah, in northern California . . . then San Francisco. . . . He had a special "burden" for people without a purpose in life. . . . Starting with a bunch of drifters of varying ages, he built a bustling church that drew five thousand people to its morning services and evening sermons each week. . . . During his early ministry . . . his concern for the poor and the non-white was genuine by every indication. . . . (On November 18, 1978, I learned that Jim Jones had orchestrated the mass suicide of 913 people, including children, who had moved with him to Guyana, South America. Reports of perverted sex, drugs, and brainwashing masterminded by Rev. Jones surfaced quickly. . . . He disguised his mental illness by cloaking it with Christianity, the perfect mask for a madman.) . . .

[While Miles was on the road, Rose Marie, unbeknownst to him, had an unexpected change of heart and was "born again" at an Assemblies service. After returning to the church a few times, she heard two ladies whispering about the fact that Miles was not at her side.] "Well, it's probably because he's too busy with his, uh, 'other interests.' " . . .

[She asked the pastor about such rumors and he told her] "it is a known fact that he has a mistress in Florida and was seen exiting a motel room with her." . . .

[I happened to phone her at that time, and she began screaming and yelling, repeating what the minister had told her.] Bewildered, I tried to reason with her. "Rose Marie, please, there is absolutely no truth in any of this. I can prove my whereabouts at all times."

By now, Rose Marie's anger had reached its peak. . . . "I'm going through with the divorce."

[Then I discovered that the same reverend who had slandered me to my wife behind my back was also having me privately investigated. I learned this from a New York police officer who attended a service I delivered. It seems the investigator had contacted the NYPD for information.] "And what have they found about me?" I asked one of the cops.

"They found out that you were clean. But . . . doesn't that minister's church preach against drinkin'?"

"Yes," I answered. "Very much so."

"Hmmmm. We found out in the course of things that that reverend is a closet alcoholic. He's got quite a stash down in his basement."

[Soon afterward, Miles was contacted by the head counselor at "The 700 Club" (Pat Robertson's Pentecostal organization). He claimed to know for a fact that Miles was having sex with the married, pregnant, eighteen-year-old daughter of an Assemblies pastor in Pennsylvania.] He added, "It's our job to stop your ministry until this thing is straightened out."

I phoned Pat Robertson, head of the Christian Broadcasting Network, and host of "The 700 Club." He refused to take my calls. I was encouraged by Pat's secretary to attend a meeting where I should "make that settlement." That was the first mention of anything to do with money. . . .

"I see that the entire matter has come to a 'settlement.' What did you have in mind to 'preserve my ministry'? Maybe a hundred thousand?"

"That would show you were sincere and of good faith," she replied, failing to pick up on my irony. . . .

Meanwhile, a friend of mine managed to corner the pregnant young woman at a Christian meeting, and she admitted after being unable to answer a few pertinent questions that the entire story was a hoax. "But," she said, her face brightening again, "it made my husband jealous and more attentive, so it was all worthwhile." . . .

Due to this slander spread by a pastor's daughter, three large church revivals and the Pittsburgh Charismatic Conference canceled me. . . . [Then] I preached a week long revival where everyone in the sanctuary wound up on the floor, "slain in the Spirit." People would approach me for prayer and then collapse on the floor in a heap as I raised my hand to pray for them. Several people said they saw a halo of light around my head.

Word spread quickly about the awesome display of mysterious, spiritual power going on at [that] Assembly of God. Skeptics attended out of curiosity and wound up on the floor with all the others. While these manifestations were occurring, I felt extraordinary emanations of energy radiating from my body. . . . I prayed that the "anointing of this church" would reach out into the highway and compel someone "who needs Jesus" to turn around and come into the church. . . . Minutes later, six hippies walked in, asking, "What's going on? We were driving down the highway in our van, and something made us turn around and come in here." I explained what had happened and our guests . . . gave their hearts to God. . . .

At the airport, I still felt that odd, surging sensation going through my body. The metal detector sounded as I walked through. Even after removing my belt and shoes, it buzzed. In exasperation, the security people let me through anyway. This phenomenon recurred each time I tried to board a plane within a day or so after leading a service. . . .

I had seen enough corruption in the Assemblies of God [including personal monetary gains by the superintendant via his funneling of millions in church funds through one small bank which made him chairman of the board of directors, and also led to land deals he made a killing on] to make me realize that this was no place for me. [Miles did not wish to represent them as an official Assemblies minister.] Instead of accepting my resignation, they told me to pray about it. While I prayed they voted behind my back to officially dismiss me. The charge? Having a previous marriage in my background [Rose Marie was Miles's second wife.] . . .

[Then] Reverend Zimmerman [the "Pope of Pentecostalism"] pursued a . . . letter writing campaign of Assemblies ministers denouncing me to various publications. . . .

I began spending more of my time at PTL. My own television show, "You Are Special," appeared on the PTL satellite network and on a number of regular television shows around the country. . . .

[At PTL Miles grew especially disillusioned. Charles and Francis Hunter began publicizing various spiritual "fads" in their books and on "PTL Club" shows. The first was "angels."] Angel books flooded the market. . . .

[The second fad was demons, popularized by] Reverend Russell Olson. Olson discovered demons in the PTL transmitter tower, in all the offices in the Heritage complex, in the C.B. radio in Tammy's car, and in the tires of Jim Bakker's car. No mention was made of the PTL health club. Apparently the steam room was demon-free. . . .

[The third craze was "prophecy scriptures."] "The Lord just gave me a scripture for you," an evangelist would say to someone he picked out. The scripture, selected at random or by some sort of divining ritual, would be recited and was expected to have some deep, personal meaning to the person given it, relating to some problem or situation in his or her life. Even though it closely resembled gypsy fortune-telling, prophecy scriptures took off among the Christians. Suddenly everybody had the "gift." . . .

Then came the announcement that the Hunters had learned the secret of teleportation! "They've been able to leave their bodies and visit places around the world in a flash to deliver the message of Jesus! It's biblical, and they are teaching about it!" . . .

[John Wesley Fletcher—the evangelist-healer whose preaching converted the actor, Efrem Zimbalist, Jr.—was discovered administering oral sex to a male companion Fletcher brought with him to PTL. Fletcher was also the minister who shared Jessica Hahn's body with Jim Bakker, and covertly joked about it with Jim on national television]: "We need more 'rest' like that."

Since one of the production staff discovered Fletcher [unquestionably engaging in a homosexual act], and the entire male security staff came as a delegation to Jim to complain about homosexual advances from Fletcher, Jim had no choice but to ban him from the Heritage U.S.A complex, citing the severe drinking problem Fletcher also had as the reason. . . .

Young people who came to attend the Heritage U.S.A. school of evangelism quickly paired off. It became a common occurrence to round a corner and interrupt two young people in an intimate embrace. These couples were not just girls and boys. Boys and boys were even more prevalent. Hushed talk about "the pretty boys" could be heard in many corners of the complex, especially the executive offices.

Gospel groupies came to Heritage U.S.A. in droves, to take jobs and try to make it with the visiting evangelists. One morning, a security guard informed me that a nineteen-year-old girl who worked in the kitchen had tried to slip past the guardhouse into the mansion where I was staying. . . .

Amidst these goings on, we all exchanged questioning glances when Jim Bakker hired David Taggart as his personal aide . . . and held many a "private conference" with David in Jim's office with the Jacuzzi. . . .

[A cameraman Miles had worked with—"a real good-looking young man"— was hired by PTL.] "When he got to PTL he found out that his *first* job was to be a 'pretty boy' for the executive staff. His *second* job was to be a cameraman. . . . He left." . . .

[For quite some time] I continued to be very protective of Jim and Tammy. Gradually, the sordid truth about the greed and lust of the televangelists came out, making all of us who had cooperated with them look like fools. . . .

After my appearance on an emotionally charged PTL broadcast [part of a month-long "Emergency Save-the-Satellite" telethon], Jim's brother, Norman, invited me to lunch. . . .

"Norm," I said after a sip of coffee, "do you think we'll make it through this emergency?"

"There's no problem," he said with a shrug. "The money's all there."

"What?"

"We have the money."

My mind reeled. There were still two weeks of telethon to go and on camera, at least, everyone was in a tizzy. That very morning, Jim and Tammy were crying hysterically, wailing about the end of [the PTL satellite network] being near. And the money was—all there?

"What about the crisis you had about four months ago, when they were going to shut down Heritage U.S.A.? How did you come out on that crisis?"

"Oh, there was no crisis." Norm spoke unconcernedly. . . . "We had the money all along. It was in another account. So, when they demanded money over here, this gave us a tool to raise money on, and something for the people to rally around."

"You had the money all along?" I kept on, fatuously flogging the dead horse. "There . . . was . . . no crisis?"

"That's right," Norm answered. He expressed no shame when he told me this. This was business.

I began to understand the significance of the direct mailing phase of PTL's fundraising efforts. My stomach knotted up a bit more when I learned that the emotional "personal" letters that the "partners" received over Jim's and Tammy's signatures were never written or dictated by them. They were carefully composed by highly skilled, psychologically trained professionals at a fundraising corporation. Careful statistical monitoring of the response to previous letters made it possible to predict the effectiveness of each ploy in stimulating the faithful to give, and to give generously. The ministry paid $20,000 for each of these scientifically designed letters. The "PTL Club" ordered four and five of these letters at a time, and predetermined the exact month to declare a "financial crisis." What sickened me even more was to learn that these "emergency" fundraising appeals were skillfully timed to arrive in the mailboxes of the faithful at the same time that their social security and welfare checks would arrive . . .

I refused to appear on the program anymore. . . .

My health broke . . . horrible attacks of anxiety and fear. . . .

[Miles returned to the circus.] They welcomed me back with great love. . . . Not one of them asked me where I had been for the last few years or what had happened. . . . I appreciated and respected the circus more than I ever had before. . . .

The break [with the ministry and the church] had been difficult, but once it was done, I felt free . . . like a captive released from prison . . . reborn—into real life. . . .

There were some beginning difficulties when word got out that I was making a comeback in show business. The church wanted me silenced forever. In Toronto, Ontario, a woman who identified herself as a Woman's Aglow member grabbed me by the arm. Fortunately, security guards were close at hand and threw her out. More Woman's Aglow members intervened with the Shriners to try to convince them that I would be bad for their circus. In Detroit, when the newspaper reviewers mentioned my name, a group of Christians rented an entire box of seats at the front. When I made my exit at the end of the show, they all stood up with their Bibles in their hands and made a thumbs-down gesture at me. But these tactics fell flat. Most intelligent people witnessing them simply had their notions about Christians being mentally disturbed reinforced. . . .

Ed Cohen [a psychologist and ex-seminarian who, like me, went through the "born again" experience] wrote, "Jesus and Paul did not hesitate to divide families over religion, and the biblical program for conduct within the family is unrelievedly hierarchical, militating much more strongly against than for spontaneous human give-and-take."[2]

The Christian church preaches the importance of family and marriage . . . as long as *everyone* in that family is *totally* in agreement with the church and its pastor. . . . If a member of the family resists the control or financial demands of the church, or balks at the church generally, the church will do everything possible to separate the troublesome wife, husband, child, or parent from the family in order to protect the faith. This is precisely what happened to Rose Marie and me. . . .

The church destroys open, responsible human relationships and turns them into fantasy ones. Cohen puts it this way, "Biblical pseudo-psychology [teaches] that humans are incapable of truly caring for one another without a God-obsession in the forefront of consciousness." They also teach that, "What may seem like loving kindness from an unbeliever is really God . . . jerking [the unbeliever's] strings."[3]

It would appear that one does not necessarily have to be an emotional cripple upon entering the church to be transformed into one after a steady diet of church indoctrination. . . .

I lost God in church. Maybe by leaving the church, I will get back to God. If I do, it will be a private matter. I believe religion was meant to be private. When Jesus ministered to individuals in the fields and in the homes, all went well. It was only when He got involved in the synagogues—the organized church—and tried to minister there that He got into trouble.

Notes

1. See also Annie Laurie Gaylor's, *Betrayal of Trust: Clergy Abuse of Children* (Madison, Wis.: The Freedom from Religion Foundation, 1988)—ED.

2. Edmund D. Cohen, *The Mind of the Bible-Believer* (Amherst, N.Y.: Prometheus Books, updated paperback edition, 1988), p. 174.

3. Ibid., pp. 212–13.

Robert Moore:
From Pentecostal Christianity
to Agnosticism

I began studying Branham's prophecies in great detail. . . . I feared that if Branham [the famous Pentecostal Christian healer/prophet] could be wrong on one point he could be wrong on others, perhaps many others, and if *he* could be wrong, so could other prophets and preachers (like Oral Roberts and Billy Graham), theologians, seers . . . perhaps even the Bible itself.

—Robert Moore

Robert Moore is the environmental director of the Natural Arch and Bridge Society in Phoenix, Arizona. He presently writes articles for local environmental publications, and for *SPAN*, the Bridge Society's newsletter. His eye-opening piece, "The Impossible Voyage of Noah's Ark," was published as issue 11 of the journal *Creation/Evolution*. Concerning his personal religious quest, Moore has written, "The more I have searched for God, the harder he has been to find. At this point I don't consider myself an atheist in the hard sense, since I have not searched every little corner. But I am frankly very skeptical of chancing upon him now. I sincerely doubt God's existence, but I do not dogmatically deny it." The following is Moore's account of his journey from "Branhamite" Pentecostal Christianity to agnosticism.

French philosopher Albert Camus wrote, "A man's work is nothing but this slow trek to rediscover . . . those two or three great and simple images in whose presence his heart first opened."

I don't know how true that statement is, nor to how many it applies, but when I look back over my own life, a life characterized by seemingly radical flip-flops, I can trace a couple of unifying themes that seem to supply some semblance of integrity.

My heart first opened at the age of nine, in a small town on the edge of Joshua Tree National Monument, California. It opened in the presence of the natural beauty of the Mohave Desert, and under the pressure of a guilty conscience inflamed by the revivalistic preaching in our tiny "holiness" church.

Growing up in a Christian home, spending many hours in fundamentalist services, I became convinced of my sinful, hell-bound condition and asked Jesus to save me. He probably did, but a child evangelist he did not create; I was shy—almost in today's terms, a "nerd"—and I preferred to keep my faith to myself as a quite private affair.

Five years passed. During my freshman year in high school President Kennedy was assassinated, the Beatles appeared on the "Ed Sullivan Show," and Martin Luther King, Jr., led the March on Washington. The phenomenon of the sixties had begun in earnest. My experience of it, and the rebelliousness it spawned, was characteristically inward, and sparked by a mere chance event.

I stumbled upon the word "determinism" in one of my parents' Sunday school papers. The denial of free will was a strange new idea, and an intriguing one, so I tried to learn all that I could about it via the limited resources of the school library. (I did not have access to any free thought literature at that time, living as I did in a tiny town of eight thousand, with a "library" no larger than a good newsstand.)

The question of "determinism" haunted me for over a year. I wrote a term paper in the tenth grade in which I denied the existence of free will. And I finally reasoned myself into a sort of naive behaviorism.

But I didn't stop there. I quickly made the transition from behaviorism to a mechanistic universe to a godless universe, and by the age of sixteen I fancied myself an atheist. (At that time I had no knowledge of religious determinism, i.e., Calvinism.)

As with my earlier Christianity, I kept my unbelief a very private matter, continuing to attend church and feign a half-hearted piety. I was astonished to eventually learn that there were not only other atheists, but even an organization of them!

Before I had time to digest that information, things changed radically once again. In my senior year I met a young lady I would someday marry, and soon we were "going steady." I was in love, and I daydreamed about our long and happy future together.

There was one little snag that troubled me, however. She was a devout Christian. Every other church-going teenager I knew was sanctimonious on Sunday but indistinguishable from the "world" when at school, which made my hypocrisy easy. She was the lone exception, "born again" and not in the least ashamed of it, no matter where she was.

Her exemplary life and my love for her were more than my superficially rooted, adolescently rebellious atheism could endure, and one evening, trapped at an awkward moment at a "Teen Challenge" meeting, I sighed deeply and "prayed through" once again. (I not only reconverted, but I forced myself, with immense effort, to "speak in tongues.")

I plunged into my new-found faith with unbridled enthusiasm, reading all the literature about it that I could get my hands on. My girl, needless to say, was delighted, and her family now began to accept me as well. Her parents were the most astonishingly devout people I had ever encountered, and I wondered if there was ever a minute of the day when they weren't thinking about Jesus.

Soon even Pentecostalism was too lax for them, and they became involved—and I along with them—with the followers of Reverend William Branham (1909–1965), a famous faith healer. The Branhamites, or "Message Believers," as they call themselves, maintained that Branham was the forerunner of the Second Coming, "Elijah the Restorer," as prophesied in the Old Testament [Mal. 4:5–6]. His "message" was brought to reestablish apostolic faith at the "end time."

Far from revolutionary, the contents of this "restoration" amounted to little more than a few oddball doctrines culled from various sources and grafted onto a Pentecostal vine. His followers have added an elaborate and ever-growing hagiography that has become their primary source of inspiration.

Their most distinguishing trait, however, is a moral code as stringent as any in America. Such distractions as television, rock 'n' roll music, and even amusement parks were looked upon as sinful, and any hint of sex outside marriage—even merely gazing "lustfully" at pretty girls—is *verboten.*

Branham was especially hard on women, forbidding them to cut their hair (which is grounds for divorce!), use makeup, or wear slacks or short skirts. A woman is "only a piece, scrap, made of a man, to deceive him by. . . . She is the lowest of all animals that God put on the earth," he thundered. Yet rather than feeling shackled, most Message women wear their unconformity as a badge of honor, enjoying the stares they garner in the local malls.

In spite of their odd beliefs, they are for the most part honest, hard-working citizens, and their inclusion in *Bob Larson's Book of Cults* seems unfair. [The best study of Branham and his followers is C. Douglas Weaver, *The Healer-Prophet, William Marrion Branham* (Macon, Ga.: Mercer University Press, 1987).]

I married in 1970, had two children, and for the next eight years of my life became active in a Message church. I had planned to attend college and study science, but Branham disparaged higher education as a wedge between the soul and its savior, so I settled for a prosaic position with the post office.

I struggled mightily to live up to my church's onerous ideals, but failure dogged me constantly. As if to compensate, I redoubled my studies of Branham's tape-recorded sermons, and in 1973 I published a four-hundred-page compilation of excerpts entitled *Quotations of William Branham.* It is still being reprinted, and thousands of copies have been distributed throughout the world.

But once again disillusion was lurking. As Christ's forerunner, Branham was, naturally, a diligent "student of prophecy." He predicted that the "rapture of the church" would occur no later than 1977, and that prior to that a series of major events would take place, among them the unification of *all* denominations under the umbrella of the World Council of Churches, the rise of the papacy to world hegemony, and the sinking of Los Angeles in an earthquake.

By 1975 it was becoming increasingly clear that time was running out. I was alarmed. I had planned on leaving this "vale of tears" before I turned thirty! I was also chagrined at the apparent lack of concern among my fellow believers.

I began studying Branham's prophecies in great detail, researching arcane subjects like ecumenism, California coastal geology, the wealth of the Vatican, and the following year I wrote my findings in a sixty-page letter that I gave to a few close friends, in which I announced that I was leaving the Message.

My family and friends were stunned. My wife cried and pleaded with me to recant; my friends begged me to reconsider and warned me of the dire consequences of even a tiny bit of doubt. They pleaded with me to repent and return.

To them the entire 1977 snafu was merely a matter of our finite lack of understanding ("for now we see through a glass darkly" as Paul said in 1 Corinthians 13). Life for them went on as before. But I feared that if Branham could be wrong on one point he could be wrong on others, perhaps many others, and if *he* could be wrong, so could other prophets and preachers (like Oral Roberts and Billy Graham), theologians, seers . . . perhaps even the Bible itself.

I felt shattered and betrayed by my religious faith. I had devoted all of my adult life to propagating it. I had sacrificed what I know could have been a very successful college career. I had spent my spare time studying the Bible and Branham's sermons, rather than indulging in "worldly pleasures." I had even neglected my body somewhat, anticipating a "new body" in 1977.

Others had left the Message before me, usually because its moral demands were too tough, and had merged comfortably back into a more "normal" church. But I was determined not to make another mistaken commitment (or to listen to the rationalizations that came forth as the days of 1977 ticked by).

I was now living in Phoenix, and thus had access to major libraries, so I embarked on an intense study of religion from every aspect. I delved into archeology, higher criticism, comparative mythology, philosophical theology, psychology, apologetics. I remembered my adolescent atheism, and even while still clinging to the tattered remnants of my faith, I felt myself being inexorably drawn back in that direction.

I called myself an agnostic, mostly for my wife's sake, but I began attending meetings of the organization whose very existence had confounded me a dozen years earlier. I debated Christians and quickly learned how weak and incoherent most apologetic arguments really were. I proudly told myself that I was superstitious no more, a free man at last. Yet happiness and satisfaction continued to elude me.

I soon discovered that atheists were not much different than anybody else, including fundamentalists. I found out that their highly touted "freedom of thought" was circumscribed with numerous taboos, and that their lives were mostly very conventional and mundane. In fact, I came to see the seemingly wide pendulum swings of my life as minor variations on a single theme: the fundamentalist need for an absolute standard of truth (the Bible, the prophet, Reason), a humorless, moralistic attitude toward life, intolerance of differing opinions.

In the spring of 1981 I read a book that I had purchased for only fifteen cents, entitled *Critique of Religion and Philosophy,* by the late Prof. Walter Kaufmann of Princeton University. As the chance encounter with the word "determinism" had irrevocably altered my life years before, this volume plucked from some discards left me profoundly moved. Through it I discovered existentialism and the philosophy of Friedrich Nietzsche. I began to see the role suffering played in one's self-awareness, and I could adumbrate the deep longing that lay at the root of both religion and philosophy.

At the same time, my love of nature, that had been a minor theme for me for many years, became a significant force in my life. I joined several environmental organizations and became an active advocate for a more livable planet. I spent as much free time as I could backpacking and camping in the wilderness, of which Arizona had a generous supply.

I continued to study religions and philosophy, and did some writing on the former, including an article titled "The Impossible Voyage of Noah's Ark," which filled an entire issue of the journal *Creation/Evolution* [issue 11, 1984].

My wife clung tenaciously to Branhamism, which made for substantial conflict in our marriage.

Ironically, at a time when existentialism was urging me to create my authentic self, I fell into some of the phoniest relationships and situations of my entire life, which perhaps goes to show that most of our existence is just a series of poses, imitations of an ideal that fall woefully short.

I often became despondent. I would look around myself at my evaporating dreams, wondering where to turn next. I had tried nearly everything—Christianity (in several varieties), scientific rationalism, political activism, "tree hugging," even drugs—but questions like "Who am I? What should I do? Why am I so unhappy?" wouldn't go away. Life frequently seemed pointless, a farce that mocked all one's achievements with death.

In mid-1989 I met a person who would qualify for a *Reader's Digest* "most unforgettable character" story. She was a stunningly beautiful Korean woman who had a strange spirituality about her that I had never seen before. We became close friends. She, too, was deeply unhappy, and we often talked about the passions that seemed to be our undoing. I wanted to share my personal philosophy with her, but before I could she moved away and vanished from my life. Our brief friendship touched something deep in my being and was deeply unsettling. My inauthenticities, the *ad hoc* nature of my "philosophy," my overall dissatisfaction, resurfaced once again.

As Kierkegaard wrote, "Perhaps there lives not a single individual who after all is not to some extent in despair, in whose inmost depths there does not dwell a disquietude, a disturbance, a discord."

I returned once more to the university library. Several years earlier I had planned a thorough survey of Western philosophy, but soon gave up at the sheer enormity of the task. Now I would try again, this time focusing on those personal questions that demanded a response.

Luck was with me, as I seemed to select just the right volumes I needed in pursuit of my quest. I think I finally began to "get it" when I read a book by Robert Solomon of the University of Texas that opened up the obscure world of Martin Heidegger to my wondering eyes.

Today those questions that dogged me throughout my life have been largely resolved. This is far from smugness, however, as they have been superseded by other questions on other levels. I don't feel as if I have "arrived," but I have crossed a watershed, and my erratic life seems retrospectively to have been a long preparation for the present.

I now see both atheism and Christian fundamentalism—as well as most other religions and philosophies—as attempts to organize the chaos of the world about us into some workable and reassuring order. Some efforts are more successful than others, but none can claim the status of the One Truth.

Atheism prides itself on its strict devotion to Reason and science, and its iconoclastic toughness. But it pays a heavy price for such cybernetic cleanliness: concepts like love, beauty, joy, loneliness, kindness, etc., become airy epiphenomena floating about the "reality" of atoms in motion. Yet when it comes to actual, day-to-day living, few people would value the invention of a new plastic or the spectrum of a distant star above these mere "effects."

As Prof. Philip Wheelwright wrote, "A person of intellectual sensitivity is plagued by the sense of a perpetual Something More beyond anything that is actually known or conceived." The hapless atheist, however, is forced to plug every loophole lest some clever theologian find a way to smuggle the supernatural in through the back way. Consequently, while paying lip service to art, romance, human dignity, the only thing that *really* exists remains mute matter, and life is correspondingly impoverished.

Yet to the fundamentalist I hastily add: Neither have you found this "Something More." I need not repeat the many pointed and valid criticisms of fundamentalism, from its ugliness (as H. L. Mencken brought to people's attention) through its morality of resentment (as Nietzsche pointed out) to its scientific absurdity.

These are damning enough, but the point I wish to focus on now, a defect shared by most religions, and a telling one in the course of my own "convictions," is its laziness, a spiritual sloth engendered by the immensity of life's burdens. In Nietzsche's words, "Weariness that wants to reach the ultimate with one leap, with one fatal leap, a poor ignorant weariness that does not want to want any more: this created all gods and afterworlds."

The fundamentalist is "wearier" than most, for, having made a desperate leap, he usually burns his bridges behind him, forever closing certain regions of his life to doubt or inquiry.

Paradoxically, he then becomes as thoroughgoing a rationalist as his free-thinking opposites, forcing everything into his system and allowing no experience or event to transcend it. Even his god is thoroughly domesticated, and his sacred poetry is caricatured in such things as "creation science."

We can begin to move beyond these inadequate formulations and toward a more satisfying position by attending to these words of Prof. Kaufmann: "Man is the ape that wants to be a god. . . . Man is unhappy in his skin and cannot shed it. He wants to abandon himself and attain a higher state of being."

This "ontological hunger," this yearning for transcendence, is built into the very fabric of what it means to be human, for desire always runs ahead of itself, imagining other possibilities, new situations.

An animal will take care of its biological urges; a person seems driven to believe that there is always something better for him, usually just beyond his reach. Desire thus also makes us conscious of our finitude—the limitations imposed by our bodies, by past mistakes and missed opportunities, and most of all by death—which widens the abyss between what we are and what we long to be. To this personal shortfall must be added the seemingly limitless amount of suffering and misery that is the common lot of humankind; such tragedy, and my impotence before it, can lead to deep alienation and a feeling of helplessness.

There are a number of responses to such a despairing mood, but two stand out as the most common. The first is to simply give up, stop thinking, and join the common herd. This means becoming a stable, happy member of society, a solid citizen, family-oriented, and most of all a fervid consumer. One's life is filled with products, one's free time with entertainment. One can be curious about almost anything except about that inner void that has hopefully been exorcised. If the specter should return, our modern therapeutic services are available to restore us to the well-adjusted status we deserve. Such a bovine existence is compatible with either atheism or fundamentalism, and cuts across all strata of society, from janitors to movie stars to rocket scientists.

On the other hand, one can affirm the hunger for transcendence in a mood of romanticism. This attitude, associated with early nineteenth-century literature and poetry, emphasizes feelings over reasoning, nature over technology, spontaneity and freedom above order, often with a longing for faraway places and distant times. Today this mood is found most often among New Agers and radical environmentalists, although it also appears in certain forms of religious otherworldliness.

Romanticism represents a step up from cowish complacency, a move forward on the road to personal discovery. But it is essentially an arrow fired into the void, and it needs to be fleshed out with specific content or it will dissipate aimlessly into sentimentalism.

The quest for Something More, the call to rise above one's present level of living, may seem most fully satisfied on a starry night at the beach, among the ruins of some forgotten civilization, or standing before a painting by Van Gogh.

But long before we find ourselves captivated by profound self-reflection—if indeed we ever do—we find ourselves already fully "thrown" into the world, already deeply engaged in activities, projects and relationships with those around us. We are called to give an account of ourselves, we are made to feel responsible, long before the question "Who am I?" ever arises. Indeed, the question itself is usually prompted by our encounter with others. Even the very language in which reflection proceeds is, of course, a thoroughly social phenomenon.

This Call: "Rise up higher," as mediated through others, is usually felt most acutely after a failure in our relations with others—normally romantic, but also often involving one's career, family, or personal goals. If these failures result in a period of soul-searching, the discoveries one makes are often very painful.

We find out how thoroughly our allegedly independent opinions, attitudes and even emotions are a product of our cultural environment; we learn how much our own behaviors are governed by familial conflicts that occurred when we were too young to even know what was happening; we see how overwhelmingly contingent our lives have been up until now, yet how this past now binds and limits our futures. In short, we discover, in Hans-Georg Gadamer's words, how "our being, effected by the whole of history, essentially far surpasses the knowledge of itself."

Yet we are called upon to give an account of and to transcend our shortcomings. How easy to once again turn to therapy, to take a class in self-esteem, to say "I'm O.K., you're O.K.!" How much harder it is to take seriously the Socratic claim that "the unexamined life is not worth living," to not shrink from the immensity of the task, but to take up the burden of one's existence one step at a time. This means, in fact, to embark upon a lifelong project.

There are no final solutions, and no shortcuts, but there can be a sort of homecoming. As noted above, desire always outruns itself, so the only way a person can be "whole" is to quench the fires in his or her soul.

But if we maintain the passion, if we continue to stand over against ourselves in an attitude of relentless self-questioning, we can begin to build an integrity that, while acknowledging the many limits of our present situation, nevertheless assumes full responsibility for it and fashions an autonomous existence that answers for itself absolutely.

This integrity is, in the words of Edmund Husserl, "that which man *qua* man, in his innermost being, is aiming for, that which alone can satisfy him, make him 'blessed.' "

Such a life is lonely, but not isolated, as it is tested continually before and with others. It is ironical, as claims to absolute knowledge and definitive answers have been abandoned, and one is always prepared to say, "Perhaps I was wrong." One's relationships are also touched with irony: empathy with others, lack of seriousness with oneself.

Having given up everlasting life in a far-off heaven, one can yet experience eternity-as-depth here and now, one can satisfy—temporarily—that ontological hunger in "that high noon instant in which one recognizes that one is where one was destined to be, that one was born to be here, a presence that is accomplished in itself," as Alphonso Lingis has written.

My own life is finally finding its way home. My heart first opened in that naively vague mixture of nature-love and fundamentalism of my childhood. Throughout the years the romantic yearning of the former and the guilt and self-contempt of the latter have struggled within me. Now I am at last bringing them together in a hopefully worthwhile integrity.

Unfortunately, such a life is often not highly visible or successful in worldly terms, but may appear withdrawn and contemplative. Perhaps that is necessary, but not necessarily forever. I am still active in environmental causes, and currently am a director of the Natural Arch and Bridge Society. I also hope to write some more in the philosophical direction that I am currently traveling. This short autobiography is a step along that road.

Charles Templeton: Inside Evangelism

> When finally I shook free of Christianity, it was like being born again. I
> began to see all of life differently. The things that had once seemed important
> now seemed trivial. And things I'd never seen the meaning of or the essence
> of I began to appreciate for the first time.
> —Charles Templeton (in a telephone conversation with the editor)

Charles Templeton's careers have been many and varied: syndicated sports cartoonist, evangelist, pastor, television and radio personality, author of a dozen
novels, screenplays, and nonfiction, and political candidate. He has held three
of the top news jobs in Canada: executive managing editor of the *Toronto Star,*
news director of the CTV Television Network, and editor-in-chief of *Maclean's*
magazine. Two of his novels deal with religious issues, *Act of God* and *The
Third Temptation.* His autobiography, *An Anecdotal Memoir,* provides an intimate
glimpse into his varied careers. He is currently writing a book on agnosticism
tentatively titled *Farewell to God.* The following account focuses on Templeton's
twenty-one years in the Christian church in Canada and the United States, during
which time he preached in fourteen countries to audiences of up to seventy thousand.

In 1936, at the age of nineteen, Charles Templeton left his job as sports cartoonist
for the *Toronto Globe* to become a minister in the Church of the Nazarene.

He had been reluctant to attend the Nazarene church where the rest of his
family had been converted, but one night he went through a "profound change."
He had returned home from a party at 3 A.M. His life seemed "empty, wasted,
and sordid." "It was as though a black blanket had been draped over me. A sense
of enormous guilt descended and invaded every part of me. I felt unclean." He
prayed at his bedside, "Lord, come down. Come down. Come down. . . ." Then
"a weight lifted off and an ineffable warmth began to suffuse every corpuscle in
my body." Afterwards he prayed, "Thank you, Lord. Thank you. Thank you. . . ."
As the birds began to chirp outside he "began to laugh . . . out of an indescribable
sense of well-being at the center of an exultant, all-encompassing joy."

He was ordained by the Church of the Nazarene after reading only "half
a dozen books and submitting to an oral examination by a group of local preachers."

Templeton spent three years as an itinerant evangelist, preaching in churches from Ontario to California. "In Minden, Louisiana, I was preaching on the subject of 'God's Perfect Love' as a tornado touched down, disintegrating the segregated African Methodist church across the street, killing eight members of the congregation, including the pastor. . . ."

During this period, he preached in a town in Michigan where there wasn't much to do during the day. He began reading in the library of the pastor with whom he was staying, a library that included Thomas Paine's critique of Christianity, *The Age of Reason,* Voltaire's *The Bible Explained at Last,* Bertrand Russell's *Why I am Not a Christian,* Robert Ingersoll's *Some Mistakes of Moses,* and books on Gandhi, David Hume and Thomas Huxley.

The arguments of these men stunned him. For about six weeks he stopped preaching. "The way back was tortuous and slow."

He met his future wife, Constance Orosco, during an evangelistic campaign in Grand Rapids, Michigan. "She was the singer and I was the evangelist. We were married six weeks later."

Together, they took all their savings, $600, and rented an empty church in Toronto. "Within six months it was impossible to find a seat in the Sunday-night service unless you were on hand by 6:45. Every week hundreds were turned away at the doors."

The board agreed with Templeton to enlarge the church. But before the morning of the rededication, an arsonist set the building ablaze. Public sentiment was so positive that enough money was pledged in one service to rebuild the church.

It was during the time spent as minister of the Avenue Road church in Toronto that Templeton witnessed two cases of instantaneous healing. Not to say that he is in favor of mass healing rallies, which he has always viewed as a health hazard rather than a blessing "since they leave behind an emotional wreckage and illnesses often worsened by neglect."

The two instances that Templeton witnessed occurred in private. In neither did he expect a healing to occur.

In the first, an infant suffering a birth defect—a muscle that was misattached, causing the baby's head to be twisted to one side—was healed within minutes after Charles laid his hands on the child and prayed. The child's condition prior to and after the healing was documented at the time by hospital physicians. *New World,* a Canadian version of *Life* magazine, ran the story and a full-page picture of the mother and child.

In the second instance, Templeton prayed for his aunt after exploratory surgery revealed that her stomach cancer was both malignant and inoperable. As he laid hands on her and prayed, he says he "felt something akin to an electrical charge flow through my arms and out my fingers."

Within hours his aunt, who had been bedridden for weeks, was up and about. The cancer did not return, the pain from the adhesions ended, and she lived for another forty-two years.

Despite his opposition to "the public healing services of contemporary evangelism—wherein "the 'healers' are often simpletons or rogues or both"—Templeton says he is convinced that "what may loosely be called faith healing is an area of medicine with unrealized potential."

Templeton first met his long-time friend Billy Graham in 1945 at a Youth for Christ rally in Chicago. He had been invited to attend by Torrey Johnson, the pastor of an evangelical church in that city, and the founder of Youth for Christ. That night, hundreds of young people in an audience of twenty thousand responded to Billy's invitation to come forward and receive Christ.

Templeton returned to Toronto and immediately began his own Youth for Christ rallies. They soon became "the largest of the more than one thousand weekly rallies in North America."

Youth for Christ International was formed, and Billy Graham was chosen as the group's official evangelist. Together, Templeton and Graham alternated as preachers in London, York, Manchester, Glasgow, Aberdeen, Edinburgh, Dublin, Belfast, Copenhagen, and Stockholm.

Returning home, Templeton continued to preach at Youth for Christ rallies and at his church in Toronto. Frequently he would fly to Chicago, Detroit, Los Angeles, St. Louis, and other cities to preach in stadiums and major auditoriums. One Easter sunrise he preached to fifty thousand in the Rose Bowl.

Back home in Toronto, he arranged yearly rallies in Maple Leaf Gardens. "Much of what we did was show business. Spectacle. The thousand-voice choir was dressed in white except for a number in black forming a cross at the center. There were five grand pianos, an international pageant in full costume, vocal soloists, a trumpet trio, the Octette, and to climax it all, Connie's 'The Lord's Prayer.'

"For Christian young people the Gardens rallies were pop extravaganzas. They were participants in something larger than life. Surrounded by thousands of their fellows, holding a common faith, they found a tangible justification of their religious commitment."

Then Templeton's doubts began to resurface. "Following our return from Europe, I had been fighting a losing battle with my faith. I had been so busy that there had been little time to take stock. But in the occasional quiet moments, questions and doubts resurfaced. There was a shallowness in what we were doing, a tendency to equate success with numbers. There seemed to be little concern with what happened afterwards to the youngsters who responded to our appeals. Billy, too, was troubled by it, and we talked about it many times. It undoubtedly contributed to his move from Youth for Christ to conduct his own campaigns.

"But my dilemma was of a different kind. I was discovering that, as I matured, I could no longer accept many of the fundamental tenets of the Christian faith. I had been converted as an incredibly green youth of nineteen. I had only a grade-nine education and hadn't the intellectual equipment to challenge the concepts advanced by my friends and mentors. I *wanted* very much to believe. There was in me then as there remains now an intense, inchoate longing for a relationship with God. In the beginning, I accepted the beliefs of the people around me, but I read widely in every spare minute; on planes and trains and in bed. Slowly—against my will, for I could perceive the jeopardy—my mind had begun to challenge and rebut the things I believed.

"I had never believed all that fundamentalists believe—the Genesis account of creation, for instance, or the monstrous evil of an endless hell. But now the entire fabric was coming apart."

At this time a friend suggested to Templeton that he quit preaching and return to school if he wanted to continue to be useful in the ministry. He was "startled" by his friend's suggestion: What would happen to the various projects he had founded over the years?

After "brooding, appraising, praying" he concluded that what his friend had sensed was true. His faith was disintegrating. "I lacked the intellectual training to deal with the questions that were beleaguering me. If I continued as I was going, I would soon become a hypocrite, mouthing what I no longer believed."

He applied to Princeton Theological Seminary but was rejected—his ninth-grade education being less than the bachelor's degree requisite for attending. After a personal appeal to the president of the seminary, he was admitted as a "special student."

A month before he enrolled at Princeton, Templeton visited Billy Graham in Montreat, North Carolina. "Billy and I talked long about my leaving Youth for Christ. Both of us knew that, for all our avowed intentions to keep our friendship alive, our feet were set on different paths. He was as distressed as I was. We both knew that I was not simply giving up Youth for Christ, I was leaving fundamentalism."

Over the years, Templeton and Graham had often discussed their beliefs. "Once we spent two days closeted in a hotel room in New York City, exchanging experiences, discussing the Bible and theology, and praying together."

It was at one such meeting that they debated the Genesis creation account. Templeton couldn't accept it. But Billy defended it, pointing out, "When I stand before the people and say, 'God says,' or 'The Bible says' . . . there are results. People respond. I don't have the time or the intellect to examine all sides of each theological question, so I've decided, once and for all, to stop questioning and to accept the Bible as God's Word."

"But Billy," Templeton protested, "you can't do that. You don't dare stop thinking. Do it and you begin to die. It's intellectual suicide."

There are accounts in a few biographies of Billy Graham that claim this particular exchange between Graham and his friend led to a temporary crisis in Billy's faith.

Here was Templeton, about to leave for seminary, but not wanting to part from his old friend. " 'Bill,' I said, 'face it: we've been successful in large part because of our abilities on a platform. Part of that stems from our energy, our convictions, our youth. But we won't always be young. We need to grow, to develop some intellectual sinew. Come with me to Princeton.' "

Graham replied that he could not because he was president of Northwestern Bible College, a small fundamentalist school in Minneapolis. He suggested that they seek admission to a seminary somewhere outside the U.S. "Oxford, for instance." As a measure of his sincerity, Graham held out his hand. There is no doubt in Templeton's mind today that if he had shaken Billy's hand "the history of mass evangelism would be different than it is." But, he "couldn't do it." He could not give up the opportunity to enter Princeton for the possibility of a chance to enter Oxford later.

"Not many months later," Templeton recalls, "Billy travelled to Los Angeles to begin a campaign that [with the aid of a newspaper magnate's publicity blitz—ed.], would catapult him overnight into national prominence."

While at Princeton, Templeton hoped to resolve some of the questions that were eroding his faith. "Paramount among them was the question: Who was Jesus of Nazareth? Was he a moral and spiritual genius or was he, as the Christian chuch has always held, 'very God of very God'"? In his search for answers he found the "stacks of relevant material in the library" to be of more value than his classes and conversations with his professors.

But his searching was not merely intellectual. "I knew that faith is more a matter of the spirit than of the mind." So, in his second year, Templeton began to fast one day a week "in imitation of Mohandas Gandhi—who remains one of the formative influences on my life."

Every night he walked for an hour on the golf course back of the seminary, straining to get in touch with God, "to grasp something of what the theologians have described as 'the mysterium tremendum.' "

One night as he stood beneath the stars, looking skyward, he went through what he later realized was a mystical experience. "I was caught up in a transport. It seemed that the whole of creation, the trees, the skies, the very heavens, all of time and space and God Himself was weeping. I knew somehow that they were weeping for mankind: for our obduracy, our hatreds, our ten thousand cruelties, our love of war and violence. And at the heart of this eternal sorrow I saw the shadow of a cross, with a silhouetted figure on it . . . weeping."

Templeton sought to repeat the experience. He studied the writings of the Christian mystics and eventually realized that such experiences had no special significance—members of various religions have had similar experiences. Indeed, Henry Wadsworth Longfellow was able to go into a transport at will merely by repeating his name aloud.

Leaving Princeton, Templeton had reestablished his faith. He had "found a measure of certainty through a conscious act of commitment."

He was ordained into the ministry by the Presbyterian Church, and the National Council of Churches hired him in July 1951 to conduct "preaching missions." He travelled from city to city across the United States and Canada under their auspices, which included most of the churches in each city he visited.

To avoid "the scandal of love-offerings," he put himself on a yearly salary of $7,500. It was traditional for an evangelist to be paid all the money contributed during the closing night of a campaign, when the largest crowd is in attendance, which could amount to thousands of dollars. When it was publicized that Templeton was receiving a meager salary for his services, *Time* magazine used the opportunity to shaft Graham. Billy had just completed a campaign in Atlanta, and *Time* ran a picture of him. Over his shoulder was a mail sack bulging with the love offering presented to him on the closing night. To his credit, Billy immediately put himself on salary at $15,000 a year.

Two significant differences between Templeton's and Graham's evangelistic campaigns remained. Billy spoke a lot about heaven and hell, and asked converts to come forward. Templeton seldom spoke about heaven, never preached on hell, and "deliberately avoided" applying any emotional pressure. At the end of his sermon, he would announce that an afterservice would be held for any who wanted to make a commitment, and would then dismiss the meeting. Those who wanted to remain had to move against the flow of the thousands leaving. Each night, hundreds chose to stay.

The other difference between their campaigns, when they preached south of the Mason-Dixon line, was that "in the beginning Billy's were segregated, mine were not."

As the crowds attending Templeton's campaigns grew larger, so did the newspaper coverage.

In the August 1953 issue of *American* magazine Edward Boyd wrote an article titled "Religion's Super Salesman." Boyd commented, "I have just seen the man who's giving religion a brand-new look; a young Canadian by the name of Charles B. Templeton. Passing up the old-style hellfire-and-damnation oratorical fireworks, he uses instead a persuasive, attractive approach that presents religion as a commodity as necessary to life as salt, and in doing, has set a new standard for evangelism.

"Dispensing with . . . tricks from the old-time evangelist's repertoire, he is winning converts at an average of 150 a night, and—what is something new in modern evangelism—they stay converted.

"At a recent two-week stay in Evansville, Indiana, for example, a count showed that Templeton had drawn a total attendance of 91,000 out of a population of 128,000. A survey taken six months later showed that church attendance was 17 percent higher than it had been before he'd come.

"He is booked two years ahead, a situation that the biggest Broadway hit can't boast, and the demands for his service are ten times greater than can be met. Moreover, observers who have closely followed his progress say that Templeton has not yet begun to hit his stride."

However, during this period Templeton began to experience pains in his chest and arms, sudden sweats at night, and a pounding of his heart that would shake his bed.

He was examined by a doctor who could not find any physiological causes for the problems. One specialist, however, told Templeton that his symptoms might be a psychosomatic disorder, some conflict or unresolved problem in his life. The physician added that unless the problem was resolved, the symptoms would continue and new ones could arise, adding to his discomfort.

Templeton knew what the problem was—doubt. "How does a man who each night tells five thousand to ten thousand people how to find faith confess that he is struggling with his own?"

Following the closing service at a campaign in Harrisburg, Pennsylvania, described in the press as "the greatest crowd ever to gather in the history of Harrisburg," Templeton made the decision: he would no longer conduct campaigns. He accepted a position as head of the Department of Evangelism for the Presbyterian Church, U.S.A. He taught at seminaries and universities and wrote two books, one of them being *Evangelism for Tomorrow*.

During this period, Templeton spoke at Yale for a week, meeting afterwards with various students. One was the outstanding man in the senior class. He was also the captain of the debating team and an avowed atheist. The two of them debated the truth of Christianity alone in a borrowed office. At the end neither had convinced the other. The student conceded, however, that Templeton had made "a hell of a good case."

Templeton's first reaction was elation, but he realized that he too had a concession to make—his arguments no longer convinced himself. "In the heat of discussion I believed them, but, alone, I knew that I had been role-playing."

During this time Templeton was hosting the CBS network's religious television program "Look Up and Live" (1952–55). Not long after his debate with the Yale student, Templeton quit the television program and "gave up the ministry."

About his irrevocable decision to leave the ministry Templeton states, "There was no real choice. I could stay in the ministry, paper over my doubts and daily live a lie, or I could make a break. I packed my few possessions in a rented trailer and started on the road home to Toronto."

Thus began his various careers as writer, editor, producer, politician. "The only activity I will not return to is the Christian ministry; I am and will remain a reverent agnostic."

Photo by Robert Smolich

Farrell Till: From Preacher to Skeptic

Away from the carefully orchestrated environment of Bible-college campuses where professors could explain away [biblical] problems . . . I was able for the first time to see that the "explanations" I had accepted before were not really explanations but merely unlikely conjectures.

—Farrell Till

Farrell Till was a minister and missionary for the Church of Christ. Today he is an agnostic and an outspoken opponent of the fundamentalist doctrine of "inerrancy," i.e., that "the Bible was originally composed without errors of any kind." He has debated this topic, both in print and in public, with fundamentalist ministers, and he publishes a periodical also devoted to this topic, the *Skeptical Review*. The following is Till's account of how his views changed.

Although my parents were not faithful churchgoers themselves, I was born into a family that had its religious roots in the Church of Christ on both sides. As a child, I was dutifully taken to Sunday school by my mother and cousins. I heard the doctrine of biblical inerrancy proclaimed in Bible classes and from the pulpit, so I grew up believing what I had been taught: the Bible was a perfectly harmonious book from cover to cover; over forty men, writing over a period of 1,500 years, living in different cultures and speaking different languages, had produced a collection of sixty-six books that contained no inconsistencies or contradictions. I really believed it!

In the fall of 1951 I enrolled at Freed-Hardeman College in Henderson, Tennessee, a junior college that was supported at the time by the Church of Christ. The next year, I transferred to Harding College in Searcy, Arkansas, also a Church of Christ college (now a university), where I later received both my bachelor's and master's degrees.

I was a conscientious Bible student, and I remember being disturbed by variations in the synoptic Gospels[1] that made me wonder about the perfect harmony of the Bible. There were always highly esteemed professors on the campus, however, who could explain away the inconsistencies and make me feel ashamed for allowing the thought of a possible discrepancy in the Bible to even enter my mind.

My zeal to spread the truth of God's inspired word led me to become a missionary, so in August 1955 my wife and I left for France, where we spent five years in a futile effort to free people there from the heresy of Catholicism.

During that time, I continued to study the Bible at a furious pace. I was determined to become as knowledgeable concerning the Bible as some of the professors and preachers I had admired when I was in college. I collected translations of the Bible in English and in French and spent long hours comparing what a particular passage seemed to be saying in one version as opposed to others.

I once committed the gospel of John (American Standard Version) to memory and could recite it from beginning to end without a single bobble. If anyone would read a randomly selected passage from the New Testament, I could tell him what book and chapter it was from and could do the same with some Old Testament books. I wrote articles for Church of Christ publications. I staunchly defended the inerrancy doctrine. In a word, I was a biblical fundamentalist through and through.

During this period of my life, however, something was happening. I had begun to see that discrepancies and inconsistencies were in other books of the Bible, besides the synoptic Gospels, only now I was away from the carefully orchestrated environment of Bible-college campuses where professors could explain away the problems. In fact, I was able for the first time to see that the "explanations" I had accepted before were not really explanations but merely unlikely conjectures. I found myself on an irreversible trajectory toward agnosticism.

By 1963, my agnosticism had become so profound that I left the ministry. Since that time I have worked as an English teacher with twenty-six of the years spent at Spoon River College in Canton, Illinois.

Although I abandoned my first profession, I did not abandon my interest in the Bible. I have studied it just as conscientiously as before but in a different way. I can no longer recite the gospel of John from memory or identify the book and chapter of any randomly read New Testament passage, because my studies have been directed toward critical analysis of the Bible rather than gimmickry intended to dazzle pulpit audiences.

I thought at first that I could find logical explanations for the apparent discrepancies in the Bible, because they were surely just "apparent" discrepancies. The Bible was, after all, the verbally inspired word of God, so if I had found problems in it, there had to be solutions to them.

The longer I studied the Bible critically, however, the more I realized that I would never find solutions to the problems I had identified, because there were no solutions. The Bible was not the verbally inspired, inerrant word of God; it was just a collection of contradictory, discrepant books that had been written by superstitious ethnocentrics who thought that the hand of God was directing the destiny of the Hebrew people.

During the Reagan years, I became concerned about the resurgence of Christian fundamentalism and the trend in government to curry its favor. Events in Iran and other Middle Eastern countries demonstrate what can happen once religious fundamentalists gain political control.

So I decided it was time for someone to challenge the outrageous claims that Christian fundamentalists were making for the Bible. This began with letters to the local newspaper and soon progressed to public debate challenges.

Church of Christ preachers are famous for their readiness to defend their beliefs, so I thought that arranging public debates on biblical inerrancy would be as simple as letting former colleagues know of my willingness to meet them. I soon found that I was mistaken. My challenges were generally met with silence, and it took me over two years and two hundred letters to find a Church of Christ preacher willing to defend the inerrancy doctrine in public.

My first debate on the subject, in fact, was with a Presbyterian minister who was intellectually ill-equipped to defend his position. Since then I have had six oral debates on biblical morality and the inerrancy issue and three written debates on inerrancy. One of the written debates was published in *Christian News,* a Lutheran newspaper published by Herman Otten, a conservative Lutheran maverick. The other written debates were *The Laws-Till Debate: An Unfinished Discussion of the Bible Inerrancy Doctrine* (unfinished because my opponent quit) and *The Jackson-Till Debate on Biblical Inerrancy: Is the Bible Reliable?* I have two written debates in progress with Church of Christ preachers that will probably become finished debates too, because I have not had responses to my last submissions in over a year in one case and nine months in the other.

I recently conducted an oral debate in Portland, Texas, on the issue of prophecy fulfillment. My opponent was H. A. "Buster" Dobbs, editor of the Firm Foundation, a conservative Church of Christ publication. I am also scheduled for a second debate at the same location in May 1994. My opponent for this debate will be Jerry Moffitt; the issue will be the resurrection of Jesus.

In January 1990 I began publishing the *Skeptical Review,* a quarterly journal devoted entirely to examining the fundamentalist doctrine of biblical inerrancy. Each edition features a pro/con exchange on some issue related to biblical inerrancy. This gives readers the opportunity to examine both sides.

In 1991 I published a thirty-seven-page manuscript that examined biblical prophecies, *Prophecies: Imaginary and Unfulfilled.*

Note

1. The "synoptic Gospels" are the first three gospels, Matthew, Mark, and Luke, which agree to a much greater extent with each another than they do with the fourth gospel, John. Since the synoptics parallel each other in their descriptions of Jesus' words and actions, it is also easy to see where their descriptions *vary.*—ED.

Part Six

Testimonies of
Former Fundamentalists
Who Are Now Atheists

The modern freethinker does not attack Christianity; he explains it.
—Morley, 1874, according to the *Oxford English Dictionary*

Let God alone if need be. Methinks, if I loved him more, I should keep him—I should keep myself, rather—at a more respectful distance. It is not when I am going to meet him, but when I am just turning away and leaving him alone, that I discover that God is. I say, God. I am not sure that is the name. You will know whom I mean. . . .

Doubt may have "some divinity" about it. . . .

Atheism may be comparatively popular with God himself. . . .

When a pious visitor inquired sweetly, "Henry, have you made your peace with God?" he [Thoreau] replied, "We have never quarrelled."
[reported by Brooks Atkinson]
   —Henry David Thoreau [quotations found in
    Henry David Thoreau: What Manner of Man?
    by Edward Wagenknecht
    (Amherst: University of Massachusetts Press, 1981)]

Dan Barker: Losing Faith in Faith

I did not lose my faith, I gave it up purposely. The motivation that drove me into the ministry is the same that drove me out. I have always wanted to *know*. Even as a child I fervently pursued the truth. I was rarely content to accept things without examination, and my examinations were intense. I was a thirsty learner, a good student, and a good minister because of that drive.

—Dan Barker

Dan Barker is the public relations director of the Freedom From Religion Foundation, Madison, Wisconsin, and also staff assistant and regular contributor to *Freethought Today,* "The only freethought newspaper in the United States." He has written two books for children, *Maybe Right, Maybe Wrong: A Guide for Young Thinkers* and *Maybe Yes, Maybe No: A Guide for Young Skeptics.* He is married to Annie Laurie Gaylor, the chief editor of *Freethought Today.* Dan frequently lectures on freethought topics and debates opponents. The following piece is taken from his most recent book, *Losing Faith in Faith.*

I was one of Christ's disciples for over seventeen years, and my subsequent self-excision was/is traumatically painful.

My dad was a professional musician during the 1940s. At one of his concerts he met a female vocalist and, as things go, they went (lucky for me). They married, and when I was a toddler, they both found true religion. Dad threw away his collection of original Glenn Miller recordings (ouch!), turned his back on his former "sinful" life, and enrolled in seminary to become a minister. He didn't finish because of the strong demands of raising three boys. But he lived his faith through his family and through lay ministry in local churches.

My folks' spirituality was so strong that they often found it hard to find a church that met their needs. So we church-hopped for many years. I can't remember all the churches, but we were Baptist, Methodist, Nazarene, Assemblies of God, Pentecostal, fundamentalist, evangelical, "Bible-believing," and charismatic.

For a number of years we formed a family musical team and ministered in many Southern California churches—nothing fantastic—Dad played the trombone and preached, Mom sang solos, I played piano, my brothers tooted various instruments, and we all joined in singing those famous gospel harmonies. It was a neat experience for us kids.[1]

My childhood was filled with love, fun, and purpose. I felt truly fortunate to have been born into the "truth." And at the age of fifteen I committed myself to a lifetime of Christian ministry.

My commitment lasted seventeen years. It gave my life a feeling of purpose, destiny, and fulfillment. I spent years trekking across Mexico in missionary work— small villages, jungles, deserts, large arenas, radio, TV, parks, prisons and street meetings. I spent more years in traveling evangelism across the United States, reaching and singing in churches, on street corners, house-to-house witnessing, TV, college campuses and, wherever an audience could be found.

I was a "doer of the word and not a hearer only." I went to a Christian college, majored in religion/philosophy, became ordained and served in a pastoral capacity in three California churches. I personally led many people to Jesus Christ, and encouraged many young people to consider full-time Christian service.

I served for a while as librarian for Kathryn Kuhlman's Los Angeles choir, observing the "miracles" firsthand. I was even instrumental in a few healings myself. For a number of years I directed the "King's Children," a local Christian music group that performed quite extensively, including a brief term of hosting a local Christian TV show.

For fifteen years I worked with (and still do) Manuel Bonilla, the leading Christian recording artist in the Spanish-speaking world. I am his main producer/ arranger and working with him has given me the opportunity to learn the skills to produce many more Christian albums, including some of my own.

I have written over a hundred Christian songs which are either published or recorded by various artists, and two of my children's musicals continue to be best-sellers around the world. (*Mary Had a Little Lamb,* a Christmas musical, and *His Fleece Was White as Snow,* for Easter. I think you can see the religious symbolism in the titles: Christ, the unspotted lamb of God who became the final sacrifice for sin. Both published and distributed by Manna Music.)

I could go on listing my Christian accomplishments, but I am already beginning to bore myself. I think you can get the picture that I was very serious about my faith, and that I am quite capable of analyzing religion from the inside out.

Last Friday evening I directed a Bible study in my own home. I opened it to all comers and announced that I would welcome all points of view with the purpose of critically examining the documents with skepticism rather than faith. The eight people who arrived (to my astonishment) were Christians who had been informed of my present atheistic stance and were curious about my intentions. My closest ally was my brother, a theistic agnostic. One fellow, a theologian, informed me that his purpose in coming was to convert me back to the faith. (He failed.)

It was a fun, lively evening and much information was exchanged, but I noticed something interesting. They were more concerned about *me* and my atheism than they were about the Bible. The discussion kept coming around to an analysis of my conversion from the faith. They were intrigued that someone who had been so strongly religious could so radically "stray" and not be ashamed. They kept probing for some deep psychological cause, some hidden disappointment, secret bitterness, temptation or pride. They were like spiritual doctors trying to remove a tumor or a blinding cataract.

One fellow suggested that I had been blinded by Satan—the Devil being so intimidated by my strong Christian witness that he needed to neutralize the enemy, get me out of commission. That was very flattering, but it misses the point.

The point here is that the merits of an argument do not depend on the character of the speaker. All arguments should be weighed for their own sake, based on their own evidences and logical consistencies.

Before the Bible study even commenced one fellow said, "Dan, tell us what caused you to lose your faith." So I told them.

I did not lose my faith, I gave it up purposely. The motivation that drove me into the ministry is the same that drove me out. I have always wanted to *know.* Even as a child I fervently pursued the truth. I was rarely content to accept things without examination, and my examinations were intense. I was a thirsty learner, a good student, and a good minister because of that drive. I always took things apart and put them back together again.

Since I was taught and believed Christianity was the answer, the only hope for "man," I dedicated myself to understanding all I possibly could. I devoured every book, every sermon, and the Bible. I prayed, fasted, and obeyed biblical teaching. I decided that I would lean my whole weight upon the truth of Scripture.

This attitude, I am sure, gave the impression that I was a notch above, that I could be trusted as a Christian authority and leader. Christians, eager for substantiation, gladly allowed me to assume a place of leadership, and I took it as confirmation of my holy calling.

But my mind did not go to sleep. In my thirst for knowledge I did not limit myself to Christian authors but curiously desired to understand the reasoning behind non-Christian thinking. I figured the only way to truly grasp a subject was to look at it from all sides. If I had limited myself to Christian books I would probably still be a Christian today. I read philosophy, theology, science, and psychology. I studied evolution and natural history. I read Bertrand Russell, Thomas Paine, Ayn Rand, John Dewey, and others. At first I laughed at these worldly thinkers, but I eventually started discovering some disturbing facts—facts that discredited Christianity. I tried to ignore these facts because they did not integrate with my religious worldview.

For years I went through an intense inner conflict. On the one hand I was happy with the direction and fulfillment of my Christian life; on the other hand I had intellectual doubts. Faith and reason began a war within me. And it kept escalating. I would cry out to God for answers, and none would come. Like the battered wife who clings to hope, I kept trusting God would someday come through. He never did.

The only proposed answer was *faith,* and I gradually grew to dislike the smell of that word. I finally realized that faith is a cop-out, a defeat—an admission that the truths of religion are unknowable through evidence and reason. It is only indemonstrable assertions that require the suspension of reason, and weak ideas that require faith. I just lost faith in faith. Biblical contradictions became more and more discrepant, apologist arguments more and more absurd, and, when I finally discarded faith, things became more and more clear.

But don't imagine that was an easy process. It was like tearing my whole frame of reality to pieces, ripping to shreds the fabric of meaning and hope, betraying the values of existence. It hurt. And it hurt bad. It was like spitting on my mother, or like throwing one of my children out a window. It was sacrilege. All of my bases for thinking and values had to be restructured. Add to that inner conflict the outer conflict of reputation and you have a destabilizing war. Did I really want to discard the respect I had so carefully built over many years with so many important people?

I can understand why people cling to their faith. Faith is comforting. It provides many "answers" to life's riddles. My Christian life was quite positive and I really see no external/cultural reason why I should have rejected it. I continue to share many of the same Christian values I was taught (though I would no longer call them "Christian"—they are my values); and many of *my* close friends are decent Christian individuals whom I love and respect.

Christians feel deeply that their way of life is the best possible. They feel their attitude towards the rest of the world is one of love. That's how I felt. I couldn't understand why people would be critical of Christianity unless they were inwardly motivated by "worldly" Satanic influences. I pretended to love all individuals while hating the "sin" that was in them, like Christ supposedly did. (We were *taught* that Christ was the most loving example.)

It was a mystery to me how anyone could be blind to the truths of the Gospel. After all, don't we all want love, peace, happiness, hope, and meaning in life? Christ was the only answer, I believed, and I figured all non-Christians must be driven by other things, like greed, lust, evil pride, hate, and jealousy. I took the media's caricature of the world's situation as evidence of that fact. For me to grow into one of those godless creatures was almost impossible, and I resisted all the way. (I have since discovered that ethics has nothing to do with religion, at least not in positive correlation.)

There was no specific turning point for me. I one day just realized that I was no longer a Christian, and a few months later I mustered the nerve to advertise that fact. Since then I have been bombarded by all my caring friends and relatives. I appreciate their concern and I sincerely wish to keep a dialogue open.

As an example, while I was typing this account I received a long-distance call from a former Christian friend who had heard about my "defection." It is hard to handle calls like that. She was stunned, and I am certain that she is at this very moment in prayer for me, or calling others to join in prayer. I love this person, I respect her and do not wish to cause any undue harm. She told me that she had read an article I wrote to my local paper. (How it got to her area is a mystery.) I understand her concern and I sympathize with her since I know exactly what she is thinking.

I was a preacher for many years, and I guess it hasn't all rubbed off. I would wish to influence others who may be struggling like I did—influence them to have the guts to think. To think deliberately and clearly. To take no fact without critical examination and to remain open to honest inquiry, wherever it leads.

Note

1. Today, Barker's mother and father are also freethinkers! Bill Lueders wrote a cover story about Barker, "Losing Faith," that appeared in "Wisconsin," the *Milwaukee Journal* Sunday supplement, July 28, 1991. Barker explained that after his mother became a freethinker "she struck upon the joyous realization that, for the first time in her life, she could love everyone— even homosexuals and people of other religions whom 'Christians aren't supposed to love.' "

And *Freethought Today* published a piece by Barker titled "With Perfect Hatred" (October 1991), in which he stated:

> Many Christians took exception to my mother's statement, claiming that "God hates the sin, but loves the sinner."
>
> I have to question their sincerity. Does a true believer want his or her child to marry a homosexual, Moslem, or atheist? Would they vote for an atheist for political office? Would they invite them into their inner circle of fellowship at their church? They talk a lot about love, but their actions demonstrate something less. What they really mean by "love" is "concern that sinners will change their evil ways to become just like me." This is hardly love.
>
> Besides, the Bible does not support the "love sinner, hate sin" idea. 2 Chronicles 19:2 says, "Shouldest thou help the ungodly, and love them that hate the Lord? Therefore is wrath upon thee." Psalm 5:5–6 says that God "hatest all workers of iniquity . . . the Lord will abhor the bloody and deceitful man."
>
> Psalm 139:21–22 states, "Do not I hate them, O Lord, that hate thee? . . . I hate them with *perfect hatred.*" The prophet Hosea (9:15) quotes God: "For there I hated them: for the sickness of their doings I will drive them out of mine house, I will love them no more."
>
> In Luke 14:26, the loving Jesus warns: "If any man come to me, and hate not his father and mother, and wife, and children, and brethren, and sisters, yea, and his own life also he cannot be my disciple." (A Baptist minister on the TV show "Milwaukee's Talking" claimed that I was taking this out of context, but the Greek word here is miseo which means simply "hate," not "love less than me," as some suggest.)
>
> I know it is possible to find verses that say "God is love," but this only demonstrates that the Bible is contradictory.
>
> In Leviticus 24:16, the Bible says that freethinkers like myself should be executed: "He that blasphemeth the name of the Lord, he shall surely be put to death, and all the congregation shall certainly stone him." Leviticus 20:13 mandates the same fate for homosexuals: "If a man also lie with mankind, as he lieth with a woman, both of them have committed an abomination: they shall surely be put to death; their blood shall be upon them." None of this sounds much like love, does it?
>
> My mom is right. Atheists and agnostics are not obligated to radiate "perfect hatred." Isn't it nice to be nice?

M. Lee Deitz:
My Conversion from Fundamentalism

I was addicted to fundamentalism. . . . There came a period, however, when I began to think. . . . I recall reading about a leader in the Youth for Christ movement resigning and reporting that he no longer believed as he once did. I thought that was very strange and at the time felt that I could never doubt the Bible and the promises of Jesus Christ. . . .

However, I began to doubt. . . . Tennyson wrote, "There lives more faith in honest doubt, Believe me, than in half the creeds."

—M. Lee Deitz

M. Lee Deitz majored in ministerial studies and Christian theology at Bob Jones University. He was president of his class, chaplain of a literary society, winner of an annual sermon contest, and also Bob Jones University's "Man of the Year." Currently he is president of Greenville's Secular Humanist Society, and a member and lay speaker at Greenville's Unitarian Universalist Church. The following is an edited transcription of a "sermon" he has delivered on numerous occasions, titled "My Conversion from Fundamentalism."

This sermon topic, "My Conversion *from* Fundamentalism," is not meant to be sensational, though I have been known in the past to use sensationalism in the pulpit. I remember a sermon I once preached, entitled "Hell's A-Popping." In announcing the sermon I would say, "Be sure to wear your asbestos suit because you will feel the flames!" Little did I know that asbestos was dangerous to your health. I suppose that if I were preaching that sermon today, I'd say, "If the flames don't get you, the asbestos will!"

A little about my background. I was reared in what a fundamentalist would label a "non-Christian" home, one in which my parents were not dedicated and there was no real pattern of church attendance. For a while we were Presbyterians, then Southern Methodists. One of my brothers converted to the Baptist church, and we all seemed to follow that direction. He was baptized, a first for our family. In time, we had what could have been considered a "Christian home."

We attended and joined a Southern Baptist church. In the 1950s there was no reason for a church to go "independent," or "fundamentalist," as they do today, since most churches were very conservative. Only a few saw the need for separating from the mainstream because of its "creeping liberalism." This liberalism was portrayed by them as creeping into Sunday school literature, college classrooms, and ruining the morals of the population at large.

College professors were teaching a "new orthodoxy," hence the term, "neo-orthodox," which was coined at that time. Those who reacted most strongly to this gave birth to what is known today as the independent or fundamentalist movement.

I remained devoted to my church throughout high school. I taught Sunday school, sang in the choir, and attended every service. I was known as "the preacher" or "the deacon" at school. I was not voted the "most popular student," nor did I win that award, but *everyone* knew who I was. My senior year I was president of the Laurens County Youth Association, a countywide Southern Baptist association.

My role models began to crystallize. I listened to the leading fundamentalists of the 1960s, Dr. Oliver B. Greene, Dr. Harold B. Sightler, Dr. John R. Rice, Dr. John W. Rawlings, and others, carefully studying their books. I jumped in all the way and believed that I had been "called to preach the Gospel." I formally announced this at my home church one Sunday morning. An unusual morning it was, the church was filled and my entire family was present. I walked forward after the service and dedicated my life to the ministry.

College was much on my mind. I could not attend Furman University in Greenville, South Carolina. It was liberal. The modernists, as we called them, had taken over Presbyterian College in my home town. And any state school was *no place* for a "Christian," whose faith would thereby be put in danger of "shipwreck"! The only choice for me was Bob Jones University in Greenville, South Carolina. It stood without apology for the Bible and the "old-time religion." I attended from 1961 to 1964, graduating May 27, 1964.

During the course of my studies at Bob Jones, I was licensed to preach. We would go out in small groups and preach on street corners, in prisons, nursing homes, missions, and churches. I was chosen to speak to Baptist Boys, a Sunday school class of six or seven hundred. I was also elected president of my class, chosen "Man of the Year," and won the annual sermon contest.

After college, I returned to my home church and became the assistant pastor, music director, youth director, Sunday school teacher, and author of the Sunday school literature. During this time I founded a statewide youth organization called "Truth for Youth," run by myself, an assistant, and several officers. We had monthly rallies (I was instrumental in getting Sen. Strom Thurmond to speak at one of our patriotic rallies), and we organized banquets as substitutes for the junior/senior proms.

Our group of churches taught that their youth should not attend proms, where wicked things like dancing, holding hands, and other activities would surely bring down the judgment of God on their participants. "Christian" youth were not to be a party to such shenanigans, therefore the banquet. This was the highlight of the year, but it was made clear that we would rather a youth not attend *our* banquet if she or he intended to also become tainted with the worldly pleasures of the prom.

Youth for Truth also produced a monthly newsletter. And we held an annual convention that featured big name-speakers, a speakers' tournament for the youth to participate in, and lots of food. At the same time, I was conducting revival meetings throughout the Southeast as far away as Mississippi, recording a weekly radio broadcast, and functioning as secretary of the Carolina Baptist Fellowship, which consisted of a group of fundamentalist Baptist churches. My itinerary was full. I was addicted to fundamentalism.

There came a period, however, when I began to think. I left my home town and moved to Greenville. There I continued my Truth for Youth ministry, but as I think back, I recall that my *interest* in fundamentalism began to wane. I married, having met my wife in one of the largest fundamentalist churches in the state. We had two children and my church activities again increased. I taught Sunday school and my wife and I were very active in the church.

After our divorce I ceased attending church except for the times I went with my children. Later, I completely stopped attending for a period of four or five years. God became very distant to me.

However, one day in January 1987, I'm not sure why, I looked up the Unitarian church in Greenville. I joined in March of the same year, made many wonderful friends there, shared experiences, listened, and was eventually "delivered" from fundamentalism after going without it "cold turkey." I took part in the "New U" program, served on the board for a year, and now find the church a very important part of my life.

Why the change? And how does one go from one extreme to the other, from fundamentalism of the Bob Jones University type to Unitarian Universalism?

Way back when, I preached that the Bible was an infallible, inspired, "God breathed" book. Every jot and tittle were the very words of God. You've seen the bumper sticker, "God Said It, I Believe It, That Settles It!" That was my mentality! To question the Bible was a sin. God was not the author of doubt.

I recall reading about a leader in the Youth for Christ movement resigning and reporting that he no longer believed as he once did. I thought that was very strange and at the time felt that I could never doubt the Bible and the promises of Jesus Christ.

However, after reading and thinking, I began to doubt. Tennyson wrote, "There lives more faith in honest doubt, Believe me, than in half the creeds."

Surely I was not alone in my doubts? My fundamentalist role models, were they not just as human as I? Could they not question?

The death of Christ, the sacrifice that He supposedly made, was it true? The Christian church says Jesus died for the sins of all. Then he rose again after merely three days in the grave, exactly as he had predicted that he would (if you accept the Gospel writers' testimonies of what Jesus supposedly said). My friend, I would give *my* life for a good cause if I *knew* I was coming back in three days! I pondered, where is the sacrifice?

Jesus said, "Ask and ye shall receive." In the churches I had attended we would pray about things we wished to see happen. If whatever we were praying for happened, everyone would give God the praise. If it did not, then it "just wasn't God's will." But, with such handy explanations available for *either* result, it reduced prayer to "six on one hand, half a dozen on the other." What will be, will be. So why pray? Why not just do your best and hope for the best?

I also realized that I was praying to someone for whom I might have to make an *excuse*! And I refused to believe in a God for whom I had to make excuses, like, "Maybe it just wasn't His will," or, "God will act in His own time, not ours," or, "We just do not have enough faith." The excuses you hear in fundamentalist churches go on and on, *ad nauseam.*

Jesus promised, "If any two of you shall agree and ask . . . it shall be done" [Matt. 18:19]. That's a promise! What do you want? Ask for it and "it shall be done." That doesn't work, and you know it.

Compare what is written in the Letter of James 5:15. "If there are any who are sick . . . call the elders. . . . They will pray and the prayer of faith shall save the sick, and the Lord shall raise him up." That doesn't work either.

"Take no thought for your life . . . (food, clothing, etc.) all these things *will be given unto you*" [Matt. 6:25, 31–33]. Tell that to the poor, the hungry and the homeless!

In fact, I will say what I believe millions want to say, but are afraid to say, "Jesus, I no longer believe you. You made promises that you have not, and cannot, keep!"

"But Lee," my fundamentalist friends might say, "aren't you afraid that lightning will strike when you make a statement like that?"

I am now afraid that lightning will strike me if I do *not* tell it the way I see it! You see, my friends, these promises are taught to little children in Sunday school as *truth*! They are promoted as divine teaching by a Savior who cares and loves, as promises that God can and will perform. I say, as one who has tried and tested these promises, they are empty and delivery has yet to be made. Much like Santa Claus and the Easter Bunny, we find that they are tales for children that only excited us for a few years.

Let me read to you a news release dated March 22, 1990, from a speaker at the 1990 Bob Jones University Bible Conference. Dr. Douglas McLachlan encouraged fundamentalists to return to "authentic Christian living":

"Dr. Douglas McLachlan, chairman of Bible studies at Northland Baptist Bible College in Dunbar, Wisconsin, said in an interview, 'Fundamentalists need to maintain a vigil against the danger of acquiring a hunger for affluence and acceptance. The danger begins when we start rejoicing and finding our source of joy in things other than God Himself. Dangers lurk when we put things ahead of the desire to please God. Christians need to get themselves back into the mindset and heartbeat of New Testament Christianity and seek to duplicate them in the twentieth century.' "

What is "authentic Christian living"? Well, Jesus is at the root of it all, so, keeping *his* commandments is certainly a priority. There are Ten Commandments in the Hebrew Bible, often referred to as the "top ten," but Jesus added some 180 commandments himself. I cite a few: Love your enemies and pray for those who persecute you. [Matt. 5:44]; Do good to them which hate you [Luke 6:27]; Forgive if you have ought against *any* [Mark 11:25]; Condemn not [Luke 6:37]; Swear not at all [Matt. 5:34].

If fundamentalist evangelists, and the Religious Right, emphasized *those* commandments of Jesus, they might be left speechless!

Or consider the following commandments. Who has kept them? And if any man will sue thee, and take away thy coat, let him have thy cloak also [leaving you naked] [Matt. 5:40]; Take no thought for your life . . . (food, clothing, etc.) [Matt. 6:25, 31]; Store not up for yourself treasures on earth [Matt. 6:19]; Give to him that asketh thee, and from him that would borrow of thee turn not thou away [Matt. 5:42]; Sell what you have and give to the poor [Luke 12:33].

Or how about even greater demands?: Pray without ceasing [Luke 21:36]; Be ye therefore perfect [Matt. 19:21]; He that loveth father or mother, son or daughter more than me is not worthy of me [Matt. 10:37]; If any man come to me, and *hate* not his father, and mother, and wife, and children, and brethren, and sister, yea, and his own life also, he *cannot* be my disciple [Luke 14:26].

And what about the commandments of the Apostles? Paul, the chief Apostle, says, "Owe no man anything" [Rom. 13:8]. Are Christians obeying this teaching?

I could go on and on, but you get the picture. I saw the inconsistencies in the lives of Christians who claimed they were living "authentic Christianity."

As for the Bible, the supposed source of all fundamentalist teachings, the inconsistencies and contradictions it contains are unreal! The First Epistle of John says, "Whosoever is born of God *cannot* sin." In the *same book* it says, "If any man sin, we have an advocate with the father." Which is true, can you sin or not?

The God of the Bible says in Exodus 20, "Thou shalt not kill." Yet in Joshua 11:6 He commands the Israelites to kill the Canaanites. Joshua himself killed King Hazor.

Women in the Bible are viewed as the property of men. "Thou shalt not covet they neighbor's house, nor his *wife,* nor his maidservant, nor his ox, ass, nor anything that is thy neighbor's." In the New Testament, "Let women keep silent in church" [1 Cor. 14:34]. One of the worst things that has ever happened to women is the church and Christianity!

Abraham and Jacob both owned slaves. The New Testament seems to teach that owning slaves remained acceptable even for Christians [1 Tim. 6:1; 1 Pet. 2:18; Eph. 6:5].

The Ku Klux Klan uses the Bible, claiming that it provides the foundation for their teachings.[1] On the other hand, the NAACP is also biblically oriented.

You can endorse capital punishment, or show why it should be abolished, based on verses found in the Bible. You can endorse the production of nuclear weapons, or seek to have them banned, based on verses found in the Bible. I say that any book that can be interpreted in a thousand different ways can not have any authority!

I once studied Unitarianism as if it were a cult. But now that I am free of fundamentalism and have had the opportunity to study both Unitarianism and fundamentalism from a different angle, I see that fundamentalism is the cult.

A cult has certain peculiarities, things one can and cannot do, things one must believe and pledge allegiance to. In the world of fundamentalism we were told how Christians were to dress, how Christians should talk, where we should and should not go. We were told to read the Bible, pray and "forsake not the assembling of ourselves together in the house of God." There was a veritable catalog of rules.

Many times as a fundamentalist preacher I would preach and then give what we called an "altar call." This was to invite people to come to the altar of the church and "get saved." It was as simple as "trusting Jesus." And he would "take away all your burdens, as if a weight had been lifted from your shoulders."

My friend, since I have left fundamentalism; since I have gotten rid of Jesus Christ and his phoney religion; since I am no longer associated with the fundamentalist movement, *now I am free! The burdens have truly been lifted!*

I submit to you that Jesus Christ *never* saved *anyone* from *anything*! He does not save, he enslaves. He does not bring peace, he brings conflict. He does not bring freedom, he brings bondage. I'm talking about the Jesus Christ of the New Testament, who is supposed to do all these great things for the human race. I believed in that Jesus. I trusted that Jesus. I gave a great portion of my life and energy to that Jesus and he kept none of his promises that he made to me in "His Word."

If Jesus saves, what does he save you from? Lying? There are good people who claim no part of Christianity who do not lie. Does he save you from adultery? You know what my comment to that is? You can only save yourself from that. Does he save you from cheating? Lots of young "born again" students aren't saved from that, though they have "accepted Christ as personal savior," and were baptized and have "Godly parents" who pray that God will lead their children in the "straight and narrow" path. Even so, they will occasionally cheat on a test, experience sex, lie a little, and yes, maybe even steal; but, they are supposed to be *saved* from all that. The same can be repeated concerning adults in the business world, or wherever one may find an occasion to "sin."

Frankly, I do not know a lot of "saved" folks. But I do know a lot of Baptists, Methodists, Presbyterians, etc., who are really Unitarians in their general attitudes, both moral and spiritual, toward life. Those people, in my opinion, are simply attending the wrong building on Sunday mornings!

What do I believe today? I believe in my strengths, weaknesses; whatever they are, they are mine. I believe in the inherent worth and dignity of every individual. Fundamentalists do not believe that. They classify people based on their lifestyles and other criteria. I believe in a free and disciplined search for truth and meaning. I believe in the freedom of religious and nonreligious expression. I also believe that we each should have the freedom to question each other's beliefs. But fundamentalists take things further than that. They will never feel secure until the entire country believes exactly as they do.

I believe that the Bible is a human document, just as Shakespeare's plays are. Religion is a human enterprise; it is the human race that has created religions out of the unique self awareness that drives us to ask questions about our origins and our destiny. I believe human beings are responsible for their own destinies. Heaven and hell are our own creations—in this life. I see no evidence of a deity at work trying to ease the sufferings of mankind. Half a million children, not to mention the adults, were killed in the Holocaust. If there were a God anywhere, surely He would have stopped that slaughter.

On March 16, 1990, another South African uprising took place. Watching the news that evening I saw a little South African child, maybe five or six years old. Anguish and terror were written all over his face, and his little eyes were filled with tears. I thought, where is this God who "loves all the little children of the world, red and yellow, black and white, they are precious in His sight"? What should we do, go there and find that little boy and say to him, "Son, Jesus loves you and cares about you"? No, the fundamentalist answer would be, "God has a great plan and purpose in all the conflicts of the world, and in the sweet by and by, we'll see the whole picture and be glad that it all happened that way."

I believe the Ten Commandments are, in general, a good code of ethics, whoever wrote them.[2]

One of the dictionary definitions of God is, "One of various beings, conceived of as immortal, as over some phase of life. Any person or thing much loved." I believe that the God attribute in each of you here today is greater than any God portrayed in the Bible.

God, Whoever, Whatever, Whereever He, She, It or They may be, is what you imagine God to be. You give God credit for the things you want God to have credit for—the rest you would have rejected anyway.

Amen.

Notes

1. Rev. Thom Robb, the grand wizard of the Knights of the Ku Klux Klan (who is also an ordained Baptist minister), recently bought forty acres of scenic Ozark Mountain greenery near Zinc, Arkansas, where the Klan is planning to build a family-oriented Bible camp resort. "Three flags already fly over the campgrounds: The Stars and Stripes, the Confederate battle flag and the white and gold Christian banner." (Ginny Carroll, "Coming Soon: Klub KKK," *Newsweek,* July 8, 1991).

Moreover, "Popular old-time religion evangelists, such as Billy Sunday and Bob Jones, Sr. (the founder of Bob Jones University), though not Klansmen themselves, endorsed Klan principles and accepted their gifts of love. . . .

"After a revival in Andalusia, Alabama [in the late 1920s], Bob Jones happily accepted a donation of $1,568 from Klansmen [a relatively large sum in those days!]. And at a revival in Dallas, Reverend Jones looked the other way while Klansmen distributed their flyers." (Wyn Craig Wade in *The Fiery Cross: The Ku Klux Klan in America* [New York: Simon and Schuster, 1987], chapter 6, "I Found Christ Through the Ku Klux Klan," pp. 176–77).

2. However, see Joseph Lewis's *The Ten Commandments: An Investigation into the Origin and Meaning of the Decalogue and an Analysis of its Ethical and Moral Value as a Code of Conduct in Modern Society* (New York: Freethought Press Association, 1946) for an in-depth look at some of the commandments' obvious shortcomings, ethically and sociologically speaking. Lewis's book was recently reprinted by Independent Publications, Box 102, Ridgefield, NJ 07657. See also W. W. Davies's *The Codes of Hammurabi & Moses,* placed in parallel arrangement with copious comments, index, and Bible references, which was recently reprinted by H. H. Waldo, Bookseller, P.O. Box 350, Rockton, IL 61072.—ED.

Timothy William Grogan:
Lies, Damn Lies, and Boredom

As I read more and more, I realized the persons that I considered ripe only for damnation were among the greatest, most clear-thinking minds of humanity. These humanists were humanistic! They even had a sense of humor, something entirely foreign to books on theology. How can you have a good laugh when you think your family and friends will, in all probability, wind up in a sulphurous inferno?

—Timothy William Grogan

Timothy William Grogan sits on the board of directors of the T. W. Grogan Company, an Ohio real estate firm, and has done graduate work in clinical psychology at Cleveland State University. Prior to that, he was voted "Most Outstanding Undergraduate Student" by the faculty at Cleveland State.

One of the problems with being an ideologue of any stamp is that the higher you elevate something in importance, the more boring it threatens to become. Where before life was a multifaceted feast for the soul and senses, afterward your vision is carefully tunneled, ambiguities crucified, and your laughter circumspect and self-conscious.

Not that boredom was the only reason I left the fold of God and became a card-carrying humanist. Let's just say boredom was the spur that began prodding me into checking out the foundations of fundamentalist Christianity. Besides, as Jean Paul Richter once remarked, "A scholar knows no boredom."

Let's face it, theology in general and fundamentalist theology in particular is one of the most boring disciplines extant. There is nothing new to teach, there is nothing new to discover. A sharp, inquisitive mind quickly falls victim to casuistry and is channelled into defending "revealed truth."

Fundamentalists are hopeful that such an intellectual backwater can compete with modern science on the one hand, and MTV on the other—Scylla and Charybdis never looked so good. After all, I think that MTV Europe had a strong hand in bringing down the mighty Soviet Empire. How can pastor Billy Joe Bob who holds a viewpoint as prudish as that of a Soviet commissar on almost any subject

(God excepted) hold onto his flock at prayer meetings with young women who look as good as Sophia Loren did at twenty cavorting around on your local cable television network? How can theology compete with this kind of entertainment?

It's part of the strategy of religious proselytizers to approach people when they are most vulnerable to conversion. Vulnerability has a lot to do with age (you want to get them when they are young) and transition points (you want to get them right after a major change in life: a death, college entrance, or a divorce). In one meeting it was said by a veteran Campus Crusade for Christ leader that converting anyone after *high school* posed great difficulties. The category I fell into was "alienated freshman college student." With a liberal overdose of wine, women, and song my central processing unit was not too inclined to critical thinking. It was at this mental equivalent of the Quatta Depression that I had my first encounter with Campus Crusade for Christ, an army of well-scrubbed white bread from Middle America with a superficial knowledge of the Protestant Christian Bible.

To be honest, I was set up. Before I became an alienated college student, I was an alienated high school student. In my alienation I read a lot of gibberish that people in the New Age movement still think is terrific. Disillusionment set in when Edgar Cayce's prophecy that in 1970 Atlantis would rise off the coast of Bimini (wasn't that where Adam Clayton Powell used to hang out?) didn't pan out.

Foolishly, I kept seeking ready-made answers to the "meaning of life" until I hit on a nonsensical piece of doggerel, *The Late Great Planet Earth,* by a part-time clergyman (and no-time scholar), Hal Lindsey. I know now that I was conned by a bunco artist (who also managed to con himself). Lindsey's work is without any redeeming social value and ought to be considered the scholarly equivalent of pornography. That probably explains why it sold over twenty million copies since it first went to print and was the best-selling "nonfiction" book in America in the 1970s.

Lindsey's thesis was that the Bible foretold current events and had foretold in particular that the end of the world was at hand. While being somewhat coy when it came to setting exact dates, Lindsey suggested that the end would take place approximately forty years after 1948, the year the modern nation of Israel was founded. Sorry, Hal, the end of the world was supposed to take place in 1988, yet we're still here. Lindsey also asserted that the Old Testament foretold the life and work of Jesus and the fulfillment of prophecy proved that Jesus was the second person of the Trinity.

Being utterly unsophisticated, I was taken in by this—to be polite—line of argument. I immediately accepted Jesus into my heart, an action based on a spurious interpretation of a passage in the Book of Revelation (3:20). At this time I was just a naive believer in the ethics of Jesus. Having no knowledge of theology, that intellectual discipline that Thomas Hobbs called "the kingdom of darkness," it was easy for me to be indoctrinated. It was when I met the friendly representatives from Campus Crusade for Christ that my theological education began in earnest.

Initially, I had believed that all "true Christians" were united in doctrine and understanding of the Bible. My self-education in the field of Christian doctrine soon taught me that so-called "true Christians" disagreed on a host of issues. Even at the lower echelons of CCC there were disagreements regarding so-called spiritual gifts, church membership, baptism, free will, etc., etc. For example, when I was involved in CCC I was told to stay away from people in the charismatic movement. People in that movement, who "spoke in tongues," were, according to my teachers at CCC, stretching the boundaries of orthodoxy. Being a skeptical sort, I immediately found a group of charismatic Christians and began to learn about their beliefs.

As I studied the Bible and the beliefs of the charismatic Christians I realized that they seemed to be entirely in keeping with the teachings of the Bible. The problem that I had was not so much with "speaking in tongues," but with the other "gifts of the Spirit" that were allegedly at work among these groups.

Throughout my year-and-a-half tenure with the charismatics I heard dozens of prophecies and saw many putative healings. The problem was that *none* of these prophecies or healings turned out to be genuine. Oddly enough, it seemed as though I was the only one in the group who found this at all strange. I also discovered that the Roman Catholic Church had embraced the charismatic movement and had their own prophecies and healings. I decided then that enough was enough and bid farewell to my charismatic fellowship.

Back with CCC, I was studying the Bible and meeting a lot of like-minded people. I kept reading the Bible on my own and wanted to find out everything I could about Christianity. When Josh McDowell, a well known speaker with CCC came to the campus to speak about the "Resurrection: Hoax or History?" I was thrilled. I wanted to believe only the truth and here was Josh McDowell, our champion, our David, against the academic Goliath. As soon as possible, I acquired all the books that "Josh" had written and began reading them.

Unfortunately for Josh, I had acquired a rather nasty habit in childhood of reading the bibliographies of the books prior to reading the text. Uniformly, the persons cited by McDowell as authorities did not hold to any kind of inerrancy of the Bible or many other theological verities that CCC claimed were necessary for salvation. The question occurred to me, "If these people, cited by McDowell as acknowledged experts in history, biblical studies, and archeology, don't believe in the inerrancy of the Bible then why should I, a self-acknowledged babe in the woods, believe it?"

When I looked at some of the quotations used by Mr. McDowell in their original context it became apparent to me that he took a great deal of care in isolating quotations that supported his view of the Bible, many times *ignoring the overall viewpoint* of the authority whose material he was using. For example, he would often quote distinguished American archeologist William F. Albright without acknowledging that Albright would have never accepted the fundamentalist notion that the Bible was without error. The technique of using out-of-context quotations in a seeming attempt to conceal the true views of many of the scholars cited was later perfected by the Institute for Creation Research, which some of my skeptical friends liked to call the "Institute for Quotation Research."

As I kept studying, a thought crossed my mind. "Why is it that none of my learned professors in the university, some of which had advanced degrees in New Testament, accept the doctrines taught by CCC?" In my search for the answer to this question I also thought to ask why "the truth" of salvation preached by CCC was rejected by intelligent and learned people. In my search for the answer to this question I stumbled on a book entitled *The Five Points of Calvinism: Defined, Documented and Defended.* This work answered my question as to why the most brilliant and learned people rejected Christian faith as I saw it: sin. The reason the "wise of this world" do not find the Lord is that *God planned it that way.* God for some mysterious reason chose some and rejected others to eternal damnation. Brains and competence were actually hindrances to salvation (1 Cor. 3:18–19).

What I had actually stumbled into was Calvinism, that charming system of theology that bears the name of one of the strangest men in human history. When I was involved in Calvinism the faults of Calvin the man were not known to me. Later, reading Stephan Zweig's *The Right to Heresy,* a book about the dreary life of those unfortunate enough to be under the government of Calvin, I discovered another instance of a superbly educated individual succumbing to the intellectual virus that I now consider Christianity to be. According to Calvinism or Paulinism (the apostle Paul held similar views) the only reason that persons have objections to Christianity is *sin,* both original and actual. If someone questions the authority of the Bible on any topic, the *real* motivation behind the questioning is rebellion and a hardhearted refusal to submit to the will of God.

Believing that I was one of God's "elect," I felt assured that no matter what, "all things worked together for *my* good" (Rom. 8:28), and my confidence in God and the truth of the Scriptures increased geometrically. Voraciously consuming all the Calvinistic theology I could get my hands on I built myself an entire library of buncombe. At the time I was proud of my library for it contained the works of John Owen, Jonathan Edwards, and a host of other celestial worthies. I now consider the books by these men to have been some of the most retrograde and destructive pieces ever written. It seems hard to believe now that humans could really only a few centuries ago have murdered each other wholesale in disputes over such obscure topics as the meaning of the Greek word, *baptizo.*

I was particularly proud of my collection of works on hell and the extent of the atonement. I used to brag to other Christians that I had the largest collection of books on hell in the state of Ohio. My favorite sermon was entitled, "Future Punishment of the Wicked: Both Intolerable and Unavoidable," by Jonathan Edwards. I recommend this rant to anyone who has any doubt of the mind-warping effects of religion on one of the most brilliant minds America ever produced. (The entire text can be found in Edwards's complete works, Banner of Truth edition.)

The books I had on the extent of the atonement defended the Calvinist position that God does not love all men, and that the blood of Jesus only paid for the sins of the elect. The Calvinist logic is inescapable. If Jesus paid the debt for sins, then either all must be saved, or he paid the debt only for some. Some theologians try to slip between the horns of this dilemma by saying that Jesus paid the debt for everyone's sins, yet some will still be punished in eternal hell. Not because of any of the usual sins, all of which Jesus has already died for— but because of the newly added sin of *not believing in Jesus.* But how could Moses, David and all the other believers mentioned in the "Old Testament" believe in Jesus since he had not arrived, and how could God punish people for "unbelief" who had never heard of Jesus throughout the centuries?

Those were the "burning" questions I pondered when I was a Christian. When not pondering, I was leading Bible studies, preaching to nursing home residents, or haranguing the homeless at the local city mission. I even told a group of seven-year-old Sunday school students that they were headed for one of the upper cantos of hell if they didn't repent and turn to Jesus. I saw the expressions of shock on those who heard about my preschool sermonette, and was never asked back to teach any preteenage classes. As you can imagine, I was quite a controversial figure, and, as a result, I bounced around from church to church, giving pastors and their flocks fits. I didn't want to be controversial out of malicious intent but out of a passionate desire to do the work of God and to believe and act on as much truth as possible.

Staying active, I joined the right-to-life movement, became vice president of the local chapter of the Bible Science Association (which I now call the "B.S. Association"), and I continued rooting out heresy wherever it reared its ugly head as if I were John Calvin revivified.

Being of a social activist nature (I had been in the antiwar movement in high school), naturally I wanted to apply my new-found faith to a this-worldly perspective. I reasoned that since I had theology proper down pat it was now time to move on to the practical application of what I had learned.

Turning to the New Testament was somewhat of a disappointment, since it had no real plan of social activism. The entire book seemed to be strictly status quo. The rule of kings was assumed and they were viewed as having been appointed by God ("Submit yourselves to every ordinance of man for the Lord's sake: whether it be to the king, as supreme; Or unto governors, as unto them that are sent by him for the punishment of evildoers, and for the praise of them that do well" 1 Pet. 2:13–14). Slavery was also taken for granted, something I found quite puzzling. I later discovered that every branch of the Christian church condoned or actively promoted slavery up until the Quakers started making a stink about it. The Quakers, of course, suffered hatred and persecution at the hands of orthodox Christians in early America.

In the midst of my reading I happened to pick up *By What Standard?* by R. J. Rushdoony. This was my introduction to the theonomy movement, a loose knit collection of Calvinist fanatics who believe that the law codes purportedly spelled out by YHWH [Yahweh], the central tribal deity of the ancient Hebrews, were perpetually binding on all men.

Not all the law codes of course were binding on Christians, but those of the "moral law" as opposed to those in the "ceremonial law" (a distinction not found in the Bible). At last I thought I had found the key to conquering the world for Jesus. What was needed was Christian evangelism and Christian government joined into one unbreakable union. I was not aware that this mixture had been tried before and led to the total destruction of old Roman civilization and a thousand years of barbarism. (For the details, consult Joseph McCabe's essay, "How Christianity 'Triumphed,' " reprinted by Prometheus Books in 1993 in a volume titled *The Myth of the Resurrection and Other Essays.* McCabe was a Catholic monk and scholar before becoming a freethinker.)

For a few years I thought this was great. Now I had "the truth" in both the systematic and practical side. Then doubts began to gnaw at this adamantine foundation. I started to see that all my theological theories of various sorts were only that—theories—and that there were multiple theories available for almost any Christian doctrine. These facts seemed to be too relativistic, but my studies in church history seemed to bear the thesis out. As one German historian said, "The history of Christianity is the best school for atheism." I also saw that various groups of Christians throughout history had no compunction about using the sword or faggot to do a little friendly persuasion. My doubts were of a fairly minor nature at this point. Soon I was to enter doubt's boundless sea.

In 1985 I received the shocking news that an acquaintance of mine who had attended Brown University had become a Quaker! She had apparently taken a class entitled something like "The Literary Origins of the Gospels," and had imbibed some nonsense about literary criticism and form criticism of sacred writ. As a self-appointed champion of the faith, I immediately took up the gauntlet and decided to read everything I could about the opposition. It was as if I were Patton and I was going to read all the books by Rommel. So this great contest for my intellect was joined.

I proceeded in my typical fanatical way to obtain everything in print from an atheistic, naturalistic, or agnostic viewpoint. I acquired all the back issues of *Free Inquiry* and the *American Rationalist.* I went to the library and looked at all extant issues of the *Humanist,* photocopying everything I couldn't purchase. As I read more and more, I realized that the persons I considered ripe only for damnation were among the greatest, most clear-thinking minds of humanity. These humanists were humanistic! They even had a sense of humor, something entirely foreign to books on theology. How can you have a good laugh when you think your family and friends will, in all probability, wind up in a sulphurous inferno?

That's the thing about Christianity in its modern forms. No one really believes it that much, otherwise the forty million or so who claim to be born again would have long ago reduced this country to a Lebanon writ large. I for one am glad few Christians are really serious about many of the teachings connected with their religion.

The upshot of my reading was that I could not find any respectable intellectual defenses for my Christian faith. The authors of most of the books available assumed that they were writing to believers who would never read books by atheists, but instead would rely on the shepherds of the flock to deal with the heathens.

So I commissioned an author I respected by the name of Bob Morey to write the definitive modern Calvinist work against the atheist position. I gave Bob $2,500 to cover the cost of his research and loaned him my IBM PC to do the typing.

After about a year of work, Bob came out with a book entitled *The New Atheism and the Erosion of Freedom.* This book did not convince me that the atheist position was wrong and contained many factual errors to boot. The book also made extensive use of the *ad hominem* argumentation that is the basis of much Christian apologetic. I had a great deal of respect for Bob's intellectual acumen and talent. If he couldn't write a good book defending the faith against the unbelievers, who could?

I continued to search for some good Christian arguments that didn't depend on Aquinas or Augustine, but I could never find anything in contemporary fundamentalist writings to equal the magnificent labors of D. F. Strauss [author of *The Life of Jesus Critically Examined, Christian Dogma,* and *The Christ of Belief and the Jesus of History*], Pierre Bayle [*An Historical and Critical Dictionary* which included a form of biblical criticism in the entries concerning Scriptural events], H. S. Reimarus [*Apology for or Defense of the Rational Worshipper of God,* from which was also derived his famous *Fragments*], or contemporary thinkers like Walter Kaufmann [*The Faith of a Heretic* and *Religion in Four Dimensions*], Kai Nielsen [*Ethics Without God, Why Be Moral?,* and *Philosophy and Atheism*], or Antony Flew [*God and Philosophy, The Presumption of Atheism,* and *The Logic of Mortality*].

After a year of intensive study I resigned my position in the church, since I could no longer intellectually accept the cobweb of historical and philosophical falsehood that Christianity is based on. I also abandoned my belief in God since the concept of God seems to lack a definite meaning and seems generally to be without rational warrant. I am now a happy unbeliever and intend to stay that way.

People occasionally ask me about the future of religion in the United States. I believe that a vague religiosity will continue to permeate the body politic for decades to come. Most persons in the born-again circles have little inclination to challenge their own thinking, in fact most have not even read the New Testament once! It is interesting to speculate on the reasons why "so many believe so much based on so little." Perhaps it is just another manifestation of the human tendency toward the comfortable, and conforming, along with a large dash of intellectual inertia. In the end, most who leave fundamentalism will not exit it via any "dark night of the soul" experience. Rather, they will just get bored with it like a worn-out joke.

There are many books worth recommending to the inquisitive, but, since brevity is a virtue, I recommend Robert Moore's magnificent little tract, "The Impossible Voyage of Noah's Ark," published as issue 11 of the journal *Creation/Evolution.* It destroyed my confidence in the historicity of the Flood story in Genesis and *caeteris paribus* the rest of the Bible. I also recommend A. J. Mattill, Jr.'s little jewel, *The Seven Mighty Blows to Traditional Beliefs,* which systematically dismembers the apologetic basis for fundamentalist versions of Christianity, Islam, and Judaism in just thirty-nine pages!

Photo by Erika Mitnik

Jim Lippard:
From Fundamentalism to
Open-ended Atheism

Around 1984 I began using a Phoenix computer bulletin board system called Apollo (602-246-1432), which had a number of active atheists on it. At first I did not contribute a lot to the ongoing discussions, but eventually I became one of the most outspoken people on the BBS. Watching some of the Christian-versus-atheist arguments moved me further away from Christianity. Although I initially defended Christianity, I found that its opponents generally had the better arguments.

My *Skeptical Inquirer* subscription led to mailings from Prometheus Books, and so I discovered books such as B. C. Johnson's *The Atheist Debater's Handbook* and George Smith's *Atheism: The Case Against God.* By the time I read the latter book, I was a confirmed born-again atheist. . . .

I've come to find that many so-called "believers" are less dogmatic and more inquisitive than many "skeptics." There are distinctions to be drawn between different kinds of claims and claimants, and it is a mistake to class all "believers" as suckers who will believe anything in the *Weekly World News*.

My present thinking has involved applying skepticism to organized skepticism, which has resulted in an increased tolerance for those with views other than my own in the religious, political, and scientific realms. I think that the existence of God, for example, is something that rational people can disagree about.

—Jim Lippard

Prior to entering his senior year of high school, Jim Lippard became the youngest employee at the Distributed Systems & Communications Center of Honeywell Information Systems in Phoenix, Arizona, to perform operations and administration work on their computer systems. He received his M.A. in philosophy from the University of Arizona in 1991, and is presently a doctoral candidate in philosophy. He has debated "creation scientist," Walter T. Brown, Jr., in the pages of the journal *Creation/Evolution* (no. 25, Fall 1989 to no. 27, Summer 1990). He is also the author of the booklet *Fundamentalism Is Nonsense*. The following was composed especially for this volume.

321

I've gone through some major changes in my beliefs in the last fifteen years, many of them just in the last few. I've gone from fundamentalist Christian to militant atheist to tolerant atheist, with many steps in between. Today I consider myself an atheist with respect to traditional conceptions of God and an agnostic with respect to others.[1] My view of religion and the religious is neither as positive as it was fifteen years ago, nor as negative as it was seven years ago. Rather than explaining everything with God or explaining everything with science, I am now more content to accept that I don't have all of the explanations.

My initial upbringing was not particularly religious. I don't remember attending church on a regular basis as a child; instead, churchgoing was typically what the family did on Christmas and Easter and when the grandparents came to visit. (Since they live in Indiana and my immediate family is in Arizona, this was not terribly often.) My two sisters and I did, however, occasionally get sent off to vacation Bible school during the summer.

When I was in fifth or sixth grade, my parents separated and things changed. My mother turned to the comforts of religion. Since she had custody of me and my two sisters, we were given a heavy dose of religion as well.

We would move from church to church, never finding the one that my mother thought was quite right. We spent a long time (several months, at least) at a Franciscan church called "The Casa," which I remember as being friendly and low-key, not much in the way of theological issues, no Bible-beating, no fundamentalism.

At some point early in this increased attention to religion, while my sisters and I were visiting my grandparents in Indiana, I was baptized and made a public profession of faith at their church. I never felt any magical feelings of conversion, but I had been told that I shouldn't rely on my feelings as a sign of conversion. I did what I believed was right.

Sometime after our return from Indiana, around 1977, my family began attending an evangelical fundamentalist church in north Phoenix called the Northwest Missionary Church (which became Northwest Community Church). The pastor there was a man named Pat Shaughnessy. He had one leg, the other having been blown off by the Alphabet Bomber. Pastor Pat was supposedly the closest survivor to the bomb, which went off in an airport locker. He also claimed to be a former juvenile delinquent. These two facts about his life gave him plenty of material for entertaining sermons.

My sisters and mother went through the same process at this church that I had at my grandparents' church—public baptism as part of joining the church. I wasn't baptized again, but I did attend the meetings for new members to learn the doctrinal stances of the church and became a tithing member.

I attended Northwest Community Church until I went off to college. My experience as a fundamentalist Christian took place entirely during this period. It was at this church that my mother met my stepfather (at various times an usher, a deacon, and Sunday school teacher), but not where they married because Pastor Pat refused to recognize the validity of their divorces.

The church became the center of our lives. We spent more and more time there—first just Sunday mornings, then Sunday evenings as well, and then

Wednesday evenings. I would attend Sunday school, morning and evening services, and Wednesday night youth group or Bible study. I attended Boys' Brigade (which vaguely resembled Boy Scouts) for a time, as well. Most of my friends at school, however, were nonfundamentalists and even non-Christians.

In the late seventies and early eighties, I began to actually read the Bible and take interest in theological and philosophical issues. During this time I spent part of a summer at Eagle Lake Camp in Colorado (run by the Navigators) at which some interesting forms of indoctrination were used, such as role-playing situations where I and other campers were placed in the role of captured Christians in an anti-Christian, near-Armageddon time period, defending our faith against inquisitor-captors. I specifically remember being challenged by a role-playing "evolutionist" leader and using opposable thumbs as an argument against the "evolutionist's" claim that humans were descended from apes.

Several events occurred while I was in high school that set the stage for my disillusion with fundamentalism. A creationist, Buryl Eads, came to speak at our church and my mother bought me an autographed copy of his book *Let the Evidence Speak*. I was utterly convinced, and during my sophomore year of high school at the Jesuit-run Brophy College Preparatory, I wrote a paper for a Western Civilization class defending young-earth creationism. My instructor for the course was impressed that I had the guts to defend my views, and said so to my mother in a parent-teacher conference. I suspect, however, that he didn't agree with my conclusions (and he offered a few objections in comments on my paper that gave me pause).

A second, related event was that I tried to argue with some friends that creationism was true and evolution was false, based mainly on what I had read in Eads's book (and the lack of good counterarguments in our high school biology text). I was surprised to find that they were not easily swayed. Instead, they offered objections that I was unable to answer.

A third event was that I viewed a program on the Trinity Broadcasting Network about "backward masking" in rock music. Again, I completely bought it—after all, I could hear the messages with my own ears. This led to conflict with a friend of mine, who offered some good arguments for why at least some of the messages were in the ear of the hearer.

Finally, during high school I had noticed that many of my fellow Sunday school classmates seemed to be ignorant hypocrites. I found that I was one of those best able to answer the Sunday school teacher's questions, despite the fact that I was really not all that well-versed in the Bible. At church camps, when rooming with other high school males, I heard them tell about their drinking and sexual escapades. Yet these ignorant hypocrites seemed to be on better and closer terms with the leaders than I was.

There were no doubt many other such events, but these were typical. They provoked me into research about the things I believed in order to see if they could really stand up. I eventually concluded that they didn't.

Around my junior or senior year of high school I began to encounter some difficulties with the Bible—in the multiple creation accounts, for example. I began to have some doubts, and to actively seek out flaws in my religious beliefs. I began asking questions in Sunday school to which the teachers did not have satisfactory answers. (At one point, this led to the high school pastor meeting with me for breakfast several times to discuss things with me, trying to make sure I kept the faith.)

In Sunday school I befriended a guy named Steve who seemed to share some of my doubts. We would make comments to each other throughout sermons and Sunday school about the material being covered, and these comments tended to be disparaging. A Sunday school lesson on the evils of rock music and the use of "backward masking" I found particularly implausible. I remember bringing in a newspaper article critiquing "backward masking" claims to the Sunday school teacher.

In 1983 I answered a direct mailing and started subscribing to the *Skeptical Inquirer.* (My previous encounter with skeptical writings came about as a result of my interest in UFOs. At one point in grade school, I had started a UFO club that lasted only a few weeks, but which led me to read Philip Klass's debunking work, *UFOs: Identified,* at the public library.) My interest in the supernatural and paranormal, which had been cultivated by reading books of "strange but true" stories ordered through school from the *Weekly Reader,* had not been tempered by skepticism and I wanted to correct that. I found the *Skeptical Inquirer*'s debunkings of various paranormal phenomena to be much more convincing and satisfying than the paranormal "explanations."

That same year I became the youngest employee (age seventeen) at the Distributed Systems & Communications Center of Honeywell Information Systems in Phoenix, doing operations and administration work on a couple of their GCOS computer systems. The following year, I transferred to the Multics Development Center to become a PL/I programmer on the Multics system—a superior precursor to UNIX—which had been my career goal for the previous three or four years. I hadn't expected to achieve it by age eighteen, though.

By the time I graduated from high school in 1983, I had stopped attending church. I moved away from home to attend Arizona State University—not too far from home—as a computer science major.

Around 1984 I began using a Phoenix computer bulletin board system called Apollo (602-246-1432), which had a number of active atheists on it. At first I did not contribute a lot to the ongoing discussions, but eventually I became one of the most outspoken people on the BBS. Watching some of the Christian-versus-atheist arguments moved me further away from Christianity. Although I initially defended Christianity, I found that its opponents generally had the better arguments.

My *Skeptical Inquirer* subscription led to mailings from Prometheus Books, and so I discovered books such as B. C. Johnson's *The Atheist Debater's Handbook* and George Smith's *Atheism: The Case Against God.* By the time I read the latter book, I was a confirmed born-again atheist.

In 1984, I was interested enough in skeptical activities to fly to Stanford University for the annual conference of the Committee for the Scientific Investigation of Claims of the Paranormal (CSICOP). At the conference I ended up in an argument with someone about gnosticism and thereby met Gerald Larue, professor of biblical history and archaeology at the University of Southern California, who overheard and stepped in on my side. (In my discussion with Prof. LaRue he strongly encouraged me to pursue graduate studies, something I had not really considered at the time. I expected to get my computer science degree and continue to work as a programmer.) At that conference I put my name on a list of people interested in forming a local skeptical group in their area, but nothing ever came of it until I took steps of my own (two years later) to start one. After two and a half years of computer science courses that I found to have little relevance to my computer programming job, and growing dissatisfaction with my job as Honeywell began to phase out its Multics system in favor of the vastly inferior GCOS system, I changed my major to philosophy. The result was a dramatic improvement in my shaky grade point average.

In 1985, I began collecting biblical errors and contradictions. By early 1986, it was a booklet of about ten pages. I spent much of 1986 researching Christianity and reading everything critical on the subject I could find. I put out six different editions of my resulting pamphlet during that year (originally titled *Fundamentalism Is Nonsense,* then retitled *Some Reasons Not to Be a Christian,* and then reverting to the former title). In May of that year I ended up going on a late-night radio talk show to promote the pamphlet. I was invited for one hour, but the topic proved to be a hot one, and I was invited to stay for another hour, which I did. The discussions continued, and I was invited to stay for yet another hour, but by this time it was well past midnight and I elected to go home and sleep. (The discussion remained on the subject of atheism for the remainder of that talk show host's program.)

During 1986, a copy of my pamphlet was given to Pastor Pat of my parents' church. He wrote to me, telling me that I'm "just one in a long line of men throughout history that Satan has used to attack the Bible" but "long after [my] hammer is worn out, the anvil will still endure." He didn't bother to address any of the points in my pamphlet.

A copy of my pamphlet sent to the Dallas-based Church of the SubGenius led to a review published in the Fall 1986 issue of *Whole Earth Review* magazine. Another review appeared in the publication *Factsheet Five.* The *Whole Earth Review* article ended up in Ted Schultz's book *High Weirdness by Mail,* which contained an expanded review of my pamphlet. I continued to sell a few issues every week by mail order (presently $4 postpaid), though I have not revised it since December 1986 and it no longer accurately reflects my views (for example, it argues for the nonexistence of a historical Jesus based on the arguments of G. A. Wells). (I have written up an errata sheet which contains some notes on my present position, and periodically I do a little bit of work to transform it into a book-length manuscript, though never very seriously.)

In 1986 I also started the Phoenix Skeptics, which initially met on the ASU campus and in the home I rented with an atheist friend I'd known since high school. The group didn't really get off the ground until 1986, when we started publishing the *Phoenix Skeptics News* (now the *Arizona Skeptic*) and received some assistance from CSICOP in finding members. By early 1988, the Phoenix Skeptics had over a hundred members.

One of the group's first acts was to challenge Glenn Dunahew of an ASU organization called Christian Life to support claims he made in a lecture about backwards messages in rock music with a blind test. Instead of letting him tell the on-campus attendees of a Phoenix Skeptics meeting what to hear, we had everyone write down what they thought they heard. The result? Everybody had different "messages," which didn't match what Dunahew said was present.

In February 1987, three Phoenix Skeptics members who were also members of an ASU group called Americans Promoting Evolution Science (APES) debated two members of Christian Research Associates in Colorado. The debate, sponsored by the Campus Ambassadors Christian group, pitted Dan Davis of CRA (supported by David Horner) against Mike Norton of the Phoenix Skeptics (supported by Jamie Busch and myself). Although the audience was filled mostly with Christians, the post-debate vote favored the evolution side.

In December 1987 I did two or three radio shows, a lecture on psychic detectives for a criminal justice class at ASU, and a TV interview with critical comments on a big local New Age expo. Our group received favorable coverage in a lengthy article in *New Times,* Phoenix's weekly paper.[2] By this time I had become a fairly hard-nosed atheist and skeptic.

In 1987 I attended my second CSICOP conference, this time in Pasadena, California, and met more skeptics from the Phoenix area who helped get the Phoenix Skeptics moving. I also got a chance to meet James Randi, Paul Kurtz, and Mark Plummer (then CSICOP's executive director).[3] I had recently been reading about CSICOP's involvement in the "Mars Effect" test controversy, and asked Plummer about it. He didn't give me details, but said it was a bad situation that CSICOP had probably not handled properly.[4] I ended up pursuing the matter further during graduate school, and have since compiled a lengthy chronology of the major events and publications involved in the controversy.[5] My study of these events drove home the point for me that skeptics are just as susceptible to error and failings such as "groupthink" as believers are.

In 1988, evangelical Christian philosopher William Lane Craig came to speak at my parents' church. They invited him to their house for dinner, specifically to get him to try to bring me back into the fold, I think. Craig himself had more sense than that, and we had a friendly conversation and have since periodically corresponded. My parents gave me copies of several of his books, and he arranged to have a copy of J. P. Moreland's philosophical Christian apologetic work, *Scaling the Secular City,* sent to me by its author. I learned that evangelical Christians need not be stupid. Craig and Moreland appear to me to be very intelligent despite my extensive disagreement with their religious beliefs.

In 1988 I received a B.A. in philosophy from ASU and decided to pursue graduate studies in philosophy. I chose to attend the University of Arizona in Tucson, and quit my job doing systems programming for the Multics Development Center. In 1991 I received my M.A. in philosophy from UA. Since then I have received a couple of fellowships from the Institute for Humane Studies as a result of my interest in classical liberalism and have begun work on a dissertation regarding the epistemology of testimony—how can we be justified in believing things that we learn secondhand (which is how we obtain most of our knowledge).

My interest in this issue led me to subscribe to the *Journal of Scientific Exploration,* published by the Society for Scientific Exploration (SSE), an organization devoted to scientific investigation of anomalies as opposed to debunking absurd claims. While some SSE members are people the *Skeptical Inquirer* would characterize as "believers," I've come to find that many so-called "believers" are less dogmatic and more inquisitive than many "skeptics." There are distinctions to be drawn between different kinds of claims and claimants, and it is a mistake to class all "believers" as suckers who will believe anything in the *Weekly World News.*[6]

My present thinking has involved applying skepticism to organized skepticism, which has resulted in an increased tolerance for those with views other than my own in the religious, political, and scientific realms. I think that the existence of God, for example, is something that rational people can disagree about.[7]

Notes

1. I actually prefer different terms: "positive atheist" for disbelief in gods, "negative atheist" for nonbelief or agnosticism. See Michael Martin, *Atheism: A Philosophical Justification* (Temple University Press, 1990), for a discussion of types of atheism.

2. Dewey Webb, "Debunk Stops Here: The Phoenix Skeptics Declare Open Season on the Paranormal," *New Times,* December 2–8, 1987, pp. 22ff.

3. I later had cause to criticize some Australian skeptics, including Plummer. See my "Some Failures of Organized Skepticism," *Arizona Skeptic,* vol. 3, no. 1 (January 1990), pp. 2–5; "Postscript to 'Some Failures of Organized Skepticism,' " *Skeptic,* vol. 5, no. 3 (November/ December 1991), pp. 1–3; "How Not to Argue with Creationists," *Creation/Evolution,* vol. 11, no. 2 (no. 29, Winter 1991–92), pp. 9-21; "How Not to Respond to Criticism: Barry Price Compounds His Errors," unpublished manuscript, May 17, 1993.

4. The "Mars Effect" controversy began with studies by Michel Gauquelin that showed a correlation between the position of Mars in the sky at time of birth and sports ability. Various skeptical groups have tested the claim; CSICOP's tests are surrounded with controversy. (See Jeremy Cherfas, "Paranormal-watchers Fall Out over the Mars Effect," *New Scientist,* vol. 92 (October 29, 1981), p. 294; Irving Lieberman, "Raging Skeptics," *Omni,* vol. 4, no. 5 (February 1982), p. 94; Patrick Curry, "Research on the Mars Effect," *Zetetic Scholar,* no. 9 (March 1982), pp. 34–53; Richard Kammann, "The True Disbelievers: Mars Effect Drives Skeptics to Irrationality (parts 1 and 2)," *Zetetic Scholar,* no. 10 (December 1982), pp. 50–65; George O. Abell, Paul Kurtz, and Marvin Zelen, "The Abell-Kurtz-Zelen 'Mars Effect' Experiments: A Reappraisal," *Skeptical Inquirer,* vol. 7, no. 3 (Spring 1983), pp. 77–82; Suitbert Ertel, "Update on the 'Mars Effect,' " *Skeptical Inquirer,* vol. 16, no. 2 (Winter 1992), pp. 150–60.)

5. "Skeptics and the 'Mars Effect': A Chronology of Events and Publications," a work in progress.

6. I elaborate on this point in a short essay, "The Proper Role of Skeptical Organizations," which was posted to the Usenet sci.skeptic newsgroup on February 17, 1993, and summarized in Michael Epstein's "The Skeptical Perspective" column in the *Journal of Scientific Exploration,* vol. 7, no. 2, Fall 1993.

7. There exist recent defenses of theism (by philosophers such as Richard Swinburne, Alvin Plantinga, and William Lane Craig) that are not adequately countered by most atheists (but see J. L. Mackie, *The Miracle of Theism* (Oxford University Press, 1982), and Michael Martin, *Atheism: A Philosophical Justification,* op. cit., for good responses to some of these recent defenses).

Harry H. McCall:
"Who Do Men Say That I Am?"

> Having grown acquainted with a world built on mathematics and physics, Christianity increasingly appeared to me to be based on arbitrarily measured, intolerant, unquestioning faith.
>
> —Harry H. McCall

Harry H. McCall is a member of the Society of Biblical Literature and served as president of the South Carolina Academy of Religion during 1993–94. He is also a member of the Greenville Secular Humanist Association, which is located in Greenville, South Carolina. McCall attended Bob Jones University (1971–72), where he was elected to the student post of "assistant prayer captain." But he received 100 demerits (during double-demerit week) when another student informed the "discipline committee" that McCall had been listening to a "secular" radio station. (Regardless of the fact that McCall had been listening to a Christian hymn at the time, the rules at BJU forbade listening to any radio station other than the university's own WMUU.) Rather than submit to the penalty of being restricted to campus, McCall left BJU. He attended Central Wesleyan College (1972–76) where he received his B.A. in biblical literature. Then he began taking graduate-level courses at Columbia Theological Seminary in Atlanta, Georgia. However, since McCall continually signed up for courses of historical and doctrinal interest, and refused to sign up for courses in "Pastoral Studies" to "prepare him for the Presbyterian ministry," the dean informed McCall that he would not earn his master's degree. Again, McCall left. The following is from a speech he delivered at the South Carolina Academy of Religion's annual meeting in 1987, in which McCall addressed the question, " 'Who Do Men Say That I Am?': Defining Christianity."

Like "Christian," the central character in Bunyan's *The Pilgrim's Progress,* necessity compelled me to leave familiar surroundings in search of a definitive understanding of my faith. Like Christian, I also encountered both helps and hinderances along the way.

In my case affirming a particular creed did not allow me to "lay my burden

329

down," or to complete my pilgrimage of understanding. The theologian Paul Ricoeur, of the University of Chicago, came along and dimmed the lights of the "Celestial Kingdom" as I drew near its gates. His work *Essays in Biblical Interpretation* (Philadelphia: Fortress Press, 1980), raised questions I had never before encountered.

My pilgrimage was prompted partially by my employment in the pragmatic world of electronics. In that world I grew to understand the functions of active and passive devices in both large and small contexts. Not merely Ohm's basic law, but Ohm's law as it relates to complex network analysis—from a simple Kirchhoff Law to Fourier Theorems. I was thereby forced to work objectively with a consideration for openness and tolerance dictated by precise parameters.

Having grown acquainted with a world built on mathematics and physics, Christianity increasingly appeared to me to be based on arbitrarily measured, intolerant, unquestioning faith.

Many today would like their Christian beliefs to be stamped with "higher" approval. Faith is not enough. But a faith that is "USDA Choice," "untouched by human hands," and "vacuum-sealed for your protection" sucks up adherents left and right. Creedal statements assure believers that their particular faith exists in a "tamper-proof package."

Ultra-conservative churches are growing in response to popular demand. Even formerly liberal churches are recognizing the benefits of stressing only the most orthodox beliefs as defined by some of the earliest church councils.

Entering the Cafeteria of Theology such churches load their trays with the sweet fatty foods most nominal churchgoers were taught to enjoy as children. These churches avoid a protein-enriched historical understanding of the Bible and of theology that may upset the finicky stomachs of their members. But a balanced diet is necessary for theological growth and the growth of tolerance and diversity.

Put another way, the faith of ultra-conservative Christians as well as most nominal ones is being nurtured in an ecclesiastical greenhouse, its glass tinted to accommodate the denomination's doctrinal department, carefully filtering out all harmful historical facts.

For instance, four years ago I was attending one of the larger churches in Greenville. The adult Sunday school class was being taught from the denomination's quarterly booklet. The lesson was on Jesus' conflict with the Jews and their traditions, which the teacher said were the legal codes of the Old Testament. The following Sunday, I brought my copy of the ancient Hebrew lawbook, the Mishna [the written text of the Talmud], to class, and a few minutes before the class let out, I passed it around and gave a short introduction to Rabbinic Judaism. Members of the class told me that although they had been in church school most of their lives, they had no idea what the Talmud was.

At the next departmental teachers' meeting, which I was asked to attend, I was told that "Sunday school literature is written by very qualified men and does not need to be supplemented in any way."

This ultimatum was put into practice next quarter when we began studying the early chapters of Genesis, and I brought my copy of Pritchard's *Ancient Near Eastern Texts Relating to the Old Testament* to class. I found myself completely ignored by the teacher.

In retrospect, I feel that Sunday schools operate much like the Essene Community once did at Qumran in Jesus' day. In both cases the interpretation of the text is guided by a "pesher" method so as to arrive at a subjective meaning agreeable to the doctrine of the "interpreter."

There appear to be two major attempts to define Christianity, one from a pietistical perspective, and the other from a liturgical perspective. I believe they both fail.

Pietistical or Low Church Christianity

This subgroup is convinced they can make biblical New Testament Christianity live today through faith. For them, traditions are evil and even damnable. The church is seen as passing through different ages or "dispensations." Most in this subgroup refuse to acknowledge the Catholic Church's credibility, portraying it as an evil, apostate church doomed to fulfill eschatological woes in the near future.

Pietistical biblical faith is denominationally controlled and/or maintained by publishing houses that print materials reinforcing a certain theological diet. Although a few in this subgroup view higher education in religion as detrimental to the faith and sometimes advocate a Chinese-Communist-style Cultural Revolution for all intellectuals, most concede that the overall benefits of higher education are beneficial, so long as the degree is pursued at a seminary that promotes the views of their particular denomination.

Such "higher" institutions of religious knowledge are limited in scope and advocate a puritanical ideology. A case in point is the Bob Jones University history professor who told his class that a truthful church history has never been written.

Pietistical Christianity includes the televangelists. The modern teleparishioner can enjoy the theology of his choice in the privacy of his own home, and when it is time to "pray and ask God what He would have you do for this ministry," the teleparishioner's offering plate is an 800 number linked to operators' pools working computer terminals who take prayer requests as fast as the number of the teleparishioner's VISA or MasterCard.

For the innovative radio or TV evangelist, the statement of Jesus to "Look on the fields for they are white and ready to harvest" has taken on new meaning. The dollar has come to symbolize and do what God cannot.

As the success of these ministries mushroomed, so did financial responsibility. The televangelist who used to request money to get on TV soon found himself requesting yet more money to stay there. With financial responsibilities mounting—often at over a million dollars a week—the need to cut through the religious jargon and have God talk directly to the faithful through a preacher/medium became a necessity. To date, Oral and Richard Roberts, Jimmy Swaggert, and Ernest Angley have been granted revelations even the pope and the president of the Mormons would envy.

However, all has not been well. Pat Robertson, whom God told to run for the presidency of the United States, lost. Jim Bakker was convicted of tax evasion and mail fraud. Jerry Falwell almost went bankrupt. And, in order for the university which he founded (Liberty University) to remain on the federal aid program, he recently had to waive religious and intellectual restrictions placed on the university's professors. Previously, they were required to abide by doctrinal statements, and could only publish materials that did not conflict with university doctrine. Now they are "at liberty" to do so.

Swaggert, with major budget overruns, broke down and cried on national television blaming viewers for halting his personal anointing to proceed with the "Great Commission." Then he was caught paying a woman to act out some of his sexual fantasies while he watched.

Reverend Tony Leyva, a southern TV evangelist who used to wear a Superman costume and carry a Bible, nicknaming himself "SuperChristian," and who was also in the *Guinness Book of World Records* (for four years) for preaching the longest known sermon (seventy-two hours straight), was hired by Georgia television station WXTX-TV to replace Jimmy Swaggert's show with his own. But before the ink dried on the contract, Leyva was arrested by the FBI, along with three of his fellow fundamentalists, on charges of transporting boys across state lines for the purposes of prostitution or criminal sexual activity.

Oral Roberts, facing a sharp decline of teleparishioners complicated by mounting university costs, closed his dental and law schools. And the "City of Faith" went bankrupt, despite the fact that Roberts raised eight million dollars by claiming that God had put a price on his head.

Crusading revelator and faith healer W. V. Grant was dropped from syndication when the Amazing Randi demonstrated that Grant's "revelations" came from a miniature microphone in his ear and not from God.

Last but not least, Ernest Angley, upon heeding God's call to hold a healing crusade in Munich, Germany, was arrested and jailed for practicing medicine without a license.

Of course, whenever one ministry loses teleparishioners, other TV ministers swoop down on its time slot, stealing the sheep and their funds.

Liturgical or High Church Christianity

This subgroup includes the largest Christian bodies in the world, the Catholic and Orthodox faiths, and also the Reformed churches, which are usually distinguished from the pietistical/low churches in being able to trace their origins directly to the Reformation.

This subgroup maintains its distinctness by requiring clergy to be theologically trained and by maintaining a large division between the role of the clergy and the role of the laity.

Because of this subgroup's tight liturgical uniformity, a parishioner from a denomination on the east coast of the United States could attend a church of the same denomination on the west coast and not notice any change in the order of worship or materials employed in the liturgy.

In this respect, high church Christianity operates like a business franchise, in that the laity is assured of "the service you have come to expect," as Hertz

Rent-a-Car puts it. Such standardization also promotes overfamiliarity and boredom.

However, I see a growing plus for this subgroup. Wile the congregation liturgically repeats dogmas outlining benefits in the spiritual world up there, seminaries have been hard at work preparing the clergy to counsel and help people down here. Proof of this can be found in the enrollment listings at seminaries, where usually there are as many doctor of ministry candidates as there are masters of divinity.

My Search for a Definition of Chrisitianity

We all know what "Christianity" is, don't we? I decided to phone church leaders and ask *them*, "What is Christianity?" After eleven calls I began to feel it was "God's will for my life" that I not know what I had been doing on Sunday morning for the past thirty-five years.

This confusion can be traced back to the question of who Jesus was. Neither John the Baptist, the disciples, nor the Jewish people could comprehend what this "son of man" was up to so as to define him. Many biblical scholars agree that even the confession of Peter that, "You are the Christ" is an anachronism.

Even glossing over the difficulty of defining Christianity, there remains the question of determining its truthfulness in a world filled with ambiguous experiences. For instance, Oral Roberts had a dream in which God told him that his daughter-in-law, Patti, would be killed in a plane crash if she ever left his ministry. Patti did leave the ministry, distressed at the way her husband, Richard Roberts, was being turned into a clone of Oral, and the way they rationalized their jet-set ways of life. But the year Patti left his ministry, she did not die in a plane crash, while Rebecca, Oral's own daughter, did. [See Patti Roberts's autobiography, *Ashes to Gold*.]

In 1982, fundamentalist preacher Lester Rolloff (who had appeared a year earlier on "60 Minutes" stating his defiance of what he called "Texas' Godless juvenile home system") along with four girl singers on their way to lead a revival, tried to fly a twin engine plane through a storm. The mistake proved lethal. After a wind shear ripped off a wing (what may be termed an "act of God"), all five plunged 18,000 feet to their deaths. I am sure that minister Rolloff was convinced he was immune to such a disaster, especially since he was obeying "God's will" in holding revivals.

Two years after Rolloff died, a 747 filled with Japanese on a Buddhist religious pilgrimage to Hawaii also encountered a wind shear, which violently rolled the plane over and caused it to plunge almost five miles earthward. Amazingly, the Japanese pilot was able to recover control with only tail section damage. Success of this otherwise doomed flight was attributed by the plane's passengers to their "songs and prayers offered to the Buddha"!

A related illustration of the ambiguity of the truth of any one religion: Many church leaders insure church property against "acts of God." "Stepping out on faith" or "trusting in the Lord" is a little easier to do when you know your church can be rebuilt in case it's struck by lightning, or, biblically speaking, "fire from heaven." No matter how deeply most denominations revere the Bible, they realize that to take it literally could prove disastrous.

The Bible is not fact, it is tradition. Tradition makes Christianity function. Thus in Christianity it is tradition and not the ambiguities and limitations of what may be known about the historical man Jesus that is honored. This tradition does entail facts, but the tradition dictates the facts and not vice versa.

Christianity is so dependent upon tradition that pressure from the tradition extends into the world of objective critical scholarship. For instance, Rudolf Bultmann, the famed Protestant theologian and scholar, just about dropped the term that he usually used, "myth"—as when he was busy "demythologizing" Christianity. His later works focused on the traditional-sounding term, "kerygma." It is more traditional to rekerymatize Christianty than to demythologize it!

Also, Frank Cross curtsied to tradition in choosing not to call Hebrew mythology "myth" when compared to Canaanite mythology. Instead, he named it "epic," as in his major work, *Canaanite Myth and Hebrew Epic.*

Oxford historian Michael Wood, in his book *In Search of the Trojan War,* began his quest as a nonbeliever. He doubted if the epic poetry of Homer was based on a historical siege of Troy, or if there ever existed a Mycenaen named "Agamemnon." After all, Homer lived perhaps five hundred years after the "fall" of Troy. Wood was suprised to discover that many descriptions in Homer's epic were substantiated via evidence from archeological digs. Wood's quest had brought belief, but not in the gods depicted by Homer, which remained a mere accretion of Greek traditions. It is in this sense that I appreciate the traditions formulated and employed by Jews, Catholics, and Orthodox Christians, which adapted and changed as they grew.

I asked Keith Nickle, a former student of both Karl Barth and Oscar Cullmann at Basel, Switzerland, who now pastors a church in Tennessee, and James M. Robinson, professor of religion and director of the Institute for Antiquity and Christianity at Claremont, California, to comment on Christianity's basis in tradition.

Nickle, being a pastor, had learned to be cautious when speaking to parishioners on this subject. He would only share his historical-critical knowledge of the New Testament with personal friends he knew would welcome such discussion.

Robinson, teaching in a college environment, was not as hesitant. He believed scholars had not only the right but the obligation to demythologize Christianity. He told me he had been criticized for not including the resurrection in a book he was writing on Easter. He then confirmed to me his conviction about Christian myths such as this and said he had no intention of including it.

I find myself sympathetic to the positions of both Nickle and Robinson, but the time comes in all objective religious scholastic careers in which one must choose between religiosity and truthfulness. "Jesus" is so obviously a product of human imagination coupled with arbitrary faith that I chose to simply acknowledge the obvious rather than remain religious.

Photo by A&R Studio

David N. Stamos:
Why I Am Not a New Apostolic

In [a] . . . philosophy course I came across a book that was to spark a profound change in my life. One of the required texts was Walter Kaufmann's *Critique of Religion and Philosophy*. While reading this book I came across a passage wherein Kaufmann mentions Albert Schweitzer's thesis that in the Gospels Jesus predicts that the end-time including his glorious Return will occur before the end of the generation around him. And when I read that I was stunned! It totally contradicted one of my church's most central teachings. Indeed I had never heard nor read anything like it before. And yet I couldn't dismiss it offhand. Its connection with Albert Schweitzer made this difficult, since I had already grown to tremendously respect the man for his work on Bach and also for his humanitarian work. Since Kaufmann gave no biblical references, and since I was busy enough with my university studies, I decided to let the matter rest for the time being and to pursue it some time later when I had the time. But a germ had been planted, and I was not aware of it at the time, nor of its immense personal consequences.

—David N. Stamos

David N. Stamos is currently working on a Ph.D. in philosophy at York University in Toronto. The title of his dissertation is "The Ontology of Biological Species: An Essay in the Spirit of Russell." He also sells freethought literature, including his book *Forbidden Truths: A Refutation of Christianity,* through Sophia Veritas Publications. The following is a reprint of Stamos' essay, "Why I Am Not a New Apostolic."

Ever since Bertrand Russell came out with his celebrated 1927 essay "Why I Am Not a Christian," it has become fashionable for skeptical authors of like mind to offer variations on Russell's theme. I have encountered, for instance, "Why I Am Not a Jew," "Why I Am Not a Methodist," "Why I Am Not a Presbyterian," "Why I Am Not a Fundamentalist," and "Why I am Not a Mormon." But whereas Russell's article is purely an intellectual and theoretical treatise, the latter are largely autobiographical, chronicling the life experiences of their respective authors in their break from their inherited religions. As such they have come

337

to comprise a unique and relatively new genre in literature, a genre which has its antecedents in the nineteenth century and perhaps even a little earlier but which has only come of age in the present century, a genre which, for lack of a better name, might be called *emancipation from religion literature.*

To add to the growth of this modern genre I offer my own autobiographical piece concerning my break from my inherited church, a church I'm sure few readers will have heard of, and fewer still actually know of, the New Apostolic Church.

Since this church is so little known by the general reading public I feel it is incumbent upon me to provide some prefatory remarks on the nature and constitution of this church. The New Apostolic Church is one of the many sects that may be grouped under the general heading of Protestantism, although New Apostolics will never acknowledge this. It is a worldwide church, established in over a hundred countries, and is centered in Germany. Its total world membership is between one and two million.

As with most Christian denominations, the New Apostolic Church believes it is the only true and valid church of God today. All others are necessarily invalid. Thus salvation is only open to New Apostolics. There is, of course, nothing surprising or particularly interesting in this. What is interesting, however, is the history of its origin. The New Apostolic Church claims to be the reestablishment of the original apostles' ministry of old, a ministry, they claim, that ended with the death of the last of Jesus' apostles, Apostle John. It is on this claim of the reestablishment of the apostles' ministry that they base their validity. According to them the original apostles were commissioned and empowered with the ability to dispense the Holy Spirit. Being sealed by the laying on of hands of a living apostle is according to them a prerequisite for salvation, which they liken to a modern immigration visa, and which they base on certain New Testament passages. Accordingly, with the death of the last apostle, Apostle John, the means of salvation were no longer available to man.

Thus began a spiritual dark age, an age, however, which came to an end in our modern age. About the year 1830 as a result of fervent prayer among various groups of believers in Scotland and England, believers longing for salvation, a most amazing event occurred, the second outpouring of the Holy Spirit, an outpouring very much like the original outpouring at Pentecost as recorded in Acts. Combined with divine revelations the result was the reestablishment of the apostles' ministry in 1832.

The church grew and spread rapidly. However, as is common with many denominations, a major schism lay not far ahead. The new apostles stuck to the belief that the new church should have only twelve apostles, no more and no less. They believed that the promised Return of Christ would occur within the time of their ministerial activity and moreover there were New Testament passages which seemed to support the establishment and maintenance of specifically twelve apostles. Congregations in Germany and Holland, however, allegedly inspired by God, disagreed with the limiting of the apostles' ministry to twelve and eventually broke away. This separation took place in 1863 and was the natal hour of the New Apostolic Church.

Naturally, as the decades passed and the hoped-for Return of Christ failed to occur, the original reestablished church progressively dwindled. Its last apostle died in 1901. The church, interestingly, still has not died. There remain in England nine congregations. However, in virtue of its lack of apostles it remains a shell of its former self.

All of this is standard church history as taught within the church. However, subsequent research on my own part has brought to my knowledge that the reestablished church was called the Catholic Apostolic Church and developed from the revelations of one Edward Irving (1792–1834), a famous Scottish Presbyterian minister excommunicated in 1830 for a tract declaring Christ's human nature as sinful. He and his followers, known as Irvingites, developed out of the revivalist and millennarian circles which gathered round one Henry Drummond (1786–1860), a politician and eventual Irvingite leader, and came to constitute the Catholic Apostolic Church. The first apostle was appointed by Drummond in 1832 and the full college of twelve held their first "council" in London in 1835. Drummond also helped finance the new church and in 1834 was ordained "Angel for Scotland."

All of this does not particularly discredit the New Apostolic Church of today but it does make me wonder with suspicion now why the church was so selective in what it told us of its origin. Could it be that with further research either or both Irving and Drummond could prove discreditable characters, from matters such as Irving's heretical tract on Jesus' sinful nature? Whatever the reason I would certainly like to find out.

At any rate, to finish off my brief description of the New Apostolic Church, it is centered in Germany and is very hierarchical. At the top is the chief apostle, headquartered in Germany. He is considered Christ's chief ambassador here on earth. Beneath him the world is divided among district apostles, who have apostles beneath them. Their word is considered the word of God. Beneath the apostles are bishops, elders, evangelists, priests, deacons, and finally sub-deacons.

New Apostolics are extremely millennarian. They firmly believe we live in the end time and that Christ's glorious Return is imminent. The only thing holding back this event is that the last soul comprising the elect 144,000 firstlings has not yet been found and sealed with the Holy Spirit. When that happens the firstlings, also known as the Bride of Christ (who, incidentally, will be taken only from the ranks of the New Apostolics), will be resurrected into heaven for the wedding feast while the horror that is Armageddon will commence on earth for three years, resulting in the death of approximately one-third the world's population. New Apostolics not virtuous enough to have made it as firstlings will be saved the horrors of Armageddon by being divinely transported into a safe place in a desert. After Armageddon, during the Thousand Years of Peace, the 144,000 firstlings will rule the world as a theocracy of kings and priests.

The firstlings, incidentally, will not all come from living New Apostolics. Many will come from the ranks of departed New Apostolics. Indeed some souls may become New Apostolic while in the realm of the departed. The most interesting (and, now that I think about it, laughable) example is that of Abraham Lincoln. During a service for the departed ones, maybe fifteen or twenty years ago, a sister had a vision in which she saw Abraham Lincoln being sealed by an apostle.

This vision was quickly authenticated and it became widely accepted throughout the church that Abraham Lincoln is now a fellow New Apostolic.

Into this church I was born. And into this church I invested the first twenty-six years of my life. My mother's side was completely New Apostolic, my father's side non-practicing Greek Orthodox. My father allowed my mother to raise me and my older sister with the beliefs and practices of the church. On Sundays my mother would take us to church in the morning and again in the afternoon. My father would spend the day trapshooting and drinking beer.

As a child, belonging to this church did not seem particularly odd or uncomfortable. However, during my teenage years it made quite a difference. It really set me apart from my peers, which is hardest felt at that age. For instance, I went through high school with short hair. Today, of course, there would be nothing odd about that. But during the early and mid-seventies long hair was definitely the thing and anyone with short hair was simply a nerd. Indeed with this church taboos abounded. No long hair on males, as already noted, and no short skirts on females. No jeans, at least at church functions like picnics and gatherings. No going dancing, no going to movies, no going to bars or worldly parties, no premarital sex, no drugs (I'm still thankful for that), no joining organized sports or clubs, etc., etc., etc.

It was difficult, but I toed the line. I toed the line because I truly believed. And they made it easier by having a very well organized Young People group, which had activities practically every week. Indeed the largest activity, and the most interesting and fun, was the annual Day of the Youth, in which young people from the church all over North America would meet for a weekend in Kitchener, Ontario.

At any rate, the purpose of the Young People organization was to keep out as much as possible deleterious worldly influences and to promote marriage within the church. Fortunately, now that I look back, I never married while a member of the church. Had I done so, the concatenation of events which led to my eventual apostasy might never have happened. At any rate, it would have made it much more difficult to leave the church. As it was, my break was much more clean.

Though I toed the line as a youth, there was predominantly one area in which I deviated. At the age of sixteen I got into bodybuilding, which I have continued with much dedication up to the present day. Naturally the church frowned upon it, but my original purpose was not to enter competition or any self-glorification. Early as a child I had contracted chronic asthma which persisted throughout my youth. When I was fifteen I had heard that working out with weights was very beneficial in reducing or even eliminating asthma. And so I shortly afterward got into it, my original motivation receding into the background as the years went on, as I increasingly learned of the many benefits to be derived from bodybuilding. Anyway, as I look back upon my life now, I can say with certainty that asthma and religion were the two biggest curses in my life. (The third would be an alcoholic father.)

Particularly interesting is the mind-set or mental disposition that is developed from being born and raised in such a religion. It was an immense exercise in alienation and deprivation of proper socialization. Indeed much of this came from the church's Manichaean outlook. We were constantly influenced to think in black-and-white terms. This Manichaeanism was even reflected in the church's official dress, in males' black suits with black ties and white shirts, in females' black skirts with white blouses. The teachings were particularly forceful. All along we were taught, for instance, that "we are in this world but not of this world," that we are a different species from the rest of this world, that only New Apostolics are children of God, the rest are children of Satan. We were taught, moreover, to despise and devalue the things of this world, and that the meaning of life is afterlife. Indeed we were given a tremendously inflated and false sense of importance. Perhaps the most laughable example of this is that we were taught that a sub-deacon, the lowest rung on the hierarchical ladder, has a more important office than the Catholic pope, because the pope does not belong to the true church and we do. It has been eight years now since I alone tore myself away from this church. And it has been a constant fight ever since to purge from myself the vestiges of this psychology, the feeling of distance from my fellow man and the residual instinct that I am a superior creature compared to the rest of mankind. No doubt working in a roadhouse bar for a number of years (first as a doorman and then as a bartender and manager) has helped me considerably to reunite myself with the human species and to make up for the lost socialization of those earlier years. But what a price to pay!

But this is all with hindsight. At the time, while I was still a believing part of the church, I was unaware of the harm that was being done to me. I truly believed and I was happy, in spite of all the sacrifices I had to endure. Moreover I was becoming an integral part of the particular congregation to which I belonged. At sixteen I was made the assistant organist; at eighteen the organist and assistant choir leader. I was also made a sub-deacon at roughly the same time. Often during Wednesday night services and Sunday afternoon services I would be called upon to serve for five minutes behind the altar. On Tuesday and Thursday nights there was door-knocking, like Jehovah's Witnesses but not as extreme or obnoxious, which I often participated in. Friday nights were often a Young People gathering, Saturday nights either Brother Meeting or Tri-District Youth Service in Hespeler, Sunday nights usually Young People choir practice or Bible class. And then of course there were the church services, twice on Sundays, once Wednesday nights, followed by choir practice. I enjoyed it all and lived it fully.

In looking back now, however, I can honestly say the only thing I miss is playing the organ. I loved being organist. I loved playing services, weddings, and funerals. I loved it and I loved the compliments. I especially remember an apostle telling me once that what I did was more important than preaching. I put everything I had into it and they adored it. Indeed the only reason I did not pursue music as a career was because I deeply feared that such a pursuit might destroy my love of it, and I didn't want to lose that love. I especially loved before and after the services. People would come in an hour early just to hear me practice Bach or Mendelssohn or Rheinberger. And before the service I would play the most elegant and appropriate pieces and arrangements, sometimes my own extemporizations. And when the service was over I would end with a flourish piece, usually Bach. The zenith of this career was when, at the age of twenty, I was first permitted to play an organ solo in the Christmas concert on the massive pipe organ in the central cathedral in Kitchener. I played Bach's most famous piece, his "Toccata" from Toccata and Fugue in D Minor. I'll never forget the feeling I had as I played the last chord, having just played the piece flawlessly, and having blown everyone's mind, including the district apostle. I'll also never forget accidentally hitting the lowest note on the keyboard during the opening prayer in a district service. And indeed I'll never forget the last time I played the organ in church. I knew it would be my last time and I played Bach's "St. Anne Fugue."

It is the only thing I miss from my church days. Playing Bach at home might sound just as good, but it's not the same. Indeed it can't be.

With such an emotional investment all my life it seemed nothing could have pulled me away from the church. I loved it. It was my life. And no one could change my mind. But as life will sometimes have it, with all its twists and turns, a very unusual set of events was about to transpire. And it would change my life forever in the most radical way.

In September 1977 I began undergraduate studies at York University in Toronto. Because I was late with a correspondence math course to complete my grade 13, I was late in applying and then registering at York. When I finally did register, most of the courses I wanted were filled up. So my advisor suggested I take a literature course on the classical world. He said, "You're Greek; you might like it." I hemmed and hawed a bit. I wasn't interested in the subject and didn't like a lot of reading. Nevertheless I gave in and took the course. And I loved it! The first philosopher we took was Plato, reading his *Apology*. I immediately fell in love with philosophy and Plato and was very active in the seminars. And, interestingly, I naturally tried to harmonize Platonic teachings with my church's teachings. I saw no inherent contradictions.

In my second year I took more philosophy courses but maintained my original goal of getting a degree in business administration, a degree perfectly satisfactory with the church, since many of its leaders were German businessmen.

In my third year at York, as per schedule, I began business school proper. And I hated it! What I hated was not so much the work but the values and the mentality they immediately tried to inculcate in us. We were the elite of the university, business and making money and profit the most important things in life, etc., etc. After two months I had had enough, realized this was not for me, and dropped out. I decided to resume studies in the spring and finish my degree in philosophy, which I loved.

It was in one of these subsequent philosophy courses that I came across a book that was to spark a profound change in my life. One of the required texts was Walter Kaufmann's *Critique of Religion and Philosophy*. While reading this book I came across a passage wherein Kaufmann mentions Albert Schweitzer's thesis that in the Gospels Jesus predicts that the end-time including his glorious Return will occur before the end of the generation around him. And when I read that I was stunned! It totally contradicted one of my church's most central teachings. Indeed I had never heard nor read anything like it before. And yet

I couldn't dismiss it offhand. Its connection with Albert Schweitzer made this difficult, since I had already grown to tremendously respect the man for his work on Bach and also for his humanitarian work. Since Kaufmann gave no biblical references, and since I was busy enough with my university studies, I decided to let the matter rest for the time being and to pursue it some time later when I had the time. But a germ had been planted, and I was not aware of it at the time, nor of its immense personal consequences.

It was not until after I had finished my B.A., however, during a long stint of unemployment, that I began my research into the matter. For the first time in my life I actually read the New Testament. Hitherto, as with most Christians, I had relied on what I was taught in church. And I couldn't have been more shocked! Not only did Kaufmann's book prove correct, not only did Schweitzer's thesis seem clearly vindicated, but I discovered so many more problems connected with the New Testament, not only internal contradictions but also major external ones, contradictions between what my church had always taught me and what was taught in the Bible. And here my church was teaching as it always had, not only that the Bible is God's true and holy Word, but also that only the New Apostolic Church is truly based on the Bible!

More and more I wrestled with these problems. And the more I wrestled with them, the more it became obvious to me that they were irresolvable and would not go away. Eventually I conceived the idea that someone should put them all together in one book and that I would attempt to do this. This was in January 1983, six months before my eventual break with the church. This short manuscript gradually grew and evolved into my first book, *Forbidden Truths: A Refutation of Christianity,* which I eventually published myself in November 1989, under the imprint Sophia Veritas Publications. ("Sophia" is the Greek word for wisdom, "veritas" the Latin word for truth.)

Why I waited six months before I quit the church was a matter of timing. For one thing I wanted to give God, if He existed, a chance to get me off the wrong track, even to push Him into giving me a miracle. Second, I wanted to wait until my mother had her holidays; I knew that my apostasy would be very traumatic for her.

My final church service was Sunday afternoon, July 31, 1983. I knew it would be my last. I had planned it that way.

Also, two days previously, on Friday, I had mailed out eight copies of a letter I wrote to the clergy. In this three-page, tightly knit letter I outlined all the problems I had with church teaching and why I was leaving. I cited many Bible contradictions. I pointed out the major discrepancy concerning the Second Coming of Christ. I pointed out Jesus' teachings on money and material possessions and how these contradicted most New Apostolics, especially our leader for North America, District Apostle Michael Kraus, a millionaire many times over, the founder and president of Kraus Carpet Mills. These I pointed out and many more. And I challenged them, since they supposedly had a monopoly on truth, being official bearers of the Holy Spirit, to answer my questions. And I told them that if they could answer my questions to my satisfaction, in writing, then I would return to the fold, and if not, then they would never see me again.

These eight letters I mailed to a good cross-section of the clergy, all of whom knew me, some very well. The list included Michael Kraus, the top man in North America, two apostles, one bishop, one evangelist, two priests, and a fellow sub-deacon who was my best friend.

Of these eight letters I received only three replies, one from an apostle, one from a priest, and one from the sub-deacon, my best friend. Each of these letters ignored my arguments and only tried to make me feel foolish and stupid. "Woe to those on the wrong side of the fence," wrote one. To the first two I replied that this was not good enough, that I wanted answers to my questions, and in writing. The third letter was followed up by a personal visit, in which we stayed up all night discussing these issues, but to no avail. Filled with the Holy Spirit, my friend, with tears in his eyes, in the end could not answer my questions. Finally, to my two replies to the apostle and the priest, only one replied, the apostle. He said he could see that they've lost me to the world's philosophies but that their door would be always open to me (until the end-time, of course).

All of this made for exceptionally interesting reading, both their letters and my replies. At any rate, it was at this point that my strongest suspicions became certainties. I knew then and there that I had done the right thing, that my loss was really a gain, my falling really a rising.

Indeed in an ironic way I had predicted the outcome. I'll never forget the last time I served from behind the altar. It was a Wednesday night. I spoke about those types of insects that prefer the dark, that scurry away when you turn on the light. I compared these insects to people who fear the truth. Naturally they all thought I was talking about people from outside the church, people from the world. Little did they know I was talking about them.

Though indeed I came more and more to consider my falling a rising, the transition period was nevertheless not an easy one. I not only gave up a set of beliefs, I gave up all my friends and social life. Plus I was filled with profound disillusionment, not knowing in which direction to turn. I was filled with a tremendous vacuum. My life seemed meaningless. What had filled my life with meaning, what I had believed all my life, crumbled to dust, and by my own hands.

I fell into a period of great depression. I don't think a day passed without my thinking about suicide. The topic of death became almost an obsession with me. I did not stop with my investigation of my church. I quickly turned to even greater matters, the existence of God and life after death. I read voraciously, both pro and con. It was all a matter of logic and evidence. The art was to try to be as objective as possible. Love of truth demanded this. And after intensive study on both topics I felt forced to give the nod to negative conclusions on them both, especially belief in God, a little less so but still strongly life after death as well.

It was a difficult period in my life, lasting perhaps two years. But what immeasurably helped me through this period of religious withdrawal were two things: my intellectual discipline, philosophy, and my physical discipline, bodybuilding. Both served me extremely well. And I did it all alone. To this day I feel that what I did was cure myself of a very difficult disease and addiction.

Naturally it would have been better had I never had it in the first place. I still envy those I meet who've never been afflicted.

And yet it turned out to have a very positive effect too. I feel much better about myself now: happier, freer, saner—I feel mature. But equally important, if not more, in losing my belief in the other world it made me think all the more intensely about this world. The almost simultaneous effect was that I came to acknowledge and accept the most profound philosophy of life ever propounded, a teaching in which life (life in this life) receives its greatest preciousness and sanctity. This teaching is Albert Schweitzer's teaching of Reverence for Life, in which life receives its highest affirmation, and life is filled once more with meaning and hope.

Photo by Evanston Photo Studios

Howard M. Teeple:
I Started to Be a Minister

My first taste of historical study of the Bible shook me up psychologically, but the experience was invaluable. I am greatly indebted to Professor Schulze, for his teaching opened my eyes to the fallacy of fundamentalism, thereby changing the direction of my life.

—Howard M. Teeple

Howard M. Teeple is the executive director of Religion and Ethics Institute in Evanston, Illinois, and has taught religion at Bexley Hall, West Virginia Wesleyan College, and Northwestern University. He is listed in *Who's Who in Religion, Who's Who in the Midwest,* and *Who's Who in the World.* His works include *The Literary Origin of the Gospel of John, The Noah's Ark Nonsense,* and *The Historical Approach to the Bible* (for which he was awarded a certificate of recognition by the National Conference of Christians and Jews in 1982). He has recently completed his magnum opus, *How Did Christianity Really Begin?* The following is excerpted from his autobiography, *I Started to Be a Minister: From Fundamentalism to a Religion of Ethics.*

I was born in our family's Oregon farmhouse, December 29, 1911. . . .
On my eleventh birthday my parents gave me a copy of the King James Bible; it was well worn by the time I finished high school. . . .

When I was twelve my parents became concerned that I had not been baptized. They had our Methodist minister in Salem perform the ceremony one Sunday. About that time they went through a pietistic period that lasted two years; in the winter evenings the three of us would take turns at reading from the Bible, followed by our kneeling beside our chairs and praying aloud.

Several factors lead me into fundamentalism. My parents attended some of the revival meetings conducted by traveling evangelists. My untrained, but well-meaning Sunday school teachers taught me that all of the Bible is true. I joined the David C. Cook organization for youth, the IAH ("I Am His," i.e., Jesus') Club and wore the IAH ring.

After responding to an advertisement in the *Christian Herald* magazine, I took a correspondence course in Old Testament theology from the Moody Bible Institute in Chicago. The course was distinctly fundamentalist in point of view, accepting the premise that if one's soul is to be saved for heaven, it is fundamental, or necessary, to believe certain fundamentalist doctrines, including the inerrancy of the Bible. By the time I graduated from the eighth grade I was definitely a fundamentalist.

Yet even then, I could not help observing that some very fine people were not fundamentalists. In fact, some were not even Christians, including two wonderful teachers I had. Another non-Christian, our neighbor, donated more of his time to help others in need in Spring Valley than anyone else in the school district. . . .

In high school, my third year of Latin consisted of the translation of Cicero's orations, taught by a marvelous teacher, Joy Hills. In addition to guiding the translation, she led the class in discussing moral and philosophical questions commented on by Cicero. She demonstrated by her life and teaching that a non-religious person can have high ethical principles. . . .

At Leslie Church, I was an active member of the Epworth League [which included spending summers at a camp filled with Methodist youth from many different churches]. . . . At the final evening service each year an appeal was made for us to prayerfully listen for the Spirit of Jesus to call us to a life of Christian service as a minister or missionary. In 1931, just after graduating from high school, I responded to the appeal. I did not hear a voice, but I felt an urge, which I regarded as a divine "call" to become a minister. Therefore I "went forward" with a few others and stood before the altar. . . .

I received a Local Preacher's License, granting me authority to preach sermons in Leslie. . . .

One Sunday, our minister asked me to preach at a small country church six miles away that was supported by Leslie Church. I decided to include something I had read: "Lord, help us to hate the sin and love the sinner." I mixed it up and prayed, "Lord, help us to love the sin and hate the sinner!" One gentleman in the congregation roared with laughter. . . .

Unaware of the fundamentalist-modernist controversy in Christianity, I bumped into it unwittingly. I was visiting a tactful liberal Methodist minister who shocked me when he said that the Psalms were not necessarily written by David. He said, correctly, that the author ascriptions in the Bible were added long after the Psalms were written.

At one monthly meeting of ministers that I attended a fundamentalist asked the modernist minister of the First Methodist Episcopal Church whether he was a fundamentalist or a modernist. The minister at First Methodist replied, "I am modern enough to believe in all that is fundamental!" Again, I did not understand what was involved.

At freshman enrollment at Willamette University I conversed with a law professor who mentioned favorably the theory of evolution. "But it can't be true!" I remarked. "The Bible says the world was created in six days." He tactfully changed the subject, and I imagined I had refuted a law professor. . . .

A course required of freshmen at Willamette then was "Bible History," taught by an ordained Methodist minister with a Ph.D. in religion from the University of Chicago. It was my first taste of historical study of the Bible. It shook me up psychologically, but the experience was invaluable. I am greatly indebted to Professor Schulze, for his teaching opened my eyes to the fallacy of fundamentalism, thereby changing the direction of my life.

I felt—perhaps erroneously—that laymen would not stand for it if I preached what I was fully convinced was the truth. On the other hand, I could not conscientiously preach what I knew was false. Therefore, at the close of my sophomore year, I abandoned the goal of becoming a minister. Some of the laymen at Leslie Church blamed the university; I blamed the laymen and the fundamentalist movement.

In my junior year I took a two-semester course, "Records of the Life of Jesus." The professor, Herman Clark, emphasized two points. "First, do not read commentaries or other books that interpret the gospels or the life of Jesus. After you have finished the course, you will be free to read whatever you wish. I want you to form your opinions on the basis of the source material alone, the gospels.

"Second, each of you is at liberty to think and believe whatever you want. You will be graded on how well you study the text, not on whether you agree with me, your church, or anyone else. . . .

After all the students declared what they thought, he resumed lecturing. "I want to tell you how Dr. Sharman produced the book we will be using, *Records of the Life of Jesus*. He was the son of American Methodist missionaries in China in the late 1800s. He became honorary lecturer in the Department of History at Yenching University in Peking. He used several Bibles and cut the synoptic Gospels into portions based on their parallel subject matter. He arranged the portions into three columns, Matthew, Mark, and Luke, so that if the same story occurs in two or three of these gospels, the different accounts are located side by side on the page for easy comparison. In the same way, he arranged the sayings and the gospel authors' descriptions. Material that occurs in only one of the synoptic Gospels is printed accordingly in that gospel's column. You will notice that the Gospel of John is not included; the reason is that it is so different from the other three that only in a few places does its material parallel that in the others. This textbook was first published by Harper Brothers in 1917.

"This type of book is called a synopsis. Other biblical scholars have compiled synopses too, but only Sharman has labeled the portions with letters of the alphabet to facilitate group discussion. Thus I might ask you, 'In Section 18 compare Portion C in all three gospels. How do they differ?' "

Professor Clark would ask a question about the text; we students would speculate as best we could; then he would give us a few pertinent facts and we could see how mistaken we had been when we lacked essential information. All the students were enthusiastic about the course, especially its method and the freedom allowed in discussions. By the end of the course the students, including myself, generally accepted the liberal point of view, although we differed among ourselves in our selection from the gospel tradition of what is authentic, that is, of what is an accurate report of what Jesus said and did.

The course left me wanting to know more. What did Jesus actually say? What did he actually do? Just how did Christianity really begin?

Soon after graduation I began reading books and examining the New Testament more closely. I borrowed books from the Oregon State Library, Willamette University's library, Salem Public Library, and Portland Public Library. The goal at first was merely to satisfy my curiosity.

In particular, one book I read, *The Search for the Real Jesus,* by Chester C. McCown, professor of New Testament and director of the Palestine Institute at the Pacific School of Religion in Berkeley, was very helpful. He summarized the efforts during the preceding one hundred years to find out what Jesus actually said and did—the same quest that I was beginning. By using the bibliographies and notes in the books I read, along with the card catalog in libraries, I compiled a list of two hundred relevant books, most of which I read. I still have the well-worn sheets of that list. . . .

[After marrying Gladys Windedahl, a librarian at the Salem Public Library] we began traveling to libraries around the country to learn more about Christian beginnings. We visited Professor McCown at Berkeley. Churches, museums, and religious sites were also of interest to us, for we wanted to learn all we could about religion, past and present.

In Los Angeles we found an abundance of odd religious groups to visit. One of them was the International Church of the Foursquare Gospel, founded by Aimee Semple McPherson. . . . In their service and in the service at the Bible Institute of Los Angeles the dominant theme was "the Lord is coming soon." [This was in the mid-to-late 1940s.] Gladys and I were shocked by the extent to which fear of atomic bombs and of war with the Soviet Union was being used by fundamentalist churches to scare people into joining. . . .

I was impressed by the sensible approach to religion at the First Unitarian Church of Los Angeles. . . .

At the First Congregational Church in Phoenix the minister called upon the congregation to confess its sins, based on 1 John 1:8-9, "If we say we have no sin, we deceive ourselves, and the truth is not in us. If we confess our sins, . . . he will forgive our sins and cleanse us from all unrighteousness." The congregation recited in unison the Confession of Sin, and then the minister commanded it to "Go and sin no more." But when the routine was repeated the next Sunday, the whole congregation was again regarded as sinners!

I was attracted to the University of Chicago because some of the best books I had read were written by some of its professors: Edgar J. Goodspeed, Shirley Jackson Case, Harold R. Willoughby, and Donald W. Riddle. . . . We attended free public lectures delivered by experts . . . and continued to visit all types of churches. . . . By this time I had decided that writing books on religion should be my vocation. . . . I also grew convinced that I should become a Unitarian minister . . . but my application at the seminary was rejected. I failed the art and architecture section of the entrance exam and gave the wrong name as a reference, someone who disagreed with the president at the Unitarian seminary.

Then I applied and was admitted to the Ph.D. program in the New Testament Department at the University of Chicago—established by Edgar J. Goodspeed in 1892, when the university was founded. The program involved a thorough historical approach, designed to produce professors and scholars. It began with ancient history, Greek and Roman religion, classical Greek language, and the archeology of Greek and Roman cities. Next, it moved to the Hebrew, Hellenistic Greek, French, and German languages [the latter two being the ones in which many scholarly publications were printed—ED.], to the historical environments of the Old and New Testaments, and to early church history and literature; then came the intensive study of the text of the Bible. Finally, a year was required for a doctoral dissertation, which had to be an exhaustive investigation of one historical topic in the field.

By contrast, the Ph.D. in Bible through the university's Divinity School involved pastoral studies instead of historical background and a pastoral or theological topic instead of a historical one in the dissertation. . . .

I received my Ph.D. in September 1955 at the age of forty-three. I was older than some of my professors! . . .

The summer spent completing my dissertation, Gladys and I joined a Methodist Church in the process of integration. The main reason for our return to Methodism was that there was so much Christian prejudice against Unitarianism we realized I had little chance of obtaining a teaching position in religion if that was my denomination. Among Christian churches Methodist was my first choice, partly because of my early training and partly because I admired—and still do—many good things the denomination has done. Also, we realized that intellectual growth in religion can be promoted both inside and outside Christian churches. To quote an old hymn, "Brighten the corner where you are."

Next we moved to Atlanta, where I began work for scholars from America and Great Britain on the International Greek New Testament Project at Emory University. The project was dedicated to "establishing the text" of the Gospel of Luke by collating, comparing, and contrasting the earliest Greek manuscripts found in European, Asian, and African libraries. We would also be employing techniques of textual criticism upon individual manuscripts to detect editorial insertions, deletions, all textual variants, etc.

As part of the International Greek New Testament Project, I examined manuscripts for seven weeks in eleven libraries in France, Spain, Italy, Switzerland, Germany, and Holland. . . .

At the Vatican, I handled and examined Codex Vaticanus. This famous manuscript, once stolen by Napoleon, is still the earliest (around A.D. 350) and best extant manuscript containing most of the New Testament. . . .

The results of the project were recently published by Clarendon Press in Oxford. . . . It took thirty-five years! [Teeple only worked on the project for two years.] . . . The project collated a total of 238 manuscripts containing all or part of the Greek text of the Gospel of Luke in addition to the versions and patristic quotations of all the other New Testament gospels and letters. . . .

In 1957–58 I was a visiting instructor in religion at Bexley Hall, a seminary of the Protestant Episcopal Church and located in Gambier, Ohio. At first all the students wondered, "What's this Methodist doing on the faculty? We want to learn Episcopalianism, not Methodism."

Because they did not trust my biblical interpretation, I assigned each one a separate small project to investigate in the New Testament. With that system they did not have to believe my teaching; they were tested in examinations on how much information they found. When they found the evidence themselves, they paid attention to it.

Because the Episcopal Church has its roots in the Church of England, I selected for the course on the Gospel of John a textbook written by a British professor, C. K. Barrett. The students soon accepted me and we became good friends. At the end of the school year some students gave me a copy of the Book of Common Prayer and inscribed it with a tribute to me in appreciation.

Some students were obsessed with the idea that theology is the most important aspect of religion, but I emphasized the idea that ethics is the most important. This, of course, is not a new issue in religion.

Once, a student and I were standing in the hall, debating this issue, and I pointed to the Golden Rule in the Sermon on the Mount, the fact that one of the two great commandments in Mark 12 is "love your neighbor as yourself," and especially the pericope, or unit, in Mark 10:17-22. In this last passage a man asks Jesus what he must do to "inherit eternal life." In his reply Jesus does not even mention theological doctrines or belief in himself. Instead, he lists six of the Ten Commandments and adds the injunction to "sell what you have and give to the poor."

My student objected, "But that's just Judaism!"

I replied, ironically, "Well, isn't that just too bad!"

He, like others, pointed to the Gospel of John, in which Jesus is presented as demanding belief in himself as Son of the Father. The student was unaware that this gospel presents Jesus in terms of Hellenistic mysticism, a type of thought foreign to Jesus and his original historical environment. . . .

My visiting professorship at Bexley ended when the professor on sabbatical whom I had temporarily replaced, returned. So I obtained a position teaching at West Virginia Wesleyan College in Buckhannon, named after the famed preachers and founders of Methodism, John and Charles Wesley. There I drove out fifty miles from the university once a week to teach modern biblical scholarship to mountaineers with Methodist Local Preacher's Licenses—some middle-aged, some young, many lacking a high school education!

I rightly assumed that virtually all were fundamentalists. Although the Methodist publications were rather conservative, they were not fundamentalist. But some of the tiny churches did not use Methodist materials in their Sunday school. Fundamentalists traveled around the mountains, urging Methodist churches not to use the materials published by their own denomination, but to use David C. Cook Sunday school materials instead.

These people even stood on the street corners in Buckhannon, preaching and teaching, urging passersby to use "a black-backed Bible" (King James Version), not a "red-backed Bible" (Revised Standard Version). In some mountain churches not only was education regarded with disdain, but also the practice of the preacher was not to prepare his sermons. Instead, he stepped up to the pulpit, opened the Bible, read aloud whatever passage his eyes landed on, and preached from that text, relying on the Holy Spirit to tell him what to say. . . .

The topic of my first teaching session was, "In what languages was the Bible originally written?" That topic was more controversial than I had expected, for a few students thought that the Bible was originally written in God's own language, namely, King James English! . . .

The topic of the second session was, "What are the sources of the English translations of the New Testament?" For this I showed slides I had made as a result of my experience in the project in Atlanta. The slides showed examples of the types of Greek New Testament manuscripts and of the ways in which scribes changed the text when they transmitted it through the centuries. The slides demonstrated that the King James Version is not translated from the original text because its translators had access only to late manuscripts containing altered texts.

At the close of the first session I had not been sure whether the course would be a success or not, but the manuscript slides in the second session turned the tide in the right direction. After viewing the slides, a student, Mack Boggs, came to me after class and said, "I'm just beginning to realize how little I know about this!" I replied, "Cheer up, you have taken the first step essential for learning. You are on your way!" . . .

At the end of the course, the students gave me an expensive briefcase as a token of appreciation. I was almost embarrassed to accept it, for I knew that with their tiny incomes they could hardly afford it. The initial chasm between mountaineers with little education and very conservative religion, on one side, and a teacher liberal in religion, with a Ph.D. in Bible, on the other side, was bridged. Most important, several of them decided to go on to college and seminary; one of them was Mack Boggs.

About a month after I began teaching students at Wesleyan [which Teeple did when he was not driving out to teach the preachers], two fundamentalist students decided that my "Basic Christian Faith" course was not conservative enough in doctrine, so they went to Dean Schoolcraft and asked that I be dismissed from the faculty. His response was to loan them his copy of Albert Schweitzer's book *The Quest of the Historical Jesus* and to ask them to read it, which they did.

The dean never told me what had happened behind my back, but after the two young men were intellectually awakened by him, they told me themselves and apologized. We became very good friends, and they became staunch advocates of the historical approach to the Bible. . . .

The students at Wesleyan were admirable. . . . At the beginning of each course I announced the basis of grading, and I emphasized that all students would be graded on the amount of their knowledge of the facts, and not on whether they agreed with my beliefs or with traditional doctrines. "What you believe is your own business," I said.

My most outstanding student was Arnold Nelson from Long Island, New York. . . . We had much in common, for he, too, had started to be a Methodist minister and had abandoned the plan when he learned how far behind churches were in their understanding of the Bible and Christian origins. . . . Today he is a practicing psychologist in Winston-Salem and a member of the board of directors of the Religion and Ethics Institute.

One student was very disappointing. She had read some of Ayn Rand's books and accepted her philosophy of selfishness ["ethical egoism"]. The student strongly opposed social action, and said she agreed with William F. Buckley that compassion and helping people does not belong in religion. Ironically, she was majoring in religious education and was a leader in the campus Methodist Youth Movement. She was in my "Christianity and the Social Order" course, and we spent a whole class period debating the question, "Should the church be concerned with social welfare?" Everyone else answered, "Yes."

One student reported that in his small pastorate in the mountains he had seen children brought to church without shoes because their parents could not afford them. He asked, "Shouldn't the church be concerned about such conditions?" We failed to convince the young lady. . . .

After leaving Wesleyan I spent a year reading and analyzing the early Christian writings outside the Bible. I asked myself these questions: What issues did the authors discuss? What problems in the churches were they trying to solve? I found enormous variation; different writers offered very different explanations or solutions to the same issue or problem. They even disagreed on doctrines. I recorded the views on each issue, typing them on filing cards. The cards furnished important source material for my recently published book, *How Did Christianity Really Begin?*

[Later] I returned to school to become a librarian and worked for years in that field, at the same time continuing to research the subject of Christian origins and have original research published in the *Journal of Biblical Literature, Novum Testamentum,* and *Wesleyan Studies in Religion.* I also reviewed books for the *Journal of the American Academy of Religion, Library Journal,* the *Journal of Religion,* and the *Journal of the Society of Biblical Literature.* . . .

I began a thorough effort to determine whether one writer or several produced the Gospel of John. . . . At first glance the question of authorship appears to be insignificant. What difference does it make? Why spend time on it? Actually, it has a major impact upon such matters as what Jesus did or did not say and do, why conflicting traditions about him arose, and what was going on in the churches when the gospels were written. The variety in the text is trying to tell us something. Are we listening?

I began my research by reading the investigations conducted by others, or if I could not obtain the original studies, summaries of them by scholars. In four years I examined all the scholarly works on the subject I could find, a total of 316. Some were in English, some in French, most in German. . . . [This research provided the basis for Teeple's book *The Literary Origin of the Gospel of John,* the first half of which summarizes the studies made by others, and the second half reports his own research.] . . .

In 1977 I retired from Chicago State University with the status of full professor emeritus at the age of sixty-five. . . . But, five years before that, I had founded the Religion and Ethics Institute (REI) "to promote the discovery and distribution of sound historical and scientific knowledge in the fields of religion and ethics. . . ."

Several factors had convinced me of the need for such an institute. . . . The churches were not teaching enough of what scholars know. . . . And, most of the books, magazine articles, and newspaper reports pertaining to the Bible are either in harmony with conservative Christian views or are unfounded sensationalism. . . . Radio and television programs, too, have generally ignored biblical scholarship.

The initial board of REI consisted of a professor of religion at Brown University . . . one at Boston University . . . one at Northwestern University (and book review editor of the *Journal of the American Academy of Religion*) . . . a professor of philosophy and ethics at Chicago State University, and myself. Presently there are nine members on the board. . . . It has been broadened to include representatives of various professions and a variety of religious viewpoints.

After the pseudo-documentary film *In Search of Noah's Ark* was broadcast on NBC, Christmas eve, 1977 . . . I wrote *The Noah's Ark Nonsense,* and REI published it in 1978. . . . At the same time that I was writing, Professor Lloyd R. Bailey at Duke University wrote *Where Is Noah's Ark?* as a rebuttal to the film; and it was published by the Methodist publisher, Abingdon Press.

[Lloyd R. Bailey has since published a second book on the topic of the Flood story found in Genesis, *Noah: The Person and the Story in History and Tradition* (University of South Carolina Press, 1989). See also Bailey's *Genesis, Creation, and Creationism* (Mahwah, N.J.: Paulist Press, 1993)—ED.]

As a result of writing that book . . . I was interviewed by twenty-six disc jockeys in the United States and Canada and by WGN-TV in Chicago.

In 1982 REI published my book *The Historical Approach to the Bible.* Like my book on the Gospel of John, it was eight years in the making. The first half surveys the rise of historical interpretation of the Bible, and the second half describes briefly the main methods of the historical approach. . . . It received a certificate of recognition in 1982 from the National Conference of Christians and Jews.

In 1986 REI produced "The Quest to Understand the Bible," two half-hour videotaped programs on the rise of modern biblical interpretation, based on my last book.

Reflections

In 1910–15 two wealthy American brothers distributed three million copies of a series of twelve booklets titled *The Fundamentals.* "Fundamentalism" as a movement can be traced to the distribution of those booklets, which elucidated seven "beliefs" a person must maintain in order to be a Christian. One, of course, was the belief that the whole Bible was verbally inspired and infallible. . . . None of the seven requirements were ethical principles.

The movement itself originated as a reaction against modern linguistic and historical interpretation of the Bible. . . .

Fear that new information may upset old beliefs is not confined to fundamentalists, however. . . . In the late 1800s, Wescott and Hort, Anglican clergymen at Cambridge, who worked together for thirty years to produce a Greek text of the New Testament that was closer to the original [as Teeple's colleagues and he had done on the International Greek New Testament Project] wrote letters to each other in which Westcott asked Hort to guarantee in advance that their investigations would not weaken Christian faith in the divine revelation of the Bible. Hort replied that he could not continue to work with Westcott "if you make a decided conviction of the absolute infallibility of the New Testament." Westcott yielded, and the two friends completed the project. Intellectual progress in religion comes from Hort's integrity, not from Westcott's timidity.

An interesting aspect of the history of biblical interpretation is that many of the reliable methods and essential source materials have been discovered only since 1850. The earliest biblical manuscripts and many significant archeological remains have been found in the twentieth century. In the same period the most advanced studies of the Bible and related ancient literature have been conducted. Thus this century has brought increased demand for change in religious beliefs, and laymen have had difficulty in adjusting to so much new information. . . .

While surveying the rise of the historical approach to the Bible, I observed that no valid method of interpretation was ever discovered by spiritual revelation. All were found by the hard work of uncovering facts and thinking intelligently about them—in short, they were discovered by scholarship. . . .

Study of the background of early Christianity gave me an awareness of the non-Christian contributions to Western culture made by the ancient Near East, from Jews, Greeks, and Romans.

Through Judaism we inherited indirectly from the Sumerians, Babylonians, Hittites, Canaanites, and Egyptians. Our heritage from Judaism, including ethics, is found not only in the Hebrew Scriptures, but also in the Apocrypha, Jewish Psuedepigrapha, Dead Sea Scrolls, and Mishnah; some of that heritage came to us through the early Jewish Christians.

From the Greeks we inherited democracy, philosophy, ethics, art, and the beginnings of science. From the Romans we inherited law, government, and ethics. Later we received part of our cultural heritage from another source: In the Middle Ages Arabs contributed science, mathematics, and principles of grammar.

Americans often speak of "our Judeo-Christian culture" as though that were our only heritage. That is inaccurate and unfair, for we are indebted to many cultures. No man is an island, and neither is a culture. Religious conservatives often use "pagan" as a smear word, but that, too, is unfair. Paganism, like Judaism, Christianity, and other world religions, contained both desirable and undesirable features. . . .

At the beginning of Christianity there was a general movement in the Mediterranean world toward a deepening concern for personal ethics. Stoic and Cynic philosophers, especially Epictetus and Marcus Aurelius, gave moral advice and maxims which are still worth reading. A similar concern is expressed in certain books of the Jewish Apocrypha, Pseudepigrapha, and Dead Sea scrolls.

Unlike the Gospel of John, the synoptic Gospels present Jesus as emphasizing ethics in his teaching. I compared the synoptic Gospels' ethical teaching with that in the contemporary Jewish literature, and I found that nearly all the ethical principles in the synoptics were already in Judaism. . . .

Regrettably, Christians soon were so involved in theological disputes that ethics became secondary. When the Apostles' Creed and other statements of what is essential for Christians were formulated, no mention was made of ethical conduct. Although through the centuries ethics was not discarded, priority was given to faith and ritual. . . .

Throughout history humanity has found that both truth and ethics are essential in the secular realm. When truth and honesty did not prevail in family relations, in commerce, or in covenants or treaties between tribes and nations, trouble resulted. When a man murdered his neighbor or stole his property, the consequences were so undesirable that laws were made to punish the guilty and to try to prevent future occurrences. The actual source of the Ten Commandments was not divine revelation at Mount Sinai, but the secular experiences of the people. The laws were given authority by ascribing them to "the Lord," even as the Babylonian king Hammurabi gave his legal decrees authority by ascribing them to the sun god Shamash. . . .

Although some individuals succeed by unethical means, their success may be only temporary and may spoil their personality and/or their peace of mind. The more I see of life, the more I am convinced of the practicality of ethics for both the individual and society.

In the last two decades conservative Protestantism has grown rapidly in the United States, but at the same time morality has declined. The situation suggests (as a Gallup poll indicated) that churches do not have as much influence on the conduct of their members as they did formerly. Wouldn't the churches' ethical teachings be taken more seriously if they were not associated with theological beliefs we do not really believe? . . .

When I was seven my chief playmate, Ted, a beautiful white collie dog, died of old age. Father hitched our horse Dolly to a sled, loaded Ted's body on it, and drove half a mile down into the river-bottom portion of our farm. There, in sandy soil under three Douglas fir trees, we buried Ted, with my tears. Father simply said, "You were a good dog, Ted; we'll miss you." Best funeral I ever attended—no theological nonsense, just love.

Frank R. Zindler: Biography

I did not leave the church without having had quite a number of discussions with my Lutheran pastor. My earnest questions received what I considered to be transparently inadequate non-answers.
—Frank R. Zindler

Frank R. Zindler is a member of the American Association for the Advancement of Science, the New York Academy of Sciences, the Ohio Academy of Science, the American Schools of Oriental Research, and the National Center for Science Education. He also manages the Dial-an-Atheist service in Columbus, Ohio, many messages of which appear in *Dial-An-Atheist: Greatest Hits from Ohio,* published by American Atheist Press. He has produced his own version of "American Atheist TV Forum" on the cable-access channel in Columbus. He has debated fundamentalist Christians and creationists such as John Morris (*The Question of Noah's Flood: A Debate*), John P. Koster (*Does God Exist?*), and Duane T. Gish (*Is Creationism Science?*). All three debates are available in written form through the Society of Separationists. The following is Zindler's "Biography."

Reared during the 1940s and early 1950s on a farm in Michigan, I thought that I wanted to be a Lutheran minister.

Being the assistant organist for an ultra-fundamentalist Wisconsin Synod Lutheran church in Benton Harbor, Michigan, I took an active part in church activities and studied my catechism diligently.

Graduating from the eighth grade in a two-room country school while yet twelve years old, I received a scholarship to attend a Lutheran seminary in Wisconsin. My father having been killed shortly before in a freak electrical accident, my mother was unwilling to let me leave home. A deal was struck. If I would continue to work on the farm, I could attend the seminary's collegiate division after graduating from high school, that is, if I still wished at that time to become a minister.

Benton Harbor High School proved to be the best thing that ever happened to me. For a while, I tried to learn all the subjects being taught at the seminary in addition to overloading on college-prep courses in high school. I studied my King James Bible intensely. My Latin teacher helped me learn Greek on the side. Jewish friends helped me learn a smattering of Hebrew. My grandparents helped me learn German.

Most days after school I taught music at the Cady School of Music. Fortunately, I was quite tall for my age, and none of my students suspected that I was only thirteen years old.

Although biology was normally considered to be a sophomore course, I took it at the beginning of my high school career. Taught by an easy-going basketball coach, the course was not too challenging academically. However, one day the teacher said something that made me conclude that we would eventually cover the evil subject of evolution, a theory condemned by the Wisconsin-Synod Lutherans. Thinking it was necessary to head the devil off before he could harm the class, I resolved to refute Darwin for Jesus' sake. (As it turned out, the teacher never brought up the subject of evolution the entire year!)

On the Origin of Species was tough going for a thirteen-year-old, but I eventually got through it. By the last page I was convinced that Darwin was right and Moses was wrong. Or, at least the Old Testament could not be taken literally.

Church attendance tapered off rather quickly after that, and the study of science became an all-consuming passion through high school. Further study of the Old Testament led to my rejection of it on moral grounds. The deity described therein seemed to be orders of magnitude worse than Hitler, of very recent memory at the time.

Of course I did not leave the church without having had quite a number of discussions with my Lutheran pastor. My earnest questions received what I considered to be transparently inadequate non-answers.

"Why did Jehovah order the Israelites to exterminate the inhabitants of Ai [Josh. 8:1–2] as they had the people of Jericho? At Jericho [Josh. 6:21], 'they utterly destroyed all that was in the city, both man and woman, young and old, and ox, and sheep, and ass, with the edge of the sword.' Why were innocent people massacred?"

My pastor's exact answer has been forgotten, but it hinged on the notion that in Old Testament times God used a different method in dealing with sinful people (the Canaanites practiced child sacrifice, you know) than he did after sending his son as a sacrifice.

Then I pursued the matter further, asking, "How can something that is wicked today ever have been good?"

The preacher answered that what God does is by definition "good," and all of this is a mystery beyond the scope of mere mortals to comprehend.

"But the babies and small children had done no harm," I persevered.

"True," replied the pastor. "But I'm sure that God knew that if they had grown up they would have been as wicked as their parents."

Not all of my doubts were camped on such high moral ground. One was of purely prurient interest. Somewhere I had read that the "groves" mentioned repeatedly in the King James Bible were really phallic pillars pertaining to a fertility cult popular in the Israelite world.

Visibly shocked that a "nice boy" like me would even be thinking about such things, my pastor denied this, saying that groves of trees were the subject of discourse.

I suggested that we look up one of the passages in his Hebrew Bible. The Hebrew word in question was *Asherah,* and I pressed the preacher to look it up in the large Hebrew-English dictionary that graced a shelf in his library. The entry was a long one, giving many different meanings for the term. With glee, I pointed to one of the definitions that had to be given in Latin. *Asherah* was defined as *membrum virile.*[1] The pastor knew I was taking Latin that year.

I do not remember any further apologetic from him on the *Asherah* question.[2] I no longer had any respect for that "man of the cloth," nor could I trust anything he said.

I completed high school in the spring of 1956, maintaining the highest academic average in what was hitherto the school's largest graduating class. The only jarring note derived from the fact that I had been completely uninterested in athletics and was, therefore, considered unfit to be valedictorian. I had to settle for salutatorian honors.

Armed with several large scholarships (including a chemistry scholarship awarded for isolation of the rare element rubidium from beets), I entered Kalamazoo College intending to become a physicist or biochemist.

Although Kalamazoo College seemed still to be loosely affiliated with some religious denomination at the time, practically everybody there was an atheist or agnostic. Even the dean of chapel appeared to be a heretic. I finished my freshman year still clinging to an anemic sort of New Testament Christianity. I took top honors in biology.

Although in retrospect it seems that it was inevitable that I would become an atheist before graduating from college, the circumstance that actually induced me to reject belief in gods and the supernatural was quite unexpected and fast-acting. The end of faith came in one of those late-night "bull sessions" that were so characteristic of dormitory life in those days.

More in jest than seriousness, a friend asked me, "If God is omnipotent, can he build a wall so sturdy that he cannot tear it down?"

In a flash it became clear, the concept of a being characterized by infinity in any way was inherently self-contradictory. If God were infinite, He would have to be present in the devil as well, which contradicted His supposed infinite goodness. If He was not in the devil, however, He was less than infinite in extension, since there was a part of the universe in which He was not! At the age of eighteen, I became an atheist.

Changing my professional plans almost on a yearly basis, I moved from college to college, finally obtaining a B.S. in biology from the University of Michigan in 1963 after earning enough semester hours in everything from linguistics and music theory to zoology to seem qualified for a doctorate in miscellanea.

In the fall of 1963 I took a job teaching biology and chemistry at New Buffalo High School on the eastern shore of Lake Michigan. Although I proved extremely successful as a teacher, the principal insisted that a man as tall as I should be coaching basketball, so I took a better-paying job at Holland High School, farther north on the Lake Michigan shore.

Although Holland was home to the Dutch Reformed Church and a wide variety of other "reformed" churches, I taught biology and earth science from a strictly evolutionary point of view. Not surprisingly, despite my popularity as a teacher, I came to grief upon the barrier reefs of local censors and guardians of the faith.

A public meeting was held—the modern-day equivalent of a witchcraft trial—at which I was accused of teaching atheism in my classes. Fortunately, many of my best students were present and testified that the charges were not true—that the folks bringing the charges could not distinguish between the teaching of evolutionary biology and the teaching of "atheism." Nevertheless, the distinction led to vindication, and soon after the "trial" the Holland Board of Education granted me tenure.

Shortly after that I was able to end my career as a high school teacher, because I had been awarded eleven graduate fellowships by the National Science Foundation. The fellowships were in physics, chemistry, geology, and several areas of biology. Not actually being able to participate in all the fellowships at the same time, I had to select two and reject the rest. One fellowship allowed me to study molecular biology and evolution at New Mexico Highlands University; the other allowed me to earn a master's degree in geology at Indiana University, doing fieldwork in Montana and the northern Rockies.

Upon receiving my master's in the summer of 1967, I taught biology, geology, chemistry, and many other courses at Fulton-Montgomery Community College at Johnstown, New York, where I ultimately became chairman of the Division of Science, Nursing, and Technology.

Although I had become well-known as an atheist-activist shortly after my move to New York, for nearly fifteen years my position at the college was never threatened on that account. Promotions came faster than for most faculty, and I was even nominated by the college president for the Chancellor's Award for Excellence in Teaching.

Then, in 1978, I joined Dr. Madalyn Murray O'Hair in her lawsuit to remove religious graffiti from American currency [the phrase, "In God We Trust"].

When the case was appealed to the United States Supreme Court, all hell broke out in upstate New York. The Fulton County Board of Supervisors passed a resolution condemning me for what they considered un-American activities, and they demanded that I be "eliminated." Fortunately, I had tenure. The minor fact that I had done nothing illegal also helped.

I could not be fired, although I was removed from my position as division chairman—the administration having to abolish all other chairmanships as well to do so! During all this time, I pursued doctoral studies at SUNY Albany in the field of brain physiology, completing all course work and exams before political pressures forced me to discontinue my dissertation research.

Great pressure was applied to make me resign. My favorite courses were abolished, and I was made to teach supposedly less satisfying courses.

The college president who had defended my academic freedom and freedom of speech was fired (for a variety of reasons), and an openly hostile Dutch Reformed ex-coach (shades of Holland and New Buffalo combined!) was made the new president. Funding for the Science Division was cut back drastically, and local politicians made it clear that as long as I stayed at the college, the entire science program would have to pay the price. Some even wanted to close the college.

In the fall of 1982 I took a job as a linguist and editor in the Biochemistry Department at Chemical Abstracts Service in Columbus, Ohio. During my first year in Columbus, I had to learn to read biochemical literature in sixteen languages.

Shortly after accomplishing that, Madalyn O'Hair asked me to establish an Ohio chapter of American Atheists. The first meeting took place in June of 1984. From then until now, my life as director of the Ohio Division of American Atheists has been a dizzying whirl of debates, radio and television appearances, and speeches before the Ohio Legislature. We have picketed popes, right-to-single-celled-lifers, Christian Science promoters of child sacrifice, and Moslem censors.

I've also been kept busy writing my monthly column, "The Probing Mind," for the *American Atheist* magazine, and writing books. *The Probing Mind,* a collection of my articles, and *Dial-An-Atheist: Greatest Hits from Ohio* have been published by American Atheist Press. For the next several years I will be occupied with what I expect to be my *magnum opus, Inventing Jesus,* a book that shall explain how Jesus, a purely fictional character, came to have a biography.

Notes

1. "Virile member," or "erect male organ."
2. Editor's note: The translation of *Asherah* as "groves" in the King James Bible is incorrect. It stands against the fact that the Old Testament often refers to the "making" of *Asherim* (the plural of *Asherah*), and also to the "building" and "erection" of *Asherim,* which would not be appropriate for trees [1 Kgs 14:15, 23; 16:33; 2 Kings 17:10, 16; 21:3, 7; 2 Chr. 33:3]. In Jeremiah 17:2 the *Asherim* are described as lying "by" green luxuriant trees, and therefore not trees themselves. 2 Kings 23:7 states that male cult prostitutes were in the house of the Lord "where the women wove garments for *Asherah.*" Again, trees would hardly have worn garments. 2 Kings 23:4 mentions vessels being made "for Baal, for *Asherah,* and for all the host of heaven," thus implying that *Asherah* was the name of a divinity.

Indeed, archeologists have discovered that *Asherah* was the wife of the Caananite god, El. She was a goddess of fertility and love (including sacred prostitution) whose worship was widely spread throughout Syria and Canaan. Her name was also used interchangeably for the cult object(s) that symbolized her, the primary object being a wooden pole. Other cult objects might include a stylized tree-like image, or a figure of the goddess herself.

See John Day, "Asherah in the Hebrew Bible and Northwest Semitic Literature," *Journal of Biblical Literature,* vol. 105, no. 3 (1986): 385–408, Or see *Harper's Bible Dictionary, The Interpreter's Dictionary of the Bible,* the *New Catholic Encyclopedia, Westminster Dictionary of the Bible,* or the *Theological Dictionary of the Old Testament,* edited by G. Johannes Botterweck and Helmer Ringgren.

Part Seven

Testimonies of
Former Fundamentalists
Who Played Major Roles in
Liberalizing the Religion
of Their Day

Scholarship that examines the Bible with a critical eye, as if it were an ordinary book capable of containing errors, has not been around for very long. In fact, the roots of today's critical biblical scholarship can be traced to the Enlightenment, a period no more than three hundred and fifty years ago, when the invention of the printing press allowed such "heretical" ideas to be spread abroad for the first time. The churches opposed Enlightenment thinkers, such as Matthew Tindal, Hermann Reimarus, and Francois de Voltaire. But after two hundred years of opposition, many Christian scholars began to employ the "historical-critical" method of studying the Bible, as David F. Strauss did in his classic work, *The Life of Jesus Critically Examined* (1835–36). For the last one hundred and fifty years the controversy between Bible "critics" and their less critical counterparts has continued to rage and abate, as exemplified in the stirring testimonies that follow.

—Edward T. Babinski

Photo courtesy of Killie Campbell Africana Library, Durban

John William Colenso: The Heretic

What hours of wretchedness have I spent . . . while reading the Bible devoutly . . . and reverencing every word of it . . . when petty contradictions met me.

I was taught . . . to stamp out . . . each spark of honest doubt, which God's own gift, the love of Truth, had kindled in my bosom. And by many a painful effort I succeeded in doing so for a season. . . .

The [more liberal views of Christian thinkers, like S. T. Coleridge and F. D. Maurice] which have lately opened before my spiritual eye . . . almost startled me at first by their extent and magnificence.

—John William Colenso

John William Colenso's controversial work, *The Pentateuch and Book of Joshua Critically Examined,* appeared four years after Darwin's (even more controversial) *Origin of Species.* The following brief biography of Colenso is based primarily on Jeff Guy's *The Heretic: A Study of the Life of John William Colenso 1814–1883,* which was published on the centenary of Colenso's death.

When John William Colenso was sixteen his letters dealt "almost wholly with spiritual matters. . . . He was expressing an interest in becoming a minister in the Church of England, and was assisting the local clergyman in his duties, visiting the elderly and infirm, distributing tracts, and showing a grim evangelical concern for the state of their souls."[1]

Graduating from Saint John's College, Cambridge, England, in 1836 with very high honors in mathematics, Colenso was elected a fellow of St. John's. Afterwards he took holy orders and was made a deacon in 1839.

At this time Colenso's faith was "strongly influenced by the thinking of the evangelical movement which so profoundly affected the character of the Victorian era. . . . The foundation of belief lay in the Bible as the literal word of God."[2]

Sarah Frances Bunyon, whom Colenso met in 1842 and later married, introduced him to the religious views of Samuel Taylor Coleridge, the poet-philosopher-theologian,[3] and F. D. Maurice, professor of divinity at King's College, London.[4] (The religious perspectives of those men did not necessitate the belief that the Bible was the *literal* word of God.)

On January 19, 1843, Colenso wrote to Francis, "The views [of Coleridge and Maurice] which have lately opened before my spiritual eye, though surely resting on the same Grand Principles as those I seem to recognize in all my earliest Lessons, ('cribbed, cabined and confined' as they now appear to have been by the narrowness of the channels in which they were constrained to flow by the prejudices and ignorances of those who held & published them), almost startled me at first by their extent and magnificence, and left me for a while apparently fenceless and shorn of that vigour and strength, which erewhile sustained me in my ministerial labors."[5]

Six days later Colenso wrote again to Francis, "I do think it quite possible to make an idol of the Bible—and as Maurice says in one of his Sermons . . . they who send us to a book, though it be the best book in the world, *for all our teaching,* soon forget that our faith is not in the book, but in Him of whom the book speaks. *Practically,* I believe, I should have assented to this statement a year ago—theoretically, I have only more distinctly recognized the truth of it of late months. But I cannot doubt, that the 'oracles of God' while they reveal to us distinctly some Truths, which we should never have learned elsewhere, yet in other respects repeat in articulate language the very sounds which have been secretly whispered to our own Souls—and have been familiar to those who in every nation have found God and wrought righteousness—even though they had not the written word."[6]

And one week after that, in yet another letter to Francis, Colenso wrote about a sermon he had recently heard. "[It] filled me with exquisite astonishment, at the wonderful agreement of the Truths the Preacher declared to those which have of late, through your instrumentality mainly, but, I trust, under God's blessing, been stirring and refreshing my heart."[7]

The preacher had said that, "The Spirit of the present day is of the World, earthly, selfish and cold—and the truths of God lying 'bedridden in the dormitory' of our memories—he spoke of Socrates in noble, truthful approbation— and closed by saying that we should not be following the teaching of the Spirit by worshipping the Bible as an Idol—that there were difficulties in the Sacred Scriptures which never could be reconciled or removed—and that it is not the letter of the Word, but the Spirit which breathes throughout it, which we are to look for and listen to."[8]

"Maurice's writings convinced Colenso of the significance of missionary endeavor which worked towards revealing the light already in all men."[9] In 1853 Colenso was consecrated bishop of the newly created diocese of Natal in South Africa, and became a missionary to the Zulus. He worked zealously for their conversion, preparing a grammar and a dictionary in the Zulu language, writing manuals of instruction, and translating portions of the Scriptures. In his day he was the one missionary bishop in South Africa who translated the Scriptures into the languages of the tribes to which he was sent to minister.

In doing so, Colenso began to "appreciate fully . . . objections and difficulties [raised by the Zulus] . . . [and was] brought again face to face with questions, which caused me some uneasiness in former days . . . [which I used to] content myself with silencing, by means of the specious explanations, which are given in most commentaries. . . .

"Here, however . . . amidst my work in this land, I have been brought face to face with the very questions which I then put by. While translating the story of the Flood, I have had a simple-minded, but intelligent native,—one with the docility of a child, but the reasoning powers of mature age,—look up, and ask, 'Is it all true? Do you really believe that all this happened thus,—that all the beasts, and birds, and creeping things, upon the earth, large and small . . . came thus by pairs, and entered into the ark with Noah? And did Noah gather food for them *all,* for the beasts and birds of prey, as well as the rest?' . . . I was thus driven, against my will at first . . . to search more deeply into these questions."[10]

Having searched more deeply, Colenso wrote part one of *The Pentateuch and Book of Joshua Critically Examined,* which was published in Britain in 1862 (see appendix A for excerpts). "It caused a sensation. Within a week the second edition was ready for sale and arrangements had been made for the publication of a further two editions making a total of some ten thousand copies. . . . The public was confronted with the picture of a bishop . . . stating that the Bible—the foundation of Christian belief and teaching—was not true."[11]

Due to the ideas expressed in part one of *The Pentateuch* (and in Colenso's *Commentary on the Epistle to the Romans,* 1861) Metropolitan Bishop Gray of Capetown, South Africa, put the bishop of Natal on trial for false teaching and excommunicated him at the end of 1863.

One year later, Colenso's book on the Pentateuch was condemned by both houses of the Convocation of Canterbury. Archdeacon Denison cried, "If any man asserts such things as are asserted in this book, Anathema Esto! Let him be put away!"[12]

The press caricatured Colenso as a pedantic mathematician (he had had several textbooks on mathematics published prior to becoming Bishop of Natal). That "natives" provoked his critical study of the Pentateuch was another source of ridicule, as in the limerick:

> A bishop there was of Natal,
> Who took a Zulu for a pal,
> Said the Native "Look 'ere,
> Ain't the Pentateuch queer?"
> Which converted the Lord of Natal.

Colenso appealed to a higher ecclesiastical court, namely, the Crown, and the judicial committee of the Privy Council, who pronounced his deposition by the Metropolitan Bishop of Capetown null and void. So Colenso maintained his bishopric at Natal, however, he was not allowed to preach or commune with the rest of the Anglican body in South Africa, who set up a rival bishopric in Maritzburg to take the place of Natal.

A book was produced to counter Colenso's views, *The New Bible Commentary by Bishops and Other Clergy of the Anglican Church* [i.e., the "Speaker's Commentary," ed. F. C. Cook]. Colenso found it a "most discreditable work in the present state of Biblical Criticism,"[14] and responded with *The New Bible Commentary by Bishops and Other Clergy of the Anglican Church Critically Examined* (six parts, London, 1871–74).

Due to the severe ridicule Colenso was subjected to, the latter parts of his work on the Pentateuch aroused progressively less interest. His seventh and final part of *The Pentateuch* was published in 1879. Colenso died four years later.

"It was not long before the Church of England came to accept that theories of literal interpretation and scriptural inerrancy could not be upheld. But of course it was 'the Church' that came to that conclusion; those who directed its thinking, not an individual colonial bishop with a mathematical training and eccentric views on the virtues of blacks. The change in viewpoint, when it came, had to come from the hierarchy itself, making clear that it controlled the Church's ideas, and where and when change could take place."[15]

Besides being a Bible critic, Colenso "was a warm friend of the Zulus . . . In 1875 he visited England to obtain justice for a native chief against the local authorities, and in the war with Cetywayo in 1879 and following years he stood boldly for right treatment of the [Zulu] king and his people regardless of the fears and selfish interests of the colonists."[16]

"In the 1890s some Zulu ministers were reported to have said . . . Bishop Colenso 'was the last of the race of true white man friends.' . . . In 1900 John Khumalo, who had been educated at Ekukhanyeni, stated that he believed the school had been closed because it had worked in the interest of Africans: 'These things displeased the Europeans and the school afterwards ceased to exist. Nothing which espouses our cause ever seems to prosper; Colenso himself did not prosper . . . Colenso left no message except the earnestness he threw into his work. . . . The original missionaries opposed Colenso, and used their influence against him. In these circumstances he gave no message but he left us an energetic example. . . . His deeds on behalf of the natives, his questionings, discussions, the briefs he held, were themselves of the nature of light; they tended to produce light; they tended to glow. The circumstances in which he laboured may pass and vanish from view, but his example is a beacon of light.' "[17]

Notes

1. Jeff Guy, *The Heretic: A Study of the Life of John William Colenso 1814–1883* (jointly published Pietermaritzburg, South Africa: The University of Natal Press, and Braamfontein, South Africa: Ravan Press, 1983), p. 5.

2. Ibid., pp. 8–9.

3. Coleridge rejected the doctrine that held the field in nineteenth-century England, namely, that every word in Scripture was verbally dictated by God. This doctrine seemingly reduced the inspired writers to mere ventriloquist's dummies. Instead, he emphasized how the Scriptures were a point of "correspondence" between God's Spirit and man's. He also argued that Christianity was primarily ethical and believed in the possibility of a unification of Christendom on a wide basis of common tenets, which earned him the title of "Father of the Broad Church Movement."

4. "Maurice's teaching was built around a humanitarian, Christian, universalism. . . . Christ, the perfect man had already redeemed the world, and it was the task of Christians to work against the evil and sin which obscured the true nature of the Kingdom of Christ." Guy, *The Heretic,* p. 25.

5. Ibid., p. 27.

6. Ibid., p. 99.

7. Ibid., pp. 27–28.

8. Ibid., p. 28.

9. Ibid., p. 25.

10. J. W. Colenso, *The Pentateuch and Book of Joshua Critically Examined* (London: Longman, Green, Longman, Roberts & Green, 1862), from the preface.

11. Guy, *The Heretic,* p. 121.

12. Ibid., p. 132.

13. Ibid., p. 133.

14. Ibid., p. 189.

15. Ibid., p. 188.

16. "John William Colenso," in *The New Schaff-Herzog Encyclopedia of Religious Knowledge* (Grand Rapids, Mich.: Baker Book House, 1958), vol. 3, p. 155.

17. *The James Stuart Archive,* vol. 1 (Durban and Pietermaritzburg, South Africa, 1976), ed. C. de B. Webb and J. B. Wright, pp. 259–61, as quoted by Jeff Guy, p. 352.

Photo courtesy of Illinois State Historical Library

Robert G. Ingersoll:
Why I Am an Agnostic

Having spent my youth in reading books about religion—about the "new birth," the disobedience of our first parents, the atonement, salvation by faith, the wickedness of pleasure, the degrading consequences of love, and the impossibility of getting to heaven by being honest and generous—and having become somewhat weary of the frayed and raveled thoughts, you can imagine my surprise, my delight when I read the poems of Robert Burns.

—Robert G. Ingersoll

Robert G. Ingersoll, the "Great Agnostic," was born in 1833 in Dresden, New York, the son of a Congregational minister. He grew to become an attorney and a famed orator, addressing moral, political, and religious issues. In fact, he was heard by more Americans than any human being before the advent of motion pictures, radio, and television. Following his death in 1899 his speeches and interviews were collected in a twelve-volume set, *The Complete Works of Robert Ingersoll*. His birthplace in Dresden, New York, was recently restored and is today the Robert G. Ingersoll Museum. What follows are excerpts from an autobiographical piece, "Why I Am an Agnostic," in which he analyzed the religious ideas that surrounded him during his youth.

I was raised among people who . . . knew that they had the truth. In their creed there was no guess—no perhaps. . . . They knew that there could be no salvation except by faith, and through the atoning blood of Jesus Christ.

All who doubted or denied would be lost. To live a moral and honest life—to keep your contracts, to take care of wife and child, to make a happy home, to be a good citizen, a patriot, a just and thoughtful man—was simply a respectable way of going to hell.

God did not reward men for being honest, generous, and brave, but for the act of faith. Without faith, all the so-called virtues were sins, and the men who practiced these virtues, without faith, deserved to suffer eternal pain. . . .

In those days ministers depended on revivals to save souls and reform the world. . . . The emotional sermons, the sad singing, the hysterical amens, the hope of heaven, the fear of hell, caused many to lose the little sense they had. . . . In this condition they flocked to the "mourner's bench"—asked for the prayers of the faithful—had strange feelings, prayed and wept and thought they had been "born again." Then they would tell their experience—how wicked they had been, how evil had been their thoughts, their desires, and how good they had suddenly become.

They used to tell the story of an old woman who, in telling her experience, said, "Before I was converted, before I gave my heart to God, I used to lie and steal, but now, thanks to the grace and blood of Jesus Christ, I have quit 'em both, in a great measure."

Of course all the people were not exactly of one mind. There were some scoffers, and now and then some man had sense enough to laugh at the threats of priests and make a jest of hell. Some would tell of unbelievers who had lived and died in peace.

When I was a boy I heard them tell of an old farmer in Vermont. He was dying. The minister was at his bedside—asked him if he was a Christian, if he was prepared to die. The old man answered that he had made no preparation, that he was not a Christian, that he had never done anything but work. The preacher said that he could give him no hope unless he had faith in Christ, and that if he had no faith his soul would certainly be lost.

The old man was not frightened. He was perfectly calm. In a weak and broken voice he said, "Mr. Preacher, I suppose you noticed my farm. My wife and I came here more than fifty years ago. We were just married. It was a forest then and the land was covered with stones. I cut down the trees, burned the logs, picked up the stones, and laid the walls. My wife spun and wove and worked every moment. We raised and educated our children—denied ourselves. During all these years my wife never had a good dress, or a decent bonnet. I never had a good suit of clothes. We lived on the plainest food. Our hands, our bodies are deformed by toil. We never had a vacation. We loved each other and the children. That is the only luxury we ever had. Now I am about to die and you ask me if I am prepared. Mr. Preacher, I have no fear of the future, no terror of any other world. There may be such a place as hell—but if there is, you never can make me believe that it's any worse than old Vermont."

Well, while the cold weather lasted, while the snows fell, the revival went on, but when winter was over . . . the boats moved in the harbor again, the wagons rolled . . . and business started again, most of the converts "backslid" and fell again into their old ways. But the next winter they were on hand, ready to be "born again." They formed a kind of stock company, playing the same parts every winter and backsliding every spring. . . .

In my youth I read religious books—books about God, about the atonement, about salvation by faith, and about heaven and hell. . . .

I read John Calvin's *Institutes of the Christian Religion,* a book calculated to produce . . . considerable respect for the Devil [as compared with respect for the kind of God Calvin depicts—ED.].

I read William Paley's *Evidences of Christianity* and found that the evidence of ingenuity in producing the evil, in contriving the hurtful, was at least equal to the evidence tending to show the use of intelligence in the creation of what we call good. . . . On every hand there seems to be design to defeat design. . . . The same God made the eagle, the vulture, the hawk, and their helpless prey. . . .[1]

I read Jonathan Edwards's *Freedom of the Will,* in which the reverend author shows that necessity has no effect on accountability—and that when God creates a human being, and at the same time determines and decrees exactly what that being shall do and be, the human being is responsible, and God in his justice and mercy has the right to torture the soul of that human being forever. . . .

I read Jenkyn on the Atonement, who demonstrated the wisdom of God in devising a way in which the sufferings of innocence could justify the guilty. He tried to show that children could justly be punished for the sins of their ancestors, and that men could, if they had faith, be justly credited with the virtues of others. . . .

But all of theology was not in prose. I read John Milton [the Puritan poet who wrote *Paradise Lost*] with his celestial militia, with his great and blundering God, his proud and cunning Devil, his wars between immortals. . . .

Among such books my youth was passed. All the seeds of Christianity were sown in my mind and cultivated with great diligence and care.

All that time I knew nothing of any science—nothing about the other side, nothing of the objections that had been urged against the blessed Scriptures, or against the perfect Congregational creed. Of course I had heard ministers speak of blasphemers, of infidel wretches, of scoffers who laughed at holy things. They did not answer their arguments, but they tore their characters into shreds and demonstrated by the fury of assertion that they had done the Devil's work. And yet in spite of all I heard—of all I read, I could not quite believe. . . .

Having spent my youth in reading books about religion—about the "new birth," the disobedience of our first parents, the atonement, salvation by faith, the wickedness of pleasure, the degrading consequences of love, and the impossibility of getting to heaven by being honest and generous, and having become somewhat weary of the frayed and raveled thoughts, you can imagine my surprise, my delight when I read the poems of Robert Burns.

I was familiar with the writings of the devout and insincere, the pious and petrified, the pure and heartless. Here was a natural honest man. I knew the works of those who regarded all nature as depraved, and looked upon love as the legacy and perpetual witness of original sin. Here was a man who plucked joy from the mire, made goddesses of peasant girls, and enthroned the honest man. One whose sympathy, with loving arms, embraced all forms of suffering life, who hated slavery of every kind, who was as natural as heaven's blue, with humor kindly as an autumn day, with wit as sharp as Ithuriel's spear, and scorn that blasted like the simoon's breath. A man who loved this world, this life, the things of every day, and placed above all else the thrilling ecstasies of human love.

I read again and again with rapture, tears, and smiles, feeling that a great heart was throbbing in the lines.

The religious, the lugubrious, the artificial, the spiritual poets were forgotten or remained only as fragments, the half remembered horrors of monstrous and distorted dreams.

I had found at last a . . . man . . . who despised his country's cruel creed, and was brave and sensible enough to say, "All religions are auld wives' fables, but an honest man has nothing to fear, either in this world or the world to come."

One who had the genius to write Holy Willie's Prayer—a poem that crucified Calvinism and through its bloodless heart thrust the spear of common sense, a poem that made every orthodox creed the food of scorn, of inextinguishable laughter.

Burns had his faults, his frailties. He was intensely human. Still, I would rather appear at the "Judgment Seat" drunk, and be able to say that I was the author of "A man's a man for 'a that," than to be perfectly sober and admit that I had lived and died a Scotch Presbyterian. . . .

And then I read Shakespeare. . . . I compared the Plays with the "inspired" books, *Romeo and Juliet* with the Song of Solomon, *King Lear* with Job, and the Sonnets with the Psalms, and I found that Jehovah did not understand the art of speech. . . .

The sacred books of all the world are worthless dross and common stones compared with Shakespeare's glittering gold and gleaming gems.

Up to this time I had read nothing against our blessed religion except what I had found in Burns, Byron, and Shelley. . . .

And . . . I read the *Age of Reason* by Thomas Paine . . . [who] came to this country just before the Revolution. He brought a letter of introduction from Benjamin Franklin. . . . In Philadelphia, Paine was employed to write for the *Pennsylvania Magazine.* We know that he wrote at least five articles. The first was against slavery, the second against duelling, the third on the treatment of prisoners—showing that the object should be reform, not to punish and degrade—the fourth on the rights of women, and the fifth in favor of forming societies for the prevention of cruelty to children and animals.

From this you see that he suggested the great reforms of our century. . . .

[Lastly, Paine] gave his thoughts about religion—about the . . . Scriptures. . . . [His work on that subject], the *Age of Reason,* filled with hatred the hearts of those who "loved their enemies," and the occupants of every orthodox pulpit became . . . a passionate maligner of Thomas Paine.

No one has answered—no one will answer—his argument against the dogma of inspiration, his objections to the Bible.

I read Voltaire . . . the greatest man of his century, and who did more for liberty of thought and speech [see Voltaire's essay "On Tolerance"—ED.] than any other being, human or "divine," . . . who filled the flesh of priests with the barbed and poisoned arrows of his wit and made the pious jugglers, who cursed him in public, laugh at themselves in private. . . .

I read Zeno, the man who said, centuries before our Christ was born, that man should not own his fellow-man: "No matter whether you claim a slave by purchase or capture, the title is bad. They who claim to own their fellow-men, look down into the pit and forget the justice that should rule the world." . . .

I read about Socrates, who when on trial for his life, said, among other things, to his judges, these wondrous words: "I have not sought during my life to amass wealth and to adorn my body, but I have sought to adorn my soul with the jewels of wisdom, patience, and above all with a love of liberty."

I read about Diogenes, the philosopher who hated the superfluous—the enemy of waste and greed, and who one day entered the temple [of the Greeks], reverently approached the altar, crushed a louse between the nails of his thumbs, and solemnly said, "The sacrifice of Diogenes to all the gods." This parodied the worship of the world—satirized all creeds, and in one act put the essence of religion.

Diogenes must have known of this "inspired" passage: "Without the shedding of blood there is no remission of sins."

I compared Zeno, Epicurus, and Socrates, three heathen wretches who had never heard of the Old Testament or the Ten Commandments, with Abraham, Isaac, and Jacob, three favorites of Jehovah, and I was depraved enough to think that the Pagans were superior to the Patriarchs—and to Jehovah himself. . . .

Then came the question. . . . Is there a being of infinite intelligence, power and goodness, who governs the world? . . .

Suppose we had a man in this country who could control the wind, the rain and lightning, and suppose we elected him to govern these things, and suppose that he allowed whole states to dry and wither, and at the same time wasted the rain in the sea. Suppose that he allowed the winds [of hurricanes and tornadoes] to destroy cities and to crush to shapelessness thousands of men and women, and allowed the lightnings to strike the life out of mothers and babes. . . . Yet, according to the theologians, this is exactly the course pursued by God. . . .

This God must be, if he exists, a person. . . . Who can imagine an infinite personality? . . .

We are told that he is infinitely wise. If he is, he does not think. He who knows all conclusions cannot think. Thought is a ladder—a process by which we reach a conclusion. He who knows all conclusions cannot think. . . .

If God is infinite he does not want. He has all. He who does not want does not act. The infinite must dwell in eternal calm.

It is as impossible to conceive of such a being as to imagine a square triangle, or to think of a circle without a diameter.

Yet we are told that it is our duty to love this God. Can we love the unknown, the inconceivable?

Can it be our duty to love anybody? It is our duty to act justly, honestly, but it cannot be our duty to love. We cannot be under obligation to admire a painting, to be charmed with a poem, or thrilled with music. Admiration cannot be controlled. Taste and love are not the servants of the will. Love is, and must be free. It rises from the heart like perfume from a flower.

For thousands of ages men and women have been trying to love the gods, trying to soften their hearts, trying to get their aid. . . . [Instead, I believe] man must protect himself. He cannot depend upon the supernatural. . . . He must protect himself by finding the facts in Nature, by developing his brain, to the end that he may overcome the obstructions and take advantage of the forces of Nature. . . . If there be gods we cannot help them, but we can assist our fellow-men. We cannot love the inconceivable, but we can love wife and child and friend. . . .

Is there a God?

I do not know.

Is man immortal?

I do not know.

One thing I do know, and that is that neither hope nor fear, belief, nor denial, can change the fact. It is as it is, and it will be as it must be. We wait and hope.

Notes

1. I submit to interested readers some futher quotations that exemplify how "design exists to defeat design" in nature. For instance, in another of his works, Ingersoll argued:

> The scientists tell us that there is a microscopic animal, one who is very particular about his food—so particular, that he prefers to all other things the optic nerve, and after he has succeeded in destroying that nerve and covering the eye with the mask of blindness, he has intelligence enough to bore his way through the bones of the nose in search of the other nerve. Is it not somewhat difficult to discover "the signature of beauty with which God has stamped" this animal?

Orson Scott Card, the Hugo-award-winning science-fiction writer, sometimes preaches "secular humanist revivals" at the science fiction conferences he attends. One of the points he raises is given below:

> One time when I was preaching a "secular humanist revival" meeting in Huntsville, Alabama, I ran across a copy of a book called *Investigating God's World* [by DeWitt Steele; part 2 by Herman and Nina Schneider; Beka Book Publications, a division of Pensacola Christian College, Florida, 1977]. It's a creation science textbook for fifth-graders. This is the kind of book that they want "equal time" for. . . .
>
> "How marvelous is your body," says this book. "Nothing about its working has been left to chance. Everything works just as planned by God. Only He had the wisdom to design the blood-clotting mechanism." (p. 144)
>
> To which I say, "How marvelous is the polio virus. It is perfectly designed to attack healthy children and kill them or leave them crippled for life. Everything works just as planned by God. Only He had the wisdom to design the polio virus."

Charles Darwin stated he could not imagine that a "benevolent God" instilled within the cat the instinct to torment little woodland creatures for long periods before killing them, nor created wasps that inject their eggs into the bodies of caterpillars, the eggs hatching and the larva eating their host alive. What must such creatures tell us of God's "character" as "creator"? That any means at all justifies the end?

A. J. Mattill, Jr., in his book *The Seven Mighty Blows to Traditional Beliefs* (Gordo, Ala.: Flatwoods Free Press, 1986) trotted forth another prime example: "Anyone who has watched a shrike attack and slowly kill a screaming cardinal by pecking its skull open and eating out of it will not find it difficult to understand Charles Darwin's shift in theology. At least it will be plain why the shrike, so beautiful in appearance, is popularly called the 'butcher bird' and 'brainsucker.' "

Science writer David Quammen discussed a species of bedbug in which the males *bugger other males* to ensure that the seminal fluid of the *buggering male* is injected into the female, and not the seminal fluid of the male who is embracing the female ["An African Bedbug Buggers the Proof-by-Design" in *The Flight of the Iguana* (Delacorte Press, 1988)]. Quammen concluded that "If *X. maculipennis* is another instance of God's widsom made manifest in the works of creation, I suspect that the sort of god manifested is not the one [that 'scientific creationists'] want."

In a similar vein the author of an article on ticks published in the *New Yorker* (September 12, 1988), wrote,

Ticks are found in incomprehensible numbers throughout the world, and man has probably been unpleasantly aware of them since his beginnings. Human detestation of the tick easily surpasses that aroused by snakes and spiders. "Ill-favored ticks," Pliny the Elder (A.D. 23–79) cried out in his *Natural History,* "the foulest and nastiest creatures that be." . . . It is hard to think of the tick, which lives on the blood of other creatures but is itself food for none, as a deliberate creation, as one of the creatures in Genesis "that creepeth upon the earth," and to believe that it had a Creator who "saw that it was good."

Mark Twain held a similar opinion of the fly, and asked his readers to ponder again and again the problems raised by its malefic existence:

Can we imagine a man inventing *the fly,* and sending him out on his mission, furnished with these orders: "Depart into the uttermost corners of the earth, and diligently do your appointed work. Persecute the sick child; settle upon its eyes, its face, its hands, and gnaw and pester and sting; worry and fret and madden the worn and tired mother who watches by the child, and who humbly prays for mercy and relief with the pathetic faith of the deceived and the unteachable. Settle upon the soldier's festering wounds in field and hospital and drive him frantic while he also prays, and betweentimes curses, with none to listen but you, Fly, who get all the petting and all the protection, without even praying for it. Harry and persecute the forlorn and forsaken wretch who is perishing of the plague, and in his terror and despair praying; bite, sting, feed upon his ulcers, dabble your feet in his rotten blood, gum them thick with plague-germs—feet cunningly designed and perfected for this function ages ago in the beginning—carrying this freight to a hundred tables, among the just and the unjust, the high and the low, and walk over the food and gaum it with filth and death. Visit all; allow no man peace till he get it in the grave; visit and afflict the hard-worked and unoffending horse, mule, ox, ass, pester the patient cow, and all the kindly animals that labor without fair reward here and perish without hope of it hereafter; spare no creature, wild or tame; but wheresoever you find one, make his life a misery, treat him as the innocent deserve; and so please Me and increase My glory Who made the fly." ("Thoughts of God," early 1900s)

We approve all God's works, we praise all His works, with a fervent enthusiasm— of words; and in the same moment we kill a fly, which is as much one of His works as any other, and has been included and complimented in our sweeping eulogy. We not only kill the fly, but we do it in a spirit of measureless disapproval—even a spirit of hatred, exasperation, vindictiveness; and we regard that creature with disgust and loathing—which is the essence of contempt—and yet we have just been praising it, approving it, glorifying it. We have been praising it to its Maker, and now our act insults its Maker. The praise was dishonest, the act is honest; the one was a wordy hypocrisy, the other is compact candor. . . .

We hunt the fly remorselessly; also the flea, the rat, the snake, the disease-germ and a thousand other creatures which He pronounced good, and was satisfied with, and which we loudly praise and approve—with our mouths—and then harry and chase and malignantly destroy, by wholesale. ("God," 1905)

To cite A. J. Mattill, Jr., again (from the unpublished manuscript version of *The Seven Mighty Blows to Traditional Beliefs*), "What kind of 'creator' would have 'specially designed' the kea, a New Zealand parrot, which swoops down on a lone sheep and tears open its flesh at the exact spot to get to the kidney fat, leaving the sheep to die in agony? Or a chacma baboon, which catches a pigeon, denudes it of its feathers, lets it go, recaptures it, pulls out its legs, and then decapitates it? Or a great horned owl, which will decapitate fifteen adult terns but eat only one? Or a mink, which wipes out whole families of muskrats in a senseless killing frenzy? Or the copper-colored fly (*Bufolucilla silvarum*), which deposits its eggs in the nostrils of toads and frogs, after which the larvae, when they hatch, blind and devour their hosts? Or tapeworms that grow up to eighty feet long in the intestines of human beings—

tapeworms with twenty to thirty hooks or suckers to prevent them from being swept away by the passage of food. Or female praying mantises which eat the male during copulation? Or a male lion, which eats the offspring of another male when he gains control of a pride? Or sand sharks and mackeral sharks which produce cannibal fetuses with sharp teeth to devour younger fetuses, until there is only one left to be born?"

And what kind of 'creator' would have 'specially designed' the following ghoulish plan of procreation: "There are medical experts who believe that as many as a quarter of all those born as single children began life as twins. What happens, they speculate, is that in the struggle for room, position and food, one twin 'wins' and the other is literally overcome, reabsorbed into the thrumming uterus, or into the body of the stronger twin.

"A friend of mine, during an operation, was found to be carrying the vestigial remains of her own twin in a mass of tissue inside her. They found vertebrae, limbs, fingers" (from "Born Rivals" by Gregg Levoy, *Psychology Today* [June 1989]:67).

Photo courtesy of Unitarian Universalist Association

Charles Francis Potter:
The Preacher and I

Strange as it may appear, the Baptist doctrines of the priesthood of the believer and the right to individual interpretation of the Scriptures were what led me out of the Baptist faith. My careful studies, from the time I was in Sunday school until I was graduated from seminary, led me gradually to leave the Baptist religion *about* Jesus for the Unitarian religion *of* Jesus, and to change from thinking of Jesus as my personal Saviour to thinking of him as my religious and ethical teacher. But, once started on the path of honest research and scientific weighing of the evidence you must continue. . . .

—Charles Francis Potter

Charles Francis Potter ran the gamut of change in religion from fundamentalist Baptist to modernist Baptist to Unitarian-Universalist to humanist (and paranormalist). He debated the famous fundamentalist Baptist preacher Dr. John Roach Straton in Carnegie Hall and on the radio (1923-24). Clarence Darrow asked Potter's aid in preparing for his famous cross-examination of William Jennings Bryan at the Scopes trial in Dayton, Tennessee (1925). In 1929 Potter founded the First Humanist Society of New York, whose advisory board included at various times such notables as Julian Huxley, John Dewey, Albert Einstein, Thomas Mann, and Harry Elmer Barnes. Potter's published works include *The Great Religious Leaders, Is That in the Bible?*, *Humanism, a New Religion, Humanizing Religion, Technique of Happiness, The Lost Years of Jesus Revealed,* and *Beyond the Senses.* The following was excerpted from his autobiography *The Preacher and I.*

O ne early memory is of my father being baptized by immersion in the Baptist church in the summer of 1888 when I was not yet three years old. I still retain the vague sense of alarm, that this man in the black robe was doing something unseemly to my own father. That is all I can remember. My mother says I protested loudly, right out in meeting: "Naughty man put Papa down in the water!" and that my cry shocked the congregation. . . . I regret that it was necessary for me to . . . shock the congregation much more when in young manhood I had to leave the faith, because I had to follow the truth wherever it led me. . . .

I had been put into Sunday school at the age of eighteen months [the "Infant

Class"]. . . . The only tangible memoir of that period I have is a little book . . . which I received as a prize for memorizing sections of Scripture. I was then two and a half years old. They certainly caught me young. . . .

When I was six years old . . . [I received] a Bible for Christmas. It was a beauty. . . . A printed paper with it said it was "Divinity circuit, Oxford paper, red under gold edges, with seven maps of Bible countries."

Before I was seven years old I had completed the New Testament and some parts of the Old, especially the Psalms, all of which I loved and many of which I memorized. . . .

By that time I was well along in Sunday School, and was often disturbed to find that my teachers didn't seem to know their Bibles as well as I knew my little fat one. (All my life since, I have noted frequently that few people who are supposed to know the Bible really do know it well.) . . .

In all my Bible-reading, questions constantly arose which my Sunday School teachers more often evaded than answered. When they couldn't say anything else, they fell back on: "You'll just have to take that on faith." Those "faith" questions piled up in my mind.

I was driven to a closer study of the Bible. I lived with the book. . . .

For Sunday school . . . we had "quarterlies" that examined a certain portion of Scripture. . . . [They included] notes and questions-and-answers. . . . [There were separate quarterlies for the primary, intermediate, junior and adult classes.] . . . I would manage to borrow copies of all four and read them carefully. Then I would get out my little Bible and read the [verses] between last Sunday's lesson and this Sunday's, for a lot was left out that seemed to me important. Then I was ready for my teacher, who often had only skimmed through one quarterly. I took Sunday school very seriously, and I was rather chagrined that my teachers didn't seem to, while many of the other boys in my class had obviously never even looked at their quarterlies. . . .

I got some mental exercise from the preacher's sermons, which I attended faithfully morning and evening every Sunday. I always had my Bible with me, looked up his text as he announced it, and followed his exposition of it, marveling at how much he could get out of one or two verses. I learned a great deal about the Bible that way, but I could not always agree with his exposition of the text. He was too busy to talk with anyone about the long morning sermon afterward. . . . One thing I noted: he always seemed to shout loudest in his sermon when he wasn't too sure of his point. And those were the places I always wanted to ask him about.

All the time, of course, I had in the back of my mind that some day I might be a preacher myself. When I was not yet three, according to my mother, I used, of a Sunday afternoon, to stand up in a chair and, pretending the back of it was a pulpit, I preached to my parents. . . .

Before I was seven [I was] testifying and even leading meetings [in the Junior Christian Endeavor]. . . .

I became an insufferable pest to my Sunday school teachers, for my questions were growing more difficult for them to answer. I brought them the discrepancies, inconsistencies, and even downright contradictions I found in my Bible.

Besides, the secular knowledge I was avidly accumulating was making me more critical of the orthodox Christian frame of reference which I had been given. In addition to my school work, I often read during the week two books from our Sunday school library and two or three from the city public library. . . . Mother called me a bookworm. . . .

I ran plump into my first doubt . . . when I was nine years old. I wanted my mother to have a silk dress. It doesn't sound like much now, but at that time I might just as well have wished for the moon. Silk dresses were far beyond the reach of our family budget, for my father's weekly wage, although he was . . . the most skilled worker in the shoe factory, averaged throughout thirty years only twelve dollars, of which one tenth, a dollar and twenty cents, went regularly to the church. I now had three sisters, so there were six to be fed, clothed, and housed on ten dollars and eighty cents a week. How my parents got along on that, paid medical bills beside, and bought and paid for our house and land, is something we wonder about every time we children meet now. I suppose the answer is that they did it by *not* buying silk dresses.

But one of my aunts had a silk dress, and I thought my mother should have one. She worked hard, doing all the washing, mending, ironing, and baking, to say nothing of keeping the house clean. Of course Dad and we youngsters helped where we could. But if anyone ever deserved a silk dress to wear Sundays to church, my mother did. So I determined to get her one.

All the money I could earn digging dandelions, picking berries, and shoveling snow wasn't much, and it all had to go toward buying my necessary shoes and clothes anyway. I would have to get Mother's dress some other way.

Then I had a bright idea. The minister had recently preached a sermon on Faith, based on a text which said that whatsoever you prayed for in faith believing would be granted unto you. This was God's promise in the Bible. The sermon made a great impression on me, and now I determined to get that silk dress for my mother by prayer in faith believing.

I thought it over quite a while, figuring just how to go about it. I couldn't expect just to get down on my knees and pray and then have the dress come floating down out of the sky. Of course, God *could* do that, for one of the Bible verses I had heard frequently was that with God all things were possible. But I finally worked out what seemed a better way.

The cellar was my private retreat, the place where I could most likely count on being alone. . . . It may seem strange, but in my boyish way I felt closer to God there somehow. I did quite a bit of my praying down there, even when I was chopping wood, for my beloved Bible said, "Pray without ceasing." I couldn't quite do that: I didn't see how anybody could. But I prayed a lot for a nine-year-old boy.

It was in the cellar that I staged the little prayer ceremony to get Mother the silk dress. I can remember the scene yet in every detail. It was all very serious to me. I decided to have something like an altar. Of course it wouldn't be a real altar; that would be too Roman Catholic. We didn't have an altar in our Baptist church, but we did have a communion table right below the pulpit.

There was a little table in our cellar. . . . Carefully I brushed the little table clean and set it behind the chimney where I could not be seen if anyone happened to come to the cellar door. Then I took a wooden ninepin, which I had previously carefully washed, and set it up exactly in the middle of the table. Making sure no one was in the vicinity, I knelt beside the little table right on the dirt floor of the cellar, closed my eyes, and prayed fervently to God to please change that wooden ninepin into solid gold so that I could sell it and buy my mother a silk dress. I prayed that prayer very earnestly again and again, and finally concluded very reverently, "For Jesus' sake, Amen!"

When I opened my eyes, the ninepin still looked the same in the dim light behind the chimney. I rose and took it to the cellar door for a more careful examination. As I lifted it, my heart sank, for it wasn't heavy like gold. And when the outdoor light revealed it as the same scarred wooden ninepin with faded red paint around its neck, something very serious happened to me inside. I felt sick and lost and lonely.

I sat down on the chopping block and carefully thought over the whole thing. I had done the entire action in good faith and for what seemed to me a worthy object. I hadn't asked for a single thing for myself selfishly. But nothing had happened. . . .

Later in the day Mother seemed to sense that something was wrong with me. I tried to keep it all from her, but at bedtime, as usual, I had to tell her. She was wise enough not to laugh at me, or even smile, and seemed really touched about the silk dress. She told me not to mind, and that some day I would grow up and earn money enough to buy her a wonderful silk dress, and her old brown woolen dress would do nicely for a long time yet.

But I couldn't let it go at that. The dress had been important to start with, but something else was more important now. What about prayer and faith and God's promise?

She tried to explain that God didn't do things that way, but that didn't satisfy me, and when she saw I was really upset, she took me to the minister the next Sunday and asked him to have a talk with me. . . .

He was shocked that a nine-year-old boy should question God's ways and tried to put me and my mother off by saying that when the boy grew up he would understand. But, although I was trembling at my own temerity, I stood my ground, insisting that I had done just what the Bible said, and I reminded him of his sermon on the subject. Finally he said: "God's promises never fail. The trouble with you, young man, was that you didn't have faith enough. You'll have to excuse me now, however, as it is the Lord's Day and I'm busy."

On the way home I said to Mother: "So that's the window they climb out of! If you get what you pray for, God has answered your prayer. If you don't get it, they say your faith wasn't great enough. Well, my faith was just as great as it could possibly be, and I was just terribly disappointed when that ninepin didn't turn into gold. I guess you just have to *work* for what you want in this world."

I could see that Mother was disappointed in the minister and rather worried about me. She chose her words carefully.

"Well, Charlie boy, you mustn't lose faith in God. There are lots of things

I don't understand, and I wouldn't wonder if there are a good many the minister doesn't understand, either. When you grow up to be a minister yourself, perhaps you'll understand more. And meanwhile, what you just said about working for what you want is pretty good common sense. After all, God helps those that help themselves. But don't let anything turn you from God and religion."

But a doubt about religion had entered my mind, and thereafter, although I was still a pious little soul, I did a lot more thinking for myself and took what that minister said with several grains of salt. Then was when I began branching out in my reading. And I always had more questions for my Sunday school teacher to answer than she had time to look up.

A few months after the ninepin episode I made another discovery which was even more disturbing to my faith.

We raised peas, and usually had the earliest green peas in the neighborhood, which found a ready market at fifty cents a peck. Every pod was precious, and one of the strict prohibitions was against picking and eating raw the tasty morsels.

I can still remember clearly the occasion when I was crossing the garden and my mother called to me from the kitchen door.

"Charlie, you know you're not allowed to eat those peas!"

"But I didn't touch 'em."

"Tut! tut! I saw you stoop down and pick a pod just now."

"I stooped down and picked up a stone to throw at that old tomcat that chases our hens."

"Now, Charlie, it's even worse to lie than it is to steal. You come right in here."

Into the front parlor she marched me and stood me directly in front of "The Ten Commandments," which she had "worked" with her own hands in colored worsted yarns on perforated cardboard. It hung in an impressive gilt frame. . . . We children were punished by being made to stand before the "Law," hands behind back, and read aloud the entire Decalogue, emphasizing especially the commandment we had broken. So I knew what to do when Mother said: "Read 'em out good and loud, so'st I can hear you in the kitchen, and keep it up till I tell you you can stop. Bear down on the ones you broke."

I felt resentful, for I had neither stolen nor lied, and I felt hurt that Mother had not believed me, but I was well trained to obedience, so I read the Ten Commandments through aloud rather mechanically several times without putting much thought into the reading or the "bearing down." After all, I had long since memorized the whole twentieth chapter of Exodus containing the longer form of the Decalogue, so this shorter form seemed pretty easy. I didn't have to read it, or think of it, so my mind wandered. . . .

My mouth was still repeating the Decalogue, but suddenly I stopped, for I had noticed for the first time something rather important.

From the kitchen, however, came the admonition: "Go right along, Charlie, don't stop yet."

"But mother, it's something awful! There isn't any 'Thou shalt not lie' in the Ten Commandments!"

She hurried right in, saying: "Why, of course there is: there must be." Then, as she scanned the prohibitions carefully, she half whispered: "Well, I never!"

But soon she brightened up again and said: "It's all right. There's one there that says "Thou shalt not bear false witness against thy neighbor.' That will cover it all right. That means 'Thou shalt not lie.' Keep right on reading. You can't skin out of your punishment this way. Go on till I tell you you can stop."

"I'll go on reading," I said, "but I still don't see what this has to do with the neighbors." . . . At nine years of age, in much mental tribulation, I was already an embryonic higher critic, commencing to question the sacred completeness of the Ten Commandments and the infallibility of the Bible. . . .

At the age of fourteen . . . I was made a Sunday school teacher. . . . I suspect that [my teacher] got the Sunday school superintendent to make me a teacher "to answer questions instead of asking them all the time."

[Potter was licensed to preach at the age of seventeen at Marlboro Baptist Church in September 1903. A little later, while studying at Bucknell to become a fully ordained minister, he functioned as a "stand in" minister at a few Baptist churches, one of which was a good-sized church in Pennsylvania. Potter ended one sermon] with an appeal to the unconverted that they make the Lord their shepherd immediately. Somewhat to my surprise there were several converts, and I was still more disconcerted . . . when a quartet of deacons . . . wanted to know if I would be interested in becoming the minister of their church [an offer Potter politely refused]. . . .

[My] sermons worked out so well that . . . two other churches wanted to call me as pastor. . . . At [one] church, when I demurred on the ground that I wasn't educated enough, and had six or seven more years of college and seminary ahead of me, the senior deacon, with real tears in his eyes, begged me: "Cast your lot in with us now, young brother, before them hired critics in the colleges spile your good Bible preaching!" I have several times since wondered if the old man hadn't a great deal on his side of the argument. But he didn't suspect that I was already an amateur higher critic. . . .

[I] attended the meetings of the ministerial students [of the Pennsylvania Baptist Education Society]. . . . But the meetings were very dull prayer and testimony exhibitions. When one of the upperclassmen proposed that we have a little doctrinal debate at each meeting and asked for suggestions as to suitable subjects, I was much relieved and proposed we debate the Virgin Birth.

There was a tense moment. . . . But . . . the Senior spoke again: "That subject is not debatable among Christians, for the Virgin Birth of Our Lord is prophesied in the Old Testament, related in the New Testament as a historical fact, and is one of the cardinal doctrines of the Christian faith."

Freshman or not, I couldn't let that go by, and replied: "May I submit, sir, that the subject is highly debatable, and has been often debated since the early church fathers, that the alleged Virgin Birth prophecies in the Old Testament are recognized by the best scholars to have reference to events of the time when they were written, that the New Testament passages in Matthew and Luke, commonly called the infancy narratives, were probably later additions, since the earliest gospel writer, Mark, knew nothing of any Virgin Birth; neither did Paul, nor John, nor Jesus himself. As for its being called a cardinal doctrine of the Christian faith, that's exactly what we ought to debate."

Before I was halfway through my little maiden speech, several of the fellows began to clap, and by the time I had finished, they were stamping loudly on the floor, and shouting, "Fight! Fight! Fight!" There is nothing a college group likes better than a good scrap, physical or verbal, and other students, hearing the shouts, came running to the scene. A fight among the ministerials was too good to be true.

The Senior tried to dismiss the subject, and the alarmed president of the ministerial association tried to dismiss the meeting, but the crowd wouldn't let them. We argued for more than an hour. Other upperclassmen got into the debate; it wouldn't do to let a Freshie trim the Senior. But I held my ground, for I knew my Bible as well as any of them, and I knew the subject, both sides of it. Most of the fellows seemed to think that I had the better of the argument, but I was dubbed "The Unitarian" for months after that, an appellation I strongly resented, claiming to be as good a Baptist as any man in college. At the next meeting of the ministerial association, it was announced that the officers had decided to have no debates at the meetings, and soon no one was attending but the officers.

When I debated the same subject exactly twenty years later against Dr. John Roach Straton in Carnegie Hall in New York City, I won with the same arguments. And by then I *was* a Unitarian, and proud of it. . . .

[After graduating *summa cum laude* from Bucknell, Potter attended Newton Theological Seminary in Massachusetts, a Baptist institution less than twenty miles from his home.] When I was a boy I didn't know there was any other Baptist seminary. Yet I was reluctant to go there . . . in spite of my early conditioning Newtonward. I thought it was too conservative.

The reason for my thinking so had a peculiar origin. Newton, I found out later, was suspected by Massachusetts Baptist laymen of being a hotbed of what was called "the higher criticism," a somewhat ambiguous term for the teachings of certain advanced scholars of England, France, Germany, and the United States who refused to take the Bible as literally and verbally true, and regarded it as a collection of ancient Hebrew, Aramaic, and Greek literature, accumulated through a dozen centuries, and containing both true and mistaken ideas.

But the Newton men [who preached in Potter's home church], well aware of the alleged heresy, were so careful to allay the fears of the laymen and so adept in the practice that I got the idea Newton was rather orthodox and old fogy. Most of these Baptist preachers had gone to college and seminary from country towns . . . or, from . . . the maritime provinces, and while they learned enough modern theology and historical criticism of the Bible in seminary to pass their examinations and get their degrees, they were too canny to preach it in their pulpits and thereby endanger their livelihood. One minister, very popular in [my home town] and in later larger pastorates, frankly advised me in private thus: "If you want to get ahead and climb to the top in the Baptist ministry, forget what you learned in seminary, and just preach interestingly what the people want to hear." . . .

What gave me a jolt [at the seminary] was the discovery that the King James version of the Old Testament might be beautiful poetry and prose, but was as inaccurate a translation as was ever sold to a trusting public. The salty, vivid, rough Rabelaisian Hebrew text has been expurgated, polished, refined, and smothered with euphemisms. Careless translations [of words and phrases by the authors of the KJV] abound. . . .

You may be sure too, that as soon as I grew sufficiently familiar with the Hebrew language to understand and love it for its stern loyalty to truth as the writers understood the facts of life, I made careful search as to the exact meaning of that commandment about bearing false witness, for allegedly breaking which I had been punished by my mother when I was nine years old. Thirteen years had passed since I had stood before the framed Ten Commandments wondering why, if God meant, "Thou shalt not lie," He didn't come right out and say so instead of that roundabout "Thou shalt not bear false witness against thy neighbor."

Careful examination of that verse, Exodus 20:16, in the Hebrew, and comparison with its parallel in Deuteronomy 5:20 (the chapter from which the Catholics take their slightly different Ten Commandments) and checking both against the Septuagint (the ancient Greek translation of the Old Testament) revealed that the verse simply forbids bringing a false witness to testify falsely against one's neighbor: in other words, it prohibits perjury by proxy. In the Ten Commandments there is no prohibition of lying in general, whether you take the version of Exodus 20 or the one in Deuteronomy 5. Moffat's translation is good: "You shall not give false evidence against a fellow-countryman." It would be nearer the Hebrew if he had written: "You shall not *offer* false evidence, etc."

If I had wondered as a boy why God didn't tell Moses to include in the Ten Commandments one against lying . . . I was given another jolt when I found that, even at Newton, the idea that Moses had had anything to do with the Ten Commandments of Exodus 20 and Deuteronomy 5 was looked on as rather naive. It was admitted that he may have given a primitive decalogue to his followers, but if so, that set of ten words was more like the one in Exodus 34, which had commandments about observing feasts, about dedicating the first-born of all living things to God, and forbade the seething (boiling) of a kid in its mother's milk. The Ten Commandments of Deuteronomy 5 were composed or compiled by the author of the Deuteronomic Code in 621 B.C., six centuries after Moses had died. The Ten Commandments of Exodus 20 are later still, dating from about 450 B.C.

But there was another code, known to scholars as the Holiness Code, found in Leviticus, chapters 17 to 26, which dates between the other two, about 550 B.C. It . . . comes right out against lying. Leviticus 19:11 says: "Ye shall not steal, neither deal falsely, neither lie one to another." . . .

Every B.S. candidate had to pass professor Anderson's New Testament course, and one requisite of that course was the completion, to Andy's satisfaction, of a "Harmony of the Gospels," a task compared with which any one of the Labors of Hercules was an infantile amusement. To reconcile the four canonical gospel accounts with one another is an impossibility, as all would-be harmonizers have discovered, from the second-century attempt by Tatian with his *Diatessaron*, which the church refused to accept except in Syria, down through the centuries until today. In our own day Stevens, Burgess, and Goodspeed, usually working in teams of two owing to the difficulty of the task, have published alleged harmonies, but have usually apologized for the use of the word, admitting that all they could do was to present more or less parallel arrangements of the similar passages. In Stevens and Burton's 1893 edition they state frankly in the preface: "We have made no attempt to harmonize what is not harmonious, but simply to exhibit the facts." In other words they were forced in all honesty to let the printed page show the many discrepancies along with the agreements.

In the recently published (1950) harmony by F. W. Crofts, *The Four Gospels in One Story,* he admits that "an absolutely accurate harmony is impossible." There are "contradictions between details"; the teachings of the four writers differ; "no one can be sure of the exact order" of the events because that order varies in different gospels, and no one can tell whether or not similar episodes are separate incidents or merely differing accounts of the same incident. . . .

It wouldn't do, either, simply to take Stevens and Burton and copy their arrangement, for Andy didn't agree with it. Those who got by worked out a sort of compromise system, inserting Andy's variations on Stevens and Burton.

But [my friend] Chipsie Wood was a perfectionist; no makeshift or compromise for him. In his room . . . he showed me the huge cardboard chart on which he was trying to reconcile Matthew, Mark, Luke, and John. He had given each evangelist a column, in which he had listed each episode or saying or parable or miracle in the order in which that writer had recorded them. Then Chipsie had drawn lines connecting, we'll say, Matthew's story of the cleansing of the Temple with Mark's and Luke's accounts. All three of them place that event on Monday of Passion Week, the last week of Jesus' life. But John locates it in the early ministry of Jesus, immediately after the first miracle, the turning of water into wine. So, was John wrong in his placing of the event, or are Stevens and Burton correct in assuming that there were two almost identical cleansings of the Temple? That was a simple problem for the harmonist compared with others. . . .

The chart labored over for many weeks by the president's son was a huge cobweb when he showed it to me, and he was exhausted and disgusted. He quit the ministry and has been a successful librarian for over forty years. His father left the presidency of Newton at the same time and returned to the pulpit. Chipsie said he quit the ministry because he didn't have the brains to be a minister. But it wasn't the brains that he lacked: he had more mental ability and intellectual acumen than his father or his brother, then a preacher and later president of a fundamentalist "Bible College." Chipsie just couldn't compromise and preach half-truths that he only half believed. He said to me rather ruefully and with a sigh that night as we stood looking at the tangled lines of the chart: "Well, Pottie, if Matthew, Mark, Luke and John didn't know what Jesus said and did, well enough to agree on it, I'm sure I don't, and I'm not going to fake it, not to please anybody."

As for myself, I had no thought of leaving the ministry just because the gospel accounts could not be harmonized. I did my best to arrange them in as harmonious parallels as possible, and let it go at that. I had become aware of the principal gospel discrepancies in my Sunday school days, long before I ever entered the ministry, and had accepted and discounted the fact of inaccuracies in Matthew, Mark, Luke, and John along with many others in the Bible. My repeated discoveries later of errors in the Scriptures and in Christian teaching, far from tending to make me quit the ministry in disgust, only increased my desire to preach—to tell people the truth about the Bible and lead them away from their petty literalism and orthodoxy to a more reasonable and intelligent liberal faith.

[Potter left seminary two years early, and served as a minister for seven years. His fine character and preaching swelled church attendance. He returned to Newton Seminary to complete his degree while serving as minister in a Baptist church located near the seminary. His return to seminary was prompted by his desire to find "the answers."] . . . I was beginning to question the very foundations of Christianity as I had been taught it in Baptist circles, and it was getting harder to choose sermon subjects because there were so many tenets about which I no longer felt sure. . . .

One of the big questions that had troubled me since I was a lad . . . was Messianic Prophecy. In Sunday School we had been taught that certain verses in the Old Testament were definite predictions of the coming of Jesus and what he would be and do. For instance, Isaiah 7:14 predicts: "Behold, a virgin shall conceive, and bear a son, and shall call his name Immanuel." This was taken as a direct prophecy of the birth of Jesus, and a confirmation of the virgin birth doctrine. Moreover, there could be no doubt that it was a divine foretelling because, referring to the conception of Jesus by Mary, Matthew says, chapter 1, verses 22, 23: "Now all this was done, that it might be fulfilled which was spoken of the Lord by the prophet, saying, Behold, a virgin shall be with child, and shall bring forth a son, and they shall call his name Emmanuel, which being interpreted is, God with us."

When I pointed out to my Sunday School teacher that the child was not called Immanuel or Emmanuel, but Jesus, and that the word Immanuel, in either spelling, did not occur elsewhere in the New Testament, she said that Immanuel meant "God with us" and since Jesus was really God and would be with us if we were good and believed on him, the prophecy was really fulfilled very nicely, wasn't it? And when I shook my head no, and asked her if she had read the rest of the prophecy in Isaiah 7 about the child, and did she think it fitted Jesus, she said I mustn't be so obstinate and should learn to take some things on faith.

Dr. Brown offered a two-term course on messianic prophecy, a thorough study of the Hebrew text of all passages alleged to be prophecies of the coming of Jesus or even reference to him. Although the majority of the men went into the course believing at least to some extent in messianic prophecy, and several of them fought strenuously to find foundation for that faith, we were unanimous at the end in agreeing that the so-called Old Testament predictions of Jesus were better accounted for by the events of the period during which the prophets themselves lived. And the author of the New Testament "Gospel According to Matthew" stood out as a Christian writer, so anxious to prove to the Jews that Jesus was the Messiah they had long been looking for, that he lost all sense of proportion and accuracy, twisted quotations to serve his purpose, and revealed himself as an earnest but unscrupulous propagandizer.

The Matthews we always have with us. . . .

Another big problem, both biblical and theological, which had given impetus to my desire to return to Newton for further study, was the Parousia. Dr. Anderson, every other year, offered a six-month course in that, open only to upperclassmen and graduate students who were thoroughly conversant with [New Testament Greek]. The Parousia is a technical theological term for the Second Coming of Christ. More fully stated, it is the future visible return in bodily form from heaven of Jesus, the Messiah, to raise the dead, hold the last judgment, and set up formally and gloriously the kingdom of God on earth.

Matthew 16:28 (corroborated by Mark 9:1 and Luke 9:26) had Jesus saying: "Verily I say unto you, There be some standing here, which shall not taste of death, till they see the Son of man coming in his kingdom."

Again, Matthew 24:34 (confirmed by Mark 13:30 and Luke 21:32) reports that after a vivid description of the end of the world when the tribes of the earth "shall see the Son of man coming in the clouds of heaven with power and great glory," Jesus solemnly promises: "Verily I say unto you, This generation shall not pass, till all these things be fulfilled."

I shall never forget the last session of the Parousia class when dear Andy, his voice choked with emotion and a tear or two bothering him, reviewed and summarized the course, and then said: "Much as I dislike to, I must in all honesty make a statement. By the records we have, which you and I have faithfully examined during these months of study, there can be no doubt that Jesus expected to return in bodily form in glorious appearance with an angelic escort before that generation of disciples to whom he was speaking passed away. His disciples so understood him, for not only do all three synoptic Gospels repeatedly so report his words, probably the best attested of all his sayings, but Paul's letters and the other epistles reveal that the early church fully expected such a messianic second advent.

"But he did not so return!" (Here, I remember Andy pausing dramatically and rather sorrowfully, then continuing.) "So, young gentlemen, we are left with this dilemma, painful as it may be to face it. We are compelled to say that either Jesus was mistaken, or the gospels are untrustworthy. Either alternative is terrible for a Christian. How can we conceive of our Lord and Savior as making a solemn promise which he failed to keep! On the other hand, if we impugn our witnesses, how do we know whether or not the rest of the gospel records are true!"

We had already examined the possibility that what Jesus meant by the coming of the Kingdom of God was his own resurrection, or the coming of the Holy Spirit at Pentecost, or the destruction of Jerusalem, or the death of the Christian, which is the "end of the world" for him, but none of these casuistic and equivocal interpretations can stand up in a careful study of the Greek text of all the relevant scripture passages. . . .

[As a result of my return to seminary] I found the answers to some of the big questions that had been bothering me. I wasn't afraid of any subject now: I spoke with confidence and my audiences were steadily growing. The church was packed full Sunday morning and evening and even Friday night prayer meeting. . . .

It was the sister of one of the deacons . . . who inadvertently got me out of . . . the Baptist ministry. [The deacon] had been bragging to her about my preaching, and sort of dared her to leave her heretical Unitarian church some Sunday morning and attend our service. On the way home he asked her what she thought of that for preaching, and she replied: "Best Unitarian sermon I ever heard!"

That did it. The deacons promptly called me on the carpet. . . .

When I told my wife: "They say I'm a Unitarian!" she came back with: "Well, perhaps you are! Why don't you find out?"

[The next morning Potter marched into the national Unitarian headquarters in Boston, and spoke with the national secretary of the organization, who asked him to preach a sermon on the spot about what he thought about Jesus, his life and teachings, and why Potter thought he was important today.]

When I got through, he clapped his hands, and when I asked him what was the difference between a Unitarian and me, he said: "There just isn't any, my boy."[1]

[Potter began to serve as a Unitarian minister, and enjoyed much success in that role. Eventually, he was chosen to lead the West Side Unitarian Church in New York City. In New York he met and debated the fundamentalist Baptist minister Dr. John Roach Straton on four topics: whether or not (1) the Bible was infallible, (2) God made the earth and man by evolution or creation, (3) the virgin birth was an essential Christian doctrine, and (4) Jesus was more than a man. The very interesting story of these debates, highly popular and newsworthy in their day, along with many of the original arguments posed by both parties, is preserved in Potter's autobiography.[2]]

During the first debate [over the infallibility of the Bible], held in Dr. Straton's Calvary Baptist Church, a little incident occurred in the Sunday school room which was used for the overflow. You could hear there, but you couldn't see very well over the low partitions which separated the room from the main auditorium. The incident was told me by two persons, unknown to each other, who were in that room, and their accounts were identical.

A little boy, about seven or eight years old, could hear but not see me as I was giving my main address on the pulpit platform. But he was resourceful. Collecting Sunday school class Bibles from the corner of the room, he piled them on a folding chair and climbed to the top of the rather precarious pyramid. Then, addressing a woman who was evidently supposed to be taking care of him, he asked: "Who's that talking?"

And she replied: "That's Dr. Potter."

After listening a bit, he turned and asked her, in evident surprise: "Are those things in the *Bible*?"

"Yes, they are," she admitted, "but Dr. Potter isn't explaining them right."

He listened some more and then said: "Aw, why don't God strike him dead?"

The woman muttered something to the effect that God hadn't yet, but He ought to. The boy, having soon lost interest in the peculiar antics of adults, as eight-year-olds are apt to, began playing around on the floor, making considerable noise, to the annoyance of many. Suddenly the woman seized the lad, and said sharply: "Ssh! Keep quiet! Daddy's going to speak now!"

[George Douglas Straton, that little boy in the Sunday school room, eventually attended Potter's old seminary, Newton, and received his Bachelor of Divinity degree in 1941, and later, his Ph.D.] He became a Professor of Religion at a college in Ohio, a liberal, but not considered a humanist. . . .

Dr. Straton's eldest son, Rev. Hillyer H. Straton, became a leading Baptist preacher and policy maker, and wrote *Baptists: Their Message and Mission.* . . . He is still orthodox, but by no means a fundamentalist . . . What he preaches and writes in his interesting style is so far ahead of his father's faith that it is much nearer the position of some whom his father fought as modernists. . . . I have it on good authority that Hillyer thinks Douglas as obstinately firm in his liberalism as his father was in his fundamentalism.

I consider the Straton boys as typical of the young people who have come out from fundamentalism. I know a number of that generation and those who were a little older at the time of the debates. Those who have been to college or even high school may be some sort of modernist, but they have only an amusement interest in fundamentalism. . . .

A year or so [later,] one of my friends who was a traveling salesman told me that all through the South the four debates were being sold in a one-volume edition, *with my speeches left out!* I couldn't believe it, but I have lately found a copy in a public library. I consider the following introductory paragraph truly unique in the history and literature of controversy. "In this volume the main addresses and the rebuttals from the orthodox side are given in four debates held in New York City between Dr. Charles Francis Potter, the Unitarian pastor, and myself. Dr. Potter's addresses are not given, as his line of thought is sufficiently indicated in my side of the debates."

I should not complain. After all, our entire knowledge of the second-century philosopher Celsus's critical and scholarly *True Account* (of Christianity) is what we can reconstruct from the Christian Father Origen's indignant tract *Against Celsus.*

One consequence of the debates for me was a decided trend or even push toward a more liberal point of view in religion. Statements which I made on Carnegie Hall platform were deemed very radical by Baptists and by some of the Unitarians. Yet those very statements seemed to me to be mild, compared with my own emerging opinions. While I was defending modernist Christianity, I became aware of rising doubts about Christianity itself, even the Unitarian version. I knew there were men in the hall who looked upon modernism as I looked on fundamentalism and who could give me a hotter debate on the other side than Straton did from the conservative side. . . . The debates started a train of thinking which resulted in my becoming a thoroughgoing humanist within five years. . . .

[When high school teacher John Scopes was put on trial in Dayton, Tennessee, in 1925 for having taught the theory of evolution, Potter was there as news correspondent. The famous attorney who defended Scopes, Clarence Darrow, asked Potter to type out a list of embarrassing incidents and verses found in the Bible. Darrow was planning to put the prosecuting attorney (the famous fundamentalist and politician, William Jennings Bryan) on the stand and cross-examine him, and wanted as much ammunition as possible. As things turned out, Darrow did not use any of the items on Potter's list, except one.—ED.]

I kept a copy of my list, however, and it later became the nucleus of my book *Is That in the Bible?*, subtitled "A Classified Collection of the Odd, Amusing, Unusual, and Surprising Items of Human Interest in the Bible," which became a best-seller in fundamentalist areas, unexpected by me yet causing me no chagrin at all.

The one question which Darrow did use from my list concerned the serpent in the Garden of Eden legend. I suggested that since the Bible account asserts that, as a punishment for having tempted Eve, God condemned the serpent to crawl upon its belly the rest of its life, the question would naturally rise in the mind of a literalist as to how the snake traveled before that time, since it is anatomically impossible for snakes to proceed any other way.

Questioning Bryan on this point on the seventh day of the trial, Darrow forced him to say that he did believe the story to be literally true, and then asked if Bryan thought the snake had previously "walked on his tail." The mental image of a snake pogoing along in such fashion was too much for the audience. The roar of laughter which arose from evolutionists and fundamentalists alike at Bryan's obvious discomfiture angered Bryan so much that he turned on his tormenting questioner a look which should have blasted him, but didn't, and then said to the judge: "Your Honor, I think I can shorten this testimony. The only purpose Mr. Darrow has is to slur at the Bible, but I will answer his question. I will answer it all at once, and I have no objection in the world. I want the world to know that this man, who does not believe in God, is trying to use a court in Tennessee. . . ."

Darrow here interrupted: "I object to that. I am examining you on your fool ideas that no intelligent Christian on earth believes." . . .

[Potter encountered a nearby group of Christians who spoke in tongues], which was usually followed by more violent physical manifestations of the presence of the "Holy Sperrit," rolling, jerking, and leaping, so that the church people called them Holy Rollers, but they claimed they were the Sons and Daughters of Jesus Christ and were the only true Christians since the "Sperrit" proved his presence by the gift of tongues.[3]

I ventured to talk with the young man [the group's leader]. There was not much response until, at a venture, I asked him what he thought of William Jennings Bryan. That did it. He reacted as if I had touched a hidden spring. He opened his eyes wide and said with quiet intensity:

"Mr. Bryan is a very dangerous man, a heretic, a in-fi-del, and an unbeliever in God's word." . . .

I asked this fanatic how he made out Bryan was an infidel, and was promptly told: "Mr. Bryan believes the world is round."

"Don't you believe the world is round?"

"No, suh, ah'm a Bible Christian."

"Where in the Bible does it say that the world is not round?"

"I reckon you don't know your Bible very well, mistuh, eff'n you don't know that. . . . It tells in the Psalms," he explained patiently, "about the four corners

of the yarth [It is not in the Psalms but in Isaiah 11:12 and Revelation 7:1—
ED.] and how come a round thing can have four corners, suh?

"And it tells in Matthew's gospel [4:8] how the devil took the Lord up into
a high mountain and showed him all the kingdoms of the yarth. . . ."

He was trembling now in his phrenetic zeal and I hoped he would finish
his point before going off into another spell. But he kept on, shaking his finger
now in my face as he reached his triumphant climax. "And, stranger, no matter
how high that mountain was, he couldn't see the kingdoms on t'other side, eff'n
the yarth was round! Now, could he?"[4]

I agreed that the Bible people evidently thought that the earth was flat. He
was thereby apparently encouraged to reveal his big news, after looking around
to be sure no one was listening.

"I'll tell you something, stranger, will rejoice your heart. We all have got
a bill all drawed up for the legislature to pass. This bill says for to throw out
them in-fi-del geography books now in our schools that are pollutin' the minds
of our innocent children by larnin 'em agin Scripture that the yarth is round,
and for to put into the schools good Christian books that foller the Bible teachin'
that the yarth is flat, as anyone can see."

"Very, very interesting," I said. "Have you any chance of getting the bill through?"

"We got up'ards of three thousand voters' signatures already on our petition
for the bill," he bragged, "and two senators has promised to interduce and back
the bill soon's we git some more names. We'll git 'em all right."

"You probably will," I said, as I turned away.

[In 1929 Potter founded the First Humanist Society of New York, whose
advisory board included, at various times, such notables as Julian Huxley, John
Dewey, Albert Einstein, Thomas Mann, and Harry Elmer Barnes.—ED.]

Strange as it may appear, the Baptist doctrines of the priesthood of the believer
and the right to individual interpretation of the Scriptures were what led me
out of the Baptist faith. My careful studies, from the time I was in Sunday school
until I was graduated from seminary, led me gradually to leave the Baptist religion
about Jesus for the Unitarian religion *of* Jesus, and to change from thinking
of Jesus as my personal Saviour to thinking of him as my religious and ethical
teacher. But, once started on the path of honest research and scientific weighing
of the evidence you must continue, and when I found that Jesus was obviously
mistaken in his Second Coming ideas which reflected the apocalyptic thinking
of his times, I reexamined some of his other ideas. His advice to give to anyone
who asked seemed poor social ethics, for it perpetuated the begging business.
His praise of the Good Samaritan was all right as far as it went, but a Better
Samaritan would have cooperated with others to have the Jerusalem-Jericho road
policed, while the best Samaritan would have tried to remedy the social system
which drove many men to robbery in order to live and feed their families.

So the religion *of* Jesus, even his improved Judaism, no longer seemed adequate.
His Heavenly Father was an improvement on Jehovah, but being taken care
of by a celestial super-being, however kind he might be, did not seem to be
a very high type of religion. I did not want to be given my daily bread: I wished
to earn it by fair labor with my fellows. . . .

Finally, when I watched my own three sons make the adjustment from belief in a personal Santa Claus to faith in the Christmastide generosity of their relatives and friends, I came to the realization that you can still believe in truth, beauty, and goodness without personifying them into a god to worship. . . .

[Christian worship] is carefully designed to produce feelings of guilt, inferiority, and subservience. When one praises and adulates an infinite almighty being called God, the tendency is to fawn before him and deprecate one's self. In fact, the oriental attitude of debasement of self and flattery of the chief is considered the expected and polite thing when praying or praising God. The Christian sings:

> I am weak, but Thou are mighty;
> Hold me with Thy powerful hand.

The most popular hymn in the Baptist church of my youth began:

> Alas! and did my Saviour bleed,
> And did my Sov'reign die?
> Would He devote that sacred head
> For such a worm as I?

I sung it so often it is a wonder I didn't wriggle on the way home from prayer meeting. . . .

Prayers [go hand in hand with such a mode of worship]. They are in essence the begging of favors, material or spiritual, from a monarchic deity. The classical prayer consists of, first, the ascription of praise, to put God in good humor; then of thanksgiving, to show that you are properly grateful for former favors; then of petition, the real prayer, which is often frank begging. In modernist churches, it is true, this oriental monarch prayer has been somewhat sublimated: it is not so anthropomorphic in its conception of deity, but it still has many vestigial relics of its origin. Different humanist groups will appreciate and use the values of meditation and aspiration without the accompanying flattery and favor-seeking of theistic prayer-forms. . . .

If hymns, sermons, and prayers are all aimed to make the worshiper feel that he is guilty, that he was conceived in sin and shaped in iniquity and that there is no health in him, he will get into a bad state mentally if the salvation medicine doesn't work with him, and it often does not. . . .

There is a nice question of ethics involved in the first place, whether it is right to make a man sick or sicker in order to get him to take the medicine you are peddling, and of method in the second place, for it is debatable if the technique really eliminates as much guilt as it creates. . . .

In the decade which I have spent in New York City there has passed before me a procession of puzzled people in those office consultations and interviews which . . . are called "the Protestant Confessional."

It wasn't that these unhappy maladjusted persons did not have enough religion: they had too much of the wrong kind. They were trying to solve the problems of an industrial age by a religion developed by a pastoral people. In *democratic*

America they were bowing their heads to an oriental *monarchic* god and wondering why that contradictory arrangement wasn't functioning happily. . . .

The task before humanism, as I see it, is to release man's soul from bondage to the fear of God. The fear of God is not the beginning of wisdom; it is frequently the end of it, psychologically speaking. Souls have been warped and stunted by the inhibitory fear complex and deity obsession. . . .

In the future there will doubtless be plenty of literalists and fundamentalists in religion. But I have long discerned a trend among thoughtful people toward what I call humanism, faith in man. Not faith in man in the sense of worshiping man instead of worshiping God, but faith in the supreme value and self-perfectibility of human personality, individually and socially . . .

[Furthermore,] a humanist who refuses to explore the field of extrasensory perception lest it destroy his faith is in the same class as the old-time religionist who refused, for exactly the same reasons, to read Thomas Paine or hear Robert Ingersoll. . . . The field of extrasensory perception may even include prayer and faith, when prayer is dominant desire for good and faith is confident outreaching growth toward a better life in a better world for everybody. The humanist should be neither creed-bound by supernatural theistic revelation nor sense-bound by any materialism though it be labeled scientific. . . .

Notes

1. Unitarians believe in one God, as opposed to the paradoxical Christian "Trinity." They also have doubts "as to Jesus' divinity" (to quote Benjamin Franklin's opinion of Jesus). And they are noteworthy for their acceptance of modern scientific theories, and the historical approach to the Bible. Their preaching aims to increase a person's moral consciousness, not their fear of God's punishments. For instance, the famous Unitarian preacher, Hosea Ballou, once said to a Presbyterian minister: "You are going around trying to keep people out of hell, and I am going around trying to keep hell out of people." Neither do Unitarians fear the specter of "eternal damnation." They believe in "a God who is a gentleman . . . a heavenly father who will leave the door latch unlocked until the last child gets home" (to quote Robert Ingersoll, who was not a Unitarian, but an admiring agnostic).

It is of interest to note that though Unitarians comprise only a tiny fraction of the American population, twenty-two of the sixty-three tablets in memory of great Americans in the Hall of Fame at New York University (circa 1951), bear the names of Unitarians, included among whom are John Adams, John Quincy Adams, Louis Agassiz, Ralph Waldo Emerson, Benjamin Franklin, Nathaniel Hawthorne, Oliver Wendell Holmes, Thomas Jefferson, Henry Wadsworth Longfellow, Horace Mann, and Daniel Webster. If, as fundamentalists believe, Unitarians go to hell, then, as Potter replied, "Hell must be the dwelling place of a distinguished company of eminent Americans."

For further information on Unitarianism I suggest reading the enlightening and amusing works of Dr. F. Forrester Church, the warm-spirited and liberal minister at All Souls Universal Unitarian Church in New York City, whose titles include: *The Devil and Doctor Church, Entertaining Angels, The Seven Deadly Virtues, Everyday Miracles: Stories from Life,* and *God and Other Famous Liberals.*—Ed.

2. *The Preacher and I* (New York: Crown, 1951), pp. 137–244.

3. Potter was not the only reporter at the trial to visit ultra-fundamentalist "Holy Roller" Christians. See H. L. Mencken's description of them in his article, "The Hills of Zion," published

in *A Mencken Chrestomathy* (New York: Alfred A. Knopf, 1926). Here follows an excerpt from Mencken's article:

> The preacher stopped at last, and there arose out of the darkness a woman with her hair pulled back into a little tight knot. She began so quietly that we couldn't hear what she said, but soon her voice rose resonantly and we could follow her. She was denouncing the reading of books. Some wandering book merchant, it appeared, had come to her cabin and tried to sell her a specimen of his wares. She refused to touch it. Why, indeed, read a book? If what was in it was true, then everything in it was already in the Bible. If it was false, then reading it would imperil the soul. This syllogism from Caliph Omar complete, she sat down. There followed a hymn, led by a somewhat fat brother wearing silver-rimmed country spectacles. It droned on for half a dozen stanzas, and then the first speaker resumed the floor. He argued that the gift of tongues was real and that education was a snare. Once his children could read the Bible, he said, they had enough. Beyond lay only infidelity and damnation.

4. For further discussion of verses in the Bible that presuppose a flat earth, see the final note accompanying Edward T. Babinski's testimony in this book.

Henry Preserved Smith:
The Heretic's Defense

The ordinary commentaries [on Scripture] to be sure left much to be desired.
They were filled with pious platitudes, they passed in silence over difficulties,
or else they read into the biblical text what was not there. . . . I was only
gradually coming to a sense of the real nature of the Bible.

—Henry Preserved Smith

Henry Preserved Smith graduated from high school in Dayton, Ohio, in 1864,
a year before the U.S. Civil War ended. Abraham Lincoln was president, Samuel
Clemens (Mark Twain) was twenty-nine years old, Thomas Alva Edison was
seventeen, and the fundamentalist/modernist controversy that divided many
American Protestant denominations in the 1920s and 1930s would not occur for
fifty-six years. Smith's career as a Bible scholar presaged that controversy. His
works included *Inspiration and Inerrancy, A Critical and Exegetical Commentary
on the Books of Samuel (The International Critical Commentary), Old Testament
History, The Religion of Israel,* and *The Heretic's Defense: A Footnote to History.*
The following is excerpted from *The Heretic's Defense.*

I took my religion as it came to me without violent reactions of any kind.
My parents were . . . New School Presbyterians . . . Calvinists. . . . I . . .
attended services and Sunday-school. When I was sixteen years old our pastor
asked the young people of his congregation to come together, and laid before
them the duty of confessing Christ. About thirty of us responded and were received
into church membership. This was without excitement of any kind. We had had
Christian training in the Sunday-school as well as in our homes, and, while conscious
that we were sinners, none of us had acute pangs of remorse, or, on the other
hand, the raptures which some feel in making the great decision. Such was my
own experience, and, as we were going through the Civil War, it seemed to me
that my Christian profession was like the patriotic young man's enlistment in
the army—motivated by a desire to do one's duty to his country, but a quiet
resolution without flourish of any kind.

The religious influence of the home was continued in college. Marietta, to which I first went, was the college of the combined New School and Congregational churches. Ohio was and is full of colleges, each Christian denomination having its own . . . [grounding students] in the correct intellectual faith, which, of course, meant the creed of the particular denomination. . . .

At Marietta we had marked religious interest during my stay there. The thrill I experienced at seeing my friends come out on the Lord's side was much like what I felt when I knew of a friend who had decided to enlist in the Union army. At Amherst [the second college Smith attended] there had been a revival the year before I entered, and the religious tone of the college was thereby heightened.

For myself, I can say that I sympathized with the atmosphere I found both at Marietta and at Amherst. I was faithful in attendance at all the religious services and did not find them burdensome, took part also in the class prayer-meetings, and in general made my faith manifest. There was, however, nothing spectacular or even distinctly emotional in my conduct. . . .

My idea of the ministry was formed on what I had observed of the pastor's duties. . . . To teach men their duty, to enlighten them as to the ways of God, to sensitize the conscience and induce a decision for a truly Christian life seemed a worthy end of effort. . . . Attempting to make a just estimate of my own abilities and attainments, it did not seem extravagant to conclude that I could qualify for such service. There was no thought of making a sacrifice, but a calm endeavor to do the best in my power. This was also the temper of my classmates, so far as I can judge. Out of the fifty-six who graduated at Amherst in 1869, twenty studied theology.

Lane Seminary was the theological school of the New School Presbyterians, and I naturally went thither. . . . We got the lessons assigned us, but had little ambition to explore fields of knowlege which lay outside of the bounds fixed by the churches (Presbyterian or Congregational) to which we belonged. Preaching was to be our main work, and one object of our study was to get subjects for our discourses. . . .

The preaching must . . . confirm the system of doctrine held by the denomination to which the preacher belongs. It was on this theory that the theological seminary organized its curriculum. We at Land had four professors. . . . Professor Nelson began his course in theology by discussing the inspiration of Scripture, and the conclusion to which he came was in these words: "The Scriptures being the Word of God, whatever the Bible affirms must be true."

[One] event which occurred during my seminary course may be noticed as of some possible interest for the reader . . . a series of meetings held by E. P. Hammond, a revivalist well known at that time. . . . After one of the meetings I noticed a young woman who had a concern . . . and on approaching her I found that she could not make up her mind to give up dancing, which was what her church would require. I simply said: "I would not let it stand between me and my Savior." Then after a word of prayer I left her. I did not see her again, but one of our men reported a few days later that he found a young lady happy in her new choice, and, on asking her if she was Mr. Hammond's convert, received the reply that she was Mr. Smith's convert. . . .

As to the people reached by the meetings . . . they were for the most part those who had had Christian training in Sunday-school, the church, or the family. The great unchurched mass was not sensibly affected, and while some effort was made to approach them, no appreciable result was reported. . . .

The psychology of religion was as yet an unknown science, but our observations might have led to some understanding of it had we had a guide; but none was forthcoming. One of our men, the one with the smallest mental equipment of our number, got a clue to his lifework. He did not see why he could not do what Mr. Hammond (who had neither Greek nor Hebrew) was doing. He therefore entered on the career of an evangelist, and I believe had considerable success.

I was licensed to preach by the presbytery of Dayton in the spring of 1871, and that summer I preached to two small churches in northern Ohio. The people were extraordinarily kind, and wanted me to promise to come back to them as their pastor after completing my theological course. I did not think it wise to bind either myself or them, but I mention the matter here to show that nothing in my experience thus far gave me reason to think that I had made a mistake in choosing my profession. . . .

[Smith graduated from Lane in 1872, then spent two years in Europe, including two semesters of religious study in Berlin] still expecting to become a pastor. . . . My chief gain was acquisition of the German language and some insight into German theological thought of the conservative kind (notice), for I still had the dread of rationalism with which Presbyterian theological students were inoculated.

Returning home . . . I was invited to teach a year at Lane. . . . This opened a door to me, and I entered it, perhaps following the line of least resistance. . . . I was then asked whether I would try [teaching] Hebrew. . . . I agreed . . . stipulating that, after a year [of teaching], I could have a year abroad for better preparation. . . .

I was ordained to the ministry [in 1875] by the presbytery of Dayton, on the theory that one who was to instruct theological students should himself be in the sacred office. . . . My trial sermon before the presbytery was on the text "All Scripture is given by inspiration of God," and it is perhaps characteristic of ordinary theological method that in preparing the sermon I did not inquire into the phenomena of Scripture itself, but took my material largely from a . . . thoroughly dogmatic work.

At this point . . . I could with a good conscience call myself a conservative. I was willing to give due weight to every argument in favor of the tradition of the church. . . . In going abroad for my second period of study, I hoped to prepare myself the better to defend the Bible from its objectors.

My first year's teaching of Hebrew passed without incident. . . . I spent the next year at Leipzig University in Germany. The reason I chose that university was that its theological faculty had the reputation of orthodoxy. Franz Delitzsch, who had the chair of Hebrew, was the leading conservative scholar on that subject in Germany. . . . [Smith heard him and also] Luthardt, another representative of conservative Lutheran theology. Although Delitzsch was conservative, his historical sense was leading him to make some slight concessions to the newer criticism. But these were not enough to disturb his students. . . . All of them [were] brought up in the tradition of the churches and were conservative in their

preferences, but all were [later] compelled to modify their views by the facts of
Scripture brought out through their study.

Returning to Lane. . . . Our students were not much affected by rationalism,
and their chief concern was to get enough Hebrew to enable them to pass the
examinations for licensure and ordination. . . .

The ordinary commentaries [on Scripture] to be sure left much to be desired.
They were filled with pious platitudes, they passed in silence over difficulties,
or else they read into the biblical text what was not there. . . .

I was only gradually coming to a sense of the real nature of the Bible. . . .

The Confession of Faith, to be sure, affirms that the original Hebrew and
Greek have by God's singular care and providence been kept pure in all ages.
But the facts show that this is not true of every detail. For example, the Hebrew
of 1 Sam. 13:1 reads: "Saul was *one* year old when he began to reign and he
reigned two years over Israel." The language is perfectly plain and means exactly
what I have given. But the absurdity of the statement is too evident to require
comment . . . something has fallen out [of the original text]. . . . As to parallel
passages, one may compare David's Psalm in 2 Sam. 22 with the copy in Ps.
18. The differences in some cases show at least scribal errors. A comparision
of the books of Chronicles with the parallel passages in the earlier historical books
[1 and 2 Kings] leads to the same conclusion . . . [which] falls short of the dogmatic
demand for an inerrant Bible. . . .

That [this type of] textual criticism is disturbing to one who thus reads his
Bible needs no demonstration. Indeed, it came to view when Cappellus proved
that the vowel-points were not part of the original Hebrew text. Buxtorf in his
reply admitted what would happen to the doctrine of verbal inspiration if consonants
only were inspired. When Walton published, in 1657, his great Polyglot, giving
the ancient versions a place alongside of the Hebrew, and also supplementing
the work by a list of various readings, he called forth a bitter attack from John
Owen, the defender of Presbyterian orthodoxy. Owen deprecated the publication
of facts which might militate against the authority of Scripture. Walton's reply
entitled *The Considerator Considered* is still worth reading. . . .

As for myself, the facts forced me to admit the necessity of textual criticism. . . .

In 1880 the *Presbyterian Review* was founded . . . [an] organ of discussion
for varying views. . . . One of the earliest papers published [in the *Presbyterian
Review*] was on inspiration, written by Dr. Hodge and Dr. B. B. Warfield. Professedly it was an argument for verbal inspiration and consequent inerrancy of
the Scriptures. But it made one significant concession; it predicated this inerrancy
of the text which resulted, *after* the original had been recovered by textual criticism.
It did not seem to occur to the writers that they were going contrary to the
Confession, which as we have seen, affirmed the purity of the copies in our hands,
or, on the other hand, that they were postponing to an indefinite future a reliable
Bible. All that now concerns us is to note that even the most conservative scholars
were compelled by the facts to admit the necessity of criticism of the *text*. The
inquiring mind might well ask whether the facts alleged by the *higher* criticism
are not equally compelling. . . .

The study which is called, rather unfortunately, the higher criticism . . . is the preliminary to all reconstruction of the past.

In attempting to date an ancient document we are obliged to take cognizance of the fact that many books or fragments were published anonymously or even under pseudonyms. The carelessness of many ancient writers in attaching [pseudo] names to their productions is something we of this day find hard to understand. When we seek certainty we want to know the name of our informant. Hence, the attempt to assign the Old Testament books to men whose names are known to us . . . Joshua by Joshua, Judges and Samuel by Samuel, Kings by Isaiah or Jeremiah, or by the two together. . . . The lack of foundation for such a [view] must be evident to any serious student. We must admit that most of the Old Testament books are without the authors' names. It does not follow that we cannot date them. An anonymous book betrays its origin by the vocabulary it uses or by allusions that it makes [each only proper to a certain period of history]. . . .

One further consideration is in place. The ancient writer rarely had what we would call the historical interest. This is preeminently true of the Israelite authors. Their purpose was distinctly religious; they would warn or exhort their fellow men, drawing lessons from the past. It stands to reason that this motive must be carefully considered, because it may color the picture which the author draws. At least it may determine the choice he makes of the material to use. . . . The religious ideas of one generation may not be those of later times. . . . [O]ne age builds on the foundations laid in earlier times. The endeavor to thus date and arrange the Old Testament material brings to light another fact. Many of the books are evidently composite. The idea of literary property being unknown, each writer felt that he could make what use he pleased of his predecessors. Palpable proof is given by the books of Chronicles, whose author embodied in his work whole sections of the earlier historical books [1 and 2 Kings]. All this is so self-evident to us of the present day that it seems superfluous to dwell upon it. But the history of exegesis shows how slowly it came into the minds of professed biblical students . . . [The article by Hodge and Warfield in the *Presbyterian Review*] was followed by one by Dr. Briggs, who argued that Hodge and Warfield's precise and emphatic view of inspiration imperiled the doctrine of inspiration by bringing it into conflict with a vast array of objections along the whole line of Scripture and history. . . . Dr. Briggs showed that many of the best known divines [seventeenth-century Puritan theologians] of the Presbyterian Church refused to admit (what Drs. Hodge and Warfield asserted) that one proved error invalidated the claim of Scripture to be inspired . . . [In fact, Briggs went on to assert] that American theologians, even of the most orthodox type, had departed from the faith of the fathers. This he set forth at length in a volume entitled *Wither?* published in 1889. . . .

Then I reviewed Wellhausen's *Prolegomena to a History of Israel*. My article appeared in the *Review* April 1882. The force and brilliancy with which all the data were presented in Wellhausen's book . . . made me see that concessions to the [higher critical] method must be made. . . . (1) Differences of style imply differences of author. (2) The historical circumstances in which an author wrote are apt to be reflected with more or less definiteness in his work. (3) The ethical and religious conceptions of his time will also influence his work.

Innocent as these appear, they imply that the processes of historical inquiry may and indeed must be applied to our sacred books. . . .

One Presbyterian newspaper [after reading my review] recommended that no more theological students be sent to Germany. . . .

[Throughout this time] my relations with my colleagues and pupils continued to be cordial. . . . I was loyal to the church. . . . My opening sermon the next year had all the approval of the most conservative members. I tell these things, not as boasting, but to show that I was not radical or aggressive, and in spite of the Wellhausen paper was not looked upon with suspicion by the great majority.

A storm broke over Professor Briggs because of his inaugural address, January 20, 1891 [delivered on the occasion of his appointment to a post at Union Theological Seminary]. . . . He asserted that the scholastics and ecclesiastics of Protestantism "enveloped the Bible with creed and ecclesiastical decisions and dogmatic systems, and substituted for the authority of God the authority of a Protestant rule of faith." He claimed that inerrancy was a barrier to the divine authority of Scripture. . . .

[After the speech, the Presbyterian General Assembly tried to veto Dr. Brigg's appointment.] Dr. Llewelyn J. Evans and myself opposed the veto. . . . We might have added that the demand the Assembly made, that critical investigation of the Scriptures should always vindicate the doctrine of our church was exactly what the Roman Catholic Church required, but something from which Protestantism had revolted. . . .

[The Assembly carried out its resolution] but its promoters were angry that it had met with opposition. . . .

The Presbyterian Ministers' Association . . . suggested that I [and Dr. Evans] read a paper on inspiration. . . . Our essays were published in a pamphlet titled *Biblical Scholarship and Inspiration* [Cincinnati, Ohio: Robert Clarke & Co., 1891]; and republished under the title *Inspiration and Inerrancy* [Cincinnati, Ohio: Robert Clarke & Co., 1892].

The temper in which we were heard is illustrated by one of the papers written in reply. The heading is: "The Down-Grade Theology; the Down-Graders Squarely in Conflict with Christ." We were accused of forcing a conflict on the church, when all that we had done was to exercise our right as presbyters, and then to accept an invitation to explain our position. . . .

[At this time, Dr. Briggs was tried for heresy. At his trial] I affirmed Dr. Briggs's liberty and duty to oppose Bibliolatry [worship of the Bible] if he discovered it, and I asked: "Haven't I heard that in Scotland the New Testament is put at the door of the house to keep the spooks away?" Several voices answered: "No!" But Dr. Ormiston, a highly respected and widely known minister, rose . . . and declared that he, a Scotchman, had known that to be done. . . .

[The result of the heresy trial] was that the directors of Union Theological Seminary stood by Dr. Briggs, and in 1892 the seminary rescinded the agreement which gave the Assembly the power to veto their professors. . . .

Logically, of course, the party which prosecuted Dr. Briggs must prosecute me. . . .

Private letters urged me not to teach errancy. . . . I responded . . . "Suppose that one of my students calls upon me in class to explain an apparent discrepancy in Scripture. You wish the assurance that I will tell him that the discrepancy *must* have come in transmission. Unfortunately, I have given enough attention to textual criticism to know that not all the discrepancies can be accounted for in that way." In the same connection I pointed out that the concern of the exegete is with the meaning of the text he studies, the present text, that is. The existence of original manuscripts in which no discrepancies occurred is a speculative hypothesis which he has no interest in affirming or denying. As a matter of fact, and as I pointed out, I had always been exceedingly careful—perhaps too much so—not to unsettle the faith of my students. . . .

My heresy trial began November 1892. . . . The belief of the [investigating] committee may be stated this way: It is a fundamental doctrine of the Presbyterian Church that the Holy Spirit so controlled the writers of Holy Scriptures as to make their utterances absolutely truthful when interpreted in their natural and intended sense.

Passing over the word *intended,* by which we may conjecture that the committee endeavored to leave a way open by which to escape from the rigor of their own doctrine, we note what I called attention to in my response—that a fundamental doctrine of the church ought to be stated in so many words in the Confession. But we do not find it so stated. The passages cited in support of the proposition magnify the excellence of the Word of God in Scripture as a source of belief and practice, which was just what I had always emphasized. The only passage which seemed to teach what the committee asserted was the following:

> By this faith a Christian believeth to be true whatsoever is revealed in the Word, for the authority of God Himself speaking therein; and acteth differently upon that which each passage containeth, yielding obedience to the commands, trembling at the threatenings, and embracing the promises of God for this life and that which is to come. . . .

The passage . . . is from the chapter on saving faith, and defines what the one who has that faith will do. He will accept not the whole text of Scripture but whatsoever is revealed therein. And this is asserted to be commands, threatenings, and promises. Had the Westminster divines meant that every believer must read the whole Bible with the conviction that its every statement is true in the natural sense of the words—if that had been their intention, they should have ruled that every candidate for admission to the church should profess faith in the inerrancy in Scripture. It is well known that this has never been the rule of the church. It never occurs to a pastor to tell an inquirer that first of all he must accept the inerrancy of the original autographs before he can call himself a Christian.

To support their claim the committee cited seventy-one texts from the Bible itself, with references to eight others, and it was a part of my duty to examine all these in detail. I may spare myself that labor here, only remarking that many of the passages were irrelevant. Those which mentioned the Word of God had no reference to the text of Scripture, but meant the word as spoken by the prophets. Their inspiration I had never denied, but we were now concerned with the text of Scripture, which contains much besides prophetic discourses.

Among the specifications in the indictment one stated that I affirmed that the last twenty-seven chapters of the Book of Isaiah were not written by him. I need not dwell upon this charge. Almost every commentator who has written on Isaiah for half a century or more holds to the composite nature of the book. If they are all wrong, there is no such thing as biblical science. The great prophet of the second half of the book has not attached his name to his work, but that he did not live in the time of Hezekiah is manifest in every chapter.

More offense was perhaps taken at my treatment of the author of the Book of Chronicles. After pointing out the discrepancies between his book and the Books of Kings I attempted to account for them in this way: "Remembering that the Chronicler was much farther away in time from the events narrated, we find it natural that he should have an exaggerated idea of the resources of his country in the days of her glory." The problem here is one of the most difficult presented to the historian by the Old Testament narrative. The two pictures of the history of Israel given in the Books of Kings, on the one hand, and in Chronicles, on the other, are irreconcilable. Attempts to harmonize them are unsuccessful. Orthodox historians have usually taken the later material (Chronicles) as the basis of their work, and have presented a story untrue to the facts. Perhaps it would have been better for me to advocate the exclusion of Chronicles from the canon. But that would have opened up the whole question of the formation of the canon, into which I did not propose to go. I had no intention of impugning the good faith of the Chronicler. He was a child of his time, and in fact throws a welcome light on the conceptions of post-Biblical Judaism. His value as a teacher of faith and morals must be judged in accordance with the facts of the record, and those facts are as I stated.

In reply to my objections the committee reproduced the usual dogmatic argument, depending for the most part on the now superannuated work of James Bannerman, *Inspiration: The Infallible Truth and Divine Authority of the Holy Scriptures.*

Their most astonishing statement was that only an inerrant Scripture can have power to accomplish in the human soul the work for which the revelation has been given; that is, the work of conversion and regeneration. Since by their emphasis on the original autographs the committee conceded that there are errors in our present text, they virtually confessed that our present Bible has lost the power of converting sinners.

Throughout their argument the committee confused the inspiration of the prophets, the orators who delivered God's message, with the impulse which led the scribes to preserve not only that message but also the history of their own times. The claim of the *speaker* to speak for God is admitted—certainly I had never questioned it. But so far as I know there is no text in which the *writer* of the historical books claims the prophetic inspiration.

Yet the prosecution went so far as to claim that the denial of inerrancy was equivalent to the unpardonable sin—the sin against the Holy Ghost. When it came to that I protested that they were merely attempting to arouse prejudice, and I challenged them to amend the charges by inserting one accusing me of that sin. Thereupon they explained that they only meant that my position led logically to that sin.

I then pressed them to tell whether they agreed with their authorities, Drs. Hodge and Warfield, who asserted that one proved error would not only refute their doctrine but would invalidate the Bible's own claim to inspiration. But they were under no obligation to answer my question, and it was ignored.

They reached the climax of their argument when they compared the higher criticism (for it was really this that they were fighting) to the genie in the *Thousand and One Nights* let out of the jar by the fisherman. In me they thought that the dreadful ogre might be crushed, and they besought the presbytery not to let the opportunity slip. That they overrated my importance and also the power of presbytery is sufficiently evident by this time.

As I have intimated, there never was any doubt as to the result of the trial. The final vote suspended me from the ministry of the Presbyterian Church. . . .

Then came six years (1907–13) at the Meadville Theological School. . . . Then I served as a librarian at Union Theological Seminary from 1913 to 1925. I had opportunity to observe the increasing importance of the library as a part of the seminary equipment. The method of instruction has changed from the few-book to the many-book. The student is expected to engage in research on his own account and to familiarize himself with a wide range of literature. The library must put him in possession not of a few "standard works" but of all that has been written on his subject. . . . The existing debate between Fundamentalists and Modernists emphasizes the need of a complete outfit of documents on all sides of the questions under discussion, and what is true of this particular exigency is likely to verify itself numberless times in the future. No institution could be better fitted to meet the problems that must arise than is our interdenominational seminary, where emphasis is laid on the essentials of Christianity but where freedom of scholarship has been and will continue to be heroically defended. . . .

Looking back, I find much to be grateful for. First, the loyal support and loving companionship of my dear wife; next the friendship of colleagues; then the opportunity to serve Christ and His church; finally the privilege of contributing something to the advance of science. . . .

And now the reader who has had the patience to follow me thus far may ask the question that others have asked: "Was it worth your while to unsettle the faith of the simple-minded Christian believer by your discussion of critical questions?"

The answer must be the answer to the general inquiry whether education has any value. It would be possible to argue that the *sancta simplicitas* of the peasant woman who brought her fagot to the fire that burned John Huss should not be disturbed. In like manner the good lady who complained to Dr. Roberts that the Lane Seminary professors were taking her Bible away from her might conceivably be let alone in her belief in every statement of the sacred Book; or the member of the Assembly of 1894 who protested that he accepted the whole Bible "from Generations to Revelations" might be spared by the scholars. But it is plain that in these cases the remedy is in their own hands. No one can take the Bible from them. All they have to do is let the higher criticism alone. But the teacher has others to consider. The minds of our young people are keen to know all that has been discovered. Set them to read the Bible, assuring them that it is the inerrant Word of God—that God is "inverbate" in it as He was incarnate in Christ—and they will at once raise questions that you will find difficulty in answering.

A minister asked me once whether he ought to give his people some information concerning the higher criticism. My reply was: "Better for them to get it from you than from the Sunday newspapers." This is one of the facts we have to face—the eagerness of the public press to exploit sensation of any kind. The only way is frankly to give a historical view, showing how the self-revelation of God perfected itself through the experiences of fallible men—in diverse portions and in diverse manners—till it reached its climax in Christ.

Appendix A

The Pentateuch and Book of Joshua Critically Examined by J. W. Colenso (London: 1862)

Part 1
(Excerpts)

There was a time in my own life . . . when I . . . could have heartily assented to such language as the following, "The Bible is none other than the *Voice of Him that sitteth upon the throne!* Every book of it—every chapter of it—every verse of it—every word of it—every syllable of it—(where are we to stop?) every *letter* of it—is the direct utterance of the Most High!" . . .[1]

Such was the creed of the school in which I was educated. God is my witness, what hours of wretchedness have I spent at times, while reading the Bible devoutly from day to day, and reverencing every word of it as the Word of God, when petty contradictions met me, which seemed to my reason to conflict with the notion of the absolute historical veracity of every part of Scripture, and which, as I felt, *in the study of any other book,* we should honestly treat as errors or misstatements, without in the least detracting from the real value of the book! But, in those days I was taught that it was my duty to fling the suggestion from me at once, "as if it were a loaded shell, shot into the fortress of my soul," or to stamp out desperately, as with an iron heel, each spark of honest doubt, which God's own gift, the love of Truth, had kindled in my bosom. And by many a painful effort I succeeded in doing so for a season.

But my labours, as a translator of the Bible, and a teacher of intelligent converts from heathenism, have brought me face to face with questions, from which I have hitherto shrunk. . . .

I am not speaking . . . of a number of petty variations and contradictions

. . . which may be in many cases . . . explained by alleging our ignorance of all the circumstances of the case, or by supposing some misplacement, or loss, or corruption, of the original manuscript, or by suggesting that a later writer has inserted his own gloss here and there, or even whole passages, which may contain facts or expressions at variance with the true Mosaic Books, and throwing an unmerited suspicion upon them.

However perplexing such contradictions are, when found in a book which is believed to be divinely infallible, yet a humble and pious faith will gladly welcome the aid of a friendly criticism, to relieve it in this way of its doubts. I can truly say that I would do so heartily myself.

Nor are the difficulties, to which I am referring, of the same kind as those, which arise from considering the accounts of the Creation and Deluge . . . or the stupendous character of certain miracles, as that of the sun and moon standing still, or the waters of the river Jordan standing in heaps as solid walls, while the stream, we must suppose, was still running, or the ass speaking with human voice, or the miracles wrought by the magicians of Egypt, such as the conversion of a rod into a snake, and the latter being endowed with life.

They are not such, again, as arise, when we regard the trivial nature of a vast number of conversations and commands, ascribed directly to Jehovah, especially the multiplied ceremonial minutiae, laid down in the Levitical Law.

They are not such, even, as must be started at once in most pious minds, when such words as these are read, professedly coming from the Holy and Blessed One, the Father and 'Faithful Creator' of all mankind: "If the master (of a Hebrew servant) have given him a wife, and she have borne him sons or daughters, *the wife and her children shall be her master's,* and he shall go out free by himself" (Exod. 21:4), the wife and children in such a case being placed under the protection of such other words as these: "If a man smite his servant, or his maid, with a rod, and he die under his hand, he shall be surely punished. *But,* if he continue a day or two, he shall not be punished: for *he is his money*" (Exod. 21:20, 21).

I shall never forget the revulsion of feeling, with which a very intelligent Christian native, with whose help I was translating these last words into the Zulu tongue, first heard them as words said to be uttered by the same great and gracious Being, whom I was teaching him to trust in and adore. His whole soul revolted against the notion, that the Great and Blessed God, the Merciful Father of all mankind, would speak of a servant or maid as mere "money," and allow a horrible crime to go unpunished, because the victim of the brutal usage had survived a few hours!

But I wish, before proceeding, to repeat here most distinctly that my reason, for no longer receiving the Pentateuch as historically true, is not that I find insuperable difficulties with regard to the *miracles,* or supernatural *revelations* of Almighty God, recorded in it, but solely that I cannot, as a true man, consent any longer to shut my eyes to the . . . manifest contradictions and inconsistencies, which leave us, it would seem, no alternative but to conclude that . . . the Pentateuch, as a whole, cannot possibly have been written by Moses, or by any one acquainted personally with the facts which it professes to describe, and further, that the (so-called) Mosaic narrative, by whomsoever written, and though imparting to us, as I fully believe it does, revelations of the Divine Will and Character, cannot be regarded as *historically true*. . . .

The number "600,000 on foot, that were male beside children," is given distinctly in Exodus 12:37, at the time of the [Israelites] leaving Egypt; then we have it recorded again, *thrice over, in different forms,* in Exodus 38:25–28, at the beginning of the forty years' wanderings, when the number of all that "went to be numbered, from twenty years old and upward," is reckoned at 603,550; and this is repeated again in Numbers 1:46; and it is modified once more, at the end of the wanderings, to 601,730, Numbers 26:51. Besides which, on each occasion of numbering, each separate tribe is numbered, and the sum of the separate results makes up the whole.

Thus this number is woven, as a kind of thread, into the whole story of the Exodus, and cannot be taken out, without tearing the whole fabric to pieces. It affects, directly, the account of the construction of the Tabernacle . . . and therefore, also the account of the institutions, whether of the priesthood or of the sacrifice, connected with it. And the multiplied impossibilities introduced by this number alone, independently of all other considerations, are enough to throw discredit upon the historical character of the general narrative. . . .

Now [if] the men in the prime of life, "above twenty years of age," Numbers 1:3, were more than 600,000 in number, we may reckon that the women in the prime of life were about as many, the males under twenty years, 300,000, the females under twenty years, 300,000, and the old people, male and female together, 200,000, making the *whole number,* together with the "mixed multitude," Exodus 12:38 [over 1,400,000 people, and thus, comparable to the total population in any one of the following large metropolitan areas in the United States: Cincinnati, Columbus, Milwaukee, Kansas City, New Orleans, or San Antonio, based on 1988 estimates in the *1991 Information Please Almanac.*—ED.].

The 600,000 [Hebrew] warriors alone being [comparable to the total population in any one of the following large metropolitan areas: Grand Rapids, Fresno, Oxnard-Ventura, El Paso, New Haven, Omaha, Toledo, Akron, Allentown-Bethlehem, Las Vegas, or Raleigh-Durham].[2]

[In the Israelites' march out of Egypt, Exod. 12:37–38] . . . the able-bodied warriors alone [all 600,000 of them, marching fifty men abreast], would have filled up the road for about *seven miles*. . . . the whole multitude would have formed a dense column more than *twenty-two miles long,* so that the last of the body could not have been started till the front had advanced that distance, more than two days' journey for such a mixed company as this. . . .

And the sheep and ["very much"] cattle, these must have formed another vast column, but obviously covering a much greater tract of ground in proportion to their number, as they would not march, of course, in compact order. . . .

What did this enormous multitude of cattle . . . feed upon? . . . The sheep and oxen could not live upon the manna [that God sent to feed the Israelites in the desert after they had escaped the Egyptians], nor could the people *drink* manna; and Numbers 20:5 and Deuteronomy 8:15 show that the rock [which miraculously spouted water in the desert] did not follow them throughout the desert. . . .

Could they have been supported in the wilderness by . . . insignificant wadies . . . which a drove of a hundred oxen would have trampled down into mud in an hour? . . . [Even given the assistance of a small running stream of water that followed them wherever they went] what would such a stream have been to [1,400,000 people]?

[Allowing only enough space per person as] *the size of a coffin* for a full-grown man, we must imagine [the Hebrew] encampment . . . [to have been] more than a *mile and a half across* in each direction, with the Tabernacle in the center. . . .

[Therefore] the refuse and ashes of . . . Tabernacle sacrifices would have had to be *carried out for a distance of three-quarters of a mile,* as stated in Leviticus 4:11–12 and 6:10–11, "And the skin of the bullock, and all his flesh, with his head, and with his legs, and his inwards, and his dung, even the whole bullock, shall he (the Priest) carry forth *without the Camp,* unto a clean place, where the ashes are poured out, and burn him on the wood with fire. Where the ashes are poured out, there shall they [the refuse that was not burnt up in the original offering] be burnt. . . ."

[Granted that the Hebrew people might faint and perish in the desert if each was only granted a coffin's worth of space, let's try enlarging the camp to] *twelve miles* [across], that is, about the size of London [in 1851], as it might well be, considering that the population was as large as that of London, and that in the Hebrew tents there were no first, second, third, and fourth stories, no crowded garrets and underground cellars! In that case, the offal of the [Tabernacle] sacrifices would have to be *carried a distance of six miles.* . . .

[Where, in the wilderness, did all the bulls, sheep, lambs, rams, goats, turtle-doves, pigeons, oil, flour, and first-fruits, come from that the 1,400,000 Israelites were commanded to give to the Priests to sacrifice?]

If indeed, such supplies of wood . . . for such [a] multitude [of burnt offerings, and burning of sacred wastes outside the Camp, and for cooking enough food to feed hundreds of thousands] . . . could have been found at all in the wilderness.

And now let us ask, for all these multifarious duties, during the forty years' sojourn in the wilderness, for all the burnt-offerings, meat-offerings, peace-offerings, sin-offerings, trespass-offerings, thank-offerings, etc., of a population of 1,400,000, besides the daily and extraordinary sacrifices, how many Priests were there?

The answer is very simple. There were only *three,* Aaron (till his death) and his two sons, Eleazar and Ithamar, Numbers 3:10. . . .

The very pigeons, to be brought as sin-offerings for newly born children, would have averaged, according to the story, more than 250 a day. . . .

Can it be believed that such a system was really laid down by Jehova Himself, which, if properly carried out by pious Israelites according to the Divine Command, would have involved immediately absurd impossibilities like the above, and required instant modification? . . .[3]

They could not . . . all have gone outside the Camp . . . a distance of *six miles* . . . for the common necessities of nature, as commanded in Deuteronomy 23:12–14. There were the aged and infirm, women in childbirth, sick persons, and young children, who could not have done this. And, indeed, the command itself supposes the person to have a "paddle" upon his "weapon," and, therefore, must be understood to [exclude females, children and elderly males], or rather, apply only to the 600,000 *warriors*. But the very fact, that this direction for ensuring cleanliness, "for Jehovah thy God walketh in the midst of thy Camp; therefore shall thy Camp be holy; that He see no unclean thing in thee, and turn away from thee," would have been so limited in its application, is itself a very convincing proof of the unhistorical character of the whole narrative. . . .

[At the very least, it is reasonable to assume that the total number of people involved in the Exodus would have been double the number of Hebrew warriors, or "600,000" times two, since we would have to include women, children, elderly, and the "mixed multitude." That would make at least 1,200,000 people. Bombay, India, one of the most densely populated cities on earth, has 120,000 people per square mile (1989 estimate). If the Exodus encampment was as densely populated as Bombay, India, it would have had to extend over an area of at least *ten square miles*.

[That the Hebrews could survive in the desert packed together as densely as the populace of Bombay is extremely doubtful. A much less densely populated "encampment" spread out over a *much larger area than ten square miles* would be a minimum requirement.

Yet the larger the encampment, the more miles the (three) priests would have had to walk to dispose of the refuse from the vast multitude of sacrifices. And the more miles the Hebrew warriors would have had to walk to take care of each and every call of nature, "outside the camp."—ED.]

[How could Moses have "called all Israel, and spoken unto them," Deut. 5:1, or, how could Joshua have "read the words of the Law before all the Congregation of Israel, with the women, and the little ones, and the strangers that were conversant among them," Josh. 8:34–35, so that all Israel—1,400,000 people—might have heard?] Under favorable circumstances, many thousands, perhaps, might hear the voice of a speaker. But imagine the whole population of London addressed at one time by one man! . . .

[How could more than half a million warriors—"the whole Assembly,' "all the Assembly," "all the Congregation," Lev. 8:1–4, Exod. 12:6, 16:2–3, Num. 1:2— be "gathered together *unto the door* of the Tabernacle?" ("All the Assembly" is not to be confused with smaller groups, like the "elders," or "princes," which are clearly distinguished from "all the Congregation," or "all the Assembly," Num. 10:3–4 and 16:19, 25.)] Presumably this was to witness a ceremony taking place in a tent eighteen paces long and six wide, which could only have been seen by a few standing at the door. . . . Supposing, then, that "all the Congregation" of adult males in the prime of life had given due heed to the Divine Summons, and had hastened to take their stand, side by side, as closely as possible, in front of the whole *end* of the Tabernacle, in which the door or entrance was, they would have reached, allowing eighteen inches between each rank of nine men, for a distance of more than 100,000 feet—in fact, nearly *twenty miles!* . . .

While it is conceivable that a later writer, *imagining* such scenes as these, may have employed such exaggerated expressions as occur in the above passages, it cannot be believed that an *eye-witness, with the actual facts of the case before him,* could have expressed himself in such extravagant language. . . .[4]

But how thankful we must be, that we are no longer obliged to believe, as a matter of fact, of vital consequence to our eternal hope, each separate statement contained in the Pentateuch, such, for instance, as the story related in Numbers 31!—where we are told that . . . Israelite [warriors] . . . slew *all* the males of the Midianites, took captive *all* the females and children, seized *all* their cattle and flocks, and *all* their goods, and "burnt *all* their cities, and *all* their goodly castles," without the loss of a single man!—and then, by command of Moses, butchered in cold blood all the women and children, except "All the women-children, who have not known a man by lying with him" (v. 18). These last they were to "keep alive for themselves."[5]

How is it possible to quote the Bible as in any way condemning slavery, when we read here, verse 40, of "Jehovah's tribute" of slaves, 32 persons, who were given to Eleazar the Priest, while 323 were given to the Levites, verses 46–47?

Who is it that really dishonors the Word, and blasphemes the Name of God Most High?—he who believes, and teaches others to believe, that such acts, as those above recorded, were really perpetrated by Moses under express Divine sanction and command, or he who declares that such commands as these could never have emanated from the Holy and Blessed One, the All-Just and All-Loving, the Father of the spirits of all flesh. . . . We are bound not to [believe] so by the express authority of the Divine Law, which we hear in our hearts, which is written in our consciences, and answers there to the voice which speaks to us from without, Deuteronomy 13:1–3.

Part II
(Excerpts)

The following instances will tend to confirm the conclusion in Part I, that large portions . . . of the Pentateuch, and . . . of the book of Joshua, were written at a much later date than the age of Moses and the Exodus.

It is generally admitted that Deuteronomy 34, which relates the death and burial of Moses, and contains the statements, "but no man knoweth of his burial place *unto this day,*" v.6, "and there arose not a prophet *since* in Israel like unto Moses," verse 10, must have been written [by someone other than Moses]. . . .

Also, such passages as the following could hardly have been written by Moses himself:

"Moreover, the man Moses was very great in the land of Egypt, in the sight of Pharaoh's servants, and in the sight of his people" (Exod. 11:3).

"Now the man Moses was very meek, above all the men which were upon the face of the earth" (Num. 12:3).

"These are that Aaron and Moses, to whom Jehovah said, Bring out the children of Israel from the land of Egypt according to their armies. These are they which spake to Pharaoh, king of Egypt, to bring out the children of Israel from Egypt: these are that Moses and Aaron" (Exod. 6:26–27).

"And if ye have erred and not observed all these commandments, which Jehovah hath spoken unto Moses, even all that Jehovah hath commanded you by the hand of Moses, from the day that Jehovah commanded Moses, and henceforward among your generations," etc. (Num. 15:22–23).

It can scarcely be doubted that such statements as the above must have been written by someone who lived in an age after that of Moses.[6]

In Deuteronomy, transactions, in which Moses himself was concerned, are detailed at full length, as by one referring to events *long past*. . . . See Deuteronomy, chapters 1–3, especially such a passage as Deut. 3:4–11 [which ends with the verses, "For only Og, king of Bashan, remained of the remnant of the giants; behold, his bedstead was a bedstead of iron; *is it not in Rabbath of the children of Ammon?*"—implying it is "still to be seen," at a time long after Moses' day]. . . .

We may notice . . . the frequent occurrence of the expression "unto this day," in places where it could have had no meaning, unless the "day" referred to was considerably later than the time of Moses or Joshua, Deuteronomy 3:14, 34:6; Joshua 4:9, 5:9, 7:26, 8:29, 9:27, 10:27, 13:13, 15:63, 16:10, 14:14. . . .

Again, such expressions as the following indicate a later date than that of Moses. "And the Canaanite *was then in the land*" (Gen. 12:6). "And the Canaanite and Perizzite *dwelt then in the land*" (Gen. 13:7). These words . . . imply that, at the time when they were written, the Canaanite was no longer dwelling in the land, as its owner and lord. [The *Israelites* pushed out the Canaanites (who were "then in the land") but only *after* Moses had died.] . . .

"That the land spew not you out also, when ye defile it, *as it spewed out the nations which were before you*" (Lev. 18:28). This implies that the Canaanites were already exterminated when these words were written. [That would have been *after* Moses' death]. . . .

"These be the words, which Moses spake unto all Israel on the other side *Jordan,* in the wilderness" (Deut. 1:1). "*On the other side Jordan,* in the land of Moab, began Moses to declare this law" (Deut. 1:5).

On this . . . Bleek writes . . . "These words could only have been written by one who found himself on *this* side Jordan, and, therefore, after the death of Moses and the possession of the land of Canaan." [Moses died when the Israelites were still living on the wilderness side of the Jordan. So, for someone to call the side with Moses and the wilderness, the "other side," they would have had to have been speaking from the side that Israel settled on *after Moses' death.*] . . .

"And, *while the children of Israel were in the wilderness* . . ." Numbers 15:32 . . . written when the people were no longer in the wilderness, and therefore, not by Moses. . . .

Again, names of places are often used familiarly, which could scarcely have been known to Moses, much less to the Israelites generally, at the time of the Exodus, some of which, indeed, are modern names, which, according to the story itself, did not even exist in the time of Moses [see Colenso's work for specific examples]. . . .

Exodus 30:13 and 38:24–26 . . . mentions a "shekel after the shekel of the Sanctuary," or, as some render the words, a "sacred shekel," before there was, according to the story, any Sanctuary in existence, or any sacred system established in Israel. This appears to be an oversight, as is also the command to sacrifice "turtle-doves or young pigeons" in Leviticus 14:22, *with express reference to their life in the wilderness,* arising from a writer in a later age employing inadvertently an expression, which was in common use in his own days, and forgetting the circumstances of the times which he was describing.

These passages show also plainly the unhistorical character of the narrative, since in the first and last of them the phrases in question are put into the mouth of Jehovah Himself. The story, therefore, could not have been written by Moses, or by one of his age, unless it be supposed that *such* a writer could be guilty of a deliberate intention to deceive. But it is quite conceivable that a pious writer of later days (when the Temple was standing) might have inserted such passages in a narrative already existing, which had been composed as a work of devout imagination, in the attempt to reproduce, from the floating legends of the time, the early history of the Hebrew tribes, for the instruction of an ignorant people. . . .

"And the sun stood still, and the moon stayed, until the people had avenged themselves upon their enemies. Is not this written in the book of Jasher?" (Josh. 10:13).

First, it would be very strange that, if Joshua really wrote [the book of Joshua], he should have referred for the details of such an extraordinary miracle, in which he himself was primarily and personally concerned, to another book, as the book of Jasher. But in 2 Samuel 1:18 we read, "Also he (David) bade them teach the children of Judah the use of the bow. . . . Behold, it is written in the *book of Jasher.*"

Here, then, we have a fact *in the life of David* recorded in this same "book of Jasher." The natural inference is, that this "book of Jasher," which prob-ably . . . contained a number of notable passages in the history [of Israel], was written not earlier than the time of *David,* and the above passage [found] in the book of Joshua was written, of course, after that [and not in Joshua's day].

Notes

1. Burgon in his book *Inspiration* asserts this to be the creed of orthodox believers. It probably did express the belief of many English Christians in Colenso's day.

2. According to Deuteronomy 7, the Hebrews were commanded to "utterly destroy . . . *seven* nations *greater and mightier*" than them. "Thou shalt make no covenant with them, nor show mercy unto them."

Using the biblical number of Hebrew warriors, "600,000," as an indication of Israel's "greatness and might," try multiplying *that* by "seven." You arrive at 4,200,000 as the warrior population of the *seven* "greater and mightier nations." And you would have to double *that* number to include the *women and children* and elderly of the seven nations the Hebrews were told to "utterly destroy," thus achieving the population of Tokyo, about 8,000,000.

How can anyone believe that 8,000,000 people once lived in that arid, geographical area? There is *no* archeological evidence based on the sizes of ancient cities, or based on cemetery populations, that such a huge population existed at that time. Even the modern nation-state of Israel with scientific farming techniques, desalination plants, food importing, apartment buildings, sanitation, a lower infant mortality rate due to medical care, constant immigration, etc., has only attained a population for that general area of 4,371,478 (estimated as of mid-1989), which is still only *half* of the number of people that God asked the ancient Hebrews to "utterly destroy."

So the number of Hebrew warriors stated plainly in the Bible, "600,000," is unbelievable in light of what it would imply about the population of the "seven nations . . . greater and mightier!"

3. "Testimony of the [earliest Hebrew] Prophets is unanimous in *disputing* that the Divine ordinance of sacrifice [was given to Moses] in the wilderness. Amos implies that it did not exist, 5:25; Jeremiah states that it was not due to Yahweh's command, 7:22. There are frequent statements of the futility of sacrifice in the Prophets' own day, cf. Isa. 1:11, Jer. 6:20, Hos. 4:13, 5:6, 8:11, Am. 4:4, Mi. 6:6–8. Nor can it be supposed that the seasonal feasts described in the Pentateuch were observed before the conquest of Canaan [i.e., while the Hebrews were still in the desert and had not yet taken up agriculture]" (T. H. Robinson, *Prophecy and the Prophets in Ancient Israel,* 3d ed., first published London, 1923).

4. Though it has taken centuries for them to admit, many evangelical and even fundamentalist Christian scholars have come to *agree* with Colenso's criticism that the *numbers* of Israelites in the wilderness, attested to in the Bible, are highly inflated.

One such scholar is W. M. Flinders Petrie, who wrote in his book *Egypt and Israel* (London: Society for Promoting Christian Knowledge, 1911), "There are . . . two wholesale checks upon the total numbers. The land of Goshen recently supported 4,000 Bedouin living like the Israelites, or at present holds 12,000 cultivators. To get 600,000 men with their families out of that district would be utterly impossible. Also on going south the Israelites had almost a drawn battle with the Amalekites of Sinai. The climate of that desert peninsula has not appreciably changed; it will not now support more than a few thousand people, and the former inhabitants cannot have exceeded this amount. How could the Israelites have had any appreciable resistance from a poor desert folk, if they outnumbered them as a hundred to one? Again, we are compelled to suppose that the Israelites were not more than a few thousand altogether. Thus we see that more cannot be got out of Goshen or into Sinai."

Petrie added that, during the Hebrew's sojourn in the wilderness, "Moses judged all disputes, which might be possible among 600 tents, but not among 600,000 men; and [only] *two* midwives were employed . . . while there would have been 140 births a *day* on the greater number stated.

"The whole subject of Levites and firstborn [in the book of Numbers] cannot fit anything in the Exodus period. But it might well fit to the population when there were about 300,000 in Palestine. The dedication of the firstborn would be likely to arise in Palestine [i.e., *not* with Moses in the Sinai wilderness], since the Canaanites [the residents of Palestine prior to the Hebrews] sacrificed their firstborn; and the separation of a sacred caste [viz., the tribe of priests known as the "Levites"] would also be a gradual growth. We must look, then, to the time of the Judges as the source of these changes, and of the census document of Levi, which was incorporated *afterward* in the Book of Numbers."

Even the evangelical scholar F. F. Bruce has admitted that he agrees with Flinders Petrie's analysis of the situation. Namely, that the large numbers found in the Bible in connection with the Exodus are incorrect.

Among recent evangelical attempts to deal with such large number quandries, fundamentalist readers might wish to note the recent doctoral dissertation by David Mack Fouts of Dallas Theological Seminary (Hal Lindsey's alma mater), titled *The Use of Large Numbers in the Old Testament, with Particular Emphasis on the Use of 'elep*, 1992. Fouts admits that, "Textual anaylsis of the Hebrew word for 'thousand' reveals no significant lessening of the enormity of the numbers, a problem which remains despite the reading chosen." Furthermore, "At no time in ancient history did the population of Palestine approach the numbers demanded by accepting the census figures of the Old Testament at face value." How then can a fundamentalist believe in a Bible without error? His solution is that the Hebrews employed "literary hyperbole" in their recounting of the Exodus numbers, and other large numbers found in the Old Testament. "It was not uncommon for royal inscriptions at that time to inflate the number of troops killed or captured and the amount of spoil taken." He then analyzes the majority of biblical passages containing large numbers, and notes similarities between those passages and the "royal inscriptional genre" of other ancient Near East countries with respect to large numbers, figurative language, and military conquests.

"Literary hyperbole" may sound like a neat hypothesis to a fundamentalist forced into that admission, but consider what questions it leaves unanswered:

(a) If the Old Testament was written by "eyewitnesses," why didn't they cite actual numbers instead of exaggerated ones? Does God need to duplicate ancient "literary genres" when he *directly* inspires His servants to preserve sacred history?

And what about the Genesis "creation" story? Its similarities to other ancient Near Eastern creation accounts are legion. (See my manuscripts on the subject—ED.) Might it not be an error to take the creation account in Genesis literally? Especially since it may be seen as lying within the ancient Near Eastern "literary genre" of mythological creation accounts?

(b) If the author(s) of Exodus inflated numbers, might not the unbelievably large numbers recorded in Genesis as the "ages of the Patriarchs" also be examples of literary hyperbole? The ages recorded in Genesis resemble in many ways the even higher ages recorded for Babylonian kings listed on ancient cuneiform tables. The difference being that the Babylonians believed their ancient kings were direct descendants of the gods and therefore could live *tens of thousands of years,* while the Hebrew patriarchs were mere mortals and therefore could not live past *one thousand years* since that number of years is a perspective proper to God alone (Ps. 90:4).

Shouldn't that make fundamentalist Christians who believe in a "young earth"—based on adding up the *numbers* of years each Patriarch supposedly "lived," from Adam until today— question their "biblical" basis for believing the earth is only six thousand to ten thousand years old? After all, those ages might be another example of literary hyperbole.

(c) If the numbers given for the Exodus, which are perhaps the most indisputable numbers in the Bible, and which are repeated in a host of realistic seeming contexts, turn out to be mere hyperbole, then how can any reader determine which numbers, or even what "overly spectacular" descriptions of *events,* may or may not be the result of a biblical author employing literary hyperbole or other ancient Near Eastern "literary genres"?

It seems that fundamentalist/evangelical scholars like David Fouts are beginning to retrace the intellectual footsteps of "liberal" Christian scholars! But, of course, they are not allowed to do so by actually *reading* and *citing* liberal sources like Colenso, but by having to rethink the same old problems from scratch at a fundamentalist university. To a fundamentalist scholar, that is called "progress in religion." Nonfundamentalists might call such progress "catching up with where the forerunners of biblical scholarship were a hundred years ago."

5. Compare Numbers 31 with the following saying attributed to Genghis Khan, "A man's greatest work is to break his enemies, to drive them before him, to take from them all the things that have been theirs, to hear the weeping of those who cherished them, to take their horses between his knees and to press in his arms the most desirable of their women." Is the account in Numbers 31 the "Word of God," or of Genghis Khan?

For a contemporary review of the historical and archeological evidence concerning the biblical Exodus/Conquest traditions, see William H. Stiebing, *Out of the Desert? Archaeology and the Exodus/Conquest Narratives* (Amherst, N.Y.: Prometheus Books, 1989). See also Neil Asher Silberman's article, "Who Were the Israelites?: Recent Discoveries Suggest That the Military Conquest of the Promised Land as Described in the Book of Joshua Simply Never Happened," *Archaeology,* vol. 45, no. 2 (March/April 1992), pp. 22–30.

6. The Pentateuch was written in the third person, not the first. It reads, throughout, like a tale told *about* Moses, and not written *by* Moses. In fact, whoever wrote the Pentateuch, they did not make any great effort to disguise the fact that, in their opinion, Moses "wrote" only *portions* of the whole, such as the following:

(a) *An account of the war against Amalek.* "And the Lord said unto Moses, Write this for a memorial in a book . . . for I will utterly put out the remembrance of Amalek from under heaven" (Exod. 17:13–14).

(b) *A list of places where the Israelites pitched their tents.* "And Moses recorded their starting places according to their journeys by the command of the Lord" (Num. 33:2). (Even so, Numbers 21–33 differ in their descriptions of the route the Israelites followed from Mount Hor into Canaan.)

(c) *The Book of the Law of God.* "And Moses wrote this law. . . . Moses . . . made an end of writing the words of this law in a book" (Deut. 31:9, 24). Unfortunately, we do not know what this original "law" may have consisted of. Perhaps its essence may be found in Deuteronomy 12–26, or parts thereof.

(d) *The Song of Moses.* "So Moses wrote this song . . . and taught it to the sons of Israel" (Deut. 31:22; 32:1–43.)

(e) *The Book of the Covenant.* "And Moses wrote all the words of the Lord. . . . And he took the book of the covenant. . . . And the Lord said unto Moses, Write thou these words; for after the tenor of these I have made a covenant with thee and with Israel" (Exod. 24:4, 7; 34:27). "The Book of the Covenant" is not the entire book of Exodus, but only chapters 19–24. Scholars believe it to be the most ancient legal collection in the Old Testament.

The belief that Moses wrote the whole Pentateuch arose later, after the Pentateuch itself was completed, probably during the Babylonian exile. Afterwards, this view of Moses being the author of the whole was attributed to Jesus also. Thus it became binding both in Judaism (in which it was stressed that the true author was God and Moses merely a scribe) and in Christianity. But doubts soon arose among both rabbis and church fathers, as early as the second century, as to whether Moses could have written the whole Pentateuch. These early Bible scholars ran across the same passages Colenso did, and asked similar questions.

Appendix B

The "*Roman* Road to Salvation" or the "*Synoptic* Road to Salvation"? Belief or Ethics?

Fundamentalist Christians often quote verses found in the apostle Paul's letter to the Romans in order to convince a potential convert to "call on the name of the Lord and be saved by faith." They call it "the Roman road to salvation." However, by stressing only Paul's letter to the Romans, they neglect the record of *Jesus'* statements on "how to inherit eternal life," which are found in the three earliest Gospels, Matthew, Mark, and Luke, the "synoptic Gospels." Those three Gospels represent, much more so than Paul's letters, the original teachings of the historical Jesus.

Was *belief* the primary concern of the historical Jesus, or was he primarily concerned with *ethical behavior*? What do the three synoptic Gospels have to say?

According to Mark 10 and Matthew 19, Jesus told an inquirer precisely how to inherit eternal life. Jesus' answer in order of priority was (1) obey the commandments, (2) sell all you have and give it to the poor, and (3) follow me. Even "follow me," is not the same as "believe in me." And when the inquirer turned away Jesus immediately focused on the importance of giving away one's riches (ethical behavior), and not on the idea of following him.

In Luke 10, Jesus was asked once again, "*How might a person inherit eternal life?*" In this case Jesus answered, "Love God, and your neighbor as yourself." This echoed the ethical teachings of several rabbis of Jesus' day, including Hillel.

And, according to Luke, Jesus capped his answer with the parable of the Good Samaritan, a person who practiced *ethical behavior,* yet whose religious *beliefs* were derided by others. (Samaritans were despised for not accepting the books of the Prophets into their holy canon, just the books of the Law.) The Good Samaritan parable emphasizes that God is more interested in ethical behavior than correct belief.

Also consider Luke 19, in which the story is told of a rich man who, after meeting Jesus, decides to give half of his goods to the poor "and if I have taken anything from any man by false accusation, I restore him fourfold." Whereupon Jesus said to him, "This day is *salvation* come to this house." Again, ethical behavior, not belief, was viewed as the primary means of salvation.

In similar fashion, Jesus taught in Matthew 5 to 7 that, "Not everyone who says to me, *Lord, Lord,* shall enter into heaven; but he that *does* my Father's will."

In a preceding verse, Jesus explained, "Whatever you want others to do for you, *do* for them, for this is the Law *and* the Prophets." Ethical behavior again!

Jesus continued in Matthew, "Many will say to me in that day, '*Lord, Lord,* haven't we prophesied in *your name*? . . . cast out devils? . . . done miracles?' And then I will say to them, 'I never knew you. Depart from me, you who practice lawlessness.' Therefore, whoever hears these sayings of mine and *does* them. . . ."

Notice Jesus' deemphasis of his own "name," of "miracle-producing" faith, and his emphasis on "practice" and "doing," i.e., ethical behavior.

Other examples from the synoptic Gospels include Matthew 25, where the "sheep and goats" are separated based on their ethical behavior, not their belief. That parable depicts behavior as the basis for God's judgment.

Or consider Jesus' teaching to "pray in this way." "If you forgive men their trespasses, your heavenly Father will also forgive your trespasses." There is nothing in the "Our Father" about the necessity of believing in Jesus in order to be forgiven your trespasses. What is required is to forgive others. Again, ethical behavior.

Neither does the parable of the prodigal son demonstrate the need for belief in order to be forgiven. Nor do Jesus' words, spoken while being nailed to the cross, "Father, forgive them, for they know not what they do."

Robert G. Ingersoll, the great agnostic, summed the matter up nicely when he said, "Who can account for the fact, if we are to be saved only by faith in Christ, that Matthew forgot it, that Luke said nothing about it, and that Mark never mentioned it except in two passages written by another person?"

Appendix C

Assorted Quotations that Address Various Aspects of Fundamentalism

On the Fundamentalist View of the Bible

Beware the man of one book.

—Latin proverb

"Those who say they believe the Bible 'from cover to cover' are not aware of all that is between the covers."
—Dr. Ralph Brown, former Chairman of the Bible Department
at West Virginia Wesleyan College in Buckhannon

"As Weber remarks, 'Despite the claims that lay people could study the Bible for themselves, their [fundamentalist] teachers rarely let them.'. . . .

"Weber concludes, 'There is something incongruous about fundamentalists who say that they can read the Bible by themselves, then pore over Scofield's notes [in the Scofield 'Reference' Bible] in order to discover what the text really means.'. . . .

"To make matters worse, every one of the fundamentalist interpretations I have cited. . . . would be challenged by certain self-described fundamentalists, and every challenge would appeal to 'what the Bible really says' on the matter."
—Kathleen C. Boone, *The Bible Tells Them So:*
The Discourse of Protestant Fundamentalism
(New York: State University of New York Press, 1989)

"As James Barr perceptively concluded in his 1977 study, *Fundamentalism.* . . . the fundamentalist is no literal reader of the Bible. Rather, he will use every logical or factual means at his disposal to avoid what the Bible literally says in order to harmonize what he thinks to be its meaning with what he thinks to be logical, factual, or historical reality. This he does in obedience to his belief in what he calls biblical inerrancy, or infallibility."

—Bruce Vawter, "Creationism: Creative Misuse of the Bible," in *Is God a Creationist?*, ed. Roland Mushat Frye (New York: Charles Scribners' Sons, 1983)

"Once the defender of the inerrancy of the Bible allows himself to meet the critic on critical grounds and not on grounds of *a priori* principle, he is lost. He finds himself involved in more and more complicated and improbable conjectures in order to save the Bible's inerrancy, and he is vulnerable at so many points, that the effort to defend every weak position becomes impossible or rather incredible. He is caught, one might say, in a Ptolemaic system of epicycles and yet more epicycles. It can hardly be a coincidence that the fundamentalist tradition has not produced one biblical commentator of sufficient status as to be recognized throughout the scholarly world."

—R. P. C. and A. T. Hanson, *The Bible Without Illusions* (Philadelphia: Trinity Press International, 1989)

"If there are atheists, who is responsible but the mercenary tyrants of souls . . . which have the God of purity and truth pronounce: 'Believe a hundred things [in the Bible] either manifestly abominable or mathematically impossible: otherwise the God of mercy will burn you in the fires of hell, not only for millions of billions of centuries, but for all eternity.' "

—Voltaire, *Philosophical Dictionary,* entry under "Atheist, Atheism," Second Section

On the Fundamentalist View of Hell

"When all has been considered, it seems to me to be the irresistible intuition that infinite punishment for finite sin would be unjust, and therefore wrong. We feel that even weak and erring Man would shrink from such an act. And we cannot conceive of God as acting on a lower standard of right and wrong."

—Lewis Carroll, "Eternal Punishment," in *Diversions and Digressions of Lewis Carroll*

"Nothing but the most cruel ignorance . . . ever imagined that the few days of human life spent here, surrounded by mists and clouds of darkness, blown over life's seas by storms and tempests of passion, fixed for eternity the condition of a person's soul. If this doctrine be true then this life is but a net in which Jehovah catches souls for hell. . . .

"Do I believe in eternal punishment? Well, no. I always thought that God could get his revenge in far less time." (*Some Mistakes of Moses*)

"I have received your letter of Feb. 16, in which you say that you want to meet me in Heaven. You certainly will if you are there." (*Letters of Robert Ingersoll*)

"When hundreds prayed outside Ingersoll's house, hoping for his conversion, he remarked, 'It reminds me of the boy who squeezed his girlfriend's hand. It made him feel good and it didn't hurt her.' "

—Robert Ingersoll

"Given the pains and problems, both physical and psychological, that accompany day to day existence: headaches, backaches, toothaches, muscle strains, scrapes, cuts, burns, bruises, rashes, PMS, fatigue, hunger, odors, colds, viruses, cancer, genetic defects, deformities, ugliness, a multitude of embarrassing circumstances, miscommunications, confused signals, mental preoccupations, dashed hopes, unrequited love, boredom, hard labor, repetitious labor, accidents, fires, earthquakes, typhoons, floods, tornadoes, hurricanes, old age, the limitations of each person's knowledge, the narrowing of one's mental horizons with age, the atrophying of one's memory with age, etc.—given all those things we each must abide—I cannot see how any human being deserves 'eternal punishment' after they die. Instead, we should all be awarded 'medals' for having passed through life with our sanity left relatively intact. . . ."

—Edward T. Babinski

"It is quite obvious to the canny observer that most Christians . . . do not believe in Christianity. If they did, they would be screaming in the streets, taking daily full-page advertisements in the newspapers, and subscribing for the most hair-raising television programs every night of the week. . . . Nobody, save perhaps a few obscure fanatics, is *really* bothered by the idea that . . . [most] people are sinners and unbelievers, and will probably go to hell. So what? Let God worry about that one!"

—Alan Watts, *Beyond Theology* (New York: Vintage Books, 1973)

On the Fundamentalist Insistence that "Ye *Must* Be Born Again"

Conrad Hyers spent three years at a leading fundamentalist university where he was dissuaded by professors and fellow students from reading William James's book, *The Varieties of Religious Experience*. But he read it anyway. He loved the book, especially James's astute distinction between "once-born" and "twice-born" Christians. The university only recognized the latter variety as genuine Christians.

Reading the book helped relieve Conrad of some of the shame he felt at not having a "twice-born" testimony to share with his fellow students. You see, he could not remember ever having not been a Christian, or having not been "saved." His own recollections about having "gone up to the altar to receive Jesus" when he was "five years old" were supplied by his mother, years after the event. Furthermore, Conrad came from a long line of preachers. After reading James, he decided that he was a "once-born" Christian. He loved God from the first. Therefore, he did not need the "you are depraved" type of "twice-born" sermon preached to him, since he had never "slipped" that far to begin with.

Twice-borns, are of course, always reliving, or trying to re-create in the ears of their listeners their "lost-now-found" experience.

Years later, Hyers was studying comparative religion and ran across two rival schools of Zen Buddhism that also exemplified James's categories of "once-born" and "twice-born" religious experiences. In the first school, the one that Hyers recognized as the "once-born" school of Zen, students were taught to calmly accept and love both themselves and others, having this love grow within them, organically and solidly, and not to seek after some cataclysmic experience of Zen bliss. In the second school, the "twice-born" school of Zen, students were taught to concentrate upon the many unendurable Buddhist hells, envisioning them intimately, until a great letting go, a great physical and emotional release, a satori of enlightenment, peace, and forgiveness overwhelmed them.

—Edward T. Babinski, based on personal conversation with Conrad Hyers

"A second birth may be a great blessing for those in the depths of psychic turmoil, but it is hardly therefore the ideal for all. And the attempt to provoke such an experience in others by artificially inducing crises, conflicts, and doubts may be a thoroughly irresponsible form of cruelty. It is as if one were to be made to feel sinful and guilty for not having felt sinful and guilty, in order that one might experience release from sin and guilt and no longer feel sinful and guilty! As Alan Watts has suggested, this can be like walking about in lead boots until totally exhausted in order to have the exhilarating experience of taking them off again."

—Conrad Hyers, *Once-Born, Twice-Born Zen:*
The Soto and Rinzai Schools of Japan
(Wolfeboro, N.H.: Longwood Academic, 1989)

"The dark side of Christianity's claim to relieve guilt is how much unnecessary guilt fundamentalist dogmas foster. As that Christian martyr Dietrich Bonhoeffer once stated: 'The church must stop trying to act like a "spiritual pharmacist"— working to produce acute guilt, and then in effect saying, "We just happen to have the remedy for your guilt here in our pocket." '

"Furthermore, the Doctrine of Original Sin plays havoc on those whose self-trust and self-image are not supported by society at large. It is a veritable weapon in the hands of those bent on controlling others."

—Edward T. Babinski

On the Peculiar Forms of Egotism that Fundamentalist Christians are Sometimes Prone to Exhibit

"Try as they might to be humble, to avoid the pitfalls of intellectual pride— largely because the Bible tells them to, perhaps—fundamentalists are dogmatic and doctrinalistic because their doctrine of the text forces them to be. They are reading an inerrant text; what they read, and therefore by definition what they *interpret,* must be inerrant."

> —Kathleen C. Boone, *The Bible Tells Them So:*
> *The Discourse of Protestant Fundamentalism*
> (New York: State University of New York Press, 1989)

"According to fundamentalist apologists the only 'inerrant' text was the one originally written by God's prophets—what we have today is a 'very nearly inerrant' copy of an originally 'inerrant' text. So, their interpretations of that text are at most 'very nearly' inerrant. But that doesn't seem to dampen a fundamentalist's intellectual pride, nor the dogmatism of their interpretations.

"Perhaps fundamentalists need to pause in their headlong plunge to convert the world and consider just how many changes their originally 'inerrant' text may have undergone over time. For example, a comparison of the most ancient New Testament texts with later copies of those same texts has revealed that the following sections are *later additions,* which did not appear in the original manuscripts: (1) the entire last chapter of Mark, which lists Jesus' resurrection appearances and the immunity of believers to serpents' bites and poison; (2) the scene in Luke's Gospel where Jesus sweats blood and is comforted by angels; (3) the espisode in the Gospel of John where Jesus saves the life of a woman caught in the act of adultery; and (4) the passages in the First Epistle of John that clearly endorse the doctrine of 'the Trinity.' Christians added all of the above sections to the original 'inerrant' documents! Obviously, if Christians have, as the evidence shows, added and/or changed New Testament documents once they had already been composed, then what about *before* they had been composed? How many additions and/or changes to the 'story' might have taken place *before* the New Testament authors first laid their pens down on papyrus, i.e., when the Jesus tradition was still in an *oral* stage of rapid ferment? Such questions make belief in the 'inerrancy' of the Bible appear questionable, to say the least.

"Furthermore, in the earliest decades and centuries after Jesus' death, Christians wrote *many* Gospels besides the ones traditionally attributed to Matthew, Mark, Luke, and John. These other Gospels contained extraordinary stories and details about Jesus' life, and the lives and adventures of the Apostles, even stories about Jesus' infancy and youth, which later generations of Christians eventually declared spurious. Which goes to prove that the writings of early Christian authors are not to be deemed entirely trustworthy simply because the authors were Christians who lived during the earliest decades and centuries of the church.

"Such considerations, taken together, should dampen even the most hard-line fundamentalist's intellectual pride, and the dogmatism of their interpretations."

> —Edward T. Babinski

"The faith in which I was brought up assured me that I was better than other people; I was 'saved,' they were 'damned'—we were in a state of grace and the rest were 'heathens.' . . . Our hymns were loaded with arrogance—self-congratulation on how cozy we were with the Almighty and what a high opinion he had of us, what hell everybody else would catch come Judgment Day."

—Robert Heinlein, *Stranger in a Strange Land*

"Look at the songs of Fundamentalism (always a good index of popular religious life): 'That will be glory for me,' 'I shall see Him face to face,' 'My sins are gone,' 'I'm so happy . . . ,' 'I'm saved, saved, saved,' 'Love lifted me,' 'He holds my hand,' 'Now I belong to Jesus,' 'Safe am I . . . ,' 'My Lord is real, yes, real to me. . . . ' Shall I extend the list, or is the point clear enough? These distinctive products of the Fundamentalist movement show its undeniable individualism. Do children still sing that shameless chorus: 'For me, for me, for me, for me'? Is not this original sin set to music and taught to the young?"

—Daniel B. Stevick, *Beyond Fundamentalism*
(Richmond Va.: John Knox Press, 1964)

"The inordinately selfish are particularly susceptible to frustration. The more selfish a person, the more poignant his disappointments. It is the inordinately selfish, therefore, who are likely to be the most persuasive champions of selflessness.

"The fiercest fanatics are often selfish people who were forced, by innate shortcomings or external circumstances, to lose faith in their own selves. They separate the excellent instrument of their selfishness from their ineffectual selves and attach it to the service of some holy cause. And though it be a faith of love and humility they adopt, they can be neither loving nor humble."

—Eric Hoffer, *The True Believer: Thoughts on the Nature of
Mass Movements* (New York: Harper & Row Publishers, 1951)

"When a man has been 'born again,' all the passages of the Old Testament that appear so horrible and so unjust to one in his natural state, become the dearest, the most consoling, and the most beautiful of truths. The [fundamentalist] Christian reads the accounts . . . with the greatest possible satisfaction. . . .

"[According to the Bible, 'God'] gave . . . an order to kill children and to rip open the bodies of pregnant women. . . . The pestilences were sent by ['God']. The frightful famine, during which the dying child with pallid lips sucked the withered bosom of a dead mother, was sent by ['God']. . . . ['God'] drowned an entire world with the exception of eight persons. The old, the young, the beautiful and the helpless were remorselessly devoured by the shoreless sea. . . .

"To one who [supposedly] 'loves his enemies,' the groans of men, the shrieks of women, and the cries of babes, makes music sweeter than the zephyr's breath. . . ."

—Robert Ingersoll (cited in *Ingersoll the Magnificent,* ed. Joseph Lewis)

"Every other sect supposes itself in possession of the truth, and that those who differ are so far in the wrong. Like a man travelling in foggy weather they see those at some distance before them wrapped up in the fog, as well as those behind them, and also people in the fields on each side; but near them, all appears clear, though in truth they are as much in the fog as any of them. . . .

"All the heretics I have known have been virtuous men. They cannot afford to be deficient in any of the other virtues, as that would give advantage to their many enemies; and they have not, like orthodox sinners, such a number of friends to excuse or justify them."

—Benjamin Franklin (quotations found in Seymour Stanton Block,
Benjamin Franklin: His Wit, Wisdom and Women
[New York: Hastings House Publishers, 1975])

"It is much easier to give people hell than your heart. . . . Passing out pamphlets is a lot easier than changing yourself into a loving, joyful person. . . . This effortless, just-say-yes-to-Jesus salvation is very attractive to our fast-paced, instant gratification world. But the truth is that changing into more God-like creatures takes tremendous effort."

—Gerard Thomas Straub, *Salvation for Sale: An Insider's View of
Pat Robertson's Ministry* (Amherst, N.Y.: Prometheus Books, 1986)

"You can fool yourself into thinking you are more 'God-like' because 'in the name of Jesus' you were 'saved' from alcoholism, or drug addiction, or committing grievous crimes. But that is not where 'God-likeness' begins and ends, it just means that you have finally awakened to behaviors that will naturally make you a healthier and happier person. Meanwhile your new insistence that everybody believe as you do may be reinflating your old ego just as fully as it was before, perhaps more so, making your new beliefs and behavior less 'God-like' than you suspect.

"I am reminded of a cartoon showing two short-haired, clean-shaven young men in suits carrying Bibles, smiling at a man who has just opened his front door in answer to their persistent knocking. One young man is saying to the man in the doorway: 'Good morning! I wonder if we might blatantly disregard your privacy for a few minutes in order to further our own personal goals?' "

—Edward T. Babinski

On Fundamentalist Christianity's Encounter with Other Religions

"The more I studied other monastic traditions, the more points of contact did I find. . . . The deeper you go into your own tradition, the more you will understand the other traditions. . . . From the similarities between monastic forms of life all over the world it became clear to me that the monk is not a 'super-Christian' or a 'super-Buddhist.' . . . Rather, one discovers monastic life as one possibility of being human. . . .

"We are not talking about the uniqueness of Zen, the uniqueness of Christianity. Each Christian's religion, and each Buddhist's religion, will be unique. Each person has to realize it uniquely. . . .

"Nowadays there are 'catholic' [in the sense of 'universal,' 'inclusive,' and 'all-embracing'] Buddhists, catholic Hindus, catholic Christians, even catholic Catholics! Not every Catholic, unfortunately, is a catholic Catholic. That is the problem.

There are also what, for lack of a better term, I call 'fundamentalists.' That is the other category. There are fundamentalist Buddhists, fundamentalist Christians, and even fundamentalist Catholics. . . . Nowadays, the catholic Buddhists and catholic Christians, just to mention two large groups, feel much closer to one another than they feel to the fundamentalists within their own traditions. And the fundamentalists of each tradition can't even get along with the other fundamentalists of that *same* tradition."

—Brother David Steindl-Rast, "The Monk is a Radical,"
The Laughing Man, Vol. 2, no. 2 (1981)

"During an evening session at Osage [Tibetan] Monastery in Oklahoma a number of outsiders were present for the film and questions and answers. Near the end someone who was obviously a Fundamentalist rose and very solemnly asked the Tibetans whether they had yet met the 'Lord Jesus Christ, King of Heaven and earth . . . ,' adding many more scriptural titles. The [Catholic] Brothers present translated for Geshe, and then one of the [Buddhist] monks responded with a beautiful simplicity and directness: 'No, we have not met the Lord Jesus Christ, but we are very happy to be with so many of his disciples whom we love very much.' The audience broke into a relieved and joyful applause."

—James Conner, O.C.S.O., "Western Monasticism Meets the East,"
The Catholic World (May/June 1990)

"It is forbidden to decry other sects; the true believer gives honor to whatever in them is worthy of honor."

—Decree (inscription on a pillar) commanded by Asoka,
Buddhist Emperor of India (died 238 B.C.)

(Compare this decree with the biblical passage below—ED.)

"If your brother, son, daughter, wife you cherish, or your friend who is your own soul, entice you away secretly, saying, 'Let us go serve other gods' . . . you shall kill him; your hand shall be *first* against him to put him to death."

—Deuteronomy 13:6–9

"The broad-minded see the truth in different religions, the narrow-minded see only the differences."

—Oliver Wendell Holmes

"May I be no man's enemy, and may I be the friend of that which is eternal and abides. . . . May I never devise evil against any man; if any devise evil against me, may I escape . . . without the need of hurting him. May I love, seek, and attain only that which is good. May I wish for all men's happiness and envy none. . . . When I have done or said what is wrong, may I never wait for the rebuke of others, but always rebuke myself until I make amends. . . . May I win no victory that harms either me or my opponent. . . . May I reconcile friends who are wroth with one another. May I, to the extent of my power, give all needful help . . . to all who are in want. May I never fail a friend in danger. . . . May I respect myself. . . . May I always keep tame that which rages within me. . . . May I never discuss who is wicked and what wicked things he has done, but know good men and follow in their footsteps."

> —The Prayer of Eusebius (a pagan who lived some
> two thousand years ago, quoted in Gilbert Murray,
> *Five Stages of Greek Religion* [London: G. Watts and Co., 1946])

"Do not return evil to your adversary; Requite with kindness the one who does evil to you, Maintain justice for your enemy, Be friendly to your enemy."

> —Akkadian Councils of Wisdom (from the ancient Babylonian
> civilization that existed centuries before Jesus was born)

"Shame on him who strikes, greater shame on him who strikes back. Let us live happily, not hating those who hate us. Let us therefore overcome anger by kindness, evil by good, falsehood by truth. Do not hurt others in ways that would be hurtful to yourself."

> —Buddhist wisdom (written centuries before Jesus was born)

"Return love for hatred. Otherwise, when a great hatred is reconciled, some of it will surely remain. How can this end in goodness? Therefore the sage holds to the left hand of an agreement but does not expect what the other holder ought to do. Regard your neighbor's gain as your own and your neighbor's loss as your own loss. Whoever is self-centered cannot have the love of others."

> —Taoist wisdom (written centuries before Jesus was born)

"People were Christian before Christ ever existed. People were humanistic before Humanism was ever organized. People were loving before LSD was ever discovered. I dug defecating before I ever knew it was a Zen thing to do."

> —Timothy Leary, from Paul Krassner, "The Cynic Route from
> Crazy SANE to Loving Haight," *The Realist* (1967)

On Fundamentalists and Their Doubts (or Lack Thereof)

"The rivers of America will run with blood filled to their banks before we will submit to them taking the Bible out of our schools. . . . When the consensus of scholarship says one thing and the Word of God another, the consensus of scholarship can go plumb to hell for all I care."

> —Billy Sunday (American evangelist) speaking at a
> 1912 revival meeting in Pittsburgh, Pennsylvania

(Compare this with the quotation below—ED.)

"All great religions in order to escape absurdity, have to admit a dilution of agnosticism. It is only the savage, whether of the African bush or the American gospel tent, who pretends to know the will and intent of God exactly and completely."

—H. L. Mencken, *Damn! A Book of Calumny* (1918)

"A man's greatest work is to break his enemies, to drive them before him, to take from them all the things that have been theirs, to hear the weeping of those who cherished them, to take their horses between his knees and to press in his arms the most desirable of their women."

—Genghis Khan

(Compare the actions of Genghis Khan with the actions of the children of Israel described below.)

"And [the children of Israel] warred against the Midianites, as the LORD commanded Moses; and they slew all the males. And they slew the kings of Midian. . . . And the children of Israel took all the women . . . their little ones . . . their cattle . . . all their flocks. . . . and all their goods. And they burnt all their cities. . . .

"And Moses said . . . 'Kill all the males among the little ones, and kill every woman that hath known man by lying with him. But all the women children [who are virgins], keep alive *for yourselves*. . . . And ye shall wash your clothes on the seventh day, and ye shall be clean [sic].' "

—Numbers 31

"There were doubts. The Old Testament God's habits of desiring the reeking slaughter of everyone who did not flatter him seemed rather antisocial, and Frank wondered whether all the wantoning the Song of Solomon did really refers to the loyalty between Christ and the Church. It seemed unlike the sessions of Oberlin Chapel and the Miller Avenue Baptist Church of Cleveland, Ohio. Could Solomon just possibly refer to relations between beings more mundane and frisky? Such qualities of reason as he had, Frank devoted not to examining the testimony which his doubting sniffed out, but to examining and vanishing the doubt itself. He had it as an axiom that doubt was wicked, and he was able to enjoy considerable ingenuity in exorcising it. He had a good deal of self-esteem and pleasure among the purple-broidered ambiguities of religion."

—Sinclair Lewis, *Elmer Gantry*

"Take as an example a person who's been brought up in a fundamental Christian faith. That is, a sect in which he believes that every word of the Bible has to be taken literally. Thus, the world was created in six days, there was a worldwide deluge, a Noah and an ark, God did stop Earth's rotation so that Joshua and his bloodthirsty genocidal Hebrews could have enough daylight to defeat the bloodthirsty Amorites. Eve was seduced by a snake and in turn got Adam to eat the fruit of the tree of knowledge of good and evil. Jesus did walk on water. And so on. Like others in his sect, he ignores the vast accumulation of data establishing the fact of evolution. He reads the Bible but does not see that, though the Bible nowhere states that the Earth is flat, it clearly implies that the Earth is flat. Nor does he take literally Christ's injunction to hate your father and mother. He ignores those. Puts them in a separate compartment of his brain. Or erases them as if they were on a tape.

"But some fundamentalists do come across evidence that they'd like to ignore. Iron stikes flint, and the spark falls on flammable material. The fire is off to the races, as it were. He reads more of the evidence, perhaps loathes and curses himself for his 'sinful' curiosity. But he learns more and more. And he becomes a liberal Christian or an atheist or agnostic."

> —Philip Jose Farmer, *Gods of Riverworld*
> (New York: Putnam and Sons, 1983)

"No matter how assured we may be about certain aspects of our belief, there are always painful inconsistencies, exceptions, and contradictions. This is true in religion as it is in politics, and is self-evident to all except fanatics and the naive. As for the fanatics, whose number is legion in our own time, we might be advised to leave them to heaven. They will not, unfortunately, do us the same courtesy."

> —*Steve Allen On the Bible, Religion, & Morality*
> (Amherst, N.Y.: Prometheus Books, 1990)

On Fundamentalists and Their Seriousness

"Humor is one of the most valuable things in the human brain. It is the torch of the mind—it sheds light. Humor is the readiest test of truth—of the natural, of the sensible. . . . Ministers have always said you will have no respect for our ideas unless you are solemn. Solemnity is a condition precedent to believing anything without evidence."

> —Robert Ingersoll

"The test of a good religion is its ability to laugh at itself. . . . A good joke is the one ultimate and sacred thing which cannot be criticized. Our relations with a good joke are direct and even divine relations."

> —G. K. Chesterton (a Christian, but *not* a fundamentalist)

"Once upon a dream, a Serious Person took me to a very high mountain and showed me all the sorrows of the world, and all the sadness, and all the pain. 'I will give you all of these,' he said, 'for I want you to understand what a bad world it is in which we live.'

" 'I have tried all my life to have these things,' I said, 'but I am afraid that I have failed miserably. Whenever I have gotten some sorrow, I make the mistake of sharing it with a friend and there is never enough of it to go around. I lose it all just about every time I do this. Sometimes I get very sad but then some beautiful song or person comes along and it gets stolen from me. And what's worse, I rarely realize what is happening until it is too late. Pain is just about as bad. I have found that time will destroy it unless you work tirelessly at keeping it. So you see I have been a complete failure at collecting the important and serious things in life.'

" 'Then what do you have to show for your pitiable existence?' the Serious One asked.

" 'Not much.' I said, rather ashamed of myself by now. 'I have a lot of friends, but they are friends with other people as well, so I guess they are not really mine. I have some music and songs but other people play them too so I guess they are not mine either. I often look up at the stars and the moon at night, but I suppose anybody can do that. I once thought I had a lot of love, but I have found that love is everywhere, so it appears that I only have a small part of the grand total. I don't know what I can do about the situation. Do you think you could really give me all of these things?'

" 'No. I am afraid it will take some hard work on your part and I can tell that you are just not up to it. There is nothing I can do for you.'

"And with that the Serious One left me for more promising prospects."

—Cecil Wyche, "The Failure"

"Having spoken with a few students at Bob Jones University [a fundamentalist institution], I learned that the university's founder—who now lies buried on campus—once replied, 'Over my dead body,' to the question of whether kissing would ever be allowed on campus. The students then told me of their whimsical plans to sneak out of their dorms one night, and kiss their girlfriends while leaning over the founder's grave."

—Edward T. Babinski

Appendix D

A List of Additional Testimonies
by Former Fundamentalists
and Related Resources

This appendix is divided into four sections that reflect the four major divisions of this book: Former fundamentalists who are now (1) moderate to very liberal Christians, (2) adherents of alternative spiritualities, (3) agnostics, or (4) atheists. The entries in each section are arranged alphabetically by the author's last name if the author's testimony is found in this book; if not, then the entry is arranged alphabetically by the title of the article or book being mentioned.

Resources for Moderate to Very Liberal Christians

Dewey M. Beegle (whose testimony appears in this book) has authored *God's Word Into English, The Inspiration of Scripture* (expanded and retitled, *Scripture, Tradition and Infallibility*), *Moses, the Servant of Yahweh,* and *Prophecy and Prediction.* For information on purchasing copies contact the author at 407 Russell Ave., Apt. 613, Gaithersburg, MD 20877–2831.

"Breaking Away: When Fundamentalists Leave the Fold" by Hilary Abramson (*Sacramento Bee Magazine,* June 22, 1986) is a newspaper article that describes the experiences of several former fundamentalist Christians.

Breaking Free: Rescuing Families from the Clutches of Legalism by David R. Miller (Baker Books, 1992). A psychology professor at Jerry Falwell's Liberty University—a fundamentalist institution—has written a book based on his six years as a faculty member at *another* fundamentalist institution. Although that *other* institution remained nameless in his book, many have deduced that his anecdotes were derived primarily from his experiences at Bob Jones University. Such anecdotes include the story of a woman being forced to wear hose at all times, a chapel speaker telling his audience that all men who parted their hair down the middle were homosexuals, and a college professor who advised students to beat unruly wives. The author did not wish to simply single out BJU for his critique of legalism. He cited his experiences as typical of what goes on at many like-minded legalistic Christian institutions such as Pensacola (Christian College) or Hyles-Anderson College.

According to the author: "There are a lot of little Christian Hitlers out there, but they're not all in one place. There's a lot of country churches that run about 200 on Sunday with some sociopath who's doing terrible things to people from the pulpit."

Called to Preach, Condemned to Survive: The Education of Clayton Sullivan by Clayton Sullivan (Macon, Ga.: Mercer University Press, 1985) is a religious autobiography in which Sullivan describes the fervor of his late adolescence, his experiences at seminary, and his life as a Southern Baptist preacher and college professor in the pre- and post-integrated South.

Of his early religious fervor he wrote:

I assumed that the Christian religion was "true" and devoid of intellectual difficulties. And I assumed there was an "obvious" Christian message that could be grasped intellectually. Lacking the ability to transcend and to evaluate the culture in which I was raised, I assumed Southern society was "Christian." Indeed, I believed that the states of the Old Confederacy constituted the geographical center of Christendom, and I believed that the Southern Baptist Convention embodied quintessential Christianity. In my mind, the Southern Baptist Convention was an organization in which I invested undiluted trust and which increasingly became the source of my identity.

Sullivan's hard-won "education" came later at seminary and during his years as a pastor and college professor. His most recent book is *Toward a Mature Faith: Does Biblical Inerrancy Make Sense?* (Decatur, Ga.: SBC Today, 1990). For ordering information write: Baptists Today, 222 East Lake Drive, Decatur, GA 30030.

It is of interest to note that prior to writing his critique of biblical inerrancy, Sullivan had invited fundamentalist spokesmen to debate the matter with non-fundamentalists, and to have their essays published side by side in book form, but "(despite many letters written and a fortune spent on long-distance phone calls) I could not locate recognized inerrantist spokesmen willing to join in such a debate."

Christ the Tiger by Thomas Howard (Wheaton, Ill.: Harold Shaw Publishers, 1979) is the author's spiritual autobiography and describes how his aesthetic sensibilities, together with the maturing effects of his varied experiences, led him out of narrow fundamentalism into a more mainstream Episcopal-Evangelical faith.

Confessions of a Conservative Evangelical by Jack Rogers (Philadelphia: Westminster Press, 1974) describes many personal episodes that led the author to leave behind the cocoon of party-line conservatism and strict inerrancy for a theologically and politically more progressive evangelical Christian faith.

A Critique of the Fundamentalist Doctrine of the Inerrancy of the Biblical Autographs in Historical, Philosophical, Exegetical and Hermeneutical Perspective by Reverend John Schoneberg Setzer is a 426-page doctoral dissertation (Duke University, Religion, 1965) written by a minister who journeyed from a more conservative toward a more liberal Lutheran faith. See also his later work, *What's Left to Believe?* (Nashville, Tenn.: Abingdon Press, 1968).

For information on how to obtain a copy of Setzer's dissertation write University Microfilms International, 300 N. Zeeb Road, Ann Arbor, MI 48106, or phone (toll-free) (800) 521-0600. (The UMI catalog number for the dissertation is 65-7281.)

Fundamentalism by James Barr (Philadelphia: Westminster Press, 1978) is a critique of the ways in which fundamentalists defend their "maximally conservative" views of the Bible's authorship, miracles, and inerrancy by misappropriating insights gained through historical-critical scholarship. Barr demonstrates that the openness of the historical-critical approach and the tentative nature of the information drawn from that approach is incompatible with the wholly orthodox and dogmatic conclusions that evangelicals seek to draw from it. Barr includes examples from fundamentalist/evangelical professors and publications. Barr was formerly an evangelical and member of Inter-Varsity, who later became Oriel Professor of the Interpretation of Holy Scripture at Oxford University.

Fundamentalists Anonymous, or FA, is "a nationally recognized support system for those who want to overcome the baggage of a dysfunctional religious experience and experience a happier, richer and more successful life." It was founded by Richard Yao and Jim Luce in 1985. As their literature explains: "FA is not anti-Christian or anti-religion but neither is it a front for any church or religion." "FA does not proselytize satisfied fundamentalists. We only work with those who have voluntarily approached us." "FA does not discuss theology in its meetings." Membership, including a subscription to their newsletter, is $30 per year, and may be obtained by writing FA at P.O. Box 20324, Greeley Square Station, New York, NY 10001; or phone them at (212) 696-0421.

Richard Yao briefly summarized his own experiences in an address he delivered at the American Psychological Association National Conference in New York City, August 29, 1987, and later published in booklet form as *Addiction and the Fundamentalist Experience: An Introduction to Fundamentalists Anonymous*:

> I grew up in an independent baptist fundamentalist church in Manila, in the Philippines. As soon as I was old enough, I was sent to the "Christian" school run by the church. It was extremely authoritarian, rigid and regimented. It was total immersion. I spent most of my waking hours either in the school

or in the church. I was guilty, fearful and anxious. I was very unhappy. They promised the "abundant life" but all I had was an endless nightmare. Gradually, I decided I had to leave. But all my friends and most of my family were in the church. Covertly, I began to make some friends outside the church. And when I left the fold, these friends became my informal support group. Years later, when I wonder why I made it and many of my friends didn't, I realized that this informal support system made all the difference for me. It gave me the courage to break out. And it sustained and helped me on the journey. Thus the idea for FA.

Richard Yao is presently seeking to have his book *Shattered Faith* published, which has received enthusiastic advance reviews from psychologists and from clergy of mainline Christian churches.

Give Me That Prime-Time Religion: An Insider's Report on the Oral Roberts Evangelistic Association by Jerry Sholes (New York: Hawthorn Books, 1979) is a tremendous eye-opener written by a man who worked with Oral Roberts for three and a half years as his television producer and writer.

Hawking God: A Young Jewish Woman's Ordeal in Jews for Jesus (1992) by Ellen Kamentsky tells the inside story of Jews for Jesus, a multimillion-dollar, fundamentalist Christian missionary organization whose goal is to convert as many Jews, worldwide, as possible. This book reveals their means and methods along with how and why one bright young talented member (who was also the *Newsweek* "poster child" for Jews for Jesus!) chose to leave. Available from Sapphire Press, P.O. Box 533, Medford, MA 02155.

The Hellfire Preachers by Pauline Blankenship is a novel based on the real-life experiences of a woman who grew up in a fundamentalist church in east Texas. Inquires concerning availability and price should be mailed to: Aardvark Publishers, 612 N. Story Road, Suite 105E, Irving, TX 75061.

I Once Spoke in Tongues by Wayne A. Robinson (Wheaton, Ill.: Tyndale House, 1973) is an amusing and touching account of the author's origins in the Pentecostal Holiness Church, his long quest for the "gift of tongues," and his subsequent disenchantment with it. He now writes to mediate between Pentecostals and mainstream ecumenical Christians.

Marjoe, the Academy Award–winning documentary film (1972), tells the story of a famous child evangelist who had preached to over fifty million people by the time he had reached the age of six, yet who was no longer in demand by the time he had reached adolescence. He reentered the evangelistic arena as a young man, but finally decided to leave it a second and final time. The movie was filmed during Marjoe's last few evangelistic campaigns, when he had already decided that he was going to leave the ministry. *Marjoe* is now on video. For information on how to obtain a copy, write: RCA/Columbia Pictures Home

Video, 2901 W. Alameda Ave., Burbank, CA 91505; or visit your local video store.

Besides the movie, there is the book *Marjoe: The Life of Marjoe Gortner* by Stephen Gaines (New York: Harper & Row, Publishers, 1973), which focuses on Marjoe's early life and adolescence. For instance, Marjoe's mother trained him to memorize his first sermon when he was three years old. It took five hours of training each day for four weeks. If Marjoe's attention dwindled, his mother ran his head beneath a cold water tap, or suffocated him with a pillow. The lesson to remain alert was learned quickly. The book breaks off right where the movie begins, when Marjoe was beginning to have doubts about spending the rest of his adult life as an evangelist.

Marlene Oaks (whose testimony appears in this book) is the author of *Old Time Religion is a Cult,* copies of which may be obtained from the author at 117 N. Pomona Ave., P.O. Box 41, Fullerton, CA 92632. She is also available for lectures.

Robert M. Price (whose testimony appears in this book) is the author of *Beyond Born Again* (a copy of which may be purchased by mailing $11.95 to Apocryphal Books, 216 Fernwood Ave., Upper Montclain, NJ 07043). Dr. Price is also the author of a 4-to-8-page monthly newsletter called *The Epistle,* dealing with Christian religious and theological topics, (for a subscription, mail $10.00 to the First Baptist Church, Church St. and Trinity Place, Montclair, NJ 07042). Recently he began publishing a journal titled *Higher Criticism.* He is also the director of the Religious Transition Project, "a counseling service for those dissatisfied with authoritarian religion, and who seek alternatives." For further information write the First Baptist Church at the above address.

Rescuing the Bible from Fundamentalism by John Shelby Spong (San Francisco: HarperCollins Publishers, 1991), is a repudiation of fundamentalist approaches to reading and understanding the Bible, and introduces alternative approaches that "resurrect" eternally insightful biblical themes and messages.

Spong is the Episcopal Bishop of Newark, New Jersey, and was a fundamentalist Christian in his youth. After a gradual (and relatively painless) widening of his intellectual horizons in college and seminary, he served at his first church in Durham, North Carolina, located beside the campus of Duke University. He has this enlightening story from his experiences there:

> I spent the first three years of my ministry preaching to young college students who were coming out of Baptist and Methodist southern fundamentalist backgrounds, hitting that university, and having their religious presuppositions collide with their knowledge. It was a wonderful place for me to start my ministry. I tried to say then, as now, that you don't have to abandon Christianity when you abandon fundamentalist aspects that you grew up with. There is something more there for you. You don't have to abandon being an educated modern man or woman just to be a Christian. . . .

The youth in the congregation consisted of undergraduates, but the bulk of the adult population were graduate students. They either had a Ph.D. or an M.D. or were in the process of working on one, so it was a highly stimulating intellectual climate. We had a club of young adults that met every Sunday night, and the program was that I would have to defend my sermon of the morning. I did that for three years. . . . I didn't suggest then, and I do not suggest now that I have the final word or the infallible truth. I do suggest that I am an honest pilgrim. . . .

Once I had a professor who told me, "Any God who *can* be killed, *ought* to be killed." The meaning of that deliberately provocative phrase is simple: "If I can kill your God, if I can shake your faith, by my pursuit of truth, then your faith needs to be shaken because clearly it isn't capable of holding you up." When I stopped being defensive for God a lot of freedom entered my life. When I stopped realizing that God needed Jack Spong to defend God, I was freed. You know, during a lot of my life I really thought I was there defending the truth of God. If God needs me, God is in bad shape. If that's what I'm worshiping, some God who needs my pitiful little mind to defend the divine power. . . . So I don't deal with that. I'm not upset when people have different points of view. I like listening to them. If they've got credibility they might easily convert me. I think God is real, and I think I journey into that truth in some way every day of my life. I don't want to lose contact with that. But if I meet God, I've got to meet God as a citizen of the twentieth century, because that's who I am. I can't be a first century man or woman.

Spring Break Missionaries: Growing Up in Christian America 1976–1983 by Dwayne Walker is a true story based on the author's experiences in fundamentalist schools and churches. Walker mentions a teacher who encouraged gay bashing, how students were forced to write letters to Congress, how Jerry Falwell took over a large church under the guise of helping it, and how one preacher stood up to Falwell and bitterly paid the price. Available from H. H. Waldo Booksellers, phone (800) 66 WALDO.

Mike and Karla Yaconelli (whose testimonies appear in this book) are editors of *The Wittenburg Door,* a magazine for people who have "given up fundamentalism, but haven't given up their faith or their sense of humor." The magazine's present title is simply *The Door,* and those wishing to obtain copies of back issues, such as the ones listed directly below, or who wish to subscribe, should write: *The Door,* 1565 Cliff Rd., STE3–450, St. Paul, MN 55122–9956.

"I Was a Teenage Fundamentalist: Reflections From a Few Who Spent Their Youth Among Religious Conservatives and Lived to Tell About It," *The Wittenburg Door,* no. 50 (which appeared in the late 1970s), contains brief reflections by former fundamentalist—now moderate evangelical—Christians such as Clark H. Pinnock and Richard Quebedeaux.

The Wittenburg Door, no. 102 (April/May 1988), is devoted to "Those Wacky Southern Baptist Convention Goers," and focuses on the fundamentalist vs. moderate controversy in the largest of all American Protestant Christian denominations. It also contains the article, "Joe Bob Goes to the Convention," in which

Joe Bob Briggs, the famous movie reviewer and humorist, tells how he "got saved," and adds the admonition, "The only way to be a decent Baptist is to have 40 other raving Baptists around you to keep you from straying into something dangerous, like Hari Krishna or the Methodist church."

Further "*Door* Stuff" such as the books *The Door Interviews, Fearfully & Wonderfully Weird: A Screwball Look at the Church and Other Things From the Pages of The Wittenburg Door,* and *The Door Compilation, Vol. 1,* and tapes of Mike Yaconelli's sermons (Mike is the pastor of Grace Community Church, Yreka, California, "the church for people who don't like to go to church") are available through Subscription Inc., 1565 Cliff Rd., Suite 3, 450, St. Paul, MN 55122; or phone toll free: (800) 827-1746.

Mike Yaconelli is also the author of *Tough Faith* (Elgin, Ill.: David C. Cook Publishing Company, 1976), in which he discusses Evangelical Christianity's reluctance to face difficult issues and unanswerable questions posed by suffering and paradox. He opts for a faith that will be honest with feelings and faithful to truth.

Reverend Miles Wesner, a former fundamentalist, and his wife, Maralene, an award-winning teacher, are the founders of Diversity Press, which publishes a wide variety of materials on Christian beliefs and teachings viewed from a psychological and intellectual point of view. "Our material is primarily for hurting people who have more questions than answers. We *never* present our views as what 'must be believed.' " They also produce a newsletter, *New Perspectives.* Write them for more information or a free catalog of their publications: Diversity Press, P.O. Box 25, Idabel, OK 74745-0025.

Resources for Adherents of Alternative Spiritualities

William Bagley (whose testimony appears in this book) is the author of *The Easy, Rapid, and Peaceful Pathway,* volumes one and two, and is presently composing volume three of the *ERP Pathway* series. For more information concerning his publications, or meditation and therapy sessions, contact him at 94868 Elk River Rd., Port Orford, OR 97465.

The Flight of Peter Fromm: A Novel by Martin Gardner (Amherst, N.Y.: Prometheus Books, 1994) is the story of a fundamentalist Christian youth who tries to convert an atheist college professor. The attempt backfires, and the youth winds up adopting more and more liberal Christian views. John Updike praised Gardner's "amazing knowledge of everything from Pentecostal sects to obscure fictional works on the adventures of the post-Crucifixion Jesus." The author, Martin Gardner, is a former fundamentalist Christian who was raised in Oral Robert's backyard, Tulsa, Oklahoma, and whose faith was challenged in college, especially his faith in the veracity of "scientific" creationism. Mr. Gardner went on to become a leading debunker of "pseudoscience," and also the mathematical puzzle columnist for the *Scientific American.* His present faith in God, and criticisms of Christianity, are elucidated in his book *The Whys of a Philosophical Scrivener* (New York: Quill, 1983). In that book he states:

> I outgrew [Protestant fundamentalism] slowly, and eventually decided that I could not call myself a Christian without using the language deceptively, but faith in God and immortality remained. Much of my novel, *The Flight of Peter Fromm,* reflects these painful changes.

"A Humanistic Approach Toward Religionists: Creating Empathy for the Apostate" by Tod E. Jones (*The Humanist,* January/February, 1989, pp. 25 and 46) discusses what a truly humanistic response toward people coming out of religion should be. Jones is a former Church of Christ preacher who is today a member of the Unitarian-Universalist Church of Little Rock, Arkansas. In the above article he states:

> After having made Christianity the basis of my life for six years and preaching in the Church of Christ for two, my subsequent apostasy was one of the most emotionally tortuous experiences with which I have ever had to deal. . . .
>
> As a humanist and apostate from Christiantiy, I often feel the tension that exists between a zealous desire to criticize the faults of religion and an earnest sensitivity to the circumstances of those who adhere to religion. . . .
>
> Just as a gardener would not hastily pull a grown weed in a crowded flowerbed, knowing that even the ugliest plant has permeating roots, we should not hope to purify our neighbor's mind by performing a philosophical lobotomy. . . .
>
> Christian ministers exhort their congregations to hate the sin but love the sinner; as a preacher who has changed ideological pulpits, I would encourage us all to hate the lie but love the deceived.

"A Personal Note" by John Hick in *Odysseys to Dialogue,* ed. Leonard Swidler (New York: Edwin Mellen Press, 1992) mentions how Professor Hick

> became a Christian by conversion whilst a first year law student. The converting power was the New Testament picture of Jesus Christ. During a period of several days of intense inner turmoil the Christ-centred world of meaning, previously dead to me, became overwhelmingly alive as both awesomely demanding and irresistibly attractive, and I entered into it with great joy and excitement. And as is so often the case in youthful conversions, the Christian friends who encouraged and supported me were more or less fundamentalist in their beliefs, so that the set of ideas which I received as part of my initial Christian package was Calvinist orthodoxy of an extremely conservative kind.
>
> A little over a year later I left these circles to serve—this was during the Second World War—in the Friends' Ambulance Unit in Britain, the Middle East, Italy and Greece. When I returned, to study philosophy as a preliminary to training for the Presbyterian ministry, I was still theologically very conservative but was beginning to be aware of a lack of intellectual integrity in fundamentalist circles, in that any potentially unsettling questions were regularly suppressed rather than faced. My philosophical training at

Edinburgh, and then at Oxford, made it impossible to be satisfied with an ethos in which clear thinking and the honest facing of problems were viewed as lack of faith, and I moved out of the evangelical student movement. I remained, however, for nearly 20 more years fully convinced of the truth of the basic doctrines of Trinity, Incarnation and Atonement more or less in the form in which I had first learned them. I remember being shocked by theologians who questioned these traditional formulations in just the way that some conservative Christians are shocked by my own questioning of them today. . . .

Encounters with remarkable individuals of several faiths, people whom I cannot but deeply respect, and in some cases even regard as saints, have reinforced the realization that our very different religious traditions constitute alternative human contexts of response to the one ultimate transcendent divine Reality.

Professor Hick's book, *An Interpretation of Religion: Human Responses to the Transcendent* (Yale University Press, 1989), earned him the coveted 1991 Louisville Grawemeyer Award for its "significant contribution" to religion. His most recent work is *Disputed Questions in Theology and the Philosophy of Religion* (Yale University Press, 1993).

"Tennessee Baptists turn to Judaism for New Inspiration: Christian Fundamentalists Seek Roots of Their Faith; There Goes the Steeple" by R. Gustav Neibuhr (*The Wall Street Journal,* March 20, 1991) tells the story of a fundamentalist Baptist minister and congregation who went from being believers in the deity of Christ, the Trinity, and the saving power of Jesus' sacrifice, to being believers in the "one God" of Israel and in the necessity of following the simple laws God revealed to Noah for all mankind. The minister and congregation repudiate the pagan superstitions that have crept into Christianity over the centuries, such as Christmas and Easter celebrations, and church steeples. They no longer believe that Jesus was "God" since they are convinced that the origins of such a belief lay in pagan and Hellenistic ideas which intruded themselves into Judaism itself. They prefer to be known as Gentile "God-fearers" or "Noachides." They share fellowship with and conduct Torah studies with, their Orthodox Jewish counterparts. The Noachide group in Tennessee is part of a world-wide Noachide movement that holds annual conferences. They also offer taped lectures by leading Noachide teachers, rabbis, and college professors. The tapes include topics that critique fundamentalist interpretations of the Bible. There is even a videotaped testimony, *Turning to Torah: The Jerry and Alice Klapper Story.* Besides producing a newsletter, *The Gap,* a list of books, tapes, and videos is available by writing: Echoes of Emmanuel, P.O. Box 442, Athens, TN 37371–0442.

Resources for Agnostics

The introduction to *The Age of Unreason* recounts Thomas S. Vernon's journey from liberal Baptist minister to humanist. Vernon's other works include *Unheavenly*

Discourses and *Great Infidels,* all of which are available through m & m Press, P.O. Box 338, Fayetteville, AR 72702.

Dead Fundamentalists: Or, Who Will Be the Casualties in America's "Culture War"? is a 26-page booklet that contains the testimonies of about five former fundamentalists. It also contains cartoons. For a copy, mail $2.00 to Yendi Boox Publishing, Inc., P.O. Box 18679, Indianapolis, IN 46218. They also offer for sale a variety of antifundamentalist "stick and runs" and "buttons."

Freethinker's Directory, 3rd ed., by David Briars is a handy booklet listing free-thinking organizations and publications in the United States and abroad. For a copy of the *Freethinker's Directory,* send $7.75 to H. H. Waldo, Bookseller, P. O. Box 350, Rockton, IL 61072; or phone (800) 66WALDO.

Fundamentalist Christians might be surprised to learn how few *freethinking* groups there are, compared to the vast multitude of conservative Christian groups and organizations in the United States. Based on my own reckoning, the number of people who congregate in churches in Greenville County, South Carolina, just on Easter Sunday and Christmas, far outnumber all the self-avowed secular humanists who meet in conferences, all year long. This proves that if many Americans still "resist Christianity," it has nothing to do with the "conspiratorial" efforts of some sparsely attended "secular humanist" conferences. After all, you don't have to be a dyed-in-the-wool secular humanist before you accept or teach evolution. Neither do you have to be a secular humanist in order to doubt the truthfulness of any number of Christian doctrines, dogmas, and/or biblical inter-pretations. Fundamentalists can't accept the slightest doubts or rejection of their beliefs so they imagine every doubter to be "a pawn in a giant Secular Humanist conspiracy," nay, a "Satanic conspiracy," which they see lurking behind the teaching of evolution and behind the slightest doubts directed at *their* religious beliefs.

It is much nearer the truth to view fundamentalist and conservative Christians as the ones who are *conspiring* to take over the school boards, and the local, state, and national governments of the United States, via organizations like Pat Robertson's Christian Coalition.

From Seminary to Skepticism (The Lonely Journey) by Allan Powell is available from the author. Send $10.00 to 3 Bittersweet Dr., Hagerstown, MD 21740; or phone: (301) 797-4916. In his book, Mr. Powell mentions:

There are those who all too readily make the charge that those who once "had the faith" and then desert it really never had it in the first place. This may be the case, but if it is, these charges must deal with the explanation of why those deserters do so in such a reluctant manner. . . . The gnawing doubts which started in the seminary did not bring about an immediate break with the church—only a break from the ministry. These doubts later came to include some basic elements of traditional Christianity and yet it was fully ten years before the umbilical cord was severed. . . .

Kevin Henke (whose testimony appears in this book) has several computer diskettes available that contain his lengthy and detailed critiques of many "scientific creationist" arguments: *The Origin of Theses* and *Science/Creationism Reviews.* These can be obtained through the National Center for Science Education, P.O. Box 9477, Berkeley, CA 94709–0477. Write them for a free catalog of publications, and for information on how to subscribe to *NCSE Reports* and *Creation/Evolution Journal,* which report on the creationist movement, and provide answers to the arguments of "scientific creationists."

"An Honest Search for Truth" by Stephen Hutchenson, *OASIS Newsletter,* vol. 6.0, no. 15 (Winter 1993): 15–16, is the testimony of a fundamentalist Christian and "staunch believer in 'creation science' [of the Institute for Creation Research variety]" who became an evolutionist.

Hutchenson explains how he "rested his mind content in my [fundamentalist] beliefs for nine years." "Having been deeply indoctrinated through years of church attendence," his "senses had been dulled." The "flame of intense curiosity I had as a child, flickered feebly amidst the winds of religious dogma and piety." Then, after encountering one book in particular, his curiosity began to burn again, "intensely like a brush fire." It was Philip Kitcher's *Abusing Science: The Case Against Creationism.* After that Hutchenson "set upon the local library like a lion sets upon its prey," and began buying and reading a host of books in an attempt "to separate fact from speculation, and reasoned thought from superstition."

The *OASIS Newsletter* is produced by the Ontario Association for the Support of Integrity in Science Education. Copies may be obtained by contacting the editor, Richard J. Wakefield, OASIS, P.O. Box 617, Beaverton, Ontario, Canada L0K 1A0.

The Humanist, published by the American Humanist Association, publishes articles by both religious and secular humanists (mostly of the latter kind). For subscription rates write: The Humanist, 7 Harwood Dr., P.O. Box 146, Amherst, NY 14226–0146.

Robert G. Ingersoll (whose testimony appears in this book), has several books that have remained in print over the years. Write: Prometheus Books, 59 John Glenn Drive, Amherst, NY 14228–2197; or call toll free (1) 800–421–0351 (24 hours); or American Atheist Press, P.O. Box 140195, Austin, TX 78714–0195; or phone: (512) 458–1244. They will each mail you a free catalog of their publications.

Of particular interest to former fundamentalists may be Ingersoll's letter-debate with the Presbyterian minister, Rev. Henry M. Field, D.D., republished in 1988 by American Atheist Press under the title *Faith or Agnosticism? The Field-Ingersoll Discussion.* Equally of interest is the 1993 reprint by Prometheus Books of three spirited debates Robert Ingersoll engaged in with leading churchmen and statesmen titled *Reason, Tolerance, and Christianity: The Ingersoll Debates.*

Ingersoll's birthplace in Dresden, New York, is today a national museum. Write the Robert G. Ingersoll Memorial Committee for further information: Headquarters, Box 664, Buffalo, NY 14226–0664; or phone: (716) 636–7571; or contact the Dresden Chapter, Box 77, Dresden, NY 14441; or phone: (315) 536–1074.

Jesus Doesn't Live Here Any More: From Fundamentalist to Freedom Writer by Skipp Porteous (Buffalo, N.Y.: Prometheus Books, 1991). The tale of a former Pentecostal/Charismatic minister who eventually left the ministry to found an organization that monitors the activities of the religious right, and attempts to raise public awareness of such activities, via radio and television interviews, and via his newsletter *The Freedom Writer: The National Newsletter that Defends the Separation of Church and State.*

Porteous also produces *Walk Away: The Newsletter for Ex-Fundamentalists,* which contains testimonies by former fundamentalists.

Dan Barker's testimony (from Christian minister to atheist and one of the leaders of the Freedom from Religion Foundation—see Dan's testimony in this book) appeared in *Walk Away,* vol. 1, no. 3 (Fall 1989).

Edmund D. Cohen's testimony (from born again Ph.D. psychologist, and later, a student at Westminister Theological Seminary, to the agnostic author of *The Mind of the Bible Believer*) appeared in *Walk Away,* vol. 3, no. 2 (Spring 1991).

John Seigel's testimony (from president of the Omaha South Camp of Gideons International to agnostic) appeared in *Walk Away,* vol. 3, no. 4 (Fall 1991).

Jim Hoyne's testimony (from Moody Bible Institute graduate to a believer in spirituality without dogmatic restrictions) appeared in *Walk Away,* vol. 4, no. 1 (Winter 1992).

Janet Lincoln's testimony (from Wheaton College student to doctor of psychology and atheist) appeared in *Walk Away,* vol. 4, no. 2 (Spring 1992).

For further information on how to receive Mr. Porteous' autobiography, or any of his other publications, write *The Freedom Writer/Walk Away,* P.O. Box 589, Great Barrington, MA 01230.

Let There Be Light (New York: HarperCollins Publishers, 1993) by Philip Appleman is a collection of poems written by a modern-day Voltaire. Their author takes fundamentalist and conservative Christian religion to task. Appleman also happens to have been a former believer. In his youth as a member of the First Christian Church of Kendallville, Indiana, he attended Sunday school regularly where he "heard all the standard Bible stories many times, and fidgeted through a multitude of sermons." He adds, "It took a lot of reading to free myself from my intense Protestant upbringing, but—speaking as a poet—it was very important, partly because liberation from one ideology helps you to evaluate the others, too."

Readers who enjoy Appleman's smart satirical poetry will no doubt also enjoy two novels by James Morrow, *Only Begotten Daughter* and *Towing Jehova,* which satirize and question biblical beliefs, and Morrow's *Swatting at the Cosmos,* which includes "Bible Stories for Adults No. 17: The Flood," a Nebula Award-winning short story. (Morrow is a former Episcopalian, a religion he refers to as "Christianity light.")

Jim Lippard (whose testimony appears in this book) debated the "creation scientist" Walter T. Brown, Jr., in the journal *Creation/Evolution,* no. 25 (Fall 1989) to no. 27 (Summer 1990). For information on how to obtain copies of those issues of *C/E,* write the National Center for Science Education, P.O. Box 9477, Berkeley, CA 94709-0477.

Austin Miles (whose testimony appears in this book) is the author of two books available from Prometheus Books, *Don't Call Me Brother: A Ringmaster's Escape from the Pentecostal Church* and *Setting the Captives Free: Victims of the Church Tell Their Stories.* Write: Prometheus Books, 59 John Glenn Drive, Amherst, NY 14228-2197; or call toll free (1) 800-421-0351.

Mr. Miles will soon be publishing a newsletter for "those who have been hurt by the church and are trying to get their lives back together." Mail inquiries concerning the newsletter to P.O. Box 685, Oakley, CA 94561.

The Mind of the Bible Believer by Edmund D. Cohen (Amherst, N.Y.: Prometheus Books, 1986) contains Cohen's testimony, from fundamentalism to agnosticism (pp. 376 ff). See also his short testimony in *Walk Away,* vol. 3, no. 2 (Spring 1991). Write: *Walk Away,* P.O. Box 589, Great Barrington, MA 01230.

Miracle (Random House, 1978) is Doston Rader's novel about an esteemed evangelist who, unbeknownst to his public, is also a foul-mouthed drinker and adulterer. Prophetic in its tawdry revelations, this novel appeared *before* the televangelist scandals of the 1980s. According to an article in *Time* ("Three Irreverent Authors," May 22, 1978), Dotson "wrote his hate-filled book about American Evangelicals because they are so filled with hatred." It should be noted that Rader's father, grandfather, and great-uncle were all travelling evangelists. Richard Nixon was "saved" at a meeting where Dotsons's great-uncle preached. Doston was raised "on the road" by his father who wanted him to become a preacher. Instead, Dotson became a journalist whose pieces often appear in the nationally syndicated *Parade* magazine.

Robert Moore (whose testimony appears in this book) is the author of a "special issue" of *Creation/Evolution Journal,* one that pursues questions which naturally arise whenever someone tries to take the biblical account of "Noah's Ark" seriously and scientifically. Such questions are so numerous and insoluble that Moore's article is titled "The Impossible Voyage of Noah's Ark," Issue 9 (Winter 1983). Write the National Center for Science Education, P.O. Box 9477, Berkeley, CA 94709-0477 to find out how to obtain copies of Moore's entertaining and well-researched piece, one that has proved instrumental in making a number of creationists pause to reconsider what they really believe, or are able to believe, concerning the story of "Noah's Ark."

"Gene Roddenberry: Writer, Producer, Philosopher, Humanist," David Alexander's interview with Roddenberry published in *The Humanist* (March/April, 1991, pp. 5ff), describes how the man who would later create "Star Trek" and "Star Trek: The Next Generation" attended a Baptist church in El Paso, Texas, every Sunday with his mother until he was about fourteen years old, when he decided to finally pay attention to a sermon and was completely astonished because what they were talking about were things that were just crazy. It was communion time, where you eat this wafer and are supposed to be eating the body of Christ and drinking his blood. My first impression was, "This is a bunch of cannibals they've put me down among!" . . . The connection between what they were saying and reality was very tenuous. How the hell did Jesus become something to be eaten?

I guess from that time it was clear to me that religion was largely nonsense—largely magical, superstitious things. In my own teen life, I just couldn't see any point in adopting something based on magic, which was obviously phony and superstitious. . . .

And then the God you consider in your teenage years is the guy who knows you masturbate. This has tormented so many people. . . .

In *The Man Who Created Star Trek: Gene Roddenberry* by James Van Hise (Las Vegas: Pioneer Books, 1992), Roddenberry is quoted as saying:

How can I take seriously a god-image that requires that I prostrate myself every seven days and praise it? That sounds to me like a very insecure personality. . . .

I don't dislike religion, but I am in considerable fear of what today's brand of it can lead to.

Salvation for Sale: An Insider's View of Pat Robertson's Ministry by Gerard Thomas Straub (Amherst, N.Y.: Prometheus Books, 1986), a former "born again" and "pentecostal" television producer, tells of his experiences working as the executive producer of Pat Robertson's "The 700 Club," and explains his subsequent disenchantment with fundamentalism and televangelism.

Charles Templeton (whose testimony appears in this book) is the author of a novel about Christian evangelism and evangelists that draws upon his own experiences, *The Third Temptation*. He is currently composing a book that outlines his agnostic views, tentatively titled *Farewell to God*. See also Templeton's autobiography, *Charles Templeton: An Anecdotal Memoir* (Toronto, Ontario: McClelland and Stewart Limited, 1983), especially the section titled, "Inside Evangelism."

Farrell Till (whose testimony appears in this book) edits the *Skeptical Review,* which critiques the fundamentalist claim that the Bible is "totally truthful and accurate, and does not contain a single contradiction." Till has also published a manuscript titled *Prophecies: Imaginary and Unfulfilled* (1991), and continues to debate fundamentalists, making copies of those debates available to his readers. For further information contact *The Skeptical Review,* P.O. Box 617, Canton, IL 61520–0617.

Resources for Atheists

Dan Barker (whose testimony appears in this book) is the author of *Losing Faith in Faith: From Preacher to Atheist* (Madison, Wis.: Freedom From Religion Foundation, 1992). To obtain a copy of Barker's book, write for information from the Freedom from Religion Foundation at P. O. Box 750, Madison, WI 53701–0750; or phone: (608) 256–8900.

Mr. Barker has also written two books for children, *Maybe Right, Maybe Wrong: A Guide for Young Thinkers* and *Maybe Yes, Maybe No: A Guide for Young Skeptics,* which are available from Prometheus Books, 59 John Glenn Drive, Amherst, NY 14228–2197; or call toll free (1) 800–421–0351 (24 hours).

Mr. Barker is currently editing a collection of testimonies by former ministers of all denominations who left their churches and their Christian faith.

M. Lee Deitz (whose testimony appears in this book) is a former "Man of the Year" at Bob Jones University, and today president of the Secular Humanist Society of Greenville, S.C. He can be contacted for speaking engagements by writing him at P.O. Box 1744, Greenville, SC 29602–1744.

Free Inquiry magazine sometimes publishes testimonies by former Christians. Write: Free Inquiry, Box 664, Buffalo, NY 14226–0664.

Freethought Today, "The only freethought newspaper in the United States," has published a number of testimonies by former conservative Christian believers, including:

"From Fear to Freedom: Finding a Way Out of the Ministry" by Bob Arends (a former Methodist/Evangelical Christian) in *FT* (March 1993).

"Free At Last: An Ex-Minister's Story" by J. Walter Gunnarsen (a former fundamentalist Christian) in *FT* (August 1987).

"From Faith to Reason: Pentecostal Pastor to Atheist" by James R. Pierce in *FT* (January/February 1991).

"From Preacher Boy to Village Atheist" by Delos B. McKown, Ph.D. in *FT* (April 1987). (Dr. McKown is also the author of a semi-autobiographical novel, *With Faith and Fury,* available from Prometheus Books.)

"Testimonio: How Bible Study Made an Unbeliever Out of Me" by Hector Avalos (former child evangelist and Pentecostal Christian, and now a college professor and atheist) in *FT* (August 1991).

See also the booklet published by the Freedom from Religion Foundation in 1982, *Rejecting Religion: Four Award-Winning Essays from the 1982 Freedom from Religion Foundation Scholarship Competition,* which contains the testimonies of a former conservative Lutheran and a former Methodist/Presbyterian.

To discover how to obtain copies of the testimonies mentioned above, or to subscribe to *Freethought Today,* write the Freedom from Religion Foundation at P.O. Box 750, Madison, WI 53701–0750; or phone: (608) 256–8900.

Some of My Best Friends Are Christians (Chicago: Open Court, 1974) and *Personal and Controversial* (Boston: Beacon Press, 1973), both by Paul Blanshard, describe his transformation "from Christian fundamentalist to humanist atheist, from stodgy Puritan to sexual rebel, from doctrinaire socialist to socialistic pragmatist . . . from the rural conservatism of my youth to the hesitant radicalism of my declining years."

In *Some of My Best Friends Are Christians* Blanshard critiqued specific aspects of his former Christian faith in detail. (He was the pastor of the First Congregational Church of Tampa, Florida.) *Personal and Controversial* is his autobiography, which describes his life spent as a pastor and later as a journalist. He summed up his beliefs in the final chapter, "An Atheist's Apology."

Blanshard was also the author of the controversial exposé *American Freedom and Catholic Power* (1950), along with *Communism, Democracy, and Catholic Power* (1951), *God and Man in Washington: The Church-State Battlefront in Congress, in the Supreme Court, in the Presidential Campaign* (1960), and *Religion and the Schools: The Great Controversy* (1963). Still in print is his anthology of the views of famous freethinkers such as Bertrand Russell, Charles Darwin, Voltaire, and Robert Ingersoll, titled *Classics of Free Thought* (Amherst, N.Y.: Prometheus Books, 1977).

David N. Stamos (whose testimony appears in this book) is the author of *Forbidden Truths: A Refutation of Christianity,* which may be ordered, along with copies of his insightful essays, through Sophia Veritas Publications, 20 Baywood Road, Unit 18, Etobicoke, Ont., Canada M9V 4A8.

Howard Teeple (whose testimony appears in this book) founded the Religion & Ethics Institute in 1972 "to promote the discovery and distribution of sound historical and scientific knowledge in the fields of religion and ethics." The Institute has published several of Teeple's works: *The Historical Approach to the Bible, The Noah's Ark Nonsense,* and *How Did Christianity Really Begin?* For a complete list of books and audiovisual products that the Institute has to offer, or to become a member and receive their newsletter, write them at *REI,* P.O. Box 5510, Evanston, IL 60204.

Why I Left the Ministry and Became an Atheist by G. Vincent Runyon is the testimony of a former Methodist Minister. It was first published in 1959 but was recently reprinted by Independent Publications, Box 102, Ridgefield, NJ 07657. Write them for a complete list of publications.

Frank Zindler (whose testimony appears in this book) is the author of *Dial An Atheist: Greatest Hits from Ohio,* published by American Atheist Press, P. O. Box 140195, Austin, TX 78714–0195; or phone: (512) 458-1244.

He has debated fundamentalist Christians and creationists such as John Morris (*The Question of Noah's Flood: A Debate*), John P. Koster (*Does God Exist?*), and Duane T. Gish (*Is Creationism Science?*). Copies of all three debates, along with a large number of his "Probing Mind" columns, are available from the Society of Separationists, P.O. Box 8457, Columbus OH 43201–0457.

Mr. Zindler also has written a book that will soon be available, titled *Inventing Jesus.*

Index